FRANCEY

DEIRDRE PURCELL

Francey

M

MACMILLAN

LONDON

First published 1994 by Macmillan London Ltd

an imprint of Macmillan General Books Limited
Cavaye Place London SW10 9PG
and Basingstoke

Associated companies throughout the world

ISBN 0-333-58319-1

1 3 5 7 9 8 6 4 2

A CIP catalogue record for this book is available from
the British Library

Typeset by CentraCet Limited, Cambridge
Printed and bound in Great Britain
by Mackay's of Chatham plc, Chatham, Kent

For Adrian and Simon
with all my love

Acknowledgements

Thanks to my family, Adrian, Simon and Kevin.

My most profound gratitude too to my friends and professional colleagues – amongst them in particular, the two Pats, Brennan and Scanlan – who helped with so much moral and practical support.

To Jane Wood, my editor – I'll miss you, Jane!

Thank you to my agents, Charles Pick and Treasa Coady, to Macmillan's Suzanne Baboneau, Hazel Orme and Peta Nightingale, and to Edwin Higel of Brookside for his indefatigable professionalism.

In the matter of detail research, thanks to my brother Declan, to my mother and father, to Canon Bradley at St Patrick's Cathedral, to Michael Cuddihy, to Roger Cronin, Flan Clune, Peter Thursfield and to Jacqueline and Aoife Duffy.

Finally, thanks to Fran at the information desk at Eason's O'Connell Street and to Dennehy and Dennehy, the 'rescue squad' from Mountjoy Garda station.

Chapter One

'Jesus, Mary and Joseph, you're enormous!' Hazel Slye shaded her eyes against the glare of the neon which illuminated the ballroom. Accepting Francey's help, she climbed down off the bandstand on to the dance floor and, the top of her blonde beehive trembling somewhere between Francey's navel and his breastbone, craned her neck to meet his eyes. 'You're *huge!*'

Francey grinned. 'I know – and before you ask, the weather's fine up here, thank you very much. Long time no see. I just thought I'd come and say hello.'

'This is amazing.' The singer's eyes, one green, one blue, rendered even more startling by two thick encirclements of kohl, were wide. 'How'd you remember? You must have been – what was it? Five or six or something?'

'About that.' It was on the tip of Francey's tongue to say something about being unable to forget those eyes but in case she might misunderstand his motives for approaching her, he resisted. 'I might return the compliment,' he said instead. 'You seem to remember me too.'

'Jesus, sure how could I miss you! Except for the hair you're the spit of—' She seemed to think better of what she had been going to say. 'I can't get over it!' she said, 'Young, er . . .'

Francey saw that while she might have recognized him out of his father, it would have been asking too much of her to remember his name. 'Francey,' he supplied, 'Francey Sullivan.'

'Sullivan? Oh yeah, that's right.' Hazel hesitated then recovered. 'Young Francey as I live and die . . . Just as a matter of interest, how tall are you?'

'Six seven or thereabouts.' Francey was used to this.

'My God! Here,' the singer tugged at the skirt of her short rhinestone-clad dress, 'let me get me coat and we'll go for a few drinks and have a chinwag.'

'Isn't it a bit late?' Francey, conscious of the last few pence jingling in his trousers' pocket, had not bargained for this. 'Don't you have to go with the band or something?'

'Them?' Hazel waved a dismissive hand, 'I can see them any time. Hey, Vinnie,' yelling over her shoulder, 'don't hang on for me.'

'Suit yourself.' The saxophonist who had led the showband did not look in their direction. 'See you on the Quays tomorrow, and for Christ's sake don't be late, Queenie, I'm warning you.'

'Wait here for me.' Hazel ignored the admonition and thumped Francey's forearm. 'I won't be a sec. Me coat's at the back of the stage.'

Feeling exposed as he waited under the neon, which had come on with the last note of the National Anthem, Francey tried to suppress his customary unease in situations like this. It had taken a great effort of will to force himself up to the bandstand to catch Hazel's eye. But having seen by chance the poster advertising the appearance of the showband with which Hazel was the lead singer, he knew he had been presented with the opportunity he had been seeking for years. Although it was virtually the only way to meet girls in Dublin, he rarely attended dances; in the press of bodies his unusual size made him feel as conspicuous as a giraffe clumping about in the midst of a herd of deer.

Height apart, Francey's main difficulty in life was that, at the age of twenty-five, he had not found a milieu in which he felt comfortable. Although he adored his family, in particular his mother, and admired – absently – the wild and beautiful terrain of the Béara peninsula in West Cork which was his home, there was no place for him in Lahersheen. His stepfather was a good, industrious farmer but their landholding was too small to keep two grown men fully occupied. In truth, Francey had been glad of this; farm work interested him not in the least, especially when *émigrés*, back in the parish for holidays from cities all over the world, brought news of excitement and adventure from outside.

But having at last made the break, Francey had found little of either in the Dublin of the early sixties, cramped as he was into cheap digs with five others like himself, all of them tyrannized by rules about how much hot water they were allowed for shaving and about not leaving teacup rings on the dingy furniture. And although his work in a large builders' supply store was steady and well paid for someone as unqualified as himself, he found it boring and stultifying. If there was excitement to be found in Dublin, it was for others and he had so far not identified its location.

Sometimes, when drinking his solitary pint in a pub and observing the raucous camaraderie of the beer-bellied dockers and builders and the men who laboured for Dublin Corporation, Francey had wished with all his heart that he, too, could have had ordinary aspirations and that he had not had the secondary education that landed him in a tight white collar behind the counter in Ledbetter's Hardware.

He had hated boarding school and to escape from the bell-driven dreariness of the daily routine, had developed an addiction to books, had devoured thrillers, romances, classics, even comics, and, since boarders were not allowed into the fleshpots of the local town, anything in print that a day pupil could procure for him from the public library. He had developed methods of concealing this passion as the priests were in the habit of confiscating any book not on the curriculum of the Department of Education. His current reading was a re-reading: the dog-eared paperback copy of *David Copperfield* reposed at present in the inside pocket of his jacket.

He touched it now, as though for reassurance as he watched the poor stragglers, who, not having clicked, walked purposefully out of the ballroom pretending they had arranged to meet someone outside. Francey knew the expression only too well, that desperate look of renewed defeat which tried to present itself as jaunty insouciance. For once, he thought gladly, he was not one of them. In fact, in the eyes of others, his shift was the Shift of all Shifts, the singer in the band.

Francey, who was not shy by nature, more by habit and self-conscious interpretation of the incredulous glances cast at his size, decided he might as well enjoy his public success, however transient. He pulled himself up to his full height, basking in the curious glances of those saddest of all hangers-on, the women who still loitered in front of the bandstand in hopes of pulling one of the band members as the instruments and music stands were being dismantled.

In stepping out of the way of a youth who was pushing a hillock of cigarette butts and sweet papers along the floor in front of a wide sweeping brush, his eye was caught by the glitter of a girl's hair-comb in the debris. Having been brought up in a household full of girls, Francey wondered how many hours the comb's owner had spent getting ready for this dance. Illusion was all, he thought. In an instant

3

this fairyland of possibilities had transformed itself into a dump for false dreams, echoing and clashing as drum kits were packed away and chairs stacked. The plum-painted walls, so cosy and welcoming under pink and red spotlights, were now seen to be tacky with dirt and, for the first time, Francey noticed the strips of leatherette hanging off chair seats and backrests, the flakes off the surfaces of Formica tables. The revolving crystal which had flashed rainbows over faces and shoulders was only a lifeless globe with chips missing and even the silvery blue stars which had winked on the façade of the bandstand were dull, the black paint under them streaked with grey.

'I'm wallfalling for a jar,' Hazel was back, 'and I want to hear all about your mother and the girls and everyone. We'll go to Collins's.'

'All right.' Francey wondered if he had the price of even one drink, let alone two. Normally he would not have dreamt of going out on the night before payday. To get into the dance at all he had had to take his chances with the ticket-seller on the door knowing that men, particularly 'respectable' young men, were always in short supply at Dublin dances and were frequently allowed in for half-price if they came late.

'Hold on a sec.' Hazel turned away from him and lowered the cigarette in her mouth over the flame of a lighter. She took a long, deep drag. 'That's better,' she said, reminding Francey of an exotic little dragon as she exhaled twin plumes through her nostrils. 'Come on.' She steered him out through the tiled foyer of the dancehall and into the street. 'How long have you been up here?'

'About three years now.' His own breath vaporizing against the October fog, Francey allowed himself to be towed along by the arm. 'I could never take to farm work.'

'I don't blame you. As for the weather in that place!' Hazel shivered.

'It's not that bad. Béara has its share of good weather too, you know. I can't remember what it was like the day you were there —'

'Have you a car?' Hazel interrupted.

'No.' Francey smiled at the notion that someone on his salary could aspire to such luxury. 'Sorry.'

'Ah, it doesn't matter, we'll walk.' A few yards further on, she stopped to sign autograph books for two girls whose hair was backcombed into lacquered mounds as high as her own. Noticing the awed looks the two were casting at Francey as she passed their books back to them, she seized his arm again and laughed gleefully into their faces: 'Youse can't have him, I saw him first. Thanks anyway, girls,' she called as she pulled Francey into motion again, 'see yiz around.'

Next evening, Francey arrived at the meeting point on Burgh Quay just after a quarter to six, half an hour early for his appointment with Hazel and the High Rollers. Butterflies square-danced around the walls of his chest and stomach, but despite a sleepless night and a half-day's work, he did not feel tired: on the contrary he felt energized and alert. This trip was the most exciting prospect he had been offered in the three years he had spent in the capital and he was torn between an instinct to retreat to safety and wild delight that at last he was doing something special. At the same time he feared that by infusing a single, simple outing to a ballroom in Limerick with such high drama he was being ridiculous.

Francey had always nurtured a desire to be different, to make a mark.

All his life he had felt that he was destined not to be an ordinary Joe like most of his schoolfriends, the height of whose ambition had been to land a safe job in the banks or, in the case of the brainboxes, as doctors or solicitors. When he was young and walking the roads around Lahersheen, he would turn around to catch some neighbour's child making faces at him behind his back and would comfort himself with the notion that some day in the future, that urchin, while boasting about having been a neighbour of the Great Francey Sullivan, would smart with regret that he had not been nicer to Francey while he had had the chance.

He did not yet know at what he would be Great. All he knew, as surely as he knew his own name, was that some day that name would be known the length and breadth of Ireland. Patting his pocket to make sure his book was there in case of disaster – suppose Hazel did not show up? – he wandered across to the centre of Butt Bridge where he could keep an eye on vehicles approaching from both directions.

Given his natural parentage, he had always thought that the most promising possibility for a fulfilling life would be to do something in showbusiness. The only periods during which he had been close to happy at school had been while taking part in the half-hearted

5

productions of Gilbert and Sullivan classics and abridged Shakespearean adaptations the priests had mounted.

Again, having no showbusiness role models except his absent father, Francey had never been able to work out any practical way into the profession and, in reviewing his suitability for it, was forced to admit that his skills were fatally limited. He could parse Latin, castrate a calf, drive a tractor, snag turnips or bake bread; he was in possession of a first aid certificate of competence issued by the Knights of Malta; he could identify nuts, bolts, washers and wires and knew the difference between raw deal and untreated mahogany, none of which could be seen as fit training for life around the stage.

But now he dared to hope: Hazel Slye had liked him. Maybe if he asked her, she might have a few suggestions as to how he could go about breaking out – or in. 'Too much of a dreamer' had been written in the 'comments' column of his school report on more than one occasion. So be it, he thought now. Secretly, Francey was proud he was a dreamer. Dreamers had to dream before dreams came true.

He reached the middle of the bridge and glanced up and down the Quays but could still see no sign of the custom-painted minibus Hazel had described to him. The evening was crisp, frost nipping at the corners of the darkness. As the city wound itself into the homegoing rush hour, all around him was cheerful cacophony: the honking and tinkling of car horns and bicycle bells, the shouts of newsboys, 'Herry-aw-May-aw-*Evenin' Press*', the ringing of pedestrians' heel-tips as, hunched into their collars, they smiled cheerful Friday expressions. Lights blazed from every window in the offices of the *Irish Press* nearby; men just released from work walked gratefully into the warm embrace of the Scotch House beside it; across the river on Eden Quay, the Astor and Corinthian cinemas were discharging the afternoon patrons, many of whom walked straight into Mooney's pub alongside.

Fog was forecast for the midlands which they would have to cross on their way to the gig but although the city air smelled as acrid as it usually did on an October evening, it was still relatively clear. Downriver of the bridge, under skeletons of dockside cranes and the gasometer which squatted like a drumlin against the smoky sky, he could just make out the black shape of the tiny passenger ferry which, like a busy water-beetle, criss-crossed the Liffey between two wharves; nearer where he stood, *The Lady Miranda* was taking on a cargo of

6

Guinness for export to England while tied up opposite her, two cattle boats rode low in the water and played host to the relaxed activity of a handful of stevedores and jobbers. Facing upriver again, he could see the brightly lit double-decker buses streaming to and fro across O'Connell Bridge under the Bovril sign that radiated multi-coloured sunbursts of neon, while further up, he could just about see the ant-like scurrying of pedestrians across the arched iron tracery of the footbridge called the Ha'penny.

Francey hung over the parapet, staring down into the full-tided Liffey, its silky black surface sprinkled with pale lozenges from the streetlights along the quays. Now that he was twenty-five, he thought, he had better get a move on if he was going to do anything momentous. Straightening, he checked his watch: he should get back to his waiting station.

He arrived at the same time as the minibus, which was smaller than he had expected but there was no mistaking its *Hazel and the High Rollers* bodywork in canary yellow, festooned, even along the laden roof-rack, with painted dice and pictures of Hazel. The only High Roller inside the vehicle at present, however, was the driver, a balding, burly character whom Francey did not remember seeing on the previous night.

He hung back, watching over the next ten minutes or so as one by one, the six male musicians arrived. Devoid of their black-on-peach stage suits, they looked rumpled, unhealthy, pale – and ordinary. There was a flurry of activity when a group of passing girls accosted one of them on the pavement as he was about to climb into the bus; Francey remembered him as a guitar player who also sang, alone and in duet with Hazel.

After the girls had left, Francey saw this man peering in his direction. A second later he was coming across the road, weaving like a boxer in and out through the clog of traffic. 'Are you Francey?' he asked when he came within earshot. Then, looking Francey up and down, he answered his own question, 'I suppose you could hardly be anyone else!'

'That's true.' Francey smiled.

'You're even bigger than she said. I hope you'll fit!' the musician smiled back, motioning with his head that Francey should follow him back across the street to the bus.

'She's not here yet?' Francey yelled above the noise of a lorry which ground past them when, marooned together on the crown of the road, they were half-way across.

'Late,' the musician yelled back. 'As usual.'

Francey followed his guide into the belly of the bus. Despite its outward appearance, inside it was surprisingly roomy and well appointed, with twelve upholstered seats behind the driver's, arranged two and one on each side of a narrow aisle. Each set of four or two seats faced its mirror image over a table and already there was a poker game in progress across the top six. 'This is Francey,' the guitarist called through the cigarette smoke. 'He's with Queenie.' Only two of the men looked up and greeted Francey; the others muttered, 'How'ya,' without raising their eyes from their cards.

The High Rollers' lack of interest in Francey allowed him to relax but his reception had been so casual he could not help wondering how many other men Hazel had brought along with her on these country odysseys. Squeezing himself into one of the single seats on the back row, he pulled out his paperback and was attempting to read it by the dim overflow of light from the street outside when Hazel at last climbed aboard. She was dressed in jeans and a tight yellow cardigan buttoned up to the neck, and although her hair was backcombed to last night's height, the part of her face Francey could see beneath enormous sunglasses was clean of make-up.

'Well, good *night*, Queenie,' one of the High Rollers called from the front of the bus.

'Nice shades!' said another. 'Hard night?'

'Come on, give us a break, fellas.' Hazel flashed a quick smile at Francey, climbed over his legs and hung her stage dress on a hook inside one of the windows. Then, collapsing into the seat row opposite Francey's, 'How'ya! I hope these yokes here looked after you all right?'

'Grand,' Francey began but was interrupted by the driver who glared in mock irritation down the bus over his shoulder.

'Can we go now that Her Majesty has arrived?'

'Aw, come on.' Hazel removed the sunglasses and rubbed her eyes. 'I wasn't all that late. Was I, Francey?' she appealed.

Not knowing what to say, Francey shook his head as the driver slammed the bus into reverse gear and eased it out into the traffic.

Hazel whipped a chiffon, leopard-patterned headscarf out of the holdall she carried and draped it over her beehive, tying the ends

8

under her chin. 'Don't be lookin' at me hair like that,' she admonished Francey, although he had been doing no such thing. 'If it's good enough for Eileen Reid it's good enough for me,' naming another female showband star from whom she had obviously copied the style. 'Nothin' much'll happen until we get as far as Egan's in Portlaoise,' she advised, 'we'll be stopping there for a cup of tea. So you might as well relax and enjoy the scenery.'

Francey forbore to point out that he was unlikely to see much through the pitch darkness. Instead, he smiled. 'Thanks for inviting me, I'm enjoying it already.'

'Don't get carried away! Talk to you later.' She opened her bag and quaffed a long drink from a bottle of what looked like water, raised the armrest between her pair of seats and swung her legs on to the one beside her own. Then, making sure her hairdo was supported and not squashed against the window glass, she snuggled her back and shoulders into a comfortable position and closed her eyes. Her head was already jerking sideways in half-sleep as the bus crawled through the traffic on the Quays towards Islandbridge; she was snoring open-mouthed before it reached Inchicore.

Safe in the knowledge that he was for once unobserved, Francey studied the woman across the aisle. Hazel looked far less outlandish than she had on either of the previous occasions he had met her and, even allowing for the dimness of the light that spilled over her from the bicycle lamp, a lot younger than her years. One of the buttons on her cardigan had come undone, affording a limited view of her splendid cleavage. She certainly had a beautiful body, thought Francey, secure in the knowledge that being at the back of the bus, no one would see the direction of his gaze.

Then an odd thing happened: he began to feel warm and protective, as though Hazel Slye was a pup or an orphan lamb put in his charge. Where women were concerned it was a feeling new to him and he remembered how comfortable he had felt talking with her the previous night in Collins's shebeen; apart from his sisters, his mother and his mother's friends, she was the first woman for many years who had, after her initial remarking on it, seemed to accept his size and to talk to him as though he were an ordinary human being and not a freak.

Francey knew that girls were intimidated by him. He was not only tall, his body was large in proportion: although he carried no superfluous fat, on the last occasion he had weighed himself the scales had registered seventeen and a half stones. It was a standing joke within his family that seen from a distance, Francey looked normal.

The weather forecasts had been accurate and, hampered by the thick fog that pressed in around them as they entered the Naas dual carriageway, progress of the bus was slow. Francey felt sleepy as they lolled along; he attempted to doze but when he had been sitting for more than an hour and a half in the same position, his muscles began to ache and he would have welcomed the opportunity to get out and stretch his legs. He was just about to try to stand up when Hazel at last unwound her own legs and arms, opened her eyes and yawned. 'Y'all right?' she twinkled across the aisle.

'Fine, thanks.'

'Where are we?' She peered through the opaque window. 'Jesus, I can't see a thing. Where are we, Mick?' she called up the bus.

'The Curragh,' was the laconic reply from the driver, whose shoulders were rounded with tension as he peered through the windscreen against which the wipers squeaked.

'Is that all?' Hazel was disbelieving, then, attempting to wipe a clear circle on her window, 'Jesus, this is desperate – we'll never get there at this rate.'

'Go back to sleep, Queenie,' the driver yelled, irritated now, 'I'm doing my best. It's like driving through mushroom soup.'

'Hmmph!' Hazel opened her voluminous holdall and took out a large square mirror which she propped up on her table and illuminated by throwing a switch: 'Battery-operated,' she explained to Francey. Discarding the scarf on the seat beside her, she inspected the extent of the depression in the beehive. She teased it up again with her fingers then took an enormous spray-can from the bag and hooshed clouds of lacquer all around her head, adding overpowering scent to the tobacco fug inside the bus and constricting the back of Francey's nose and throat; he felt if he did not get some fresh air soon he would choke – his calf muscles were threatening to cramp. He tried to shift to a more comfortable position as the bus regained a little speed on the other side of the town, then asked Hazel if he could open a window. 'Sure,' she replied, 'go ahead.'

But the release catch on the sliding window beside Francey's seat was stuck. He was seated at an awkward angle to it and, twisting his torso, he raised himself a little and knelt on one knee to give himself purchase, to no avail. The window stayed shut.

'Here, try mine.' Hazel indicated the one beside her.

Levering himself up, Francey leaned across her. Her window slid aside with ease – but as it gave, the bus, still accelerating, went round a bend and to save himself from falling sideways on Hazel he was forced to grab on to the table.

'Well done!' She thumped his arm. 'Sit here for a bit, why don't you?' she invited, removing her scarf and patting the place beside her.

'Thanks,' he said as simultaneously the driver swore – 'Oh Christ!' – and braked hard.

This time Francey, still on his feet, was thrown completely off balance, falling heavily on to the table top and sliding forwards to hit the seat opposite. For a millisecond, through the screeching of the tyres, he was conscious of the other band members also shooting forwards, of playing-cards scattering, Hazel's mirror spinning off her table and shattering on the floor of the aisle. He felt Hazel pinned under his left knee and heard her scream, a high-pitched sustained piercing of the eardrums just as he felt sharp pain in his midriff where the tabletop cut into it.

The milliseconds continued to tick themselves off as he struggled to take his knee off Hazel.

The bus slewed sideways, and skated and shuddered through the smell of burning rubber.

Then it cannoned to a halt.

The impact sent Francey, already sprawled across his table, further against the back of the seat opposite so his neck was twisted into the angle made by the seat and back-rest. As he waited for the sound of tearing metal, convinced his end had come, the only thought which flashed through his mind was that this would teach him to have ideas above his station . . .

The expected sound did not arrive. Instead, the bus teetered on the wheels along its right side and corrected itself. But the momentum created a pendulum effort, and as everything in the vehicle – bags, playing-cards, instruments which were not secured outside to the roof-rack – crashed around the occupants' heads, the right-hand wheels left the road. Except for the driver, who still clung to the steering wheel, the impact had thrown everyone to the left side of the

11

minibus, which, for another precarious moment balanced on its two left-hand wheels. Then, under the combined, imbalanced weight of its passengers, it toppled over and landed on its left flank, engine roaring and wheels still turning.

Francey was thrown backwards; his head cracked against the road through the open window, his torso landed on Hazel. He was conscious – even as his head struck, even through the chaos of screaming and men's swearing – of the crunch of his elbow against Hazel's face and of the awful sound of bones breaking.

Silence for a fraction of a second and then bedlam.

Francey tested his limbs: sore but nothing broken. As he tried to heave himself off his back, using the seatbacks to his right for traction, he separated the sounds and identified the high-pitched, terrified lowing of cattle. They must have ploughed into a wandering herd.

Hazel stopped screaming and began instead a constant low keen. At least, Francey thought, his brain snapping with clarity as he continued the effort to right himself, she was still alive. He had to get her out, but immediately reconsidered. If her back was broken, should he move her at all?

He managed at last to pull himself off her and, crawling over the backrest that barred his way, punched at the doors of the bus which gave easily. Still on hands and knees, he crawled into the foggy air and stood upright, gulping in the air.

He was followed in quick succession by three of the High Rollers, unhurt but shaken. 'Hazel's bad,' Francey gasped, 'we've to get an ambulance. How are the others?'

'I don't know.' Only one of the men seemed able to answer. One of the other two stumbled to the grass verge and began to retch; the other was leaning against the overturned minibus, his hands cradling the side of his head.

Trying for a moment to ignore Hazel's moans, Francey surveyed the scene. As far as he could see in the fog, the accident had occurred just where a bend in the road straightened out. The engine continued to run and the right-hand wheels turned lazily as the bus lay across three-quarters of the roadway; two of the injured cattle, ghostly in the beams of the headlamps, blocked the remainder. 'We have to clear this or something else will hit us.' Francey took charge. 'In the meantime, one of us will have to find a telephone and get the ambulance and someone else will have to go to the other side of that bend to warn traffic. Will you go for a phone?' he asked the musician who most seemed to have his wits about him.

'Where?' Instinctively, the man had accepted Francey's self-designated position as leader.

Francey looked around. A little off the road and about eighty yards away, he saw a faint light. Although there was no guarantee it was in a house, he decided to gamble. 'Try over there,' he said pointing, 'and if they don't have a telephone, ask them for help anyway. And we need a tractor,' he called after the man who was swallowed up by the fog within seconds.

'Will you go to the other side of the bend? Warn traffic?' He took the shoulders of the man beside him who was still holding his head.

'All right.' The man's whisper was hardly audible.

Francey watched as, staggering a little, the man went off round the bend but was diverted by the muffled sound of an engine approaching from the straight side of the road. He ran towards it, waving his arms. The driver of the car, which was travelling very slowly, saw him in time and stood on the brakes. Two men got out and within seconds were joined by the occupant of a second vehicle, a small van. This driver volunteered to go into the town to bring out a doctor and to make sure the ambulance was on its way. He jumped back into the van and lowered the window. 'And I'll organize something for those beasts,' he shouted, negotiating his way along the grass verge and around the stricken animals which were still blaring. As far as Francey could make out, both had broken legs; several other cattle which appeared uninjured plunged about in the ditches on both sides of the road, adding to the confusion.

Francey heard a shout from the car driver, who had dashed around to the back of the bus. 'Give us a hand here,' the man called. 'There's a few badly hurt people inside. And we have to turn off the motor – there's a desperate smell of petrol.'

Grateful that other people seemed now to be sharing the responsibility, Francey, whose knees suddenly felt as though they contained no bones, managed to obey, walking as fast as he could round the bus. The car driver was already inside, crawling over the seats and reaching for the ignition key. As far as Francey could tell, the sounds coming from inside were made by only two people, Hazel and one of

the men; the other three, including the driver, were either unconscious or dead. Refusing to dwell on that possibility just yet,
Francey climbed back inside.

When he reached Hazel he saw she had fallen diagonally across
the large opening of the window so that except for her legs, she was
lying on the stones of the road. Both arms were raised above her head
at a peculiar angle and he saw that they were pinned under the
bodywork of the bus around the frame. She was also caught by her
mound of hair: blood streamed down her face from an open wound
all along the hairline.

More blood oozed from her mouth and her nose was probably
broken; another three inches, Francey thought, and her skull would
have been crushed. He was more worried by the dark stain that spread
down one leg of her jeans and covered an entire thigh. He feared an
artery might have been severed and looked around frantically for
something to use as a tourniquet. He was trying to manoeuvre in the
confined space to reach one of his shoelaces when a pattern caught
his eye. The leopardskin scarf was draped across the edge of the table.
Retrieving it, he stretched it into a string, knotting it around the top
of her thigh. But as he did so, she stopped moaning. 'Hazel!' he cried.
'Hazel, can you hear me?'

She was unconscious.

She had to be removed from the bus – and fast. 'The woman's
trapped, we have to get her out of here,' he shouted at the car driver
in front of him who was lying on his belly in an attempt to check the
condition of one of the musicians slumped head down across the back
of his seat. The driver wriggled backwards. 'Will you take this' –
Francey indicated the knotted scarf – 'keep it as tight as you can. I'm
going to see if we can't raise the bus off her.'

'All right.' The man braced himself and took the ends of the
chiffon.

By the time Francey emerged on to the road, the man originally
dispatched for the ambulance was back. 'They're telephoning,' he
gasped, 'but they don't have a tractor. They're ringing a neighbour
up the road —'

'Give us a hand, get everyone,' Francey interrupted. 'Hazel's
trapped. Get everything movable out of the bus.' As the man began
to throw bags and instrument cases out onto the road, Francey ran

14

round and started to release the ropes which held the drum kit, music stands and PA gear to the roof rack.

'What are you doing?' By this time a man and a woman from another car had joined them. The speaker looked incredulous.

'There's a woman trapped in there,' Francey said, undoing the last of the tethers, 'we have to lift the bus off her.' As he finished speaking, the freed drum kit fell off the rack and crashed onto the tarmac.

'It's impossible,' the man shouted. 'There's someone coming with a tractor – and maybe she shouldn't be moved. She could have a broken back, or neck –'

'We can't wait. She's losing a lot of blood. And her feet and legs are all right so her back isn't broken.' Francey peered into the bus. 'Hold on,' he called to the car driver, whom he could just about see, 'if this works, you're going to be thrown about a bit. Keep hold of the scarf if you can. Could we have a bit of a hand here?' he barked at the group of bystanders, which, augmented by the fresh arrivals, milled around the scene. Without hesitation, everyone rushed to his side to help.

Squeezed into a ragged line with Francey at the centre, everyone, including the woman from the most recently arrived car, took handholds where they could and began to strain. 'Wait,' Francey ordered. 'All together, please, on a count of three.'

'Stand by,' he called to the man holding Hazel's tourniquet. 'Now,' he took a deep breath, 'one, two, *three* . . .' They strained in unison for the best part of ten seconds and although the bus, which unladen must have weighed over a ton, shuddered a little, it did not give.

'Wait a second.' Francey released his hold on the roof rack and straightened. Stepping back, he tried to direct every iota of his concentration into the task, narrowing the focus until he saw his strength as a black-tipped arrow directed at the metal bar in front of him. He took a step forward and took as much air into his lungs as he could.

'Again,' he ordered, taking his portion of the bar in his hands. 'Now! One, two, *three*!' Bending his knees to allow his thighs to take the strain, he lowered his chin almost to his chest and envisaged power flowing towards the bus through the top of his head. To each side of him he was conscious of the grunting of the helpers.

And then Francey sensed the slightest of movements under his hands.

He made one supreme effort. His thighs trembled, his shoulders, neck, upper back and forearms screamed against the punishment he was inflicting on them, his lungs burned and cords of pain stretched behind his closed eyes. Then he roared, a visceral, nether-worldly bellow which seemed to come from deep below his tortured feet. The sound went on and on until he believed his chest might shatter.

Everything went black.

When he came to, he was kneeling on the verge, one cheek flattened against the cold grass, pins and needles shooting like firecrackers up and down his forearms, back and legs. The roofrack was bent and half torn off.

The bus was upright.

Chapter Two

One hour merged into the next during the rest of that night and half the following day. At teatime, discharged from hospital where he had been kept overnight for observation, Francey went back to the digs and found himself being given a hero's welcome. It was only then the reality of what had happened began to sink in.

In many ways, his dream about being famous had come true, but not in the way he had imagined.

As he let himself in through the front door, he was met by his landlady, beaming her own congratulations at him while passing on telephone messages of concern and praise from his family and friends in Lahersheen – and from his employers in Ledbetter's. The crash had been mentioned on wireless bulletins and had been front-page news in all the newspapers. And because he was a native of the county, the *Cork Examiner* had splashed the story across four columns with his part in the saving of Hazel and the other injured band members written up in flattering terms.

The next day, Sunday, he woke too late to make even one o'clock Mass at High Street, last resort of laggards and nightshift workers. The Lord would forgive him, he thought, testing the pain in every muscle and sinew in his body. As he stretched so that his feet hung over the footboard, he replayed not only the crash but what had brought him to it, and also the first time he had met Hazel Slye. It had been the one and only time he had ever met his real father and was the reason he had sought her out at the dance.

George Gallaher, according to Francey's mother, was an itinerant actor from Scotland. Accompanied by Hazel, he had visited the farmhouse in Lahersheen one hot summer's day in 1944, more than nineteen years ago. Francey, then only six years old, had more or less accepted his mother's introduction of George as her cousin. But since, in those wartime years, visitors from outside the close-knit community were few and since he had never in his short life encountered such an extraordinary couple as George and Hazel, he had studied them all the time they were there. He had been blessed with the gift of almost perfect recall not only of the detail in conversations but of pictures and scenes, and even now, nearly twenty years later, could have described what Hazel had been wearing that day. He remembered every line of his 'cousin's face and massive physique: the way the hot sun lit the leonine, artificially auburn hair, the horizontal creases on the back of the green suit jacket which stretched between the shoulder blades.

Francey's longing for the presence of a 'real' father had begun as something vague, a small feeling, no bigger than a hazelnut, some-where beneath his breastbone. He was not unhappy in the care of his stepfather – Mossie Sheehan had been a generous and solid presence for most of his life – but he had never felt that Mossie was anything but a substitute. Over the years the hazelnut of longing had grown to fill his body; it was not painful, just ever-present, like the thump of his heart.

Now he hoped the conduit to his father would be Hazel.

After the dance, the place to which she had led him had proved to be a small hotel in a side-street on the fringes of the city centre.

'What are you havin'?' Unperturbed, Hazel had waved a greeting to several groups of people huddled chummily together in a sort of sitting-room beside the front lobby, then bustled up to a hatch behind which a young man dispensed drink.

'Just a bottle of Phoenix, please.' On the evidence, Collins's appeared to be a small private hotel patronized by middle-aged men in suits. It was hopping with activity. He could see no vacant seats anywhere near him and, aware as usual of several pairs of eyes scrutinizing him, fixed his eyes on a worn spot on the carpet and endeavoured to carapace his head into his body. Long practised in the art of conversation with people far smaller than himself, when Hazel returned with his beer and a vodka and tonic for herself, he braced himself against the wall and inclined his head like a confessor to listen as she chattered on about showband life, about how difficult it was to be on the road all the time, how she could never afford to take a proper holiday. Since the conversation seemed to require only the occasional nod of empathetic assent, Francey rode on the mono-logue and on the buzz of talk from the other patrons in the room and allowed himself to fantasize. Perhaps this was the opening he had been waiting for? *Francey and the* . . . what? So what if he could neither sing nor play an instrument. He could learn . . .

As if she had divined his tentative imaginings, he heard that Hazel was complaining about the proliferation of low-talent, high-profile showbands which were springing up 'like feckin' mushrooms' all over the country, more than seven hundred of them competing with each other. 'Think of it, Francey!' she exclaimed. *'Seven feckin' hundred!* In a country as small as this . . .'

As she chattered on, he again let his attention wander from her words, instead watching the mobility of her small features. If Hazel's eyes were distinctive, in Francey's memory, George Gallaher's had been just as remarkable, so blue as to be almost violet. And it was when, at the age of eleven, he saw those eyes staring back at him from a mirror that the truth finally dawned on him that this Scottish actor had not been a cousin. He had kept the discovery to himself, not wanting, even at that age, to create any more problems for his mother. Instead, he had, with little success, pooched around amongst her private letters and papers in an effort to find more about his true parentage. It was not until his twenty-first birthday that he had broached the subject openly and learned the truth of his birth: that his mother had fallen in love, been seduced, and then abandoned. Even then, although he had tried to work up a head of hatred for George Gallaher, he could not manage it. His mother's personality was strong, therefore Gallaher had had to be so charismatic as to be irresistible. He had believed her, however, when she had said that not only did she not know where he was now but she never wanted to hear from him again as long as she lived.

Watching Hazel that night in Collins's Hotel, Francey had longed to broach the subject of George Gallaher; other than his mother, the singer was his first real link to his father. But since this would have involved certain other, more delicate questions about her own relationship with him, he had decided it was too soon yet. Instead, when it was his turn to speak, he had complimented her on her singing and had, more for conversation's sake than enquiry, wondered at why she had switched from acting to singing.

'Just look at me,' Hazel had taken her cue and went along with the change of subject, 'I'm not exactly going to be cast as Joan of Arc, am I? Thank God for backcombing and stiletto heels.' She swizzled her drink with one long red nail. 'If it wasn't for the hairdo I'd be invisible. There aren't many parts for midgets.'

Francey had gazed down at her: 'Come on now, I know you're small but you're not that small —'

'Lookit,' she had retorted, 'I'm four foot eleven in me stockin' feet. I got fed up of acting. Singing's steadier – and anyway the acting experience isn't wasted. Acting comes in handy for putting the songs across . . .' She had gone on then to tell him the story of her life in showbusiness. Apparently she had started out as an actress and dancer in the old fit-ups – which was where she first came across George Gallaher. But as the numbers of fit-up companies had dwindled under the onslaught of competition from cinema, Hazel had found work more and more difficult to come by and, seeing the success of the showbands, had taken singing lessons.

'That's fantastic!' Francey said at the end, lost in admiration for her guts.

'Sure I'm a genius!' Hazel smoothed wrinkles out of the dress which had ridged up over her abdomen. 'I only hope it lasts.'

'Of course it will – all the ballrooms are packed.'

'They are at the moment,' Hazel replied, 'but I'm an old dog for the hard road and I take nothing for granted.'

'How old are you?' It was out before Francey could stop himself.

'Jesus – get you!' Yet Hazel did not seem insulted. 'You don't put a tooth in it, do you?' She grinned. 'Thirty-six,' she said, 'old enough to be your mammy. I don't feel like your mammy, mind you,' she added, with no trace of coquettishness.

Hardly believing his luck, Francey rushed to tell her that he was twenty-five. Then, nursing the last of his beer, he struck while the iron was still hot. 'Do you mind if I ask you if you're married?'

Hazel considered for a moment or two then told him she was separated. 'He was a civil servant,' for once her eyes were serious, 'pens, Pioneer pins, Fáinnes – the lot. I thought I wanted to get away from showbusiness. I was wrong – bored out of my tree. I haven't seen sight nor light of him for years.' Seeming to tire of the subject, she drained her glass. 'D'you want another Phoenix or will you have a real drink?'

Francey was a little shocked at Hazel's matter-of-fact acknowledgement of her marital state. Separation was a condition spoken about in confidential, sometimes snide, whispers. 'Where is he now?' he asked, trying not to let his attitude show.

'Haven't a clue,' she shrugged, 'probably wearing out his knees in some church somewhere. Last I heard he was still in London. He's Irish,' she explained, 'but we met there when I was still an actress. One of these days I hope he'll get around to divorcing me. I've asked him to but, of course, it's against his feckin' religion. How about yourself?' She raised painted eyebrows. 'Girlfriend?'

'No.' Francey decided he could be truthful with her. 'Women take one look at me and they think I'd break them,' he said, 'and I can't dance, so there's no joy there.'

'They don't know what they're missin'!' Hazel patted his arm. 'Size isn't important, you know!' She fluttered false eyelashes as thick as brushes but when it was clear he did not get her double-meaning intent, gave him a thump. 'Jeez, you *are* wet behind the ears, aren't you?'

Too late, Francey got the joke and tried to recover but Hazel cut off his attempts: 'Never mind, love, you're gorgeous. Women are suckers for blonds, you wait and see! If I was a few years younger now —' She stopped, cocking her head to one side like a small audacious bird. 'Come to think of it . . .' she added, then seemed to make a decision.

It was then she had invited him to come along on the trip to Limerick.

Smiling at the memory, Francey stretched again in his bed but then, like an abrupt smack across the head, the moment of the crash, the squealing, the juddering, the terror, hit him all over again and he began to sweat. Rather than let it play over and over, he made a determined effort to crawl out of bed.

Downstairs, he found his landlady was still inclined to treat him as though he had singlehandedly saved the city from marauding Vikings. She had good news for him, picked up from the wireless: all those injured in the crash – despite Francey's fears none had died – were now off the critical list in hospital.

He wondered if he should try to visit Hazel, then decided against it: she would not yet be in the mood for visitors and, anyway, she would be inundated with people as soon as she was well enough to see them. Instead, as it was a fine day, he caught the bus to the Phoenix Park and, trying to ameliorate the pain in his stiff muscles,

21

spent the next two hours walking through the glory of its autumn dress.

When he got home the fresh batch of messages included one from Hazel. The hospital had telephoned on her instructions: she would like him to come to see her. When he enquired next day, however, Francey found that the visiting hours in the hospital did not fit in with his work schedule and it was the following Sunday when he knocked and then pushed open the door of Hazel's room. She was alone and asleep.

Sitting in a chair beside the bed, Francey studied her. Every inch of visible skin was black and blue, her plastered arms were held in traction on pulleys above her, strapping covered all he could see of her torso except for her bare shoulders and upper chest, and white padding concealed the stitches along her hairline, upper lip and bridge of her nose. Over the bandages, her blonde hair, what he could see of it, was somewhat like he remembered from the visit in 1944: short and tufted, it resembled a spiked helmet. She looked like a small, crucified mummy.

The hospital was south-facing and, as it was a clear day, sunlight shafted in through the wide windows of the room as though it were high summer. Francey found himself beginning to sweat and checking that Hazel still showed no signs of imminent consciousness, got up from his chair and went to the window in search of some air. The Bons Secours hospital had been built on the crest of a hill, and the grey city below, sunk in Sunday slumber, its factory chimneys innocent of smoke, was spread before him as far as the rounded, purplish backs of the Dublin mountains. They seemed further away than they were, an illusion that Francey, an honorary Dubliner, knew denoted a continuation of the fine weather.

From behind him, he heard a groan and turned round to find Hazel gazing at him through eyes streaked with blood. Far from being grateful, she seemed angry.

'How are you feeling —' he began but she interrupted him.

'You fell on me, ya big lug!'

'Sorry, I couldn't help it. I did the best I could — '

'Joke — joke!' Hazel tried to smile but to add to her afflictions, one of her top front teeth was missing. The effect was macabre and she knew it: to Francey's alarm, she burst into tears.

'Don't!' He glanced at the door, hoping for rescue from a nurse

22

or another visitor. He did not know her well enough to cope with this. 'Please, Hazel,' he begged, 'please don't cry.'

'I can't help it. I know I look like the Creature from the Mummy's Crypt – oh!' she wailed. 'Me head, me head!' The suspended plaster casts jerked above her as though she had forgotten she could not use her arms.

'Will I get a nurse?'

'It's all right,' Hazel groaned, 'don't mind me. Everyone tells me I'm lucky to be alive. I suppose I am too.' She swallowed hard. 'Mop me face, will you? There's hankies on the locker.'

Francey did as he was bid, using a tissue to blot up the moisture from the wet places between bandages.

'Lookit, Francey,' Hazel said more quietly, when he had finished, 'thanks for what you did. You're the talk of the place. You know I'm grateful – did you get my message?'

'I did, but don't thank me, I only did what anyone else would have in my place.'

'I'm an atheist but thank God you were with us.'

'Are you feeling a bit better now? Are you sure I shouldn't get someone?' Francey was afraid she was going to cry again.

'I feel as if I'll never be normal —'

'Of course you will, your hair will grow again,' he added, hearing how feeble it sounded. 'Here, I brought you these.' He proffered a bunch of white chrysanthemums, which, by contrast with the drifts of roses, lilies and orchids that covered her locker and windowsill or stood in pots on the floor, seemed cheap and wan.

'Thanks.' Hazel's voice was constricted as she remembered just in time to keep her lips closed when attempting to smile.

'You must be tired.' All Francey wanted now was to leave. 'I'll just put them here.' He crossed to the windowsill and left his offering to droop in their cellophane beside a crowd of showy tiger lilies.

'I love chrysanths.' Hazel's gaze followed him. 'Sorry I'm not in better form,' she added, closing her eyes. To Francey's consternation another big tear rolled down her cheek. Her eyes opened. 'Can you come again? Please? I know I've been rude and I really am grateful and I would like to see you again – Tarzan!' The wisecrack sounded forlorn through her swollen lips.

'Well, if you're sure . . .'

'I'm sure. And it doesn't matter what time you come in, the nuns are lovely here. I'm sleeping a lot but if I'm not awake, just give us a thump.'

Promising to come back the following evening, he left her then.

On the way down towards the bus-stop his attention was caught by a group of children who were playing aeroplanes on the wide green lawn that fronted the hospital. Arms held wide, coats streaming open from their shoulders, as they raced around one another, their cries floated up to him like the notes of wind-chimes. One child in particular took Francey's eye: dark-haired, a little apart from the others, he buzzed around within his own private circle, throwing handfuls of golden leaves in the air and letting them rain down around his head.

The little boy reminded Francey of Dessie.

George Gallaher's visit to Lahersheen that summer afternoon in 1944 had impacted not only on his son but on one of Francey's stepsisters who had been so smitten she had gone with him and Hazel Slye to join their company as an actress. Kathleen had come back pregnant. The baby had been absorbed into the family and Francey had adored him. But when Dessie was six years old, Kathleen, volatile at the best of times, had left Lahersheen and had taken Dessie with her. Neither had been heard of since, despite the family's best efforts at tracing them through the Guards, the Salvation Army, through the bigger armies and networks of Irish clergy and emigrant groups in England, America and even Australia.

Francey had been inconsolable. Yet, even after he had learned that Dessie too was George's son, he remained caught in hero-worship fed by mythical stories of Celts and Greek gods untroubled by monogamy, and could not find it in his heart to blame his father. Instead, the truth served only to increase his fascination with the absent – or dead – George.

As he walked down the hill towards the bus-stop, the conviction that this was not a false start, that his life was changing – had changed – grew apace.

Up to now, Francey's routine in Dublin had been seldom varied: he had worn tracks between work and digs, work and digs, Mass on Sunday mornings, Croke Park on a Sunday afternoon if there was a match on, a few drinks in a local pub on pay night and a rare outing to a dance on a Saturday.

The encounter with Hazel had forced him to face that Francey

Sullivan's solitary state was of Francey Sullivan's own making. At the age of twenty-five he had allowed himself to become a reclusive, unattractive drone.

Time to take advantage of the opportunities presented. And not only in the matter of finding his father.

'How'ya!' Nearly four weeks after Hazel Slye's admission to the Bons Secours hospital – five weeks after the accident – her chirpy greeting for Francey as he pushed open the door of her room was characteristic of her old self. As usual at this time of day, tea-time, she was alone. No family ever came to see her, which she explained away by telling Francey she had none. 'I'm an orphan,' she had said. 'Maybe you could lend me some of your lot. As far as I can see, you've enough relatives to populate half the country.'

Although her blue eye was still a little bloodshot, the bruising on her face had faded to slight traces of yellow around her cheekbones and her plastered arms lay in a relatively natural position on the coverlet on both sides of her. The removal of the head bandages and suturing displayed five weeks' growth of dark roots in her bleached hair, however, and she looked like a scrappy, multicoloured mongrel. Today, she told Francey as he pulled up the chair, she was to have the remainder of the strapping removed from her ribcage prior to going home on the morrow. 'And I'm gettin' these feckin' plasters off early next week. Can't wait.'

'That's great, you won't know yourself. You're obviously feeling better.' Francey placed a small bag of iced caramels on the locker.

'Like a lark.' Using her legs as propellants, Hazel scooted higher on her pillows. 'The nuns can't get over what a great healer I am! Comes of being a dancer, I suppose, not to speak of all that good living!'

Francey grinned. In the weeks he had been visiting her he had got to know from comments she had let slip that Hazel's lifestyle would not have been what the priests in school would have called virtuous. 'I'm supposed to be out walking,' she went on, glaring at the door, 'on that stupid feckin' corridor but I'm sick of it, I've feckin' grooves worn in it. Here I've a present for you,' Hazel indicated with a flick of her head, the pile of scrapbooks on the floor beside her locker.

'Is that them?' Francey's eyes lit up.

'Well, they're not brass bands, stupo!' she relented. 'You'll have to search through them yourself. I just told Vinnie to bring them all in.' The saxophonist's relationship to Hazel had never been made clear to Francey. Obviously, however, he had free access to her flat and knew it well enough to know where she filed her cuttings – kept, she had informed Francey, so that when she came to write her life story she would have all the material she needed.

'You're sure you want to find that old humbug?' she asked now, watching as Francey picked up the pile of books. 'You're sure you're not better off without him? He's nothing but a . . .' Unusually, words failed her.

'I can't explain it.' Francey sat back in his chair, balancing the pile on his lap. 'It's just something inside me.' It had taken more than a fortnight of visiting to pluck up enough courage to ask Hazel if she had any information on the whereabouts of his father; he had still not asked about her own involvement with George. Perhaps it was the naïveté of a six-year-old but he had always assumed that when they came to Lahersheen, George and Hazel had been a couple, a notion which she seemed to confirm – 'that fecker's going to be one of the juicier bits of me book' – when she had mentioned that amongst her cuttings were press and magazine accounts of George's wedding. He felt he could ask her now. 'I never asked you about –'

'About me and him?' Hazel had an uncanny habit of anticipating his questions. 'Half the women in Ireland were in love with that man during the war,' she said. 'You've got to remember that there wasn't much entertainment in those days and those touring companies played to packed houses all over the country.'

Francey took a deep breath. 'Including Kathleen?'

'Particularly Kathleen,' Hazel replied. 'And before you ask, I blame meself for a lot of what happened there. I'm sure your mother blames me too,' she added. 'I promised your mother I'd look out for her if she was let come to Killarney that time.'

'Oh, I'm sure she doesn't blame you.' Francey had no idea whether or not his mother resented her. 'She loved Dessie,' he added sadly, 'we all did . . .'

'It was a little boy?' Hazel's eyes were sympathetic. 'I never did hear.'

Although its urgency was long dissipated, Francey's distress at losing his young half-brother still prodded from time to time. Like

26

Francey, Dessie had loved all animals and seemed to have a mysterious attraction for them so that, from the time he could walk, he was never to be seen in the yard or in the fields without at least one dog at his baby heels. The most poignant memory was of a tender-hearted little boy bundled up in oilskins and out in the farmyard at an old table, laying crumbs for the wild birds; the crumbs kept blowing away in the wind but he persisted, gathering them up again and again until Francey's mother had intervened and brought him back indoors. One of the family jokes was that the wrong brother had been named after Saint Francis of Assisi.

'That business with Kathleen finished me with that fecker,' Hazel said now, 'but I swear to God I didn't know she was pregnant until well afterwards. I swear it, Francey. I'd a' killed him! I heard it in London, actually. You know your mother was sending solicitors' letters to Equity trying to find him?'

'I didn't know that.' The contemporaneous details and aftermath of the affair between Kathleen and his father were still unknown to Francey. 'And what happened? Did she get hold of him?'

'Don't know,' Hazel replied. 'I wasn't exactly bosom pals with the creep at the time. Does your mother know what you're up to now?'

Francey had spent many an hour wondering about the answer to that question. But the urge to find George Gallaher was stronger than loyalty to his mother's feelings. He would cross that emotional bridge after he found his father – if and when he did. 'I'm not sure she'd be all that thrilled,' he admitted to Hazel, 'but she'd understand, I'm sure.'

Hazel looked at him for a few seconds and then wriggled her shoulders into the pile of pillows. 'What you want should be in number five or six.'

Francey saw the books were numbered on the outside, one to ten. He discarded all but the ones she had mentioned and opened the top one of the two. He found them almost immediately: two pages of photographs, most in black and white. One, the largest and in colour, was full-length. Francey's father was as he remembered except for the hair. In his memory it had been the mane of a lion or the coat of one of the reddish-brown collies employed as cattle herders around Lahersheen, but in these pictures his father's head was streaked in shades of grey like the back of a silver fox. The amazing green outfit of that day was replaced by a dark, beautifully cut lounge suit, a shirt which replicated one of the paler greys in George's hair and immaculate black shoes. The smile was the same, however, and so was the heroic stance, the breadth of shoulder and chest.

Carrying a small posy of white roses, the woman at his side wore a strand of creamy pearls, an elegant charcoal-coloured dress and jacket, and high-heeled shoes. She seemed older than George, and even in her youth she may not have been pretty in the conventional sense, but her large jaw was firm, her blues eyes were clear and wide and, although not smiling, she seemed to exude calm self-confidence.

As he gazed at the photograph, the walls of the sunny hospital fell away from around Francey, leaving him isolated with his father. He tried to identify his emotions and found that other than being somewhat shaky, he felt little. With an avenue to George Gallaher open at last, he had been expecting to feel excited or at least apprehensive.

'Well?' Hazel's voice seemed to come from far away.

'It's – it's him all right.'

'I know it's him, stupo. What do you think?'

'He hasn't changed . . .' He continued to study the photograph. The date Hazel had pasted in her scrapbook, *May 1951*, was written under it. 'It was twelve years ago, though,' he faltered, 'maybe he's changed now. He could even be dead.'

'He could be,' Hazel agreed, 'but you'll never know until you go looking for him, will you? How are you going to do that, by the way?'

Francey had not thought much beyond going to London and finding his father in some theatre there. But, discussing it now, Hazel thought it unlikely George was still acting. 'He was gorgeous but he was an awful actor and he's hit the jackpot now, hasn't he? He doesn't need to work at all.

'If you take my advice,' again she levered herself higher on her pillows, 'you'll go to one of the newspapers in Fleet Street. The wife's not only loaded, she's a public figure – doesn't it say there somewhere that she's a bigwig in a few charities? These society pages keep track of people like her. And go in person, it'd be useless trying to do this on the telephone.' Gap-toothed, she grinned. 'Try some young girl on the front desk. Throw yourself on her mercy – smile at her, ya big lunk!'

Although he was getting used to it, Hazel's frankness about how

28

attractive she thought him to women was still such a novelty that Francey blushed. He was not quite clear on the nature of the relationship between the two of them: although it was lovely to have such a chatty and approachable woman friend, after an initial frisson of anticipation that she could turn out to be someone special in his life, he had decided that he was forcing the issue, that because of the unusual circumstances and the easiness of it all, he was making more of the friendship than perhaps was warranted.

As for Hazel's attitude to him, it had been hard to ascertain whether or not she found him attractive or thought he was just attractive in general. Most of the time she maintained a sort of joshing camaraderie with him which he found difficult to place into a separate category from the constant wisecracks that passed like tennis balls between her and her professional colleagues. The difference in age between them was something which did not seem to bother her. And the more he got to know her, the less it worried him.

'Can I take this book with me?' he asked now, gazing down again at the picture of the face he knew so well from so many imaginings. 'Go ahead,' Hazel chirped, 'but be careful with it. That's me fortune in there. Watch them all headin' for the hills when word gets out I'm writing me autobiography.'

Francey had some annual leave coming to him from Ledbetter's and as winter was a slack time for the firm he had little difficulty in getting time off to go to London.

Finding his father's home address had proved easy. One of the charities mentioned in the caption under the wedding photograph was a fund-raising organization for a children's hospital; Hazel had rehearsed Francey in the pretence that he was an Irish cub reporter whose first time this was to cross the Irish Sea and who had been sent over to write a feature on the hospital because it sometimes helped Irish children to come across for urgent treatment. He had taken her coaching, down to plastering what he felt was an excruciating smile all over his face, and within hours of arrival in London, he had gone to the reception desk of one of the newspapers in Fleet Street.

The smile, false or otherwise, had seemed to work and the girl on duty had enlisted the aid of one of the reporters in the newsroom who in his turn had supplied Francey with as many names and home addresses of the directors of the charity as he could find. Mrs Julia Dill Smith Gallaher's address was on the list and the reporter was able to confirm that Francey's stepmother was married and not a widow.

George, therefore, was still alive.

Tired from the overnight journey, Francey spent the rest of that first day in a haze, wandering around in the rawness of the November day, eating in fish-and-chippers and aware that as always he was attracting curious glances. He went to a railway station and found out how best to get to the village of Little Staunton – by train to Leamington Spa followed by a bus trip – and then booked himself into a rundown hotel in one of the pillared and terraced squares which seemed to run one into the other all over the city.

But next morning, after a sleepless night during which he had not even been able to concentrate on reading – his present volume was *The Crock of Gold* – he found himself suffering from a severe attack of nerves. He was almost afraid to meet his father. Suppose when he did, he found that the object of so much of his childhood fantasy was, as Hazel continued to opine, nothing but a shyster?

He had promised Hazel, who loved London, that after fulfilling his mission he would sightsee a little. He rationalized that he might as well do it beforehand rather than afterwards and that he could use the time to gather his thoughts and plan what he was going to say when at last he was face to face with George. He booked into the hotel for another night.

But on the third day after his arrival in England, he woke full of resolve. Carrying his belongings – and the scrapbook – in his small, brand-new suitcase, he took an early-morning train and, following directions from a porter on arrival at Leamington Spa, identified the correct bus for Little Staunton.

Chapter Three

Throughout the obsequies, George Gallaher had maintained what he hoped was a pensive expression. At least the rain, he thought, made it easier to look glum.

Now, as the clergyman droned on, he risked a look around the circle of mourners: under the black canopy of streaming umbrellas, all heads were bent towards the coffin, all bodies stiff with proper respect. The embassy people, George noted, were professionals at this sort of thing, even if they were American. Their dark raincoats were the crispest, their black ties the most cleanly knotted.

His own family was conspicuous by its absence. George's exhausted mother had died when he was fourteen and six months later, after a row with his father, George, who was the youngest of nine, had left his swarming Glasgow tenement without a backward glance. Already tall and precociously attractive, he had set out to hitch to London. The third lift proved to be with a travelling repertory company and by the time the lorry had reached the outskirts of the capital, George had his first job. Or jobs as it turned out: the general stage manager had defected to a rival group the day before and with a shuffling of the pack, George found himself acting as general dogsbody and walk-on actor. Within weeks he was playing small parts.

He never contacted his family again and anyone who asked was told he was an orphan. As time went on George came more and more to believe his own story, 'seeing' the Spartan conditions of the Scottish orphanage in which, according to his own imagination, he had been so brutally raised. The story went down well with women; it was never challenged because, except for one short-lived television advertisement for a holiday resort, George never achieved eminence, and publicity about him was non-existent. When he married Jool – which did make the national press – the reports concentrated on her

31

wealth and background and referred to him as a bit-part actor who had found himself in the right place at the right time.

The vicar trailed to a merciful halt and George shifted his attention back to his wife's remains. Cheerio, old thing, he thought. After the initial shock of finding himself entering into wedlock at the age of fifty-three George had become quite fond of Jool.

For a few seconds, the hum of raindrops against taut umbrella fabric was the only sound as everyone waited for someone else to move first. Glancing around, George realized it was up to him; he cleared his throat and took a small step backwards, allowing the rest of the mourners to follow suit and to break up into smaller clusters.

Over the next few minutes, George conducted himself as behoved a grieving widower, standing with head bent to accept the final condolences from the vicar, the embassy people and then, in ones and twos, from Jool's friends and fellow charity-board members who came up to him to touch his arm and to pronounce the formulaic words. Most declined his offer of refreshment although a few of Jool's closer cronies did accept. He himself had moved around so much, and had formed so few deep friendships, that his own chums were in reality only acquaintances, all of whom thanked him for his invitation but regretted they had to rush away.

The last to approach George was Jool's solicitor. 'I'll be in touch in the next day or two, Mr Gallaher,' the man said having extended his sympathies, 'when everything settles down.'

'Thank you,' George replied, 'I'll be looking forward to it.'

He certainly would, he thought. He had always acknowledged without guile that he had landed on his feet when he met Jool but he had no idea how much she was actually worth and was curious to find out. All he knew was that his wife had been one of the wealthiest women in New England. She had been born rich, her first and second husbands, both dead, had been richer still. Jool was an Anglophile who, long before she met George, had decided to leave her empire in New England in the care of her boards of directors and trustees and to make her home in England; this impulsive decision followed the death of her second husband while they were both attending a matinée performance of *The Tempest* in Stratford-on-Avon.

Jool's third husband, released at last to walk towards the Rolls-Royce which was parked nearby on one of the gravelled walkways, noticed now that the representatives of his wife's family, what was left of it, were bunched self-consciously together, unsure of what to do next. He crossed the sodden grass. 'You must come back to the manor for refreshments,' he invited, 'please do. You've come such a long way . . .' George's titling of the enormous ranch-style house Jool had had built for them after they married had started off as a joke between them but then she had ordered a brass plate for the gate pillars, naming the place Inveraray Manor in honour of her new husband's Scottish upbringing.

'If you're sure . . .' The expression on the face of Jool's widowed brother-in-law, well into his seventies, cleared.

'I insist,' said George, 'and there's plenty of room in my car. Please join me. You can tell your driver you'll send for him later.'

'Okay.' The small group – the brother-in-law, his son, and a middle-aged woman who was apparently a cousin – moved across to where their chauffeur waited beside the rented limousine. Someone touched George's arm. In responding, he found himself looking at his thirty-five-year-old son. Colin Mannering's personality was incomprehensible to his father. Not having made his acquaintance until the boy was well into maturity, George had not taken to him.

George freely acknowledged that he had led, and continued to lead, a charmed life up to and including his marriage to his wealthy wife. When Colin turned up not too long after the wedding, he had been forced ruefully to accept that at long last he might have to face the consequences of his actions. In the light of Jool's steady gaze, not to do so would have seemed so irresponsible and churlish that in her eyes, he knew he could well lose his lustre. But although his son proved charming, with perfect manners, and although he seemed not to hold any grudges against his father for parental laxity, George privately considered him a nuisance. Colin was just too damned eager to please, like many of his acquaintances who had also been in public school.

Jool had been the one who had smoothed over the cracks. With the straightforwardness of her New England upbringing, George's wife had accepted the young man as the product of her husband's youthful indiscretion, had welcomed him to the family fold, and had been delighted when, soon afterwards, Colin had produced his wife and young son. After the initial shock, George, who found conversation difficult with his son, had taken care that, as much as possible, Jool was around during Colin's subsequent visits. Now that she was dead, he wondered how he would manage and hoped that Colin was not going to become a frequent fixture around the place. 'Are you coming back to the manor?' he asked.

'Of course, Dad – if we're invited.'

As usual, there was something about the way Colin said it which set George's teeth on edge. 'Of course you are, silly boy,' he retorted. 'You know the way. How are you, my dear?' Turning to Colin's wife, he flashed the smile which had dazzled women all over the British Isles for more than forty-five years. Then he remembered where he was and in what circumstances and wiped it off his face.

'I'm very well, thank you.' Fleur glanced at Colin as if worried that she had spoken without permission. This was not the first time George had received the impression that she could be afraid of her husband, but he had never delved. To do so might have forced him to take uncomfortable action. He smiled at both of them then turned away towards his Roller, thinking as he walked that Fleur's parents had been prescient in naming her: there was something flower-like about her.

In other circumstances, he thought, he would not have minded a turn with her: underneath that reserve, he had sensed she might be quite a little goer. They all were, of course, once you got them organized. The opportunity had not arisen, however, unless one counted the abortive occasion when, under the influence of the demon drink, he had been a little premature, initiating proceedings while Colin was still within the precincts. Thinking back on it later he had had to admire the way Fleur had disposed of him, sandbagging, as if she had not noticed what he was at.

Probably just as well, he mused as he opened the door of the car and beckoned to his in-laws-once-removed. The situation was complicated enough as it stood and in any event Jool, who had made it clear that where women were concerned the trail had ended with her, might have divorced and disinherited him. And where would that have left him now?

George had been astonished at his own self-control during the twelve years he had been married. With the exception of one or two tiny incidents – well, maybe two or three but nothing of any significance – he had managed to stay faithful to his wife. Twelve *years* when up to then he could not have lasted twelve weeks with the same woman.

His dead wife's relatives seemed shy and disinclined to talk as the car purred away from the manicured graveyard and, after making sure they were comfortable, George took advantage of his status as chief mourner and made no effort to engage them. Instead, as they moved along the small roads, he gazed out at the dripping countryside.

After a minute or two, to his surprise, he found that the dreariness of the day suited his mood, and that the flat, empty feeling inside his chest, a most unaccustomed sensation, could be given a name and was actually sadness.

What was more, the seriousness of his expression for once owed little to the years spent as a ham actor. George almost enjoyed the novelty of the feeling. His brain, however, was already speculating about what life held for him next. At sixty-five years of age, he felt physically as though he were still in his forties. Nature had been kind to him: he had never been seriously ill, had all his own teeth and hair and other than a certain slackness in the skin around his waist and upper arms and finding it a little more difficult to get out of bed every morning, felt as fit as he ever did.

Jool, doughty old bird that she was, had appreciated this. Eight years older than he, she had acted as though all her birthdays had come at once when he had agreed to marry her. Once, when they were on holiday in Italy, he had asked her why she had chosen him. She had looked at him for a long, speculative minute. 'In many ways you're the kid I never had,' she had replied finally. George had been about to protest but she had held up her hand to silence him. 'Don't take it wrong, Georgie,' she had said fondly, 'it's a compliment. I was happy with my other husbands, both of 'em, but they were older than me. I like having a young man on my arm, someone to look after. And you're not bad-looking, you know!

'And I've presided at two funerals,' she had continued, 'I don't want to be the star attraction at a third. It's you who'll be seeing me out, George.'

'Nonsense.' George had kissed her then, with genuine fondness. Every woman he had ever known had acknowledged his looks. But Jool had been prepared to put something behind the pretty words, like her wealth. And she was the first woman he had ever met whom he had respected. Maybe it was because she was older and represented the mother he had known so little.

How right she'd been about the funerals, George thought now, continuing to be surprised at the revelation of how much he would miss Jool. Maybe he had loved her, after all.

He had drifted through life unencumbered by emotional involvements, and that women had frequently mistaken his sexual advances for invitations to love had not impinged on him much. He had always regarded these involvements, and the tearful outpourings when he moved on, as inconveniences, the price to be paid for pleasure. By his own lights he had always been scrupulous enough. Before Jool, when he was with a woman he had given her his full attention for as long as it lasted, but had always been careful not to create any false expectations, making it clear from the start that he was not interested in anything permanent. It was not his fault, he reasoned, that they never seemed to believe him.

The affair with Jool had been a different matter. She had taken one look at him in her no-nonsense way when they met at a charity party to which George had been dragged by an acquaintance and had decided that he was for her. For some reason he could never afterwards quite fathom, he had acceded.

He was being unusually self-analytical today, he thought, discarding the prompt that the American woman's attraction had perhaps lain in her money: although it was pleasant not to worry, money meant as little to him as emotion. He accepted that he had many faults but greed had never been one of them. Perhaps he had agreed to Jool's proposal because he was bored with the continuing procession of younger women and their sentimental demands. Jool had had the good grace never once to utter the word 'love' or, even worse, the deadly duo, 'in love'. And this admirable trend had continued after they were married: she had never mentioned 'relationships', asked what he was thinking about, or bothered him with trivialities like seeking reassurance about her appearance.

She had made only one demand: no other women, in public or private. 'If that's agreed, Georgie,' she had said on the evening she had proposed, 'you'll find you'll have a very good life. You'll find we'll rub along fine – neither of my other two husbands had any complaints – and you'll never again have to worry about cash. Ever. For the rest of your life.' George had studied her handsome determined face and stout, comfortable body, and had heard himself agreeing.

Perhaps, he thought with some surprise, he had just been tired at

36

the time and had recognized the need for a little luxury and pampering to cushion his middle age.

The Rolls slowed going round a bend in order not to frighten a skittish colt and its rider and George summoned up a reassuring smile for his guests. They smiled back, leaving him free to turn away again to watch the slow pass of the fields and leafless, dripping hedgerows.

His bride had been as good as her word. The twelve years of their marriage had been genial and, once he had put his mind to it, George found it easy to resist the blandishments of other women. Even his little indiscretions had been so slight that none had gone beyond a single night and had occurred only when Jool was thousands of miles away and could not possibly have found out. He had plenty at home to keep him occupied: his own bedroom and dressing-room con-nected with Jool's and he enjoyed his excursions into his wife's sumptuously appointed boudoir where she made love with him warmly but as efficiently and with as little fuss as she did everything else in her life.

George became lord of his manor. He learned to ride and spent his time loafing about the stables or land which came with the house, pottering in the village of Little Staunton three miles across the gentle countryside or taking short trips into London where Jool arranged several club memberships for him. The matter of money was amiably disposed of through the medium of the local bank manager who managed all Jool's petty cash accounts and who had standing instruc-tions that her husband was to be given whatever he asked for. George had never abused this happy state of affairs: but if he wanted or needed something – clothes, a Land-rover, a new horse or a replace-ment car – he bought it.

The chauffeur again slowed down, activating the remote control which opened the gates at the end of the driveway to the house. George, glancing behind him to see if the in-laws' limousine was following, saw instead the sleek yellow nose of his son's MGB. He frowned: he had always operated on the principle that if you did not think about it it would not happen but in this instance, his instinct told him he would have to stay alert if things were not to become bothersome; he was not so stupid as to think that Colin's reasons for coming out of the woodwork after the wedding – when Jool's wealth had been written up in the press – were spurred solely by filial devotion. 'Leave the gates open for the others,' he tapped the chauffeur on the shoulder, 'and don't bother to wait to close them after they've come through. I'm sure people won't want to stay all that long,' he added in hope. All he had ever wanted, George told himself plaintively as the Rolls led the procession of cars up the driveway of Inveraray Manor, was a quiet life.

It was just after noon when Francey found himself travelling in the village taxi through a pair of wrought-iron gates that gaped open onto a pristine driveway. The driver was uncommunicative, although Francey was conscious of the curious glance the man had thrown him as he was given the address of Inveraray Manor. Strung up as he was, however, he told himself the look was just the customary one of strangers who saw him for the first time.

Now, as the car's wheels hummed along the tarmac between two sets of white post-rail fences, he watched out for the first glimpse of the house and worried that the driver's interest in him had perhaps been aroused because he was not appropriately dressed for calling on the gentry. Never mind, he thought, remembering his mother's exhortation whenever she sensed in him an incipient inferiority complex about his size or anything else. 'Always remember, Francey, that one of your ancestors was a king.'

Expecting a turreted English mansion, or even a castle, he was taken aback when Inveraray Manor came into view. Spread in an easy crescent shape around an ornamental lake, the building was of redbrick, single-storey but with several irregularly pitched roofs, and half-timbered, in what Francey supposed was an effort to make it look older than it was – or maybe as a nod to its manorial status. For as far he could tell it was quite new.

Circumnavigating the lake, complete with fountain playing ten feet into the air and parapet decorated with concrete fol-de-rols, the taxi-driver halted his vehicle between two Mercedes limousines, uniformed drivers at their wheels. Two other cars which Francey, who had a passion for automobiles, recognized as a Bentley and a Rover, were parked nearby, while four others, a Rolls-Royce, a Landrover, a Jaguar and an MGB, a model he had always coveted, were parked in front of the doors of a quadruple garage separated from the far end of the main house by a neat but wintry rose garden. He had stumbled into a ritzy party.

As the driver leaned over the back rest of his seat to open the passenger door for him, Francey, his stomach fluttering, hesitated. He had little wish to embarrass his father, but he was conscious also that he had to start back for Ireland the following day. 'Thank you.' He paid the driver and got out.

Sensing curiosity from the two chauffeurs, Francey, pretending confidence but wishing he could hide the suitcase, went to the recessed front door, which was guarded by a sculpted pair of dwarf conifers, and rang the bell. He heard no jangling from within but assumed that in such a well-tended place – every sapling along the driveway had worn a wire skirt against predators – there was no possibility of a malfunctioning doorbell. He waited.

'May I help you, sir?' The man who opened the door was middle-aged and beautifully presented in a black suit, white shirt and black tie.

'I – I'd like to see Mr Gallaher,' Francey stammered.

The man's eyes flickered to the suitcase and Francey divined his thoughts. 'I'm not selling anything,' he said quickly. 'I'm genuinely here to see him.'

'Do you have an appointment, sir?'

'I'm afraid not.' Francey became conscious of the creases in his good suit, the rain-darkened shoulders.

'I'm not sure if Mr Gallaher is receiving callers at present, sir,' the man's features remained smooth, 'but if you would care to wait inside?' He stepped back and opened the door a little wider. Despite his spine-stiffening exercises of a few moments before, as Francey passed into the hall he was all too conscious of being outclassed.

'If you would follow me, sir.' The door clicked shut behind him and he was led through a pair of pillars into a small open lobby. 'Wait here, please.' His guide indicated a club chair. 'Whom shall I say is calling?'

'Sullivan,' Francey supplied, 'Mr Francis Sullivan.' The man inclined his head and moved away, his footfalls quiet as cat's paws on the marble floor.

Francey thought he detected the sound of voices, but so far away that he had no idea how many or of what sex; he did not sit down

39

but moved across to the wall of picture windows which ran along one side of the lobby to look over the ornamental lake and empty green paddocks.

He was too tense to notice much about his surroundings; nevertheless the overall impression was one of easeful space. The décor was muted with a preponderance of beiges, creams and buffs; a large abstract painting in shades of apricot and peach hung on one wall and, beside him, a graceful arrangement of lilies in a white china bowl cascaded over an onyx table bound with silver. Soft, rain-filled light filtered through skylights in the high roof. In an extraordinary admixture of styles, the roofbeams were exposed but painted in pale ivory to blend in with the general scheme.

'I'm sorry, sir.'

Francey wheeled. 'Yes?' He had not heard the emissary come back.

The man paused, then: 'I'm not sure if you're aware, sir, that Mr Gallaher has been recently bereaved.'

'No, I'm sorry to hear it.'

'The lady of the house, Mrs Dill Smith Gallaher, was buried less than an hour ago. Perhaps you saw the obituary in this morning's *Times* or *Telegraph*?'

Francey stared at him, then shook his head. He had never been one for reading newspapers, save for the sports pages of the *Cork Examiner*. 'When did she die?' he asked.

'The day before yesterday,' the other man replied. 'It was a quiet funeral, sir, perhaps this is why you noticed little stir in the village. She had left instructions that there should be no fuss. This is why she was buried so quickly. It was her wish.'

'I see . . .' Francey was floundering, unsure of what to say next. George's wife had apparently died just as he was enquiring about her in Fleet Street. And now he knew why the taxi-driver had cast such a curious look at him.

He realized that the functionary in front of him was still speaking. 'Mr Gallaher's apologies, sir,' the man said, 'but as I'm sure you will understand, he is not receiving outside visitors today. If you'd care to leave an address and telephone number?'

Francey had been so wound up about this visit that all his imaginative energies had been focused on the point where he and his father would come face to face. He had been prepared for not being

40

able to find George or for the possibility that George was dead, but once those barriers had proved surmountable, he had not catered for any other impediment.

'Sir?' The man in front of him was holding out a small pad of paper and a silver pen.

Francey made up his mind. Now that he had at last found George Gallaher he was not going to be balked. 'Did you give him my name?' he asked.

'I did, sir. But Mr Gallaher was quite emphatic.'

Francey noticed that there was no mention of him calling back at a more convenient time. He reminded himself of the long tiring journey by boat and train, the two nights already spent in a dingy hotel, the money the trip had cost him, down to the purchase of the suitcase, and which he could ill afford. He also thought of the contrast between this opulence – real art, servants, Rolls-Royces – and the careful money management his mother had always had to practise in the small farm cottage in Lahersheen. Not to speak of the dingy room he himself had to share in the Dublin digs. The timing was unfortunate but, he reminded himself, he was not intent on making trouble.

He straightened his back and shoulders which brought his height to a good twelve or thirteen inches above the stature of the valet or whatever he was. 'Please go back to Mr Gallaher,' he made sure he was not talking too quickly, 'tell him I'm very sorry for his trouble – I mean, I'm very sorry about his wife's death – I had no idea. But tell him I've come a long way and that as I'm not going to be in England long, I have to see him today. I understand perfectly that he's tied up at the moment. I don't mind waiting.' He sat in the club chair, crossed one knee over the other and pulled the James Stephens classic out of his pocket as if he intended to sit it out for as long as it took.

'Very well, sir.' The other man's expression did not flicker as he glided away.

When the butler came into the drawing-room to announce the new visitor, George had not at first recognized the name. Then, as the man waited for instructions, the word 'Sullivan' echoed like cannon-fire in the hollow of his brain. That Irish girl ... That Elizabeth Sullivan. That strange and beautiful place in the middle of nowhere where she lived with those gangs of children; the serious little

41

towhead who was his son. He even remembered that the son was called not Francis, as he had been announced, but Francey.

Then there was that young black-headed daughter, Kathleen she was called, who wanted to be an actress and who had followed him to Killarney for the summer season there. The solicitors' letters, which, like bloodhounds, had followed him for a while all over England, Scotland and Wales . . . Many times during that period George had regretted with all his heart the stupid tribal impulse which had led him to agree to visit that stupid farmhouse with his stupid ancestral train-set as a gift for his son. He must have been mad. 'What does this fellow look like?' A small flame of hope fluttered in his breast: perhaps the name was just coincidence.

The butler doused the flame. 'He's very tall, sir,' he said, 'with – ah – light-coloured hair.' The man's expression was so impassive his face might have been made of wax.

This visit meant trouble. Instinctively, George glanced across the room towards Colin. Under no circumstances should his two sons be allowed to bump into one another. He heard himself say he could not possibly receive any visitors today, that surely the butler could make the fellow understand?

But as he watched the man's back retreat across the drawing-room carpet, he thought perhaps he should be a little more careful, that by giving a little now, he could deflect a full-blown drama. 'Lewis,' he called just as the butler closed the door. Hurrying over, he issued instructions that Mr Sullivan should leave an address and telephone number where he could be contacted.

'Certainly, sir.' The butler melted away.

George, reassured that Lewis would handle things in his usual tactful manner, resolved to get in touch with the Irish lad as soon as things settled down. Maybe bring him over for a little visit. Give him a bit of money.

Taking advantage of his temporary separation from his guests he went to the sideboard and, under the pretext of pouring himself another snifter of Cognac, tried to think. Why now? If only Jool were still around, she'd know what to do.

Then it hit him. Of course! The boy must have read about Jool's death in the newspapers this morning.

Another one out of the woodwork.

Probably looking for money, too.

Well, it was one thing to be generous, it was quite another to give in to blackmail. George felt the glad onrush of self-righteousness. Drat the impertinence of the fellow! Could he not have waited at least until the poor old girl was cold in her grave?

By the time he rejoined the guests, grouped together on an arrangement of sofas at the far side of the room, George had convinced himself that he had been absolutely right to turn Francey Sullivan away from his door.

But within minutes the butler was again hovering in the doorway. 'Excuse me.' His nerves jumping with annoyance, George apologized to Jool's brother-in-law with whom he had been talking and again walked across the room. 'What is it now, Lewis?'

'I'm sorry, sir, but the young man is most insistent. He says he'll wait until you are free.'

'Did you outline the circumstances?' The traces of the Scottish burr which still laced George's accent always became more pronounced when he was upset.

'I did, sir.' While the butler stared at the middle button of his jacket, George could almost hear his own brain buzzing with the effort of thinking what he should do. He was just about to put his brandy balloon on a side table to give himself another moment when he felt a touch on his arm, 'Is it anything I can help with, Dad?' and found himself looking down into his son's eyes, shaded somewhere between light brown and pale green and reminding him as always of canal water. 'No, it's all right, thank you, Colin,' he said. 'I—'

'Not to worry, you have enough to do here with your guests. I'll go.' Before George, or the butler for that matter, could intervene, Colin had slipped through the doorway behind him.

George had had such a peaceful, Jool-run existence for the past twelve years that his reactions were rusty. Stunned, he watched through the open doorway as Colin Mannering clicked down the hallway but could think of nothing decisive to do or say which might avert or ameliorate the double horror of an unmediated encounter between his first and second sons.

He realized the butler was waiting for further instructions but his voice was sticking in his throat.

'Thank you, Lewis,' he managed to croak.

*

Within the club chair, Francey's body felt as confined as the figure in a child's jack-in-the-box. He shot to his feet as he heard the quick footsteps approaching. Those were not the butler's feet. Now that the moment was on him he wanted to run away as fast as he could. This had all been a mistake.

'May I help you?'

On seeing Francey, the eyes of the man who came into view widened and returned to normal so quickly that, when analysing and rerunning the meeting afterwards, Francey wondered if he had imagined it. His heart, which had threatened to strangle him, dropped a few inches towards its normal berth as he answered, 'I'm looking for Mr Gallaher.'

'And you are?' asked the man, whom Francey, accustomed to making snap judgements as to others' height, thought to be probably around six feet one. Slim, his complexion was sallow and his eyes were peculiarly colourless. Francey decided that this was another brush-off and became angry. 'Francis Sullivan,' he replied after a moment or two. 'And you?'

'I am Colin Mannering, Mr Gallaher's son.'

'Oh!' Francey was taken aback. He should have remembered: Hazel had warned him that he and Dessie were not George's only sons – and that for all she knew there could even be more than the three of them. He'd had the newcomer pegged as a secretary of some sort and it was only now that Francey saw the resemblance to George Gallaher around the mouth and chin. 'I'm terribly sorry about your mother,' he extended his hand in sympathy.

'Stepmother,' the newcomer corrected, 'thank you.' He accepted Francey's hand and shook it. Outside, the horn on one of the cars sounded, in such a truncated way that it was obviously by accident. A door thumped shut somewhere in the bowels of the house and, for a moment or two, Francey was at a loss as to what to say next. But when the other man did not seem inclined to speak, he repeated the phrase he had used with his first interlocutor, again deliberately slowing his speech. 'I've come a long way,' he said.

'It's simply not convenient now,' the other replied, 'I'm sure you can understand. If there is anything at all I can do—'

'I'm afraid not.' Francey was determined he was not going to be put off, 'I have plenty of time. I won't take up too much of your father's.'

'It was he asked me to come to talk to you,' Colin Mannering insisted but Francey was still not deterred.

'I'm sorry,' he replied stubbornly, 'I made it clear to the other man that this is personal.'

They stared at one another and it occurred to Francey that he was standing in front of his half-brother. Before he could register the implications, Colin Mannering spoke again. 'Maybe you could tell me what you want?'

Francey took it as an innuendo that he was here for some personal gain and flushed with anger. Mannering had obviously guessed his identity from his appearance – from the wedding photographs, Francey already knew his own resemblance to George Gallaher was not only around the eyes – but he was certainly not going to confirm it. His heartbeat was quite steady now. 'I'm not looking for anything,' he said, 'I just want to meet Mr Gallaher and I'm not leaving this house until I do.' But it was against all his upbringing to be impolite to strangers. 'I'm sorry about coming on such a sad occasion,' he added, softening his tone, 'but I had no way of knowing. And I'm leaving England tomorrow to go back to Ireland so I must see Mr Gallaher today.' All his nervousness gone, he stared deep into the ditchwater eyes below his. 'So I'd appreciate it, now, Colin, if you'd go and tell him that.'

'Whatever you like – I'll go and tell him,' Colin Mannering replied, smiling so openly now that Francey, caught off-guard by the suddenness of the transformation, felt the antipathy must have been imagined.

'Thanks,' he said uncertainly.

His half-brother inclined his head a little to one side and spread his hands – he had graceful, tapering fingers, Francey noticed – and said, man-to-man, 'But I must tell you, Francis, that my father is, as you would imagine, quite preoccupied.'

'No hurry.' Francey took back the initiative. He resettled himself in the uncomfortable chair and opened his book. 'I've all day.'

Prepared for a long wait, he stood up in sudden panic when, within minutes, he again heard footsteps approaching – more than one pair. He barely registered the return of Colin Mannering, however, as, a few seconds later, he and his father were facing one another.

For a few seconds of silence Francey felt the chips could fall in any direction. Although supremely nervous, he was determined not to make the first move. He seemed to win the contest because it was his father who moved forward, holding out his hand. 'I'd recognize the colour of that hair anywhere,' he said. 'How's your mother?'

Through his agitation, Francey, who had been expecting hostility, was surprised to see how defensive the other man seemed. Now that this moment had arrived, his own emotions staggered between extremes of jubilation and panic. He forced himself to smile and brushed at his strawberry blond thatch with his left hand while his right took George's. 'She's grand,' he said.

'That's good,' George broke the handshake and stepped back a little. His eyes slid away from Francey's and Francey stopped smiling. This man had breezed in and out of his own life and his mother's, leaving the two of them to fend for themselves. Not to speak of how he had behaved towards Kathleen and Dessie.

'Why'd you do it?' he burst out, not caring about the presence of a third party. 'Why'd you do it to her, to us?'

'I did write, you know —' George still would not meet his eyes.

'This is a surprise, I'm sure you know that, Francis,' Colin Mannering inserted himself into the moment; in Francey's ears his half-brother's voice sounded panicky. 'As far as I'm concerned,' Colin went on, 'you're very welcome, you've got to make allowances – we weren't expecting – I mean I didn't know I had a brother —'

'That makes two of us.' Francey kept watching his father.

'I wrote more than once,' George appealed, looking directly at him at last. 'Did your mother not tell you?'

'Leave my mother out of it. She doesn't know about this, about what I'm doing.' All of Francey's carefully rehearsed phrases had vanished from his memory and he was playing by ear. 'This is my own idea.'

'We all have a lot to talk about. Shall we go somewhere more comfortable?' Again it was Colin Mannering.

'I wouldn't doubt it's your own idea,' George replied, ignoring the intervention. 'I know your mother wouldn't send you on her errands.' Francey noticed he still spoke with a trace of a Scottish accent.

'Dad?' Colin raised his voice a little. Francey glanced in his direction: his half-brother was definitely agitated.

'What?' George acknowledged his eldest without looking at him.

46

'This isn't the place for this conversation,' Colin begged. 'Shouldn't we offer Francis some refreshment after his long journey?'

George's forehead creased with irritation. 'I believe my butler told you it was a very bad time.' He addressed Francey with something approaching haughtiness but Francey, whose senses were so alert they seemed to hum, recognized that it was he who had the upper hand.

'I'm very sorry about your loss,' he said, 'but I didn't know about it. I couldn't have —'

His father seemed to come to some decision. To Francey's astonishment, the frown on his handsome face was replaced by a grin. Wide, sunny and impossible to resist, it showed what Francey's mother had seen in this man. 'You're a credit to your mother, Francey,' he said. The transformation was so unexpected that Francey, bemused, took an involuntary step backwards.

George cocked his head to one side. 'Just look at the size of you! You're quite a specimen, aren't you?'

Francey, finding himself charmed, tightened the book he held in his left hand to help him to hang on a bit longer. 'We've got to talk,' he said.

'Of course,' George replied. 'I'm sorry we didn't get to know one another before now.'

'Then why didn't you get in touch with us? You knew where we were!' But he had never been able to sustain anger for any length of time and everyone present knew the heat had left the moment.

'It's not my place, of course, Dad,' Colin rushed in again, 'but would you like me to look after your other guests while you and Francey have your chat?'

'Oh, yes, the others.' George's forehead creased again, this time with doubt. 'I have a lot of guests in the drawing-room,' he appealed to Francey.

'I said I'd wait.' Francey swallowed. As the emotion drained away he was beginning to feel weak and jittery.

'You understand why it wouldn't be feasible to take you in there,' George went on, 'none of them know you. But I'm sure they couldn't be staying much longer.'

'Please . . .' Looking into the mirror of his father's violet eyes, gleaming with sincerity, Francey found himself reassuring him. 'I said I don't mind. If you like I can go away and come back later. It's just that today is my last day and that's why I insisted —'

'We understand perfectly, don't we, Dad?' Colin came so close that Francey moved back a further step or two. He felt he was taking part in an odd gavotte. 'Are you sure you don't mind, Francey?' The relief on George's face was clear.

'Of course not, take your time.' Francey meant it. His mission was under way and the hardest part was over.

Five minutes later, led there by the butler, he was seated in the palatial kitchen, a glass of beer and a plate of canapés in front of him, in the company of an efficient woman – a cook or a housekeeper – who was too busy to pay much attention to him. Two uniformed girls came and went through a swing door and, after the first time, paid as little attention to him as the cook.

Never one to pass up the opportunity to eat, Francey larruped into the canapés. They were beautifully presented in contrasting colours and flavours, some of which he recognized, but many, including the fishy taste of something which looked like blackberry jam, he did not. As he ate, he imagined himself relating this part of the adventure to Hazel. He heard her laugh as she envisaged him consigned to the bowels of the house with the hired help. Patience . . . he admonished himself, it's early days yet – you mustn't get touchy.

It was too soon to divide the maelstrom going on in his head into separate strands. Letters from Johanna, the sister to whom he was closest and who had gravitated from a normal job in a Chicago shoeshop to a hippie commune in Montana, were full of advice as to how he should find what she called his 'still centre of existence'. But at present, this still centre of existence, whatever it was, was proving elusive and instead, phrases such as 'the condemned man ate a hearty breakfast' continued to roll like marbles around the inside of his head.

He had finished the canapés and was drinking the remains of his second glass of beer when from the front of the house he heard the faint sound of starting car engines, how many he could not tell. From where he sat, looking out over the pruned skeletons in a garden of immaculate rose beds, he could see the garage and the undisturbed vehicles in front of it. The guests, or some of them, had to be the ones who were leaving.

The butler came back into the kitchen. 'Mr Gallaher's apologies for keeping you waiting so long,' he said, 'but if you'd care to come with me now?'

48

Francey thanked the cook for the impromptu meal and followed his guide out of the kitchen and into a long corridor which, studded with doors at regular intervals, seemed to curve from end to end of the house. Yet another uniformed maid – how many did this house support? – nodded at them in friendly fashion as they passed.

A polished mahogany door faced them at the end of the corridor. 'In here, sir,' the butler knocked discreetly, turned the handle and stood back.

Francey walked into an enormous room, the walls of which, except for the one containing the door he had just come through, seemed constructed entirely of glass. He got no time to form more than an initial impression of the décor – furniture in shades of apple green and pale blue on a creamy white carpet – because his father, who had been standing by a free-standing fireplace made from silvery metal, came forward immediately to greet him.

As he did so, however, Francey realized that, behind him, two other people were present. One was Colin Mannering, drink in hand. The other was a woman so beautiful that on the instant he saw her, Francey's heart rose into his throat.

Chapter Four

'You'll stay to lunch?'

Francey hardly heard his father's invitation. 'Th-thank you,' he stammered, trying to keep from staring at the exquisite creature who was sitting on the couch beside Colin Mannering.

She had waist-length, lustrous black hair and an oriental cast to her features, with high cheekbones, full mouth and dark, almond-shaped eyes. Her legs, what Francey could see of them, tapered to delicate ankles and feet; her plain black dress was cinched to a double handspan at the waist and in the rainy light which bathed the room, the pearls at her throat glistened like drops of milk. Every detail of the wedding photograph that had brought him here was etched on his brain: this could be the necklace worn twelve years ago by George's bride.

'You haven't met my wife, Fleur,' Colin Mannering said. 'Fleur, this is your new brother-in-law, Francis Sullivan.'

'Hello.' The woman's face was expressionless as she greeted him, her voice was husky. She did not seem surprised at finding herself with a new relative and Francey assumed she had been forewarned.

'H-how do you do?' he stammered, and to prevent his confusion from showing, turned away to smile at his father, uttering the first inanity to pop into his brain. 'This is a lovely house —'

'Yes, isn't it?' George went to a long sideboard on which were displayed bottles, decanters, glasses, ice buckets, swizzle sticks and cocktail embellishments, enough to stock the bar of a small hotel. 'Let me get you all a drink,' he boomed. 'I see you have one already, Colin. A sherry for you, m'dear?' And when Fleur nodded, he smiled at Francey. 'And what's your poison, son?'

'A beer please.' Behind him, Francey was aware of the woman's presence: it pulled at him like strings of spun glass.

'Here you are.' George gave Fleur the sherry then put the beer in

50

Francey's hands. 'Bottled, I'm afraid. We haven't risen to a tap yet but Jool says – ohhh! Sorry . . .' He looked nonplussed.

To fill the silence that descended on the room, Francey trawled for something appropriate to say. 'Was your wife ill for long?' was what came out.

'About a month,' Colin volunteered. 'Cancer of the pancreas – it was a shock to all of us, I can tell you, because she was a healthy woman. But she took it well. In fact, it was she who was comforting us . . .' He trailed off.

Francey thought it wise not to say any more. He sipped his drink and noticed that the flames in the free-standing fireplace seemed not to crackle but to emit a low, continuous hiss – the wood was not real. Second by second the renewed silence intensified until Colin again broke the impasse by turning to his wife: 'How's your drink, darling, all right?' The resonances of the endearment sounded to Francey as though his half-brother had struck a piano key that was out of tune.

'Very nice, thank you.' As she spoke Francey noticed her English was a little accented. He was having difficulty in schooling his expression so as not to show his susceptibility to her, so he gazed into the pale depths of his beer.

'Why don't you sit down?'

'Won't you join us?' George and Colin spoke simultaneously.

'Sorry.'

'Sorry.'

The second concurrence served to break the ice. 'Come on,' George took Francey's arm and led him towards where the other two were seated, 'enough of this. Lunch won't be long – apologies for incarcerating you in the kitchen like that but to be honest I don't know how I would have presented you to my American in-laws just at the moment!' He grinned and, indicating that Francey should join him, sat one end of a long curving couch which faced the Mannerings.

Feeling huge and clumsy in the luminous presence of the wife, Francey sat down. He was a little surprised that, contrary to his father's initial demeanour of being less than enamoured at his untimely arrival, George seemed now to have accepted his presence with equanimity.

'So here we are.' As if he had heard the unspoken thought, George glanced around the four of them as though initiating a lodge meeting.

'*The Bustle in a House*,' he intoned, '*The Morning after Death, Is solemnest of industries, Enacted upon Earth* – How's your Emily Dickinson, Francey?'

'I beg your pardon?' Unlike fiction, poetry, learned by rote in school, was not a subject which had fired Francey's imagination.

'Never mind.' George remained blithe. 'Well, well! You never know what's going to happen when you wake up in the morning, do you? "Hear the voice of the Bard! who Present, Past, and Future sees . . ." That's William Blake.' He addressed Francey in the manner of a kindly schoolmaster. Then his tone sharpened as he peered at them all from under his splendid eyebrows. 'Quite the little family, eh? Might as well get used to each other, I suppose.'

'What time is your flight tomorrow, Francis?' Colin glanced around with a look of unease, confirming Francey's growing impression that although his half-brother could attempt to be masterful when unchallenged, he folded at the first sign of discord or disapproval.

'Tsk tsk!' George's expression lifted and he clucked mock disapproval. 'Don't be so rude, Colin, we're just getting to know our new relative.' He turned to Francey. 'You'll stay awhile, of course?'

'I'm not sure,' Francey demurred. 'I'm not flying as it happens,' he explained to Colin. 'I'm taking the night-time mail boat from Holyhead.'

'Ahh – Holyhead!' George seized on the possibility of safe anecdotal passage across the psychological minefield which had spread itself in front of him. He slapped his knee. 'God be with the good old days of Holyhead. Did I ever tell you about my first trip to Ireland, Colin?' He launched into a long account of his maiden voyage across the Irish Sea with a touring repertory company.

In other circumstances, Francey would have been fascinated. But when his father was a few paragraphs into the story, he saw there was little required of him beyond passive attention and barely kept up with the narrative. Instead, he tried to read the people around him.

His memory had not played tricks on him: without doubt his father was attractive. George Gallaher's voice was deep, with the command and clarity of an organ. Listening and watching, Francey wondered at Hazel's dismissal of the man's talent; as far as he could tell, the rolling cadences, the expansive, expressive gestures, should be indicative of a powerful stage personality. George did not look sixty-five – the twelve-year-old newspaper cuttings had put him at fifty-three then – and his dark suit glided around his bulky but taut frame as though made for it.

Which it probably had been. George's son cast a covert glance at the corrugated lap of his own suit, the sleeves and legs of which had been let down to the end and fitted with false hems. Bought and worn with such pride in Dublin, it now looked cheap and stretched to ripping point. Francey also became conscious that the warmth of the room had released the fabric's damp reek.

He judged Colin Mannering to be in his early to mid thirties although with his unlined skin it was difficult to tell. Colin's neat head was cocked a little to one side as he listened to George's story and in Francey's opinion he smiled a little too readily at every high point of the anecdote: it was almost as though each reaction was on cue. But then, observing that the chuckles sometimes arrived a fraction of a second before they should have, he recanted. This was not the first time Colin had been the audience for this story. Francey admonished himself not to make too many premature judgements about anyone in this room, least of all his half-brother. He wondered how he would feel if, having thought his rich father was his alone, he had discovered a previously unknown pretender.

Did Colin Mannering know he had a second half-brother? Francey decided that on balance he did not: the initial shock – the widening of the eyes – Colin had displayed at their meeting in the lobby was proof enough that George Gallaher had not confided much about his colourful past.

Lest he betray the effect she was having on him, Francey dared not look at the fourth member of the company, who was sitting at an oblique angle to him. But once, as his father chuckled at something which struck him as particularly amusing and Colin laughed along, he risked a quick glance at Fleur Mannering.

It was obvious that she too had heard George's story before. Her eyes never left George's face as she sat decorously, her beautiful legs at a slight angle to her lap, one hand holding a sherry glass, the other curled around a small clutch bag. Although the lips were fuller, her half-smile reminded Francey of the print of the *Mona Lisa* which, along with Van Gogh's *Sunflowers* in an identical frame, hung to the left of the twinned photographs of Pope John XXIII and John F. Kennedy over the fireplace in the dining-room of his digs in Dublin.

But there the resemblance ended. In Francey's view of the beauty stakes, Fleur Mannering left da Vinci's model at the starting gate.

He realized his father was coming to the climax of his story and forced his attention away from her. 'And to make a long story short' – George's laughter rolled around the room – 'the ship was bucking about so much that the crutch kept sliding away from under the poor old bugger, remember he had only one leg, and I had to pick him up in my arms. But before I could get him to the rail, he spewed like a catherine wheel and everyone else was sliding around in it and holding on to each other . . .' His resounding laugh was infectious and, as Francey joined in, it occurred to him that except for George's confusion of tenses with regard to his wife, not once since he had come into this drawing-room had his father betrayed any emotion about his bereavement.

In fact, the tenor of the entire conversation puzzled him. At home in Ireland, funeral parties were long-lived and lavish, encompassing not only the bereaved family and in-laws of the deceased but all the friends and the people of the entire neighbourhood. And although the talk was eclectic and jocose, it arose out of the life and doings of the person whose existence was being commemorated, or at the very least skirted around them. The detachment displayed in this drawing-room, he thought, must be a manifestation of the famous English stiff upper lip.

Further rumination was cut short by the announcement of lunch.

On entering the dining-room, Francey stopped dead just inside the door. He felt he had walked off the world. To his left, the lake outside the window wall was now illuminated by concealed spotlights so that on this dull, rainy day, the fountain in the centre cast serene rainbows on to the lily pads on the surface, burnishing them as though they were tropical water-hyacinths.

But it was not the lake alone that cast the magical, almost mystical aura through this room. The furniture, appurtenances and décor, if not unique, were so far outside Francey's personal experience as to be surreal. The floor was tiled, but beneath several inches of translucent, floodlit lucite, its surface roughened. The ceiling sloped upwards, from a height of ten feet or so over the door, to eighteen or more at the opposite end of the room; living foliage tumbled from containers placed along a ledge just below its apex to become entangled with other plants snaking upwards from giant ceramic urns placed at intervals along the floor. Behind this jungle of riotous, entwined greenery, a wide and gentle waterfall babbled down the pale marble of the wall.

The dining table in the centre of the room was a slab of solid glass at least eighteen inches thick and lit from beneath to show its whorls, bubbles and natural imperfections; it was supported on four shining columns of what Francey assumed was steel, the seats of the pale ashwood chairs around it were upholstered in mottled, sand-coloured velvet, shades repeated in the underfloor tiles. Crystal and silver glittered in a matching ashwood sideboard, the doors and top of which were also made of glass, which, although thinner than that of the table top, was as solid as oak.

The most extraordinary feature of this extraordinary room, how-ever, was the aquarium, about thirty feet long and eight feet high, which had been built into the wall opposite the windows; full of darting, radiant fish and sumptuous weed, it, too, was lit to great effect. It seemed to end in a sort of undersea grotto and it was only after a few seconds that Francey saw that this was *trompe d'oeil*, painted on a door to the corridor outside.

Mesmerized, he felt weightless, as though floating through an underwater infinity of light and sound. Unsure of whether he liked the sensation or not, he realized his host was watching for his reaction. 'It's amazing!' he breathed.

'Nice, I agree.' George smiled with satisfaction as he sat at the head of the table. Francey took the seat to his left, Fleur was put opposite him, Colin beside her. 'This was Jool's favourite room,' George added, as he shook out his napkin.

'I'm sure it was.' Francey was still looking around him. 'It's like what you'd see in – in . . .' He was at a loss to identify an appropriate setting for this phenomenal manifestation of fantasy and wealth, and, having nothing with which to compare it, could not make up his mind whether it was the height of good taste or an excrescence of vulgarity.

'A lot of the ideas came from Fleur,' George smiled at her, 'and at the risk of being immodest, some of my own ideas were included, too. Jool engaged an interior designer, of course – several, as a matter of fact – but Fleur's the one with the inspiration. Isn't that right, my dear?'

Not a muscle in Fleur Mannering's face moved as she acknowledged the compliment. 'Thank you.'

'Do you live in Dublin, Francis?' It was Colin's turn to shake out his napkin as one of the uniformed girls Francey had seen earlier in the kitchen began to serve soup.

Fleur bent her head over her place setting as though accustomed to being publicly snubbed by her husband. It was not the first time Francey had noticed this and, on her behalf, he had difficulty in keeping his voice level. He had already decided that if she had had anything to do with its design, 'vulgar' was the last adjective to be applied to this room. 'Dublin?' He picked up his soup spoon so that he would not have to look at Colin. 'Yes, I do, for the present.'

'Oh?' Colin arrested his own spoon in mid-air. 'Are you thinking of moving?'

Francey, who had had no intention of moving anywhere, found himself saying, 'That remains to be seen!' then knew that the remark had arisen from spite. Sensing that Colin would be none too pleased to have a new half-brother living on his doorstep, he had wanted to get at him because of the way he had insulted Fleur. But knowing the reaction was juvenile, he repented. 'Ah no,' he glanced at Colin, appeasing him with a smile, 'I'm happy enough where I am.'

'And how's little Tommy, Fleur?' To his relief, George Gallaher, sitting back in his chair to facilitate the serving girl, diverted the conversation.

'He's very well,' Fleur replied. 'He's with his nanny today. I – we did not want to upset him with the funeral.' Her eyes remained downcast as they all started to eat and Francey was conscious of an insane desire to reach across the shining table to stroke her feathery eyelashes. He took his first mouthful of the reddish soup; like some of the canapés earlier, the flavour was unfamiliar: rich and sweet, it was reminiscent of the lobsters he used to bring home to his mother from the pots he and some of his friends set now and then from small boats in the Kenmare river.

For a while, the rush of the water and the muted ringing of spoons on china were the only sounds in the room as everyone concentrated on eating.

'Tommy is my grandson, Francey,' George explained then between mouthfuls.

'Yes,' Colin took up the running, 'he was Jool's pride and joy,' he chuckled, 'he's some kid. He's got a wonderful imagination. I must show you some of the stories he wrote for Jool while he was staying here. You wouldn't believe it, Francey. It wouldn't surprise me if he became a writer when he grows up – I'll show you some photographs later. Or, better still, we have stacks of home movies.

'I know!' His spoon suspended above his plate, Colin beamed at his father. 'If you don't mind, Dad, I'll set up the screen and if Francey's not going until tomorrow night, why don't we all stay here tonight and we can watch them together? And that way we can get to know one another too.'

'Oh . . .' George's expression became unsure.

To Francey, his father's dubiousness about this arrangement was all too transparent and although he would dearly have loved to spend a night getting to know not only George Gallaher – with whom he had a great deal to discuss – but Fleur Mannering, he demurred. 'I'd better be getting back—' he began but, to his surprise, his father immediately overrode him.

'Good idea,' George said, his voice hearty now.

'But what about Tommy?' Francey's father then addressed Colin and Fleur. 'Don't you two have to get back to London?'

Colin hastened to assure him that Tommy would be happy enough with his nanny.

'Good.' George grinned widely as though his first reaction had never happened. 'It's all settled then, Francey!'

'Are you sure it wouldn't be too much trouble?'

'Of course not!' Although Fleur said nothing, the chorus of the other two was solid and Francey was too new in this company to discern what lurked under the surface of the relationships. There were so many levels of intercourse here that he was at sea. He had no wish to become a buffer or to enter areas to which he did not have an emotional map. 'I'll stay,' he said. 'That's if you're absolutely sure it's not too inconvenient.'

'Terrific.' George signalled that the soup plates should be taken away.

The remainder of the meal, while crackling with undercurrents in Francey's overheated perception, passed without outward incident. The food, thick slices of roast beef with all the trimmings, was delicious, and George and Colin both exerted themselves to be charming; Colin, he saw, could be acerbically witty when he tried.

Even Fleur seemed to relax a little, contributing little but smiling a lot. She seemed curiously passive, almost doll-like, yet to Francey this only increased her aura of mystery and allure.

Finding it impossible to behave as it seemed he should – as if this were an ordinary social lunch at which he was an unfamiliar yet honoured guest – Francey longed to escape to solitude. He listened as George described the attractions of the house, its eleven bathrooms, its circulating air system which kept it warm in winter and cool in summer so there was no need to open windows, how this cut down on the task of cleaning . . .

Both George and Colin then plied him with questions about Ireland and about Dublin and even about his job, treating the profession of counter clerk in a builders' supply store as a fascinating occupation; they did not notice his lack of enthusiasm for two-by-fours and masonry nails and, between them, filled most of the conversational gaps. In reply to his polite reciprocal questioning, Colin revealed that his own business was 'import-export', a profession Francey knew nothing about and which Colin, seemingly, cared little to describe.

To Francey's relief, no one wanted Cognac or liqueurs after the meal and he was glad to accept his father's suggestion that, after his tiring journey, he should lie down for a while in one of the guest bedrooms.

The room to which he was shown, bigger than the entire ground floor of the house in Lahersheen, was just as heavy with central heating as the rest of the house but welcoming. Whatever about her exuberant taste, Francey thought, George's wife had certainly had a way with lights: this room too owed much to Edison. His mother would have died had she seen the wattage of electricity being consumed by the dozen table lamps and uplighters highlighting the roofbeams which, Francey now realized, were exposed all over the house. He also noticed that the bedside table on each side of the bed supported not only its inevitable lamp but a telephone and wondered if two were necessary in case the guest could not roll from one side of the vast mattress to the other in time to catch an incoming call. His suitcase, resting in the centre of the enormous, white-carpeted floor space, looked poor and inadequate and in the face of all this order, Francey was glad no one could see his higgledy-piggledy packing methods, the squashed paper bag full of his laundry.

The butler informed him that dinner would be at eight o'clock and withdrew.

Francey took off his jacket, brushed it with his hands and smoothed the shoulders over the back of a small curved chair by a writing desk. Afraid of marking the carpet, he took off his shoes as well and then, after a failed effort to open the three floor-to-ceiling windows which were sealed, he crossed to the bathroom. This was territory unglimpsed except in the pages of magazines in the dentist's waiting room. Such was the grandeur and shining cleanliness of its mirrors, marble surfaces and tiles, of the gold taps which gleamed in the washbasin and in the bath sunk into the floor, that Francey wondered if he would have the nerve to use it.

The flow of adrenalin that had sustained him for the past few hours had ebbed, and fatigue sapped his arms and legs. He went back into the main bedroom and stood by the bed, wide enough to accommodate his entire family, piled high with pillows and covered with a tailored counterpane the colour of buttercups. Loosening his tie and his belt, he stretched out on it, discovering to his surprise and pleasure that it could accommodate his length with inches to spare. For the next few minutes, he attempted to identify the thoughts and emotions which revolved like carousel horses in his head, but on top of the full meal he had just eaten, the combination of tiredness, warmth and insulated silence proved overwhelming and soon he dozed off.

Barely half an hour later, covered in sweat, he woke feeling uneasy and disoriented. Gradually, as he saw the tangled pillows around him on the yellow bed and recognized the contours of the room, he remembered where he was. Instantly, the image of Fleur Mannering's beautiful face materialized between his eyes and the roofbeams above his head.

Before he could fall asleep again, Francey sprang off the bed and padded towards the bathroom, taking off his watch as he went. It was four o'clock. He undressed and ascertained how to turn on the shower – familiar from American movies – and stepped into its hot, healing benediction. With hands braced on either side of the shower head he stooped under the powerful jets of water, letting them wash over the back of his head and neck. What was he going to do?

His deepest instincts pushed him to run fast, to get out of here as quickly as possible. And yet, as he raised his face to the warm flood, he dwelt on the hours and hours he had spent as a child playing with his clockwork train-set while dreaming it would magically grow big and transport him to wherever his father was. He recalled the occasions when, confined to his room for some childish misdemeanour, he had been angry with his mother or his stepfather, and had imagined his real father striding over the brow of Knockameala to rescue him. He had wanted this meeting for too long now not to follow through. And now that he had at last met George, his brain bubbled with questions, many of them accusatory and beginning with the word 'why'. He would have to stay, to get the full story from George's side of the fence.

After five minutes or so, he felt calmer.

He turned off the shower and stepped into the silence of the bathroom. But as he towelled his hair, several images of his oversized self mocked him – *Oh, yes? Who do you think you're fooling?* – from all around the bathroom. Although he had experienced crushes before, and although from his incessant reading he knew well the manifestations of a *coup de foudre*, Francey had never known what it was to be bowled over by a woman. Compared to this boiling, thunderous feeling of shock and excitement, all his previous attractions to women seemed as hollow as blown eggshells.

He was reluctant to face it, but it was not only George now, it was Fleur too.

And yet how could such an exquisite creature look twice at someone like him – even if she was not married? The incontrovertible fact was that, forbidden or not, he wanted her so much that mere mouthing of her name raised goose-bumps on his arms. He dried himself harder, scrubbing at his skin as though to slough off the shame and confusion of his fascination with someone else's wife. When his skin was red and tingling and he could no longer use the towel as flagellant, he discarded it in a basket he assumed was for the purpose and went back into the bedroom. The beginnings of a headache throbbed somewhere at the back of his neck and his sinuses were clogged by the warmth of the suite. He had to get some fresh air.

From the jumble in the suitcase, he took a pair of slacks, a fresh shirt and a new Aran jumper knitted for him by his mother's friend, Tilly Harrington. But as he pulled the latter over his head, the smell of oiled wool and turf fires brought him back to Lahersheen and he longed for his mother and home.

Complex though the array of blood and marriage relationships was within the four walls of the small farmhouse, it was an arena he knew. Francey felt now it would be a long time before he could begin to understand the differences between his own culture and that prevailing in Inveraray Manor or even in England. Hazel had been right, he thought, as he laced on his shoes. Sleeping dogs were perhaps better left to lie.

He let himself out of the bedroom, making as little noise as possible. Since the doors to all rooms seemed to open on to the central corridor, it was easy to find his way back to the kitchen from which he knew that a door led into a small greenhouse and that this, in turn, led into the open. On the way he met no one and when he got into the kitchen, found that although several machines hummed and swished, it was empty. And elderly man working at a potting bench in the greenhouse raised his head and saluted him as he passed through. Francey returned the greeting as at last he got out into the air.

Although the ground was still damp, at least the rain had stopped and a few ragged patches of watery blue showed through the shifting clouds. Francey welcomed the freshness but shivered at his own stupidity: he had thought that the climate in England would be warmer and drier than that of Ireland and had not brought a coat. Warm though the jumper was, its loose weave admitted the stabbing wind.

He blew on his hands and paused a little to take his bearings. The back of the house was as well kept as the front; clean gravelled pathways traversed the lawns and from where he stood, he could see vegetable gardens and a children's playground containing a swing set, miniature carousel and a large square frame which stood horizontally about three feet off the ground and on which was strung what seemed to be a flexible piece of fabric or even rubber. He wondered if it could be some sort of American device to facilitate sunbathing.

What was obviously a stable block, set round a quadrangle and entered through gates under an archway, stood a little to his right. Seeing some activity in the yard, Francey hesitated but then curiosity got the better of him. For one brief glorious period during his childhood his family had owned a beautiful black gelding named Lightning to which, at the age of six, Francey had become passionately attached. But the accident that had claimed the life of his eldest half-sister had also killed the horse, which she had been driving at the time and, much to Francey's disappointment, their mother had never been able to bring herself to acquire another.

When he saw the two animals in the stableyard as he approached, he gasped in amazement. These horses were the biggest he had ever seen; compared with them, Lightning, even from the distance of his childhood, was only the size of a foal. Each of the pair being groomed by two stable-hands was a black with a blazed face and four white socks, its hooves concealed by skeins of long creamy hair. Both pricked their ears with interest at his arrival.

'Afternoon, sir!' One of the grooms straightened when he got as far as the gates.

'May I come in?' When the groom nodded, Francey let himself in, latching the gates behind him. 'They're magnificent,' he indicated the horses, whose heads towered over him, 'obviously a matched pair?'

'That are that,' the groom replied, stooping again to a foreleg.

'Are they a particular breed?'

'Shires,' said the man. 'This here's Goliath and that's Samson.' He indicated the second of the pair. 'There's not many of 'em left now, a few brewery teams, a few in America. There's a lot of 'em was slaughtered hereabouts in the last few years and the Squire's the only one keepin' 'em in this part of the country but now I dunno . . . We's just doin' our job, keepin' 'em in trim like . . .' He trailed off, applying himself energetically to the untangling of the silky hair around the horse's massive foot.

'May I see the others?' Francey patted Goliath's shining neck and looked beyond him towards where he could see several more heads looking in his direction over the half-doors of the stalls.

'Go ahead,' the groom invited, 'but watch Amazon. She's inclined to take a nip now and again.'

The two rows of stalls were located opposite one another at each side of the yard, attached at right angles to what had to be an administration block. Many were empty but eight sported an engraved brass plaque beside their doors. As well as Samson and

Goliath the yard played host to Trojan, Ulysses, John, Richard, Jumbo and Amazon. Francey gave the mare a wide berth but patted and tickled all the others. They blew in appreciation and tossed their wonderful heads; Trojan extended his neck and nuzzled Francey's breast pocket. 'He's partial to chocolate,' the second groom called, 'but he's on a diet.'

'How big are they?' Francey stood back to admire them *en masse*.

'Varies,' the man replied. 'Trojan there's nineteen one – he's a big 'un, one of the biggest in the world, I reckon. He weighs well over the ton and ten stone mark. The mare's the smallest in the yard – she's just over seventeen two. She's in foal for next May. Fancy a little Shire to take home to Ireland, sir?'

'I'll see.' Francey grinned. News travelled fast.

'We got an Irishman here,' the first groom interjected, 'head lad, Mick O'Dowd. He's on a day off today, though.'

'I see. Well, thanks for letting me look around. Good luck with the horses,' Francey called as he let himself out of the yard.

'Yes, well, if there's any left. It's Mr Gallaher's decision, they're his animals.' The first groom wiped his forehead with the back of his forearm. 'Thought we might as well prettify 'em anyway.'

Francey felt better: the calm, stolid strength of the animals had put things in perspective. In a hollow to his left, about a quarter of a mile away, he saw a small wood and walked towards it. Once on its outskirts, he found that the little playground was not the only evidence of a child's influence. In a cultivated tableau setting of dwarf trees and shrubs at the entrance, a group of Disney characters, Bambi, Pluto, Mickey and Minnie Mouse, were playing with their friends the woodland creatures. Rabbits, squirrels, hedgehogs and moles gambolled in lifelike poses; exquisitely coloured birds perched above their heads or swung on wires between them. Beyond the tableau, a little windmill rotated its blades over a miniature waterwheel; the brook powering it had been dammed at one point so it spread into a shallow pond, complete with stepping stones and wooden bridge and nearby, the plaster figures of what Francey presumed to be Jack and Jill, stood holding hands in front of a wishing well.

Then, through an archway of evergreen trees to his right Francey spotted the curve of a narrow path. This path, however, was not made of gravel: it had been constructed of brick and painted bright

63

yellow, and where it began, half-hidden behind the bole of one of the trees, stood a bright red signpost on which was written the single word *OZ*.

This could not be resisted. Enchanted, Francey stooped through the archway and set out, like Dorothy, to follow the yellow brick road.

Although on either side of the little pathway there was evidence of continual clearance work, by contrast to the rest of the land around Inveraray Manor nature had been left undisturbed within the precincts of this old forest. Francey walked slowly, savouring every step of the road as it twisted and turned back on itself like a snake. He watched the play of intermittent sunlight as it filtered down through the latticework canopy of bare branches above his head, took deep lungfuls of the pungent air and rediscovered as he had in Dublin's Phoenix Park that even in winter forests play their own music.

Every so often, through the trees, he caught glimpses of red-spotted Disney toadstools; here, a startled plaster doe looked up from her grazing, there, an owl gazed across at him from a branch. His company multiplied: the Tin Man, gleaming with polish, beamed at him across the top of a five-barred gate which guarded nothing, the Scarecrow drooped away from him over a small patch of what looked like turnip tops, the Cowardly Lion hid from him behind a bush which was far too inadequate for concealment. Around his feet, Munchkin bakers, seamstresses, cobblers, candlemakers, mothers and naughty children, even a dog-catcher tugging a sad little mongrel on a lead, went about their business.

Whoever had laid out this fairyland had had a child's heart and unlimited money. On the evidence of the room with the glass table, it had to have been George Gallaher's wife.

The yellow brick road ended not at the Wizard's castle, but at an enormous treetrunk, fallen – or felled – so long ago it was covered in lichen, ivy and moss, its base buried in mulch so thick it was impossible to determine where the wood ended and the earth began. Several strong branches rose vertically from it at one end and nestled into them was a little wooden treehouse.

In the treehouse sat Fleur Mannering.

Francey had been so taken with the journey and its distractions that he did not see her until he was about four feet away.

64

'Oh! Sorry – I didn't notice . . .'

'That's all right.'

Notwithstanding the racket in his heart, once again Francey noticed Fleur's capacity for lack of surprise. 'I come here quite often,' she said. 'Tommy's grandmother had the trail laid out for him as a surprise for his seventh birthday.'

'I see. How old is he now?' Francey, who was having to stoop under some of the overhanging branches, was supremely conscious of his damnable height.

'He's nearly eleven. He'll miss his grandmother.'

'Of course.'

'Did you really like the dining-room?' Fleur stepped out of the treehouse. She was wearing a full-skirted astrakhan coat with a wide shawl collar of fox fur and, with gloved hands holding this around the lower part of her face, gazed at him with an expression of impish enquiry.

'Oh, yes,' Francey said uncertainly, 'it's wonderful.' Then feeling this was not what she wanted to hear, amended it. 'At least I think it is.'

She smiled at this. 'Jool – Tommy's grandmother – had some unusual ideas. So does George. I managed to restrain some of them.'

'Like what?' They had begun to walk deeper into the wood, beyond the end of the yellow brick road. The mossy undergrowth silenced the sound of their passing.

'For one thing,' Fleur continued to smile, 'George wanted the table to be the aquarium so the fish could be seen swimming below the knives and forks when you were eating. Jool thought this was a wonderful idea. She thought this, too, would be nice for Tommy. He is deaf, you see, and she wanted to fill the house with delights for his other senses.'

To Francey's thrilled ears the archaic phrasing sounded wonder-fully exotic. Then he was ashamed of his lack of compassion. 'I'm sorry,' he said simply. 'Has he been deaf since birth?'

'Yes.' Fleur indicated an archway created through the pruned but intertwined branches of two birch trees. 'Shall we go this way?' Her matter-of-fact answer and change of subject shook Francey as he followed her, having to stoop through the branches. 'You should see his room here,' Fleur continued over her shoulder. 'As well as being

65

colourful, everything in it which doesn't move is either furry, soft, or convertible to something else. I do so love your sweater,' she added. 'It is Irish?'

'Yes. A friend knitted it for me, one of my mother's friends,' he corrected himself in case she would think he had a girlfriend. 'She sounds – sounded – lovely, my father's wife, I mean . . .' He held back a trailing branch so it would not snag Fleur's hair, which was caught beneath her collar except for one thick strand looped through the paler fur. It took all his self-control not to take it between his fingers.

With a small inclination of her head, Fleur acknowledged his gallantry. 'She was a magnificent person. Tommy will miss her, so shall I.'

They walked on in silence. Except for the narrow trail on which they found themselves, this part of the wood had been left untouched and although he had to duck frequently, Francey did not know whether he wanted them to walk like this for the rest of his life or get back to the house and safety as quickly as possible. Of necessity they had to walk quite close together and to pick her up would be so simple. All he had to do was to extend his right arm; it would take less than a quarter of a second. Like the jerky action of some of the ancient films he had watched in the dance hall in Eyeries, the nearest village to Lahersheen, he could see himself picking her up, putting her down, picking her up, putting her down; he knew how light she would be, the scent of her skin . . .

It was a relief when, arriving at a narrow part of the trail, he was forced to walk behind her and, by pretending to examine the berries on a holly bush, allowed her to get some yards ahead of him. To inject some sense of reality into himself, he scrunched the thorny stems of the shrub between his hands, scrawbing the skin so it hurt.

He was sucking his index finger as he caught up with her when they came out into a little clearing. Here, again, was evidence of Jool's love for her step-grandson: a child-sized maze, constructed from fence posts and chicken-wire through which were trained thick walls of evergreen ivy. 'This was for Tommy, too?' Francey felt sure Fleur must hear the effort he was putting into making his voice sound commonplace.

'Yes.' She stopped and tucked one of the leaves in among its fellows. 'I don't know what I'm going to do now.'

It was so unexpected that Francey was caught off-guard. 'Time will heal —'

He began the time-honoured cliché of condolence but she interrupted, 'No, I'm afraid not.' She looked away over the top of the maze towards another bright signpost which pointed the way back towards *OZ*. 'I'm sorry you arrived at such a time,' she said. Francey was convinced she had been about to say something else but had thought better of it.

'I'm sorry too,' he replied, 'but I didn't know. Perhaps I shouldn't have hung around but I've been wanting to meet my father for a long time.'

'Of course.' She hesitated. 'You really didn't know?'

It hit Francey that she, probably like all of them, thought he had turned up at this time looking for money. He had already started to revise his opinion about her passivity. 'I swear it,' he said. It had become extremely important that she believed him. 'I couldn't have known —'

'The newspapers, surely?'

'It would not be in the Irish papers, definitely not. It was only in the last few weeks I found out my father was married to the American lady. And it was because —' he stopped. He knew why he was unwilling to mention Hazel Slye: again he did not want to give Fleur Mannering the impression that there might be a woman – any woman – in his life. 'It's a long story,' he said, 'but you've got to believe me. I didn't know even where my father was until I saw his twelve-year-old wedding photographs in an old newspaper. An English newspaper.'

'I see.' Fleur considered. She smiled at him then. 'Your father is a most unusual man.'

'So I see. He wasn't very happy to see me.'

'Perhaps.'

If Fleur was of average sensibilities she would have reassured him, Francey thought, but he knew now that she was far from average in any sphere and was not surprised at her refusal to follow social niceties. 'I suppose I don't blame him.' He looked away into the heart of the little maze. 'I did arrive without warning, after all. Maybe I should have telephoned in advance.'

'Perhaps.' Fleur pulled the collar of her coat so high it concealed most of her face.

'I think I like him, though,' Francey confided, 'and I've a lot I want to ask him.'

'Everyone likes George.' Briefly Fleur glanced at him. 'Perhaps we should be getting back to civilization. No doubt they will be wondering where we have to got to.' Leaving the maze, she walked towards the signpost.

'Do you mind my asking where you're from?' Francey blurted as they entered another little trail.

'I was born in Bangkok. I'm half Thai.' Fleur's tone warned him not to ask further then she softened somewhat. 'My father was French, that is why my mother called me Fleur. I never knew him, of course, so you and I have something in common, at least until now.' She walked on, giving Francey no opportunity to reply to this revelation.

They came to a footbridge fashioned from logs lashed together over a shallow stream. The floor of the bridge was slick and damp and Francey insisted on going first, taking her hand to help her across. Although she accepted the help, her gloved fingers warm against the scratches on his palm, he saw she was as poised as a ballet dancer and had no need of it.

Within a minute or so they were back at the treehouse and she went a little ahead of him as they walked back towards the manor. Just as they emerged from the wood Francey felt that if he did not say or do something significant right now she would move for ever out of his reach: 'Mrs Mannering – Fleur!'

She turned round in surprise. 'Yes?'

The call had been intuitive and faced with her enquiring expression, words failed Francey. He forced himself to say something – anything. 'N-Nothing . . .' he said. 'I mean,' to recover, he mouthed the first question that entered his head, 'will I be seeing you at dinner?'

'Of course.' They were standing close together in a patch of weak sunlight, so close that he could smell the scent of apples from her hair. He thought he saw a gleam of amusement in her eyes but the trace vanished as quickly as it had appeared and he could not be sure.

Then Francey heard himself compound the idiocy of the dinner question by saying something about seeing her there.

Fleur put a hand on his arm. 'Shall we go, then?'

As they moved off, he did not care at all if she had seen what he was feeling, whether or not she despised him for it. So be it, he thought, watching the way her hair gleamed blue-black in the chequer-board light patterns through the trees.

He had learned one thing about Fleur Mannering, however: at first sight she may have appeared to be somehow in thrall to her weak-minded husband but Francey would have bet his last ten pay packets that this was not the case. Fleur was her own woman. The thought fuelled his guilty excitement.

Such was the impact of the telephone call George Gallaher had just received that he did not replace the receiver but sat staring at it as though the Bakelite of which it was made contained something astonishing.

He was seated at the desk in his study, another of Jool's fantasy rooms, which she had built and urged him to furnish to his own taste more out of fondness for him than practicality. Because George's business acumen – or even interest – was virtually non-existent, the room had been outfitted not with any real purpose in mind, but with the aid of his actor's imagination as to how a rich man attended to business. Leathery and gentry-squirish, the surfaces on its solid furniture gleamed from non-use as though they were still new. Jool had had the grace never to ask George what he did when he retired to this room but colluded with the notion that he used it as his bookish retreat from the world. A casual perusal of the glass-fronted bookcases, however, would have disclosed several sets of identical titles. George's books had been purchased by the yard from a London bookshop.

Carefully, as if it were as delicate as a piece of bone china, George now placed the receiver into its black cradle, the click loud in the double-glazed hush. The call had been from Jool's solicitor who had telephoned, he said, to prepare George for the surprising nature of Jool Dill Smith Gallaher's will. George had questioned him, of course, but the solicitor would not reveal anything, merely asked that everyone in the family be present.

Including the newest member, Francey Sullivan.

George stood up from the immaculate desk and went to the window, looking out over the lawn. Hands behind his back, he rocked forwards and backwards on the balls of his feet and reflected that perhaps life was at last about to catch him out. First Colin, now Francey. And the dratted legal eagle had mentioned the third son as well, the progeny of that fling in Killarney so long ago; the way things were going, he would not be surprised if this kid, too, turned up on the doorstep.

George made a silent and rueful hats-off gesture to his deceased wife who had evidently known far more about him than she had ever indicated. What a classy lady, he thought; most women could never have kept such ammunition to themselves. George knew his Jool well enough to know she would not disinherit him but the solicitor, while not saying it in so many words, was preparing him for having to share the loot. He did not worry too much about this – there was plenty to go around after all – no, what he did worry about was that he might have to become familial. He wouldn't put it past Jool, whose main regret in life was that she had been unable to have children of her own, to insist that he take belated responsibility for his offspring. Fat chance, he thought. They were all grown up now, anyway. And at the age of sixty-five, he himself was not exactly in the first flush of energy . . .

His stream of thought was interrupted by his catching sight of movement at the far side of the crescent behind the lake. 'Well, well, well!' He whistled the words through his teeth. Francey and Fleur . . . How interesting.

George smiled in admiration at his new son's speed. Maybe the chap was not such a country hick as he appeared on first meeting. He watched as the two figures stopped just outside the perimeter of the wood. Too far away to see if they were touching, he saw they were definitely standing very close together. On the surface, it seemed they had already become as thick as thieves.

Dinner was preceded by an uncomfortable little cocktail session in the drawing-room. Francey knew it was not the time to air his questions and, in any event, George had sunk into introspection, sipping his whisky without making much effort at conversation, leaving it to stumble along amongst the other three. Not yet having a reliable barometer as to the complexities of his father's personality, Francey felt intuitively that he was being watched with unusual keenness but told himself that, under the circumstances, this was only natural.

Fleur and her husband again sat side by side on one of the sofas but within five minutes of their arrival in the room, Francey's impression of something askew in their relationship was reinforced. Colin dominated the talk, superficial though it was, and his wife's subdued demeanour bore little relation to the behaviour of the gentle yet self-possessed young woman Francey had met in the woods earlier in the afternoon. Fleur Mannering was not herself in the presence of her husband and behaved as though he had some hold over her.

It was a relief when dinner was announced.

The chandelier suspended over the glass dining table had been dimmed, allowing interplay from the décor lighting both inside and outside. As he went into the room, Francey felt once again that he was entering a sort of undersea grotto. All four diners made for the same places they had occupied at lunch: it was one of the phenomena that had always fascinated Francey, how people sought repetition and familiarity. Even in his hardware shop in Dublin, tradesmen and customers on a repeat visit tried to go to the same salesman and always endeavoured to stand near the place at which they had been served before. 'May I ask what soup this is?' he asked after five minutes or so, more to break the unnerving conversational hiatus than out of interest. While he liked it, the soup, pale and creamy, was redolent of something he had never tasted or smelt before.

'It's garlic soup.' George did not look up.

'I see.' Francey, who since his arrival into the dining-room had not once dared to look directly at Fleur Mannering, could not understand why he now felt so calm. It was as though he were a spectator at this table, waiting for the other players to make their moves. 'It's delicious,' he said, taking a half spoonful and swallowing it as silently as he could.

'Did you enjoy your walk in the wood this afternoon?' George suddenly glanced up from his plate.

Involuntarily, Francey looked towards Fleur, whose eyes widened – with alarm? with warning? – before returning to passivity. 'It was very interesting,' he replied. He turned from George to Colin, whose face showed nothing, and then back again to his father. 'It's – it's like

71

fairyland,' he stammered. 'Your wife was a woman of great imagination.'

George smiled. 'She certainly was that,' he agreed, placing his spoon beside his soup plate which was still half full. He gazed around the table. 'And she's not finished with us yet.'

'What?' Colin suspended his eating.

'You'll hear on Monday,' George answered. 'I'm as much in the dark as you are at present but I had a telephone call late this afternoon from Jool's solicitor.'

'Yes?' Colin paused in the act of spooning soup.

'We'll all just have to wait.' George smiled around at them all. 'You too, Francey,' he added, turning towards his second son. 'Apparently,' George announced, 'you're in the will.'

'I couldn't be!' Francey, still reeling from the revelation that George had seen him with Fleur, was doubly shocked.

'It's true.' George, his eyebrows twitching with amusement or chagrin – Francey could not tell – looked around the table. 'My Jool did her homework, it seems. When I told the solicitor chappie you'd turned up, he seemed not at all surprised. Said it would save a bit of trouble. He said you should be there too, my dear,' he addressed Fleur.

'Of course.' Fleur continued to eat. Of all of them at the table, she was the only one unaffected by George's startling news – or by what was going on in the sub-stratum.

'But I have to get home. My job—' Francey could not take in the news about the will.

'You can telephone tomorrow morning, I'm sure your boss will understand.'

Francey glanced at Fleur, who was just finishing her soup, and then at Colin whose spoon lay forgotten. His half-brother's mouth was hanging open.

George cranked up his smile to its full capacity. 'Well, now,' he said to the company in general, 'what a complicated little group we are . . .'

Chapter Five

'*Dear George, I have left a private letter to you in the safety deposit box in the bank in Little Staunton.*'

As he read from four thick sheets of writing paper covered in Julia Dill Smith Gallaher's resolute hand, the solicitor might have been reciting a grocery list.

'And in that, George [he continued], *I tell you what it meant to me to have you as my husband in the Fall of my years. But I want this present letter read aloud in connection with my will. It's not that I want to air our private life, George, it's that I want no ambiguity or anyone putting his or her own interpretation on what they think I meant. I want to let you in on my thought processes and why I've set out my will the way I have. (By the way, this letter is being written* after *the will, which was drawn up and witnessed over a full day's consultation in my solicitor's office. And as you know, Mr Solomons is a well-respected man from a firm which has served me well both personally and in business here and back in the States.)*'

The solicitor, who was seated at the head of the glass dining table, took a mouthful of water from the crystal goblet in front of him. As he did so, he kept his eyes averted from the other end of the table and his small tense audience. All chairs were angled towards the top and, as a result, Francey, who felt he was an interloper, could not see any of the other faces. He studied the whorls and thick spirals under the polished surface of the glass. For the rest of his life, he thought, this glass table would have momentous significance for him.

'*I've thought a lot about what I mean* [the solicitor replaced the goblet and resumed the reading], *and the man, or his deputy, who will be reading this to you, can confirm that I'm not a babbling old fool but that I've considered this very carefully.*

'As you well know, George, one of the privileges of being wealthy is freedom to spend the damned money. But there is responsibility which goes with this privilege. And believe it or not it's quite a problem to know what to do with it when your time here is over. The last thing I'd want is for squabbles to break out among those left behind. I've seen it amongst some of my contemporaries back home and it's a horrible sight. And, of course, the lawyers take all in the end.

'So I got to thinking about it when the doc gave me the news that I should get my affairs in order, as they so charmingly put it on this side of the Atlantic. I tried to understand what money should be used for, what the Lord intended when he made some of us rich and more of us poor. Some of the conclusions I came to were obvious: of course money should be spread around; those of us who can help should do so and you'll find that in the will none of my charities is forgotten. Business is important too: think of all those employees feeding their families and dreaming their own dreams. So of course I also have a duty to protect what you like to call my business empire and you'll find that this is taken care of.

'But even after all of these things are looked after, there will still remain a substantial amount of disposable assets and cash. Perhaps what I've decided to do may surprise you a little but I hope you won't be disappointed. I'm sure, knowing you, that you will take it in the spirit in which I've intended it. You've heard me say many times that the most important empire of all is family, haven't you, George? Unfortunately, the Lord did not see fit to give me children of my own. But He gave you three. Or maybe there's more I don't know about? Sorry, George, it's just my little joke.

As though oblivious of the electric silence in the room, the solicitor took another precise mouthful of water. Francey, now so embarrassed that he felt he was growing into his chair, kept his eyes fixed on the man, a small, balding figure whose paunch, gold-rimmed half-glasses and bow-tie encapsulated everything he had always imagined about the lifestyle and affluence of those in the legal profession. He fancied he could feel the shock waves emanating from the chair behind him which was occupied by Colin Mannering. Even though

74

Colin seemed to bear him no personal ill will, it would be stretching credibility to expect him not to be upset. Up to a week ago, George's eldest son had thought that apart from George himself, he and his family had sole claim to his stepmother's fortune. Now here was news that not only had he to share the throne with one, but with two pretenders. As the solicitor began again to read, he resisted the temptation to look round.

'But the more I thought about meeting my Maker, [Mr Solomons continued after what seemed an interminable pause], *the more I got to thinking about my life and why, just when I thought I was going to be a lonely old widow, the Lord sent you to me. And then it came to me. He wanted me to have a family after all. When we married, George, your three kids became my three kids, even if I had the privilege of meeting only one of them. We've to take care of them, George, they're family.*

Now please don't be upset that I know about your other two sons. Even before Colin came into our lives, I've known about all three of your boys right from the outset. And I think when you reflect on this, you will accept that as a widow in my position (remember all those people depending on those businesses in the States) I would have been derelict in my duty if I hadn't found out as much as I could about you before I entrusted my life to you. After all, George, you might have been a confidence trickster! So I set to finding out about your past life, or lives, which, I assure you, did not surprise or shock me one bit. To tell you the truth, with your looks and in your profession, my dear, I think I would have found it more astonishing had I discovered you had been a good boy for all of your first fifty-three years!

Now, to the sons themselves and the reason for this letter. I think you will know already that they feature in my will. You may find it strange that I never did anything to bring your sons to us while I was still alive. Well, one reason was I didn't want to embarrass you, dear. And you know also that I have always been a God-fearing woman and I felt that the Lord, in His wisdom, would do what He wanted with us all in His own good time. However, I must tell you that in spite of what I've just said, I was trying to find your youngest son, Desmond. Now it is over to you, and I feel sure you will do the right thing. Perhaps, dearest George, this is the way the Lord wants you to face up to your responsibilities.

'You'll have Colin with you, I'm sure, for the reading of the will, and now I can tell you that Desmond's last-known whereabouts were in London. I'm afraid he was not in the greatest of circumstances and, to my sorrow, sometime in 1959, which was four years before the writing of this letter, he vanished just as I was about to sort out some way to help him. Since then, however, even the best people in the business have not been able to find him. You'll find details of what I know and who to contact attached to the will as an appendix.

'Your middle son, Francis (whom everyone calls Francey, by the way) is in Dublin, Ireland. You'll find his current address attached to the will too. He's a fine young man by all accounts, George, you'll be proud of him. When you meet him, tell him so and tell him old Jool is sorry she missed meeting him – that's of course provided he doesn't turn up voluntarily and providentially before I go. What joy that would bring me!

'Now to my darling little Tommy. What can I say about him? I want you always to protect that boy, George. I've taken care of him financially, but I want you to look out for him every other way. The responsibilities of a grandfather are every bit as serious as those of a father.

'Sorry to spring all this on you. But if you remember, near the beginning when we first met, I said to you that I thought of you as a big kid. And maybe that's why I feel it's my job to make sure about the welfare of the three boys and Tommy. Don't take this badly, dear, I loved you for the fun you brought me. (Read my private letter.) And as you'll see in the will proper, you are well taken care of.

'I want everyone who hears this letter to know that I loved you all. And Colin, I'm not sure if you ever knew about your brothers. I hope you'll be happy with them if everything works out as I hope it will. Be good to your dad.

'Finally, people, you'll find I've left other letters too, one for each of you, Colin, Fleur, the three boys, my dearest Tommy, who in my last years gave me more happiness than I could have imagined. (I'm sure he won't think anything of it now so maybe you should

keep it for him until he's old enough to know what he meant to his
old Gran.)

I must say that it's an odd feeling writing letters you know will
only be read after you're no longer around. And I did shed the
occasional tear while composing them. But I had great fun too,
imagining reactions. God bless you all. In conclusion, George, I
remain always, with loving care, tenderness and gratitude for the
great times we had together, your wife, Jool.

'I shall now proceed to the reading of the will, unless any of you
have questions? Folding the sheets of writing paper, the solicitor
looked over the tops of his half-spectacles. Unbidden, the notion of
what Hazel might ask – *Hey! How much?* – entered Francey's head
and he felt the absurd inclination to giggle. Oddly, it was since
meeting Fleur Mannering that he had found he missed Hazel. All
weekend he had tried without success to reach her by telephone,
telling himself that he needed a dose of her forthright common sense:
Hazel was the one who would be able to puncture the balloon of
unreality in which he seemed to have been encased since arriving at
Inveraray Manor – or at least to deflate it a little.

He had had plenty of time to think since George had dropped his
bombshell about him being included in the will: Colin and his wife
had returned to London early on the following morning and had
come back to the Manor only minutes before the arrival of the
solicitor; his father had spent a lot of time out of the house, where,
Francey did not know. The urge to talk to a friend had become
pressing, and not only about George and Colin and Inveraray.
Francey was longing to confide his feelings about Fleur to someone
and barring his mother, who, given her history might understand
but who would feel bound to counsel him towards caution, Hazel
was by far the best someone he could come up with. Hazel, he felt,
would be able to tell him what to do – or even if there was any hope
for him.

But each time he telephoned, Hazel's home number rang
unanswered. So, having cleared the extra few days' leave with his
employers, who proved to be understanding, and having no one to
talk to except the polite but unresponsive house staff, Francey had
spent a great deal of the weekend mooching around the stables where
he had been allowed – not without a certain amount of incredulous

teasing by the hands – to help out with some of the chores. Mick O'Dowd, the Irish head groom, who had proved to be a wizened ex-jockey in his fifties and who came from Newbridge in Co. Kildare, had been an unexpected salvation: the little man's extensive store of horse-lore was fascinating and kept Francey's mind off his own problems.

'No questions?' the solicitor asked again.

Francey risked a glance over his shoulder at his father. As he shook his head, George's expression was so rueful it verged on the comic. Francey himself felt like laughing: given Mrs Gallaher's religious nature, this entire situation could be seen as one of God's little jokes. As he watched the solicitor smoothing the will on the glass surface in front of him, he wondered what his mother would say.

Funnier still, what would Lahersheen say?

Francey could just imagine the upsurge of gossip about him when this got out. Given the way Lahersheen and Béara worked, he thought, many people there probably knew more already than he did himself.

The solicitor began to read and Francey applied himself to the dry language of the document. It made little sense to him because after the business and charity sections and several specific bequests to all of them – Francey found himself to be the new owner of one of Mrs Dill Smith Gallaher's paintings – and to several people he did not know, it spoke, not of pounds, shillings and pence, or even dollars, but of percentages.

But he did gather that if this were a lottery, Tommy Mannering was the big winner, being left in trust the house, farm and everything pertaining to Inveraray Manor, plus the bulk of his grandmother's fortune which was held in shares, bonds and securities. He was not to receive any of this, however, until after George's death. For the rest of his natural life, George was to have the income, which should be substantial, from Tommy's portfolio, plus the right to live in the Manor.

As Tommy's mother, Fleur Mannering was to have the income from a second, separate portfolio of shares which would revert to her son on her death. She was also to receive all of Jool's considerable and valuable collection of jewellery.

George's three sons were to carve up equally the balance of what were called residual assets, which were to be sold and invested by the executors, the income from which was to be delivered to the beneficiaries annually until Tommy Mannering reached the age of twenty-five when they could then dispose of the capital as they wished.

There followed a complicated set of intertwined ifs, howevers and whereases which Francey could not follow although he discerned it had something to do with safeguards built into the will in case any of them predeceased the other before Tommy got to the age of twenty-five, if anything should happen to Tommy himself, if Dessie could not be found or if any of them became of unsound mind or turned to crime.

But as the solicitor intoned Jool's name, the names of witnesses, executors and the date the will was drawn up, it was not the money that excited Francey but the ecstatic knowledge that because they were now bound up together as a family not only by blood but by money and arrangements about money, he should, *would*, have further opportunities to meet Fleur Mannering.

Then, as Solomons went on to describe what was in the appendices and codicils, including a separate provision under which money was invested to pay for the upkeep of the house, he felt he should be thinking, not of his half-brother's wife, but of Dessie. Faced with this unknown old woman's determined efforts to find his half-brother, his own had been so half-hearted as to be derisory. Now that Mrs Dill Smith Gallaher had provided him with proper leads, he would have to make a serious effort.

'I have a question.' Colin's voice cut through the shuffling of the solicitor's papers as they were replaced in their folder.

'Certainly.' Solomons snapped open the cap of his fountain pen as though to take notes.

'I'm sorry to be so blunt, but do you have any idea . . .' Colin's voice was apologetic, 'could you let us know how much this means to each of us?'

'I was prepared for that.' The solicitor took a legal pad out of the briefcase at his feet. 'As there are a number of financial transactions to be pursued, the precise amounts will not be known for quite a while – and of course the will must go through probate. But Mrs Dill Smith Gallaher and I did perform some rough – I emphasize that these are *very* rough – calculations, and the figures will depend, of course, on the exchange rates pertaining at the time the amounts are released. I would emphasize also that, in the interim, provision has been made in a separate bank account to accommodate the needs of all the beneficiaries until probate comes through. I have all the documents with me.

'But on present exchange rates,' Solomons consulted his legal pad, 'and being conservative about yields, Mr Gallaher's inherited income will derive from investments of approximately six million pounds sterling and should yield somewhere between seven and nine hundred thousand annually, Mrs Fleur Mannering will receive in her own right the income from an investment portfolio of one point three million pounds which should yield at least two hundred thousand pounds per annum, and the sum to be divided and invested on behalf of Mr Gallaher's three sons would amount to something in the region of eight point four million pounds sterling, yielding approximately one million a year, or one third of a million each. And I would remind you, of course, Mr Mannering, that when your son reaches the age of twenty-five, you will be able to have access to your share of the capital, which, all going well should be equal to, or more than, your original share of two point six million pounds.'

Francey's income from Ledbetter's was at present just over four hundred and twenty pounds per annum.

'Calm down, calm down, for Jaysus' sake . . .' Hazel's exasperated voice came and went from far away. 'I can't understand what you're trying to say, Francey. Where are you ringing from? You sound like you're in Outer Mongolia.'

It was later that afternoon and having tried to reach her virtually non-stop since he had heard the news, Francey had at last got through. 'I might as well be,' he gibbered. 'I'm in a place in the country in England. I found him, Hazel, I found him and you'll never believe what's after happening—'

'Try me.'

'I'm after becoming a millionaire.'

Faced with the silence which greeted this revelation, Francey raised his voice further. 'Are you there, Hazel? Hazel, for God's sake, are you there?'

'I'm here.' Hazel's voice became stern. 'Have you been drinking, Francey?'

'No, I haven't.' Francey was shouting now. 'For God's sake – it's true. I'm after being made a millionaire. It's in George Gallaher's wife's will. She died. Hazel, what am I going to do?'

'Look, what's your number there?' Even from this distance, Francey could hear the irritation in Hazel's voice. 'I'm going to ring you back.'

Desperately, he looked around for some evidence of the manor's telephone number. 'I can't find it,' he said, 'I'm ringing you from my bedroom here. The number's not written on the phone.'

'Well, hang up and you ring me back, then. This is a terrible line, I can't make out what you're saying, and anyway you're not making sense.' The receiver went dead in Francey's sweating hands.

Over the preceding hours, his semi-amusement at the situation into which he had been catapulted had flaked away, to be replaced by feelings of inexplicable panic and confusion. He felt he should be rejoicing at his good fortune, but also as though all props had been whipped from under him.

The Mannerings had departed for London in the immediate wake of the solicitor and he and his father had been left with just the servants for company. George, muttering that he had some business to attend to, had gone to earth in some other part of the house, leaving Francey to his own devices. He did not even know if he was expected to attend for dinner.

Before picking up the telephone again, he paced around the bedroom, trying to force himself to be calm. The quietness served to increase his sense of isolation and he wished that his feet would make some sound on the thick carpet.

By the time he reached Hazel, he had managed to inject at least a semblance of control into his voice. 'It's true, Hazel, it's really true,' he said, in response to her exasperated query as to what was going on, 'I've been left an enormous amount of money. But it's a bit complicated. I can't spend it yet. At least I can't spend the millions yet. But in the meantime I'll be getting a huge dose of it every year as an income.'

'Tell me again how much.' Francey told her. 'That's fantastic,' she said in reply, but in his ears she still sounded dubious and it was not until the best part of a quarter of an hour later that she seemed convinced that he had not suffered a rush of blood to the head. 'Right, start at the beginning, from the time you got there,' she ordered.

Francey complied, naming the family but skating over their complex inter-relationships, concentrating instead on outlining the vagaries of the extraordinary house, the multiplicity of servants, the luxury, the food, the stables and the little wonderland in the wood. Hazel listened in silence and when at last he ran down, let out a low whistle. 'Some deal you've got there,' she said. 'Have you told your mother?'

'No I haven't. You're the first one I've told. Oh, Hazel, what am I going to do?'

'What do you mean, what are you going to do, stupo? You're going to have a great time for the rest of your life, that's what you're going to do.'

'But it's so much – and, Hazel?'

'What is it?' Her voice sharpened, and Francey knew she had detected the change in his tone. He had been about to confide in her about Fleur Mannering but his courage failed him. 'Francey?' She raised her voice a notch. 'Are you still there?'

'Yes. I can't wait to get out of here,' he blurted, knowing it was only half true.

'When are you coming back?' Hazel had evidently decided not to pursue whatever it was he had been about to say and for that, Francey was grateful. 'Probably tomorrow,' he said. 'I've to ring the job. They'll think I'm lost.'

'You can tell them to get stuffed now.' She was again her caustic self.

'Oh, I wouldn't do that –' Francey began, then stopped. It had not occurred to him until now that he need not go back to Ledbetter's if he did not want to.

'Look, give us a ring when you get home and we'll have a chat about everything,' Hazel said briskly, 'all right?'

'Thanks. Oh, I forgot to ask, how are you feeling?'

'I'm not planning on entering the hop, step and jump in the Rome Olympics, if that's what you mean.'

'Good.' Francey was glad he had reached her. He felt soothed. 'Is the pain all gone?'

'I'm fine, really. The ribs are completely better and I got the plasters off me arms last Friday. You wouldn't believe the relief! I've only got elastic bandages on them now and I can use them perfectly well.'

'That's great, Hazel. I'll see you as soon as I can,' he promised.

'And tell me once more,' he could hear her take a deep breath before she continued, 'you're actually a millionaire? This isn't some kind of culchie gag from West Cork?'

He knew she was convinced now, and Francey began to enjoy his so-called predicament. 'No,' he replied, 'it's true – God, I can't believe it,' he added with wonder.

'*You* can't.' Hazel laughed. 'Well, fair dues to ya, Francey Sullivan! Bring us back a packet of Spangles – you can afford them!' The tubes of fruit drops, which were not available in the Republic, were always taken home as souvenirs of a trip to the North of Ireland or to Britain.

Francey laughed. 'At the moment I have four quid something in my pocket.'

'In that case, bring us two packets! Listen,' she added, 'isn't this a gas? Here's the two of us in it now.' She chuckled. 'When me compo comes through the two of us should go on a world cruise.'

'Bye, Hazel.' Francey replaced the receiver and went to the window of the bedroom. Little had changed outside: the undulating, immaculate fields lay under a coverlet of ragged mist; above, the sky was an unrelieved grey. He toyed with the idea of going back into the magic kingdom George's wife had created for Tommy Mannering but, seen through the window, the trees at the edge of the wood now looked dark and uninviting.

He discovered he was hungry; he had been too nervous to eat much at breakfast and, since the will-reading ended, had spent the time holed up in his bedroom trying to telephone Hazel.

'You're very quiet, Fleur.'

'Yes.' To discourage any further conversation, Fleur did not respond with so much as a glance towards the driver's seat. Anyhow, being so low on the road the MG was noisy at this speed and she was not inclined to waste energy in raising her voice.

Fleur despised weakness and had never yet met a man in whom it was not a glaring defect. As for Colin, she had never had less respect for him than during the past few days while she had observed his meek toadying to his new half-brother. Colin's puppy-like eagerness to please and collateral fear of the opposite had trawled depths previously unreached even for him.

Although at the beginning she had tried hard to develop a proper fondness for Colin, no one but Tommy had ever occupied Fleur's heart and no one else ever would. Her habit of detachment and self-reliance had been so well cultivated throughout her lifetime it was inviolable. If it had not been for the urgency of her son's needs, both at present and in the future, she would long ago have been happy to have seen the back of her husband.

'What are you thinking about?' As he touched her thigh to attract her attention, she turned her head towards the passenger window, discouraging intimacy.

'I am thinking about the noise in this car,' she said with partial truth, seeing only her own reflection in the glass, trying to imagine what lay in the cold density of the English winter night beyond it.

'Oh, Fleur, you know how I love her—'

'Yes, I do know how you love your car. But you asked what I was thinking about.'

'What's wrong?' From behind her head, Colin's voice was reproachful. 'Are you upset with me?'

'Why should I be upset? I'm tired.' Leaning back in her seat, Fleur closed her eyes as if to sleep.

'Because of what happened with the will?' Again Colin touched her.

Fleur found she had not been lying when she said she was tired. Her weariness, however, was not physical but emotional. She could not wait to get back to the warmth of their flat, the comfort of her boudoir – and her own company. 'I think your stepmother has been most generous,' she said.

'Yes, she has.' Although Fleur had kept her eyes closed, Colin was refusing to take the hint and was intent on chat. 'There's Francey, though,' he said, 'and now there's this new chap, Dessie.'

'The time to discuss this, Colin, was an hour ago with your father, or with Francey himself.' Fleur hoped her tone would discourage him. 'It has nothing to do with me. I should like to sleep, if you don't mind.'

'Sorry, but I do so hope you're not upset.' Colin subsided into merciful silence.

In the knowledge that he was unaware of how he repelled her, Fleur wished she could be more confrontational. Accustomed, however, to working only towards her goals, however distant, and in following only the rules and moves which would bring her another step towards them, she knew she must remain calm. It was because of her long-term aims that she was always careful not to let her scorn for Colin show. She was less cautious at home but it served Fleur's purpose to let her husband continue in the belief that he was the master and she the waifish stray he had rescued. When they were out together in public she wore a mask of timidity which she knew fooled everyone: the English, being unsubtle, were so easy to dupe, she thought. *Poor Fleur* . . . She could see the concern in their eyes, so pale and round, like the eyes of fish. It appeared that the only one who had not been fooled had been Jool Dill Smith Gallaher.

On the evidence of the letter, the little personal homily received along with her inheritance, Fleur knew now that Jool had seen, at least in part, through the protective web of deception she had woven about herself. The old lady had not seemed to care, however, and had had the tact not to spell it out. Yes, this was a person for whom Fleur had had respect. What was more, although her stepmother-in-law's death had left only a small ripple on the calm surface of Fleur's emotions and although she had not grieved or mourned, Jool was the only person she had come close to liking in England and, of course, George's wife had not been English.

Notwithstanding that Jool was prepared to have people investigated, no matter what those investigations uncovered, she had been able to accept people with transatlantic *laissez-faire*. Not like the English whose superficial politeness masked fundamental suspicion of anyone not of themselves: in Fleur's view, the English class system was more unbending than anything she had seen in the caste systems of the East.

She would soon be finished with it, with the English. Success in her life came down to the possession of independent means. And sooner rather than later, Fleur and Tommy would be able to shed Colin and his cold wet country.

*

Having braved the kitchen and been given a large heap of sandwiches by the sympathetic cook, Francey again spent the rest of the afternoon at the stables, drawing calm from the stolid magnificence of the Shires. Mick O'Dowd and the others seemed to accept his presence with good grace; Mick, standing on a step-stool, demonstrated the special way of interweaving the animals' manes and long tails with ribbons to make tight plaits, then left him alone with Tarzan, the laziest, most placid of the horses, to see what kind of a fist he would make of the task on his own.

Tarzan, his headcollar tethered to an iron ring fitted to the concrete wall of his stall, snoozed his way through the operation. Tall though he was, Francey found he had to use the step-stool to reach the horse's mane without straining; he tried to emulate the way Mick had so deftly interbraided the coarse hair and colourful ribbons but after just a few minutes, could see that the result was going to be a mess. He undid it all and began again. 'There now, Tarzan,' he whispered, leaning on the horse's solid withers, enjoying the feel of the muscles moving like continental plates beneath the animal's skin. He checked over his shoulder to make sure he was not being overheard and, as he worked, told the horse about the beloved black gelding of his childhood and how he used to sneak out in the middle of the night to sleep beside Lightning in the prickly straw bedding.

Tarzan nickered, redistributed his bulk from one hind leg to the other and resumed his nap. 'I love her.' Francey pushed his forehead into the horse's Promethean neck, as sturdy as the span of a bridge. 'I love her. I love her.' But Tarzan remained asleep and, feeling foolish, Francey resumed his struggle with the ribbons and the hair.

He was three-quarters the way down the mane when Mick popped his head over the half-door to check on his progress. 'You've made a horse's arse of it, if you'll pardon the pun,' he said with a grin. He let himself in and, pushing Francey aside – 'Bit of a Shire yourself, aren't you?' – hopped on to the top rung of the stool and within two minutes had undone all Francey's efforts. 'Never mind,' he said then, raking the coarse hair with his fingers, 'this is show work and we're just doing it to keep our hands in. We spend a lot of time having breaks around here.' His tone became rueful. 'As a matter of fact we're just brewing up right now, as it happens. Come on and have a cup of char. I think there's cake.'

There seemed to be six employees in the yard, who staggered their days off. The five on duty today sat around the scratched and worn table in the large tack-room with Francey as an uncomfortable sixth. Conversation was slow to start and Francey realized with a shock that to Mick and the others he was not one of them but was on the toff's side of the fence. 'Tell me about showing the horses,' he asked when the silence seemed to be stretching towards infinity.

'Don't know now whether we're just wastin' our time, keeping them up to scratch, I mean,' Mick added, after a glance around at the other men. 'We don't even know if yer man's even going to keep the bloody horses, never mind show them again, do we?'

'Oh, I'm sure he will.'

'You reckon?' A bony, fresh-faced boy, his dark hair cut in what was to Francey an outlandish fringed style, looked up from his mug. 'We've not been told a dicky-bird.' Then, boldly: 'The will was this mornin'?'

'Yes.' Francey saw every face fix on his own. 'I don't know if I'm supposed to tell you what's in it —'

'I told you there was no point askin'!' One of the older men threw the dregs of his tea into a nearby sink.

'Shut up, Wiley!' Mick O'Dowd frowned at the man then turned back to Francey. 'We'd appreciate it, Francey, if you'd ask Mr Gallaher to let us know what's going to happen. Most of us have families, you see.'

Francey told them what he knew, omitting the amounts of money and also that yet another son was to be added to the odd mélange which constituted Julia Dill Smith Gallaher's collection of heirs.

'You mean the place is not going to be sold, after all?' The relief on the men's faces was evident.

'I don't think so,' Francey replied. 'It's left in trust for Tommy, and Mr Gallaher — my father,' Francey braved all their stares, 'is to live here until he dies.'

'We reckoned old George was your father, all right, no contest.' Mick grinned. 'Not much goes on here but we don't know about it. Bet your arrival was a turn up for the books. You hear about the old lady's death in Ireland, then?' he asked, taking a sip from his mug.

'No.' Francey realized then that they, too, thought he was a gold-digger. He was getting tired of this. 'I didn't know, honestly,' he said.

'I've been looking for my father in one way or another all my life although I didn't get the opportunity to do anything about it until very recently . . .'

No one responded and Francey knew they did not believe him. Then, to his surprise, he found it did not matter to him all that much. Hazel believed him. More importantly, so did Fleur.

'This the first time you met your brother, too?' It was another of the men.

Francey contented himself with nodding and the older man stared at him. 'You're not much alike, you two, are you?'

'We have different mothers. As I told you,' Francey steered the conversation into safer waters, 'I didn't hear anything specific but I'm sure they're safe, the animals, I mean. I'll ask if you like?'

'That'd be good. If the Squire's stayin'.' Mick, who seemed to be trying to convince himself, glanced around for confirmation. 'Mr Gallaher bought most of these horses, bred a couple,' he explained then to Francey. 'This yard was built a couple of years after the house. Word in the neighbourhood was that your father was going to keep hunters like the rest of the swells around here, but it turned out we were all wrong. Your old dad fancied himself driving the buggers, all right, handy enough at it too, but only once in a blue moon.'

'Fancy himself is right,' one of the others muttered only to be silenced by a poisonous look from Mick.

'More tea?' he offered Francey. 'And when we're finished, I'll show you the rulleys if you like.' As he poured a stream of the dark brown liquid into Francey's mug, he proceeded with a potted history of the yard. 'We all had a bit of learning to do when we were taken on. Wiley here's the only one who'd ever had anything to do with heavy horses before.'

As he frequently did when conversation became unimportant to him, Francey drifted off into a daydream; a new idea for his future was germinating and, as the rest of the men chatted amongst themselves, he looked at it this way as he sipped the scalding tea.

Francey went back to Dublin the following day. He resisted George Gallaher's urgings that he should eschew the mailboat and fly, opting for the slower route.

'But why, Francey?' George had been mystified. 'You've all the money you need now. Why put yourself through all that bother?'

Francey had no adequate answer. He felt unable to explain that as yet he did not feel he deserved such self-indulgence; that the condition of being rich was too new for him to take it for granted, and brought up as he was to be thrifty, the waste of a ferry ticket seemed like a sin. 'Have it your own way.' George had shrugged in dismissal. 'Stay in touch, won't you?'

'We need to sit down and have a proper talk,' Francey had looked his father in the eye.

'Of course, of course, old chap,' George's grin was as brilliant and guileless as ever, 'any time you like. Bit busy at the moment, of course, lot on the plate . . .'

And so, promising to telephone the following weekend, Francey had set off for the long trek home.

Although he was gritty-eyed on arrival at Dun Laoghaire in the early morning, he was glad he had taken the surface route. It had given him the chance to think and to start the confusing business of sorting out his feelings and impressions of the past few days. So much had happened so quickly, however, that by the time he and his fellow passengers were disembarking, his brain was addled with images and snatches of conversation. The wealth – what would he do with it? What did all that money look like? George: what did he really feel about his father, so obviously irresponsible but strangely lovable none the less? And during that weekend, who had said exactly what? And at what point? More importantly, why?

But no matter how hard he had worked his mind, it came round over and over again to Fleur Mannering. Throughout that long night, Francey tried as hard as he could to place his headlong rush of feelings for his half-brother's wife in perspective but failed. His crush – love, lust, whatever anyone else might have called it – might have been shattering, amoral and downright inconvenient, but Fleur dominated every waking moment. He found himself continually cataloguing her beauty, her voice, her wonderful ankles, the raven's-wing hair, the narrowness of her waist and delicacy of movement; and although he tried to force himself to think about his riches, about George, about the horses – about anything other than his half-brother's wife – his stomach remained tight with love. To distract himself he even tried to work up a head of indignation about George's appalling vanishing act from the lives of himself and his family – from Colin's life, too – but his mind and heart refused to deal with anything except Fleur.

Not having eaten or drunk at all throughout the trip, by the time he was disembarking Francey's stomach was rumbling and he was so tired his throat hurt. He shouldered his bag, for once oblivious to the curious glances, and followed the thin stream of people through the freezing customs shed and out into the pre-dawn morning.

It had been raining, and there was more to come. The raucous wrangling of seagulls over scraps in the murky water near the yacht club was in sharp contrast to the human lethargy which larded the waking port. An elderly lady, so multi-scarved and galoshed that barely an inch of skin was visible, walked an arthritic terrier on the seafront near the pier, a train hooted in the nearby station, a few cars swished by on the greasy roadway. But to Francey, the dank air, spiced with salt and the sweeter condiments of sewage and diesel exhaust from the mailboat, tasted like manna. He was home.

He headed for the bus stop then hesitated and patted the fabric concealing the inside pocket of his jacket: for once there was more there than a paperback book. Before he departed his father had insisted on giving him a thousand pounds 'on account old chap'. So far, Francey had not spent a penny of it. Somehow to do so would have seemed like the violation of a sacred entity. *A thousand pounds*: even the phrase was exotic, it was hung about with bells and bunting, like a liner on a Christmas cruise. Francey had never dreamt he could aspire to so much money, let alone have it in his possession in a single lump.

Yet now he was so tired that the temptation to break into its wholeness was strong. Come on, he exhorted himself, the principles of frugality with which he had been reared were all very well but he'd have to get used to being able to afford a taxi. Then he remembered that the cash was in sterling and he had to take the bus after all.

By the time he reached Ledbetter's, the employees were beginning to arrive. Francey knew that the boss, a Protestant who was affable but who could be picky about details, was always the first in and was no doubt already ensconced. Having geared himself up for a ticking-off, he decided to get it over with. Discarding his travel bag, he made his way towards the small, glass-walled office at the rear of the store.

As he got nearer, he could see the boss and his ageing secretary deep in consultation over a ledger.

Both heads came up in response to his knock and he was bidden to enter.

'Well, Mr Sullivan, the prodigal returns!'

Francey saw with relief that the boss's upset was more pretended than real. 'I'm very sorry, Mr Grieve,' he said, 'but as I told Miss Pym on the phone, I had to stay for – for family business.'

'My condolences on your sad loss.' The store manager, who had always prided himself on taking an interest in his employees' family affairs, stood up and shook hands with Francey across his cluttered desk. 'Was it unexpected?'

'A little,' Francey replied, aware of the irony.

'Time will heal.' The boss sat down again. 'Now, as it happens, I'm glad to have the opportunity of a chat with you. Sit down, sit down. Would you leave us for a few moments, Miss Pym?'

The secretary passed on her own sympathy and left the room. Although he had been many times in this office this was the first time Francey had been invited to sit. Ill at ease, he balanced himself on the chair that the secretary had just vacated.

'You're a good man, Mr Sullivan,' the store manager began when the door had clicked shut. 'Everything I hear about you tells me that you are punctual and a hard worker. Not to beat about the bush,' he placed his elbows on the desk and steepled his fingers, peering at Francey over their joined tops, 'I'd like you to move to our new store in Santry and to offer you a promotion there. How does that sound? Of course, it would mean a raise in salary. Quite a substantial raise, if I may say so myself.' He smiled, proud of his benevolence.

Francey was thunderstruck, more surprised by this than by what had happened to him at Inveraray Manor. He had never thought of Ledbetter's as a place to make a career, more as a stopgap until his real destiny showed itself. The store manager mistook his confusion for modesty and smiled more broadly. 'I know this probably comes as a surprise to you, Mr Sullivan, but I believe promotion is not only deserved in your case but long overdue.'

'Th-thank you, Mr Grieve.' Francey found his voice. 'Could I think about it for a day or two?'

The manager frowned. 'Don't think about it too long,' he seemed a little insulted, 'there are others here, you know, who would jump at the chance I'm offering you. Santry is a coming place, you know. Get in on the ground floor there, so to speak, and who knows? You could be a department manager there within a very short space of time. As little as five years, even . . .'

Now that he was presented with it as the opportunity of a lifetime, the thought of being stuck with lumber, hardware and the innards of cisterns for any longer was so awful that Francey could not contemplate it. But he was not yet ready to relinquish his Lahersheen habit of caution about being the incumbent in a *good job*. 'I know I've just come back,' he knew he was pushing his welcome, 'but I wonder could I have today off, Mr Grieve? I was travelling all night and I'm desperately tired. I'll take it off next year's annual leave,' he added quickly.

'I can see you look tired all right,' the manager responded, 'and since you haven't made a habit of this, go ahead – make arrangements with Miss Pym on your way out. But I'd like an answer about the other matter first thing tomorrow morning, all right?'

'You have my word,' Francey promised, relieved to be able to remove his weight from the spindly chair.

'I must say,' the boss said, looking up at him, 'your attitude to my offer has surprised me. I had thought you would jump at the chance. Have you been happy at Ledbetter's?'

'Very,' Francey lied, 'I've been very happy here, Mr Grieve.'

'Well, then,' the manager persisted, 'what's the problem? Is it Santry? Do you not want to move?'

'It's just that I'm too tired to think about anything at all right now.'

'Tomorrow, then?'

'Definitely.'

As he retrieved his bag and urged his aching legs towards the digs on Berkeley Road, Francey promised himself that after a good sleep he would face all his problems in one go.

But later, as he drifted off in his lumpy bed, he heard a dim echo of Hazel's laugh as she joshed him about his dilemma: 'Some problems you have, stupo . . .'

*

Hazel had nominated Neary's in Chatham Street for their meeting that night and Francey, who was early, ordered himself a pint of Guinness. Being Tuesday, it was a quiet night, with much of the banquette seating and chairs at the side tables unoccupied, although a morose row of men lined the bar on high stools. Because of the way many of the clients were dressed – more flamboyantly than was the norm – Francey supposed that Neary's was a place frequented by people, who, like Hazel, came from the world of showbusiness.

She arrived twenty minutes later in a flurry of leopardskin and black flounces. As she made her way towards him, he noticed that, despite the support bandages on her arms, she had managed to apply not only her customary eye makeup but the false eyelashes as well plus bright red polish to her nails. 'Phew!' She flopped down beside Francey, 'the bloody taxi was late as usual.' To go with the black-and-leopardskin outfit, she was wearing black stockings and sling-back stiletto heels, emphasizing her wonderful legs. 'Mind you,' she continued, 'being half crocked doesn't help.' She glanced with disgust at the bandages then smiled at Francey. 'It's all right, though, I've got all me strength back. Well, nearly all. You'd better be careful. The physiotherapist says I'm a great healer – comes of good livin'! These hands are now registered as lethal weapons!' She shadow-boxed a little with both fists and Francey noticed that her smile was again intact, the replacement crown so good it was impossible to tell from her real teeth. Since he had last seen her she had had her hair re-blonded; she looked bright and well and he was surprised at the depth of gladness he felt at seeing her.

'You look great,' he said, meaning it. 'How are you feeling, in general, I mean?'

'Gaspin'!' Her kohl-ringed eyes crinkled.

'Sorry, what'll you have?' Francey grinned back.

'Do you have to ask, stupo?' dropping her hand she dug him in the ribs. 'With what you're worth I'll have a brandy, of course – a double!'

As he went to the bar to order Francey reflected that all was right and cheerful with the world. He had no doubt that Hazel would be able to steer him in the right direction. He could enjoy the money too: he had woken up in time to make it to a local bank to exchange the sterling for Irish currency and now that it was in the familiar colours of the large Irish banknotes, the money George had pressed on him seemed not only substantial but real. Francey relished the way the barman, sucking the air into his teeth at the sight of the twenty-pound note, held it up to the light to check its authenticity while making doubtful noises as to whether he had enough change. Being rich could easily go to your head, Francey thought happily.

He brought the brandy and another pint for himself back to the table, and as he sat down, slid two packets of Spangles beside Hazel's balloon glass. 'Hey, I was only joking,' she laughed, 'I didn't mean it.'

'I know you didn't. But I got you something else too.' Francey reached into his pocket; he had been looking forward to this moment. 'Sort of as a get-well gift,' he added, 'and also to thank you for all the help in finding my father.'

'What help?' Hazel seemed nonplussed as she looked at the small Weir's box he placed beside the sweets.

'You know.'

'Weir's?' She picked up the box. 'Are ya out of your mind, Francey?'

Weir's was the most exclusive jeweller in Dublin. Francey had been in there only once before, during the first Christmas of his employment when he had been searching for a present for his mother. On that occasion he had run out of the shop as soon as he had seen the prices of the merchandise but had always wanted to visit it again: it spoke of wealth and security. While passing it today, it had occurred to him that now he could afford to shop there. 'Why don't you open it?' he tapped the little box in Hazel's hand.

'Ohmigod!' For once stuck for something to say, Hazel stared at the little butterfly brooch glittering in the palm of her hand. 'It's marcasite and enamel,' Francey offered. 'The man said it'll last a lifetime.'

'Why'd you do this, Francey?' To his consternation tears stood in Hazel's eyes.

'Because I wanted to – er – stupo!' Alarmed that she might start to blub and make a show of the two of them, Francey tried to make light of it as she would. This was not going the way he had planned.

'No one's ever given me a present like this before.' She seemed transfixed by the little object in her hand.

'Oh, I doubt that! Don't get carried away, Hazel, it's not all *that* great, it's just a token.' But before he knew it, she had flung her arms around his neck and was hanging on, squeezing his head between her arms. She had not been lying when she said she had regained her strength. Despite her injuries her grip was like iron. After a moment, he hugged her back, aware that they were now the focus of attention in the small bar.

'Hey, Hazel, who's the new Jekyll?' Francey's worst fears were confirmed as a drunk at the counter teetered around on his stool and leered in their direction.

'Shut up, you. Not in the business a wet week and feeling entitled to speak to your betters!' Hazel disengaged herself and glared at the man. 'If I wasn't disabled I'd come over there and knock your block off!'

'Ooh, temper! Nothing like a bitch in heat!' The young man who had been good-looking until his face had collapsed into the slackness of the habitual drinker, wove an unsteady circle in the air with his free hand.

'When's the last time you got it up, ya poxy bollocks?' Slamming the table in front of her so that the glasses jumped, Hazel half rose from her seat.

'Now, none of that, Hazel!' The barman intervened from behind the counter. 'Sit down and mind your language. Finish up your drink there now, Larry, like a good man,' he addressed the drunk. 'You've had enough for one evening.'

'Come on, Francey,' Hazel struggled to her feet and grabbed her handbag, 'something smells in here. We'll go where we can have a drink in *peace*.' As she sailed past the drunk, Francey thought she might take a swing at him but to his relief she kept her head high and eyes on the door in front of her. So embarrassed that he did not know where to look, he followed her out.

'What got into you, Hazel? Was that not a bit excessive?' he asked when they were on the pavement in Chatham Street.

'I know that chancer,' Hazel spluttered. 'It's me own fault, I shouldn't have brung you to Neary's – I might have known he'd be proppin' up the bar. Come on, we'll go round the corner to Sinnott's.'

'What does he do?' Francey, tailoring his steps to Hazel's shorter ones as they moved towards St Stephen's Green, was curious as to the cause of her outburst, which seemed out of all proportion to the offence.

'As little as possible,' she retorted. 'Oh, he hangs around the showbands,' she amended, 'drives, does a bit of sound stuff, roadie work, that sort of thing.'

'But what have you got against him? I know he was rude but what'd he ever do to you?'

'Doesn't he just wish!' Hazel muttered under her breath and Francey decided it would be wiser not to pry any more.

Having had one drink in Sinnott's they went for another in Davy Byrne's and yet another in the Old Stand and then, on Hazel's suggestion, walked the few yards down Andrew Street to the Trocadero restaurant for a meal. 'Might as well, Francey, since we're celebratin' and you're payin'!' To Francey's amazement, Hazel, who had recovered her sunny humour within minutes of arriving in Sinnott's, had not flagged all evening despite her handicap. 'Best thing that ever happened to me,' she retorted when he mentioned this. 'It's the first time for twenty years I've been mindin' meself. Exercisin', not drinkin' – well not much – I'm probably in better shape now than when I was a baby.'

As the head waiter – who had embraced Hazel as though she were a long-lost daughter – led them to their table, Francey thought that this evening had been like an education to him. His social life in Dublin had been limited to a number of dismal pubs up to now and the succession of cheerful venues they had visited had been a revelation. Despite its being so early in the working week, the candlelit Trocadero, its red walls lined with photographs of glamorous clients, was alive with buzz and chatter. By the end of the meal, mellow with drink and good food, Francey felt he could do anything in the world.

Yet although he and Hazel had batted about plans and schemes for his future – many of them preposterous – he had not yet found it opportune to bring up the subject closest to his heart. Now, piling the last piece of sauté onion on to the last piece of his steak, he glanced across the booth at his companion. It was funny the way the world worked, he thought. If he had not met Fleur Mannering, he might at this moment be pursuing his initial attraction to Hazel. The light of the candle between them shot minuscule prisms of light on to her face from the butterfly pinned high on the shoulder of her black dress; it also softened the hues of her blonde hair and enlarged her startling eyes, which, he now saw, mirrored the colours in the little brooch. 'What is it?' she asked, startling him. She frequently did this, catching him in the middle of something he did not want her to know.

'What do you mean?' He played for time.

'What's on your mind? It has to do with something else you said happened to you in England, hasn't it? You were going to tell me something on the phone that time, weren't you, something else besides the money?'

Francey hedged, telling her a little about how he reacted on first seeing his father. 'But we didn't get a chance to talk properly. He said we would, though.'

Then Hazel was diverted by another patron who was leaving the restaurant and who stopped by their table to say goodbye. She seemed to be acquainted with not only the proprietor and all of the waiters in the restaurant but also most of the clientele.

'Well?' The friend having been dispatched, she turned back.

'Do you know *everyone* in Dublin?' Francey continued to stall.

'Of course not,' she grinned, 'but show business is a very tight circle and everywhere we went tonight would be one of our haunts.' As she sipped her wine, her expression became serious. 'Come on, Francey, out with it. And not about one G. Gallaher either.'

'I've met someone,' Francey blurted after a short pause.

'Thought that's what it was.' Hazel dropped her eyes to her wine. 'Well, come on,' she said, swirling the red liquid round and round and studying its movement as though to read its meaning, 'tell us the gory details.'

'She's beautiful.' Francey found he couldn't continue.

'Aren't they all?' Hazel's tone did not match the laconic words. She looked up. 'What's the problem, then, Francey?'

'How do you know there's a problem?' Francey was astounded.

'Because if there wasn't, you wouldn't have stopped with her anatomical details. Would you mind if we had another bottle?' Picking up the empty one in front of her she twisted round in her seat and held it up, showing it to one of the waiters. 'Go on.' Turning back to Francey she drained her glass in one gulp.

'I don't know where to start.'

'Try starting with the first time you saw her. That's usually a good place. It's your half-brother's wife, what's-er-name.'

'Fleur.' Francey did not bother to pretend surprise. 'How did you know?'

'How many times do I have to tell you I'm an old dog for the hard road?'

Their waiter came with the second bottle of wine and Francey had to wait until all the palaver with corkscrew and tasting was over before he could continue. 'I'm not that transparent, am I?' he asked.

'People in love usually are.' Hazel concentrated on topping up her glass.

Francey opened the floodgates, releasing every detail of every second he had spent in Fleur Mannering's company, describing the walk they had taken together in what he now thought of as the enchanted wood.

Hazel interrupted him as he was relaying his suspicions that all was not well with Fleur's marriage. 'You really have it bad, don't you?'

'I'm afraid I do.' The admission thrilled him. 'I didn't ask for this to happen, you know.' He saw that while he had been talking he had gone through his wine. He began to refill both glasses.

'Men!' Hazel said. 'What are you going to do about it?'

Francey attempted to read the expression in her eyes but could not. 'What *can* I do?' he asked. 'I was hoping you'd have some advice for me.'

Hazel made up her mind about something. 'Does she like you?'

'Oh, God, I don't know. We've known each other such a short time.'

'You can usually tell, you know.' Her mouth twisted in a one-sided smile.

'How?'

'Jesus, Mary and Joseph, what are we going to do with you?' Her tone was exasperated. 'Look, do you mind if I ask you a personal question?'

'Go ahead.' Francey braced himself.

She looked him straight in the face. 'Are you a virgin?'

'Yes.' Somehow, while he would not have admitted this to any of the so-called male friends, he did not mind that Hazel knew.

'Thought so,' she said. 'And if you weren't, do you think it'd be easier? Or would it bother you that she's married? Adultery, and all that?'

98

'Of course it would!' Francey was scandalized. 'Nothing happened between us, Hazel, nothing at all.'

'Of course it didn't, ya big lug,' Hazel replied affectionately, then put down her wineglass. 'I'm tired, let's go home.'

'What about all that wine?' Francey looked at his glass, at hers, at the bottle, still more than half-full.

'We'll bring it with us.' Hazel proceeded to pour the wine from her glass back into the bottle. 'Listen, Francey, you're rich. A few drops of wine is not going to break you.'

'I didn't mean . . .' Was he that much of a miser?

But Hazel, beckoning to their waiter for the bill, was not listening. 'And bring us a cork, Frank, will ya?' she called. 'We're bringin' the rest of the plonk home with us.'

As he counted out the money to pay the bill, Francey resolved that no longer would he worry about wasting food or drink.

They did not speak again until they were outside and approaching the taxi rank outside the Bank of Ireland at College Green. 'You take the first one,' Francey insisted, 'and here – have the wine, please.' The clean, cold air had hit him, making him realize how much he had drunk; his blood seemed a little unstable, billowing up and down his body in warm, pleasurable waves.

Hazel looked down at the bottle with some hauteur. 'Are you not going to see me home? It's customary, you know.'

'Of course I am,' he said as he opened the door of the taxi at the head of the rank and stood back to let her in.

Hazel gave her address and sat into the back seat; the taxi-driver waited until Francey was in, then gunned his engine and threw it into a wide U-turn, which threw Hazel against him. 'Hey, watch it, Fangio!' Hazel shouted as she righted herself.

'How do you know about Fangio?' Francey asked, surprised that someone from Hazel's background and with her interests would know about the racing driver.

'Why wouldn't I?' Hazel retorted. 'For a rich culchie, Francey Sullivan, you've an awful lot to learn about human beings, haven't you?' She continued to brush herself off as the taxi sped down Dame Street.

'I suppose I have,' Francey admitted. 'Now that we're talking about peculiarities,' he added, 'what's – who's a "Jekyll"? Something to do with Jekyll and Hyde? That man in the pub —'

'That chancer? That's just someone I used to know. Don't mind him. But you want to know what a Jekyll is?' She inched across the seat and threw her arms around his neck. 'You got it in one, Francey. Jekyll and Hyde, *ride* – geddit?

'It's this.' She planted her lips on his.

Chapter Six

Despite the bowls of pot-pourri, the air in the living-room of Hazel's flat smelled of stale cigarette smoke overhung with a whiff of the musky perfume she used. But Francey saw that she had to be well off: the flat, which was on the first floor, was spacious with a high ceiling. Papered in a discreet and unremarkable shade of cream, the large Venetian blind which covered the two picture windows hung between heavy velvet curtains in a buttermilk shade, and except for the kitchen – and presumably the bathroom – the whole place was carpeted from wall to wall with shag-pile carpet in a deep navy blue. The living-room also sported a piano, a radiogram and, luxury of luxuries, a television set built into a cabinet.

What interested Francey most, however, was the corner display unit, which was packed with a menagerie of stuffed animals: scores of glass, embroidered and printed animal eyes seemed to meet his gaze no matter where he moved in the room. And the animal presence did not end with the living-room: when he peeped into the bathroom, he was faced with an enormous elephant smiling at him from the top of the linen basket. His butterfly brooch, he thought, had been an inspired choice.

When they had come in, Hazel had turned on only one lamp, on a side-table beside the main sofa in front of the fireplace, and with just the light spilling in from the kitchen as an addition, the living-room was plush and attractive but, except for the animals and photographs which decorated the top of the piano, wore an air of transience. 'This is a lovely place,' he called into the kitchen into which she had vanished, 'you've great taste.'

'Thanks,' she called back. 'But I can't take all the credit. I hired someone to decorate the place. Don't know meself whether I like it or not. I'm not here all that much as it happens.'

'You like animals, I see.' Francey was still conscious of the tiers of artificial eyes boring into his skull as though their owners resented this intrusion into their domain.

'Don't you?' Hazel answered. 'I find animals are far nicer than human beings, present company excepted, of course – ah, shit!' This in response to a loud crash. 'Make yourself comfortable,' she shouted over the sounds of sweeping up, 'won't be a sec.'

Francey crossed to the piano, a polished upright which took up an alcove between the two picture windows. Most of the photographs were of the singer herself, alone or standing as one of a fuzzy, beaming row, but there were images of other individuals as well.

Many were of men and, peering at one of them, Francey saw it was signed with a name he did not recognize and inscribed 'To Queenie with love'. The feeling grew that he was out of his depth: this was the first time in his life he had been alone with a sophisticated woman in her home at this hour of night. What was on the agenda now? Restless and indecisive, he moved to the window and parting the slats of the Venetian blind, saw that the flat overlooked a park.

Lit by the yellowish glare from the sodium lights in the street, the scene looked surreal, almost sinister: black uncovered bones of trees and shrubs appeared to bloom like dark fungus from the flat grass; boxy hedges that ran like spectral railway carriages beneath the spikes of iron railings revealed an unnatural symmetry and, in the light night wind, the seats of the children's swings in an asphalt clearing moved to and fro as though occupied by languid ghosts. The park seemed to stand on tiptoe as though waiting for something awful to happen and Francey shivered. He was reminded of Kilcatherine graveyard, an ancient place near his home which for him was full of resonances, so much so that he hated going there for funerals. When standing beside someone's open grave, he could almost hear the whispering of a vast cosmic gathering preparing for his own final arrival.

He dropped the slats and turned back into the living-room. All the drink he had consumed during the evening must be pickling his brain, he decided. What the hell was wrong with him? What man in his right mind would not want to be in his position? Alone with a famous showband star – what was more, a showband star who had kissed him passionately in the back of a taxi.

Like most of his contemporaries, Francey thought of sex outside marriage as a thrilling sin but, unlike them, serious experimentation had ceased around the time of puberty when, just as his interest and drive intensified, his height began to soar. Now he vacillated between urgent desire that Hazel wanted to take things further than she had in the taxi – and vague hope that she might let him off the hook. Francey was not sure he was ready to commit a mortal sin. Since he had come to Dublin, he had been a dilatory Catholic and rarely gave his religion much thought – but was he ready to take this ultimate step? More confusing, should passion for Fleur Mannering not preclude sexual attraction to all other women? In love with Fleur as he was, it was terrible, surely, that he was even thinking about the feeling of Hazel's lips on his own. Or was it because Fleur was married and he couldn't have her? Was he just using Hazel as a substitute? Francey's heartbeat speeded up as turmoil was overcome with fresh desire.

Another thing: would Hazel laugh at his inexperience, even at his ungainly body? And then came the most urgent concern of all. Would he be able for it? Francey had read as much Henry Miller as the next man and he knew that the old rules, those they used to titter about in the school playgrounds and on the rugby fields, no longer applied.

Perhaps he should clear out while the going was good. Planted in the middle of the floor, the tops of his shoes concealed by the deep shag, Francey felt like the Pushmepullu he remembered from the book of his childhood and glanced towards the open kitchen door. Hazel was not visible although he could still hear her sweeping. 'I should be going,' he called, 'aren't you tired?'

'Fresh as a daisy!' Hazel appeared in the doorway holding two full wineglasses and a plateful of cream crackers and cheese. 'Sorry about the delay, bit of an accident with a few plates. Not to worry. Here, have some of your own plonk.'

As Francey took the wine, his agitation was such that he spilled a little from the over-full glass. Hazel grinned impishly. 'A little nervous, are we? Do I gather that someone as big as you could actually be afraid of someone the size of me?'

Francey was getting used to her unerring instinct. 'Of course not,' he lied, gulping from his glass. He noticed she had reapplied her lipstick and was indeed revitalized.

'Take the weight off your feet, then.' Placing the plateful of crackers and cheese on a coffee-table, Hazel kicked off her sling-backs and seated herself at one end of the couch in front of the empty fireplace. 'Over here.' She patted a space beside her, but on seeing his

103

expression, 'Jaysus, Francey, for the love of God, I'm not going to bite you!'

Then, as he gaped, she lowered her voice and with wicked eyes, breathed, 'That is, of course, unless you want me to?'

Francey's blood jumped. Clutching the stem of his glass he sat at the other end of the couch and crossed his legs, first one way, then the other.

Hazel watched this performance. 'Christalmighty,' she tut-tutted, 'what am I going to do with you? Would you *relax*?' She reached behind her and by turning the shade, deflected the light from the table lamp so the couch was dappled in shadow. 'Is that better?' And when Francey nodded, 'So why don't you loosen that ridiculous tie?' Before he knew it, she had closed the gap between them and was reaching for the knot.

'What's wrong with it?' His free hand flew to his neck; the tie, purchased in Hanley's of Castletownbere the previous Christmas, had been a present from one of his stepsisters.

'It's beautiful, a work of art,' the redness of Hazel's lipsticked mouth shimmered just inches away as she brushed his hand off and picked at the tie with her varnished nails, 'but it's too tight.'

'Leave it,' Francey jerked his head away, 'I'll do it myself.'

'Ooh – who's a *big* boy, then?'

'Stop it, Hazel.' Her joshing made him feel as though he was making a show of himself.

'Tsk-tsk.' She caught hold of both his cheeks, chucking them as though he was a baby. 'For God's sake, Francey, willya loosen up a bit?'

'Am I that bad?' She had not let go of his face and hers was so close his eyes could not focus on it.

'I've never met such a nervous Nellie in the whole of me twist,' she retorted. Then she kissed him gently on the lips.

'Sorry.' Francey was so jittery he had to school himself not to recoil. As Hazel pulled back to look into his eyes, he surreptitiously licked his lips: they felt greasy from her lipstick and tasted of strawberries.

'Once and for all,' again she chucked his cheeks, 'will you stop apologizing, ya gorgeous thick, you don't know how dishy you are.' Her voice became tender. 'That's why you're so feckin' attractive. That Siamese twin or whatever she is doesn't know how lucky she is.

Now, Francey,' after a second or so her voice softened, 'time to put your money where your mouth is. Do you want to or don't you?'

Francey felt impaled on her multicoloured gaze but Hazel took his silence for assent and moved even closer. 'Then would you ever give over – and put down that glass, it's not a bloody breastplate.'

When he had complied she kissed him again, harder, but stopped on the instant he began to respond. 'Take it easy, sweetheart . . .' Slowly, she undid two of his shirt buttons and slid her hand inside. 'What were those culchie girls thinking about at all, at all?' She smiled up at him, stroking a small area between his navel and breastbone to electrifying effect. 'How old are you, me old flower – twenty-five? Don'tcha think it's about time you had a bit of fun?' As she continued to stroke him, her voice was as smooth as cream.

It was going to happen. It was really going to happen. All Francey's heart-searching and questions melted in a hot flood of elation. His body, seemingly of its own volition, slid backwards until he was half lying. He turned his face into the seat back as though to blot out what Hazel was doing but as she undid more of his buttons and then the belt of his trousers, his arms crept around her slight frame. Where her hip swelled out, he could feel the ridge of her knickers, more erotic through the velvety fabric of her dress than any explicit photograph of a girl in a bikini. He pulled her towards his chest and she was astride him, her flounced black dress ruched up.

'Are you comfy?' She sounded throaty, and very near.

Francey opened his eyes: her full lips glistened just above his own. 'Hazel, Hazel,' he moaned, catching the back of her head and crushing her mouth on his.

'Not so fast . . .' Like an eel, she wriggled out of his grasp. 'I want your first time to be un-for-*gett-a-ble* . . .' Starting at his breastbone, she punctuated each syllable with a small lick, each lower than the last until, having lowered the zip of his fly, her tongue flickered just below his navel.

'It is already—' Afraid he would not be able to control himself, he tried to raise her face again to his but she resisted.

'No,' she breathed, 'the first time has to be proper. In comfort.' She slid off him and on to the floor. 'You'll thank me in later life. Come on . . .'

Francey saw little of the bedroom as he allowed Hazel to pull off his jacket and to push him backwards – 'Go in the middle there, I

105

want you right in the middle' – on to the double bed so that his head came to rest on the belly of a soft green hippopotamus.

'Lights!' She flipped the switch which brought on both bedside lamps. '*Voilà!*' She paused for a moment, looking down at him. 'Nice,' she breathed, then. 'We've no camera, unfortunately, but he-eee-re's *action*!' With one movement, she swished the trousers off his unresisting legs.

Both Francey's hands flew to protect the bulge in his crotch. 'What about getting pregnant?' It was the first time the danger had occurred to him.

'All taken care of,' she whispered, removing his hands and placing them by his side, 'nothing to worry about.' Before he could stop her she had brushed her lips across his encased erection and was back again at the base of his throat. She shushed his startled groan with a finger on his lips, then took one of his hands and placed it over one of her breasts.

She became as still as a stone.

The nerves in Francey's groin and in the palms of his hands joined together in pulsing circlets. He had been permitted to handle a girl's breast on few previous occasions; Hazel's felt warm and full and his instinct was to tear away the soft wool and the silky stuff underneath so he could squeeze and suck the malleable flesh. But wanting to delay, to postpone the exquisiteness of what was to come, he lay there, keeping tight rein on his instincts, experiencing each ecstatic second.

'How does this feel?' she asked softly. While wriggling her belly against his hip, she did something with the underlying muscles so the breast moved within his palm.

'It's –'

'Good!' Before he could reply further or take any action, she had flipped herself over and was lying beside him on her stomach, her arms stretched like a diver's above her head. 'Unzip my dress, would you, Francey?' she said, without looking at him.

Her brazenness was so sexy that Francey's breath almost choked him as he sat up to comply.

Hazel wriggled her toes with pleasure as, with fingers as unwieldy as spades he managed to lower the zip without incident. She wore no slip; her bra, panties and suspender belt were in a matching shade that Francey thought might be called magenta. He was past caring,

106

however, as first the taut white skin of her shoulders, back and waist, then the twin rounds of her covered bottom were revealed. His hands itched to remove the panties.

'Would you like to take the dress off altogether?' she invited.

'Are you sure this is all right – I won't hurt your sore arms?'

'Leave that to me, I'll scream – I hope!' As he worked the dress over her shoulders and down over her body, she helped him by undulating her arms, legs and torso, so enticingly that Francey forgot about her bandages altogether. Finally he could bear the tension no longer and having dropped the dress on the carpet beside the bed, lunged for her.

Like an otter, Hazel, still face down, scooted away to the edge of the bed. 'Hold on, hold on . . .' Then, smiling at him over her shoulder, 'One stage at a time, dear heart. Well,' she fluttered her false eyelashes, 'what do you think? Even allowing for me sexy wrappings,' semi-twisting her torso, she raised one of her arms and caught the edge of the elasticated bandage between her teeth and gazed up at Francey from under her absurd eyelashes, 'will I pass?'

'You're beautiful, Hazel.' He was not lying: at this moment she was the most seductive and enticing creature on earth, so much so that he was having difficulty getting the words out.

'It's a bit hot in here, don't you think? Let's see . . .' With sinuous grace Hazel resumed her face-down posture on the bed. Reaching behind her she patted her seat as though testing it. 'M-mmm, I think my bottom could do with a bit of fresh air – what do you think, Francey?'

He knew as he seized the slithery fabric and pulled the garment off that it was almost too late for him. 'I can't – I can't –'

'All right.' In a flash she had kicked off the panties, was off her stomach, and had pulled down his underpants, manoeuvring both of them so she was again astride him, this time skin to skin.

'Jesus.'

He turned his head away but she reached for him and pulled it back. 'Don't close your eyes,' she said urgently. 'I want you to remember everything, everything . . .' As she fed him into her, the sensation caused uproar in Francey's blood.

'That's my boy, that's my boy.' Despite her exhortations to him to keep his eyes open, Hazel's were closed as she bowed her body backwards to ride his bucking body; one hand on his stomach to help

107

steady herself, the other, the sight of which served to intensify his frenzy, was splayed over her breasts, massaging them through the lace.

'I – I –' He felt a scream bubbling up through the tumult.

'That's right, that's right,' Hazel laughed out loud, 'that's my fella, come on, come on –'

For a split second, like a neon tube about to ignite, Fleur Mannering's face flickered in and out of the detonating air above Francey's eyes. But then the base of his stomach erupted and Fleur's features dissolved in a roaring display of sight and sound which shattered the caverns of his head and chest; his body seemed to catapult outwards, rocketing alone in a private universe of sensation. The intensity of the pleasure rendered it indistinguishable from pain.

After a while, he could not have told how long, the rush ebbed, sucking away the marrow in his bones and making way for an incoming flow of a sluggish substance which felt like lukewarm treacle.

'There now.' Hazel lowered herself on to his chest and kissed him on the lips. 'That was nice, wasn't it?' she whispered. 'Bet, now, you didn't expect that when you were waiting for me in a pub earlier tonight?'

'Oh, Hazel . . .' Although it was beginning to calm down, Francey's heart was still knocking hard against his drenched ribcage; he knew his eyes were wet with tears but did not know why and did not care. 'Come here to me,' he whispered, lifting Hazel and turning both of them so they were lying facing one another and he could cuddle her close in his arms. 'I can't tell you what that was like.' With his uppermost hand he stroked her cropped blonde hair.

'You don't have to,' she chuckled, 'I had a ringside seat, remember?'

'Thank you.' As he hugged her, his muscles felt like old elastic.

'Don't thank me,' Hazel, her wisecracking temporarily suspended, closed her eyes and sighed, 'it was a privilege. It really was, Francey. I only hope –'

'What?' Francey kissed the top of her tousled head.

'Oh, nothing.'

'Come on, what do you hope?' At present he would have given – or told – Hazel anything on earth.

When she was not forthcoming, he could not find the energy to pursue her. 'I can tell you,' he said dreamily, 'you'd better look out, Hazel, you're after letting the genie out of the bottle now.'

'If you ask me, stupo, it was a long time coming – no pun intended!' They giggled and Hazel planted a kiss under his jaw, then subsided again into his embrace.

They lay like this for a little, allowing their overheated bodies to return to normal. One of her black-stockinged legs made a V on his stomach, bonding to it in mutual warmth; the rest of her body felt as though she had been built to fit his arms. Francey's imagination hovered above the two of them, seeing the incongruity of their dishevelled attire – her bra, suspender belt, stockings and arm bandages, his own shirt, loosened tie and socks – but in this state of blissful drift, it did not seem incongruous to him at all.

After a few minutes, he felt his strength returning and slipping one hand under her naked behind, he hitched her tighter to him. 'Did I make much noise?'

'You sure did.' Hazel's tone was smug. 'Me neighbours must think I have a herd of rhinoceroses in here.' In her Dublin accent the multiple syllables of the word sounded roundly delicious.

Francey laughed. 'Sorry.' As a matter of fact, he thought, he was not sorry in the least.

'If you say sorry one more time, I'll spank you.'

'You and what army?' Lightly, Francey smacked the damp rump under his palm. 'Are you comfortable enough there?' he asked, looking down at the top of her head.

'M-mmm.' Hazel shimmied her shoulders deeper into his embrace. 'I'm dyin' for a fag, though.'

'Wait a minute?' He was not ready to let her go just yet.

'All right. But I have to have one soon, all right? So tell us,' she went on, 'I'm curious about something. I know you could hardly call yourself Gallaher but where did the Sullivan come from? I seem to remember that Kathleen's name was Scollard, wasn't it?'

'Sullivan was my mother's maiden name.' Francey did not want to go into the reason why he had eschewed his first stepfather's name as it had to do with the difficult relationship he had had with Neeley Scollard. 'I've a complicated family,' he added. He was feeling lazy: his bones only now regaining their customary rigidity and the relationships at Lahersheen being difficult to untangle for an outsider, he hoped she would not press him too hard.

'You can say that again!' Hazel kissed his bare shoulder.

'Well, if it really matters to you,' Francey dropped a reciprocal kiss on the tip of her nose, 'pay attention now. As you know, my mother was pregnant when she got married to Neeley Scollard who had daughters. So those girls, Margaret and Kathleen and Goretti, they're my Scollard stepsisters, all right? And then, after me, she had two more girls, and they're my Scollard *half*-sisters. And when he died, she married again – Mossie Sheehan – and she had another girl so Connie is my Sheehan half-sister. Have you followed that?'

'Jesus, Mary and Joseph!' Hazel cackled. 'There's Scollards and Sheehans already in the house so to make things real simple, you go and call yourself Sullivan.'

'Yeah.' Francey grinned. She had not asked about Dessie and he decided not to complicate matters further by mentioning him.

But as they lapsed into quietude, he found he was thinking not of the complexities of his many-layered family but of Fleur. How would it be with her? Stroking Hazel's buttocks and back, he imagined what Fleur would feel like, how she would taste, how her bones might feel cuddled up like this in his arms. Then, within the crook of his elbow, Hazel gave a little sigh and he felt like a rotter. 'Hazel?' He squeezed her bottom.

'M-mmm?' She shifted, rotating it a little. 'If you don't want me to light up me fag do that again – that feels good.'

'That's fine then.' He obliged, massaging, compacting the soft flesh between fingers and palm, 'Because –'

'Oh, yes, keep doing that – that's gorgeous . . . Because what?' She did not open her eyes.

'The problem is,' he said, 'what do I do now?'

'What do you mean?' She looked up at him and seeing one of her false eyelashes had become unstuck, he peeled it off.

'I want it again.'

'You couldn't!' She laughed incredulously. She took off the other eyelash then raised herself on one elbow to check. 'Well, whaddya know?' she marvelled. '"The dead arose and appeared to many." You're your fa— you weren't lyin' when you were talking about genies gettin' out of bottles!'

You're your father's son. Although he knew quite well what she had been about to say, the exigency of his desire made Hazel's slip irrelevant to Francey. 'What are we going to do about me?' He made a grab for her but she eluded him and, after a good-humoured wrestling match, slipped out of his grasp and stood just out of range at the side of the bed. 'At least this time let's get our clothes off,' she said, reaching around to unsnap the catch of her bra. 'And this time, me oul' flower, let's take things a bit easier. I've meself to think about too, you know – and what's more, I'm still not in the whole of me health, you know!' Belying this last statement, she whipped off her bra and, holding it for a theatrical second at arm's length, discarded it with a daintiness that contradicted the expression in her eyes. 'What do you think? Not bad for an old lady, eh?'

Like a body builder, Hazel put her bandaged arms behind her back and lowered her shoulders, lifting her breasts so they jutted.

Francey stopped fumbling with the sleeves of his shirt. Never, even in his most feverish fantasies, had a woman behaved so provocatively.

'You like?' She was clearly enjoying his reaction.

'I like,' he choked as he gazed up at her breasts, at the archway of magenta suspender belt which framed her pubic hair, at the long fresh scar which ran under the stocking-top from just below her hipbone.

'Don't be looking at me war wounds now, Francey!' Hazel ran her finger along the scar and popped the suspender over it. Then she unhooked the belt and stepped out of the stockings altogether. She knelt on one knee on the side of the bed. Slowly, she compressed her cleavage with both hands until, to Francey's avid eyes, it looked as thin as a hair. 'Double trouble, sweetheart,' she whispered, offering her nipples, pushing them so close together that his mouth could take the two at once.

Later that first night Francey told Hazel about the job promotion offer in Ledbetter's and her advice was forthright. 'You'd be out of your brains,' she said in disbelief. 'That's not a career, that's a dead end. When are you going to realize that you don't *need* feckin' Ledbetter's any more?'

They should both have been exhausted but Francey's exhilaration was such that he wanted to stay awake as long as possible. 'But if I leave,' he asked, 'what can I do with myself? I'm qualified for nothing.'

He confessed then how he had flirted with the notion of going into the fringes of showbusiness when she had invited him to accompany her on the fateful minibus trip to Limerick. He did not tell her about his most recent idea, the one formulated in the stables of Inveraray Manor.

'H-mmm.' Hazel had not laughed as he had expected but her eyes took on a faraway look. 'There is probably something you can do,' she said slowly. 'Leave it with me. But first thing you've got to do is to go into that place and give in your notice. Do you hear me, Francey?'

Notwithstanding, it took all of Francey's courage to go into Mr Grieve's office the following day. He was still unused to the prospect of being his own master and answerable to no one. The idea of having a superior – his mother, a teacher, a boss – was deeply ingrained. The manager, who had been expecting 'good' news, was stony-faced in accepting his resignation and, having dispensed with notice – 'It is my experience, Mr Sullivan, that an employee is of no use once the decision to leave has been made' – counted out the money Francey was due.

Francey found himself out on the street as a free man within an hour of arriving at the premises, holding five pounds sixteen shillings and fourpence. He also found himself in a state not of exhilaration as he had imagined, but bordering on panic. Now what?

Before he knew it, he was in a taxi on his way back to Hazel's flat and it was only when he was describing to Hazel how the manager had reacted, the disbelief in his eyes, that he realized how much he had hated the place.

His sexual confidence had trebled and it was at his insistence that he and Hazel tumbled into bed again; the next two hours helped no end in dispelling any remnants of suspicion that he might have been a bit hasty in saying goodbye to the world of hardware and builder's supplies. Now that he had discovered sex with a willing partner, Francey could not get enough of it, and during the remainder of that week, days and nights merged into one another as Hazel continued her initiation, throwing up surprise after surprise. Francey was amazed to discover that women could have orgasms: up to now he had been aware, vaguely, that they needed to be 'satisfied' but had assumed this was something to do with the size of the male organ.

They ate at odd hours – fish and chips from the local chipper, or cornflakes, or cheese and tomatoes, everything from Hazel's fridge. He telephoned his landlady to say he would be away for a few more days and instead of going back to the digs to get fresh clothes and shaving gear, spent with abandon on new clothes and toiletries on their only outing, which was to the seaside suburb of Blackrock. He bought groceries, too, steaks and thick chops and smoked salmon. Hazel was not, she admitted cheerfully, an imaginative cook.

Francey's thousand pounds, which was a lot more in Irish money, seemed endless and he insisted on buying clothes for Hazel, too. They had taken the bus to Blackrock after a mere two hours' shopping, decided over a meal in a snack restaurant that they needed one another again too badly to waste any more time and so, leaving their half-eaten mixed grills on the table, they gathered up their purchases and took a taxi back to the flat.

Late on Saturday that week when the Blackrock groceries ran out, Francey went to the local newsagent's to buy biscuits and chocolate – and in that way he and Hazel discovered, twenty-four hours later than anyone else on the planet, that while they had been engaged in pushing back the boundaries of physical enjoyment, the world had been transfixed by the assassination of President Kennedy in Dallas. Francey brought home a newspaper and they turned on Hazel's television for an hour or so, watching the fuzzy pictures from Washington in disbelief as a shocked Vice-President Johnson was sworn in. But then they had turned off the pictures and turned their attention back on themselves.

Hazel's outside life intruded occasionally during the week: the telephone disturbed them from time to time until Francey, feeling masterful, took it off the hook when they embarked on a fresh session. The door chimes sounded now and then but the flat was equipped with a loudspeaker arrangement between its lobby and the front entrance and Hazel was able to deal with callers without seeing them. Curiosity had never been one of Francey's driving forces and he did not bother to enquire who was there; neither did Hazel volunteer to tell him.

On the morning of the seventh day, when the flat looked as though all the stuffed animals had come to life and had rampaged through it in continuous stampede, Hazel emerged from the bath-room and, looking around the strewn bedroom, announced that her cleaning lady came on Monday mornings and that, anyway, she wanted to go away to visit a friend somewhere in Sligo. 'I've me own life to get back to, bud,' she said. 'Me public's been clamouring for me, I don't think!'

Then, holding up her arms, the bandages on which were now more than a little the worse for wear, 'Even if they aren't, thanks to you, I've already missed one appointment with me specialist. I could have had these off by now. It's a miracle me poor body has stood up to all this after what it's been through.' Francey had noticed that Hazel's Dublin accent became more pronounced when she was at one end or the other on the scale of decision: when she either felt unsure or absolutely sure of herself.

Still in bed and lost in a fuzz somewhere between what the two of them had just done and what he would like to do to Fleur, he did not feel up to judging on which end of the scale she now trod and turned his head lazily. He had always known that their spree would come to an end sometime and it had lasted a lot longer than he had expected. 'Of course you've got to go and see the consultant,' he said, trying to find a way out for one of his feet through the tangled sheets. 'But,' revealing his nakedness, he ripped off the offending sheet altogether, 'if this is what we can do while you're still not in the whole of your health . . . ?'

Hazel did not respond. 'Get up, will ya?' she ordered. 'I'm going to make a bit of grub.'

It was the first time she had been sharp with him in sexual matters and Francey sat up, alarmed. 'You're not sorry, are you? I'm certainly not.'

'No.' Hazel hesitated then came across to sit beside the bed. Her face serious, she stroked his forearm. 'Of course I don't regret a minute of it, Francey. But there's no point in beating around the bush, is there? I know that your mind is elsewhere.'

'I'm sorry.' Francey trapped her hand and pressed it to his mouth. 'It's not my fault, it's something that seems to be sort of outside my control. But I can't tell you enough how great this has been—'

'Ssh.' With her fingers, Hazel pinched his mouth shut. 'Don't say any more. It's been great for me too.' She slid off the bed and left the room. Francey listened for the customary sound of clashing and clattering from the kitchen but it was a long time starting and suddenly he felt wretched. Disentangling himself from the bedclothes, he jumped out of bed and padded into the bathroom. When he stooped to look at himself in the mirror, his unshaven reflection, topped with a thatch which at present spiked in all directions, gazed back, accusing him: *What kind of a rotter are you?* He washed and shaved and by the time he was dressed and had thrown his stuff into the suitcase out of which he had lived since his arrival home from London, the aroma of rashers and sausages was strong.

'Just in time, here you are.' Hazel, whose back was to him when he arrived in the kitchen, turned round and held out a plateful of food.

'Thanks.' Francey put down his case and took it. 'Hazel,' he began, but she cut him off.

'Sit down and get that into you, Francey Sullivan, or I'll knock your block off.'

He tried again as they finished the meal but she would not hear of any discussion of relationships or imminent partings. 'For God's sake, Francey,' she said at one point, 'will you leave it? We had a good time, we both did, it was fun but it's not *Gone With The Wind*.'

'At least can I see you when you come back to Dublin?' he asked ten minutes later as she handed him his coat.

'Of course, stupo,' she said, 'ring me. But I think we could do with a decent break from each other. I'll be back sometime in the middle of next week – make it Friday, all right? Now if I don't hurry I'm going to be late. Take your bloody case out of me way and git!' She opened the door of the flat and pushed him out.

As Francey wandered the streets of Dublin in the empty day that followed, he found he missed Hazel, and not only with his awakened body. He missed her companionship, her sense of fun. To fill in time during the afternoon, he went to the motor tax office of Dublin Corporation and bought himself a driving licence. Although he had had little practice he knew how to drive in a rudimentary way; now that he had the wherewithal, he planned to acquire a car, maybe an MGB like Colin's . . . No, he thought then, not a car like Colin's but maybe an Aston Martin or a Morgan. As he looked again at the pristine red cover of the driving licence, he marvelled at how the idea of spending money was becoming easier.

As the day progressed, the void caused by the withdrawal of the physical satiety to which he had grown accustomed with Hazel was filled with renewed urgency to contact Fleur Mannering. Under the ministrations of a barber in North Earl Street, who cut his hair and then shaved him with soothing dexterity, Francey decided the time had come to make some serious decisions.

He went straight from the barber shop to the digs, where he paid off the startled landlady and divided his clothes and belongings into a suitcase and a shopping bag. The latter he left at the St Vincent de Paul depot in Mountjoy Square in the hope that the contents might be of some use to the poor of the city and then, carrying his case, he checked into a room in the Gresham Hotel in O'Connell Street.

That evening, he picked up his bedside telephone and gave George's number to the hotel operator. The butler – Francey could not remember his name – answered. And just before the line clicked dead as his call was transferred to wherever George was, Francey, pressing the receiver hard to his ear, fancied he heard a woman's laugh. His stomach flipped. It had been the most fleeting of sounds. Was his imagination playing tricks or could Fleur be there? As the seconds – and the shillings – ticked away and the earpiece remained impenetrably noiseless, he became impatient: like most Irish people, he had a horror of the expense of long-distance calls. Then he remembered that he could afford to hold on for as long as he liked. The habit of a lifetime was hard to beat.

'Yes, Francey?' At last his father was on the line. Francey was a little taken aback, George's manner was more brusque than he had expected. 'I'm just ringing up to say hello,' he said. 'Did I ring at a bad time?'

'Not at all, old man, lovely to hear from you. How did your mother react when you told her your news?'

Although George's tone softened a little Francey knew for sure now that his call was not welcome. 'I haven't told Mammy yet, as it happens,' he replied, determined not to be intimidated. After all, he had every right to call, he thought, then heard himself tell his father that he would probably go down to Lahersheen next weekend although this was something on which he had not yet decided.

'That's your business, of course.' George's voice became muffled as he covered the mouthpiece at his end for a split second – to hush someone else up? To impart information as to who was on the other end of the line? Then: 'Was there anything else, old chap?'

Francey became annoyed. Silence crackled between them and he decided he was not going to be the one to break it.

116

'When will we see you over this side of the water again, d'you think?'

Francey was glad that George had been the one to give in but could not yet bring himself to the purpose of the call. 'Soon, I hope,' he said. 'We have to sit down and talk – er – George. There's a lot I want to ask you.'

'Certainly. Go ahead.' George waited.

'Maybe the telephone is not the best place.' Forgetting his irritation, Francey swallowed and screwed his eyes shut. 'We'll leave it until I come over, all right? Are – are Colin and Fleur around, these days?' There – it was out. He clenched his toes.

Silence again at the other end of the line. Finally, 'They were here with young Tommy last weekend. Pity you weren't here then, Francey, we don't expect them again now for another wee while. Maybe we can all get together sometime during the Christmas holiday?'

'Yes, maybe,' Francey found his voice, 'I'm thinking of going over to London for a few days – you know, start the process of looking for Dessie . . .' Then he took a deep breath. 'And I thought I might look the two of them up. Have you got Colin's number handy?'

'Sure, sure. I'm bad on numbers so I have to write everything down, hold on a minute . . .' Francey's toes bored harder into his shoe-leather as he heard George rustling paper. Then he was back. 'Here it is.'

As her number was read out and he transcribed it on the little notepad beside the telephone, the pencil felt slippery in Francey's hand. 'I'm glad, as it happens, that you're coming over.' George's voice was brisk now. 'We have to make proper arrangements about transferring money to you on a regular basis. And I've earmarked your painting for you in case someone else fixes it with a beady eye. How are you for money at the moment, by the way? Need more? Is that why you telephoned?'

'Oh, no,' Francey was aghast. 'I've plenty of money left,' he spluttered, 'loads —'

'As you pointed out, Francey, it is your business, of course, but there are even more loads of it over here for you. Your income now is almost six thousand a week. I hope you've sorted something out with your tax people over there?'

'Not yet.' In the whirl of all that had happened to him, Francey had given the nuts and bolts of his financial windfall very little attention.

'Well, take my advice,' George was winding up his side of the conversation, 'get it sorted out as quickly as possible. I've said the same to Colin, by the way. I've a good accountant over here. When you come over, if you like I'll make an appointment for you. Maybe the two of you could go to see him together.'

'I'll do that,' Francey promised. Saying that they would keep in touch, they terminated the call but not before Francey had heard again that faint, fluting laugh.

After he replaced the receiver, his father's financial exhortations dissolved as Francey sat staring at the scrawl on the notepad. He had planned to telephone her straight away while his courage held, but now, remembering the silence on the line after he mentioned her name and his father's dinner table question as to whether he and Fleur had enjoyed their walk in the wood, he felt unnerved. He folded the number into his wallet.

Later that evening, as he climbed into his neat hotel bed, Francey decided that what he had said to George about going to see his mother the following weekend would have to become a self-fulfilling prophecy. The time had come to face the music at home. What had held him back was a reluctance to open up again the whole subject of his paternity. Francey's mother was better than the parents of most of his contemporaries in the matter of open communication but she, like most people, operated on the basis of 'let well enough alone' and Francey knew she would not relish any revisiting of her former notoriety. As soon as he revealed what had happened to him, not only Lahersheen but the entire peninsula would be agog, rehashing the juiciness of what had been the biggest scandal to visit the district in decades.

And he was afraid of opening up old wounds. The death of Neeley Scollard, his first stepfather who had married Elizabeth Sullivan and had taken on the rearing of himself, her bastard son, was still vivid in his mind, not only because of its awfulness but because somewhere in the back of his mind, Francey had always blamed himself for Neeley's death. He had been just six years old but just as the images from his father's visit to the farmhouse were as fresh in his mind as if they had happened yesterday, so were the scenes surrounding his stepfather's death, the awful fight between Neeley and his mother which led to his own intervention and subsequent incarceration in a Cork hospital with a cracked skull. When he had come home from the hospital, Neeley was dead and buried.

No one, not even his mother, had told Francey the full story of what had happened; nevertheless, during his primary schooldays, on being taunted with some lurid version of his family history he had fought many a fellow-pupil in her defence. All he knew for sure was that as if his mother's pregnant-out-of-wedlock state when she had married his stepfather had not been bad enough, the scandal about her which had surrounded Neeley's death had been even worse. It had involved a feud of silence with another family in the parish, the McCarthys, one of whom had vanished from Lahersheen soon after the event. As soon as he had been old enough to understand the innuendo and gossip, Francey's private reaction – and retaliatory support for his mother – had been to insist on being called Sullivan, which was her name, instead of Scollard, as he was known on his birth certificate. No one had ever been able to get him to change it back. He had so far never needed a passport but when the time came, he was going to go the full distance, changing his name by deed poll.

He turned off the lamp beside his bed: he would not think about what faced him in Lahersheen until he was forced to. He would think about poor Dessie. After his home visit he would make a full-time occupation, at least for a while, of searching for his younger half-brother.

And he also had something to look forward to: the arrangement to meet Hazel again at the flat at the end of the following week. Flopping over on his stomach in the bed, which was, as usual, too short for him, Francey deliberately conjured up some of the things he and Hazel had done to and for one another and fell asleep in the image of that first night, when Hazel had fed him her breasts.

This time, however, what he imagined was not Hazel's opulence but the cool delicacy of Fleur.

All the way back to Cork, Francey's brain clicked in slothful tandem with the wheels of the train. He had chosen to travel on a Saturday so as not to alarm his mother; if he had told her he was coming home on a weekday, she might have worried that he had been fired.

His satiated body was bathed in voluptuous memories of sex. He should have been drained, he knew, but in a way he did not understand, the week of passion with Hazel had resulted in his not feeling 'too tall' or 'huge' any more, merely 'big'; and being big was to be full of vitality, to vibrate with certainties. He was amazed at how little he worried about being a sinner and the more he thought about it, the more he felt that the Church had somehow got it wrong: surely God would not have created something so beautiful for His subjects to enjoy if He had not meant them to utilize it to the full? There was no risk of anyone getting hurt, no possibility of a baby. Hazel had a friend who knew a Protestant doctor and had had no trouble in getting the Pill.

Francey knew only one small strand of disquiet, so filmy that it brushed none but the outside reaches of his conscience and, surprisingly, it was not that Fleur was married. Francey worried about the morality of going to bed with one woman while being in love with another.

Hazel would always be a dear, dear friend, but that was all. He would continue going to bed with her if she was happy about it too, but his fantasies were now vested in Fleur. He and Hazel had discussed it during the odyssey of that week. She had been sensible and comforting, allaying his worries that he was being somehow disloyal to both women, or that he was using her.

'Of course you're not,' she had reassured him. 'This was my choice, remember?' She had kissed a spot in the centre of his chest. 'Don't worry about me, sport. I don't expect anything from you, anything at all. I've been relyin' on Number One for a good few years now.' She had been smoking and in consideration of Francey's distaste for cigarette smoke, was lying on her back to blow it away from him. And when he had reached over to hook up her chin, her expression had been candid and smiling. Over the next week, they had discussed other things too, their lives, their hopes. Now that Francey thought about it, however, he remembered that it was mainly his life and hopes they had explored.

He thought about Hazel and Fleur again now under cover of the gloom as the Cork-bound train entered the tunnel on the outskirts of the city: he thought of Fleur's breasts, what they would feel like – and then of what Hazel could do with her fingers and even her toes.

She had not been trained as a dancer for nothing, he thought, and she had kept herself in shape. All his life, or at least since he had grown so tall, he had worried about making love to a woman much smaller than himself. But Hazel had shown him ways and means to get around such disparity, teasing him that given her own delicate state at the time, their having to be careful about his size was a blessing in disguise.

Good old Hazel, he thought as the driver applied the brakes to his locomotive and the train squealed into the station. He could not have been luckier in the choice of his first sex partner. And it was great she was so mature as well.

He was tired by the time he got to Castletownbere nearly six hours later. When he had telephoned his mother to announce his visit, he had told her only that he was coming because he had some news.

But when the Berehaven bus pulled into the square in front of MacCarthy's pub his mother's answering smile as he waved to her and Margaret, one of his stepsisters, through the mud-spattered window beside his seat made him realize once again the depth of his love for her. Manipulating the parcels he had lugged all the way from Dublin, he plunged down the steps of the bus and leaned down for a hug. Lately Elizabeth Sullivan had taken to wearing Ashes of Roses, the same scent as her own mother, his grandmother Sullivan; the smell always reminded Francey of his childhood. 'How are you, Mam?' He smiled down at her.

'Never better.' Her answering smile lit up her high-boned face. Sometimes, from the distance of Dublin, Francey had to remind himself that she was forty-five years of age. In his mind she was as she had been when he was old enough to notice: a beautiful woman of the age he was now. Looking at her now, in the gloom of the streetlights, she did not look any older than Hazel Slye.

'What's in the box?' Never one to beat about the bush, having inspected him up and down – 'You look all right, anyway' – his stepsister bent down to examine the largest of the heavy packages. In many ways, he thought with amusement, Margaret reminded him of Hazel; there was no fear of anyone getting uppity or sentimental around either of them.

'It's great to see you.' Elizabeth hugged him again then stood back. 'I must say you look healthy enough.' Then she, too, gazed in amazement at the array of parcels. 'What's all the stuff? Did you rob a bank or what?'

'You'll all have to have a bit of patience.' Francey eased Margaret out of the way and picked up the box at which she had been poking.

'It's like Christmas.' Margaret took two of the smaller packages and followed Francey across the wide square towards the family's old Hillman, which was parked in front of MacCarthy's pub.

'Well, it is nearly Christmas, isn't it?' Francey waited until his mother caught up with him and opened the boot of the Hillman. She sighed as she watched him put the box inside. 'God, I love this time of year. It's funny but we always seem to get great weather coming up to Christmas.'

Francey let her go ahead of him to the passenger side of the car and helped her inside. Hesitating before inserting his bulk into the discomfort of the back seat, he stood with his hand on the roof and breathed in the smell of the town, which had not changed since he was a child: only the passing seasons added degrees of variety and pungency to the familiar cocktail of fish, diesel fuel, animal manure and turf smoke which permeated the salty air.

Darkness blended out the neglected paintwork on the buildings which stood around the square; it unified the architecture of the buildings and almost gave the lie to the old-timers who opined that Castletown had never been the same since the British, who had run a thriving naval base on Bere Island, had left. But the square was largely empty, occupied by just the Berehaven bus on which Francey had arrived, dark and empty now, plus three cars and as many horse carts. He remembered other pre-Christmas seasons, when, each evening, the horse traffic had to jostle for parking space and such was the press of bodies in the pubs round the square that doors were propped open to let in a bit of air.

The wind was quiet this evening and beyond the cars and animals, out of sight behind the chandlery building, he could hear a trawler chug slowly into her berth. The sound made him feel lonely, as though he had moved beyond the reach of his childhood. To his left, a stout woman puffed out of MacCarthy's, bringing with her a spill of yellow light and laughter but as the door closed again behind her, it acted like a candlesnuffer. Francey looked with longing at the scarred wooden door: although he knew it would be only a matter of days before he would be fretting to leave again, coming home like this always filled him with softness, and the brief glimpse of cheery intimacy was enticing.

'What's keeping you?' Margaret leaned across Elizabeth and tapped on the passenger window.

'I'm coming.' He was getting sentimental in his old age, Francey thought as he got into the car.

They lifted two neighbours as they turned the corner out of the town on to the road towards Eyeries and Francey was spared the probing of his mother and stepsister during most of the journey. Even when they let the neighbours off at Ballycrovane, he refused to divulge his news. 'Ye'll just have to wait. And anyway, I think I should tell you first, Mammy —'

'You're getting married! He's getting married, Mam.' Margaret turned to Elizabeth in excitement. 'I knew there was something different about him, the minute I saw him! The boy's in love!'

'I'm not getting married!' Knowing that amongst all these women, a wedding would outshine even becoming a millionaire, Francey was peeved. If that's what they were expecting, what he had to tell them would be almost a disappointment. 'None of you lot have managed it yet, have you?' he snapped at Margaret, then regretted it as Elizabeth remonstrated, 'Lads, lads, please.'

In reply, his stepsister ground the gears while negotiating a bad bend on the tortuous, hilly road and it was on the tip of Francey's tongue to retort that she was the one who had started it when he realized how silly it would sound. Considering how adult his behaviour had been in the past week or so, he thought, this infantile regression was extraordinary. It always happened, every time he came home.

His mother took up the conversational slack, filling him in on the doings of the district and leaving him free to watch the pass of the quiet countryside. Despite his physical discomfort – the roof of the car was too low for him so he had to sit hunched over and at an angle to accommodate the length of his legs – Francey quite enjoyed driving at night. Something about the dim, womb-like feeling of being enclosed, safe from the outside darkness, fed him with a sense of security. The sea below them was quiet, sheeny with reflected stars, and tonight, keyed up as he was about other matters, he did not flinch as he normally did when the wavering headlights of the car picked out the Celtic crosses which loured over the high stone wall of Kilcatherine graveyard directly ahead of them. 'Anyone dead recently?' he asked, giving Elizabeth another conversational opening as Margaret drove with caution round the blind half-circle under the crosses.

As they climbed the steep hill beyond Kilcatherine point, Francey checked through his rear window: there it was, stalwart pal of his youth: the fleeting white lighthouse flash from the direction of the Bull Rock. He was home.

'Wasn't it terrible about poor President Kennedy?' Margaret had recovered her good humour. 'It was the talk of the district. I was called out to Derryconnla' – Margaret was a district nurse – 'and it was on the wireless. Everyone was out on the roads, no one could believe it. Was it as big in Dublin? I suppose everyone was talking about it.'

'Oh, yes.'

'How'd you hear?' She eased the car round the last bend and started to descend the hill towards home.

'Oh,' Francey was thankful for the darkness, 'on the wireless too, I think —'

'You only *think*?' Margaret gave a theatrical sigh. 'Typical! I suppose you had your nose stuck in book. An atomic bomb could fall and you wouldn't notice.'

'U-mmm.' Ahead of him, Francey could see the hump of Knockameala against the paler sky and craned forward for his first glimpse of the house, which sat between the ridges of the mountain's broad foot. 'Who's home for Christmas?' he asked, willing Margaret to get off the subject of the late president.

'Not many yet,' Elizabeth replied. 'There's a few Yanks around already and the Harringtons are expecting cousins from England on Monday but no one you'd be interested in. It's a bit early. When are you coming home yourself? How long have you got off?'

'Don't know yet.'

His mother caught the evasion. 'Has something happened at work?'

Her perspicacity annoyed Francey. 'Of course not,' he responded, and was saved further protestations of innocence as Margaret slowed the car down to turn it through the gateway and into the farmyard. His heart always skipped at this point of homecoming and tonight was no exception: in anticipation of his arrival, every window in the two-storey house was lit.

As he unfolded himself from the car, the latest Rex, a recent acquisition, less than a year old and not yet fully trained, lolloped across the yard to say hello.

'Bloody eejit.' As she got out, Margaret brushed away the animal's exuberant greetings. 'This yoke', she complained to Francey, 'thinks cows are for playing with.'

'Hello, fella!' Francey, who had not seen this Rex before, allowed the enraptured animal to jump up on him. 'He'll be grand, won't you, boy?' He fondled the dog's ears, still soft with puppy wool and then, picking up a stone, threw it across the yard.

'Mossie'll kill you.' Margaret, watching Rex hurtle after the missile, shook her head in disapproval. 'You know very well the way he thinks working dogs should be treated.'

'Would you have a heart, he's only a baby.' Francey threw another stone for the pup.

'Baby or not,' Margaret said, 'he's going to break our hearts. This one's a wanderer. He goes missing and half the time we don't know where he is. But Mossie doesn't like tying him up during the day.'

With that, the stocky figure of Mossie himself appeared in the open doorway of the kitchen. 'Hello, Mossie,' Francey called. He was fond of his second stepfather, in an absent sort of way.

'Welcome home.' Mossie walked towards the car to help with the luggage. Then, on seeing the contents of the boot, he put his hands on his hips and stood back a little as though assessing a prospective purchase at a mart. 'Did you buy up Dublin?'

'He refuses to tell us his famous news. I bet he's won the Sweep and didn't remember to tell us at the time. Or maybe he's one of the Great Train Robbers!' Margaret seized a package and marched off with it towards the house.

'Would you all have a bit of patience?' Francey grinned. This was the good part of having money, he discovered, and he was determined to get maximum pleasure from his own generosity by making a sort of ceremony with the presents.

Before he got to the door, he and his parcels were engulfed by the sturdy arms of his second youngest stepsister, Abigail, twenty years old and home for the weekend from her job in a grocer's shop in Kenmare. 'How are ya, Francey?' she bubbled, catching him just above the waist. 'Welcome to the ancestral pile.'

'Thanks, Abby, my arms are full or I'd hug you back.' Although of all in his family he was closest to Johanna, the sister in Montana, he was always delighted to see Abigail, whose sunny personality lit up in any company in which she found herself.

'Got a kiss for me, Connie?' he called as, with Abigail in close attendance, he crossed the door into the warm kitchen.

Constance, his mother's only child with Mossie, looked up from the schoolwork spread over the big table in the centre of the room. 'Hello, Francey,' she said, her small serious face creased in a frown. 'Sorry, I'm in the middle of something here.'

'So late?' Dropping his burdens on a chair by the window, Francey crossed the room and ruffled her dark curls. 'And there was I thinking a genius like you wouldn't have to crack the books at all?'

'Stop it, Francey,' Constance replied crossly, 'it's no joke. I have *piles* of eccer this weekend.' To her mother's delight, Constance was planning to go on to university after doing her Leaving Cert in eighteen months' time, the only one of Francey's long-tailed and motley family to do so; if it worked out, and her teachers were confident it would, she would also be the first girl from Lahersheen to go. Within the preceding few years, several girls from neighbouring Derryconnla had got into teacher training college or into the lower grades of the civil service and a few had become nurses, but most of the girls in the parish, if they sat the Leaving Cert at all, took jobs in shops or went on commercial courses in Dublin or Cork and became secretaries, bookkeepers or clerks.

'Well, it's not often your favourite brother comes home from the big smoke to see you, so leave the old books for five minutes and make us a cup of tea, will you?' Francey kissed her cheek.

'Why does it always have to be *me*?' With a sigh, Constance got up from the table, crossed to the Rayburn and moved the kettle in on to the hotplate.

As his mother and Margaret hung up their coats, Francey flopped into a chair at the top of the big table which dominated the kitchen. It was too tidy, he thought. There had been a time when to get enough space on this table to do homework was a competitive struggle. 'The place looks empty,' he said.

'Yes, doesn't it?' His mother pushed a few strands of her hair back

126

into place. 'Sometimes it doesn't feel like real life any more here, with just Maggie and Connie as permanent residents. Here's the latest letters from Goretti and Hannah, they're both doing well – Goretti's moved jobs, she's now selling real estate in one of the Chicago suburbs, or so she says, and she has a new boyfriend.' She reached up to take a sheaf of envelopes from behind a small framed photograph on the mantelpiece and paused, her expression sad. 'It's coming up again to the anniversary of the time Kitty and Dessie left, you know, Francey.'

Francey looked up at the photograph which was all they had left of the two runaways. 'I know,' he said. 'And I want to talk to you about that.'

'When are we going to know what's in the camel-train?' Margaret, still engaged with the parcels in the centre of the room, called out, interrupting.

'I've to talk to Mammy first.' Francey took the letters from his mother and stuffed them into his pocket.

Chapter Seven

The smell of paraffin was pungent but not unpleasant. It wafted from the Valor heater, but also from the oil lamps Francey's mother kept in the sun-porch because she preferred their gentle glow over the harshness of electricity.

The porch, a recent addition hung with baskets of ivies and geraniums, ran the full length of the front of the house, enclosing the never-used main entrance. His hands hanging between his knees, Francey gazed through the windows in the direction of the luminous bluish halo, about a mile and a half distant, which hung over the village of Eyeries at the other side of Coulagh Bay. To the right of the village, the black wall of night was pricked by a string of tiny lights stretching all along the foreshore as far as Cod's Head and the intermittent flash from the lighthouse.

Peripherally, however, Francey was watching his mother as she sat assimilating what he had just told her. He noticed the way silver veins in her hair glinted in the light from the nearest lamp; he had always loved her hair which, still luxurious, straggled as usual from the coil in which she tried to confine it. During his childhood she had worn it unfettered and straight so it poured like honey over her shoulders and one of his earliest sense memories was of grabbing it and trying to stuff handfuls of it into his mouth.

As though reading his mind, she reached behind her neck and attempted to tidy the coil, pulling out hairpins and shoving them back in different configurations; although in many ways he felt closer to her than to any other human being on earth, she could shut him out as she did now. Elizabeth Sullivan had always been different from other mothers in the district, not only in her height and beauty. Francey assumed that the comparison arose from her middle-class city background.

Since reaching adulthood and going to Dublin, he had wondered now and then how easy – or difficult – it had been for her to settle in Lahersheen after her relatively affluent upbringing. He never brought the thought too far, however, since he knew too well that her illicit pregnancy with himself had been the cause of the forced resettlement. 'So what do you think?' He fiddled with a set of draughts on the table which stood between their respective chairs.

Instead of replying straight away, his mother stood up and crossed to the Valor to readjust the height of the flame. Francey, watching her long slim back as she bent over it, wondered why it was that, despite his age, he still felt he needed her approval.

'What are you going to do with all this money?' She turned round at last, her face serious.

'I don't know,' Francey admitted. 'It's all happened so fast I haven't had time to think about it much. But it's not going to go away and I think it would be better not to do anything hasty?' His appeal for affirmation, or advice, went unanswered as his mother's expression continued to defeat his efforts to read it.

'And George,' she continued to study him, 'your father, how's he taking the news?'

'Again, I'm not too sure about that.' He felt he was teetering along the edge of a narrow wall. There were consequences to the discovery that his father was a man of flesh and blood and not a fantasy figure, and one of them was an unexpected stirring of loyalty. One step in the wrong direction and he would be disloyal to one or the other of his parents. 'It was a shock to him, of course,' he said, choosing his words, 'to us all. But so far it's been all right, I think.'

Then to get away from the subject of George, 'And as for the other man I told you about, Colin, my half-brother, so far he's being pretty good about it too.'

'But I still don't understand. Why do you think this American woman went to all that trouble to find out about you and Dessie, all the rest of it?'

'Mammy, I haven't a clue. I think it's all to do with her not having a family of her own – I think,' he repeated, knowing that this, too, might seem disloyal to the mother who had gone through the difficult times while George and Jool were living in the lap of luxury. And while Jool's actions might have sounded logical around her own fantastical glass table it sounded more than a little unlikely in the homely rural setting of his boyhood. 'Look, Mammy,' he blurted, 'the reason I came home at all was that I really want to know how *you* feel about it.'

'I don't know how I feel, to tell you the truth.' Elizabeth sat back into her chair. 'I feel all kinds of things, some good, some not so great. But you must believe that I'm thrilled for you – truly, Francey. It's a great piece of luck. I hope you'll be very happy.'

When he had imagined this scene, Francey had envisaged whoops of joy, hugs – or at the opposite end of the scale, tearful recrimination about his contacting his father without telling her in advance. He had failed to foresee this quiet reserve. He and his mother had always been able to talk to one another although in latter years had fallen out of the habit. He took a deep breath. 'Come on, Mammy, what's the not-so-great things you're feeling?'

'I can't put my finger on it.' She twisted her bracelet. 'I should be out-and-out delighted and in a way I am – yet I feel sort of disappointed. Even resentful.' She leaned forward. 'I'm trying to be honest.'

'Resentful? Why?' Francey was on the defensive although he was pretty sure what she meant. She had every right to feel resentful.

'It's not a very pleasant feeling and I'm not proud of it.' Avoiding his eye, she got up again and went to the nearest window, clearing the condensation from one of the panes. 'After all these years,' she said, 'you'd think I'd be past caring what that man does or where he is or anything about him. I thought I was rid of him for good – but he can still get under my skin, it seems.'

'It's a long time ago, Mammy,' Francey appealed.

Her eyes were shadowed in the lamplight as she turned round again to face him. 'Of course it is, Francey, and you're the good side of George Gallaher. Thank God you don't seem to have inherited his fecklessness – that I know of anyway.' She looked up at him as though trying to read his soul and Francey could not hold her gaze. What would she have made of his lust-filled week with Hazel Slye? When he looked up again she had dropped her eyes again to her bracelet: 'I know that sounds harsh and I'm sorry, but I'm too old now to beat around the bush. And I'm only human,' she added, 'so something inside me says that it just isn't fair how George Gallaher always seems to fall on his feet. From what you tell me, having escaped all his life from any repercussions from his actions, he marries well and now, as well as being rich himself, he's handed on a plate two ready-made grateful sons, boys he never had to smack or scold or force to do their homework or sit up all night with. What's more, in one blink of an eye he's made you rich. And now that he has the incentive – and the money, of course – he might even be able to find Kitty and Dessie, something I've failed to do. Is it any wonder I've mixed feelings?' She stared at him and then smiled wryly. 'I suppose, if I'm honest, I'm jealous.'

Francey was afraid she was going to cry. 'But I had to see him sooner or later,' he urged, 'you accept that?'

'Of course I do. I just wish the whole thing didn't hurt so much, that's all.' She passed the back of one hand across her forehead. 'I'm sorry, I'm being very childish. I suppose this is some kind of turning-point, a swapping of roles. It's you who is being the mature one here.'

'Don't be hurt, please,' Francey begged, 'nothing is going to change between me and the family – *this* family, I mean. Listen, Mammy,' he added, 'this is *good* news. Anyone would think I'm telling you I'm going to be transported to Australia or something.'

'You know I want only the best things in life for you, Francey.' She lifted her chin. 'Look, there's another thing.'

After the puzzle of her initial response, Francey welcomed the sudden blaze of challenge in her eyes. 'What is it?'

'I'm afraid now you won't want to know us – me – any more. That you'll be dazzled by him. Who knows better than me how blasted attractive that bastard can be?'

Francey almost laughed with relief. 'Oh, Mammy, is that all that's wrong? I can assure you that will not be the case —'

'I can't see you coming back here to the farmhouse and settling in with the cows and the spuds!' she interrupted.

'No,' Francey admitted, 'but I was never going to do that anyway.'

With that, the challenge collapsed. 'Oh, Francey,' his mother half laughed, half groaned, 'don't mind me. I'm sorry! All right, so it's not fair but what's fair in this life? Thank God I don't believe in God or I'd think this was His little joke on me! Come on, give us a hug.' At last she smiled. 'It's great, it really is, Francey. And I'm a bloody selfish old so-and-so.'

As he bent to hug her, Francey wondered if he would ever in his life understand women. At least he could leave a few bob behind him when he left. The first time he had ever been able to do that since he had started working.

'What? You're a *what*?' Margaret screeched when Francey announced a few minutes later that it was time to open the parcels, and then the reason for them.

'What? A millionaire?' Connie's eyes were round.

'Yep. I'm a millionaire,' he repeated, delighted now.

'Lizzie?' Mossie looked towards where she was standing in the doorway which led from the kitchen in to the sun porch.

'It's true,' Elizabeth replied, 'Francey's inherited a lot of money from – from a relation.'

'What relation?' Constance flew across to Francey and caught hold of the lapels of his jacket. 'Have I a rich relation I don't know about?'

'Come on, Francey, give us more details.'

'Yeah.'

'For God's sake, Francey, are we all going to be rich?'

The three girls chimed in together, leading Francey to hold up his hands for quiet. He glanced across at his mother. 'Is it all right to tell them about how it happened?'

She nodded and turned away to the stove. Mossie went to join her and through the clamour still being made by the girls, for a fraction of a second, Francey's recently awakened eyes noted the casual way his hand dropped to caress her waist. The next instant he realized it was none of his business. 'All right, girls,' he laughed, 'enough – *enough*! Sit down and I'll tell ye . . .'

He started at the beginning, enjoying the rapt attention while he told them everything, including the part that Hazel had played in finding George Gallaher.

Margaret remembered Hazel and, naturally, was inquisitive about how he had encountered her. Francey told her, then went on to relate how he had chanced upon his father's house on the day of Jool's funeral, the story of the will – and of Colin.

'You've another brother?' Margaret looked to Elizabeth for confirmation.

Trust her, Francey thought. 'Yes,' he confirmed, 'there's three of us. All my father's sons.'

132

'Holy God, this family's gettin' more complicated by the minute!' Hearing Margaret's echo of what George had said at the glass table at the Manor, Francey grinned. 'You haven't heard the half of it,' he said ruefully.

'What's he to us, Mammy? This new brother, would he be a relation of ours?' Margaret frowned in concentration.

'No, he's nothing at all to any of us, only to Francey. I'll explain later.' She threw up her hands in mock desperation. 'Why don't you open the bloody presents and stop asking *me* these questions? Francey's the only one who can unravel this.'

Because Francey wanted the bulkiest parcel to be the biggest surprise he told them to leave it until last. His mother and stepfather hung back as the other three tore open the rest of the packages which included fancy chocolates, a bottle of whiskey, another of brandy and one of gin for his mother, Bewley's fruit bracks which he knew they all loved, silk scarves, a sheepskin rug, dyed royal blue, purchased on impulse in a butcher's shop near Hazel's flat. One of the boxes was stuffed to the brim with tinsel ropes, paper chains, glimmering glass balls, little plastic Santas and reindeer for the family Christmas tree, and a selection of cheap clockwork toys: a drumming soldier, a long-armed monkey which tumbled over the top of a miniature highwire, a dog whose yapping more resembled a squeaking hinge than a bark, a yellow rabbit which clashed tiny cymbals together and an eight-inch plastic baby, clad only in a nappy, which, when wound, scuttled along on hands and knees like a little flesh-coloured cockroach.

'I couldn't resist them.' Francey grinned, seeing their surprise at the gewgaws.

'Now,' he said, holding up one of the three packets which, unlike all the rest, were wrapped in colourful paper, 'why don't you open this?' Abigail seized the first one from him and on opening it, screamed with delight on finding a clutch of jeweller's boxes, inside which were six indentical gold watches. 'You should have seen the face on the man in the shop when I said I'd take the lot!' Francey felt proud. 'There's one for everyone. We'll have to send off Johanna's and Goretti's.' He offered the second of the three boxes: 'Here's yours, Mam, and instead of a watch I got you a Ronson lighter, Mossie.'

'Thank you.' Mossie came in from the fringes.

'Last one now, Mam. Open this one.' Francey gave her the little flat case from Weir's, purchased at the same time as Hazel's butterfly. A third item from the same shopping expedition, which he did not know that he would ever be able to deliver – it depended entirely on the progress, or lack of it, of his relationship with Fleur Mannering – reposed in the elasticated lining of his suitcase.

His mother opened the case to find a marcasite lizard with protruding tongue of silver and two tiny rubies for eyes. 'It's beautiful, Francey,' she breathed, 'I'll treasure this for ever. Thank you.' Embarrassed at the naked love in her eyes, Francey dropped his own. 'You're welcome. Now the big one,' he mumbled, hefting the last parcel towards the edge to the table. 'Be careful with it now.'

'A television set!' Connie was awestruck when Margaret finally revealed the contents. 'Wait till the girls at school hear *this*.' The Irish television service was in its infancy, and on Béara, television sets were luxuries. 'The man in the shop said he thought you'd be able to get reception all right but you'll need to put up an aerial.' Pleased at the general reaction, Francey turned to Mossie. 'Some of the programmes are very good. And they do matches from Croke Park.'

'As if this house didn't get enough visitors already,' Mossie said, scratching his head. 'I hope the chimney'll take the strain of an aerial,' he added, 'much less our brains. I believe you can get square eyes watching this thing. But thank you very much.'

Francey looked around at the debris, paper, string and straw packing. Despite the excitement and good feelings, he felt anticlimactic and lonely, as if he was a stranger here. He had to get out to be by himself for a little. 'I think I'll get a breath of fresh air before I go to bed,' he announced.

Outside the farmyard gate, he debated whether he should walk downhill towards the crossroads, with the consequent risk of running into some of the neighbours, or up towards the rounded summit of Knockameala which sheltered the house from the north-east. He was not fond of the mountain: after his first stepfather had been shot on its slopes, Francey's imagination had bestowed on it a rivalrous, even hostile personality which filled him with vague unease; he could not understand, for instance, why his mother continued to walk there and for a long time had panicked when he had come home from school to discover she was not in her accustomed place at the stove or at the kitchen table. But because he did not feel like conversing with anyone he might meet on the road, he turned his steps uphill.

Within a few minutes, he was glad he had done so, even managing to shake off his customary unease about walking in the last few footprints of Neeley Scollard. Out here, the night was not the dark wall it had seemed from behind the windows of the sun-porch, but an effervescence of starlight. The sharp air stung his cheeks and made his eyes water but, avoiding the stone cairn near which Neeley had died, by the time he had climbed as far as a little plateau and stood to take a short rest, he felt exhilarated. He had not been up here at night for years and had forgotten what a special place it could be.

Far below, the two patinated ribbons of Coulagh Bay and the Kenmare river, so quiet tonight that their customary background roar was mute, planed between the slumbering hills of Cork and Kerry; and except for the sound of his own coursing blood, the silence around Francey was so profound that it seemed to fuse in a single, singing note, like the faint echo of a flute.

The bracken, crisp with cold, crackled beneath him as he sat down to think. His own house, hidden by a fold of the mountain, was not visible from here but, standing out from all the houses scattered like sequins over the dark, undulating terrain, he could see the windows of the Harringtons' new bungalow, glowing larger than any other for miles around. Tilly and Michael Harrington, their closest neighbours, had lived for many years without complaint in their traditional two-storey farmhouse but it had caught fire a few years previously and, although the damage had not been irreparable, Tilly had taken advantage of the situation to build the new house. Francey could not decide whether he liked it: in one way he regretted the intrusion of the bungalow into the landscape and wanted everything around Lahersheen to remain exactly the way it had been all his life so he could revisit it at will.

Finding it odd that, although the temperature could not be much above freezing, he did not feel cold, he lay back in the snapping bracken, inhaling deeply. The scent out here was similar to but less complex than that of the town; the west-flowing air had travelled thousands of miles since it had last passed over land and although laced with traces of turf-smoke, salt and seaweed, tasted so pure that Francey imagined it slicing through his citified lungs like a flat-bladed sword. Staring into the depths of the sparkling sky, he wondered if there might not be a creature on some other planet out there staring back towards him and also wondering what to do with its unpredict-

135

able life. And did other creatures on other planets fall so unsuitably in love?

Did they use money up there? He let his thoughts freewheel. Now that he was rich, should he build his family a bungalow like the Harringtons'?

He lay there for a while, spending his money this way and that, on a car, on cars for everyone in the family, on a little house for himself – he was not yet so used to the notion of luxury that he aspired to anything much outside the norm – and then the cold began to infiltrate. As he sat up preparatory to going home, he noticed a small bobbing light coming up the mountainside towards him and before long, was able to see that it was a torch being carried by Abigail. 'Mam sent me up to get you,' she called. 'She says you're to come in out of this cold, that you'll catch your death. And you're to put on this beanie,' she added, reaching him.

Francey, amused, took the small woollen hat from her. Ever since his skull fracture, his mother had fussed over the temperature of his head. 'She never gives up, does she?'

Abigail shook her head. 'Mammys are the same the world over. Look,' she hesitated, 'I volunteered to come up here. There's something I want to ask you in private.'

'Sure,' Francey patted the bracken, 'sit down for a minute, it's not all that cold.' When Abigail had lowered herself beside him he looked at her expectantly. 'Well, come on, spit it out!'

Abigail hesitated, then turned her head away from him. 'It's not all that easy.'

'I'm your big brother.' Francey hugged her shoulder then it hit him that she might be about to tell him she was going to have a baby. 'Oh, Abby,' he said softly, 'whatever it is you can trust me. You can tell me anything.'

'I'm going to be a nun.' Abigail's voice was strong.

Francey's laugh of relief that she was not pregnant died in his throat. His lovely sunny sister shorn of her hair and encased in all that black? Before he could say anything, Abby looked at him with fearless eyes. 'And I need a dowry,' she said. 'This millionaire thing is the answer to my prayers. I didn't want to ask Mam and Mossie. Well, they're comfortable and all, especially since Granddad Sullivan died, but I didn't think it was fair.'

'Are you sure about this decision, Abby?'

136

'More sure about this than about my own name.' Seeing her shining, starlit face Francey knew there was no point in arguing with her and enfolded her in a bear hug. 'I can't pretend I'm not surprised. I'd no idea. And I'm going to miss you. We all will. But of course I'll give you a dowry, Abby. How much do you need?'

'It's voluntary.'

'Well, don't worry,' he got to his feet, pulling her up with him, 'the nuns'll think all their birthdays have come at once. Happy to be of service. There's a condition, though,' he added, searching her face.

'Anything.'

'You have to pray for a very special intention for me. You've to wear out your knees. To Saint Jude, if possible.'

'That bad?' Abigail smiled. 'I'll add in Saint Anne – she's great. Consider it done,' she said. 'Thanks, Francey.'

'I'm very pleased for you, Abby, if it's really what you want. Honestly,' he added. 'How did Mam and Mossie take the news?'

'They don't know yet, I'm afraid it's going to be a big shock to them. But it's not as if I'm going into the Carmelites or anything,' she continued, more to herself than to Francey. 'I think I'd like to join a nursing order.'

'I'm sure that no matter where you go, it'll be them that'll be getting the best of the bargain.' Again he hugged her.

'Oh I don't know about that.' Abigail laughed. She took his arm as they began the descent of the mountainside towards home. 'I'll begin praying for you straight away. Tonight.'

'Good girl.' But Francey wondered if, considering the nature of his special intention, his little sister's prayers would cut any mustard with the saints, no matter how tolerant they were.

To his mother's disappointment, Francey left Lahersheen early the following Monday morning. The house seemed to have shrunk around his shoulders so that wherever he turned he was always bumping into something or someone. And despite his best intentions to remain equable, Sunday's constant stream of wondering neighbours – Connie had been unable to keep the news of their material good fortune to herself – added to the continuous questions from the family, had begun seriously to grate on his nerves even before the Sunday night card party brought everyone in the entire district, it seemed, travelling to the house. If he had been told a month ago that becoming rich overnight might pose problems, Francey would have laughed. Now he was not so sure. In the midst of the crowd crammed into the kitchen, where the drink was flowing and the festive air should have been a delight, he already noticed a difference in the neighbours' attitude to him: a deference, as though having money made him wiser or gave him more insight into the world. What was also quite clear was the tinge of envy, or even resentment, with which many questions were loaded. Among the genuine congratulations – 'I always knew you had it in you, Francey' or 'Couldn't happen to a better man!' – he heard the occasional: 'Of course, the man with the big money won't want to know the likes of us, now,' or: 'Suppose you'll be leaving us now and living over?' or, more wounding, a muttered reference to his illegitimate origins.

His family was not immune: Margaret could not resist a few barbs – 'Of course, a millionaire doesn't make his own bed' – when he was still loitering over his breakfast on the Sunday morning and even Connie, after her initial exultation about all the gifts, had started to question him about what *else* he was going to do with all that money. His mother was edgy – unusual for her – and only Mossie and Abigail seemed unaffected by his new affluence.

By eleven o'clock on the Sunday night Francey had had enough and gone to bed, leaving the revellers to enjoy the rest of the party in his absence.

The following morning brought its own problems. His mother refused to take the money he offered her and when, feeling nonplussed and foolish, he insisted, fought him about it. Her unwillingness was to do with the fact that the money was coming by proxy via George Gallaher and it was only Mossie's intervention which averted full-scale war. He accepted the cash, saying they would put it towards a new tractor.

When he arrived back in Dublin late on Monday, for the first time since leaving home, Francey welcomed the protective anonymity afforded by the city. No one here cared a damn whether he had a penny or a pound. Although the shops were closed for the night, the pre-Christmas rush was now discernible, with pubs busier than normal and the coloured lights, not yet illuminated, creaking on their cables as they swung to and fro in the keen, Liffey-scented wind which swept down the tunnel of Henry Street.

Hazel was not due back in the city until Wednesday and, having nowhere else to go, Francey again checked into the Gresham.

As soon as he was shown to his room, he sat down to count his remaining money. George's thousand pounds, he found, was now down to a little less than a hundred. Three weeks ago this would have represented a fortune – almost three months' salary – now, for some reason, it looked like cause for worry. He would have to take George's advice and sort out a satisfactory way to organize his affairs. Somewhere in the middle of his chest, his heart experienced a small collision. That meant London.

Before he went to sleep, Francey composed a note to Hazel to say he had to make an unexpected trip to London and would telephone her from there.

The following morning, however, as the human babel swirled along the line of public telephones in the lobby of the Underground station it was not Hazel's number Francey rang first but Fleur's. 'I beg your pardon?' he shouted, as, with a finger in his free ear, he strained to hear what his half-brother was saying in response to his invitation to come to a restaurant for a meal that evening. Seeing Fleur with her husband, he had decided, would be better than not seeing her at all and it would give him a better chance to assess the situation in which he found himself. Yet if the truth be known, a tiny part of his brain hoped against hope that Fleur's attraction for him might prove to be ephemeral. It would be so much simpler.

Now it seemed that it might not be possible to test even this. 'You'll be away?' he shouted. 'Sorry, Colin, there's an awful lot of noise here – you'll be away tomorrow night, is that what you're saying?' He listened hard while his half-brother confirmed that indeed he would be away for a few days.

Then Colin almost floored Francey, by suggesting that he meet Fleur anyway.

Shaken, Francey was about to say, 'Are you sure you don't mind?' but he stopped himself just in time, yelling instead after an uncertain pause, 'Do you think she'd like to? Shouldn't we ask her? She could have something else on.'

'Oh, I'm sure she doesn't.' Even through all the noise, Francey thought he could hear the dismissal in his half-brother's voice. 'Be something for her to look forward to,' he added. 'She hates being alone in the house at night.'

'Is she there now?' Francey asked.

'No, but I'll tell her when she gets back. Where do you want to meet?'

'The Coliseum,' said Francey, naming the ritziest hotel he had been able to find in the brochure he had picked up at the airport.

'About eight o'clock?'

'That'll be fine.'

'She'll be there,' Colin promised. 'And we must get together ourselves when I get back. After all, we've rather a lot to discuss, haven't we, old man?'

'I'd love to,' Francey lied.

Forty-five minutes later, having checked into a small hotel in one of the white colonnaded squares in London – so different from those derelict Georgian streetscapes on the north side of Dublin – he telephoned George, who gave him the names of the firms of solicitors and accountants he had to contact in order to gain access to the money set aside for him against his inheritance.

Armed with this list, Francey spent the morning in a succession of discreet brown offices. At one point, while sipping tea from a china cup given to him by an acolyte of George's solicitor Mr Solomons, he wondered what type of service he might have received in one of these places a scant month ago. He decided that Tilly Harrington's oft-repeated proverb was true: money did talk.

With assurances of assistance ringing in his ears, he finished up just before noon with a bank draft for a hundred thousand pounds and a recommendation as to which bank should receive his custom. Ignoring the latter and going into the first one he came across, he opened an account, lodged the draft and in possession of a wallet of temporary cheques and another thousand pounds in cash – a thousand was becoming his favourite figure – emerged into the London day.

In pursuit of the perfect suit to wear for his appointment with Fleur, he spent the next hour or so wandering in and out of the shops in Oxford Street. Within each one, relentless background music rang with jingle bells and heigh-ho cheeriness, and as it came nearer to lunchtime the Christmas shopping rush swung into top gear. Girls rushed in and out as though they had five minutes left to live, and outside on the street, charity collectors redoubled their efforts, rattling boxes right under his chin.

To his surprise, in the matter of buying a suit, he found himself

140

stunned into inaction. The thick wad of cash in his inside pocket had widened his choices so much that he could not make up his mind.

He gave up the idea of a suit, bought a very expensive sheepskin jacket instead and went into a fairy-lit pub for lunch.

When he arrived at the Coliseum that evening, the area between Francey's Adam's apple and the pit of his stomach seemed to be filled with a viscous, aerated slime and it was only with the greatest effort of will that he was able to prevent himself from running to the lavatory more than once every fifteen minutes.

He was early for his appointment and sat on a velvet settee in the lobby, which was newly built and fitted out, as its name suggested, in the style of some interior designer's black and gold vision of Ancient Rome. Even the bellboys, like standard-bearers for a column of Caesar's advancing legions, carried their chalked messages on tasselled plaster noticeboards fashioned to look like scrolls of parchment.

Francey's sense of feeling out of place in the echoing opulence was ameliorated a little by the sight of the sunglasses over the eyes of the robed Arab who, twirling a set of worry beads around the index finger of his right hand, sat on the settee opposite him. When set against the pitch darkness and rain outside, the sunglasses seemed so ludicrous and affected that Francey felt superior. In fact he was so busy watching the flying worry beads that he failed to notice Fleur's arrival until the sound of her stiletto heels tap-tapping their way towards him across the marble floor tiles caught his attention – and that of every other male in the lobby.

She was wearing a coat of silky dark brown fur: of fuller cut than the astrakhan she had worn when they had walked together in the woods, its deep folds fell from her slight shoulders almost to her ankles. Her hair was concealed under a matching hat. In her leather-gloved hands she carried a small clutch bag encrusted with beads, and her delicate instep was arched like a dancer's in the high, strapped shoes. With her almond-shaped eyes and full lips, she looked like a film star or an exotic spy and Francey was filled with pride that of all the people in London it was he who had a date with her.

This was followed by alarm that he would not be able to live up to the privilege. He scrambled to his feet as she reached him. 'So sorry I'm late.' Tiny crystals of rain flashed from the tips of individual strands all over the coat and hat as she smiled up at him. 'The traffic was awful.'

Within the bulk of the coat she seemed as fragile as a china doll and all the old feelings of his own monstrosity came flooding back to trammel Francey's tongue, his new-found confidence with women proving of too recent a vintage to help him. 'You're not late at all, I'm just here myself,' he blurted, wishing he had rehearsed something suave and cosmopolitan. 'Would you like a drink before dinner?'

'No, thank you.' She hesitated. 'Perhaps we should go into the restaurant right away?'

'Of course.'

She seemed to know the topography of the hotel because she turned in the direction of the restaurant.

The maître d'hôtel greeted them with efficient charm and as he helped Fleur out of the magnificent coat, it struck Francey that import-export must be a lucrative field. He waited to take his own seat as she removed the hat, taking a tortoiseshell barrette from the top of her head and causing her hair, dense and shiny as a blackbird's wing, to cascade around her shoulders. As she sat down, she ran her fingers through it and Francey's own fingertips prickled.

'How long is Colin away for?' he asked, sitting down at last.

'A week, I think,' she replied, 'perhaps longer. Thank you, Bernard.' Giving the name its French pronunciation, she smiled at the waiter who handed her a menu.

'You know this place?' Francey took his own menu.

'Yes,' Fleur continued to smile, 'I have been here on several occasions.'

Yes, thought Francey as he perused the prices on the terrifying list of unfamiliar French words, his half-brother's business must indeed be a lucrative one. 'Maybe you could recommend something?' he asked.

'But you choose the wine, yes? Do you like fish?'

The irises of her eyes, Francey saw now, were not black but a deep charcoal grey. 'Fish?' he fibbed. 'I love it.' Although Castletownbere was one of the biggest fishing ports in Ireland, and although like most of his neighbours he used to fish with baited lines as a pastime, he ate little from the sea. In Ireland, the popularity of fish, regarded as a penitential food, had never been high.

'I like it too.' Fleur lowered her eyes to the menu and Francey, opening the wine list as though it was a bunch of nettles, discovered to his relief that it included a description of each bottle and recommendations as to with what it should be drunk. He picked a bottle from one of the lists of French whites; you drank white wine with fish, he knew that much at least.

They had been seated opposite one another at a table which could have accommodated four or even more, and he felt safe in watching Fleur as she paged through her menu. Flooded with love, he saw that she read like a child, mouthing the words as her finger moved down the columns in front of her. Tonight she was wearing a simple scoop-necked sheath in some sort of white fabric; within its weave, an integral pattern gleamed a little as though it were a watermark. Except for the pearls at her throat, she wore no jewellery, even on her wedding finger, and Francey, who thought he had observed and memorized every detail about her, could not remember now whether her fingers had been bare at Inveraray Manor. 'I love your dress,' he offered.

'Thank you.' She acknowledged the compliment without looking up. 'I had it made. It's shantung. Colin brought the material from Hong Kong.'

'Is that where he is now?'

'He is somewhere in the Far East, but he travels a lot, Shanghai, Singapore, Bangkok, even Dhaka. I do not know precisely where he is until he telephones me. Have you been to Asia?'

She looked up at last and, to Francey's embarrassment, caught his eyes on the seamless white dress where it swelled over her bosom. Acquainted as he was with Hazel's physical lushness, he had been imagining how Fleur's breasts would feel under his fingers – cool and smooth as porcelain, no doubt. 'N-no, I've never been abroad.' He willed the blood not to rush to his face. 'I've never been anywhere at all, as a matter of fact. This is only my second trip away from home.'

'Now that you have money, you must travel.' Fleur seemed unaware of his confusion. 'I hear Ireland is a beautiful country,' her voice warmed, 'so green – but there is much to see in the world besides one's homeland. And you have no wife or family so you are free. Or do you perhaps have a girlfriend?'

Francey knew she was being polite but there was something in

143

the way she asked, an excess of innocence, which puzzled him. 'No, I have no girlfriend.' As he said it, he wondered if his week with Hazel counted.

'Not *yet*, of course.' Fleur smiled at him. 'Shall we order? If you trust me, as you say, I think we shall have *moules* to start, and then the turbot?'

'That sounds wonderful.' Francey, who had no idea what any of this was, nodded with enthusiasm.

They gave the order, to include a bottle of Chablis.

'What kind of things does Colin – er – import and export?' Francey felt this was safe ground.

'He is a kind of middle man.' Fleur went on to explain that her husband used an extensive network of contacts in the Far East to broker deals for businesses back home. 'Sometimes it could be tea, sometimes textiles, sometimes toys or shoes or clothing – even, on one occasion last year, two yachts. We had a very good Christmas, the three of us, from the commission he made on that transaction.'

'It must be a very interesting life.'

Fleur flashed him an amused glance but did not elaborate. 'This is nice.' She sat back. 'A nice surprise to be asked out to dinner.'

'I hope you didn't mind the short notice?'

'Not at all. Tommy stays at his school from Monday night to Friday and when Colin is away the nanny and I rattle around in the house like lost souls. I can see you wonder why we have a nanny when Tommy is not there,' she continued, although Francey had been wondering no such thing, 'but the child is attached to her and as long as she is getting her full-time wages, she cares not whether it is for a full-time or part-time job.'

'Did you have a nanny yourself when you were a child?' Francey, whose ideas about Siam or Thailand had been formed from watching a scratchy print of *The King and I*, had wondered a lot about Fleur's background. Her manner was so exquisitely gentle that even though she had never known her father, he felt sure she must have been highborn. But when she flashed him the warning glance that he remembered from the last time he had tried to pry into her life during their walk, he tripped over himself with apologies. 'It's all right, you don't have to tell me anything you don't want to. I'm sorry, it's none of my business.'

144

'My mother did not have enough money to afford a nanny,' she said.

'I'm sorry, Fleur,' he said again, 'I'm not being nosy – it's just that I was interested, that's all.' She did not react as, in Francey's experience, most people would have by reassuring him. Instead, she picked at a bread roll.

To save her further embarrassment, he told her about his own home place of Béara, about the surprising climate, now and then as hot as the Mediterranean, more often so wild and stormy that it was difficult to put a nose outside the door. But he was relieved when their waiter brought the *moules*, which he found were plain ordinary mussels in a sort of clear soup, and extracting the orange-coloured flesh from the shells provided distraction.

Fleur at last reciprocated his confidence, opening up enough to describe the place she was born but omitting the circumstances. Reading between the lines, however, Francey could see that far from being highborn, she and her mother had eked out a poverty-stricken existence just above starvation. 'What was your name before you got married?' he asked, wanting to think of her not as some other man's wife.

'De Lys,' she replied, wrinkling her small nose in amusement.

'Come on, Fleur.' Francey smiled back. 'What was it?'

'It was my mother's name. You wouldn't remember it.'

'Try me,' Francey insisted.

'Chareonkoopta.'

The guttural sound proved too difficult for Francey's tongue. 'De Lys it is,' he acknowledged. 'Go on.'

He applied himself to his food whilst she revealed further snippets of her early life. Apparently her French father had abandoned her and her mother when Fleur had been a baby. They had been forced to move out of their comfortable house and, to support the two of them, her mother had been compelled to go out to work, cleaning the houses of the rich, and when that work was not available, doing anything that was. From the age of four Fleur herself had gone from door to door begging for old rags from which her mother made clothes for them both.

For most of her life in Bangkok, she and her mother had lived in one of the open-sided, one-roomed dwellings of the poor on the

145

banks of one of the *klongs* – canals – that fed into the river emptying into the harbour at Bangkok. 'It was always interesting to see, however,' Fleur said, in her soft voice, describing how these water-ways were the major commercial thoroughfares of the city, how the river was the teeming centre of existence for many people. As well as those who lived along its banks, it was a way of life for the rice and noodle vendors, who from small boats ladled out their steaming wares into the bowls of their customers, for the small shopkeepers who sold peanuts, vinegar and pickled vegetables from their tiny premises opening on to the water, for the men who made a living from sifting through the silt with wire baskets searching for commodities, even valuables discarded or dropped by others, even for the drunks who often had to be rescued from its wide brown waters. 'The Thai people love celebration and celebration includes alcohol,' Fleur smiled at her host while she took a small sip from her wineglass, 'and this, I'm afraid, was another way we made some money. Mother knew how to distil alcohol.'

It was by far the longest speech she had uttered in his presence and Francey was entranced by her husky voice. 'Teach me a Thai word,' he asked.

In reply, Fleur put down her glass and placing the palms of her hands together in front of her face, inclined her head a little. '*Wai!*'

'Does that mean Hello?'

'The equivalent, yes.' Her head still cocked to one side, Fleur's expression became unreadable. 'I should warn you, Francey, that a Thai smiles and says "no" when he means "yes". It is another custom of which I quite approve. The English are so boring, don't you think? Very little subtlety.'

Francey could just nod. What was she implying? He searched for a suitable reply but could not think of anything. 'I'll remember.' He wished she did not so easily push him off balance. 'Can you speak French?' he asked then to keep the conversation going.

'Yes, and some Chinese. There are many Chinese in Bangkok.' Fleur's expression cleared and she returned her attention to her meal.

In response to Francey's anodyne questions, she told him a little about some of the customs from her country, particularly those she thought he might find unusual: 'For instance,' she said, 'after an

146

occupied coffin is removed to a temple, relatives stay with it for the first night in case a black cat should jump over it – bad luck,' and she told him that the currency was called *baht* and that Thais were addicted to a form of chess called *ma kruk*. But as she continued to describe a way of life so far removed from anything he had known, or even read about, Francey, pretending to listen, was speculating about what lay beneath her unprompted revelation about the reversal of meaning for 'yes' and 'no'. He was sure she had meant him to take something out of it.

As he conjectured, he reflected on the transience of the self-confidence he had thought he had gained during the week with Hazel. This one-to-one situation, which he had dared dream about, had shaken him to the extent that, once again, he felt awkward and adolescent and as unlike a sophisticated man of the world as it was possible to be. As Fleur told how many times she and her mother had enough money for just one meal in the day, he watched how the light from the candle on their table lit the skin of her throat so that under the pearls it seemed as smooth as the curved petal of a lily.

Fleur seemed unaware of his scrutiny as she toyed with a translucent flake of pastry on her plate. 'And the climate!' she continued. 'It is very, very hot – so hot that the only time to get coolness is before the dawn. At that time, you will see everyone who lives along the river bathing in the water.'

As she talked, Fleur was aware of the effect she was having on her host. As for her spiel, it was so well worn by now, she thought, she was coming to believe it herself. At the beginning, after her arrival in England, she had been nervous about her assumed identity, all the time prepared for someone to challenge it. Now, however, she was so accustomed to the wide-eyed acceptance, even pity, of every new acquaintance as they listened to the fabricated story of her childhood that the repetition bored her. She was so pleased she would not have to trot it out for much longer.

She saw by the way Francey's rapt eyes glistened in the candlelight that he, like all the others before him, was lapping up every word. The sooner she could put her plan into action and start a whole new existence, she thought, the better.

In Bangkok Fleur's looks and body had been unexceptional,

particularly within the confines of the Lily Garden, the discreet brothel in which her mother had brought her up and to which she had been inducted as a working girl when she was just over eleven. Until she was that age and old enough to be useful, her mother had allowed one of the other girls to teach her how to read and write, but except for these rudimentaries Fleur was uneducated. Yet even at that tender age she had had a keen ear for languages and had managed to pick up a little English, French and Chinese. When her time came to take her place, she was offered to the foreign clients.

'It must have been an amazing change for you to come to London.' As Francey pushed away his plate, she saw he had eaten little.

'I did not mind the cold so much. I was prepared with warm clothing,' Fleur finished with her own food and sat back. This as least was the full truth.

'What I did not expect,' she continued, 'was the greyness. Grey in the morning, grey at noon, grey in the afternoon. Sometimes the sky here is so close to the ground that I feel I cannot breathe. I miss the colour most of all, the sky colours, the colour of the river, the bright colours of the clothing the people wear. Here it is like everyone is hiding in a cave, trying to be invisible.' She grimaced. 'Is it the same in Ireland?'

'You must come over to Ireland,' Francey urged. 'In some ways it is the same but in others, in the ways of the people there, the difference is every bit as great as you found between England and your home. You'll come? You and Colin, I mean,' he added, 'and, of course, Tommy . . .'

Fleur hid a smile. Colin's half-brother was just like all the rest, prospecting, seeing how far he could go. 'I'd like that,' she said.

'Tell me a little bit about Colin.'

This too was predictable. He was now going to try to find out how she felt about his half-brother. 'About Colin's business?' she asked innocently.

'Yes. About his – er – import-export business.'

He was so guileless she felt quite sorry for him.

As Fleur began to outline how Colin had got started, Francey felt ill with love and frustration. He was so deeply immired that all objectivity had left him and he could not tell how he was doing or whether

148

she thought him a fool. Instead of listening to the words, he found himself admiring the way Fleur's full lips formed them, the way her eyebrows remained perfectly still, the way the beautiful dress could not have suited – or fitted – anyone else on earth.

Afraid she would notice his adoration, he was able to force himself at last to pay superficial attention to what was quite a startling story, although not on a par with Fleur's own. Apparently Colin's mother had been a soubrette of a little fame and volatile temper who had beaten him without mercy for the smallest transgression, and when, resenting the curtailments on social freedom that motherhood presented, she had packed him off to boarding school at seven, Colin had been bullied there too.

It was hardly surprising therefore that on the day Francey's half-brother had learned of his mother's death in a car accident he had immediately walked out of the hated school, leaving all his belongings behind. He was seventeen, in possession of a lovely flat in Kensington and a decent amount of money. This latter Colin had left to its own devices for time while he started work as low man on the sales totem of a shoe shop in Kensington High Street.

He proved to have an aptitude for selling and in time moved from the shoe shop into Barkers, where he became assistant manager in the household linens department. Within a year, in partnership with another young man, he had set up on his own to sell good quality second-hand carpets. He learned about Oriental rugs and made his first trip to the Far East, coming back with rugs, ceramics, bales of silks, and an experimental container-load of Oriental bric-à-brac. The partnership dissolved when the other man met and married an American tennis instructor and Colin had decided to go it alone, hiring as his deputy a middle-aged clerk who, having worked for a customs clearance house, knew everything there was to know about importing goods into Britain from more exotic parts of the world.

When this man died, Colin's business – now a modest chain – was sold and he became the broker he now was, travelling the world on expenses and commission, risking none of his own money, but enabled to benefit if he saw something with profit potential. 'And this is how import-export became Colin's life.' Fleur smiled. 'Shall we order dessert?'

'Of course, this is how you two met?' But Francey saw that this was as much as he was being told. Fleur was signalling for menus.

As he perused the print, his frantic brain scrambled the words. What on earth was he going to do? Although he had been marking time for so many years, it was not in his nature to be passive and he feared he might do or say something precipitate which would break the fragile threads of communication stretching between them. 'You must miss Colin when he's away,' he said, when he felt the silence had gone on too long.

Fleur looked up from the menu and again he thought he saw that flickering gleam of amusement. 'Why do you mention Colin all the time?' she asked. 'Is it because you are attracted to me?'

Shocked, Francey began to stutter a denial but then, looking into Fleur's dark eyes, decided there was no point. 'Yes,' he said. 'I am tremendously attracted to you. Please don't worry, though, Fleur, I won't cause you and Colin any problems.'

'I can take care of myself,' she said, after a pause, 'and so can Colin.' Then, just as his heart was starting to recover from its trauma, she delivered the *coup de grâce*. 'I'm sure Tommy would love to meet his new uncle,' she offered. 'He will be home with us on Friday, if you are still in London. Why do you not pay us a visit then?'

Chapter Eight

'For cryin' out loud!' Hazel Slye, suitcase at her feet, arms full of flowers and the post she had collected from her box in the lobby, shoved a second time at the door of the apartment. It had been raining almost non-stop for the past three days and, as always happened in damp conditions, the wood had swollen. Using her shoulder, she heaved again, this time with the desired effect. Like a thwarted mule she back-kicked the door shut and dumped the flowers and post on the half-moon table in her little hallway. Although she had been absent only eleven days, the flat, gloomy because of the weather outside, smelled unused and unwelcoming. 'Great help you are!' she muttered towards her bowl of pot-pourri as she went into her bedroom to get rid of her luggage. Back in the living-room she addressed her collection of stuffed animals. 'Youse'll all have to go – crowd of wasters and dust-traps!' She marched into the kitchen and slammed around among the mugs and tea caddies.

The day had not gone well; the lift she had organized from Sligo had not materialized and she had been forced to take the long, wearisome train journey. Because of the imminence of Christmas, it seemed everyone in the country was travelling and she had found herself wedged against the window of the train beside an enormous woman who seemed to be taking everything but her milking stool with her to Dublin for the holidays. What was worse, the woman was a gabber and, because she had recognized Hazel, had to be endured with politeness. Her boring, repetitive chatter had driven Hazel to distraction and in the end she had resorted to the pretence of sleep to escape its relentless grinding.

She poured the boiling water into the teapot so fast she almost scalded her hand. She was expecting Francey that evening and had planned to be home in time to have a long bath and wash her hair. Now everything would have to be rushed.

She had calmed down by the time she had her second cup of tea.

151

With the dismal evening shut out by the blinds and curtains, the flowers distributed among several vases and a fire flaring in the hearth, the flat again looked cosy and welcoming. Pleasantly anticipatory, she turned on the taps to run her bath and then, while waiting for it to fill, decided she could face the horrors of the post.

She flipped through the envelopes: most of them were windowed and obviously bills. Several, however, were Christmas cards and there were also three letters, one with an English postmark, the other two handwritten in script she did not recognize. She took these into the bathroom with her and placed them on the cover of the linen basket within reach of the bath tub. Then she slipped off her dressing-gown, added bath oil to the steaming water, and climbed in, wriggling her shoulders as she luxuriated in the warm silky feel. She closed her eyes and let herself drift, projecting what the evening had in store. She tried to picture what Francey was doing: probably, she thought with affection, scraping a razor over his thick chops . . .

Hazel had not yet fully decided how she felt about Francey Sullivan. He was too young for her, that much was obvious. But there was a sweetness about him she had not encountered in a man before and to which she acknowledged an attraction; he reminded her in many ways of one of the wide-eyed animals in the living room, clumsy, trusting and eager to offer himself for petting. And there had been a few moments during their odyssey of sexual discovery together where she had thought she might be falling in love.

Thank God she had insisted on the break, Hazel opened her fingers and combed the surface of the water to make little waves, the separation from him had put the situation in perspective. As a result she was able to look forward to his visit this evening with merely this sense of mild excitement. If he was not interested any more, if he had managed in the meantime to come to some sort of arrangement with his little Siamese mot, well, so be it. She'd just suggest they go out for fish and chips or something. And, she thought, looking on the bright side, if that's all that was on offer for the evening, she would take it for what it was: she did not at all object to being seen out and about with such an impressive-looking hunk of youth. Hazel reached out from under the water and, shaking the excess moisture from one hand, picked up the top letter, the one with the English postmark. Tearing it open with her teeth she saw it was from a firm of solicitors in Birmingham.

'What?' The water slopped out on to the floor of the bathroom as, disbelieving, she sat bolt upright and read that she was being divorced in England by her husband. Her first impulse was to laugh but this was followed by the contrary urge to cry. If Hazel had been asked that morning whether news like this would have mattered to her in the least, she would have scoffed derisively that anything her long-absent spouse might do or say could have any effect. She hadn't given the man any but the most fleeting of thoughts for years. But for some reason, the brutal finality of the typewritten and pedantic words on the sheet of thick white paper in front of her seemed like a guillotine.

Dropping the letter on the floor, she groped for the other two. The first was from a fan seeking an autographed picture. The second was from Francey: he was not coming to the flat that evening but would be in touch soon.

It was only then that Hazel recognized her devil-may-care attitude to Francey Sullivan for the sham it was.

Teatime on that foggy Friday evening found Francey standing on the doorstep of a large house in Kensington, one of a terraced row which faced a small park. He had dithered for what seemed like hours as to whether or not he should bring the little Weir's box with him but had decided that to offer jewellery at this stage might seem presumptuous and had opted for more prosaic offerings for his hostess and her son, but the flowers he carried had been chosen with more care than he would have lavished on a bouquet for the Queen of England. He also held a bottle of wine, a carrier bag from Hamley's and another from a record shop containing a long-playing record by the Beatles singing group. Francey rarely listened to the radio and did not own a gramophone so the Beatles meant nothing to him. He had sought the advice of his concierge, however, and this record had been recommended to him as the latest rage in popular music.

He took a deep breath and pressed the bell marked Mannering, one of four set into the wall beside the heavy door. He had been surprised to find that Fleur lived in a flat; since discovering that the Mannerings were well off, it had never occurred to him that they would have less than a whole house to themselves. But when he pushed open the door in response to the disembodied instructions

153

followed by the sounding of a buzzer, the huge, carpeted foyer into which he stepped was far removed from any flat he had ever seen and more resembled his conception of the entrance to a mansion. It was larger and posher than the entrance lobby of his hotel.

Following Fleur's directions, he took the lift to the fourth floor. The door slid open on to a wide hallway. At one end was an impressive marble staircase and here was another assumption banished: up to this, Francey had no idea that a flat could cover two storeys. The walls of the hall were niched and in each indentation stood either a small sculpture or an urn full of fresh flowers, so exotic that he was ashamed of the size of his own bouquet of budded white roses and baby's breath. But as he sought a hiding place for it, Fleur, barefoot, dressed casually in white jeans and a boat-necked T-shirt in navy cotton, emerged from a doorway opposite the lift opening. Behind her came a boy whom Francey presumed was Tommy, a sloe-eyed child with his mother's glossy black hair and Oriental features. 'How are you, Fleur?' Francey thrust the flowers at her as though they might bite. 'Sorry, I see you have enough of these already.'

'Oh, Francey, thank you!' Fleur buried her face in the blooms and inhaled. 'Of course we don't have too many. One can never have too many flowers.' She turned to her son and simultaneously using her fingers to sign, smiled down at him. 'Say hello to your Uncle Francey, Tommy.'

The child, eyes wide, extended a small, delicate hand.

'How do you do?' As he took the little hand, Francey found the child's unswerving, considering gaze unsettling. It was as though Tommy was sizing him up from a brain far older than his years. 'I brought something for you.' Slowing his speech and feeling like a man offering a bribe, he held out the Hamley's bag which Tommy, first throwing an enquiring glance towards his mother, accepted gravely. When, unchildlike, he did not peek inside, Francey, still speaking louder than normal, said, 'It's a helicopter, Tommy. The lights and the rotor work and there are batteries in it and all. And since I know you love stories, I brought you this too.' Remembering Colin's boastfulness about Tommy's potential as a writer, at the last minute Francey had purchased a beautifully illustrated book of Irish legends and folk tales.

'You can speak as you always do.' Fleur stroked her son's fine hair. 'Tommy is a good lip-reader. To bring a present was unnecess-

154

ary, Francey, but we thank you, don't we, darling?' She signed and in response Tommy, sounding as though he was gargling, uttered something deep in his throat.

Francey guessing it was 'thank you', smiled. 'You're very welcome.

'And I brought a few sweets,' he added, pulling a bag of liquorice allsorts out of his jacket pocket. Although it was customary in Ireland when visiting children to offer not only sweets but money, he was unsure of how Fleur would take the gesture and stopped short of offering the usual half-crown. Tommy again made that uncomfortable sound deep in his throat and his mother hugged his shoulders. 'He is so clever, he can say many words now. Let's go upstairs.'

Carrying the flowers, she led the way and, nervous though he was, as Francey climbed the staircase behind her, he had great difficulty in keeping his eyes off the trim, jeans-covered buttocks undulating just inches in front of him. Instead, he forced himself to smile down at the boy hopping up the steps alongside.

The staircase curved on to a galleried landing. 'This is the drawing room.' Opening one of several doors, Fleur led him and Tommy through.

'Oh,' Francey cried, unselfconscious at last, 'this is beautiful.'

The room, scented with incense and decorated in the warm, complex colours of the Orient, was far larger than he had anticipated. Dominating it was a large Christmas tree, trimmed in white and lit with a myriad of transparent fairy lights. Another small tree peeped in from a balcony outside through the panes of one of two sets of french windows. The heavy tasselled curtains at these windows and over two doors in alcoves on either side of the fireplace were in a shade of dusky rose; the carpet and furniture were covered with rugs in muted shades of ochre, indigo and carmine, colours echoed in the kilims and silk tapestries with which the walls were hung. Brass, lustrous as gold, gleamed throughout the room: in the intricate pendant lampshades which glowed from three of the four corners, in the fire-irons in front of the crackling log fire – a real one unlike the one at Inveraray Manor – in the table lamps, picture frames, candle sconces, incense burners and occasional tables. Where wood was deployed it was lacquered or carved with ornate scrolls and curlicues. 'I'm glad you like it.' Fleur had been watching his reaction. 'This is more to my taste than the fantasies at the Manor. My upbringing, of course . . .'

155

'Perhaps you would like to see our nice view?' She led Francey across to one of the french windows. 'When we had this place valued, the estate agent called it a penthouse.' She laughed. 'Ridiculous American affectation, of course, since we are only on the fourth and fifth floors.'

'Are you thinking of moving?' Francey was alarmed.

'Not at present.' Fleur unlatched one of the doors and the three of them stepped out on the balcony which overlooked the park. 'My husband says it is not a good thing to sit on such an asset. I do not care.' She shrugged and changed the subject. 'It is a pity about the fog.'

There was very little to see from the balcony. Although up here the fog seemed thin, drifting in ragged strings through the tiny white bulbs on the Christmas tree to Francey's right, it concealed most of the city below. 'There was not much point in bringing you out here,' Fleur shivered, 'I am sorry. Perhaps when you come back in the summertime.'

As he turned towards her to reassure her, Francey was cold, too, but not because of the temperature. The faint light from the tree and from the murky street lamps below had bleached Fleur's face of all colour. Her monochromatic clothes and black hair intensified the wraith-like illusion and, having inherited his mother's superstitious nature, he was struck with the notion that this could be an omen. He suggested that since it was so chilly they should go back inside.

Returned to the warmth he remembered he was still carrying the wine and the bag which contained the Beatles' record. He gave the bottle to Fleur and was just about to hand the record to Tommy when he realized how close he had come to making an awful *faux pas*. Improvising, he offered this also to Fleur, telling her it was for Colin, then hoped she would not think he had brought it to appease his own conscience. 'I believe everyone who's anyone is listening to that group these days,' he said. 'They're the coming thing.' All this second-guessing was not just tiring but dangerous. *Be careful*, he admonished himself, *just relax and enjoy yourself.*

'Run along to Nanny.' Fleur signed to her son. 'I'm sure she has your supper ready.'

Tommy smiled up at Francey as his fingers flew in response. 'He asks you to come back soon and thanks you for your present,' his mother translated.

156

When the child had gone, Fleur asked Francey to be seated, went to the fireplace and pressed a bell push set into the wall. Within seconds a young Oriental girl appeared wheeling a small trolley spread with tea-things. Francey's overheated imagination fancied the girl looked curiously at him as she arranged the cups on the trolley before leaving them but Fleur seemed not to notice or to care. 'I thought we would be more comfortable in here rather than in the dining room,' she explained to Francey. 'I have tea every afternoon, it is one of the few English customs I admire.' Handing over the flowers with orders to put them in water, she dismissed the girl and began to pour.

'This is delicious.' As he bit into one of the tiny watercress sandwiches she had placed on his plate, Francey was struck by the ludicrousness of such social niceties in these sensuous surroundings. He wanted neither tea nor polite chitchat; the warmth and musky scents created a heady intimacy which laid siege to his self-control and what every nerve in his body screamed for him to do was to tip over the tea trolley and make love to Fleur Mannering in the debris. Instead, he had to nibble his way through sandwich after sandwich, pastry after cream cake, making small talk about the hotel in which he was staying and answering Fleur's polite questions about the health of his family as he had last found them in Lahersheen. Now and then she allowed the conversation to lapse and this was another thing Francey had observed about her: unlike most people, she did not seem to worry about silence.

'More tea?' After one of these lacunae, she held up the china pot. On one level – the level at which his blood was not racing – Francey felt he should be laughing at this situation. She could have been putting him through his paces as though training him for an audience of the Queen.

'No more tea, thank you.' He found courage and put down his cup. 'Look, Fleur, I shouldn't be here.'

'Why not?' Her expression was enquiring.

'I think you know why.'

'Perhaps you could tell me?'

'Don't tease me, please.'

'I don't tease.' Her eyes flickered a little, belying the words. 'I should like for you to tell me what you mean.'

Francey held her gaze. 'I'm not interested in tea, or sandwiches, or whether the plumbing works in my hotel. I'm interested in you.'

157

Fleur did not reply but dropped her eyes to the cup in her hand. She appeared to be considering this statement. At least, Francey thought, she had not reacted with anger or shock. *Don't say anything just yet*, his insides hushed. 'I know there's no point in telling you something like this,' he said nonetheless. 'You're a married woman, after all. But I had to say it and I'm glad I did. I've loved you from the first moment I saw you.'

He could not bear to look at her any longer and stared at the mantelpiece for what seemed like a lifetime, watching the second hand on a little brass clock twitching around the numerals. If he strained his ears, he could just about hear a faint, synchronous clicking and, irrelevantly, remembered the pitted chrome alarm clock on the mantelpiece at home, its self-important ticking and the cacophony of the hammer racketing between its twin bells. How simple it would be to be back home where the emotional timbre, if dull, was at least familiar.

'I like you, too . . .'

It took a moment or two for the words to penetrate his brain but then he looked across the depleted tea trolley to where she sat, composed, dressed as though on a yacht and playing hostess to one of her husband's rich clients. 'I beg your pardon?' His voice sounded faint.

'I said I liked you too.'

Wild excitement ousted Francey's inner calm. 'Do you mean it?'

'Of course.'

He was still afraid to go over to where she was sitting and do as his instinct bid him. To his amazement, however, Fleur obviated the need for him to make any move. She came across to him and, seating herself in his lap, placed both arms around his neck. 'Is this what you want?' Her long hair fell around Francey's face as she pressed her lips to his.

'Oh, God . . .' As Francey took her in his arms, he felt like weeping. She was about the same size and weight as Hazel but there the similarity ended. Where Hazel was warm and curvy, Fleur felt slight and lean yet the impression she gave was of lightness and fragility and he felt impelled to keep a check on his passion for her. He had the absurd notion that if he lost control of himself, even if he kissed her back with any sort of urgency, she might shatter like a piece of china. And besides, what would happen if the maid – or worse, Tommy – came back into the room . . .

Fleur seemed to have no such qualms. She continued to kiss him with full, cool lips, her hands playing with the short hairs at the back of his neck, doing something so pleasurable with them that he felt the rest of his hair lift upright on his scalp. Little by little, he allowed himself to respond, stroking the swell of her hip through the tight jeans, daring to move his hand to the small of her back to pull her tighter to him. She accommodated him by turning a little so that her small firm breasts pressed against his chest and one of her knees ground into his groin. 'What do you like?' she whispered.

Francey gasped. 'I beg your pardon?' Pulling back a little, he searched her grave face.

'I asked what you liked,' she repeated.

'What do you mean?'

'You don't know?'

Francey, half thrilled, half repelled, gazed at her. First Hazel, now Fleur. He had always believed it was men who were the sexual beings and that women had to be wooed exhaustively and cunningly until they at last – and reluctantly – 'gave in' to men's base desires. He found his voice. 'What about – about –'

'About Tommy?' she asked seriously.

'No – well, yes. No . . . I mean – what about Colin?'

'What about Colin?'

'He's your husband!'

'So?' Fleur smiled. 'What Colin does not know will not hurt him.'

'You mean you'll – you're willing to –'

Fleur waited, forcing him to say the words, and at last he managed them. 'You'll go to bed with me?'

'Of course. Is that not what you want? I should like to please you, however. And this is why I ask what you like.'

Francey found the matter-of-fact way she said it, its very blandness, so erotic that his entire body seemed to pulse. He could almost span her waist with his hands. 'I don't know what I like,' he whispered. 'I think I like everything.'

'You think? You are virgin?' her mouth twitched a little.

'No.' *Thank God for that at least* . . . In the circumstances, Francey knew he was blaspheming and did not care. Restraint dissolving, he kissed her extravagantly then stopped. 'Sorry.'

'So many apologies. Is this what they teach you in your country? Come!' Fleur slid off his lap.

It was too much for Francey. 'Come wh-where?' She was not suggesting they go to her marital bed?

Fleur looked down at him, her amusement now plain to see. 'Does it matter where? But as it happens, I have a boudoir, mine alone. We shall not be disturbed.' She took his hand and tugged.

'You mean *now*?' Francey's voice shook as he allowed himself to be pulled upright from the chair.

'You have another appointment, perhaps?'

Overwhelmed, he allowed himself to be led towards one of the doors beside the fireplace. 'Through the other door is Colin's office,' Fleur explained as though she were a guide conducting a tour of a warehouse.

The windowless boudoir was small and sumptuous, its tented ceiling and fabric-covered walls as colourful but harmonious as a peacock's tail. Against one wall was a *chaise-longue* covered with cushions of silk, satin and lace; against another was a davenport and a high wooden chest of drawers. An armoire and a small table, on which rested a large wooden crucifix, completed the furnishings except for what riveted Francey to the floor just inside the door: the half-tester, which dominated the room. Fleur saw his shock. 'I come here when I want to be alone,' she said, 'to think, to meditate, sometimes to sleep. Everyone in the house knows not to come in here, including Tommy and the servants.'

'Colin doesn't come in here?' Francey's perceptions were once again thrown out of kilter by a glimpse inside this strange marriage.

'I don't go into his office,' she countered, reaching up to loosen his tie. 'Now let us stop talking about me. You still have not told me what you like . . .'

The next hour or so was a revelation to Francey. He thought he had reached the limits of sexuality in his adventures with Hazel but Fleur's ministrations to his body created such acute points of pure sensuality that there were moments when he thought he might die. And, unlike Hazel, Fleur's own desires, subjugated to his, seemed minimal. Each time he was on the point of orgasm, she forced him to hold it so that his body raced like an incoming tide across the spectrum of sensation, each successive wave reaching further than the last. He forgot about Colin, about Tommy, about Hazel, George, his family, his money and even about Fleur herself, whose hands, lips, hair, flat belly, wetness, tightness and smooth muscularity fused into a conductor of pleasure until, towards the end, he lost the sense of his own body. Instead of being a collection of oversized bones, muscles and nerves, it felt clarified and refined down to a single thread of ecstasy, taut and glittering as new steel. His release, when finally she allowed it, pierced him like a long, exquisite rapier.

Afterwards, dizzy with relief and joy, he lay panting and drenched with sweat in the tangled bedclothes. Although he felt that more should be required of him than inchoate inertia, at present he was incapable of rational thought or speech. Hazel had always helped him out with a wisecrack. It took an age for his head to turn on his neck. When it did, he saw that Fleur was propped up on one elbow resting her chin in her hand. 'You are happy, Francey?' Her mouth curved in that closed-mouth Mona Lisa smile.

'Happy? Happy doesn't describe it.' He was having difficulty in focusing his eyes. 'I've never felt like this before in my life.'

He reached for her but she slithered off the bed. 'I think you flatter me.'

She went to the armoire and as soon as she opened the door a garland of lights came on over a mirror inside, revealing, along with clothes on hangers, a concealed washbasin. She wrung out a hand towel and came back to the bed, sponging Francey's face, hairline and throat with deft and gentle hands. 'Good boy,' she murmured, 'you've been a very good boy, haven't you?'

'Oh, Fleur!'

Francey attempted to grab her hands but she evaded him. 'You must continue to behave.'

'I love you,' Francey insisted, inhibitions loose as a collapsed sail. 'I love you,' he repeated, 'I love you . . .'

'Of course you do.' Fleur smiled. 'Now you must get dressed. If you like to wash, there are towels and soap.' Again she crossed to the armoire, and indicating the articles by the washbasin, slipped a flowered kimono off one of the hangers and belted it around her waist. 'Shall I ring for more tea?' Not waiting for a reply, she left the room.

Given Francey's impassioned declaration, the offer was like a slap.

161

Yet thought was still kept at arm's length by the liquidity in his bones and he could not summon up an anxious response.

But how did Fleur feel? Francey made a supreme effort to force himself to think and eventually saw that she had seemed as disengaged from their mutual experience as if she had been a pleasure-giving toy.

He climbed off the bed and, with fingers that felt like old pastry, washed himself as best he could and tried to console himself with the panacea of his own limited experience: after all, having had just one previous lover, he was hardly in a position to be over-analytical about Fleur's tastes and satisfactions. Perhaps, he thought, women's practice of sex was as individual as they were – and perhaps this was the way Fleur liked to enjoy herself. He hoped now that he had not ruined things by that incautious remark about loving her. She was so sophisticated, she might not be willing to risk making love again with such an open-hearted clod.

Retrieving his scattered clothes, he started to get dressed and as he tried to shove rubbery knees into his trouser legs, he could hear, through the open door, Fleur's soft voice giving orders, presumably to the maid. Fresh doubts assailed him: what was he to make of this? Did she not care what the maid thought? He went to the door and making sure he was concealed, peeped out. To his relief, Fleur was alone, but talking on a telephone.

By the time he rejoined her, having convinced himself that he had nothing of which to be ashamed, he was composed; the initiation, after all, had been hers. He was even able to smile at her. 'I don't know what to say—' he began.

'Then don't say anything.' She got up from where she had been sitting and went back towards the boudoir. 'I've ordered tea to come in about ten minutes. I must dress too, I shall not be long.'

'All right.' In the face of her composure, Francey's, already precarious, threatened to disintegrate but he managed to hold his grin. 'Hurry up, I'm starving again.'

And by the time the Oriental girl brought the second round of tea, complete with fresh sandwiches and cakes, Francey felt calm and happy enough to smile at her as though he had a perfect right to be where he was. The girl did not return the smile although she did acknowledge it with a small inclination of her head.

When Fleur reappeared, Francey found to his surprise that his earlier statement about being hungry was true. Her temporary absence had also emboldened him. 'Fleur?' he asked through a mouthful of chocolate and cream. 'Do you mind if I ask you something?'

'Go ahead.' Fleur cut a corner off a sandwich and toyed with it.

'What happens now?'

'Do you mean do we see one another again?'

'Yes, that's what I mean, all right.' He looked full at her, feeling that after what they had done together, he had nothing to fear by being honest. 'I couldn't bear to lose you now.'

'I think we should leave that to fate,' she said. 'And you do not gain me or lose me. These are not terms I encourage. In Thailand there is a proverb, given by the Lord Buddha: "We are never impervious to grief while there is anything we would grieve to lose." I think that is a very good saying, is it not? It is how I live my life. Now, please enjoy your meal.'

As usual, Fleur's attention had already wandered. She had an appointment for dinner that evening with a business client of Colin's, a man who was very, very rich, and she was thinking ahead about the practical arrangements. He was sending a car for her but she was wondering whether she should not send it away and order a taxi instead. Fleur was always prudent.

Soon after they arrived in England, Colin's singular brokerage business had begun to flourish to the point where he and his beautiful wife went on to the guest lists not only of businessmen but of some of the minor aristocracy. One day, about eight years previous to this evening and when Colin had again been abroad, the maid came into the kitchen where Fleur was giving the week's orders to the cook. The girl bore a large bouquet of red roses which had just been delivered by florist's messenger. It had come from a man in whose palatial Surrey mansion Fleur and Colin had been entertained the previous weekend; the card attached to the flowers asked her to telephone a certain number. She took the roses upstairs and stared at them for a long time. Then, making sure that Tommy was busy with his own affairs, she went to the telephone and dialled. The man, who was married, 'just happened' to be in London on business and at a loose end that evening; he was wondering if Fleur, by any remote chance, was free too. The ensuing discussion was delicate, laced with meanings other than those normally attributed to the words spoken and set a pattern for dozens of future conversations.

Fleur quite enjoyed the preliminaries: it gave her a sense of power and control. Sometimes, when the mood took her, she did not bother to be indirect but came straight to the point, enjoying the wry embarrassment which always greeted her exposition of what was really going on. The main thing, in Fleur's book, was to keep men guessing, to be unpredictable.

Her name was passed from mouth to mouth in certain quarters, and from then on she and Colin were invited to dinner parties and weekend stays in places far outside Colin's regular business circles. After such an occasion, during which Fleur's husband invariably boasted about some forthcoming trip or transaction abroad, the flowers, or champagne, would arrive at the door of the flat within twelve hours of his departure.

If Colin suspected that he and Fleur were being cultivated for any reason other than his own charm and talent for business – and if he wondered why these invitations continued to arrive despite the paucity of their reciprocal entertainment – he kept quiet about it. At the beginning, she watched him, had even dropped subtle hints, but Colin had reacted to none of them. Instead, he buried himself in his work and Fleur, growing in confidence, eventually decided that even if he did suspect something, her husband simply did not want to know. It had become evident early in their marriage that Colin would go to any lengths to avoid a confrontation: he collapsed like a house of cards at the first sign of anger, even disapproval. And in his own way, he adored her, she was sure of that.

He certainly did not want to lose her. The sex between them was one reason: Fleur could enslave Colin and, because of his sexual tastes, frequently and literally did. As the years went on, this relativity passed to their relationship outside the bedroom until it came to the point that when she wanted her own way all Fleur had to do was frown or intimate that she was not happy with him and might even have to consider leaving. As a result, since he already had an office, the privacy of which was sacrosanct within the flat, it had been an easy matter for Fleur to negotiate the boudoir for herself. Colin readily accommodated his wife's charming request that she needed a place to do the feminine things all girls did in seclusion.

Fleur's business transactions were always discreet and although they sometimes took place in the boudoir, it was more typical that she met her generous friends in plush, rented flats or hotel suites. Since she was paid only in gifts, she would never have dreamt of thinking herself still a prostitute.

She looked across at the huge blond man seated opposite her. He looked so pleased with himself and yet vulnerable too. The moment the thought entered her head, Fleur banished it. She never bent her self-imposed rules. No involvement. No feelings.

Francey noticed her looking at him: he had been considering what she had said about self-protection against grief. Given the streams of pleasure that still coursed through him he refused to take her words as a personal rebuff. 'What about Tommy?' he asked. 'Surely you'd grieve if anything happened to him?'

'Where Tommy is concerned,' Fleur's eyes darkened, 'there are no rules, no proverbs. I would kill for Tommy.' Her expression cleared. 'I am sorry, you touched upon a nerve. I had in mind enjoyment, physical delights, money, beautiful objects,' she waved her hand around the room, 'all you see here. It is a mistake to become attached.'

'And Colin? Are you attached to Colin?' Francey watched her reaction, but divined no responding ruffles in her serenity.

'Of course I am attached to my husband,' Fleur replied. 'He is my husband. But he, like me, like you, like all of us, is mortal. Shall I pour more tea?'

'I bet, though,' Francey persisted as he held out his cup for a refill, 'that if all this wealth and comfortable living disappeared tomorrow, you would miss it.'

'I would miss it, but it would not be a tragedy. I started with nothing and can start again with nothing. I am a resourceful woman.'

'Tell me about how you started,' Francey asked, 'how you met Colin, for instance.'

'I am sorry. That is for another time. Now, shall we talk about how we go about finding our other brother?' As they mapped out a plan of campaign involving the police, the Samaritans, the Salvation Army and the many Irish clubs and associations in London, Francey, who was again ready for sex, employed his imagination in an effort to contain his physical excitement and emotional jubilation. Mention of

165

the charitable agencies helped: he pictured the ragged derelicts sprawled with their bottles of Amicardo on the pavements of Dublin, the unfortunate beggarwoman who thrust holy pictures and cheap rosary beads into the hands of anyone venturing up the steps of the Pro-Cathedral in Marlborough Street. By the time they had agreed on what they should do first, Francey was more or less under control.

To temper his desire further he again mentioned Colin. 'He must be doing very well?' waving his hand around the luxurious appurtenances of the room.

'He is doing well.' Fleur hesitated. She seemed about to say something else but changed her mind. 'He is doing well,' she repeated. Francey took a leaf out of her book and did not press for an explanation or expansion. Instead, he made himself be quiet and Fleur said nothing more, letting the silence she liked so much develop around them so that they finished their tea without further conversation.

Despite her abstruse warnings about leaving everything to fate, he was fearful of making no concrete plans. 'I'll be off, so?' he said, hoping she would press him to stay. When she did not, he stood up and helped her to her feet, kissing the back of her hand. 'I know we're leaving our next meeting to destiny,' he said quietly, 'but may I at least ring you?' In his own great paw the bones of her hand were so delicate they felt like the spines of the birds' feathers he used to collect during one phase in his childhood.

'Of course you may.' Fleur smiled, withdrew her hand and went in front of him towards the door so he had no option but to follow.

She saw him as far as the lift and pressed the call button but did not wait for the doors to open. After a smiling but swift 'goodbye' she turned and walked up the stairs without looking back.

So it was that three hours after his arrival at the flat, Francey found himself out again in the cold, dank street. Far from being deterred by her coolness at the end of the encounter, he was now resolved that no matter what it took or how long, he would make Fleur feel about him the way he felt about her. The morality of it was difficult but he was in England now and they did things differently here. Fleur seemed not to be pushed about the implications of adultery and her husband could fight his own corner.

Francey realized that in many ways, he felt locked into a sort of contest with her. He did not understand the rules yet, but he would . . .

He looked up at the balcony and the fog-smudged glow from her fairylit tree. He felt far older than his years and confident. 'You don't know me yet, my darling,' he mouthed, 'but you will. Today was just the beginning. You wait and see. I can have as much patience as you.'

After he got back to the hotel, he had a long, hot shower and got into bed. Feeling warm and sleepy, he was drifting off into a pleasant, hazy doze when he remembered that tonight he had been meant to meet Hazel again. He hoped she had received his note. On impulse, he lifted the telephone on his bedside table and asked the operator to put him through to her number. Her telephone rang unanswered for a long time and he was about to hang up when he heard her voice, fuzzy and unclear, breathing a faint 'Hello.'

'Oh, Hazel,' he was contrite, 'I'm sorry, did I wake you up?'

'Who is this?' She slurred the words and with a shock he realized she was not sleepy but drunk.

'It's Francey.' He wished now he had not telephoned her. 'Did you get my note?'

The question was greeted by such a long silence that he thought she had not understood. 'Did you get my letter, Hazel?' he repeated, louder. 'I wrote to you —'

'I got your shagging so-called polite fucking *note*.'

'How are you?' Shocked at her vehemence, Francey could not think of anything more suitable.

'I'm fine, I'm great. Never better.' The ugly sarcasm was not helped by a coughing spasm following a noisy drag on a cigarette.

Francey waited until the coughing subsided and then asked her if she had a pencil and paper. 'I'd like to give you my number here,' he explained, and had to wait through the cacophony of Hazel dropping the receiver followed by fumbling and tearing, presumably of paper. At last she picked up the telephone again: 'Shoot.'

He gave her the number, repeating it so he was sure she had got it right. 'Ring me in the morning?' he asked.

'What time is it?' Her anger, if such it was, had lost its thrust and when he told her it was just after ten in the evening, she just grunted, 'Nice of you to te-helephone,' the hiccup ruining the attempt at haughtiness. 'Thank you.'

She hung up, and Francey was left staring at the receiver. 'Have you finished, sir?' The voice of the hotel operator cut through the dial tone, leading him to believe she had been listening in to the call.

'Thank you, yes,' he said.

He turned over and snuggled down under the clean, smooth sheets and blankets, knowing that to think or worry about Hazel's belligerence would diffuse the dreamy, lazy feeling of warmth throughout his body. Rather than let that delicious state go, he promised himself he would ring her again in the morning and was soon asleep.

His room was flooded with brilliant sunlight when he was woken by the shrilling of the telephone beside his head. Lost in a dream centred somewhere around Lahersheen, the bell cut into him like the blade of a saw and he shot upright, banging his head against the wooden headboard. 'Ow!' He rubbed his head as he lifted the receiver. 'Hello?'

'I'm sorry, Francey, I really am. I was langers last night when you rang.' Hazel's voice was subdued and nasal as she rushed on, 'I don't remember much but I do remember I was nasty to you. Sorry.'

'That's all right.' Francey slid his feet on to the floor. 'I caught you at a bad time. I just wanted to make contact and to make sure you got my note so you weren't waiting for me or anything like that.'

'Not at all.' Hazel was gabbling. 'To tell you the truth, I forgot all about our appointment. I had a few friends in and we drank too much. I'm payin' for it now, I can tell you! Me stomach thinks me throat is cut.'

Francey smiled. 'A big feed of rashers and eggs, that's what you need.'

'Don't talk about food, for God's sake. How're things going over there?' Hazel hesitated, then, 'Have you found your brother?'

'Not yet, but I'm working on it.' It was Francey's turn to hesitate: although he had spoken the perfect truth, in not mentioning Fleur or her involvement in the coming search, he felt he was being less than honest, but now that he had made love to her, he felt unable to talk about her just yet, even to Hazel. 'I'll let you know if there are any developments,' he said.

'Have you a photograph or anything? I've a few contacts over there.'

'No, the last photograph we have, Dessie was only a small child.'

'When do you think you'll be home?' Hazel's voice was approaching something nearer its chirpy norm.

'Don't know yet. To tell you the truth, Hazel, everything is so new over here, I don't know whether I'm coming or going. And you know, strangely enough, I always thought it would be great to be rich but having the money doesn't seem to change the way you feel.'

'Go on ou'a that! Some of us'd fancy our chances, Francey Sullivan.'

'It's true,' Francey insisted.

'Yeah, well, I'm sorry for you, I don't think. If you don't want it, sign it over to me and I'll show you a thing or two about how rich people *could* feel.'

'I might take you up on that.' Francey grinned again. 'I'm looking forward to seeing you again, Hazel. As I said, I don't know how long I'll be here but I'll keep in touch, all right?'

'Fine.' As she had last night, Hazel rustled paper. 'I can see here the diary's pretty full. We're starting telly rehearsals for the Christmas show this week so I've a lot on me plate. But I'll be in and out. You'll be bound to catch me sometime.'

After they said goodbye Francey marvelled at the behaviour of human beings: to listen to himself and Hazel, he thought, you'd never think that not long ago they had been rolling around in bed together for an entire week. He was lucky she was modern. Francey knew from the small amount of male exchange of confidences to which he had been privy that women were funny about sex: they used it to get their hooks into you. Hazel took it as she found it, maybe that she was older than him had a lot to do with it.

Anyway, he thought, it was great to have someone to talk to, he had never had such a good pal before. Whistling, he flung off his pyjamas and when he stepped into the shower, he was already calculating how long an interval he could decently leave before telephoning or calling again at the flat in Kensington.

He was to see Hazel, however, long before he saw Fleur again.

All that day, still savouring the wonderful aftertastes of the day before, he wandered around London like the tourist he was. He had never been happier or more excited in his life as he squandered money on taxis to take him around the sights. He bought small, expensive Christmas presents for everyone in Lahersheen and in a jewellery shop, vacillated over a beautiful, diamond-studded watch for Fleur before deciding against it. He was not sure how she would take it: it might be too soon to offer anything so extravagant and he did not want to excite any suspicion in Colin's breast. He even managed to find a suit which fitted him.

It was in that jeweller's that he noticed a strange thing happening: two of the women assistants behind the counter were displaying unconcealed interest in him and even the girl who was serving him was unusually vivacious, even flirty. Were it not that he was dressed in the same clothes he wore before he became rich, he might have put it down to the obsequiousness shown in the presence of money. Then he wondered if he should put it down to the ritziness of the place – maybe they were trained to look at men that way to make more sales? Whatever the reason he was attracting such attention, Francey found he was enjoying it and did not feel either shy or embarrassed. He stood a little straighter and smiled more than usual.

As he waited for one of the girls to wrap his purchases, he thought of the dreary dances he had attended in Dublin – had that been only a few months ago? – and the mocking expressions which had greeted his clumsy attempts at gallantry with women. It had to have been his experience with Fleur that had changed him, he thought as, having smiled a happy farewell at the women, he left the shop, still basking in the warm afterglow of their admiration.

Outside again, he found he was hungry but instead of going into a pub as usual decided to treat himself and veered towards the entrance portal of a nearby hotel. There, to his astonishment, the status of the new plane to which he had been elevated was emphasized at the front desk when he asked the way to the restaurant. The receptionist, who had long red nails like Hazel's, almost dazzled him with her smile as she directed him, and when he looked back over his shoulder, she and her female colleague were both looking after him with unmistakable interest.

To his disappointment, the waiting staff in the restaurant were all male and he had no chance again to test his new-found attractiveness. Examining it as objectively as he could, he decided the phenomenon had to be due to one of two things: either he did look better for knowing what it was to make love, or he was seeing women in a new way. Maybe that was how they always looked at men and he had been so self-conscious before he had never noticed. He ate as though he had not had a meal for three weeks and gave such a big tip to the waiter that for a fraction of a second the man's eyes widened in disbelief before the notes vanished into some mysterious inner pocket as if they were props in a magic trick. Francey decided to walk off the bloated feeling after the meal but soon passed a cinema and, always having been a fan of Elizabeth Taylor, went in on impulse to see *Cleopatra*.

What seemed like hours later, with ears still ringing from the impact of the film's noisy exuberance, he came out into the dark, frosty evening. His father, he thought, would have fitted in as one of Caesar's senior army officers: he had the physique to wear a toga and a breastplate.

Before going back to his hotel, he went into a pub for a pint. While sucking through the creamy top of the stout to get to the smoothness of the black stuff below, he looked around at the subdued clientele in the pub, which was only half full. Would he ever get to know the English? In Dublin or even Castletownbere, he thought, the Saturday before Christmas would have found any bar packed with exhausted but cheerful Christmas shoppers and workers who had started their week-long Christmas celebrations with the double week's pay on the Friday night and had not yet gone home to face the music. Here, it seemed, Christmas was not the annual bacchanalia it was at home: leaving aside the coloured streetlights and commercial hoopla, to judge by the tense faces in the shops and streets, Christmas in England seemed more of a problem than a celebration.

Home.

He would have to telephone when he got back to the hotel to tell them whether or not he was coming for the holidays. Because he knew they were expecting him as usual, it was a conversation he had been putting off: deep in his heart, Francey was still hoping for an invitation to spend Christmas at Inveraray Manor with his new second family. Central, of course, was the hope that Fleur would be there.

He finished his pint and smiled at the barmaid, who twinkled back at him and wished him a merry Christmas, then left the pub to meander home through streets quietened by the closure of business for the weekend. When at last he got into the foyer, the receptionist handed him three messages with his key.

Francey's frivolous mood evaporated. The decision to telephone

171

home had been pre-empted as all three were from Lahersheen: they would not call three times in a row unless it was urgent.

The news was awful. Mossie had slipped off a ladder while fixing the television aerial to the chimney and had been rushed unconscious to hospital in Bantry.

Before he left for the airport, Francey extracted the Weir's jewellery box from the lining pocket of his suitcase where it had spent so much time and, with the assistance of the concierge, parcelled it up in Christmas paper. He added a card on which he wrote a non-committal message and addressed it to the Kensington flat, leaving the concierge enough money for postage plus an enormous tip. He wished now that he had followed his instinct to buy the diamond watch that afternoon. Let the consequences fall where they may.

Chapter Nine

With the help of a sympathetic Aer Lingus booking clerk, Francey managed to get a seat on a star flight that night and, on arrival, hired an astounded taxi-driver off the Dublin Airport rank to drive him all the way to Bantry, arriving at the hospital as breakfast was being served to the patients.

Not to Mossie, however.

'Oh, Mammy!' Francey embraced his hollow-eyed mother, who rose from her husband's bedside to greet him as she saw him come into the small ward. 'I'm so sorry, it's all my fault for buying you that damned television.'

'Please, Francey.' She laid her head against his chest for a moment. 'It's no one's fault. It was an accident. He could have been doing anything up there, fixing slates, or the chimney, even. He's been going up there all our married life.' She let him go and, shaking her head, sat down again. 'It's no one's fault.'

'Tell me again what happened.' Francey looked down at Mossie, unnaturally clean, an oxygen mask on his face, his arms festooned with tubes leading to drip stands.

'We don't know for sure.' His mother's voice was dull and flat. 'No one saw him. All we know is that somehow he slipped off the roof ladder. He didn't even shout or if he did no one heard him. Maggie found him lying on the ground at the side of the house when she went out to call him in for his tea.' She stroked Mossie's thick forearm. 'He must have tried to save himself because part of the gutter came down in pieces around him. It was all bent.'

'How long was he lying there?'

'It couldn't have been more than ten minutes because about a quarter of an hour beforehand, I'd gone out to tell him I was putting the kettle on.'

His mother was occupying the bedside chair and, feeling impotent, Francey stood behind her watching her bent head as she

173

continued to stroke her husband's arm. Mossie was not wearing a pyjama jacket and Francey's throat tightened as he noticed the tide marks just below the elbows: whereas the forearms were freckled and brown, the biceps and shoulders were as white as those on a baby.

Francey remembered the wedding of Mossie to his mother, with all the sisters as excited bridesmaids and himself imprisoned for the second time in his First Communion suit, chiefly for the wonderful spread of cakes and goodies afterwards and the pocketfuls of money he had been given by inebriated relatives. Except for that milestone, to a seven-year-old concerned about his own busy life with school and chores, the impact of Mossie moving in had not been as momentous as it might have been and the relationship between the two of them, although harmonious, had never run deep.

Day-to-day life after Mossie's official arrival as part of the family had greatly improved, however. Francey's first stepfather had been volatile and, like all his contemporaries, employed the cane or belt to subdue any unruliness in his household. Mossie Sheehan had never lifted a hand to any of the children and looking at his still, pale face now, Francey remembered how at school he had been the envy of his schoolmates who knew, if it was discovered at home that the teacher had beaten them, that they could look forward to more of the same from their parents on the principle of adult solidarity. And Mossie had been full of surprises, initiating Francey into the joys of smoking when he was only ten – which made him so sick he forswore the habit for ever – and for one memorable birthday, building an engine-driven go-cart from the remains of an old pram and a tractor, on which Francey chugged around the fields for many months until he got bored with its top speed of about two miles per hour.

Mossie came from a long line of teachers and bibliophiles and his huge store of inherited books had outshone in quality and variety even the selection available from the public library in Castletownbere. When added to those of Francey's mother, there were so many they could not be accommodated in the house. As a result, one of the outhouses had been insulated and fitted with bookshelves, a few secondhand armchairs and a Valor heater and became known by neighbours as 'Sheehan's Folly' soon shortened to 'the Folly'. Everyone nearby borrowed books from it and Francey had learned more about the world within its stone walls than he had ever learned from the curriculum prescribed by the Department of Education.

All through his adolescence, the Folly had also proved a haven for him. He got on well with the girls but their endless prattle about periods and clothes and dances and local boys bored him to distraction and he used the Folly as a bolthole, burying himself in its books, or messing about with his clockwork trainset. Mossie had been the only one in the house to share Francey's interest in the Hornby and now and then joined him in the Folly to stand alongside him. They did not speak much but these times were among the few occasions where Francey felt a genuine sense of two-way communication with his stepfather.

At a loss for words of comfort or hope for his mother, Francey searched now for anything at all to say. But having been up all night, his thought processes were fogged by fatigue and all he could do was to lay one arm around her bowed shoulders. 'Poor Mossie,' he murmured. 'Try not to worry, Mammy. Everything's going to be all right, I'm sure it is. Mossie's a strong man. He'll pull out of this.'

It was not to be, however. Mossie's brain had been damaged in the fall and two and a half days later, just before midnight on the Tuesday before Christmas, he suffered a massive and fatal stroke. He had never regained consciousness.

By about nine o'clock on the Wednesday night, as chief host at Mossie's wake, Francey was fraught and tired almost beyond his experience, and so talked-out that he felt that if he had to be nice to one more new arrival he would scream. All day he had been at his mother's side, organizing the transfer of the body from the hospital, arranging details with the undertakers. Throughout, she had not once given way to her sorrow and in a way he had found her iron self-control to be more wearing than if she had stormed and sobbed and behaved like the widows at most of the funerals he had attended.

Following their arrival home, as the only man in the house he had been the one to greet the friends, neighbours and relatives who crossed the threshold in a continuous stream to offer sympathy. Margaret had appointed herself as chief answerer of the telephone but most of the callers asked to speak to him. It seemed as if the world now assumed him to be the head of the household, a state of affairs he refused to think about because the implications frightened him.

It did not help that, having offered the ritual yet genuine

condolences, all who came in felt the need to question him about his own exciting good fortune.

To escape the fug and clamour for a few minutes, Francey left the kitchen and went outside. Blowing into his cupped palms, he hesitated in the centre of the yard. He had planned to walk towards Knockameala to clear his head but although the most recent storm had cleared away, it was very cold and damp. On impulse, he pushed open the door of the Folly. He turned on the light and, seeing the familiar, comfortable chaos within, already felt better. In here was the physical catalogue of his life until he had left Lahersheen to go to work in Dublin.

His mother, a magpie by nature, hated to throw out anything which 'might come in useful some day' and as the creature comforts of the house had improved over the years, the Folly, planned merely to provide a home for all the books, had taken so many redundant articles, such as iron and brass bedsteads, couches, chairs, oil lamps, chamber pots and skillet hooks, that it resembled a secondhand furniture and bric-à-brac shop.

The circular weights in the bowl of some old kitchen scales clattered as he made space for himself on a tattered sofa. The walls of the windowless building were so thick he could hear no evidence of the talkative crowd still thronging the kitchen only yards away and, with a sigh of relief, he put his aching feet on the armchair opposite the sofa and allowed the peace to seep in through his senses. He had always loved the unique bouquet of the Folly: of dust, old mortar, fabric and wood, and that special, fusty aroma emanated by packed shelfloads of books. And yet, having made the break – and particularly in light of recent events – would he want to live here again? Would he have any choice? Would his mother, like the neighbours and sympathizers, now expect him to come home and take Mossie's place in looking after the farm? He could think of nothing he would hate to do more. And yet he could not escape the gloomy truth that he was the only son and the girls all had their own plans.

As he sagged into the lumpy horsehair of the couch backrest he let his thoughts wander – about death, such a familiar part of life in the country where wild animals and birds were shot, snared and trapped, and died unmourned by their own kind. He watched a strand of grimy gossamer, the remnants of an ancient cobweb suspended from the light fixture above his head, drifting to and fro.

Where, he wondered, was the spider who had once been so busy? How many generations had descended from it since the little creature had laid out its glistening trap? Why, alone of the species which shared the earth, did human beings surround the death of one of their own with such ritual and prolonged ceremony?

Despite what he had thought about the English way of death, now that he examined it, Francey was unsure as to whether in Ireland all this eating and drinking, this hospitality so blithely assumed and generously given was a burden rather than a help. Could there perhaps be a middle way?

He pictured his dry-eyed mother, who, despite numerous offers of help from friends and neighbours, insisted on presiding over the stove and kitchen table as though she were the hostess at a party and not the relict of the corpse she loved, which lay only feet away on their candlelit bed. Would she not be much better left alone to grieve in private? And was there something wrong with him that he could not feel about his stepfather's death as perhaps he should?

In his own way, he supposed he must have loved Mossie. Yet even looking at his stepfather's corpse he was conscious that his predominant feeling was not of personal grief but of concern for his mother and sisters and – more insidious, this – the selfish worry about what this might mean for his own future. He was glad that human beings had not yet developed the capacity to see inside one another's thought processes. What would others think of him had they known that even while going through the motions surrounding the obsequies for his stepfather, Francey's attention fell all the time into traps placed in its path by Fleur Mannering?

Such philosophizing – he must be even more tired than he had thought. He shook his head as though to clear his brain and instead dislodged small grey puffs from the back of the couch and had to pinch his nose so he would not sneeze.

He was so tired he was dozing off when the door was flung open. 'Here you are!' It was Margaret. 'For God's sake, Francey, I've been looking everywhere for you. You're wanted on the telephone.'

'Again?' Francey groaned. 'Could someone else not take this one?'

'This one's long distance. Come on.' Margaret turned on her heel.

Long distance? Francey's heart lurched as he prised himself off the couch. Could Fleur have found out somehow? 'Who is it?' he called after Margaret.

'I don't know, I didn't ask. It's some woman with a Dublin accent,' she called back. 'Hurry. She's been waiting for ages, I hope she hasn't hung up.'

Francey schooled his disappointment as he crossed the yard, reminding himself that since he had not informed anyone in England of Mossie's death, he could not expect any communication from there. To his relief, he noticed as he entered the kitchen that the crowd had thinned out somewhat. Conscious of his mother's stare as he picked up the telephone, he turned his back on the room. 'Hello? Hazel?'

'Francey, I'm so sorry.'

Her voice was so faint he had to press the receiver to his ear and block off the other with a finger. 'Thank you,' he said. 'How did you find out?'

'It was in the evening paper. The funeral's tomorrow after Mass at one o'clock?'

'That's right. We're having it late because we hope Goretti – one of my sisters – will get home in time from Chicago.'

'I'll be there.'

'Oh, Hazel.' Francey was alarmed about how his family, particularly his mother, would react to Hazel's exotic presence and then was instantly ashamed of his reaction. 'I appreciate the thought,' he said, cupping his hand over the mouthpiece so he could speak a little louder without being overheard in the kitchen, 'but it's not necessary. And, anyway, tomorrow's Christmas Eve.'

As he said it, it occurred to Francey that he knew so little about Hazel he had no idea where or with whom she planned to spend Christmas.

'Would you ever shut up – what are friends for?' Hazel's voice was brisk. 'We'll be there. It's nine o'clock now so we can get a good sleep and make an early start. It's so long since I've been down that way, could you give me directions?'

'It's an awful distance to come.' With trepidation as to the composition of that ominous 'we' – he could just imagine the mickey-dazzler Hazel might bring with her – Francey tried once more to dissuade her. But when she still refused to capitulate, he accepted defeat and told her how to get to the Eyeries chapel and then the Kilcatherine graveyard. 'Who'll be coming with you?' he asked, hating himself for his pusillanimity.

178

'Don't know yet,' Hazel replied, 'but I'll organize something.'

Then, to his surprise, Francey found himself looking forward to Hazel's forthright, uncomplicated presence. 'Well, if you're sure it's not too far,' he said, turning his back further on his mother's all-seeing eyes, 'it'd be great to see you.'

They said goodbye and Francey turned to his mother. For perhaps the first time that evening, she was unattended. 'Are you all right, Mammy?' He crossed the floor.

'Was that Hazel Slye?' Her face was set in tense lines.

Francey nodded assent. 'She's coming to the funeral. Do you mind?'

'Why should I mind?'

'Well, the connection with – my father. You know –'

'Francey, you're a man now. Your friends are your friends. And I'm no one to talk – you know my history as well as anyone.' Her eyes slid away, although they remained dry as she twisted the bracelet on her arm.

In response, Francey found his own eyes stinging. 'You've had enough for one day, Mammy,' he said softly. 'I'll get rid of all these people. We've a difficult day ahead of us tomorrow and you'll need as much rest as you can get.'

'What about . . .' Elizabeth indicated the bedroom. It was unthinkable that Mossie should be left without company on his last night above ground.

'Don't worry,' Francey reassured her, 'me and the girls will stay up. We'll do it in shifts. And Tilly's already said she'll stay for the vigil.'

His mother complied and went into the bedroom shared by the girls and, with the help of Margaret and Abigail, Francey managed tactfully to clear the kitchen. Afterwards, Constance, Mossie's only natural daughter and the most visibly upset, was dispatched to bed too, and Francey and the other two girls poured themselves yet another cup of tea and sat around the table, talking with Tilly Harrington, their closest neighbour and lifelong friend of the family.

Except for small movements emanating from behind the door of the second bedroom, each time they stopped talking, the silence of the kitchen seemed more profound than usual. Underlining it, as well as the tinny ticking of the alarm clock on the mantelpiece, Francey could hear the faint shushing of the turf in the range and the upward draw of air through the cavernous chimney. He was now so tired his thigh and calf muscles felt as though they had swollen to twice their normal size. 'Seems later than it is.' Abigail, lowering her voice until it was not much louder than a whisper, broke into one of these hiatuses.

'It's because we're all so drained,' Margaret muttered in response.

'This Hazel's coming all the way from Dublin for the funeral?' Abigail turned to Francey.

'She's a good friend.' Francey felt defensive as Abby's eyes quickened with further interest.

'I see. How much of a friend?'

'Leave him alone.' Margaret stirred her tea.

Francey was grateful for her support. 'I can fight my own battles, Maggie, but thanks,' he said. 'She really is only a friend,' he said to Abigail.

'I'll go in, say a few prayers.' Tilly pulled out her rosary beads and went into the bedroom where Mossie was laid out.

After she had left, Abigail changed the subject. 'I hate all this,' she said, 'it's so hard on Mammy. I wish it was over. I'm going to leave a letter in my will saying I just want to be thrown off a ship or something.'

'Nonsense,' Margaret interjected. 'You've got to think of those left behind. It does people good to have the opportunity to say goodbye.'

Francey was in no mood to discuss Margaret's psychological theories. Leaving them to it, he got up from the table and went in to join Tilly Harrington at Mossie's bedside. She was not praying, but replacing some of the spent candles, lighting the new ones off the guttering stubs. 'Doesn't he look lovely?' she breathed.

Francey, gripping the mahogany footboard of the double bed, stared at his stepfather's waxen, shadowed face and Brylcreemed hair. 'He doesn't look like himself at all,' he whispered.

'Of course he does. You're just used to seeing him differently.' Tilly caressed the pale forehead. 'He was a great man. Now, poor soul, all his problems are over.'

Without warning Francey's heart started a tattoo in his chest and he found it difficult to breathe. The curtains were pulled shut over the window, and tendrils of the still, warm air in the room seemed to be closing in around his head, invading his ears and nose and reaching down his throat to choke him. As he pulled at his collar to loosen it, Tilly noticed. 'What's wrong?' She looked at him in alarm.

'Nothing,' he muttered. 'I'm just very tired, that's all. I have to get a bit of fresh air—' He lumbered out of the room, out through the kitchen, ignoring his stepsisters' surprised expressions, and again went into the night.

His heart continued to thump as he wavered in the centre of the yard but at least the claustrophobic feeling had lifted a little. Although, according to Margaret, the weather had been 'poxy' with storm after storm during the past week, all traces of turbulence had cleared off to the west over the previous twenty-four hours and the night was clear and calm. Francey raised his face to the sparkling sky and concentrated on slowing his breathing. He was at a loss to know what had happened to him: he had attended many funerals, of relatives and people he knew well, and was accustomed to being in the presence of a corpse. As he looked down at his hands, however, he saw that the fingers were trembling like leaves.

He could not yet face going back into the house and the curious looks. Maybe he could go back into the Folly? But the thought of being encased in another room without windows, served only to restart the feelings of panic. Yet he needed some companionship. Francey crossed the yard and went to fetch Rex from the cow-byre in which he had been confined for the night. As he opened the door, the dog, after one brief acknowledging wag of his tail, erupted from the outhouse, sped like a bullet across the yard and through a gap into the hedge which bordered what the family called the hill field. At least his escape gave Francey something to do. No dog, especially one as young and untrained as this, could be left out to roam the countryside at night.

Following him, Francey climbed over the stile into the field, set out in drills of potatoes. 'Rex,' he called, trying to project while keeping kept his voice soft; the window of the girls' room was at this side of the house and he did not want to disturb his mother. There was no response and moving further into the field, straining his eyes for signs of movement, he scanned the silvered rows in the field. 'Rex!' Still seeing no indication of the dog's presence, he cursed his own stupidity and set out fast across the field, picking his way along the soft earth between the drills.

The hill field was the largest on the farm and it took him a few

181

minutes to reach the far side. Rather than go through the gate and into the road, he was forcing his way through a place in the hedge where the woody stems were least dense when, to his relief, he heard the sound of Rex's panting approach. 'Come here,' he ordered, emerging at last into the next field. 'Bad dog!'

Rex, still twenty yards away, skidded to a halt and dropped full-length on his belly in the grass. He turned over on his back with all four paws scrabbling in the air and adopted such an apologetic and humble expression that when Francey reached him, he did not have the heart to punish him but contented himself with catching him by the scruff and pulling him upright. 'Bad *dog!*' he said again.

He was glad he had tight hold, because the dog continued to whine, straining to get away again. He alternated pleading glances at Francey with alert interest in something off in the distance, almost as though he was trying to tell Francey that they had to do something important out there.

'Keep still!' Assuming the dog had flushed a fox or was in pursuit of a hare or badger, Francey felt in no mood to accommodate his games. He scooped the animal into his arms and pushed back through the hedge to walk to the house. Surprised to find himself being carried, Rex forgot his original mission and licked his new master's face so exuberantly that Francey relented. 'You're an awful scallywag!' He buried his face in the soft fur behind the dog's ear. 'What are we going to do with you at all?'

He locked Rex back in his night prison and prior to going back into the house took several deep breaths – a trick mentioned to him by Hazel as being of benefit in calming stage fright – to help him face it. At least the adventure had ameliorated the sharp edges of that unwarranted fear of just a few minutes ago.

Tilly had been watching for him because the door of the kitchen opened before he got to it. 'I was worried about you,' she said. 'Are you all right?'

'Fine, thanks, Tilly.' Francey followed her into the kitchen, 'I just needed a breath of fresh air, that's all.' More to distract her from his own behaviour than anything else, he told her about Rex's escapade but only half-way into the tale, surprised by the look on Tilly's face, trailed to an uncertain halt. 'It's all right,' he assured her, 'whatever he was after he didn't get it. And he's safe now in the outhouse.'

182

To Francey's further perplexity, this seemed to agitate Tilly. She turned to his two stepsisters, now sitting in the chairs on either side of the stove. 'Why don't you two go get a bit of a rest?' she suggested. 'There's no point in all of us exhausting ourselves. We'll take turns to watch. Francey and I will hold the fort for now and I'll call the two of you in a couple of hours.'

Neither Margaret nor Abigail demurred and when they had left the room, Tilly turned to Francey, her face working. 'Sit down, Francey,' she said. 'I'm sort of glad that happened with the dog because it's made up my mind for me. There's something I want to tell you. It's been on my conscience for ages.'

What on earth could she have to tell him about Rex? 'I hope he didn't worry any of your stock?' Francey lowered himself into one of the chairs vacated by the girls.

'No, it's nothing like that.' Tilly wrung her hands then took the plunge. 'Look, I've been trying to think of what I should do about this. And in the present circumstances —'

Mystified, Francey watched her sturdy, grey-haired figure as she paced up and down in front of the stove. The room was warm but not so warm that it could have produced the beads of perspiration that he could see studding her weatherbeaten forehead. 'Whatever it is, Tilly,' he urged, 'it can't be that bad —'

'It's not bad at all,' she blurted, plopping into the chair opposite. 'It's just that I promised I wouldn't say anything. But I feel I should. I took advice in confession but the priest wasn't able to help me much. I thought of writing an anonymous letter, but you see I swore on my sacred word of honour . . .'

Francey decided it would be better to stay silent until she got it off her chest. He did not have long to wait.

Tilly sighed. 'I think I know where Rex was going, maybe not where he was going to but who he was going to see.'

'Who?' Francey failed to see the significance. So what if the dog had struck up an acquaintance with one of their neighbours?

'Your brother's around the parish. He's been around for the last while.'

Brother? What was she talking about? At first the news was too startling for Francey to comprehend.

'Dessie,' said Tilly flatly. 'Dessie's come back. He has a dog with him.'

'Did he come for the funeral?' Then Francey realized it was a stupid question. She had said Dessie had been around for a while. 'Where?' he amended.

He felt nothing except a weird sense of the absurd. 'Where did you see him?' he repeated. 'Please, Tilly, when and where did you see him? And how come Mammy doesn't know?'

'One question at a time.' Tilly held up her hand. 'I swore to him I wouldn't tell anyone. But I can't keep it to myself any longer.'

'Promised who?' Francey forced his tired brain to concentrate.

'Dessie.'

He stared at her until the full import of what she was saying at last penetrated the dullness of his brain. Galvanized, he leaped to his feet. 'Where is he now, Tilly? Tell me. I've got to go to him.'

Tilly rose too. 'Take it easy, Francey. He may well come to you. He could turn up at the funeral tomorrow, although I don't know if he knows Mossie's dead.' She gave a long, shuddering sigh. 'Thank God it's out. It was awful not being able to tell your mother. Sit down and I'll tell you all I know.'

Stunned, Francey sat back into his chair while Tilly related how as darkness fell one evening her husband had come across a vagrant asleep under a thick holly bush beside the new road to Ardgroom. 'You know how Mick is,' she said, 'he couldn't just pass by and leave the creature be. So he woke him up to give him a few shillings.'

'How did he know it was Dessie?' Francey hardly dared breathe.

'He didn't, of course, not at first. He'd seen him before, we all have, the poor fella's been around the district for a good few days now, even weeks maybe. He'd disappear every so often but he'd always turn up again. Even your mother or Maggie might have seen him and not have known who he was. He has this awful, thin scraggly beard and hair down to here, Francey,' Tilly indicated a spot somewhere in the middle of her chest, 'and you can hardly see any of his face except his eyes. But now that I know who he is, of course, I'm kicking myself I didn't twig the resemblance. He has your eyes, you know, Francey. I suppose ye got them from your father . . .'

'Is he tall, like me?'

'Not really. A bit taller than average, I'd say, but nothing like you – it's hard to say. Any time I saw him he was sitting down or even if he was standing or walking he was a bit hunched up.'

She stopped but Francey, desperate to hear the story, urged her to go on. 'Please, Tilly . . .'

'We've all given him a few bits and pieces and scraps of food for himself and the dog but he'd never come into anyone's house,' she continued, sitting back in her chair with a weary sigh. 'He's not the first tramp we've had in the parish as you know and, like a lot of them, he seemed to want to keep himself to himself and we all respected that. Someone, I can't remember who, said they'd heard he was a poor demented young fella who had taken to the roads because he had been disinherited off a farm somewhere in North Kerry and that's what we all thought for a while.'

Tilly paused then looked Francey in the eye. 'There's no easy way to say this, Francey. But the crathur is into the drink. Mick found an empty bottle of meths beside him in the ditch.'

'I was afraid of that.' As Francey listened to Tilly, he was torn between excitement at the rediscovery of Dessie and, given Tilly's description of him, trepidation as to how to handle it.

'Mick didn't like the look of him that day,' Tilly continued. 'It was lashing – you know the way it gets around here, night was coming on and the forecast was bad. There was blood on his face, what you could see of it, it was all scrawbed from the holly, his clothes were in rags and his shoes, such as they were, were in tatters. God love him, he had tried to keep the wet out with bits of brown paper and straw but they were sopping and you could see his toes. He was coughing a lot and Mick was afraid the poor creature was sick, maybe even TB, and he didn't want it on his conscience that he might die of exposure. He had been shivering, even in his sleep, and he had his arms around the dog to keep warm. Mick offered to bring him home for a meal and warm-up by the fire or at least a cup of tea and at first he refused but then Mick said he had a couple of sound pairs of old boots at home and the fellow could have them if he came.'

As Tilly unburdened herself, Francey wanted to weep with guilt. This was the baby companion of his childhood she was talking about. He should have made efforts long before now to find him. He had never pictured Dessie as the abject, pathetic reality he obviously was. 'Not in the greatest of circumstances' to use the phrase in Jool's letter had even been a little romantic, and far from what Tilly was describing. While listening to her soft, lilting voice, he thought of all

185

the grandiose plans he had made, which now seemed so self-centred: how, foreseeing months of close co-operation, he had been looking forward to Fleur becoming involved with him in the hunt and how it would all end gloriously.

Somehow, as a result of the momentous events of recent history, the original motivation had been diluted until Francey realized he could now with justification be accused of casting himself and not Dessie in the lead role of the rescue scenario. He was the cavalry coming over the hill and Dessie was to be grateful, Fleur admiring. Furious with himself, he pounded the arms of the chair with his fists, interrupting Tilly in mid-flow. 'Sorry,' he said then, 'I'm just mad that I didn't do something sooner. Go on.'

'You mustn't blame yourself.' Now that the weight was off her own shoulders, Tilly was full of sympathy. 'Sure aren't the roads full of them, the poor souls. They all had mothers sometime.' She told him that Dessie and his dog had been brought home by Mick that evening but since neither would venture into the house, she had brought out a pile of blankets and pillows and created a bed in a corner of a stable, unused since their horse had been replaced by a tractor. She had put a flask of tea, a drop of whiskey and a meal of bread and cuts of meat nearby and left them in peace.

They were gone the next morning when she went out to check but as darkness fell that evening she looked out of her kitchen window and saw the two of them just inside the door of the stable, accompanied this time by Rex, 'And our Jack too,' Tilly added. 'The creature seems to have a way with dogs.' She had brought out food and drink again, said goodnight, and left.

When she went to the stable next day to remove the dishes from the night before, instead of finding it empty as she had expected, Tilly found Dessie sitting up with his back against the wall, still half asleep with the three dogs snoozing at his feet. She paused. 'And just for something to say while I cleared away the vessels I asked him then who he was and where he came from. It was awful, Francey,' she clasped her hands in her lap, 'he started shaking and shaking and I thought he has having some sort of a fit. It was so bad that I ran into the house and brought out the whiskey, I didn't even wait to get a glass. He put that bottle to his head and then he told me who he was. You can't imagine how bad I felt.' In her misery, Tilly hugged her arms to her chest. 'I'd *minded* that young fella when Kathleen brought him home from the hospital and now here he was – the teeth black in his mouth. It was desperate.' She bent her head and waited a moment or two. 'He started to cry –'

'Did he say why he had come home? Or where Kitty was?' Francey needed more information and could not let her become emotional. 'The last was heard of him as far as I know he was in London and there was no sign of Kitty then.'

'Things were bad for him over.' Tilly brought her voice in check. 'Some friend of his died or something and he was even beaten up a few times. He stole a few bob and came to Dublin but it didn't go well for him there either. He was taken in by the police the very first day he arrived off the mail boat. He didn't say, but judging by the meths and the way he gulped that whiskey I gave him, it was probably for the drink. And I did ask him about Kathleen but apparently he lost touch with her years ago.'

'Why weren't we told about the arrest?' Francey found safety in indignation.

'He's not using his own name.'

He leaned forward. 'But if he came home to the parish he must want to come home to the farm. Why hasn't he made himself known?'

'I think he can't get the courage,' Tilly replied. 'He hasn't been seen at our place since that day he told me. I asked, casual like, in the post office when I was there this morning and one of the women there said she saw a bearded character with very long hair out near Derryvegill yesterday so I'm sure he's still hanging around. That's only a couple of miles from your place. If he turns up, or if you find him, please don't tell him I told you? But thank God it's off my chest.' With a sigh, Tilly sat back in her chair. 'Something has to be done for him, Francey. He needs hospital, or at least a doctor.'

Francey stood up and, for something to do, took down the alarm clock from the mantelpiece and began to wind it. He was so agitated that he used too much force and the key, bent and overused, snapped off in his hands. It was the last straw. 'Now look what's after happening,' he expostulated, looking at the useless piece of metal between his fingers. 'It's no good without the key.'

'How long is it since you've had a decent sleep?' Tilly came up to him and put her arm around his waist, which was the highest part of him she could comfortably reach.

'Days, nights, weeks, I don't know,' Francey muttered.

187

'To bed with you, then. There's nothing you can do tonight about anything. You've a lot on your plate and you'll have more tomorrow.'

'I can't ask you to stay up by yourself, Tilly.'

'You're not asking me. This wouldn't be the first time I've watched through the night. Anyway, I knew poor old Mossie before any of ye.' She shepherded him to the back of the kitchen where she pulled out the settle bed, already prepared. 'When will your mother build herself an extension?' she complained as she shook out the quilt. 'I've been at her for years – get in there now,' she ordered, 'don't even bother to undress. The next time I look at you, I want to see those eyes closed and hear you snoring.'

'Thank you, Tilly.' Francey was so grateful to be taken in charge and told what to do he was even able to raise a smile. The bed was too small but it was comfortable and warm. He curled up and, like a child, pulled the quilt under his chin until he felt snug.

'Goodnight. I'll call you in a few hours.' Tilly pulled the curtains around the bed and left him, then went to check the level of fire in the stove. As she riddled it, Francey felt himself drifting off. His jumbled, disturbing thoughts assaulted him, however, and he was afraid he might have nightmares. To ward them off, guilty at the inappropriateness of it, he summoned up his favourite memory of Fleur, of twin black wings of hair lying on flawless white breasts.

But this comfort was denied him. No matter how hard he tried, Fleur's image was supplanted by the picture of Dessie, dressed in rags and with his arms around a mangy dog, trying to shelter from the rain under the thorny foliage of a holly bush.

Most of the following morning was occupied with fetching Goretti, who was due to arrive at Shannon airport so early that Francey and Margaret had to leave at half past four to be there on time. Francey's other sister, Johanna, would not be able to make it home from Montana on time. Throughout the car journeys both there and back, the revelation that Dessie had shown up burned like a torch on the tip of Francey's tongue, but he was afraid to raise premature hopes and decided not to confide in his stepsisters or anyone else just yet.

It took so long to distribute Communion at the Mass and so many people wanted to shake the family's hands outside the chapel that the cortège did not leave Eyeries until almost a quarter to three that afternoon. 'Last lap,' he consoled the four tear-stained sisters as he saw them, his mother and his grandmother Sullivan into the mourning car outside the chapel. Thinking of his own bloodlines, he wondered what peculiar cement bonded people of different – or even similar – genes together so they constituted a family?

For instance, here was Dessie, after all these years, come back presumably with the intention of contacting a group with whom he had relatively tenuous blood links. And whereas Francey remembered Dessie as a happy, outgoing baby, his mother Kathleen, who was Margaret and Goretti's full sister, seemed always to have been argumentative and unhappy and had never fitted in with anyone. As the car moved off at a walking pace, Francey found himself wondering if he had not been better off before any of this happened. Perhaps his lacklustre existence in Ledbetter's had not been so bad, after all. And Mossie would still be alive . . .

He was worried about his mother's unnatural fortitude. Whereas Connie had wept openly and the other three girls had also been crying into balled handkerchiefs, throughout the Mass his mother had stood or knelt beside him, following the prayers as though she were a robot, and Francey himself had been so intent on trying to act as a pillar of strength for her that he had not yet shed a tear either. In fact, rather than thinking about Mossie, he was on tenterhooks all the time, wondering if Dessie was at the back or outside, or if Hazel had arrived yet.

The three-mile journey to the graveyard was an ordeal. The scene outside looked so normal – half-deckers and open fishing boats bobbing around on their anchor ropes, a cat licking its paws on a gatepost, sea birds wheeling overhead – that as the cortège moved along the skirts of Coulagh Bay, he felt it was an intrusion. The weather had held and sunlight scudded along the whitecaps; it glowed in holly berries, ignited the graceful flowers of the unseasonably blooming montbretia in the hedgerows, and bounced so brightly off the bonnet of the car that it dazzled the driver.

Did the earth not know that someone was dead? Francey wished with all his heart it was raining.

He was squeezed into the back between his mother, as straight as the haft of a spade, and Constance, who, with her head on Margaret's shoulder, was sobbing her heart out. His grandmother, an elegant lady whose beauty still showed under her old-fashioned veiled hat, sat between Abby and Goretti on the seat opposite. In an attempt to comfort Constance, he put one arm around her shoulders only to be rebuffed. 'Try to pray, Connie.' Abigail, whose emotions were more controlled, tried to press rosary beads into the younger girl's hands but was just as surely repelled. Francey fixed his eyes on the foot of Mossie's coffin, visible through the rectangular window of the hearse ahead of them, and wished it could be over soon.

When they were still several hundred yards away from the cemetery, he saw the High Rollers' new minibus, distinctive in its yellow and black livery and mud-spattered from the long journey, tucked as discreetly as possible into a gateway. Hazel's blonde head hove into view as the car followed the hearse into the wide parking bay outside the graveyard gates. Accompanied by one of the High Rollers, wearing flat shoes and what was for her a drab coat, she was standing well back by the ditch as though to be inconscpicuous, and Francey saw her don a head scarf as the hearse came to a stop. Despite the sombre occasion, his heart lifted with fondness: dear old Hazel, he thought, she was making sterling efforts.

Having helped his mother and grandmother out of the car, he went across to Hazel and took both her hands in his. 'Thanks for coming,' he said. 'You'll come back to the house afterwards?'

Hazel nodded, proffering a white envelope: 'Here's a Mass card.' Francey thanked her again and went to the back of the hearse to shoulder the coffin into the graveyard.

The difference in height between himself and the three of Mossie's cousins who were carrying the coffin became evident as they entered the cemetery and Francey, conscious that the other men were forced to take most of the strain, tried to walk with bent knees as, following tradition, they followed the perimeter wall of the graveyard, moving their burden around the points of the compass. His legs were trembling by the time they arrived at the open grave and it was a relief to lower the coffin to the ground. Stepping back, he took his mother's arm and the final rites began.

When he had helped to lower Mossie into his last resting place, he stood back and pulled himself up to his full height, scanning the back of the crowd and even the fields beyond the graveyard. If Dessie was going to come, would he not have shown himself by now?

Beyond the compact mass of bowed heads in the tiny graveyard, the fields were empty.

Francey was too busy for the next few hours to think about anything other than catering for the crowds in the packed kitchen of the house which rang with the terrible gaiety that falls on a post-funeral party. He, Tilly and his sisters were rushed off their feet dispensing food and drink in vast quantities. His mother was at last prevailed upon to take a back seat and to allow others to do the work. Checking on her every so often as she sat, still as a stone, beside her own mother in the seat of honour beside the stove, Francey began to wonder if this consideration had not been a false one. Maybe she might have been better off had she been occupied. So far, apart from a brief, formal expression of condolence in the cemetery after the burial, he had not noticed any direct contact between her and Hazel. Perhaps if there were to have been embarrassing words between them, the time had passed. Francey relaxed about it.

As he emerged from the scullery with a fresh batch of sandwiches, he noticed that Hazel, surrounded by a rapt group of people, was seated in a corner fielding a stream of questions. The High Rollers were in the first rank of showbands, on a par with the Clipper Carltons, the Cadets, the Royal and the Miami, and he was reminded that Hazel was a star, a fact which did not often occur to him. He searched for her companion, the High Roller whose name escaped him. He could not see the fellow anywhere and decided he would have to rescue her himself.

Making his way over to her, he held out the platter. 'Are you all right there, Hazel? Would you like another sandwich?' and, when she demurred, 'Mammy hasn't had a chance to talk to you at all,' extricating her from the group to be rewarded with a whispered 'thank you'.

He asked where her friend was and when Hazel replied that he had gone out to the van, Francey took her hand. 'Come on with me. You don't have to talk to Mammy, I only said that to get you away from that crowd. I want to talk to you.' He unloaded the plate of sandwiches on Tilly and, ignoring the knowing glances being cast their way, excused their passage and took Hazel out into the yard. It was almost dark, and so crisp and cold that if he did not know that they never got snow on Béara, he would almost have expected flakes of white to fall around their heads. 'Come in here,' he pulled her towards the Folly. 'We'll get a bit of peace for a few minutes at least.'

If he expected her to remark on the unusual contents of the

191

building into which he ushered her he was mistaken. Hazel made space for herself on a rocking-chair and curled one foot under her as usual.

'You're great to come, Hazel, and I appreciate it,' he squatted on the floor in front of her, 'but you don't have to stay. Anyway, I'm sure it'll be breaking up soon. I'm surprised they're all still here this late on a Christmas Eve.' The words were a shock: it was difficult to believe that this should be one of the happiest days of the year. 'People shouldn't die at Christmas,' he said.

'People never do what you want them to do,' Hazel replied, an odd expression on her face. 'That's what makes them interesting. But don't worry,' she added, 'I'm not going to be a burden. Vinnie's gone into Castletownbere to book us into the hotel for the night so you'll only have to put up with me around the place until he comes back. Were you very close to your stepfather?'

Francey found himself talking about Mossie then, blaming himself for his stepfather's premature death because he had been showing off his new-found wealth. 'I'm not safe to have in a family.' He felt no need to expand. 'I wish I could turn the clock back.'

'Do you?' Hazel gazed at him. 'No money? No rich relations? No Siamese twin? How'd it go with yer woman, by the way?' she asked, her tone casual.

Having grown up surrounded by so many women, Francey knew romance was grist to their conversational mills but something – perhaps his passion for Fleur was too new? – still kept him from confiding fully in Hazel.

Or could it be that he wanted to leave a chink open so that if a suitable occasion arose, he and she . . . ? Although he despised himself for this thought, Francey found himself acting on it. 'Fine,' he said, 'we didn't see all that much of each other, to tell you the truth.'

'I see.' Hazel's pencilled eyebrows twitched.

'I'm sorry I broke our date last Friday,' he rushed on, hoping he sounded convincing, 'but I got involved in all sorts of business stuff. I'm thinking of buying a place over there. If I do, you'll have to come over and visit.' It was only when he heard himself say this that it came home to him that it was a ridiculous way to talk to a woman with whom he had made love for days and nights on end only a few weeks ago. 'Look, Hazel,' he began, 'I never thanked you —'

'For what?' She cut him off.

'For, you know . . . For that wonderful time I had in your flat . . .'

'All part of the service.' She made a small *moue*. 'I didn't have such a desperate time of it meself, you know.'

Francey leaned forward and took both her hands in his. 'I mean it, Hazel,' he insisted. 'I'll never forget it, it was like waking up out of a long sleep or something.'

'Yeah.' Pulling her hands away, Hazel uncurled herself from her chair. 'That's me all right, Sleepin' bleedin' Beauty.' She walked away and began to examine the titles on the nearest bookshelf. 'Whose are all the books?'

Although her tone remained pleasant the abrupt change of subject discomfited Francey. 'My stepfather owns – owned – most of them.' Feeling like a child seeking reinstatement, he followed her to the bookshelf. 'I feel awful that your Christmas is disrupted like this –'

'My Christmas', Hazel's tone was flippant, 'has been spent on the road for the last donkey's years.'

Francey thought he detected an uncharacteristic seriousness under the words. This was not the Hazel he knew or needed. 'What about your family, your Christmas dinner?' he asked, but felt a little reassured when she smiled up at him.

'My family is the High Rollers and I hate turkey.'

'I can't believe you've no relations at all.'

'A few oul' uncles and aunts and cousins I wouldn't be seen dead with.' Hazel shrugged. 'Not to speak of them being seen dead with me. And me husband's divorcing me,' she added.

He remembered that at some stage during their first drink together in the after-hours shebeen Hazel had said something about hoping – or assuming – her husband would divorce her, but he was abruptly unsure of her tone. She did not sound like someone who was glad or even resigned. 'How does that make you feel?' He was feeling his way here.

'I dunno.' Hazel appeared to consider. 'All right, I suppose . . . The shitehawk. Sorry,' she apologized, 'but that's all he is. Nothing for years and years and years and then a letter. One fucking page. And it wasn't even from him.' Her voice rose and her whole body tensed. 'It was from some fucking Brit solicitor.' She looked up at Francey, reminding him of a small, fierce squirrel. 'Well, he's another think coming if he thinks I'm going to take this lying down.'

Francey was astonished at her vehemence. It was as though he had pushed a button marked 'rage'. 'But haven't you been separated for years?' He stared down at her.

'That's not the point,' Hazel cried. 'That shagger left *me* —'

To his consternation, she burst into tears. He hesitated for a fraction of a second and then, lifting her out of the chair, took her in his arms as though she was a baby. 'Don't cry.' He attempted to hold her head against his shoulder with the palm of one hand.

But Hazel was having none of it. 'For cryin' out loud,' she struggled in his arms, her tears forgotten, 'put me *down*, ya big lunk!'

Bewildered, Francey lowered her to the floor as Hazel berated him. 'I'm not a shaggin' nipper,' she yelled.

'A what?' He had never heard the term.

'A *kid*!' Hazel pulled at her dress, ruched up under the coat she had not taken off since her arrival. 'I'm not a bloody *kid*. And I won't be picked up and put down like a – like a yo-yo.'

'Who's treating you like a – I'm not treating you like anything,' Francey protested, 'Hazel, I've—' He had started to say he had nothing but the height of respect for her but thought better of it. In her present mood who knew how she might react to such a prissy sentiment. 'Can I get you anything?' he asked instead. 'A drink?'

Hazel stared up at him through her brimming, curiously hued eyes. Her mascara was running – despite her toned-down clothes she was in full warpaint – and Francey remembered she had once told him she would not think of doing anything even as mundane as putting out her bins without first donning her false eyelashes. 'Please forgive me, Francey,' she said quietly. 'I'm being a bitch and I know it. It's me that should be comforting you. That's what funerals are for, isn't it?'

'I'm sorry about your husband,' he said. 'I was being stupid. It's just that I didn't know you'd care that much after all this time.'

'I don't, that's just the point. I can't understand what's got into me.' She scrubbed at her face. 'Do I look awful? I always look shockin' when I cry.'

'You look lovely,' Francey said.

'Friends?' Hazel shoved out her hand.

'After the week we spent together, I hope we're more than that, Hazel.' Francey felt gallant and sophisticated as he bent to kiss her on the lips.

194

Her response was cool and he drew away. 'Sorry,' he said, 'I know that was inappropriate. After all this is a funeral.'

'Yeah. We should go back inside? Your mother will be missing you.'

'Not just yet. I could do with a bit of a breather. Is there anything I can do about your husband? Do you need a solicitor or anything?'

'Could you go back to Ledbetter's for just one day and steal a chainsaw?' To Francey's relief she laughed, sounding more like the chirpy Hazel he knew.

He returned the smile. 'You know if you need anything, you only have to ask. I might need your help, as a matter of fact,' he added impulsively. 'I have to tell someone or I'll burst.'

He told her about Dessie's reappearance.

Chapter Ten

Five miles away, an unkempt figure scrambled upright from a hollow under a crag. A terrier-type dog, its brindled coat matted and filthy, came out too; it stretched and yawned and then, while its master adjusted the belt that was the main support for most of his clothes, settled in for a comprehensive scratch.

Chief among Dessie Scollard's extensive inventory of aches and pains was a toothache of such severity he felt as though his entire head was being used as an anvil. In an attempt to alleviate the pain, he ground his fists into his temples as he surveyed his location.

He was standing on a small isthmus bridging a natural archway above the sea, which sucked at the warren of caves below. White as ice, the evening star shone low in the cloudless sky but it was not yet dark: the sun had only just slipped below the grey pencil-line of the Atlantic horizon and the violet hues of the Kerry mountains on the other side of the Kenmare river were still visible. Shivering, immune to the calm beauty, Dessie unscrewed the top of the baby Power bottle he took out of one of his pockets and drank the last half-inch of poteen it contained, swooshing the burning liquid around his mouth in a further effort to anaesthetize the toothache before swallowing. He sucked out the last precious drops and discarded both the bottle and cap, aiming a despairing kick at them. He needed more, far more, but he doubted if he could get any tonight.

A half-mile to his right, the lights of the pub at which two days ago he had successfully begged a meal and a bottle of stout burned steadily through the winter haze. Between it and where he stood, however, the undulating bog, criss-crossed with neat fault lines of excavated turf banks, seemed unfriendly. In any event, he felt so weak that he did not think his legs could carry him that far, even if he could be assured of charity at the end. It had been more than twenty-four hours since he had eaten.

For once his mind, although possessed by the need for another drink, was clear. He sank to the spongy grass and called the dog. Waving its mangy tail it crept towards him on its belly and curled up against one of his thighs. Dessie pulled at its ears. 'What'll we do?' he whispered.

It had been a mad exercise to come to this godforsaken place. The whole idea of coming back to Ireland had been crazy. Dessie remembered little of his early childhood in Lahersheen but all the time he had been away, with his mother and afterwards, in and out of his mind had flashed an abstract image of a place full of light, movement and warmth, of warm golds and friendly yellows. The feelings that went with these memories eluded him; all Dessie knew, if he concentrated hard, was that this must have been what it was like to be happy.

He had been six – old enough to remember it – when he had been taken away, but could remember nothing of the journey, only how the picture had changed from light to dark, from yellow to sludgy brown. One moment he was home, the next he was sleeping in a dark smelly bed beside his mother, on the other side of whom was a man he did not know and who hated him. He did not even know what period of time separated the two images, and when he was old enough to ask his mother she was too far gone to remember.

Life had become a matter of endurance, of staying quiet and gulping down what food he was given, of hiding in corners away from the rows and blows. Of the two of them moving from town to town all over the north of England with a succession of 'uncles' while his mother was often so sick from drink he could not wake her. They lived in caravans and derelict houses and for one winter, in the basement boiler room of a disused factory, all the time managing to stay ahead of the clean English women and fussy men who occasionally found them and tried to separate them or force him to go to school.

Somehow Dessie had survived to the age of thirteen until one day, while living behind the shutters of a boarded-up council flat in Birmingham, the latest 'uncle' had given him an especially vicious hiding. He had waited until the man and his mother were asleep and then, taking with him whatever money and valuables he could find, had struck out on his own for London. He had never seen his mother again and although now and then when at a low ebb he missed her, the missing was visceral, like a pain in an unnamed organ of his body.

197

He did not miss anything specific about her: she had never hugged him as far as he could remember, and most times he thought of her as an old slag.

For the next three or four years he had lived on his wits, sometimes joining up with other youngsters like himself. They had all lived on the proceeds of petty theft and from this group Dessie learned the craft of shoplifting. Armed with this new skill, he had drifted away from the group to fend for himself, getting to know the night shelters and charitable institutions where few questions were asked of the homeless and destitute.

In one of these, when he was almost eighteen, Dessie met Petey McCann, an alcoholic Cavan man who years ago had been a teacher. The two of them had hit it off and, as much as ever happened in their fragmented society, become friends and, quite literally, fellow travellers. Petey was wise to the best free gaffs and when they were not available, to the driest outdoor beds in the city. He was acquainted with the network of Irish kitchen workers, barmen, waiters and hotel porters who kept the gustatory wheels of London turning and who were, in the main, pretty charitable. He knew which Irish clergy would give money without passing judgement or admonition that it was not to be spent on drink and he was on first-name terms with the staff attached to the many Irish centres. In many ways the year Dessie spent in Petey's company was, if not the happiest, at least the most stable he could remember. Like Petey himself, however, he came more and more to depend on drink.

Petey was often incoherent but shining through his ramblings was the culture of a fine mind. It was he who inspired Dessie with the idea that to tramp the roads was a noble tradition and to do so was to follow the paths trodden by the poets and bards of Ireland. And so when Petey had died under a canal bridge one cold morning a few months ago, Dessie decided that he had no future in London. He was Irish, after all, and should go home.

For a while it appeared that he had made the right decision. His *modus operandi* was simple: he tried always to be near a village or town before it got dark and he would knock on doors, persisting even in the face of occasional hostility, until he got what he needed – sometimes even a nip of whiskey or brandy to keep out the cold. He learned that convents and monasteries were invaluable resources and that it was possible to sleep undetected in an upright position on the priest's seat in the confession boxes of a church; often he was able to call on his shoplifting talent to procure a proper bottle for himself.

He acquired a dog, or rather, the dog acquired him, on a back road in North Tipperary and after that he found people were more generous than ever: the sight of a pitiful animal attached to him by a piece of unravelling twine seemed to sting the consciences and open the purses of the middle classes more effectively than the spectacle of a human being down on his luck.

It was only as he had got close to his former home that things started to go wrong. He and his dog had been trudging along the road on the outskirts of Castletownbere when he felt the violent onset of pain in a tooth which had been threatening him for some time. He had a bottle of sherry with him and managed to dull the agony for a few hours but that night it came back in full force. He had been given food and a cup of hot soup by the owner of a pub and had settled down in a shed near the bridge at the bottom of the town but he had been unable to sleep.

Next morning, not remembering anything about the town, he was unsure as to which road to take to Lahersheen and did not want to ask for fear of arousing suspicion. Then he heard the shouted offer of a lift to Eyeries from a motorist to a man on foot. The name of the village was familiar. A high-up chapel? Honeybee toffees in a cardboard box on a shop counter? He decided to follow the route taken by the car.

Ten minutes after he and the dog set out, Dessie's toothache began to ease as a result of swallowing a Mrs Cullen's Powder and dabbing on tincture of oil of cloves, both medicines donated by one of the women from whom he had begged a piece of bread and a drink. As he walked along, in an effort to remember landmarks, he stared hard at everything around him: a Marian shrine on one side of the road, two huge cypresses at the centre of the graveyard on the other, a cottage here, a farmhouse there. But if these green and brown mountain sweeps, that bright sea-line at the end of the sky were features of the way to Lahersheen, he had wiped them from his memory.

If asked, he would have been hard pressed to articulate why he was spending so much time and effort criss-crossing the district, peering over hedges and across gullies. Perhaps, he thought, just finding the place would be sufficient for him and he would not make himself known. Nevertheless, as he continued to tramp the roads and boreens, expectation bubbled like warm oil in his heart, and during the first couple of days in the parish, it seemed nothing could go wrong. A woman gave him a full packet of Aspro to dull the pain in his tooth, another gave him a small bottle of poteen. But having passed a night in a shed in the company of an ancient donkey, he and the dog woke on the fourth morning to tremendous cacophony as the corrugated roof over their heads groaned and drummed under the assault of a howling change in the weather.

The shed, one of a small, dilapidated row, had been placed to shelter its owners' dwelling house and was exposed to the full southwestern blast. When Dessie peered through a grimy window, he quailed at the thought of going out. The erupting black sea, streaked with an intricate tracery of white, flung geysers high into the air across the rocky coastline; lumpy necklaces of foam stretched high into the fields and flecked the hedgerows while further inland, thick winter grasses and branches of stunted thorn trees bent under the successive billows of rain which blew across the landscape like huge grey sails.

He had not had a drink for more than twenty-four hours, and the longing was becoming acute. At least he still had some Aspro left. Gathering a knot of saliva in his mouth, Dessie swallowed three of the sour tablets and calling the dog to him, folded it inside the breast of his coat.

At hour later, in a small shop which glowed like a beacon through the rain, he filched four bars of Fry's Chocolate Cream and a bottle of methylated spirits while the owner was in the back getting him a drink of water. He had drunk meths only once before and had hated its sweet, petrol taste, but the craving was now so bad that he did not care if it poisoned him. Still carrying the dog, he nevertheless put a decent distance between himself and the scene of his crime before daring to drink it.

He found himself on the crown of a road which, having been cut through a bog, was straight and level. The storm, unhindered, screamed like a werewolf along its length but Dessie turned his back on it and unwrapped the Fry's bars, letting the wind pluck the wrappers away. He gave one of the bars to the dog. Then, alternately tipping the bottle of spirits to his lips and taking bites of chocolate to kill the taste, he swallowed enough to dull the craving. Within seconds, however, he felt woozy and nauseous. He had drunk too much too fast, he had to lie down.

He crept under a sturdy holly bush, his arms around the dog for comfort, and with the animal licking the residue of chocolate from the hair around his mouth Dessie slid into oblivion.

The next thing he knew, he was being shaken awake. Then he and the dog were being driven in a car to a house where he was given food, a dry bed in a stable, even new boots by people he now knew as the Harringtons who had been good to him providing not only shelter and food but, most importantly, drink.

When daylight came the morning after that first night in the Harringtons' barn, memory stirred when Dessie stood at the crossroads near the Harringtons' bungalow. This was Lahersheen. Two other dogs had attached themselves to him during the night. Dessie loved their undemanding companionship but he did not like the possibility that their presence could attract undue attention to him.

He hung around for the next few days, covertly watching his family home while trying to decide what to do, but after he had trusted Mrs Harrington with the knowledge of who he was, he had taken fright, making sure never to be seen by day. Although she had assured him that his relatives were wonderful people who would respect his need for privacy he was not so sure. He was used to being alone, with no one on earth having any influence over him. Suppose they wanted to put him into some place to dry out? And if he would not agree, suppose they called in the police to commit him? The circles within which he had moved in London were rife with stories of people being signed into so-called hospitals against their will.

Then late yesterday evening, from a vantage point on the slopes of a small mountain behind his own house, he had seen a lot of coming and going in cars and on bicycles, food and drink being carried in through the kitchen door in copious quantities. This made up his mind for him. There was obviously going to be a big Christmas party. He could never show himself when there was the prospect of so many people about. Perhaps he would come back again sometime, but for now Dessie decided there was no place for him here and, taking the coast road, headed north-west for Kerry.

The weather had improved: although it was cold, the wind and rain had gone. He had lifted one of the blankets Mrs Harrington had left out for him in the stable, and with this to keep him warm and new boots to keep his feet dry Dessie slept quite well under an upturned haycart that night.

But on awakening this morning, toothache assailed him more viciously than ever before. Each step he took seemed to jolt the tooth in its socket, sending lightning bolts up behind his eye. When he had travelled a few miles, the pain became so bad it seemed again to be consuming his entire head and was now eating its way down through his shoulders into his chest and arms. This was why he had searched the wide landscape for a daytime bolthole and had spent the past few hours under a rock. If he could sleep for a bit, he reasoned, he might feel a bit better when he woke up again.

'C'mere.' The darkness was falling and he pulled the dog tighter to his torso. 'We'll have to train you to pull teeth.'

The dog licked his nose, sighed and closed its eyes. Hugging its scrawny body, Dessie considered ending it for the two of them. The gentle sound of the sea beneath him was seductive, almost hypnotic. Here it would be so easy . . . Two seconds – that's all it would take to finish all the botheration. Two seconds and there would be no more pain. As well as the agony in his tooth, his stomach ached with hunger, his nerves screamed for the emollient of a drink and he was tired in a way he could not have described.

He needed to think. Pulling the dog after him, Dessie crawled back under the boulder. After a while he again fell into a light, blessed doze. He dreamed he was in a sort of corral, four-sided, open-topped, the vertical bars constructed of fluid, pearly light. A number of large, insubstantial figures floated about outside. As though they were made from liquid, the figures merged and separated from each other at random and, although they had no discernible faces or limbs, Dessie knew they were perpetually benevolent. When he looked at them he felt calm and so weightless he could float up to them if he wanted to; all he had to do was to lift his arms and he would rise. He had no need to, however, he was contented where he was. The whole scene was flooded with golden light, the centre of which was a pulsating, rich sun just outside his corral and at his own level. The sun reached out and penetrated the inside of his body and made him feel his blood had turned to honey.

The dog in Dessie's arms, in the throes of some dream of its own, whimpered and twitched and woke him up. As usual after this dream, which had recurred on and off for as long as he could remember, Dessie's eyes were wet and the feelings of loss were so strong he could taste them. It took a second or two to recognize the black rock ceiling so close to his head, to feel the onrush of cold air, the renewed assault of pain in his tooth.

After that the decision was easy.

Dessie searched the ground and found a small rock. With difficulty because his fingers were frozen, he wound around it the free end of the twine trailing from the dog's neck and tied it in a clumsy knot. He had to do this quickly or he'd change his mind. The dog did not resist but as he carried it to the edge of the cliff it started to tremble in his arms and looked up at him, the whites of its eyes showing in the clear cold light from the stars. 'I'm sorry, boy,' Dessie whispered, 'but you'd never survive without me.' He closed his eyes and threw the dog as far out as he could. There was no sound. Just a terrible silence followed by a small splash, indistinguishable from the quiet slap of a wave on the rocks below.

He was afraid to go in from here. He could splatter on the rocks and not do the job properly. Blinded by tears, pain tearing into his head, Dessie ran along the clifftop for about a hundred yards and found a place where the rocks shelved into the sea. Headlong, he scrambled down, glad it didn't matter about the scratches and grazes on his hands, rejoicing in the tearing of his clothes. The tide was low and the last thirty yards were slick and wet. His foot slipped into a deep cleft, his ankle twisting under him. Wrenching it out, ignoring the new pain, he limped the last few yards and came to the edge where there was a drop of several feet. He did not hesitate but, summoning as much breath as he could, screamed in a way which could have been interpreted either as a cry of torment or of jubilation as he flung himself into the water.

As he hit the surface he tried to relax but he had not expected the water to be so cold. Shocked, he thrashed about. He had never learned to swim and was surprised that he was not sinking.

He took a deep breath and forced himself to go limp but as soon as the water closed over his head, could not stop himself from again reaching for the surface. Absurdly, he counted out loud: 'One, two, three,' and on the last count again let go.

*

203

'Carry on,' Francey said with sudden decision as they reached the high embankment over Derryvegill lake, 'let's drive on for another fifteen minutes.'

Because it was Christmas Eve the post-funeral gathering had dispersed earlier than it might normally have done and the house was clear of visitors by half past six. It was just after nine o'clock and the search party – Tilly and her husband, Hazel and her friend Vinnie who was driving the High Rollers' van plus Francey himself – had been scouring the countryside for an hour or more.

About three miles from the lake, following Francey's directions, Vinnie drove down a steep laneway towards Cleanderry, a small harbour hidden from the road. They had brought both Rex and the Harringtons' dog with them. 'Everyone watch the dogs,' Francey ordered as they split up. His theory was that if Dessie still had his dog with him, theirs would gravitate towards it.

He began by looking under the small, upturned boats on the beach and then, with Rex splashing in front of him in the water, stood at the edge, listening hard for any sound from either of the half-deckers at anchor about twenty yards away. The anchorage was at the mouth of a small inlet, protected from the Kenmare river by a high cliff breached to Francey's right by a natural archway. He turned on his torch and used the beam to scan the clifftop for signs of movement or unusual shapes. He whistled at Rex and with the dog leaping like a goat ahead of him, set about reaching the crag. The cliff face sloped rather than rose vertically but the going was tough. Although the earth and stones were bound by a covering of grass, the heavy rain of the previous week had loosened and softened it and Francey saved himself from slipping backwards by crawling upwards on his hands and knees and using some of the sturdier looking tussocks as handholds.

Tail waving from side to side like a pennant, Rex was sniffing the ground under the big rock when, out of breath, Francey reached the top. He cast the torchbeam around and saw an empty baby Power bottle. He sniffed: the smell of alcohol was faint but he recognized the smoky traces of poteen. He tried not to get excited: this could have been brought up here by a local. A little way away, Rex was now nosing at something else. Going across to him, Francey saw it was a dog turd. And it was quite fresh.

'Go to it – go!' With a toe, he tried to roust Rex to see if he would follow a trail but, thumping a wary tail, the dog averted his head and stayed put. 'Go, Rex!' Francey tried again. Giving a happy little bark, Rex rushed around in circles and Francey gave up. Pocketing the little bottle he shone the torchbeam to the right and left but could see no other clue that anyone had been up here recently. With the dog again ahead of him, he made his way back down to sea-level.

Tilly and Hazel were first to arrive back at the van.

'Don't get your hopes up too much, Francey,' Hazel warned as he showed the bottle to them. 'It's not as though these things are scarce.'

But Tilly took the bottle from him and turned it over in her hands. 'He had one of those with him all right,' she said. 'I filled it up for him a few times.

'Have faith,' she patted Francey's arm, 'there's always magic at Christmas.'

Rex, who had been sitting at Francey's feet, suddenly pricked his ears and jumped to his feet. Before Francey could stop him, he had bolted like a hare across the grass verge and vanished from view. Seconds later, the Harringtons' dog, Jack, approaching with the two men, veered away and raced after him.

'They've heard something.' Francey, allowing himself at last to get excited, broke into a run and followed the dogs, going back the way he had just come.

Rex's coat was well marked with white and Francey could follow his haring progress to the top of the cliff. But when the dog reached the summit, instead of going towards the area of the big boulder where they had already searched, he turned right and silhouetted against the sky, ran for a few seconds along the top ridge before plunging out of view. 'There's something up there – bring the torches.' Francey, screaming back over his shoulder, hardly felt the ground under his hands and feet as he scrambled upwards for the second time. Adrenalin flowed through his body and he was at the top of the cliff while the others were still approaching the base. Having picked his way along the narrow, treacherous ridge, he stopped to listen. Luckily, there was no wind at all this evening. 'Here, Rex,' he called then listened hard for a reply.

Nothing. Only the rhythmic sloshing of the sea against the rocks below.

'Rex?' he called again, and louder still, 'Jack! Here, boy, good boy, *Jack!*'

After ten seconds or so he was rewarded with a scuffling and soon a sheepish Jack, fearing he had done something terrible, emerged from behind a line of scrub and crawled towards him on his belly. 'Good dog.' As Francey took hold of the dog's scruff, he heard the hard breathing of another man behind him and knew it to be Mick Harrington. 'Our dog is somewhere down there,' he shouted, indicating the spot from which Jack had emerged. 'I haven't gone to look yet.'

'Let me go first, I know this coastline better than you.' Mick scrambled past him and Francey released Jack who went after his master, trotting first to the right of him then to the left but always keeping behind.

Suddenly Francey did not want to know what was behind that low, sinister line of dwarf bushes. His feet and heart like lead, he stood for a little while where he was, forcing himself to remain calm, before he followed Mick.

But it was when he saw it was not a sheer drop into the sea that Francey realized what he had feared. At first he could not see Tilly's husband or either of the dogs, and although he did not need it to see the terrain in front of him, he snapped on his torch and played the beam over the black, honeycombed rocks that descended to the sea in a series of uneven terraces, many supporting small mats of vegetation. At the limit of the torchbeam he caught a flash of white and, clambering down towards it, saw that the two dogs were moving around Mick's hunched back as he stooped over something on one of the patches of grass. Francey's fear returned to choke him. He tried to call out but his voice refused to come.

Mick stood up and with Rex and Jack frisking around his feet began to walk back towards him across the terraces. He was carrying something in his arms. 'You're not to worry,' he called, seeing Francey, 'it's just a dog.'

'Is it Dessie's?' Francey's voice croaked out from somewhere beyond his throat.

'Aye,' Mick replied, 'but you're not to add two and two and make five.' He had come almost level. 'This fella's so weak it's quite likely he fell down from above and your brother thought he was a goner and went on without him.'

206

'Is he alive?'

'If you could call it that. He was whining when I got to him but he's so far gone I don't know how the dogs heard him. To tell you the truth I think he'd be better off if we put him out of his misery.'

'No,' cried Francey, reaching out and snatching the creature from Mick's arms.

The mongrel lay without moving and Francey feared that Mick might be right. He was shocked by how little it weighed – he had lifted ducks and hens which seemed heavier. 'Are you sure there's nothing else over there? Did you look—'

'I'm absolutely sure.' Mick's reply was gentle. 'The rocks make a sort of cul-de-sac there, just beyond where I found the dog. The caves are all on the other side and even if there was anything in there we couldn't go in from above. We'd need a boat. And the current goes the other way,' he said in answer to Francey's unasked question, gazing at his feet.

Francey looked down at the half-dead creature in his arms. A piece of sodden string, tied at the end with a sort of looped handle, trailed from its neck. 'Are there any bones broken?' he asked.

'I don't think so, poor thing . . .' Mick touched the animal's head and was rewarded with a slight twitch of its tail.

'Yoo-hoo, fellas!' It was Hazel, calling from the base of the cliff. 'What are yiz doing up there? We're gettin' worried. Did yiz find anything?'

'Be down in a minute, Hazel.' Francey's voice was coming back to normal. As though willing into it the beats of his own heart, he hugged the dog but as he did so, fresh fear washed into him: the animal's coat was damp and smelled of the sea. 'Mick,' Francey said, 'be honest. Do you think he's drowned himself? This beast's been in the water.'

'I know.' Mick Harrington's voice was steady. 'Francey, I think it's time we called the Guards.'

'No.' Francey felt that to call in the Gardai would be to admit failure and he wanted one more chance to find Dessie himself. Then he felt the other man deserved an explanation. 'If the Guards come in and he's alive, he'll run again. If he's dead it'll make no difference to him to wait. Give me twenty-four hours. I'll go through the whole parish with a fine-tooth comb.'

'Of course.' Mick's slow voice was not reassuring.

Scrambling down the cliff again with the featherweight dog limp in his arms, Francey was determined that the animal should live. To keep it alive seemed at present the most important task he had ever undertaken. He made an act of faith in himself: if he could sustain this dog, he could sustain Dessie too. Until it was proved otherwise, he would not entertain the smallest doubt that his half-brother was not alive. The dog had fallen in, that was all – and Dessie had gone on without him.

They dropped the Harringtons at the crossroads but when they got back to the farmyard, Hazel insisted on coming in with him to help settle the mongrel in Rex's outhouse. 'Hot milk with a drop of brandy, that's what that fella needs,' she said as she followed Francey into the shed and watched him place the animal on an old piece of sacking.

'I heard a car. What's going on?' Margaret, with Abigail behind her, stood in the doorway.

'We were out for a drive,' Francey bent and started to undo the knot which held the string around the dog's pathetic neck, 'I was showing Hazel around and we found this fella.'

'Oh, the poor thing, he's skin and bone.' Abigail came in and bent to look at the animal, whose ribs protruded through its skin.

'It's too far gone, you should shoot it, Francey,' Margaret advised from the doorway.

'For God's sake, it's feckin' Christmas, he *can't* shoot it!' Like a dervish, Hazel whirled on her. 'Where's your Christian charity?'

'Only a suggestion.' Coolly, Margaret surveyed her, then turned and left.

'I'm sorry, Francey,' Hazel was contrite. 'Me and me big mouth, I shouldn't be puttin' me bloody oar in.'

'Don't mind her, Hazel.' Abigail smiled. 'She's a district nurse, thinks she knows what's best for everyone.'

'He deserves a chance anyway.' The knot on the makeshift collar had proved too old and tight to unravel so Francey chucked at the string itself. Its rotted strands parted easily and, giving the dog a consoling pat, he straightened up. 'Run in and heat up a sup of milk, will you, Abby?' He waited until she had left and spoke to Hazel in an urgent whisper, asking her not to reveal anything of where they had been or of what he planned to do later.

208

'I'll come back and help,' Hazel hissed in reply but Francey shook his head.

'No, you'd only attract attention.'

She looked him up and down. 'And you won't, I suppose, all seventeen foot of you?'

'People wander around these mountains all the time, with guns, snares, that sort of thing.'

'Well, do you want the lend of the van?'

The idea of trying to be inconspicuous while driving around in a vehicle painted all over with monster dice and likenesses of Hazel was so ludicrous that if he had not been so intent on his purpose, Francey might almost have laughed. On impulse he swung Hazel off her feet and kissed her.

'What was that for?' she gasped when he put her down again.

'For being you,' he said. 'Thanks for everything. You're really good.'

'Yeah,' Hazel muttered, bending over the dog and stroking the matted hair on its flank, 'Mother Mary Aikenhead, that's me.'

Abigail returned, along with Constance, the latter's tear-puffed face curious. 'There was already milk on the stove,' she said, putting the dish she held on the ground, as close as possible to the dog's head.

Francey bent down beside her and dipping his finger in the milk, wet the animal's nose with it. He had to do it twice but then the dog opened its eyes and struggled on to its belly, lapping feebly at the dish. 'Get more, Abby,' Francey ordered, 'and bring out a bit of bread too.'

'I'll get it.' Evidently glad of the distraction, Constance trotted off.

As he watched the dog's drinking becoming steadier, Francey could have cheered. It was going to be all right. He felt it in his bones. He wanted them all to go away now to let him get on with the search, but he knew he had to have patience: Margaret would not be willing to give him her car so he would have to wait until she was asleep. He knew she never took the key out of the ignition.

He hugged Hazel and told her to go back to the hotel. 'You've been a great help,' he said, meaning it. 'And thank you for coming to the funeral.' The words were a little shocking. He had become so involved in the search for his half-brother that he had almost forgotten the reason why he and Hazel had come here in the first place. He let her go and smiled down at her. 'Better not keep your man waiting.'

Hazel seemed to hesitate and in the gloom of the outhouse Francey could not make out her expression. 'Vinnie's not my man,' she said, but before Francey could say anything else, she turned to leave. 'Be sure and let me know what happens,' she said. 'Cheerio.'

'Good luck in Killarney,' he called after her, *sotto voce*.

Starting at about one in the morning at the place where they had found the dog, Francey systematically searched the country between the coastline and the village of Ardgroom and then swept a wedge-shaped area between that village and the limit of the distance he thought his half-brother could have covered in the time elapsed on the Killarney road. Everywhere he disturbed wildlife, rabbits, stoats, ferrets, shrews, even an otter and a few feral cats.

He went on full alert at seeing a drunk staggering from side to side of a boreen in Derryconnla but the man proved far older than Dessie would be.

The weather remained cold, dry and bright, the stars giving so much light that he needed the torch only to search along ditches and under the shadows cast by hedges and rocks. It was coming up to half past three when, tired but still resolute, he sat for a breather on a little grass platform over a natural spring. The profound quiet was like a blanket against his ears; above the pattering of the spring into its grassy basin beneath his feet, he could hear his own strong heartbeat, the surging of his blood, the small gurgles and clicks of his organs and bones. He tilted back his head, stared into the sky and wished he was a writer or a painter so he would have the language to describe, just for himself, this infinite brilliance.

Stars behind stars behind stars.

So many that the small high moon was relegated into insignificance. The more Francey stared into the sky, the more he fancied he could hear something new, a high sweet sound, such as he used to hear when he stood beneath a telephone pole when there was no wind, or could make for himself by wetting a finger and rubbing it round the rim of one of his grandmother's crystal wineglasses.

Where was it coming from? Francey listened harder, straining his ears, but the singing was all around, coming from the air itself or from behind the galaxies. It was a mystery, like the elusive core of the woman he loved.

For the first time, Francey gave himself permission to wonder if he would ever penetrate that core. He had always imagined that to be in love would have to be a mutual bonding, not this challenging ache he carried with him and which sharpened in moments of solitude like this. On the paltry few occasions he had been with Fleur, or had just been near her and able to watch her, the equations had seemed so simple: he was attracted to her, he wanted her, he loved her. Ergo, it would be just a matter of time before she saw she loved him too.

And if she did not see it by herself, he would be able to show her.

The sex between them meant he would never be the same again, yet Francey was forced to examine the prospect that perhaps the experience had not had the same effect on her. All his life he had read about the inscrutability of the Orient. Was Fleur's apparent remoteness a natural character trait? He longed for some learned advice. He mulled it over until he was distracted by the cry of a curlew, miles away across the bog, and closing his eyes, listened hard for an answering call. Irish poets and writers were big on curlews, he thought. They used the cry as onomatopoeic shorthand to symbolize loneliness, mourning, all the singular longings of the soul.

He was surprised to find he did not feel in the least lonely. On the contrary, under the splendour of this sky he felt he was being cared for and watched. The future, whatever it contained, was certain: somewhere up there it had already happened. These galaxies hung over Fleur, and Dessie, and Hazel and his mother and sisters, even Johanna so far away in Montana; they wheeled over Mossie in his grave; they stored all the thoughts ever thought and still to be conceived. They knew where Dessie was. Francey found that in the last few hours his fears about Dessie had been assuaged. Under this sky, he knew as well as he knew his own name that everything would work out.

The by-road where he sat led upwards into the mountains and was about a mile from Ardgroom. From this elevation, he could see the village and some of the hinterland of his own town. As it was Christmas Eve, many of the houses still showed lights as the women tended their hams and puddings. Under the clarity of this sky he could tell the difference between the houses which had 'th'electric', as

211

it was called in the parish, and those that still relied on the gentler glow of paraffin. Rural Electrification was a creeping giant, and although Francey was pleased that his family had benefited, he missed the little ceremony which had attended the lighting of the lamps each evening at dusk, the warming of the glass chimneys, the squeaking of newspaper against them as they were polished, the flare of matches, the way the smell of the oil leaked into the kitchen as a little yellow and blue fire raced the length of the soaked double-wicks.

Dessie had loved it: Francey remembered that from the age of four or so, as a special, supervised treat he had been allowed to light the lamps. Francey's half-brother had been fascinated by fire and because of this, alone among all the babies in the house, a guard had had to be erected in front of the stove. As soon as he was old enough to stand, each time the oven door was opened Dessie used to reach out from the playpen to try to touch the glow within.

One after the other, two shooting stars tumbled across their fellows towards the horizon: when he was small and still religious, Francey believed what the teacher taught him, that shooting stars were souls on their way to heaven.

Enough. He stood up and gave himself a mental shake. Stars, skies, sentimentality – he was going soft in the head. He had practical things to do. He strode towards Margaret's Hillman to resume the search for Dessie.

Two hours later, he admitted defeat and went home.

He free-wheeled into the yard and stealthily, using one of the containers he knew were kept in a little fenced-off enclosure behind the house to save Margaret having to make trips into Castletownbere for petrol, he topped up the Hillman's tank so she would not know he had been using the car. He hoped that would be sufficient but he would not put it past her to know exactly how many miles were on the vehicle's clock.

Before letting himself into the house, he went to the outhouse to check on the new dog. When he shone his torch over the half door, he was met by two wagging tails. Dessie's dog did not get up but its eyes were open and to Francey it already looked healthier.

He reached his settle bed without incident and fell into dreamless sleep.

*

212

Minutes later, or so it seemed, he was shaken awake by Margaret. 'Come on, lazybones,' she whispered. 'It's Christmas morning, we have to go to Mass – we're all going together to support Mammy.' Francey, whose body felt as though it was lined with lead, groaned that he was not going to go to Mass but Margaret was not put off. 'Don't be so selfish, we need you at a time like this,' she insisted. 'Come on, legs out, make an effort.' With practised authority, she continued to pull at his arm and Francey found himself seated on the side of the settle with his feet on the floor.

Goretti and Abigail were seated by the stove at the far end of the kitchen, talking quietly together. Francey's brain at last snapped to: he had been out all night searching for Dessie. He had to go out again today. And this time he would look for as much help as he could get. Anyway, he thought, he could not keep the news to himself for very much longer. They deserved to know. He decided to tell the girls straight after Mass and to leave it to them whether or not to tell his mother, whose silence continued to be impermeable.

Although they were all solicitous of her, the atmosphere in the packed Hillman as Margaret drove the six of them to Eyeries, was of desperate sadness. A cheering note, for Francey at least, was that Dessie's terrier had continued to make progress. Although still lying on its side in the spot where it had been placed, it did not have to be coaxed to drink the milk Francey brought it before leaving the house.

They reached the chapel with time to spare. As it was Christmas, even the laggards who always hung about outside during Mass had made an exception and, caps in hand, were standing inside the porch. As Francey passed through the confined space, holding his silent mother's arm, strong aromas of Brylcreem, soap and new serge competed for his attention. The men had been chatting but, on seeing the newcomers enter, fell silent out of respect. Francey had taken a few steps inside when his overtired brain rebounded against something he thought he had heard before the talk had died away. 'You go ahead,' he whispered to his mother, 'I'll be with you in a second.'

He went back out into the porch. 'What were you talking about before we came in?' he asked the nearest man, a wiry little fisherman he recognized as being from Derryconnla.

'Did you not hear?' one of the other men volunteered before the first could answer. 'John Montgomery from Salladerg took a fella from the sea last night.' He lowered his voice. 'He thought he saw

213

something moving in the water when he was pooching around at the mouth of that little stream at Foilathuagig trying to get a salmon for the Christmas dinner, wisha the Montgomerys don't have much, God love them, you know how it is —'

Francey did not care about the law and salmon poaching and he cut short the man's story. 'Who?' A pulse in his temple began to beat. 'Who was the man?'

'We don't know.' They were all crowding around now, glad to have a new audience for the news. 'He's not from hereabouts,' this speaker was unknown to Francey, 'by all accounts he's a young fella from north Kerry. The wife says she's seen him about a bit lately.'

Francey was afraid to ask the next question but it came out regardless. 'What state was he in? Was he alive?'

'Dunno,' the first man shrugged, 'it was touch and go last night as far as I know, God be good to him.'

'Where is he now?' Francey did not care that he was betraying undue interest.

'Why, do you know him?' asked the fisherman with quick curiosity.

'I might,' Francey said, 'I have to go and see.'

They told him that, as far as they knew, the young tramp was still in John Montgomery's house and gave him directions, then crowded out of the porch to watch Francey's dash for the Hillman.

'Don't get your hopes up,' the fisherman called after him.

Chapter Eleven

Salladerg was a segment of the parish between Cleanderry and Castleclough; the Montgomerys' cottage stood about half a mile from the area where they had found the dog. A poor place close to the shore, it was built on rock and surrounded by a tumbledown stone wall. As he got out of the car, Francey could see John Montgomery's open boat, upturned on the rocks above the waterline.

At his approach across the yard, a bantam cockerel fluttered out of a pram body and scuttled away from him across broken toys, tools, farm machinery and old bicycle frames, coming to rest on a rusting mangle. The rest of the farmyard fowl scattered out of his path as he threaded his way through fish boxes, lobster pots and discarded pieces of net to get to the kitchen door. 'Please don't let him be dead,' he prayed to no one in particular as he knocked.

The door was answered by a thin, sallow woman with some of her hair pinned up, the remainder trailing around one side of her face. As Francey introduced himself, he could see a raft of small, silent children hanging behind her. 'I came to see if I could help with the tramp,' he said.

'Oh,' the woman pulled the door wide, 'I can't wake the poor man, himself's gone for to telephone the doctor.'

Francey forced himself not to think the worst as he stepped past her into the kitchen, stooping under the low ceiling so as not to bring down skeins of coloured crêpe paper. 'He was very far gone when John brought him in,' the woman seemed grateful to have the opportunity to unburden herself, 'but I made him take off his wet clothes and gave him a blanket and seat by the fire and a sup of hot port, we had a bit of drink in for the Christmas,' she clipped up a hank of the fallen hair, 'and although he was rambling a bit, poor man and we found it hard to understand what he was saying, he seemed to be asking for more drink so we gave it to him. And before we knew where we were the bottle was all gone. But we did think he

215

was going to be all right, that's why we gave him the bed for the night . . . If I'd thought—' Still pinning her hair, she looked up at him with sudden hope. 'Do you know his people?'

'I think I might.' Francey's eyes were getting accustomed to the dim light in the kitchen which was coming from a single, tiny window. The efforts made to brighten it up for the holiday accentuated its meanness.

'Thank God,' the woman sighed, 'I don't mind telling you I was afraid we'd be left with him. I don't know whether he's alive or dead at the moment to tell you the truth.'

'Can I go below?' Francey indicated a closed door at the end of the kitchen. He resisted the urge to pinch his nostrils against the smell of cooked cabbage which vied for supremacy with that of strong disinfectant in the smoky air.

'Surely.' The woman picked up a baby which had crawled between her legs and was attempting to pull itself upright.

One end of the camp bed in the centre of the virtually empty parlour had been propped up with two fish boxes and at first Francey could not see anything human on it. Like the kitchen, this room had just one small window and nothing differentiated one end from the other in the heap of blankets and coats piled on the cot. He went closer and put a hand to his mouth to prevent himself from crying out.

He had to make an act of faith in what Tilly had told him to accept that what he saw here was Dessie. Most of the face was invisible under a mat of stringy brown hair and the eyes were closed but even had they been open, Francey doubted if he would have believed this was any kin to him or his family. Afraid he was too late, he did something he had never seen outside picture houses: he put his ear down to the face and listened for breathing. The smells were no less sour in here and he had to hold his breath to protect himself from the stench that hung like a foul slime around Dessie's head. After a few seconds he heard something, the faintest, most intermittent of somethings, but it was life.

Sensing movement behind him he looked round. All the children, seven or eight of them, had crowded in behind their mother in the doorway. 'I couldn't wake him this morning,' the woman repeated, pointing to a bowl of thin gruel on the floor beside the bed. 'That's why John's gone for to ring the doctor. Is he —'

'He's alive all right.' Francey looked back at the bed. He came to a swift decision. 'If you don't mind, I'll bring him with me. When the doctor comes, would you send him up to our house in Lahersheen?' In no doubt that word had already spread about where he had gone to in such a hurry, he was not worried about the abandonment of the rest of his family at the chapel in Eyeries. He knew his mother and the girls would not want for offers of lifts home.

'Oh I don't know . . .' the woman twisted one hand inside the other, 'do you think it's the right thing to do? My husband said —'

'I'll take full responsibility,' Francey reassured her. 'And I'd like to thank you and Mr Montgomery very, very much, whatever happens.' For the first time in his life, Francey took money out of his pocket to pay someone off.

Stupefied, the woman looked at the bundle of notes he had pressed into her hand. 'I couldn't — ' she began but Francey, feeling there was little time to be lost, interrupted.

'For the children,' he said. 'I know this poor man's people would want the children to have something nice for Christmas and they'd be very grateful indeed for all you've done.' As he spoke he was discarding the coats and cocooning Dessie in a few of the blankets. 'I'll return the bedclothes to you as soon as possible,' he said, scooping up the bundle into his arms. Then, carrying it as easily as if it was the terrier he had held last night, he hurried past the wide-eyed children out to the car.

'What'll I do with his clothes?' the woman called from the kitchen door.

'Burn them,' Francey replied, placing Dessie tenderly into the back seat of the Hillman.

He turned on the heater of the car full blast and drove as though his cargo was a consignment of rare eggs. When he got home, he carried his half-brother through the kitchen and, after the smells in the Montgomerys' cabin and emanating from the burden in his arms, was never more conscious of the wholesomeness of his own house. In his mother's bedroom, he unwrapped Dessie and placed him between the sheets of the double bed, trying not to dwell on the image of the corpse that had so recently lain there.

What Francey saw now was even more frightening. Despite his immersion in the sea, Dessie's feet, hands, and what could be seen of his neck were streaked with dirt; the threadbare, buttonless pyjama jacket he wore had fallen open, exposing ribs like bowed ladders and a hollow below the breastbone as deep as a pudding bowl, the bones of his arms and legs protruded like the shafts of a cart; one of his ankles was discoloured and swollen. His mouth was open and the tops of the black teeth were rimed with green around the gums. 'Nothing that can't be cured,' Francey murmured, and removed the inadequate pyjamas from the rag-doll body, replacing them with a pair of Mossie's, which he took from the chest of drawers nearby. When the operation was finished, he pulled the sheets and blankets up to his half-brother's chin, tucked them in, and plugged in the electric fire beside the bed, flipping the switch to ignite both bars. 'Don't go away,' he said, as he left the room.

He ran out to the yard and into the outhouse. Pushing the fawning Rex aside, he picked up the terrier and hurried with it back to the bedroom where he placed it on the bed beside the inert body. The little dog, evidently accustomed to taking life as it came, showed no surprise at finding itself in such unusual surroundings or at rediscovering its master. It put its head on its paws and looked from the mound in the bed to Francey and back again. Then it sighed, stretched full length and closed its eyes.

Francey waited until he was sure the dog had settled before going into the kitchen to wait for the doctor. Each minute passed as slowly as a century as he paced the kitchen and telephoned the doctor's Castletownbere number over and over again to no avail; each time he went into the bedroom, he found that neither man nor dog had moved a muscle since he had last checked on them. At last, hearing a car outside, he rushed to the door to find, not the doctor's car, but Mick Harrington's with Tilly in the passenger seat and a grim-faced Margaret in the back.

Francey's first reaction was of chagrin – now there would be a row about his unauthorized taking of the Hillman – but then he remembered that Margaret's was the best possible arrival. 'No time to talk,' he said, pulling open the back door, 'come on, you're needed inside.'

As Margaret got out, Mick Harrington rolled down the front window to tell Francey that the rest of the family was coming in another neighbour's car. 'Some poor tramp, is it?' he added, signalling to Francey that he had not filled Margaret in on their visitor's identity. 'Is there anything we can do?'

'No thanks, Mick,' Francey, already following his step-sister into the house, called over his shoulder. 'I'll see you later – and happy Christmas, by the way.' He did not wait for the greeting to be returned.

'I hope there's a good explanation for this.' Margaret, hands on hips, was standing in the middle of the kitchen floor. Saving the revelations for later, Francey explained as succinctly and rapidly as he could that the man in the bedroom had been pulled out of the sea the previous night, had seemed to be all right but was now unconscious. 'Thank God you're a nurse,' he finished. 'I don't know what to do.'

Margaret shrugged off her coat and hung it up behind the door then walked across the kitchen. 'Why are you getting involved with this? What's it to you? What's that animal doing there?' The questions were buried in professional outrage. Clucking her disapproval, she shooed the terrier off the bed and bent over Dessie's still face. 'Get me my bag,' she ordered, 'it's beside the dresser – and bowls of hot and cold water. Towels. And boil the kettle.' She rolled up the sleeves of her black cardigan and went to work.

The rest of the family arrived a few minutes later and while Francey's mother, her ironclad cloak of detachment intact, stayed in the kitchen, the girls crowded around the bedroom door. 'Oh my God.' The tender-hearted Abigail's hands flew to her mouth.

Margaret turned round. 'Everyone out,' she ordered. 'I need a bit of space here. Is there any sign of the doctor?'

'No. How is he now?' Francey peered over the shoulders of the girls.

'It's still too early to tell, he's very weak. He mustn't have eaten for weeks – and there's a strong smell of drink. He might even be suffering from alcohol poisoning.' Margaret turned back to her patient, 'I think when he wakes up he'll need stuff I don't have. Try to see what's keeping the doctor, will you?'

'How bad is he?' Francey's mother took off her leather gloves, folded them one inside the other, and put them away in a drawer of the dresser when Francey, followed by the girls, turned back into the kitchen. 'Is this his?' She looked down at the terrier, awake but curled up in a self-deprecating ball in a gap between the dresser and the side of the chimney breast.

'Yes, that's his, all right,' Francey said, then decided that he could no longer play God. It was not fair to the rest of them – they had the

219

right to make up their own minds how they felt. 'Mammy,' he blurted, 'I know who he is.'

'Who?' It was Constance.

'It's Dessie.'

He could have predicted the various reactions. Abigail and Goretti gasped aloud while Constance's eyes widened with excitement. 'What?'

Only his mother gave no outward sign of being affected. He moved over and grasped her arms. 'Did you hear what I said, Mammy? It's Dessie in there in the bed.' The words tumbled off his tongue but still her expression remained frozen. 'Mammy, Mammy . . .' He shook her gently, forcing her to pay attention.

As though being sucked out by an invisible hose, the blood drained from his mother's face. She made no effort to blink away the huge tears that spilled into her eyes. The slow-motion change, as her entire face seemed to disintegrate, was terrible to watch: to Francey it was like seeing cracks spread through a doomed concrete wall. But what was most terrible was that still she made no sound. 'Mammy, Mammy!' he cried, gripping her arms. 'Are you all right?'

'Leave her, leave her, she'll be fine, she hasn't cried at all, it's the best thing for her.' Margaret, unaware of the trigger for her step-mother's collapse, bustled forward from the bedroom to take charge. 'Come on, Mammy,' she said in a soothing voice, plucking her from Francey's grasp, 'sit over here by the fire. One of you make her a cup of tea, make it strong and put plenty of sugar in it,' she snapped over her shoulder while guiding her unresisting charge to one of the chairs beside the stove.

'You don't understand, Maggie,' Constance, who had wept with little respite since her father's death looked as though she was about to start again, 'she's not crying over Daddy.'

'Of course she is. What do you mean?'

'It's him in there.' Goretti pointed to the bedroom. 'Francey says that tramp in there is Dessie.'

For once Margaret could think of nothing to say as she sagged into a chair.

Francey's mother continued to weep, shoulders heaving. She emitted sounds now, awful sounds pulled from depths at which Francey could only guess. He was acutely uncomfortable, and felt the stirrings of panic that lurked at the centre of his soul and which were always ready to spring to life at the sight of someone else's grief. He knew he should put his arms around her, comfort her, do something, anything . . .

Margaret saved him by finding her tongue. 'Let her cry.' She looked at the rest of them. 'One thing at a time – is that tea ready yet?' Abigail, white-faced, brought the steaming cup from the stove and Margaret, sitting on the edge of Elizabeth's chair with one arm around her shoulders, coaxed it into her drop by drop. 'There now,' she soothed, 'that's nice, isn't it?'

The doctor knocked at the kitchen door.

Dessie woke up in stages, consciousness washing over him and then away again in long gentle waves. Shaved, bathed and surrounded by hot water bottles, his tangle of hair pulled back from his pale forehead, he was now propped up on pillows being spoon-fed a mixture of hot milk and white bread by Margaret, with the assistance of Abigail.

So far he had not spoken except with bewildered, pain-filled eyes which slid away from everyone else's as he accepted all that was being done for him. The doctor had warned that he should not be put under any stress, and although the girls were bursting with questions, they let him be. To give the doctor his due, thought Francey, seeing the man out more than an hour after his arrival, he had been assiduous, tending to his patient until he was sure there was nothing else he could do. Before he left he had bequeathed all his samples of penicillin and an assortment of other drugs to Margaret to tide her over until she could get prescriptions filled in the chemist's shop after Christmas.

Margaret would not let more than one person besides herself into the bedroom and as she and Abigail finished feeding him, Francey went into the room to take their place. 'How are you feeling now, Dessie?' he asked, sitting on a chair beside the bed. 'A little better, I hope? You gave us all a fright.'

The bloodshot eyes swivelled towards him. 'Were you here before I left?' was croaked rather than spoken.

Francey had expected something clichéd in the line of 'Where am I?' but this implied that Dessie knew quite well where he was. 'Yes, I

221

was. My name is Francey,' he replied, then realized he was speaking as though the young man in front of him was a two-year-old child. 'Do you remember me at all?' he asked, in a more normal manner.

Dessie responded by closing his eyes again.

'It doesn't matter,' Francey pulled his chair back a little in case his half-brother felt crowded. 'I remember you very well. I'm your brother. You're home now, Dessie. And we've an awful lot to talk about, but not yet. First we're going get you some help, all the help you need . . . We just want you to rest now.'

To his horror, Dessie reacted as though he had been hit, struggling on his pillows, thrashing his hands on the coverlet. He was uttering a frantic stream of words, in such an unusual accent that Francey found him difficult to understand but somehow he comprehended that his half-brother was begging him not to put him in a home.

Francey had to restrain him physically from getting off the bed. 'Relax, Dessie,' he urged, reminded of how undernourished were the bony forearms under his hands. 'We're not going to put you anywhere, rest, now – rest.'

But the other man continued to be so distressed that Francey shouted for Margaret, who rushed in and administered another injection.

Minutes later, when her patient was asleep again, Margaret stood back to look at him. 'He needs to be in a hospital,' she wrapped the used syringe in a piece of cotton wool, 'and he could badly do with a dentist but it's Christmas Day, and it's not a matter of life and death at the moment.'

'That's what he's afraid of.' Francey looked with compassion at the bag of bones in the bed. 'He thinks we're going to put him away somewhere.'

'Well, if that's the best thing for him, that's what we'll have to do.' Margaret twitched the covers over her patient.

'Can we talk about it later?' Francey was afraid Dessie was not fully asleep. *Reader's Digest* was full of articles about patients in comas who could hear and understand every word spoken in their presence.

He was conscious of an extraordinary feeling of anticlimax. For so long he had been focused, consciously or sub-consciously, on the task of finding his brother that the finding itself had become the end. He now realized he had never thought much beyond it: even after

222

Jool Gallaher's will had seemed to reveal a rather frightening vista, he had not taken on board the full implications of Dessie's state of dereliction; instead, his imagination had persisted in seeing a celebratory, prodigal-son type reunion, with everyone smiling into a happy-ever-after future.

He looked at the unkempt skeleton in front of him; eyes closed the skull under Dessie's face was all too obvious and Francey's heart sank at the task ahead. But then he thought of the cheering news he had for his half-brother: perhaps the discovery that he, too, was rich would aid his recovery. It would, no doubt, make it easier to get the best medical and psychiatric care.

He followed Margaret into the kitchen. His mother and the girls were seated at the kitchen table drinking tea and it occurred to Francey what a poor Christmas this was with the turkey forgotten and still hanging head-down from the rafters in the scullery, the cold puddings waiting under their muslin on the dresser, even his own Christmas presents lurking in their garishness at the bottom of his suitcase. 'Any chance of a drop?' he asked, then saw that on the table in front of them was one of the family albums, open at a page of snaps taken during a long-forgotten birthday party. His mother had removed one of the pictures from its corner-pieces and, tears still pouring down her face, was staring at it. Now that she had started to release all the grief she had pent up over the past few days, it seemed she could not stop. 'Don't cry, Mammy,' he begged.

'I told you before, leave her,' Margaret warned in a low voice. 'It's good that she's crying.'

His mother passed him the small square photograph she had been examining: it had been taken in the yard, in front of the open kitchen door, on Dessie's fifth birthday.

In front of the little crowd, Francey's proud half-brother displayed his birthday present, a tennis racket almost as big as himself. Behind him, beaming, stood Francey's mother holding the two-year-old Connie, and Mossie, who had one arm around Francey himself, eight years old and already gangling taller than Mossie's elbow, the other around Johanna who was tiny, almost as small as the birthday boy. At the back of the group, the Harringtons were rubbing shoulders with Margaret, Goretti and Abigail but Kathleen, Dessie's mother, stood a little apart, looking away from the camera as though already distant from this place and everyone in it.

223

Francey did not know how he was supposed to react. 'Maybe we should show him this when he wakes up again,' he offered. 'He seems to be a bit afraid of us – of me anyway – and this might help him feel we're his friends.' He passed the snapshot back to his mother.

As she reinserted the photograph into its allotted space in the album, she stoppd crying and seemed to come to a decision. 'That's a good idea, Francey,' she said, 'at least it'd be something concrete I could do. I'll bring it into him the next time he wakes up.'

Relieved, Francey poured himself some tea. The adrenalin of the morning had ebbed and fatigue had drained his limbs so that all he could think of was sleep. He added milk to the cup but was too tired to stretch for the sugar bowl which was at the far side of the table; it seemed like too much trouble even to ask for it to be passed to him. 'I'm sorry,' he yawned, as he slugged a large mouthful of the strong, bitter liquid, 'but I'm wrecked, I haven't had a night's sleep for what seems like a fortnight. I'm going to have to have a nap for an hour or so. Can I use one of your beds?' appealing to the girls.

They nodded assent and leaving the rest of the beverage undrunk, Francey went into the bedroom and without bothering to get undressed, parcelled himself under the quilt on one of the beds crowded into the room. In the wispy trails of half-dreams which drifted through his brain just before he dropped off, Dessie's haunted eyes hung in front of him as though they had been detached from his skull. Then, just before he surrendered to oblivion, a happier thought occurred as he remembered he had promised to telephone Fleur at the first hint of news. He was too tired to do it now, he would do it when he woke up . . .

But when he did wake again, refreshed, alert and hungry, the house was encased in the silence which occurs only late at night or in the early hours of morning. All around him was light breathing and in the quarter-light from the window, he saw the other beds in the room were occupied. How long had he slept?

He got up as quietly as he could and tiptoed out of the room into the kitchen. As he closed the door behind him, he became aware of a scrabbling noise somewhere near the stove. The source became clear as soon as he switched on the electric light: claws clicking on the flagged floor, Dessie's terrier trotted to and fro at the feet of his master who was rooting around in the dresser. Surprised by the flood

224

of light, Dessie turned to see who had turned it on. 'Oh,' he said, Mossie's pyjamas flapping like flags on his thin body, 'it's you.'

'Are you looking for something?' Francey took in the entire kitchen at a glance: sometime during the day or night, his half-brother had been transferred to the settle bed.

'No, nothing,' Dessie replied, his eyes continuing to dart around.

'It's all right,' Francey reassured him, 'anything you want, you just have to ask.' But as he approached, his half-brother flinched as though fearful of being hit. Francey stopped in the middle of the floor. 'Can I help?'

'I couldn't sleep, I was looking for a drink,' Dessie muttered.

'Sure.' Francey decided it was not his place to play watchdog. He went to the scullery and brought back a bottle of whiskey and two bottles of stout. 'Is this all right?' he asked, holding them up. Even at this distance, he could see the way Dessie's eyes gleamed. 'Come on,' he invited, fetching four glasses from the dresser, 'let's sit at the table.' Without waiting for a reaction, he turned his back and seated himself. Opening both bottles of stout he poured the contents into two glasses, then filled the other two with generous chasers of the whiskey. 'Are you hungry?' he asked, without looking over his shoulder. 'I sure am, I think I'll make myself a sandwich.'

'I've a toothache.' At last Dessie came and sat with him at the table, but as far away as possible on the other side. The electric light hung above the table and in its glare Francey noticed that the skin on his half-brother's shaven cheeks and neck looked raw, like the surface of a plucked chicken. Since Francey had last seen him, someone – Margaret, he supposed – had cut off some of his hair; the result had been to emphasize the gauntness of his face. As Dessie seized the whiskey glass, Francey noticed his hands were shaking.

He crossed to the door and took down Mossie's overcoat. 'Here,' he said, 'you're cold. Put this on,' adding with sympathy as Dessie complied, 'there's nothing worse than a bad toothache, would you like me to wake Margaret? She could maybe give you another injection. A pain killer or something.'

'She gave me tablets.' Dessie popped some into his mouth and drained his whiskey.

'Did Mammy show you that photograph of your birthday party – I remember that day, do you?' Francey coaxed his half-brother to talk

225

about himself and after a second refill of whiskey, the shaking stopped and Dessie drank the stout at a more normal pace while, slowly at first, he began to speak, giving Francey a halting précis of what had happened to him in the years since he had left Lahersheen.

As the story proceeded, Francey sipped his Guinness and tried to control his growing fury at what Kathleen Scollard had put her son through. Alone of all his step- and half-sisters, he had never liked Kitty and remembered her as a silent, bitter girl of uncertain temper who would thump you as soon as look at you. And even though from a young age he had made allowances for the traumatic way she had become a mother – everyone in the family had been aware of her short fuse and had treated her accordingly – he had been aware that she had never taken to maternity, leaving the nurture of her son to anyone else who cared to take it on. It had been a mystery to them all why she took Dessie with her when she had gone missing.

After a half-hour or so, when Dessie's peculiar accent was becoming slurred and even more difficult to understand, Francey went to the dresser to make ham sandwiches. Behind his back he heard the clinking of bottle against glass as his half-brother helped himself to more whiskey. Tilly Harrington had been right: foremost among his half-brother's problems was the drink. Something would have to be done about it – but not just yet, he thought, reminding himself that he was taking one thing at a time.

Not wearing shoes, he felt a nudge at his toe and looked down to see the terrier's shaggy muzzle. The dog, which had made an extraordinary recovery, was lying twitching its tail and looking up with beseeching eyes. 'Poor fella.' Francey offered it a sandwich and the little animal, snatching it before this new benefactor could change his mind, scurried with it into the furthest corner of the kitchen. Francey brought the rest of the sandwiches back to the table and dived into them, then pushed the plate towards his half-brother.

'No-nho th-thha —' Dessie's shorn head wobbled on his neck. He was abruptly and completely inebriated.

Francey became frightened. 'You should eat something,' he urged. 'You'll need something to soak up the drink. I know I always do.' But he might as well have been speaking Chinese as, without comprehension, Dessie tried to keep his head from falling on to his chest. It wobbled and jerked as though on springs as he reached again for the whiskey bottle. 'No,' Francey took the bottle, 'no, Dessie,' he put it on the floor, 'I think you need to go back to bed.'

Dessie tried to refuse but was incapable of putting one coherent word after another and Francey, half carrying him back to the settle bed, feared that his careless liberalism had ruined all Margaret's good work. She had said he might be suffering from alcohol poisoning. Suppose all that whiskey had made him worse than he was before? After he had settled Dessie, Francey rushed into the bedroom. Reluctant to wake everyone else, he had to wait until his eyes adjusted to the relative darkness before recognizing which of the sleeping forms was Margaret. 'Maggie!' he whispered, shaking her by the shoulder.

She came awake immediately. 'Wha —?'

'S-sh,' Francey hushed her with a finger to her lips, 'will you come out into the kitchen for a minute? It's about Dessie.' Not waiting for her reply, he tiptoed out of the room again.

'Is he poorly?' Margaret was behind him, belting on a dressing-gown. 'What the hell's this?' Her voice changed as she saw the bottles and glasses on the table.

'Sorry, it was my fault,' Francey admitted. 'He was looking for a drink and I thought it would be better at least if someone could be with him watching him.'

Margaret shot him a poisonous look and crossed to where Dessie slept the sleep of the dead. She picked up his wrist and held it, gazing at the dial of her wristwatch. 'Well, he's still alive, no thanks to you,' she snapped at Francey after a few seconds. 'Bring me my bag again, it's on the dressing-table in the bedroom.'

Meekly, Francey stood beside her as she administered two injections. 'What are you giving him?'

'Vitamins, potassium, nothing sinister.' Hand on hip she gazed at him. 'For God's sake, Francey, will you have a bit of sense. Giving him drink in his condition – you might as well give him paraquat and be done with it!'

'I told you —' Francey started to protest, then got angry. He was fed up being bossed around. 'Look,' he retorted, 'give me a bit of credit. I'm the one who stayed up all night to find him, I'm the one he talked to.'

'What did he say?' Margaret's curiosity overcame her censure.

'Plenty,' Francey said grimly. 'Your sister Kathleen has a lot to answer for. He's had a shocking time of it.'

'Does he know where she is?' Her stricken face collapsed Francey's anger. He might not have been close to Kathleen, but in his self-righteousness he had forgotten that she and Margaret were full sisters and not far apart in age. 'No,' he muttered, 'I'll tell you all I know.'

Margaret searched his face. 'It's not good, is it?' and when Francey shook his head she turned away. 'Tell me later,' she said, her voice muffled as she bent over her bag. 'Are you staying up for a while?'

'Yes.' Francey looked at her hunched back. He could do nothing right.

'Well, watch him,' Margaret said, still fiddling with the bag. 'The biggest danger is he could choke on his own vomit. Just watch him, all right? Call me again if there's any change or if you're worried.' She walked back into the bedroom and Francey pulled a chair near to where Dessie slept.

The terrier crept out from its corner and curled up beside his shoes.

He and the terrier watched until daylight but Dessie did not need them: apart from heavy snoring and the occasional groan or cry, he seemed to be sleeping comfortably enough, a status confirmed by Margaret when she came out to check him a little after six o'clock.

The day dawned as bright and blue as high summer and light from the new sun was streaming through the gable window at the east end of the kitchen when the doctor, calling on his own initiative, knocked on the kitchen door just before nine o'clock.

Despite the light and the fact that it was St Stephen's Day, the atmosphere in the house remained funereal: Elizabeth was not up yet and the other women of the household talked together in subdued whispers as they moved around preparing breakfast. Having admitted the doctor, Francey, fearing he would be blamed for Dessie's relapse and afraid to hear the prognosis, escaped to the Folly.

Comfortable in its low-wattage gloom, he rummaged through the shelves until he found his trainset and, clearing a space on the floor, began attaching the tracks to each other to make a large oval. As his hands worked, however, his brain was undertaking a comprehensive review of his situation. In Dessie's current condition he could hardly be brought over to England to be introduced to the other half of his family.

228

Then a thought came to him which was so wayward that he suspended the fiddly operation with the tracks and sat back on his heels to enjoy it. It would be almost worth bringing Dessie to Inveraray Manor to watch the reaction there. He pictured the electrifying effect it would have on both his father and Colin Mannering if he were to present them with Dessie in his present state . . .

Francey concentrated again on the little trainset. He must not get carried away, he told himself. Dessie's welfare must come before such foolish one-upmanship. For instance, how soon should Dessie be told about his financial windfall? With his history, should he be given control of such large amounts? It did not take a genius or a psychiatrist to work out that the money might be the means of his final destruction. Could George's solicitor, the solemn Mr Solomons, be prevailed upon to make sure he did not get his hands on too much of it at least until he was of age?

While growing up, Francey and his schoolfriends had discussed *ad nauseam* how they would spend the fortunes they were going to earn when they went to work, how they might even win the Sweep, how happy they would be if that happened, leaving them without a care in the world. Now, he thought, here he was, rich as Croesus but helpless. Money was not helping him win Fleur, it was not helping with his family – it had killed Mossie – and no amount could save Dessie unless he wanted to save himself.

No, Francey thought, winding the beautiful little brassbound locomotive, being wealthy was not all it was cracked up to be. He applied the brake and set the locomotive on the tracks. It was up to him now to use that money to advantage, he could become its boss. He could stop seeing it as something apart from himself, even as a weird social handicap: the first thing he could do was to stop feeling sheepish about it.

For the first time, Francey faced down his defensiveness about being rich: it was as though he was ashamed of it, as if, detecting the odd envious or malicious gleam in some neighbour's eye, he had been forced to cry, to himself as well as to everyone else, *I haven't changed, honestly* . . . His mother had worried that his new standing would change his life for the worse, he had had to ignore the occasional barb in the comments of some of his sisters and, now that he thought about it carefully, only Hazel and Abigail had treated his new status with, respectively, good cheer and blithe unconcern. Mossie, too, had been as unruffled as usual.

Francey abruptly missed Mossie. He had been so busy looking after his mother's welfare and the practical considerations surrounding the funeral that he had not had time to think deeply about what the loss of his stepfather might mean to him. While again acknowledging that their relationship had been in many ways superficial, Francey saw now how he had taken his stepfather for granted. Mossie's rock-like common sense and strength would have been a great help in the present crisis; he would have divined some way to put Francey's wealth to practical use to help Dessie.

Francey hooked up the little passenger carriages, guard's van and goods wagons to one another and slotted them on the tracks behind the locomotive. He let off the brake and sent them on their way and, as his brain, too, swung into high gear, again sat back, this time watching the circling train. Maybe he and Dessie should go away together on a holiday. If the two of them got away to a warm climate for a while, to a sunshiny beach in Spain or Italy, perhaps his brother could be diverted from the drink and distracted into more healthy pursuits. The more Francey thought about it, the more attractive the prospect became – and the more ambitious. They could all go, the whole family: as far as he knew, except for one trip to Dublin with Tilly Harrington to see the pantomime at the Theatre Royal, since his mother came to Lahersheen with him in her belly, she had not gone anywhere outside Cork or Kerry. But would Dessie come? Like the train, Francey's thoughts came full circle. The main problem would lie in persuading Dessie to accept help. And if he would not, what then?

Francey decided then that, for the time being, rather than do something dramatic like taking him abroad or forcing him into a hospital, which might well frighten him into going on the road again, the best thing to do was to get help for him a little at a time. Starting with a dentist. The busy clickety-clacking made by the train as it progressed around its track a second time brought him back to his childhood. The sound, so small and self-contained in the overstuffed room, the hypnotic, slow circling, sent him into the sort of trance his mother used to call a daydream. His eyes glazed over, fixed themselves on the locomotive and he found it impossible to pull them away.

A few minutes later, just as the locomotive was winding down a second time, the door of the Folly burst open and he was jerked back from his state of pleasant narcosis. 'Yiz found him!'

Francey saw that Hazel had reverted to her normal style: leopard-skin jacket over a polo-necked jumper, tight white slacks tapering to high-heeled shoes. 'Yes.' He lumbered to his feet.

'I was talking to one of your sisters, the young one,' Hazel continued, 'and she told me he was pulled out of the sea.'

'That's right, come in, Hazel.' Francey went over to her, closing the door. 'I wasn't expecting you this morning.'

'Couldn't sleep, so we're already on our way to Killarney, but I had to drop in to see if there was any news. Vinnie thinks it's the middle of the night. I've got to hand it to you, Francey, you're bloody great. Tell us what happened!' she commanded, perching herself on the old rocking-chair and curling one leg under her.

Francey told her everything he knew, warning her that a lot of it, about Dessie's interim life in England, was still third hand from Tilly. He found it a relief to unburden himself of his worries about Dessie's health and drinking habits. Hazel listened, not interrupting except with empathetic clucks and affirmations. 'At least he's young so he has a good chance,' was her comforting response at the end of the story, 'not like some I know. There's millions of them in our business,' she looked earnestly at Francey from under her false lashes, 'and I've plenty of experience of this. I know I could sort him out if you'd let me help.'

'You've done enough,' Francey said. 'Thank's a lot, but we're his family. It's up to us.'

Hazel dropped her gaze for a second and then uncurled herself. 'Well,' she said, 'I'd best be going, but if you change your mind, you know where I am. We'll be on the road until the fifth of January but we'll be playin' in and around Dublin for a week or so after that because we've a spot on *The Showband Show* on Telefís Eireann. Get in touch with me at the flat during the day if you feel like it.'

As though waiting for him to reply to this she paused for a fraction of a second before going to the door. But for Francey, too much had happened, was happening, to allow him find what it was she expected him to say. 'Thanks, I will,' he smiled at her, 'but don't go yet. Won't you come in for a while? I'm sure the doctor won't be long more.'

'Ah no,' she said, 'your poor mother has enough on her plate.'

She stopped again, this time on the threshold. 'Families are gas, aren't they?'

She let herself out but turned round just before she got into the van, parked outside the gateway, to impart a final wave. As the vehicle zoomed away like a bizarre wasp, Francey reflected ruefully that 'gas' was not quite accurate as an epithet for his family. He saw that the doctor's car was still in the yard and feeling that, in all decency, he could stay out of the fray no longer, went into the kitchen.

'Hello again, Francey.' On hearing him enter, the doctor, a smallish, middle-aged man who had been in huddled conversation with Margaret near the stove, turned round. 'I was just saying to your sister here that it's imperative the young man dry out for a while.'

'I know, but—' Francey had been about to make excuses for providing drink for Dessie but stopped. To grovel would not be helpful, least helpful to himself. Instead he pulled himself up to his full height and looked down at the doctor. 'I think we know that now,' he said, 'but we'll need help.'

'We were discussing that.' The doctor unwound the stethoscope from around his neck and packed it in his Gladstone bag. 'Hospital would be best for him in my opinion but your sister tells me you're worried about that. He's so confused and malnourished that, to tell you the truth, provided he gets proper care here it won't make all that much difference at the moment. I'll keep an eye on the situation. I'll be off, Margaret,' he added, nodding to Francey. Then, after some hesitation, 'I'm not pretending this is going to be easy. On the other hand he's still very young and the liver is a marvellous organ. He can't have done all that much damage, nothing permanent anyhow. I've prescribed a course of tablets, but what he needs is proper looking after and a lot of time. Don't make any particular fuss of him, let him come round in his own way, and don't be surprised if he appears to reject a lot of what you would see as kindness. And if you could soften him up about going to hospital—'

'Thank you,' Francey cut in, remembering Dessie's reaction when he thought he was bound for a 'home'.

'It's sometimes helpful to offer other sugars in lieu of drink,' the doctor said then, 'sweet tea, for instance, or chocolate.' Saying he would call again the following day, he left.

Dessie spent the remainder of the morning in a state that veered between fretful sleep and a wary state of vigilance. Francey and the rest of the family behaved as though it was quite normal for them to have a semi-comatose young man at one end of their kitchen. Although they had all braced themselves for an uncomfortable confrontation about alcohol, Dessie did not request any. Margaret's theory was that his body was too damaged and too confused by the plethora of medication she fed him.

Watching his mother put small pieces of cold cooked chicken into the Spong to mince them for Dessie's next meal, Francey was relieved to see how calm she was now and reflected that the emotional release of the day before seemed to have cleansed her, for the time being at least.

Now that the situation was under control, or at least in shared control, he allowed his thoughts to turn to Fleur. He had a perfect excuse now, to contact her.

Chapter Twelve

Boxing Day at Inveraray Manor began slowly and by half past ten, Fleur, wandering restlessly through the house, still had the place to herself. Unlike Colin she had always been an early riser. Even Tommy had not yet stirred and she was bored to the tips of her nails. She considered the possibility of going for a walk but on looking out, saw the tops of the far-off trees arching in the gale and huddled further into the collar of her mohair cardigan. She retrieved a champagne flute which had fallen behind one of the heavy curtains at the window and placed it on a side table so someone on the staff would see it. Then, with a sigh, she picked up a magazine and took it to one of the couches near the fire which, as usual, hissed its unvarying flame pattern through the gaps in the arrangement of logs. As she leafed through the magazine's stiff, glossy pages she wondered how soon they could leave for London. Staying in this house had become more of a trial than ever since Jool's death.

On the surface at least, George Gallaher had seemed to behave himself while his wife was alive and if it had not been for a drunken advance on Fleur herself, which she had pretended not to notice, she might have thought he was a model citizen. But since the funeral he had begun openly to flop into hedonism, twice returning to Inveraray from London with a female overnight guest in tow, and not seeming to care in the least about the presence of Fleur and Colin – or Tommy – all of whom were staying in the house on both occasions. Fleur, who was the guardian of no one's morals, nevertheless despised those who behaved without discretion.

Philandering apart, accustomed as she was to reading men, Fleur had detected early that Colin's father skipped across the surface of life like a skimming stone. With her background, however, she was not at all surprised that, superficial and shallow though he was, George was also a person on whom fortune smiled. It was not an uncommon phenomenon: while some strove all their lives without success to

234

overcome a succession of handicaps, others, no matter how venal, were born and remained lucky. It stood to reason, therefore, that he would be the one who would have been in the right place at the right time when Jool Dill Smith Gallaher had sought a third husband.

From time to time at the start, she had wondered what Jool saw in George but had in the end come to the conclusion that by the time she met him, the old lady, knowing that nothing in this life was perfect, had settled for the considerable assets of George's charm and physical beauty. Fleur had seen more than once within the sophisticated circles in which they all moved that having the delicious – and much younger – George Gallaher on her arm was quite a feather in Jool's cap and that the old lady had revelled in the green-eyed consternation her acquisition had caused amongst the less well disposed of her acquaintants.

Lifting her eyes from her magazine, Fleur gazed into the eternal flames and smiled in retrospective admiration of Jool's lack of pretension in this regard.

She had every reason to be grateful to Colin's stepmother: thanks to her posthumous generosity, Fleur could now see her scheme for the future of herself and her son come soon to fruition.

Two years after she arrived in England, in pursuit of this plan, she had begun quietly to accumulate diamonds. As they were portable and quickly accessible, she preferred them to other valuables, even to money. Her *modus operandi* was simple: she accepted gifts from rich Englishmen. And those judicious gentlemen 'friends' had proven generous.

Little by little, Fleur had managed to set up arrangements with a few retailers whereby items she received – perfumes, expensive French underwear – could be exchanged for cash at a little below what they would cost; more importantly, a dealer in Hatton Garden, once an intermittent guest in her boudoir but now happily married for the fourth time, accepted lesser jewels and precious metals from her, accumulating them for trade-in against selected diamonds. Because some of the gems were uncut, this patron had guessed quite early in their commercial relationship that she was not collecting them as a hobby or for ornamentation and Fleur, faced with his keen inquisition, had to decide to trust him.

In fact this man had become the only person in the world, apart from Tommy, whom she did trust; she discovered he maintained holiday homes in Mauritius and St Thomas and found he would be willing, when the time came, to help her find a bolthole of her own, a sunny part of the world where she and Tommy need never again see any Mannerings or Gallahers or any of their vapid friends. She was surprised at how easily the dealer had offered help: her theory was that she represented the daughter he had never had.

And so, during one of Colin's business trips, she had had a floor safe installed under the bed in her boudoir and until they were needed, her diamonds reposed in it, snug in a beaded purse which had belonged to her mother.

Fleur threw aside the magazine, stood up and went to the window, the outside pane of which was now splattered with large, sleety raindrops. Brought up in a climate which was friendly to human beings, she hated English winter weather and went outdoors in it only when it was absolutely necessary, or when she could not escape the English obsession with fresh air, when she and Colin were guests at a country-house party where it would have been impolite not to take part in the muffled-up and tweedy outdoor pursuits which were *de rigueur* on such occasions.

When Colin had brought her out of the Lily Garden to install her as his concubine in a cheap hotel room beside the river, the little purse was the only baggage she had brought with her; in addition to its sentimental value, it had been a present to her mother from a member of the British aristocracy. Colin being British, Fleur saw the purse as an amulet.

It had worked its magic because by dint of excelling herself sexually and making sure that each visit Colin made to her in her new home was better than the last, before long, he was begging her to marry him and to come with him back to England. At that time money bought almost anything in Bangkok, even birth certificates, passports and visas, and before long, Colin was able to take his beautiful young wife and six-month-old baby away from Bangkok. Neither he nor she had divulged that she was only fifteen when she first stepped on to English soil.

Now, having seen enough of the depressing grey landscape, Fleur looked at her watch; if her son did not get up soon, she decided, she would go along to his room to call him. It had been no problem to persuade Colin that Tommy was his and a little premature – the child had been born while his putative father was on an extended trip in

Malaysia – Fleur herself was so small and undernourished that her baby had been born tiny and weak. Tommy's features, although Oriental, were sufficiently mixed not to arouse Colin's suspicion and Fleur blessed the talent for languages which had given her such a wide client base.

Behind her, one of the two telephones in the room rang but as she turned to answer it the call was taken somewhere else in the house. She contemplated picking up the magazine again and then decided she would wake Tommy *and* Colin. She had to get away from here.

The bedroom she and Colin shared was the first along the corridor after the drawing-room and as Fleur entered it she saw he had already awoken. To her dismay, she saw immediately by the look in his eye that he was amorous. 'I'm already dressed,' she said, in an attempt to cut across the expected request. 'And I do want to get out of here as soon as possible. Please?' But Colin assumed his hurt little schoolboy look and Fleur, who was doing everything in her power to keep him sweet and give him no cause for suspicion, gave in. 'All right.' She sighed, unbuttoning her blouse and going to her bag to fetch what she knew she would need to satisfy him. Then she locked the door and walked towards the bed where Colin's face was already flushed with anticipation.

Ironically it was he who had first shown Fleur the way to financial independence, which now, in her book, equated with happiness.

Her mother had been dead and she had been fourteen when he had first crossed the threshold of the Lily Garden. Fleur, wearily experienced by now, thought him undistinguished, just another of the cross-section of foreign businessmen who passed through the doors seeking service. Colin's demands, too, were commonplace for an Englishman: he asked to be spanked before sex. Afterwards, she had given neither him nor his sexual proclivities any more thought than she ever did and, in any case, another client had arrived in her room within minutes of Colin's leaving. Also, because she was pregnant and had not yet told anyone so it could be dealt with, she had more pressing matters on her mind.

Colin came back the next day, however, and the next and the next, always asking for her, which, although not unprecedented, was rare enough. Although Fleur knew she was uncommonly talented in sexual matters, she had a word-of-mouth reputation and was seldom without a client, most of the repeat visitors to the Lily Garden, however, liked variety and took different girls each time.

On his fifth visit Colin's pre-intercourse requests had moved up a notch; they involved the use of implements and her dressing in the unusual English-made outfit he produced from the bag he had brought with him. He mistook her indifference for hesitation and, as an incentive, offered her a thin gold bangle in the form of a snake, its clasp set with several tiny diamonds, promising 'more where that came from' if she pleased him. That bracelet was the first proper gift she had been offered by a client and Fleur saw the opening up of further possibilities. She worked especially hard that afternoon and when Colin, who confessed to her that he had already overstayed the allotted time for his business trip by two days, vowed to return the next afternoon for one last time, she was in no doubt but that he would.

Fleur detected that Colin probably represented her last chance to escape. She was already fourteen, with perhaps only a few years of usefulness in her before she became riddled with disease – if she was not already – or even died. And although at that time she had no interest in the baby in her belly, she was not sure she wanted to get rid of it and was curious about what it might be like to have something of hers alone.

Only once before, in Fleur's memory, had one of the girls been borne from the Lily Garden by a client-turned-suitor and she knew the odds stacked against her were almost insurmountable.

She was ready for Colin when he arrived that afternoon. She smiled shyly at him as she took the bag from him then, as business commenced, shed the smile and very slowly, affecting a disdainful expression – she had discerned that this was part of the game he liked – discarded her kimono. Making sure he could see every inch of her, she sat in front of him to pull on the outlandish thigh boots and gloves, and picked up the thongs and leather apron. But then, drawing on all her hard-won acting skills, she fumbled, dropping everything to the floor and allowing her eyes to fill as though she was overcome with emotion.

Colin, whose excitement was already intense, pressed her as to what was wrong but she would not tell him. Instead, biting her lip as though to hold back tears, she picked up the equipment again, tied on the apron and went to work.

She gave top-notch service that afternoon, drawing it out until Colin, weak and shuddering, begged her to stop and release him. Fleur allowed her tears to flow then. In her halting English, she confessed to him how special he was to her, how she had lost interest in all other men, how, although she had had to conceal it, she had known from the very first moment she had touched him that he was the only man who could ever fulfil her in every way. And how she could not possibly see him again when next he came back to Bangkok because it would be too painful for her to have to treat him as just another client.

She played with him as she wept, absently, as though not realizing what she was doing. And by the time Colin came, he believed himself in love and had vowed to take her with him.

As she worked on him now, Fleur's mind was already far away. With Tommy she was walking along soft white sand at the edge of a blue sea. 'You've been naughty again, haven't you?' she admonished Colin in a severe, no-nonsense voice while her mind's eye saw the edges of the waves lap at her toes. 'I warned you what would happen if you didn't behave. Come on, bend over!' Overcoming his feigned resistance she pushed him over so he was face down on the bed. 'Now Mummy's going to have to give you a good seeing-to.' And while he groaned and shuddered with ecstasy and attempted to twist around to fondle her breast, Fleur closed her eyes so as not to see his reddening thighs and bottom or his thrashing, fettered legs but the fronds of a palm tree shivering in a tropical breeze.

A few minutes before Fleur got down to business with Colin, in his own bedroom George Gallaher woke up too, not fully but enough to know he was sliding out of the gorgeous dream he had just had. He had been romping in a field with a farmer's daughter, a girl of spectacular, Rubenesque proportions, with massive legs and huge, bouncing breasts. Snuggled into the bedclothes he kept his eyes closed and tried to hold on to the final strands of the luscious images, of the all-encompassing warmth of that soft, roly-poly belly and those magnificent haunches, but she was floating away, moving out of his reach . . .

The rude bell of the telephone beside the bed shrilled, shocking him into full consciousness, and as he groped for the receiver, the brandy from the night before made its thundering presence felt in his temples. His condition was not helped by the import of the telephone call. Five minutes later, as he hung up, George groaned aloud and, lying back into the blessed relief of his pile of pillows, placed the palms of his hands over his throbbing eyes; his stomach was at him, too, gurgling like a drain as it continued to deal with all the rich Christmas food. All in all George felt diseased.

To say that he was taken aback by the news from Ireland would be to put it mildly. Francey's revelation meant that he would have to *do* something. Was there to be no end to his trials? Lifting himself on to one shoulder again he pulled the telephone closer and dialled the kitchen to order coffee, iced water and Alka-Seltzer, then stumbled into the bathroom. 'You need a full overhaul, laddie,' he told the bleary-eyed wreck who stared back at him from the mirror. What further affliction would the day hold? It was George's experience that when a day began this badly it was downhill all the way.

After a long sojourn in the shower he felt a little better and when he went back into the bedroom, gulped the Alka-Seltzer which had been delivered in his absence, then drank draught after draught of the hot strong coffee. It had been Jool who had weaned him off tea and now George could not contemplate starting a day without drinking at least three or four measures of the beverage she had had imported specially from the States.

He really missed Jool. All right, he thought, there were times when it was lovely to range as free as the wind but there were others, like now, when real life entered the frame, that it was awful to be alone with no one to share the burdens. George, in whom self-deception was not one of his many faults, then found the humility to acknowledge that 'share' was not the correct verb. He wanted Jool to be still alive to take over this awful new situation in its entirety. Morosely, he stared into the dregs of his last cup of coffee. He supposed he had better pass the bad news on to Colin. After all, this was another relative for him too. And for Tommy.

Thoughts of Tommy, of the kid's delight in all the presents – George had bought him a table-tennis table, net and bats which they had set up in one of the spare stalls in the stable block – made him smile a little. He had not thought things through, of course, when ordering the ping-pong set – buying it was one thing, having to play the wretched game with his grandson was another – but George had found that once he had accepted his Jool-less state of paterfamilias, at least for as long as Christmas lasted, the role and duties it entailed had not been half as unpleasant as he had expected. All four of them, Colin, Tommy, Fleur and himself, had had more than an hour of uncomplicated fun in the stables before Christmas dinner last evening as they struggled to overcome the disparity in their fitness and expertise.

The Alka-Seltzer, in combination with the caffeine, was beginning to do its work and George cheered up even more as it struck him that in the matter of this imminent new arrival it was up to Colin to help, too. He should be told as soon as possible. Maybe Colin and Fleur could stay around for a while rather than go haring back to London? Knowing this was a faint hope, George nevertheless determined to ask them.

In the knowledge that his battered body could not have borne anything heavy or constricting this morning, George pulled on old, comfortable slacks, a soft cashmere sweater, a pair of slip-on shoes, drenched himself with expensive after-shave, and crossed the corridor towards the door of the room occupied by his son and Fleur.

Not wanting to wake them if they were still asleep, he hesitated before knocking, listening closely at the door for signs of life inside. Although the walls of the manor were solid and the internal doors of solid mahogany, to his amusement George heard, very faintly, the distinct sounds of sexual activity. Fairly robust activity at that, he thought enviously, suppressing the lecherous images that arose at the thought of having Fleur himself. He knew he should go away, but as he hesitated the sounds died away. George waited a few seconds more, then knocked.

After a short pause, the door was unlocked and opened by a kimono-clad Fleur, as composed as always. 'Morning, Fleur,' George said, then, 'Oh, sorry. I've obviously come at a bad time,' addressing the dishevelled Colin, who, the shade of a beetroot and swathed in bedclothes, was sitting upright against the headboard of the bed.

'It's all right,' Colin's voice was breathless and husky, 'what can we do for you?'

'That was our new family member on the telephone from Ireland,' George included Fleur, 'sends his regards. Bit of news for us, as a matter of fact.'

'What news?' To George, Fleur seemed as uninterested as always but she stepped back from the doorway to admit him.

Accepting her implicit invitation, George came a little way into the room where he noticed that the smell of sex was heavy in the heated air. 'Apparently Jool's other protégé,' he yawned as though the subject bored him, 'my son, the wild colonial boy or whatever he is, has turned up.'

'Really?' As if trying to protect himself, Colin pulled the bed-clothes tighter around him. 'Since when?'

'I'm not sure about all the gory details.' Then George decided to pull no punches. 'The two of them are coming here soon. Could you be here to help when they do?' he begged. Turning again to Fleur: 'The two of you?'

'Help with what, Dad?' Colin asked, after a glance at Fleur.

George decided to appeal directly to her. 'You know how bad I am at this sort of thing, left all that to Jool . . .' Somehow, he summoned up a smile. 'So do you think you could organize yourselves to be here?'

'I've several business meetings in London next week, Dad. Remember I told you about them at dinner last night —'

'Oh, I don't think it's that imminent,' George rushed to reassure him, 'but even if you're away when they do come, could you be here, Fleur?' Then he felt he was overdoing the appeal and moderated his approach. 'Apparently,' he added drily, 'our prodigal is in a precarious state of health and not yet fit to travel.'

'I should like to meet him, of course, but I would hesitate to do so without Colin.' Fleur's tone, gentle as ever, nevertheless brooked no argument and George thought it wiser not to make an issue of it.

'Sorry I interrupted,' he said, shooting Colin a knowing look, to be rewarded with an instant deepening of his son's high colour, 'but I thought you'd be interested in knowing you're about to meet your brother.'

'Oh, I am Dad, I am!'

'Carry on!' George left the room.

Back in his own bedroom he again dialled the kitchen, ordered another pot of coffee, then threw himself on the bed. That had been a start but not all that satisfactory. George knew there was more than a possibility that he might have to deal with Francey and Dessie on his own.

Dammit, he thought, he had to have support for this. He picked up the telephone again to ask a London friend of forty years' standing

242

to come down to Inveraray for a few days to help him out of this fix. This friend and George had hunted women together and the friendship had never been tested beyond that, but now was the time to call in a few favours. Might as well place the bugger on standby, George thought, in case the other two let him down.

As the telephone rang unanswered, though, George had to give up. He stared at the ceiling. Come what may, he was not going to face this alone.

George's face-to-face encounter with his third son was not as near at hand as he had feared. And while he was brooding over it, his second son had no time for such introversion, because over the next fortnight, Francey was so concerned with everyone else's welfare that he had little time to think about his own or about what lay ahead.

With her dowry assured, Abigail chose the night before Goretti went back to the States to inform the rest of the family about her plans to enter the convent, an announcement which threw everyone into a tizzy. Constance returned to school and Margaret resumed her peripatetic job, leaving Francey as Dessie's minder and his mother's principal companion, with the exception of the ever-faithful Tilly who came every day on some pretext or other.

As if he had not enough to preoccupy him, it worried Francey that his mother might become dependent on having him around the place: he had to protect himself from the development of hope that he might settle in as a full-time farmer. But he had so much to do that he put off any serious discussion with her about what should happen next. In an odd way, Dessie's presence helped: Elizabeth was so concerned about nursing him back to health and in dealing with the practicalities of Abby's decision that she was distracted from her grief and from almost everything else as well, including her own future.

At the beginning, Dessie was little trouble; drugged into painless quiescence by the attentive doctor and Margaret, during the post-Christmas period he hovered between drowsy consciousness and sleep, accepting everything being done for him. He was so woozy that he did not ask for drink: Margaret explained to Francey that the tablets he was being fed in large doses were to help him get over the hump of the drying-out process.

Francey eventually told Margaret the story of what had happened

243

to her sister. She bore it stoically, reacting only when he started to talk about the beatings Dessie had received at the hands of so many of his 'uncles'. 'Stop,' she held up her hands then, 'I don't want to hear any more. Anyway, you have only one side of the story.'

'Yes,' Francey felt desperately sorry for her. 'I'm sure it's a bit exaggerated.'

Margaret got up and left the room.

Life staggered on in the farmhouse. Francey's mother sank into her own thoughts and went around the house like a ghost. Many times at night, Francey, who was sleeping on a mattress on the floor beside Dessie's settle, was wakened by the sound of her bedroom door opening as she came into the kitchen to fetch something. He knew there was little he could do to assuage her sadness and although he knew the offer was inadequate, had to content himself with telling her he was there if she wanted to talk, an invitation of which she never availed herself.

During the period of his half-brother's initial convalescence, at least his passivity enabled Francey to cope with the changes in the circumstances of the farm and the legalities which had to be faced after any death. He was fortunate in that it was the season where not much work was required in the fields and the animals were housed, simplifying their care. Although he had to go through all the formal steps, in legal terms, it was going to be easy. Since the farm had been his mother's before she had married him and still was, Mossie's will concerned his own small farmhouse and few scrubby acres a mile away, which had been rented to a German couple who had arrived from the Ruhr in search of a simpler way of life. This he had bequeathed to Francey's mother; to Constance, Mossie left the grandmother clock, patchwork quilt and the few pieces of old china he had brought with him to Lahersheen; he had left his books and tools to Francey.

At the end of the first week in January, when they felt Dessie would be up to it, Francey arranged to hire a hackney from Castle-townbere to bring his half-brother to the best dentist in Cork. To take full advantage of the trip, he made a concurrent appointment with the legal firm founded by his late grandfather Sullivan to discuss legal matters concerning both his mother's and his own life after Mossie. On the assumption that Dessie would need follow-up care, they were going to stay with old Mrs Sullivan for as long as it took.

Dessie continued to be sleepy and taciturn but biddable. It was as though he had transferred all responsibility for his life and actions to others. When told where he was going and why, all he said was 'yes'. Francey hoped that, now they were alone and away from the farmhouse, he could take advantage of the trip to break through to his half-brother in some substantial way.

Dessie slept for most of the journey, and as the car travelled up the Quays along the Lee coming towards the centre of the city, Francey leaned into the back seat to wake him, but then had to wait for a second or two. Dessie's emaciation and stooped posture belied his height: taller than he had seemed when Francey first found him, he stood at around six feet one or even two and was curled into the back seat of the car like a baby. His hands were finely boned, with long, expressive fingers. Despite all his sleeping, in the sunlight that slanted over his face through the window, he still looked exhausted and very young and it seemed like murder to wake him.

As gently as he could, Francey placed a hand on his shoulder. With a start, eyes squinting into the brightness, his half-brother unfolded himself from the position in which he had been curled. Now that he was clean-shaven, George's arresting eyes were seen to full advantage in Dessie's face. For the first time, Francey saw him objectively and thought that, given time, he could turn out to be quite as imposing figure as their father. 'Are you all right?' he asked. 'We're nearly there.'

Dessie yawned – his blackened teeth shattering the illusion of beauty – and pulled himself upright. 'I'm fine,' he muttered, then, searching through his pockets, 'I'm out of ciggies. I can't go in there without a ciggie.'

Francey asked the driver to stop at the nearest shop and went in to buy a fresh supply of Woodbines. Dessie's first intelligible request after regaining consciousness had been for a cigarette and despite a dreadful, phlegmy cough, which seemed to get worse when he dragged the smoke into his lungs, had smoked almost non-stop during every conscious moment since.

The hackney driver turned round in his seat to watch as Francey handed over the bundle of little packets. 'Coffin nails,' he remarked. 'My brother in the States says they'll give you cancer.'

Because of Dessie's cough, Margaret had made a few similar noises at home, but as her half-brother's principal protector, Francey had squashed them. Although he had never developed the habit himself, he had nothing against smoking and, with the exception of his mother, everyone in Lahersheen, his stepfather and sisters – even Margaret herself – smoked like chimneys. 'What harm?' he intervened before the driver could press his point home. 'They're all mad over there in America. A few fags never killed anyone.' Dessie could smoke all he liked, he thought, provided it kept his mind off the booze.

'All set?' Francey held open the door for him when the car pulled into the kerb outside the surgery. Dessie's reply was to light up another cigarette. He got out of the car as though he were on his way to the gallows. 'Don't worry,' Francey tried to reassure him, 'they've made great progress in dentistry. It won't hurt at all.' Dessie did not look convinced but glanced around as though seeking an avenue of escape.

It had occurred to Francey that his half-brother might again disappear if left to his own devices in such a threatening environment as a dentist's waiting room and, once inside, he sat with him, leaving only when he was sure Dessie was secure in the hands of the dentist. The Castletownbere doctor had briefed the dentist by telephone about the specific problems and several sequential appointments had been blocked off for him so that Francey now had about two hours during which he could go about his own business.

As he crossed one of Cork's many bridges towards the South Mall, where his grandfather's firm had maintained offices for as long as he could remember, he stopped to watch two little boys flinging hunks of stale bread at a flotilla of swans milling about on the surface of the river. The boys, who were about seven or eight, were oblivious to his scrutiny as, with mighty concentration, they dipped into the brown paper bags they carried and distributed their largesse, which had also attracted the loud attention of a considerable number of gulls.

Francey leaned over the parapet, admiring the grace of the swans as they stretched their necks to beg and then lunged for the bread, missing collisions with each other by a feather's width. But to the little boys' disgust, the swans were slower than the raiding gulls and were missing out; in an attempt to beat the pirates, the two ran off the bridge and down a set of steps to the water's edge from where they could better target their intended beneficiaries.

The happy commotion was so far removed from the family

concerns into which Francey had been thrust that his spirits lifted. One plank of the priests' educational methods had been an effort to inculcate a sense of perspective. Francey saw now that no matter what happened to him and his two-pronged family, to Fleur, to Dessie or George or any of his sisters, even to these little boys or the bridge from which he watched them, this river would continue to unroll towards the sea like a shiny brown hair-ribbon and this cold, clear sky over his head would allow its freedom to countless future generations of birds. The notion encouraged hope.

On impulse, he went after the boys and tucked a five-pound note into each of the almost empty bags. 'To get more bread,' he explained. 'Happy New Year!' Grinning, he bounded up the steps towards the street again but before walking away could not resist looking back down at them. Their mission temporarily forgotten, they were staring up at him with open mouths and it gave him enormous satisfaction to see their round-eyed gaze of incredulity. 'Cheerio now,' he called and, whistling, went on his way. Giving away money was one of the unsung benefits of its possession. There and then Francey decided to do as much of it as possible.

Half guiltily, he also found he was enjoying the freedom of being away from Lahersheen and the crushing weight of responsibility he had found so suddenly thrust on him. He did not *mind* it, Dessie, his mother, the farm, the assumption of the man-of-the-house mantle – or did he? Francey pushed his introspection away: he would make the most of this break. It was a lovely day and he was surrounded by ordinary people doing ordinary things. For a while he could be part of it all.

Having dispatched his business in the solicitors' offices at great speed, and with still more than an hour in hand before he had to be back at the dental surgery, he decided to try his luck in telephoning Fleur from the main post office in the city. He had been disappointed not to have been offered the chance to talk to her when he had rung Inveraray on St Stephen's Day and had not had the privacy to telephone the flat since. Anyway, he reasoned, he needed to ask her if she had received his Christmas present in the post.

But as he finished dialling, Francey's confidence ebbed: he had not planned what he would say if Colin answered. As the phone rang at the other end, he decided that the only way to play it was casually: after all, they had every reason to talk, brother-to-brother, about

247

Dessie. Regardless of his lightning rehearsal, however, by the third ring his heart was thumping so hard that he panicked and almost hung up when he heard the fourth ring being cut off.

By some miracle, it was Fleur. Francey gripped the telephone hard in his sweating palm as he tried to keep his voice from betraying the ardency of his feelings. He heard himself asking Fleur how she was, how she and her family had got over the Christmas, heard all the maladroit inanities spewing off his tongue for what seemed like weeks. Her replies, in that shy voice and archaic English he loved so much, were polite and cool, so cool that Francey panicked.

Then the penny dropped. Of course! She was trying to indicate to him that someone else was listening. He changed tack. 'I wanted to talk to you about Dessie,' he said, like the conspirator he was. 'Is Colin around?'

But Fleur's voice remained remote. 'He is in Singapore, I believe.'

It was not Colin, then, who was preventing her from speaking as she would wish. 'That's a pity.' Francey decided there was no point in going any further with a conversation at such cross purposes. He gave her a quick, nervous summary of Dessie's situation as it then pertained, then, promising to telephone again soon, rang off. But as he stared at the dead instrument in his hand, he was furious at himself for the way he had handled that, at how he was feeling now. What had happened to all that self-confidence?

As Hazel had taught him, he took a deep breath to steady his nerves.

Now here was a good idea. He had not been in touch since he had seen Hazel on St Stephen's morning. She must think him ungrateful for not contacting her sooner after all the help she had given: and she had said she would be back in Dublin by the fifth.

Hazel answered on the first ring and he launched into the story of what had been happening since last he had seen her. 'That's great,' she said every so often when he paused for breath but it did not occur to Francey until he was well into his flow that she too sounded a little quiet and was stricken with remorse at his selfishness. 'I'm sorry,' he said, 'here am I going on and on and not asking anything about you. Is everything all right with you, Hazel?'

'Sure, why wouldn't it be? Everything's marvellous,' she laughed, 'and the tour was great. Packed out.' In Francey's ears, something about the laugh did not ring true. Then, in the background, he heard a loud crash. 'What was that?' he asked. 'Did I ring at an awkward time?'

'No, not at all,' Hazel replied, 'there's roadworks outside, bloody driving me mad, I've a desperate headache to tell you the truth.' She sounded so peculiar that Francey renewed his apologies and, promising to contact her again soon, said goodbye.

Outside again, he was annoyed that he had used the telephone at all: his high spirits of just a few minutes ago had evaporated. *Women!* he thought. A fellow would be better off at the North Pole or on a desert island. At least he wouldn't be on this emotional see-saw. Well, he was damned if he was going to put himself through such an emotional mangle again. Fleur could just bloody well ring *him* the next time – and as for Hazel . . . The minute he heard his own thought, Francey was ashamed of himself. He had no right to be upset by either call. It was just that where feelings were concerned, rights did not seem to enter into the situation at present.

To cheer himself up, he went into a book shop but every volume he chose for browsing screamed reminders of his plights. He noticed that even the most hard-bitten of detectives in the most racy of thrillers seemed to be falling for some dame or other; the old reliables chronicled by P. G. Wodehouse seemed far more concerned with affairs of the heart than he had hitherto perceived. And as for the classics: Francey could see little in them now other than accounts of relationships in various degrees of crux. On impulse, he bought the three most expensive books he could find in the shop, none of which had anything to do with love or romance: an enormous atlas, a massive English dictionary and a glossy, 'coffee-table' publication about Atlantic wildflowers which did not interest him in the least. For some reason it gave him grim satisfaction to hand over the outrageous sum demanded by the man at the till; the act of squandering the money seemed to soothe the *Angst*.

As he lugged his cumbersome purchases back into the street, he knew that he had just learned his second lesson, almost as valuable as the first, about money. To spend it imparted almost as good a feeling as to give it away.

Chapter Thirteen

Hazel, who had improvised the existence of roadworks outside flat, had not been lying when she told Francey she had a headache, the result of too much red wine the previous night.

She glared at the dead telephone receiver in her hand: she was sick of herself and the self-destructive course she had taken since recognizing how inappropriate it was for her to hope there could be anything other than friendship between herself and Francey Sullivan; she did not blame Francey in the least, it was all her own stupid fault. Hearing his voice had kindled such depths of rage and self-loathing that she felt like throwing the telephone out of the window right then and there.

The noise from the kitchen continued and she tumbled out of bed and pounded through the living-room towards the kitchen. 'What are you doing, Larry?' she demanded. 'What's the bloody racket?'

Wounded, the young man standing in the room turned away from the rubbish bin into which he was placing the remains of a large bowl. Last night in the subdued after-hours lighting of Collins's he had looked presentable enough and had not had more than a couple of pints. Now the unforgiving January sunshine which poured through the kitchen window was merciless with his stubbled chin, the loose, pallid skin of his chest and his none-too-clean underpants. 'It wasn't my fault,' he complained, holding up the shards, 'it wasn't put back properly into the press and when I opened it to look for a cup it fell out.'

'I've changed me mind about coffee,' Hazel retorted. 'Look, this was a mistake. Let's call it a day, all right?'

As he continued to stare at her like a whipped dog, Hazel privately castigated herself, *You're a glutton for punishment*, and wondered what had possessed her to bring this yoke home with her again. She should have learned her lesson the last time: the two of them had had a fling for a few weeks a year ago but it had not taken

250

long for Hazel to find out that Larry preferred drink to women and she had dumped him.

He stared at her. 'What?' he asked, aggrieved. 'You mean you want me to go right now?'

Even allowing for their previous history, it was unfortunate for Larry that he happened to be the one in the line of fire. 'Yes, now!' she yelled, catching him by his bare arm and pulling him towards the door. 'Get dressed and out of here.'

'Jesus,' he did not resist but allowed himself to be shoved towards the door, 'you're some tulip!'

'A worm like you would know all about flowers, of course.' Hazel knew she was being unreasonable.

'At least I'm not a cradle-snatcher,' Larry sneered. 'How's that oversized child I saw you with in Neary's not so long ago? Getting hard up, eh, Hazel? Times getting tough?'

Hazel gasped. She had forgotten that Larry had been propping up the bar that night. 'Get out!' she screamed.

'I'm going, I'm going.' With an unpleasant smile, Larry held up his hands in mock surrender.

At least, Hazel thought as she closed the door behind him a few minutes later, this time her sexual odyssey with that creep had been short. Stupid beyond belief, but short. She ran water into the bathtub and turned on the shower as well: she needed as much scalding water all over her body as she could get and as quickly as possible. She stepped in and began to scrub with a loofah. She hated herself, despised herself, revolted herself . . .

Her body was pink and sore when she stepped out of the bath again but at least she felt a little better. Her headache still thumped away but that could be taken care of with a few Alka-Seltzers or the bottle of Fernet Branca she kept for emergencies.

Hazel wished then as she towelled herself dry that she didn't have a gig that night. She wished she had never clapped eyes on Francey Sullivan. She wished she was Siamese. She wished she was young. All that day, everywhere she looked, youth socked Hazel one right between the eyes: young couples billed and cooed at one another as they strolled around, advertisement hoardings for food commodities were peopled by girls on the right side of twenty and, to add insult to injury, when she went to her corner shop to buy cigarettes and milk, the motherly woman who worked there was missing and had been replaced by a young wan whose dead-white makeup and black lips did little for her complexion. 'Where's Mrs Cotter?' Hazel demanded as she paid for her purchases.

'Sick,' the girl replied through a mouthful of chewing gum, leaving Hazel too dispirited even to ask when the other woman would be back.

She was not to be spared even at work: that night, even the crowd seemed younger than was usual for a midweek gig at the Valley Ballroom.

During the interval, she sat smoking on a three-legged chair in what was laughably called the dressing-room behind the stage. Through the thin sateen curtains which gave the band a modicum of visual privacy, her ears rang with the concerted shuffle of feet on the dance floor, the conversational roar, and the awful, out-of-tune thumping of the interval band. Her headache was coming back and she wished with all her heart she was somewhere – anywhere – else.

The rest of the High Rollers stood or sat around sucking on their drinks and as usual telling lewd jokes. 'Give it a rest, lads!' she called as they all howled at something which normally she would have enjoyed but tonight found offensive.

'What's got into you, Queenie?' The band's leader turned on her.

'Nothing,' Hazel snapped, 'it's just that I'd like you for once in your poxy lives to remember that there's a lady present.' Glowering around her, she dared one of them to try saying something about her not being a lady.

None of them did. 'Come on,' the saxophonist appealed, 'it's only a bit of fun.'

'I've had enough of it.' Hazel ground her cigarette into the concrete floor. 'It's time you all showed a bit of respect.' She went over to the table on which she had placed her vanity case, snapped it open and bent over to examine her makeup in the mirror inside the lid.

She was recurling one of her false eyelashes when Vinnie, who had helped in the search for Francey's brother, came over to her. 'It's that culchie, isn't it?' he said in a voice too low for the others to hear. 'Do you want to talk about it?'

'Of course it isn't,' Hazel muttered, 'there's nothin' to talk about . . .'

Then: 'Damn!' She had chucked the eyelash off. Staring down at it, protruding from the tongs like a furry insect from a trap, she felt like crying. 'Don't mind me, Vinnie,' she said, 'I must be due.'

'Well, if you change your mind,' he reiterated his offer, 'I'm not doing anything afterwards.'

The second half of the gig seemed to go on until she was ready to scream. Hazel was experienced enough, however, to be able to whip herself into order: none of the punters would have had any idea that she was on anything except top form as, sequins flashing in the spotlights, she swung her way through her numbers. She clicked carefree fingers to 'High School Confidential', bopped side-to-side with the others in the front line of the band during Michael Holliday's 'The Stairway Of Love' and Brenda Lee's 'Speak To Me Pretty', and tried to overcome the personal irony inherent in Lee's 'All Alone Am I' by picking a point above the dancers' heads and staring at it with soulful eyes.

The second last set, during which she shared the vocal honours with two of the men, was a slow one. Almost everyone was up, even the wallflowers, smooching around the floor under the glitter and flash of the revolving ball and, if she did not know better, Hazel would have described the scene as romantic. She was hanging back a little out of the spotlight for the Jim Reeves number, 'Put Your Sweet Lips A Little Closer To The Phone', when one particular couple caught her eye. The girl, whose mousy hair was teased out in a drooping flick, had a sweet, young face. Dressed in stiff, peach-coloured *peau-de-soie* she stared down at her feet as she and her partner passed the bandstand.

It was not difficult for Hazel to see why the girl looked so miserable. The man who was dancing with her clutched her to his chest so that she was bent slightly backwards and the point of his chin rested in the curve of her neck. His hair was lank and stringy, his face, even under the cover of the kind lighting, was greasy with sweat. He could not have been a day under fifty.

Given her present sensitivity, Hazel felt like jumping off the bandstand and shaking the false teeth out of his head. And when her turn came to take up the running with 'Save The Last Dance For Me' followed by Elvis's 'The Hawaiian Wedding Song', although she had lost sight of the couple she forced such an unusual pace that some of the crowd began a slow jive and the band's leader frowned at her over his saxophone. She did not care. All she wanted now was to get the gig over and done with and get home to bed.

On her own.

But since this was the High Rollers' first gig at the Valley since the accident, the stage was besieged with well-wishers afterwards.

Goddamn Francey Sullivan and his bloody youth. Goddamn the Siamese twin. Hazel smiled and batted her eyes and wisecracked along with the best of them until she could escape.

Francey was impatient for Dessie to be well enough for the journey to England. For George to play his part in the salvation of his son.

Despite flashing money on gifts for his grandmother and to bring home, on clothes for himself and Dessie, on taxis, on anything else he could think of, there were times during the three days and two nights Francey spent with his half-brother in the spacious Blackrock house when he had to call on all his inner resources not to abandon all hope of ever getting back to some semblance of an even emotional tenor.

He had to manage his half-brother alone; his grandmother, a genteel woman whose unflappable sang-froid and impeccable grooming had always intimidated Francey somewhat, was attentive and hospitable for the first few hours after their arrival, but although she tried her best, he saw she was not able to overlook Dessie's appalling table manners, unfettered belching and the constant pall of cigarette smoke which hung in her pale, tasteful rooms. It was a relief when, having given them the run of the house, she retired to her room for the rest of the day. For most of their visit she was either closeted there or out with friends.

Her ancient housekeeper, Maeve, whom in his childhood Francey had loved so much, might have been more of a help except that she was too old and infirm now to do much and spent a great deal of time sitting by the fire, herself a guest rather than a functionary in the house. And the new maid, although willing, was too young and inexperienced to deal with such a raw presence.

In some ways he was grateful for the continuing distraction Dessie caused him. Terrified of going back to the dentist after his first visit – he had to have two abscesses drained as well as the more routine set of extractions, filling and cleaning – his half-brother refused to budge until Francey persuaded the dentist to treat him under general anaesthetic, which he agreed to only reluctantly in view of his patient's general state of health. Yet even with that assurance it was with the greatest of difficulty that Francey managed to deliver him to the surgery again and by the time he was left in the hands of the anaesthetist, Dessie was bordering on nervous collapse.

Traumatized from the long struggle, as Francey left the dentist's surgery, he felt weak and empty as though Dessie had sucked all the energy out of him. For the first time he began to doubt his ability to reintegrate his half-brother into the mainstream of society. Or even if this was a good idea. He tried to be objective about this, as he endeavoured to work out what was the best thing to do next, and wandered the quiet back streets of the city, envying the women who gossiped over garden walls and the pram hoods which sheltered their babies from the Atlantic wind sweeping up through the hills from the mouth of the Lee. Although he heard nothing specific as he walked by, he could just imagine their concerns: the price of butter, the scandalous doings of wayward sons and husbands. Normal, everyday worries that Francey would have given a great deal to have on his mind instead of this dark crushing weight of anxiety.

To counteract the danger of descent into a sludge of self pity, he decided that lateral thinking was what was needed. First things first. The most immediate problem was Dessie.

He must not let Dessie skew his perspective. When he examined it, Francey saw there was plenty to feel good about. As he walked along MacCurtain Street past the Metropole Hotel then turned up Summerhill towards the Arbutus Lodge Hotel, he thought hard, pushed himself, using the clicks of his heels against the pavement as a rhythmic abacus to help him enumerate the positive aspects to his life. This ticking off of blessings was another habit he had been taught years ago in boarding school.

Robust health. Money. The finding in Hazel of the first good friend he had ever had. Perhaps, he thought for the first time, her being older than him was an advantage; she did not intimidate him the way younger women used to. The satisfactory culmination of the search for his father. A sturdy and dependable family on his mother's side.

And Fleur.

A hundred yards more and he was at the entrance of the Arbutus

Lodge Hotel which clung to the sides of a steep hill, its grounds sloping away from in front of it to afford an unobstructed view of most of Cork. From up here what was most striking to Francey was the lack of city noise. Anything that moved, moved without a sound. So far below as to look like Dinky's, the cars and lorries, the ponderous cranes which swung over the ships docked nose to tail along the Quays, the train progressing at a snail's pace towards the station, moved without a sound. Francey followed the skeins of the Lee, picked out the wide hulk of the Ford factory complex and counted all the church spires, raised like admonitory fingers into the overcast sky.

The entire city was wrapped in a bluish film of haze, unifying it so that the terraces of houses climbing the steep hill towards Gurranabrahar were softened and out of focus like the cityscapes in some of the French paintings Francey had seen on his one and only visit to the National Gallery in Dublin. It was only each evening, when he was so tired that he had difficulty in fending off sleep, that Francey found the peace to think about his own affairs. Lately, Hazel had seemed to intrude into these reveries, her body and Fleur's flickering in and out of one another to make a composite. It was strange because the two sexual experiences had not been at all comparable. Fleur's exquisite delicacy bore little resemblance to Hazel's rude strength and enjoyment, which, although thrilling, had been in retrospect, Francey thought, too robust, too shocking for him.

He supposed all this agonizing and soul-searching was the price to be paid for true love and yet, when on the verges of sleep, once or twice Francey found himself wishing that in some ways Fleur could be as uncomplicated and open as Hazel. It would make the management of their affair so much easier.

Francey and Dessie arrived at Inveraray Manor ten days later in the middle of a snowstorm. Francey, who had seen snow only once before during one glorious weekend in Dublin, might have enjoyed its novelty if he was not feeling so jittery. He had no idea how the next few hours, never mind the weekend, might go.

As they travelled up the driveway in the car he had hired at the airport, he was disappointed that the air was so thick with the

256

whirling flakes that they could not see the house until the last minute, depriving Dessie of the full effect of its grandeur. 'I do wish you could have seen it, it's so impressive.' He pulled the car round the perimeter of the fountain. 'Never mind, we'll see it tomorrow, I'm sure.'

He let the vehicle coast to a halt in front of the still fountain and turned off the engine. 'All set?' His voice sounded too loud in the abrupt silence which had descended on them like a shroud.

'Do I look all right?' Dessie tugged at the sleeves of his new coat.

'You look wonderful.' Fancey's heart melted with compassion at the begging look in his half-brother's eyes. 'Honest to God.' He tried to look reassuring.

Stuffed as he had been with cod liver oil, malt extract and other vitamin and mineral supplements, Dessie's appearance had already improved a great deal by comparison with the day he had been carried from the cot in the Montgomerys' cabin but he was still as thin and pasty as a Belsen survivor. The newly cleaned teeth showed huge in his wasted face, his barbered hair emphasized the gauntness of his neck, and without the awful beard, the skin which sagged in the hollows between his jaw and cheekbones should have belonged to a man fifteen years older. 'Here, have a Ritchie's mint.' Francey shoved the sweet into his half-brother's unresisting hand and waited until he was sure it was in his mouth. He had briefed George on the telephone about all of Dessie's problems, including his dependence on drink, although he had emphasized that this seemed under control for the present at least.

'Do you think they'll like me?' Dessie's voice was hoarse with fright as the two of them crunched over the snow towards the lighted front door.

'Of course they will, now stop worrying. I'll be here all the time, right behind you.' Francey noticed how the excess fabric from the new camel hair coat hung in a fold from his half-brother's curved shoulders as though from a clothes hanger. Like a mother with a child on his first day at school, 'There now!', he reached over to pull it straight and then rang the bell.

George himself answered the door. For a second or two he surveyed both his visitors in silence and Francey, immobilized by the keen violet stare, felt his own words of greeting dying away in his throat. He also became conscious of the picture they must present, the absurdity of himself and Dessie arriving on their father's doorstep in the middle of a blizzard, pathetic fallacy of a high order.

Then George stepped back to admit them. 'Come in.' His tone was sincere now. 'Good flight?'

'Great.' Francey, annoyed by the less than enthusiastic welcome and not at all fooled by the too-swift warmth, found his voice. 'What about the cases?'

'I'll have them brought in later. Come in, for Christ's sake.'

As they stepped into the warm hallway, Francey, taking Dessie's arm and feeling the tension radiating through the muscle, squeezed it to offer comfort and support. The next minute or so was occupied with divesting themselves of their coats and scarves then, 'Well, well, well,' George surveyed his newest son, 'so this is the famous Desmond.'

'That's right,' Dessie whispered.

'Well, well,' George repeated heartily, 'after all this time. How do you do?' He extended his hand. 'Although I suppose that's hardly appropriate in the circumstances —'

Dessie, lost for a reply, appealed with his eyes to Francey. 'He's a bit overwhelmed,' Francey said stiffly, still watching his father's true reaction. 'It's all a bit much altogether.'

'I can just imagine,' George dropped Dessie's hand, 'but there's no rush. The one thing we have here is plenty of space, we don't even have to see each other if we don't feel like it.' He smiled then and Francey saw once again that this wide grin, with its hint of boyish mischief, was their father's best weapon. It had disarmed him on their first meeting and now even raised a wan, answering smile in the terrified Dessie.

'Come on in and meet the rest of the family,' George urged, turning to walk away from them in the direction of the drawing-room.

Francey's stomach lurched. Fleur had said Colin was away. 'Are they here?' he asked.

'Yes' George carolled over his shoulder, 'I managed to persuade Colin to reschedule his trip. He and Fleur got in not long before you but Tommy's not here yet, he's coming down this evening with his nanny.' He threw open the drawing-room door. 'In here, Desmond.'

Over his half-brother's head, Francey's gaze flew towards Fleur who was wearing a high-necked sheath dress in pale lilac. She and Colin rose and came forward together to greet the new member of the family but as George made the introductions, Francey saw she was avoiding his eyes. Her personality was again subdued, just as it had first seemed to him. She was no doubt taking care, he thought, that her husband should not notice anything untoward. At least, that's what he hoped she was doing . . .

He compelled his attention towards Dessie, who, blushing and shuffling his feet, was attempting to respond to the overtures of the others as Francey had coached him. Then Francey, disbelieving, saw his father's eyes dart towards the drinks table and moved to intercept disaster. 'Our tongues are hanging out for a decent cup of tea,' he blurted.

To his relief, George took the hint. 'Of course. You haven't had lunch,' and rang a small handbell to summon the butler.

Francey sat on the nearest couch and like his shadow, Dessie followed, sitting so close beside him Francey could smell his peppermint-scented breath. Shadowing Francey was a habit he had developed since their return to Lahersheen from Cork; almost everywhere Francey went, Dessie followed as doggedly as the brindled terrier followed the two of them. It would have been comical if it had not been so pathetic.

Colin and Fleur resumed their seats, too, leaving only George standing in the middle of the floor like the lead character in a play. He rubbed his hands together then cleared his throat. 'I see!' he said to no one and no purpose and then was saved by the entrance of the butler.

While they waited for their tea, Francey, surprised by a swift surge of adulterer's guilt, did not dare look towards the couch where Colin and his wife sat side by side. The guilt was unexpected: up to now he had been quite confident of his every-man-for-himself stance.

'I'm glad Francey found you.' George addressed Dessie again after a long, awkward silence. 'I was going to hire an agency myself – I'm sure Francey has told you all about the letters that my late dear wife left us all. She specifically asked us, well, me, actually, to continue the search for you but this lad here beat me to it.'

Dessie checked with Francey to see what he should do or say to this and when Francey, who did not believe a word of it, just smiled encouragingly at him, Dessie smiled too and nodded with great vigour.

Francey himself was having to deal not only with the impact Fleur's presence was having on him but with his surprise that he no longer disliked Colin Mannering. What he and Fleur had done together had swung the weathercock of his feelings for his half-brother in a complete 180-degree arc. And so, while the eyes of Fleur and Dessie remained downcast, Francey found he was able to keep conversation going by engaging Colin, asking a succession of questions about his business and travels. That Colin seemed so eager to talk increased his guilt.

George took no part in the conversation as, while pretending to be gripped by Colin's outline of the peccadilloes of his trading partners in various parts of the Far East, Francey tried to solve the conundrum of his half-brother's personality. He saw that Colin was doing his level best to include the newest member of the family in the conversation, explaining the basics of his business. He seemed just like an ordinary Joe, a bit pompous, boastful perhaps, but on balance, not at all suspicious or resentful as Francey assumed might be natural in the circumstances; after all, Dessie and himself were cuckoos in what should have been Colin's well-feathered nest.

After a bit Francey was forced to conclude that Colin was reconciled to having to share his inheritance. And as his half-brother talked on, Francey saw the astonishing difference between familial-Colin and businessman-Colin. The latter's work was a field in which he obviously felt masterful. 'It's just occurred to me,' Colin turned to George, having exhausted the subject of customs officers, 'maybe we could fix Dessie up with somewhere here in England, even near the house, until he finds his feet and gets someplace for himself. Wouldn't that be a good interim arrangement, Dad? Or maybe,' he turned back to Dessie, 'you want to go back to Ireland?'

'What do you think, Dessie?' George's expression was unreadable. 'Maybe Ireland would be better for you?'

Dessie squashed closer to Francey on the couch. 'What do you mean?'

'I think it's too early to make any plans,' Francey cut in swiftly. His father need not think he was going to get rid of the problem as easily as that.

260

'We only want to do the best we can in the circumstances.' George remained bland.

Colin then came up with specific suggestions, so quick and eager that all the pieces at last fell into place in Francey's brain: what was at his half-brother's core was an insatiable desire for approval, from his father, from everyone he met. Yet there still remained the puzzle as to why Fleur seemed so timid around him. Even before her relationship with Francey, she had taken no active part in conversation when her husband was present, and was demonstrably dominated by him. She sat now with her eyes fixed on her lap as though waiting for an invitation before contributing.

As he agonized over it all, Francey only half listened to George and Colin's discussion about the possibilities for Dessie's future; his attention even strayed from Dessie's monosyllabic answers and frightened, shifting eyes.

He dragged himself back only when he heard that the talk had died away to be replaced by renewed silence.

'This is nice,' George said then, looking around the room. 'Jool would have liked this. As a matter of fact it's what she wanted, isn't it? All the family reunited . . .' Although his father's expression had become convivial, Francey, still confused about the undercurrents in the relationships within the room, could not make up his mind whether or not George was being malicious.

'Quite a turn-up, I'd say,' Colin's reaction was equable. 'I must say Jool did seem to think of everything.'

'That reminds me.' George walked to a *bureau plat* and opened the drawer, 'I have her letters here, the ones she left for you two Irish lads.'

'I'll take them.' Francey stood up. He did not want Dessie, who could not read or write, humiliated in front of these people.

A half-hour later, in Francey's room, Dessie, pulling at one of his Woodbines, was staring at the unopened letter in his hand as though it contained a reptile.

'Will I read it for you?' Francey took it and slitting the top of the envelope, saw it contained not just a letter but a small snapshot, a copy of the wedding photograph that had led him to George. He gave the snap to Dessie without comment and scanned the contents of the note. Not having read his own yet, it was the first time he had seen Jool's handwriting: he was no graphologist but it was obvious that this rounded, flowing script bespoke a generous and confident woman.

Francey had already decided that if there was anything here that could confuse Dessie further he would prevaricate about the contents. Over the past few weeks he had unfolded, a little at a time, not just the story of his half-brother's parentage but how Jool had died and how she had been kind enough to leave sufficient money to take care of them all for the rest of their lives. But Dessie somehow could not grasp the notion that he now had two families willing and anxious to help him; in the intervals of lucidity between dosages of his prescription drugs – which were being tapered off – he remained fearful and insecure, reminding Francey of a wild animal which, although hungry, refused to be domesticated for fear of a fate worse than an empty stomach. And since his half-brother had exhibited no concept of the value of money other than how far it went towards the next bottle or a dry bed for one night, Francey had not divulged to him the extent of his inheritance.

Having seen nothing in Jool's letter except kindness, he began to read aloud.

Dear Desmond [the letter began], *I hope you don't mind that I intruded into your personal life to the extent that up to a few years ago at least, I think I've gotten to know you a little. And of course if you are reading this it means my efforts will not have been in vain.*

All I want to say to you, Desmond, is that the Lord is a good shepherd and He will seek you, hound you down if necessary, until you are safely home with the rest of His flock. And He'll take care of you too, much better than you could possibly imagine. Trust Him during the dark days, OK?

I've imagined what you look like, Desmond. Tall? Those killer eyes of George's? Or are you more like your mom, perhaps? My informant about you was a person of few words and told me only that you were gentle. Gentle is just fine by me, dear.

You do have problems, Lord knows you do, but nothing that can't be cured. And never forget, will you, that I'll be up there

*watching and that you will have a friend in court! We all love
you.*

*I know you like to travel light but I thought you might make
space for a personal memento which would remind you that from
up above, old Jool is rooting for you. I would be so honoured if you
would put me in your wallet! Think of me as your Fairy
Grandma if you like.*

Much love,
Jool

'She was a nice woman,' Francey handed the note and the
envelope to Dessie.

'That's the first letter I ever got in my life.' Dessie handed it back
and lit another cigarette. 'Will you read it again to me, Francey?'
Patiently, Francey repeated the words from the note, slower this time.
He glanced up between sentences to find his half-brother, eyes
burning, followed the words, mouthing them a split second after they
had been uttered. 'What does it mean, "rooting" for me?' he
demanded at the end.

'It means being on your side, taking your side in a contest.'

'Read yours now.' Dessie settled himself on the side of Francey's
bed.

Francey's letter was longer than Dessie's and he, too, had been
given a copy of the wedding photograph. Included as well was
another snapshot that he saw with amazement was one of himself,
taken outside Ledbetter's as he was coming out through the customer
entrance. 'I'll read this quietly if you don't mind,' he said, suddenly
wary.

This was an extraordinary situation: he was about to read a letter
sent to him, in essence, from beyond the grave and which contained
evidence that the person who wrote it had been spying on him. He
had not until now taken in the implications of that. How long had
Jool had him watched – and how closely? Did she know about
Lahersheen – and Hazel?

The old lady had anticipated his reaction:

Dear Francey,

*Don't get a shock, dear, but as you can see, I'm quite up to date
on your life and I believe I know you well.*

263

Don't worry, I wasn't outside the hardware store in person, the photograph was sent me by my Dublin informant. I include it only to show you how I see you: this was my favourite picture of you. You may already have found the others, which are with my personal papers in my bureau.

In case you're worried, you were not under constant surveillance. All that was organized was that from time to time, every couple of years maybe, I checked on your progress. (By the way, you're quite a handsome young man, aren't you? And if your personality is anything like my George's, those poor Irish colleens won't have a chance!)

Maybe you're wondering why I didn't go to see you or break the news to George that I knew about you, but believe it or not, I got to love your Dad very much (even though he is an old rogue!) and we were rubbing along just fine. When you get to a certain age you believe in leaving things be.

But I don't want you believing I didn't think about you a lot, I certainly did. And from what I know of you, I believe we would have liked each other. So I'm sorry we couldn't have gotten together but as you know, God's been good to me in life and I hope you'll think kindly of me now and that what I've been able to give you materially will compensate a little for us not meeting up. And for my unAmerican activities in invading your life!

Don't forget, like I've told your two brothers, I'll be watching out for you from above. I'll be the one winking at you from behind the moon!

Think of me sometimes, won't you? I am/was a good ol' Protestant as by now no doubt you know, but I wouldn't object if now and then maybe you'd light a Catholic candle for old Jool. You're a good boy, I already know that. And Francey, I hope you don't mind the imposition but I have the feeling you are going to be the one to look out for the whole family in the end. Don't be frightened, dear, the Lord made the back for the burden. You won't always see it, but you're the one He's choosing. So look after them all, Francey, my beloved George and your brothers and specially little Tommy and his mother. I've a funny feeling they're the ones who'll need you most.

Love from your old Yankee Grandma (don't I wish!)
Jool

Moved, curious, and conscious of a strange little thrill about what he hoped was the old lady's prescience about Fleur and her son, Francey folded the note and put it back in its envelope. As he stared at his stepmother's handsome face in the photograph he now knew so well, for a few moments he feared that this woman did have the power to reach to him from beyond the grave. 'You wanted us all to be together,' he willed her now to hear, 'so here we are. Help me get through this.' The next instant he realized he was asking the impossible: Jool Gallaher would be amenable to help in the social integration of Dessie but he could not ask her to collude in adultery.

Dessie, eschewing lunch, took some of his pills and went for a sleep, leaving Francey free to pay a visit to the stables.

Eerily quiet under the snow which was still accumulating, the stableyard seemed deserted when he let himself in. Then he spotted a flicker of movement at the far end and saw it was a face peering out from a doorway. 'Hello-ooo,' he called, fascinated by the way his voice did not travel through the falling snow.

'Francey? Is that you?' Mick O'Dowd shaded his eyes with his hands as Francey approached.

'It's me all right.' Francey shook hands with his fellow Irishman. 'Still here, I see!'

'Hard to kill a bad thing. Thought it might be the guv.' Mick stepped back inside, leaving the doorway clear. 'We're all skiving today, not much we can do in this. Come in, we're just brewing up.'

'Could I see the horses first?'

'Sure,' Mick smiled, 'want me to come with you?'

Francey shook his head. 'Not unless you have to.'

'You know your way. Be sure to lock the doors afterwards. Come in when you're finished.'

Francey made straight for the nearest stall. He had a particular affinity with many of the Shires as individuals but he had found Tarzan, with his sleepy acceptance of everything being done to or for him, to be his favourite. He supposed that, in many ways, the huge horse reminded him of a solid, immovable rock in a quicksand world. 'Hello,' he called quietly as he opened the stable door.

Tarzan, leaning against the concrete wall of his stall rather like a louche barfly, opened mild eyes, regarded his visitor for a few seconds without a flicker of interest and then closed them again. 'Oh, come on,' Francey said, closing the door behind him and going over to pet him. 'Show a little love.' As he stroked the Shire's smooth haunch under the hairy horse-blanket, he remembered with a half-smile that Tarzan had been one of Hazel's pet names for him during the week of his induction into the mysteries of sex.

He talked now, letting Tarzan in on the grandiose plan that had bubbled on under the surface of his thoughts since he had first clapped eyes on these magnificent beasts. The more Francey saw of them, the more he had begun to think of acquiring some of his own for showcasing in Ireland. He was convinced that in such a horse-loving nation, a team of Shires would be a major attraction at fairs and horse shows around the country, even at the dizzy height of the Dublin Horse Show. The largest horse species he had ever seen in Ireland were the patient Guinness horses which, oblivious of the chaotic motorized traffic around them, hauled their drays up the Dublin Quays from the brewery at St James's Gate. For impact, however, those animals, although large and well cared-for, could not compare with the snoozing Tarzan and his ilk.

A rectangle of snowy light leaked through the door on to the piles of new straw and hay that insulated the stable as Francey's imagination, untrammelled by practical considerations, took full flight. Continuing to stroke Tarzan, he visualized himself as a ringmaster, flicking a long whip as, nose-to-tail, a string of these wonderful giants lumbered around a railed enclosure. 'But I'd never let it touch a hair of you,' he whispered into the horse's satiny neck, 'and you'd never have to do anything demeaning.' Instead, Francey thought, he would show off his charges' grace and strength, perhaps harnessing them to pull anvils or heavy anchors, even double-decker buses and steamrollers. He could offer them as a star side attraction in the annual National Ploughing Championships where they would not do anything as mundane as pulling ploughs like ordinary horses, but would excavate huge boulders from beneath the earth, or fell superfluous old trees from the ditches. Children could be offered rides, five or six at a time.

As well as touring around, he could establish a permanent performance home for them to which local people and tourists would travel: he could offer Mick O'Dowd a job to look after their physical welfare; he could have beautiful accoutrements and bridles specially made . . . Hazel and her High Rollers could do gigs, comedians could do stand-up, other singers and bands could come and he would even hire companies of actors to perform one-act plays . . . Maybe even his father? By the time Francey was finished he was running a miniature variety house. 'Do you think you'd like to be part of the team?' he asked Tarzan, who did not move a muscle.

Francy leaned his head against the blanket and heard the slow thud of the horse's mighty heart. 'Maybe not you,' he conceded. 'You could be the mascot. They could just look at you.'

'Everything all right?' The door opened and Mick O'Dowd's form was silhouetted against the whirling snow.

'Sure.' Francey, hoping Mick had not heard him talking to the horse, gave Tarzan a last pat and walked to the door. 'Not exactly nervous, is he?' he asked, jerking a thumb over his shoulder towards the animal.

'A bomb could go off and that fella'd sleep through it,' Mick replied cheerfully. 'None of them's what you'd call sensitive, mind you,' he added, 'and if you give them a fright, they just walk away. Amazon's the nearest thing we have to a prima donna here. She's temperamental, like most women,' he laughed, 'particularly when she's in foal. But to tell you the truth she's no problem really. And it's not nerves, only temper. You could shoot a gun in her face and provided she could see it she wouldn't spook. Don't make any sudden movements behind her, just stay in front of her where she can keep an eye on you. You go ahead,' he added, 'I'll lock up.'

But as Francey preceded the groom towards the tack-room, a movement by the door of another stable caught his eye and in the next instant he recognized Dessie's figure, partially obscured by the whirling snow. 'Dessie?' He had left him asleep, Francey thought, what was he doing out here?

'I woke up and you weren't there.' Dessie hurried forward.

'How did you know where I was?'

'I asked Colin, he said you were probably going to be here and he gave me directions.' Dessie was shivering, despite his expensive new coat.

'You'll have to stop worrying about where I am,' Francey chided. 'I told you I won't ever be far away and I'll come back.' He realized he was talking to Dessie like a mother to a four-year-old. Something would have to be done about Dessie's dependence on him, it was getting out of hand. And if he was being honest, he thought, it was also beginning to irritate him a little.

'Come on in out of this,' he urged, about to lead his half-brother towards the tack-room then, thinking it would be fair neither to the stable-hands nor to Dessie to inflict them on each other, changed his mind. 'Do you want to see these horses?' he asked instead. 'They're wonderful – oh, here's Mick!' as O'Dowd came over. 'This is one of the men who work here.' Having made the introductions, Francey received the unsurprising impression that Mick knew who Dessie was.

All three of them were now covered in snow. 'You go on in, Mick,' Francey continued, adding that he would make sure to lock each stable door after showing Dessie round.

'Make sure he doesn't smoke in there.' Mick indicated the Woodbine that, snow or not, burned steadily in the hand of this new member of the family.

'He won't,' Francey promised.

Dessie stamped out the cigarette and followed Francey around the stalls, becoming more and more entranced with each animal. The horses pricked their ears and blew with pleasure and Francey remembered what Tilly had said, that his half-brother seemed to have a way with animals. 'You like them?'

'Oh, yes.' Dessie's eyes were alight for the first time. He looked like a different person, even happy.

In his study, George stood with hands behind his back, looking out at the snow. He remembered the last time it had snowed at Inveraray. It had been two years ago, about three weeks before Christmas and Jool, who had taken Tommy along on one of her shopping expeditions in London, had come back home full of her plans to create the Disney wonderland in the little wood. She would not wait for the snow to stop but had insisted on taking George on a reconnaissance mission through the trees, picking out the locations for the models, seeing what could be achieved by damming the little streams.

At one point, having identified the fallen tree as a location for a treehouse she had turned to him, her face alight like a young girl's: 'Oh, George, it'll be perfect, perfect!' Although she was well over seventy and muffled up in furs, with eyes shining and the green-white light illuminating her skin, for an instant she had looked almost

268

beautiful. George, who had come along reluctantly, had taken her in his arms and kissed her, the first spontaneous such action in years.

'What was that for?' Jool had looked astonished.

'Because you're my wife and I love you,' George had replied, his sincerity for once unforced.

'My, my!' Jool had leaned back a little in his arms. 'Getting sentimental in your old age, George?'

'Maybe.' But the moment had passed as quickly as it had arisen, leaving him feeling uncharacteristically embarrassed. He hugged her again, quickly, and told her that as the snow was thickening, they had better been getting back inside. 'Don't want you to catch cold.'

'Heavens to Betsy,' Jool had laughed with infectious amusement, 'when is the last time you were in New England?'

George laughed along, his embarrassment evaporating, and they had held hands like schoolchildren as they walked back through the trees, coming apart only when they got out into the open. At their age, they admitted to one another, holding hands felt a little foolish.

Unspoken between them, however, as delicate as the drifting flakes around their heads, was the thought that it was too late. And although they were amiable with one another to the end, and had had sex when it suited one or both of them, it was the last time they had been so romantic together.

Although George could see the fringes of the wood now, from where he stood there was little evidence of the care and delight his wife had taken in the design and execution of her plan to delight her grandson. How would she have coped with this new intruder? The more the complications multiplied in his life the more George wished Jool was not dead.

Chapter Fourteen

After the coldness outside, the blast of warm air that hit his face as soon as he opened the back door which led into the kitchen made Francey sneeze. He closed the door fast so the heat would not escape and stamped the snow off his feet on the coir matting just inside, vowing the central heating in *his* house would be of a more moderate order. 'That's a cold one,' he said to the cook as he passed through. The woman nodded at him and went back to what she was doing, and Francey noticed the way the kitchen seemed to murmur to itself at the relaxed pace of professionals who are sure of what they are doing. He added a cook to the shopping list for new acquisitions when he had time to sort himself out with a place of his own.

He had taken the precaution of telling Mick O'Dowd that he was leaving his half-brother in the stable yard and Mick seemed to have no objection, but Francey was already beginning to worry. Who knew what went on in that brain of Dessie's?

On the other hand, the personality change that the horses had wrought in his half-brother had been so instantaneous and so extraordinary that Francey was kicking himself for not thinking of the therapeutic value of animals before this. It would have been an easy matter to borrow, or even buy, a few horses or ponies on Béara, and the farm in Lahersheen was equipped with plenty of outhouses. Better now than never, he thought, as he walked down the carpeted corridor towards his room. Maybe he should think of including Dessie in his plans for the future . . .

He was about to go inside when he saw his father coming towards him. He raised a hand in greeting, but George did not return the salute. Instead, he vanished from sight through a doorway.

Francey was taken aback: had it been his imagination or had George ducked? Acting on instinct, he determined to find out and knocked on the closed door through which his father had disappeared, opening it without waiting for an invitation.

George was standing in a large room, a study-cum-dressing-room, lined with expensive, glass-fronted bookshelves and divided by a pair of double doors through which was a fully fitted bedroom. He looked startled as Francey asked if now was a good time for a chat. 'Bit busy, actually,' he appealed.

Francey refused to be fobbed off. He looked with meaning at the shining – and clean – expanse of desk which stretched between the two of them. 'When would be a good time?'

'Let's see.' George took out a morocco-bound notebook from one of the drawers in the desk and turned over the leaves.

Francey waited for a moment or two and then lost patience. 'When's your next appointment, George?' he asked, hearing the name on his own lips for the first time. It sounded inappropriate but after this man's neglect for so many years he was damned if he was going to ape Colin by calling him 'Dad' or 'Daddy'. 'What's wrong with now?' he continued, 'I won't cut into your schedule. I'll leave the minute you have to attend to your next business.'

George, looking hunted, closed the notebook and sat in the leather wing chair behind the desk. He invited Francey to sit too. 'Go ahead,' he said. 'I've a bit of time now, as it happens.'

Francey stared at the silver-bound face that would not be out of place on the cover of a magazine. When he had envisaged this meeting, he had thought it would be civilized, even conciliatory, but now that he was embarked on it, found to his consternation that words and emotions were piling up like an unstable bundle of explosives behind his tongue. 'I don't know where to start, to tell you the truth,' he said and to his disgust his voice shook.

George remained silent.

Francey looked down at his hands, balled in his lap. 'I've been wanting to talk to you for a very long time, all my life,' he began. 'I rehearsed it, I knew your answers, I pictured what would happen . . .' When he looked up the bundle of words behind his tongue exploded. 'The first thing I wanted to know,' he cried, 'is *why?*'

He gave George no chance to reply as it all spewed out, faster and faster. 'Why did you leave us without a word for all these years? If I hadn't come looking for you would you ever have contacted me? *Ever?*' He gripped the edge of the desk. 'I thought about you, dreamed about you. I had you up on a pedestal. I thought you'd come every week. My mother never said a bad word about you ever.

Did you know that? Did you ever give her a moment's consideration? Did you think of her for one second after you left Ireland, did you think of me, of Dessie, of Kathleen?'

George attempted to interject, holding up his hands to interrupt the flow but nothing could stop Francey now. 'And don't even *think* about giving me that shite about coming to visit us that time,' he cried, 'I know only too well that you came once. *Once.*'

He jumped up from his seat and began to pace. 'I remember that time as clearly as if it was an hour ago, but I suppose to you it was just a little side excursion, eh, George? It would have been better if you hadn't come at all, do you know that? Don't think I don't know why you came. It was out of interest to see the little bastard you made, like you'd go to see a freak show. And you couldn't leave well enough alone even then, could you? What do you do then? You take Kitty away with you, make things worse, twice as bad, ninety times as bad.' He was so upset now that he ceased pacing and leaned across the desk as though to strike George. 'Do you know what we went through, all of us? Did you care, George? Do you care now?'

His father flinched away as though afraid he was going to be hit. 'I thought you said your mother was all right —'

Francey would not let him finish. 'Of course she's all right now,' he yelled. '"All right" meaning she's now widowed for the second time. She's forty-five or forty-six or whatever she is and her hands are all rough and her hair is grey and she was a solicitor's daughter. Do you know what that means in Cork City? It means well-to-do, part of the gentry. She could have had a lovely life instead of slaving to the bone in muck and dirt and storms – and instead of being the talk of the parish —' He stopped, realizing this was turning into the story of his mother and George rather than George and himself.

His father's face was wavering, expanding and contracting in rhythm with the blood that pulsed behind Francey's eyes. Somehow he saw that George was no longer smiling but looked afraid; he made a brief effort to control himself but could not. He crashed both palms on to the surface of the desk, causing a crystal ashtray to jump. 'Where do you think Kathleen is now, George?' he shouted. 'And I've left your other son, who's a mental and physical wreck, out there with the animals. Because that's the way you wanted it. Thanks to you, your youngest son thinks and behaves like an animal because that's the way

272

he was brought up. Maybe we should have left him to drown. That would have suited you, wouldn't it?'

His father stood up. 'That's enough! I'm not going to take any more of this.'

'Are you not?' As they faced one another, Francey was glad he was the taller one. 'Why, George?' he asked in a quieter voice. 'Why'd you do it?'

'If you're not going to be reasonable about this —'

'*Reasonable?*' Francey's fury began to ebb, however, as he heard the emptiness behind his father's blustering. 'Don't make me laugh.'

'I'll talk to you if you sit down.'

Abruptly, Francey resumed his seat and after some hesitation, George did too. 'I can't give you any explanation,' he said, his eyes wary as though watching for the next eruption, 'at least none that would pacify you.'

'Try,' Francey said through gritted teeth, 'anything at all will do.'

George appeared to consider. 'I don't suppose there's any point in lying or making excuses about my own life,' he said, then, 'There's no explanation at all. It's just because I'm me.'

The audacity took Francey's breath away, yet it also completed the deflation of his anger. He kept on at George for another little while but no matter how much he pushed he got nowhere and they went round and round in circles, with George exhibiting what to Francey was that most infuriating of all traits, passivity. George apologized, he accepted he had been less than paternal, he apologized again. But it all came down to a single tenet that this was the way he was and there was little he could do about it. Francey ran out of ammunition and the row petered out. 'I'm sorry, truly,' George said for the fifth or sixth time into the silence, his violet eyes wide.

The remaining blinkers fell off Francey's vision. This man would never be what he had dreamed he might be. 'What about Dessie?' he asked coldly. 'How are you planning to help him? I'm doing the best I can with him but you're the one who's responsible.'

George's eyes slid away. 'We'll have to wait and see.'

Francey stared across the table for a long minute then stood up again. 'Don't wait too long,' he said.

'Do you think he'd like a little dinner party?' Following his father's swivelling eyes, Francey saw they had lit upon a silver framed photograph of himself, his wife and a number of other people seated outdoors on a sunny day, glasses raised towards the camera. 'We could welcome him into the family, so to speak.' George looked back at his son, his face hopeful as though he had just come up with the perfect solution.

Francey laughed out loud. '*Dinner* party?' he exclaimed. 'Dessie wouldn't have a clue what a dinner party was, let alone know how to behave at one. Far from dinner parties he has lived – and me too, by the way.'

'Well, a different kind of party, then? With more people – where he wouldn't have to feel he had to be anything but himself.'

Francey stared at him. And for the first time since they had met he saw his father was unnerved. 'I'm only trying to help,' George appealed, unable to sustain the scrutiny, 'you tell me what Dessie would like – anything. D'you think he'd like a holiday, for instance?'

'George,' Francey said, cold now, 'would you just listen to yourself?'

Back in his room, he sat for a long time on the side of the bed, staring into space. Now that he had cooled down, he found he bore his father no ill will: the anti-climactic nature of the long-awaited meeting had been less frustrating than sad. George Gallaher had turned out to be as insubstantial as a puff of smoke. You could not hate or despise something that had no substance.

And his father was obviously going to do his damnedest not to be alone with Dessie and to spread the burden of his rehabilitation. Right then Francey made up his mind that he was equally going to do his damnedest to make George face the consequences of his own actions.

Francey himself felt like a coreless apple: for so long he had thought that meeting his father would be important. It may yet prove to be, he thought, but at present all he felt was annoyance that he had been such a chump. Other things, too. He felt cheap: half of his own genes had been given to him by this man; he felt lonely and miserable and ashamed, of both himself and George, of George because this was his father who had turned out to be so shallow, of himself because he felt such disloyalty. He slumped backwards on the bed, analysing his feelings until this, too, became a cause for shame: Francey had been brought up to believe that self-analysis was self-absorption and therefore egoistic and unChristian.

He swung his legs over the side of the bed and went to the window. Snow lay unbroken along the quiet fields, accumulating like little roofs along the fence rails; it drifted easily past the double glazing and lent to Francey a sense of calm and isolation. *Pure as the driven snow* . . . the old phrase washed up in his brain. He was no longer that – that was one sure thing. Then an antonym, *concupiscence*, came in: could Francey Sullivan, adulterer, hold himself in higher order than his father?

It was too soon to know whether all those dreams and fantasies he had vested in George Gallaher had been wasted, yet underneath the sadness and sense of let-down were the tantalizing puffs and bubbles of another sentiment, so novel that it took Francey a long time to recognize it for what it was. As the minutes ticked by, weight was lifting off the back of his neck to be replaced by a sensation as light as the feathers of snow outside. He was amazed to discover that his despondency had been replaced by the creeping tentacles of something else. Francey stood very still until the feeling showed itself.

Liberation. To know that there would never be a man on a white charger to come to his aid had, in an odd way, set him free. Although the experience had not been pleasant, the interview with George meant that at last he knew where he stood. Since leaving school Francey had never thought of himself as anything other than grown-up and responsible for his own actions, but he saw now that this had not been the case: all these years, unknowing, he had been second-guessing his actions because of business unfinished, or never started, with his father. If he had been asked half an hour beforehand how he might have reacted to George's rejection of him, he would have used words like 'devastated' or 'destroyed'. Never having had a relationship other than an illusory one, however, he saw now how his waiting for George had engendered a form of partial emotional paralysis.

Francey became angry all over again as he saw what opportunities he had squandered while holding himself in readiness for George – with his stepfather, for instance. Thanks to his infatuation with a fantasy he had never given a relationship with Mossie a proper chance and now it was too late.

He blamed his mother. All right, so George was charming, lovely, sexy – even Francey could see that – but how could she not have seen through him? How could she have let herself . . . For a few moments, Francey toyed with the idea of telephoning Lahersheen and having it out with her right then and there but reason prevailed: she was so upset about Mossie and off-balance about Abby's decision to go into the convent that the timing would have been desperately unfair. He knew, however, that he would have to talk to her about it sooner rather than later. And he was not finished with George yet.

Nevertheless, he felt he had to talk to someone right away. He had promised to let Hazel know how things were going with Dessie. He looked at his watch: she was on a few days off and, as it was still only mid-afternoon, should be at home.

When she answered the telephone, after the preliminaries and an updating on Dessie's integration into the Inveraray set-up, Francey poured out the whole sorry story of his altercation with George. To give Hazel her due, he thought at the end, she had never once given in to the temptation to say, 'I told you so!', a surprising display of tact for which he was grateful. 'And you'll never guess what his solution to Dessie's problems is,' he added with derision.

'Try me,' Hazel offered.

'He asked if he would like a party,' he snorted, 'I ask you – a *party!*'

'Don't dismiss it,' Hazel said after a short pause. 'If it was a small party and carefully managed, it mightn't be the worst thing.'

'Hazel!' Francey was outraged. 'Dessie would *die!*'

'Not if he knew this party was especially to make him welcome. What's he had in his life up to now to make him feel special? When did anyone even wish him a happy birthday or happy Christmas? So what's wrong with someone celebrating that Dessie is alive and kicking and has turned up at last?'

'But, Hazel,' Francey could not believe his ears, 'my father just offered that off the top of his head—'

'So what?' Hazel said. 'He said it, didn't he? About time that fecker exerted himself! Maybe you should ask Dessie himself whether or not he'd like a party.'

Francey continued to argue but the more he did, the less his words held water. He promised Hazel he would let Dessie decide.

'How's your little friend?' Hazel asked him.

'What little friend?' Francey frowned.

'Don't play games,' Hazel retorted.

Francey remembered. 'She's fine,' he said cautiously, 'I haven't seen all that much of her, as it happens. But I'm worried Colin will notice something.'

'Well,' Hazel paused a fraction, 'I suppose I should wish you good luck—'

'Thanks,' Francey replied with feeling. 'I'll stay in touch, all right?'

Hazel hung up, prolonging the click as the receiver hit the cradle. Over the previous few days she had had little to do other than brood on the shortcomings of her own character and the emotional morass into which she had let herself sink. The next gig was not until the end of the week and she dreaded the empty days that faced her. She had tried to persuade herself that her depression was a result of delayed shock in the aftermath of the accident but at last had to face the fact that this was balderdash. How could she have been so stupid as to let herself fall in love with a man so much younger than she was?

Cradle-snatcher . . . The words used by that creep Larry haunted her. Deliberately excoriating herself, Hazel re-created the fuzzy memory of the tow-headed little boy with George's eyes who had stood gazing with such intensity up at her and his father in the farmhouse kitchen that day so long ago. She had not revealed to Francey that it had been her damned idea to make that visit in the first place. Only seventeen years old but worldly beyond her years, Hazel had been having a public affair with Gorgeous George as he was known in the trade. He specialized in young girls, she knew that, but he was so charming and he had been so flattering, so sincere, so *gorgeous* that Hazel, like so many before and since, had fallen for his line. And his talent in the bed department had been extraordinary: for someone so self-centred, George Gallaher knew more about how to make love to women than anyone Hazel had ever met.

Until Francey.

Francey was too inexperienced and coltish as yet, but by the end of the week they had spent together, Hazel knew without a shadow of doubt that George had passed on his talent in this area to his son. The difference was, however, that given the right girl, Francey's lovemaking would not begin and end with sex. He was a decent, intelligent human being who was, she was sure of it, unselfish enough to sustain a good two-way relationship.

That summer – what was it, 1943, '44, '45? – Hazel, with an eye to the future, had taken it on herself to try to change George. Every girl in every town in Ireland who clapped eyes on him fancied her chances but at the time Hazel had believed that this was the real thing for her. Days of public preening and nights of private passion were interspersed with long, intense conversations in which she tried to understand her lover. He had been evasive and lighthearted through-out but, somehow, she had managed to winkle out of him some stories of his past life, including that he had a son living in some godforsaken place in West Cork.

Hazel, in the role of the caring, responsible, mature one in the relationship, had managed to persuade him to take a detour when they were on their way to play summer season in Killarney: it had also been her idea that he should bring a significant present.

But, of course, the results of that visit, as every dog in the street now knew, had been catastrophic. When Hazel had seen which way the wind blew between her lover and the benighted girl who had followed them to Killarney, she had been so outraged she had kicked George in the shins, hard enough to give him a three-day limp. And although he had had the wit not to make any further approach to her after Kathleen left, she left him, and everyone else who cared to see, in no doubt as to how she felt. It was Hazel's first great lesson in how quickly passion can turn to contempt.

She had made another awful mistake with her husband whom she had met during a variety performance in aid of the St Vincent de Paul with which he was a volunteer: it had been before the advent of the High Rollers and Hazel was twenty-two and trying her hand at singing for the first time. Since George, she had run all sorts of men through her hands, each of them as unreliable as the last but this one seemed different. He had nothing to do with showbusiness for a start: safe, solid, the rhythm method and a future with a pension, he was the antithesis of everything in the profession, and in his own way he was good-looking. After they married, he insisted she get out of showbusiness and Hazel, relieved, or so she had thought, gave it up without a qualm.

Up to the time she married, Hazel, who was an only child, had never had a real home. Born into a circus family, almost from the time she could walk she had performed as part of the family troupe of acrobats and dancers, sold tickets for the menagerie, collected money for the raffles and moved, moved, moved. Her father drowned in a boating accident when she was nine and her mother had died of consumption less than two years after but Hazel continued to perform with her cousins. The circus got into financial difficulties when she was fifteen and its abrupt disbandment, in a provincial town in Co. Waterford, was traumatic for her but not terminally so; she had always been able to bounce back from adversity and went immediately in search of work. As it happened, a company of fit-up actors were playing in Waterford city and by lying about her age and experience, Hazel, after a peremptory audition, had secured a job as an actress-dancer.

So, though the wandering life was all she had known she nurtured a fixed picture in her mind, an *Old Woman of the Roads* picture, of a little house, hearth and stool, with heaped-up fire, dresser, speckled delph and all. She pictured herself sweeping the floor with an old-fashioned broom and using wadded newspapers to polish the little windows until they shone.

This man who wanted to marry her seemed to promise such stability and for a while it seemed her little dream had come true in the flat they rented while saving up for a house – Hazel's husband did not believe in debt. She threw herself enthusiastically into homemaking and although cooking defeated her, hand-sewn curtains covered their windows and their cheap furniture sprouted with home-made cushion covers made from remnants. Hazel went shopping and discussed the price of milk and bread with other young housewives like herself, accompanied her husband to the cinema, planned with him the family they would have. Their lovemaking was chaste and, since her husband would have been shocked had she demonstrated a quarter of the tricks she had learned throughout her colourful career of love, rather dull. He taught her to angle her pillowcase in a certain way on the nights she was 'safe' so that, recognizing the signal, he could initiate sex with her without anything as raunchy as pre-coital discussion. For a while she believed she was happy.

In the end, though, the flesh crawled on her back every time she heard her husband's front door key turn in the lock. And yet, when he was the one who left, she had been, contrary to what she had told Francey, upset in the extreme. There had been many men since, but none had affected her emotionally until Francey. Or at least none to the same extent.

Every time she thought about Francey she accused herself of being ridiculous: nothing so pathetic, surely, as a thirty-six-year-old yearning for a rub of the relic from youth and vigour. But each time Hazel thought that, the counter-insurgent image of that oul' fella in the Valley Ballroom arose to enrage her. That fecker had considered himself good enough to ponce around with a lovely young girl in a peach-coloured dress. He was a man so it was all right for him, beer belly and all, was it? But not for her, who took care of herself . . . Hazel marched into the bathroom of the flat and stripped off all her clothes. She looked at herself critically in the mirror, pulling in her stomach, then letting it out again to its fullest extent to see just how much damage the years had wrought. She turned sideways to see if she had sagged in the bosom department, then turned her back to the mirror to view the cheeks of her bottom. The early dance and acrobat training had stood to her: things were not all that bad. Not sixteen any more, but nothing to be ashamed of, either, even when she let her breath out. And the scar on her thigh was healing.

She was sick of moping around and feeling helpless. She was also fed up with being Miss Goody Two Shoes: all that understanding and social workery stuff was for the birds. Action. That was what was needed. 'Right,' she said aloud to her reflection, 'it's time to come out of your box . . .'

Some way or another she was going to have to see if there was any chance for her with Francey Sullivan. It was worth one good shot and if she won she won; if she didn't, no harm done except to her pride. And pride did not butter any parsnips.

First she would have to view the competition; Hazel did not like working in the dark.

When Francey went back to the stables more than an hour after he had left them he need not have worried that Dessie might be making a nuisance of himself. He found his half-brother in Amazon's stall and, if a horse could be said to be purring, Amazon, who was becoming heavy with her foal, was the perfect prototype. She was leaning against Dessie, rubbing her massive cheek along his and making contented, whiffling noises. Although it was snowing outside, the temperature in the stable was quite comfortable and Francey would not have been surprised to learn that it, too, was centrally heated. He stood without speaking to watch his half-brother's inter-action with the mare. 'That's amazing,' he marvelled, 'that horse terrorizes everyone here.'

Dessie had not heard him come in and turned around, his expression calm. 'She's beautiful,' he turned back to Amazon and with one finger, stroked the horse's nose right between the nostrils, 'aren't you? You're my favourite.' His voice was low and soft, bearing little relation to the strangulated syllables to which Francey was accustomed.

As Amazon, eyes blissfully lidded, shifted her bulk closer to her new friend, Francey brushed an accumulation of snowflakes off his shoulders. 'I just came to see if you wanted to come back to the house, but I can see you're happier here.'

'Yes,' Dessie said, 'I could live here.'

'Well, I don't think that would be such a good idea.' Francey became alarmed. It stood to reason that after the life he had led, his half-brother would be more comfortable sleeping on straw in the company of animals than in a luxury bedroom under a satin quilt but it was something not to be encouraged. 'Our father wouldn't like it, I don't think.'

'How much money do I have?' Dessie asked without warning.

'Did I not tell you?' Francey hedged.

'No, you didn't.' Dessie left the horse's side and came over to stand looking up into Francey's eyes. In the snowy light leaking through the open door his face was different: the lines of tension had relaxed and although he still did not look healthy, he no longer seemed much older than his years.

'Well,' Francey said, 'you have a great deal of money—'

'Enough to buy these horses?'

Francey gasped. 'I don't think they're for sale.'

'Well, ones like them, then?' his half-brother persisted.

'What would you do with them?' Dessie's reaction to the horses so paralleled his own that Francey was spooked.

But then Dessie reassured him. 'I'd just have them,' he replied, 'I'd like to have them for my own.' He bored into Francey, forcing him to cut the subterfuge. 'Have I enough or haven't I?'

When Francey explained, as succinctly as he could, how much they were both worth and the conditions of the will, he again saw that his half-brother defined money not in terms of wealth, security or acquisition, but only in terms of immediate want or need. Dessie took it all in but without reaction or excitement.

'Looking after horses is a hard job, Dessie.' Francey knew before his half-brother replied that the attempt to deter him was wasted.

'How hard could it be?' Dessie smiled. 'Feed them, love them, mind them, exercise them. Like dogs.'

'There's a big difference,' Francey replied. 'There's shoes and vets and stables for the winter and land, you'd need land —'

'Have I enough money for land?'

'I've just told you. You sure have.'

'Well, then.' Dessie walked back towards Amazon and patted her withers.

'There's more to it than that, even,' Francey said, after a brief silence. 'There's responsibility. You wouldn't be able to drink the way you used to,' he went on, thinking that the cliché which spoke of striking while the iron was hot could not be more apposite than in a case where there were horses involved.

'I wouldn't drink if I had horses like this.' As Dessie turned towards Francey his eyes gleamed under the bare overhead bulb. 'I wouldn't have time, Francey. I'd be minding them all the time.'

'But you like drink very much,' Francey pressed his advantage.

'I know,' Dessie admitted, 'and I know it's a problem, but I'd be willing to get help.'

This was better than Francey could ever have hoped. 'You mean real help? he asked. 'Even in a hospital – if that's what you thought was necessary,' he added hastily, seeing the expression of fear that passed across his half-brother's face.

Dessie thought for a bit. 'Yes,' he said, 'I would, Francey. And would you help me, with the money and everything? And getting some land?' he went on as eagerly as a child.

It was only then that Francey saw the flaw in what was happening. His half-brother's enthusiasm was like a child's because emotionally that was what he was. He would promise to be good, pledge the moon in return for what he wanted. It would have been criminal, however, to dash this first sign of vitality. 'Of course I'll help you,' Francey said, 'but in return will you start right now to try to cut down on the drinking? I'm sure there'll be wine at dinner tonight,' he went on, 'that'd be a good place to start.'

'But I don't like wine!'

At the sight of his half-brother's helpful expression, Francey burst out laughing. Dessie's ingenuous face was a further lesson in how far he had to be brought along in the 'civilization' process. Everyone around him would have to remember that he took most things literally.

'What's funny?' Dessie's eyes clouded now.

For the first time, Francey threw his arms around him. 'Nothing,' he said, 'you silly old eejit.'

Dessie did not seem to know how to respond to the hug and stood immobile. 'Come on,' Francey squeezed the thin back under his armpits, 'give us a hug back, it won't break you.'

After a bit he felt his half-brother's arms rise and go around his back. He felt no pressure, however. 'Come on,' he urged. 'This is another thing you have to learn if you're to be part of my family. Squeeze!'

Fed up with being ignored, Amazon clopped forward and head-butted the two of them. Dessie laughed – another first.

'Listen, Dessie,' when they came apart Francey decided that now might be a suitable time to take Hazel's advice, 'I know you've just got here and everything is very strange,' he said, 'but George, our father, I mean, has come up with an idea that I thought I'd ask you about. He was wondering if you'd like a party – a little one,' he amended, to be fair and not to put his own slant on the suggestion.

To his surprise Dessie did not shrink with alarm as he had expected. 'Whatever you think, Francey,' he said, stroking Amazon.

'It's not what I think.' Francey hesitated. 'Do you think you'd be up to it?'

'Who'd be there?'

'I suppose the family, mostly. Did you like Colin and Fleur?'

'She's beautiful,' Dessie stood very still, 'like a – calendar.' Then, as Francey stared at him, Dessie nodded for emphasis. 'Oh, yes, she's very lovely,' adding jovially, 'it's a pity she's married.'

Francey's thoughts spun. It was not only horses then – he had overlooked that Dessie was a nineteen-year-old man whose libido, presumably, was in working order. 'To get back to the party,' he said, 'I'm sure you don't want to be bothered. It'd be so new and all, and you're not even settled. What would you think?'

'I don't mind. Whatever you like, Francey,' Dessie said. 'Would there be a cake?'

Francey wondered about Dessie's mental picture of parties. 'Do you not think it might be a bit soon?' he tried again. 'You were worried about coming over here – remember how nervous you were? That was only a few hours ago, Dessie.'

But aggravatingly for Francey, who still believed George's idea to be cuckoo, no matter how many objections he put up his half-brother viewed the prospect of a party in his honour with equanimity and Francey was forced to offer to explore the idea further with their father.

Once inside, the two of them went to their respective rooms for a rest before dinner; when next Francey checked, Dessie was sleeping soundly.

Dinner had been arranged for seven o'clock and did not include Tommy and the nanny, who, although they had arrived, had eaten earlier and separately. Now, half-way through the meal, George sat like the patriarch he was in his accustomed place at the top of the table, keeping a wary eye on the faces of his three sons through one of the silences that had infested the meal. Since the beginning, both Colin's and Fleur's manner had run true to form, Colin's chatty and eager to please, Fleur's passive. Francey, his attention divided between consciousness of Fleur's presence and protectiveness of Dessie, was so uncomfortable he was finding it difficult to taste the food.

Outside the dining-room, the snow carpet, which had hardened under a covering of frost as night came on, glistened in the overspill of light from the ornamental lake. Francey fixed his eyes on its calm beauty as the clink of cutlery against plates, the swish of the serving girl's dress, the eternal wash and gurgle of water counterpointed not only the silence but the hazardous undercurrents in the room. Seated beside Dessie he thought it ironic that his half-brother was the only one at the glass table who was not wearing some form of metaphorical yashmak.

He continued to marvel at the change in Dessie's demeanour. His half-brother was more lively than Francey had ever seen him, his gaucherie considerably less crippling. Warned in advance to follow Francey's lead with cutlery and glasses and to eat slowly with his mouth closed, Dessie sat as straight as a child on his best behaviour, speaking only when spoken to. But he did respond to the desultory but polite questions of his father and Colin with, for him, some animation. And having darted a glance at Francey, he had passed on the wine when it was offered. The main difference, Francey worked out, was that for the first time, Dessie was trying to play a social role.

The only major *faux pas* was the cigarettes: none of the rest of them smoked but throughout the meal, even between mouthfuls of food, Dessie pulled with gusto on his Woodbines and despite the size and height of the sealed room, the air stank, even though George had signalled at least four times for Dessie's ashtray to be removed and a clean one brought.

As the current silence wore on, Francey reckoned it was his turn to say something and trawled through his reluctant brain. Once more he saw Fleur was wearing hardly any jewellery except for a pair of tiny diamond earrings which flashed each time she moved and it occurred to him again that she had not acknowledged receipt of his brooch. If she had not got it, he thought, he would have something to say to that concierge.

'Your dress is beautiful, Fleur,' he said at last. Even if it had not been she who was wearing it, the dress was impressive for its own sake: heavily embroidered with silver thread, sleeveless and with a high, split collar encircling Fleur's slender neck, it emphasized the delicacy of her body. He was answered, however, not by Fleur but by her husband who informed him that it was a genuine cheong-sam he had purchased in Hong Kong. The conversation lapsed again.

'Fleur tells me you called by with a gift for Tommy. That was nice, Francey.'

Francey's nerves jangled in response and he looked sharply at his half-brother. It seemed, though, that there was nothing behind Colin's words except an attempt at taking his turn at conversation. 'Oh, it was nothing,' Francey mumbled, 'I just happened to be in town.'

He did not dare glance towards Fleur straight away but when he did, she was composed.

'Did Francey ask you about my suggestion that we should have a party for you, Desmond?' George asked after the hiatus during which the sweet course was served.

'He did.' Dessie nodded vigorously.

George waited for elaboration but Dessie pulled a deep draught from the current Woodbine and then took a mouthful of ice cream. 'So what did he think?' George appealed to Francey. 'Did you have a chance to think it over?' By concentrating on picking up his spoon he did not meet Francey's eyes.

'I still don't know,' Francey was non-committal. 'I still think it's a bit soon.'

'What a wonderful idea, Dad,' Colin chimed in. 'A little supper party, yes?' For the first time that evening he addressed his wife. 'Fleur, you know some good caterers, don't you?'

'Yes, I do,' but she did not seem all that interested as Colin and George, relieved to have something safe and concrete to talk about, discussed the project.

They discovered that St Valentine's Day was coming up. 'How about that, Dessie?' George was delighted. 'There's a good excuse for a party if ever I heard one and it would take the heat off you as well. We'd know and you'd know that it was for you but everyone could just relax and have a good time.'

'Are you sure this is what you want, Dessie?' Francey, annoyed that the idea seemed to be taking on a life of its own, cut across their conversation.

'Sure, Francey.' Dessie smiled at him with naïve trust. 'I think it would be great. I was never at a party.'

'You're welcome to stay here until then,' George offered, 'or maybe you'd prefer to go to Ireland and come back again?'

Francey saw quite clearly which option their father would prefer but would not let him off the hook that easily. 'We'll see,' he said.

Later that evening, with Dessie safe in his room, Francey walked the floor of his and not because his doubts about the party had been overruled. He had known it would be difficult to be under the same roof with Fleur and not to be able to talk to her properly or privately but had convinced himself that to see her this way was better than not at all. This was not proving to be the case. Seeing her across a table, or in the drawing-room, always in company with her husband, was so frustrating it was driving him crazy. Maybe this party would prove to be a blessing after all: surely when there were others around he would get a chance to talk to her, even to snatch a few moments alone?

What was most upsetting of all, however, and what he had not expected, was the wall of blankness which she seemed to have erected between them. From time to time during dinner he had endeavoured to catch her eye, on one occasion even addressing her about something innocuous to do with her son, but received in return only a

286

non-committal murmur directed at her plate. Francey just could not understand it: when bracing himself for the dinner he had envisaged covert embarrassment, coolness, even a feigned antipathy, but this sponge-like behaviour was beyond his comprehension. He was even beginning to doubt the veracity of the experience they had had together. He had to talk to Fleur – and urgently.

He was not to catch her alone, however, until late the following morning.

Having seen Dessie into the hands of the grooms again, he was morosely drinking a cup of coffee while trying to concentrate on the tiny print in the Court Circular of the *Daily Telegraph* when Fleur, accompanied by Tommy and the nanny, came into the room for a late breakfast.

Francey sprang to his feet. 'I'll tell them in the kitchen you're here. Is Colin coming too?'

Fleur told him that Colin had breakfasted already and was closeted with the telephone, then went on to say that they were all going back to London within the next hour or so. 'You don't need to fetch anyone,' she continued, ringing a little handbell Francey had not seen before. 'It's usually so warm in this house,' she rubbed one hand against the other, 'one does not need many clothes for Inveraray. But for once it is cold in here.'

'Will I tell them to turn up the heat?' Francey, who thought it was as warm as the Palm House in Dublin's Botanic Gardens, made as though to leave the room.

'Don't bother,' Fleur shrugged, 'as I said, we are going soon anyway.' Then she signed something to Tommy, who trotted out of the room.

Turning back to Francey she introduced him to the nanny, a tall, pale girl in her mid-twenties. It was a revelation to Francey that nannies could be the same age as himself: in books they were always old and buxom and Scottish. With Tommy out of the room, he seized his chance. 'Could I have a quick word, Fleur?'

'Of course.' Fleur walked towards the table. 'Let's sit down, I see it is snowing again.' As she pulled out a chair she looked away from him towards the whirling white flakes.

'I mean, on our own.' Francey smiled at the nanny to show it was nothing personal. 'Family business.'

'No problem at all,' the girl smiled back, 'I'll go and make sure

Tommy brings you the right sweater, Mrs Mannering.' She hurried off.

'Oh, Fleur!' In three strides, Francey was across the room and sitting opposite her at the table. 'I thought I'd never get you alone.'

Seeing that her expression remained impassive he faltered, 'I've been wanting to talk to you so badly —' He had to break off because one of the maids came in with a fresh pot of coffee, a rack of toast and a silver teapot.

Fleur, who might have been in Harrods' tea-room in the company of a maiden aunt, ordered cereal for Tommy and told the girl that she and the nanny would fend for themselves from the hotplates on the sideboard. Francey, caring little if the maid caught him, devoured Fleur with his eyes while she spoke. Her hair was pulled back off her face under an Alice band this morning and instead of a T-shirt over the jeans he remembered so well from his visit to the flat, she was wearing a madras cotton blouse. After what seemed like an interminable amount of checking under the silver domes which lined the sideboard, the maid left the room. 'Please, Fleur,' Francey begged, 'there isn't much time before we're interrupted again. You've got to say when we can see each other again.'

'Thank you for your gift,' Fleur replied. 'It was very charming.'

'Did you really like it?' Francey was again off-balance. She had a way of cutting the ground from under him; this was not the way he had expected the conversation to turn and at present he could not give a fig for social niceties.

'I liked it very much, so small and delicate.' She said nothing more, pouring tea into her cup.

'I didn't know what you'd like,' Francey hesitated, 'you don't seem to wear much jewellery.'

Fleur touched one of her earrings, the same ones she had worn last night. 'I love jewellery.'

Francey thought he heard the nanny's discreet cough outside the door and interrupted, begging, 'Quickly, Fleur, when?'

But Fleur took her time, studying him. 'Telephone me when you come to London,' she murmured finally as Francey's fear that the nanny was about to enter grew to agonizing proportions, 'any time after Monday lunch.'

'Excuse me,' the nanny was hovering in the doorway, 'have you finished?'

288

'Come in,' Fleur beckoned to the girl, then, to Tommy as well, signing, 'Come on in, darling, thank you very much.' As she smiled at her son and took the sweater from him, she seemed little older than he.

Hazel waited until Sunday night before making her telephone call to Inveraray Manor. 'How's it going, sport?' she asked when Francey came on the line.

'Great!' To her surprise Francey sounded euphoric, his voice rising and falling with excitement. 'Absolutely wonderful.'

'Whoa!' Hazel cautioned. 'So what's changed to make things so great? The last time —'

'Everything, Hazel, just everything.' Francey fell over himself to get the words out. 'Dessie's fine, he adores the horses here and he's even starting to come out of his shell a bit so that I'm able to leave him more to his own devices.'

'I'm glad things are starting to go right for you, young fella, you were starting to sound old before your time.' Then, although she kept her voice light, Hazel stiffened every muscle in her legs. 'And? Come on, Francey, what else?'

'We-e-eel —'

'Yes?' she invited.

'Fleur's here, of course.' Francey lowered his voice.

'Of course,' Hazel prompted, 'so what's happening on that front?' She forced herself to laugh. 'You can tell your auntie Hazel!'

'Oh, nothing much!' Francey's voice was fluffed with gaiety.

'I see!' she endeavoured to match him. 'Watch it there, buster, if "nothing much" happens much more you'll go into orbit – Oh, by the way,' she continued, her voice elaborately casual, 'I've been meaning to ask you, did you ever mention anything to Dessie about that party?'

'Yeah,' Francey said, 'and you won't believe it, but you were right, Hazel. You should be a psychiatrist. He's not against the idea at all.'

'Well, what do you know!' Hazel grinned – *so far so good* – then she adjusted her features in case the grin might transmit. 'So when is this whingding?'

As he told her about the party and the guest list, she was only half listening as she checked through the small diary she kept by the telephone. *Dammit*, she thought, *where was that page* . . . 'Go on,' she encouraged.

Then she saw the fates were on her side. The Rollers' Valentine's night gig was at a private party; they had the Saturday, the party night, off and the Sunday date – Sunday was the biggest dancing night in Ireland – was in Kildare, well within striking distance of Dublin. If she took a plane from Cork and flew back to Dublin she could make it with ease. 'Sounds great,' she said when Francey paused for breath. 'Are you sure Dessie'll be able for it?'

'I'm beginning to think he might be.'

'Who'll be there for you, though?' Hazel stiffened again, not only her legs this time but her back and arms as well. This was the big one . . .

'What do you mean?'

Hazel might have laughed if this had not been so crucial. 'I mean, sunshine,' she replied briskly, 'who's going to be there to give *you* a bit of moral support?'

'Well,' Francey appeared to ponder, 'the rest of the family, I suppose.'

'Well that's all right then,' she responded. 'If you're sure that's going to be enough. I mean, shouldn't you ask some of your own family?'

'They wouldn't come all this way just for a party, Hazel. Anyway,' he pointed out, 'they're in mourning.'

'Sorry.' Hazel paused. 'Hey! I've just thought of something. I'm free on Saturday night so would you like me to come over? After all I'm more or less family now.'

'Well—'

She rushed on before his doubts could take hold. 'As a matter of fact, I've to be in London some time in the next few weeks anyway. I've had a bit of good news, Francey. There's an agent who wants to take me on. I was going to leave it until we were doing the Lent tour but I could kill two birds with one stone.' With a 'dispensation' for St Patrick's night, Irish ballrooms were closed in Lent and most of the top showbands packed up and went on tour in England.

'I'm going to London tomorrow myself,' Francey said slowly. 'To see . . .' He stopped, then: 'Do you understand? I'm *invited*, Hazel.'

Hazel, who knew precisely what he was signalling, kept her reaction under control. 'That's marvellous, Francey,' she said. 'There's no keeping up with you. Be sure to let us know how you get on, won't you?'

At the other end, Francey's voice softened, 'Of course I will, you're my best friend. And you're the only one who knows anything about this,' he sounded cautious, 'so if you do come to this party, Hazel, you'll be sure to keep that in mind, won't you?'

Although she knew she had been no angel herself, jealousy gnawed at the inside of Hazel's stomach as she reassured Francey that *if* it worked out and she made it to the party, she would keep her mouth zipped.

One shot, she said to herself after she hung up, *just give me one shot*. She had one thing going for her over the Siamese twin, she thought. At least she was single.

Chapter Fifteen

Before keeping his appointment at Fleur's flat late on the Monday afternoon, Francey went shopping. He bought an enormous bouquet of blooms he could not have named, and even though Tommy would be away at school, a pair of exotic, rainbow-coloured fish, fish food, gravel, aquatic plants and a small aquarium. He took a taxi to the jeweller's shop he had patronized before Christmas and leaving everything on the back seat of the vehicle, told the driver he would not be long. To his delight, the diamond watch was still available, but as he paid for it with the first cheque he had ever written, he was unheeding of the smiles from which he had got such a kick less than a month previously.

Fleur seemed to love the watch. 'Thank you so very much,' she said, as she allowed him to fasten it on her wrist from which it hung at least an inch too big.

'I'll take it back to have the bracelet adjusted,' Francey offered eagerly but she demurred, telling him she would have it dealt with herself. Then she rang for tea.

'I don't want tea.'

'Ah, but I do.' Fleur evaded Francey's ardent attempts to take her in his arms. 'So civilized, do you not think so?'

Francey, reasoning that since Fleur had asked him here she must want him, was forced to his customary conclusion that it was her eastern background which was responsible for her sang-froid. For someone who was about to make love, her coolness was remarkable. He, on the other hand, was finding it difficult to sit still but managed to summon up what he hoped was a friendly smile for the girl – the same one as before – who brought the tea and who returned his smile with a tiny bow of recognition.

During the fifteen or twenty minutes it took to ingest dainty food he did not want and the flavour of which he could not taste, Francey tried to behave as though this was normal carry-on. Fleur's hair was caught in a thick coil at the crown of her head by a pair of combs, and she was wearing the jeans she seemed to love, and which he now thought of as 'his', with a buttoned cardigan in apricot angora. To his dazzled eyes, her hair against the pastel seemed blacker than before, the skin of her throat smoother and even more refined. She did not seem to be wearing a bra. As he put yet another morsel into his untasting mouth, Francey could already feel his hand sliding down under the softness of that wool, the warmth of the skin underneath, the firmness of the small breast. With every second, his agitation grew. She would have been blind not to have noticed, he thought, yet she gave no sign that she had.

When at last she finished, Fleur touched a napkin to her mouth then stood and smiled at him. Francey's heart seemed to expand into his stomach as without a backward glance she walked towards the boudoir. By the time he got there, which could not have been more than thirty seconds later, Fleur was already naked, except for the diamond watch which dangled from her wrist as, with her back to Francey, she loosened her hair from the combs. In the subdued lighting, the vividly coloured surroundings, her honey-skinned body looked too precious to touch, like that of a shrine goddess. She turned round and smiled. 'There you are, I did not hear you come in.'

She walked towards him, the diamonds on the watch flashing in the glow of a nearby lamp as she touched his breast pocket. 'You must remove your suit.'

'Yes,' Francey whispered, then with recovering confidence, 'would you like to help me off with it?'

She eased the jacket over his shoulders and, turning her back on him again, folded it so the lining was outside, taking her time. As she leaned over to place it on the seat of the *chaise-longue*, Francey saw she bent further than was strictly necessary so her buttocks were presented. Accepting the implied invitation he went behind her and folded her into him, one hand taking one of her breasts, the other seeking between her thighs. Fleur arched her back and froze.

He turned her round a little and lifted her. She lay supine across his arms, eyes closed and head thrown back so that he could see her entire body. She weighed as little as a child. Hearing a singing in his ears, he sat on the side of the bed and played with her, lifting her

293

hair, kissing her neck, biting gently on her shoulders. He whispered endearments as he licked the soft places just under her jaw, telling her how much he loved her, loved her, loved her . . .

Fleur's eyes opened. 'I want to please you,' she said.

'Love me, Fleur.' Francey's voice was hoarse.

'Of course,' she slipped off his lap but as he reached for her again she intercepted his hands, her eyes glinting with a flash of amusement, 'do you wish to keep your clothes on while we make love?' She reached for the belt of his trousers. 'What would you like? You must tell me.'

Somehow, Francey held on to a semblance of control. He was determined that this time he would not be the passive one, having things done to or for him. He had planned and fantasized too much about this encounter to let that happen. 'No,' he trapped her hands against his stomach, 'this time is for you. It's my turn to please you, Fleur. It's your turn to tell me what you'd like.'

'I want to make you happy.' She sat back into his lap and slid one hand out from under his and down towards his groin.

Francey groaned as he found that somehow his fly had been opened and her hand was inside it. He kissed one of her breasts. 'Don't,' he begged, 'please don't, I want this to be —' He could speak no longer, Fleur was opening his belt with her other hand, her lips were against his stomach, her tongue now doing something with his navel . . . Making a superhuman effort, he pulled her off him and rolled her on to the bed. 'You want to know what I want?' he asked, pulling at his tie, tearing at his shirt. 'I want to make love to you better than you've ever been made love to before in your life.' Fleur's dark eyes were inscrutable as, stretched on the sumptuous covers, she watched him rip off the rest of his clothes.

For the next ten minutes or so she was a willing co-conspirator in the delusion that she was the one being pleasured as, remembering some of the lessons he had learned with Hazel and finding Fleur responsive to his every initiative, Francey grew more and more daring. To his delight, she moaned and cried occasional words of encouragement, writhing under his probing fingers, lips and tongue. She seemed to enjoy everything, even the exposure and stimulation of the most intimate parts of her. But as he experimented with her body – 'Is that nice? Do you like this?' – the sights, sounds and feel of her became too much and, unable to resist any longer, shuddering with excitement, he rolled on to his back and pulled her on top of him. He heard her cry out as she impaled herself on him and, within seconds, he was coming.

A few minutes later, as they came apart and she made as though to get off the bed, he pulled her back. 'Don't go yet, what's your hurry?'

'No hurry.' She lay down beside him but he could already sense the separating of the strands that had bound them. 'Did you really enjoy it?' he asked, getting up on one elbow to search her face.

'Yes.' Her expression was serious. 'I think you must know that.'

'You didn't come, though.'

'No.' The unvarnished reply did not surprise him. He was becoming accustomed to Fleur's directness.

'Did I not do enough for you?'

'I do not come,' Fleur stated incontrovertibly.

But Francey noticed her choice of verb. She had not said she *could* not come. 'May I try again?' he asked. 'I won't be so quick this time, I promise.'

'Perhaps the next time.' Fleur lay very still which left him every opportunity and none.

Francey, registering the implied promise, decided not to force anything physical right now but satiation had made him bold. 'I want to know everything about you, Fleur,' with one finger he stroked her lovely cheek, 'everything. Sometimes, when we make love, I think I'm getting to know you and then you slip away again. Like now, for instance. I feel very close to you but I get the feeling that you're already away somewhere else in your head.'

She closed her eyes and this, together with her continuing immobility, unnerved him. He withdrew his hand from her face. 'Is it Colin? Are you worried about what we're doing behind his back?'

'I told you before, I think, that Colin and I in many ways lead separate lives.'

Warning bells sounded in Francey's head. Separate lives? Did that mean they were each free to have affairs – and did she do this kind of thing often? 'I'm not the first, am I?' He pulled back from her a little, but then, having heard the tone of possessive jealousy, regretted the outburst. 'Sorry,' he seized her in his arms, 'that was a stupid thing to say. Forget it altogether. It's just that—' He ran out of words and hugged her.

She let him hug her until he was defeated by her passivity then opened her eyes at last. 'So many questions,' she said softly.

'Sorry,' he repeated, struck with the fear that he had already trespassed beyond the boundary she seemed to set around her privacy. He could not have borne to drive her away now and at present was willing to accept all of the unspoken and puzzling conditions that hedged their relationship. Releasing her, he attempted a wry smile. 'I'll try to remember to keep my mouth shut in future. No questions. We'll just enjoy each other when we're able to, all right?'

'You're pleased with the watch at any rate?' He knew it was the most craven of questions.

'I think it is very beautiful, Francey.' She slid it over her hand without opening the catch and placed it on the pillow between them. 'I shall keep it very safe and wear it only for state occasions.' She got off the bed, and as she had done the last time they were together, padded across to the armoire and put on her kimono. Then, also as before, she wrung out a handtowel and came back to wipe the cooled sweat from Francey's face. 'Dear Francey,' she said, 'you are a very generous and kind boy.'

'I love you, Fleur.' He closed his eyes to pinch off the strange pain which darted in him as she used his name with such affection. Francey could no longer play games. 'I don't care if you're married. I don't care about any of it, I love you. I'll love you until I die.'

Fleur kissed him on the lips. 'Our time is short but good. Think of the good things.'

Then she was beyond his reach and on her way to the door.

Unlike the last time he and Fleur had been together, Francey recovered his physical and mental faculties in short order. He supposed it had a lot to do with the length of time for which they had made love: next time, he vowed, he was going to ensure he had more self-control.

While washing, he reminded himself that it would take more than determination to win Fleur Mannering and saw that again he was not just thinking in terms of an affair: he would not be satisfied until she was his. Leaving morality aside – and at rock bottom Francey was still not sure that he could – what would it take? More than sex, that was for sure. Or at least more than the sex he could offer her at present. He thought back over their encounter, which in many ways had been so good for him and yet, because this time he had had a different agenda, not quite so all-encompassing as before. He had wanted to make Fleur scream, like Hazel had.

Had he failed? She had seemed to enjoy it, yet the back of Francey's mind continued to niggle with suspicion that, far from his having won his self-imposed contest to please, Fleur had not for an instant surrendered control. She reminded him of *mála*, that infinitely malleable Plasticene he and his fellow pupils had played with in Low Babies' class in the National school. *Mála* would take any shape, any impression and yet was unsatisfying because of this. The next child to come along could with one squeeze undo all your own careful work and create his own.

He looked at his tousled reflection in the light-wreathed mirror: 'Buck up, Francey,' he mouthed, 'stop the philosophy and decide once and for all how to get what you want.' As he came back to pick up the clothes he had discarded in such a hurry, he caught sight of the watch and picked it up, weighing it in the palm of his hand.

She had been thrilled with this, that had been plain to see. It was common, he supposed, for people from a deprived background like hers to put so much store by material things. Francey had thought he had encountered poverty in the mountain cabins of Béara or the slums of Dublin but had revised his notion of what being penniless meant when he had heard first-hand just how the ragpicking poor lived in those tar paper shacks by the river in Bangkok.

It was no wonder Fleur was such a complex personality. Anyone who had escaped such a grinding existence and come to live in a world which included not only Colin Mannering and his luxury flat but George Gallaher and Jool with their fantasy manor in the country would have to have been overwhelmed by the change. It was natural she should be watchful and protective of herself. As he put himself in Fleur's shoes, Francey saw the daily fear of somehow being reduced again to penury. He decided then that if presents would help in the wooing and winning of Fleur, then so be it. At least he had the wherewithal: once again, Francey thanked his lucky stars for Jool Dill Smith Gallaher. But before going out into the drawing-room he took a few more minutes to compose himself and to plan what he was going to say. Too many times he had put his foot in it by speaking without due thought. He was not going to break through that reserve by ordinary means, that was for sure.

She was standing by the window, looking out between the

curtains into the dark evening. 'I think it may snow again,' she said without turning round. 'I wish it was summer.'

'Summer will be here soon enough,' Francey replied, 'and I don't want it to be summer before we make love again.' That brought her round but he held up his hand before she could respond and stood his ground in the doorway of the boudoir. 'Don't say anything to me this time about leaving it to fate,' he said, 'or anythng silly like that. I have to see you again. I won't be put off, you know, Fleur, so you might as well tell me now. Even if it's not for months, I need a real day to look forward to or I'll go crazy. You don't want a madman on your hands now, do you? Raving and looning on your doorstep, destroying you with the neighbours?' He grinned at her, the most confident, wicked grin he could muster. Then he walked towards her. 'You forgot your new watch,' he said, holding it up. 'Give us your wrist there.'

She held it out and he fastened it on. 'There now,' he said gaily. He turned her hand over and kissed the palm then dropped it without giving her the opportunity to respond either positively or negatively. 'I love buying you presents,' he said. 'When's your birthday, Fleur?'

'I am not sure,' Fleur said but when pushed, admitted that she thought she might have been born in November. 'Well, what date in November do you celebrate it?' Francey kept his tone airy.

'Whenever Colin is at home.' She said it as though surprised he had to ask.

'Do you believe in divorce?' He changed tack.

As she did always when faced with a sudden question, Fleur considered before giving a reply. 'It is impossible to live in a divorce culture and not to see its advantages and disadvantages,' she said.

'Which outweighs the other, in your opinion?'

'That depends on the individual circumstances.' Fleur shrugged but Francey, who was watching her closely, saw the small line of uncertainty between her eyes.

His objective had been to see if he could throw her off her stride a little and he had succeeded. Nevertheless, he continued to admire her singularity: he could not imagine Hazel, or his mother, or any of his sisters, not following up this line of questioning by asking why he had introduced such a topic. 'Never mind,' he kissed her as tenderly as he knew how, 'it's not a topic for today. We'll talk about it some other time. So when will we meet again?'

She held his gaze for a few seconds. 'Telephone me.'

'Tonight, tomorrow?' Then he saw he had gone too far and backtracked. 'Some day this week, then,' he amended as though the matter was settled. He dropped his act and took her in his arms. 'You don't know what you have here, Fleur,' he said, his voice husky. 'I'm giving you due warning.'

'If I am not here when you telephone, I shall see you at the party. I am looking forward to meeting our new brother again.' Fleur leaned back in his embrace.

'Goodbye, Fleur,' he let her go, 'I'll telephone you in a few days.'

Francey hardly dared breathe until he was out in the street again. He had hit most of his targets: she had accepted another date and he had at least introduced the subject of divorce. He was in this for the long haul and although the morality of it continued to bother him, he would have to leave that for later consideration. So far, he thought, he and Fleur had not hurt anyone and that was the main thing, surely?

Fleur, her face thoughtful, rang the bell so the Filipino could come to clear the tea-things.

Francey had caught her out with that sudden mention of divorce; her scheme included no such option. She planned to fade quietly out of Colin's life and had no wish to cause him, or anyone else, any more trouble than was inevitable. To give Colin his due, she thought, her antagonism to him was instinctive: he had certainly done nothing overt to deserve the deliberate infliction of distress. By his own lights he had been a good husband and at first, having got to know the story of his life, Fleur had surprised herself by entertaining a certain sympathy for him. Although their backgrounds were dissimilar, in many ways they were alike, loners who had clawed their way out of an unpromising start. She expected that long after he and his family were nothing more than shadows in her memory, she would remember how supportive Colin had been when, barely two months after they arrived in England, Tommy's deafness had been diagnosed.

Fleur did what she always did whenever she needed reassurance, she went into her boudoir, closed and locked the door, and checked the contents of her safe. As well as the new diamond watch, she had two other items in hand for encashment at present, one was an antique atomizer in gold and Venetian glass, the other was Francey's first gift, a curious lapel pin worked in gold, silver and turquoise, a stylized representation of some animal, at Fleur's best guess, a cat. It had arrived by post at the flat on Christmas Eve just before they had left to come down here.

Unlike the watch, the little cat was hardly worth a waste of her jeweller-friend's time, and as she gazed down at it Fleur knew she had miscalculated in the matter of Colin's brother. Perhaps she had allowed herself to be misled because he was the first Irishman with whom she had had personal social dealings; she had had no Irish clients in Bangkok, and although she had met a few Irishmen on the dinner-party circuit none had asked her out. Accustomed since the Lily Garden days to making snap generalizations about national character traits, she found she had not liked these Irish any more than the English: they were somewhat more entertaining in that they had talked more than anyone else and seemed to know a lot of jokes, but they got drunk with great ease and then tended to insult people.

Francey had until this evening reminded her of a big, clumsy St Bernard puppy, beautiful but naïve; yet underneath all that awkwardness, she had thought she had sensed an honest solidity which, for its novelty value, intrigued her. So much so, she now saw, that at the time of the walk in the wood and their subsequent dinner together, she had dropped her guard. But as he had continued to push and probe, Fleur realized she had let herself become careless. She had told him too much; this one was too close to home and what was worse, he did not seem to have enough sense or experience to know what was on and off limits. This one was in love.

And that mention of divorce had been exceptionally dangerous.

Maybe, however, Francey had done her a favour. Fleur recognized that as well as becoming incautious, she had perhaps grown a little greedy. When the diamonds she had accumulated were added to the income Jool had ensured for her and Jool's own jewels, she already had more than enough for the rest of her life. Perhaps now was the time to call a halt and to consider activating her plan.

On his return to Inveraray from London after his date with Fleur, Francey found Dessie comatose in the drawing-room, an upturned bottle of whisky on the floor beside the sofa on which he had passed

300

out. He decided not to make a fuss and carried his half-brother to bed.

Dessie had slept it off and the following morning seemed little the worse for wear. 'It won't happen again,' he said to Francey over the table in the sunny breakfast room, 'sorry.'

'Is it the party? Is that what you're worried about?'

'A bit,' Dessie said, then paused. 'To tell you the truth,' he admitted, 'that's not the reason. It's not the party at all, it's just that the drink was there and I was there too. I'm looking forward to the party, honest, Francey.'

'All those people? All that fuss and noise, everyone looking at you? Don't you think it would be better to postpone it a little, until you're feeling a little better? Or even make it smaller, just invite people to lunch or something?'

'I'm feeling fine, honestly. And won't you be there? And Father?' Dessie's eyes were wide and trusting.

His use of that nomenclature for George Gallaher seemed so surprising and anachronistic to Francey that he had to hide a smile. 'Of course we'll be there,' busying himself with his breakfast so Dessie would not think he was laughing at him.

'And won't everyone be looking at each other too? And not only at me?'

Staring across the table at him again, Francey had to admit he was projecting his own fears. Dessie was so childlike he might even enjoy this blasted event.

But he was not yet ready to let go completely. 'To get back to the drink,' he said, 'there'll obviously be a lot of it around at this party. Are you going to be able to cope with that side of things?'

'I promise, Francey, I promise. Now can we talk about something else?' It was the first hint of an attempt by Dessie to take the initiative in a conversation, a show of embryo independence which gladdened Francey so much so that he stopped nagging. The previous night's episode was a warning, however, that his half-brother's progress must not be taken too much for granted and he continued to worry.

But the rest of the week passed calmly and when compared with his former self, Dessie was so well that Francey, seeing him growing a little stronger and more confident by the day, felt justified in leaving him to his own devices for longer and longer periods. His half-brother spent almost every waking hour in the stables, even managing to lower his Woodbines intake because of the strict rules about smoking in the yard. He became firm friends with the stable hands and each time Francey went to check on him, was either engaged in horsy chores or taking tea-and-smoke breaks in the tack-room.

Free to pursue his own interests, Francey explored the Manor's hinterland in the sturdy Morris Oxford he had bought from a dealer in Leamington Spa on the Tuesday of that week. The old Francey would have thought this a risky endeavour: he had not decided, after all, where he was going to live. The new, spendthrift Francey, however, said the hell with it: if he was not going to settle here, he'd sell the car or give it away or even leave it to rot outside Inveraray Manor to drive George and the fussy butler mad. And while there was enough of the old Francey left to feel that he did not yet deserve the acquisition of the longed-for Morgan, this was buried in the file of dreams for the future.

To give him his due, George had offered Francey the use of one of the Inveraray cars for the duration of his stay; but he preferred to steer clear of any obligations towards his father and in any event believed himself not yet an experienced enough driver to handle one of the Manor's showy cars. For the present, the Morris suited him fine as he tootled around the pristine villages. Although, for Dessie's sake, Francey was being more than civil to their father, the row had caused such a setback in the advance of their relationship that Francey felt that he and George would probably never get on well. As it happened they had had little opportunity to make it up as George now seemed to spend most of his time in London.

In between excursions, Francey spent a good deal of time on the telephone, to Mr Solomons in London who was going to take over Dessie's affairs, to Lahersheen, to Hazel, whose plans to be at the party had firmed up. Now he was glad he had accepted her offer to come: he welcomed the prospect of her sturdy support in what could prove a difficult evening. He was also looking forward to seeing her face and hearing her comments when he showed her round the house: he could just imagine what she would think about the dining-room and its glass table. The one fly in the ointment was the slight danger that she might somehow betray to Fleur that she too had been to bed with him but the more Francey thought about it, the more he trusted her; she must have been through millions of such scenarios before.

He had been holding off on telephoning Fleur but on the Thursday morning the longing to contact her became acute. He decided to telephone her that afternoon, around the time she would be taking her afternoon tea, and to distract himself in the interim, he set off again in the car.

After all the snow, the weather had picked up and, for February, was quite balmy, so much so that he was even able to roll down the Oxford's window, revelling in the sharp freshness of the air, which was such a contrast to the artificially scented, sealed antisepsis within the house. Spring was well advanced this year; the birds were busy and the fields were sheeny with the beginnings of new growth.

Never pushed about scenery when he was younger, Francey found that as he grew older he was noticing more about natural surroundings. He even had to admit that he was beginning to understand what foreigners saw in the wild land and seascapes around Lahersheen. These rolling, ordered vistas could not have been more different from what he was used to at home; and it was not just topography, it was the way the country was presented and maintained. The word 'manicured' came to mind. Ireland was messy, no doubt about it: in summer, the hedgerows along even the best roads straggled willynilly to the sky, and on the smaller ones, untamed grasses and wildflowers rampaged from the verges. Except in a few of the fatter counties, fields were lumpy and uneven, cattle nosing through rocks and stones or sinking to their hocks in bogs and marshes between indestructible crowns of sedge. By contrast, these Warwickshire fields were as smooth as lawns and although there was no stock on them at present, Francey could just imagine what the cows would look like here when they were put out – jigsaw perfect.

Another eye-opener was the difference in the arrangements of the farm buildings: while in Ireland a farmhouse, known merely as 'Scollard's' or 'Harrington's' often effaced itself at the end of a boreen, here the farmer's dwelling stood proud on the road, proclaiming itself as Bull and Butcher Farm or Mickle Hill Farm.

Seeing the world through the eyes of a man in love, everything was new and enchanting to Francey, and within the past day or so, he had begun collecting Warwickshire names, writing the best ones in a little notebook for the joyful novelty of the way they felt on his tongue when he spoke them aloud, villages and little towns as well as the farms: Weston under Wetherley, Kites Hardwick, Birdingbury,

Ashby St Ledgers, Long Itchington, Leek Wootton, Bishop's Tach-brook, Bubbenhall, Hampton Lucy – who was Lucy? And when he followed the signposts to the some of the places bearing these enchanting names they proved to be little more than crossroads. Yet who in their right mind would want to live in a place called Snitterfield? Or the even more weird Wootten Wawen?

The villages – all clipped ivy, roses-around-the-porch and bandbox paint – were so like the illustrated books of Francey's childhood that as he passed through them he already knew where the post office, complete with red pillar box, would be. Little Staunton was just such a picture-perfect village and as he strolled along its wide curved street, Francey half expected Noddy or Big Ears to come popping up from behind a gate.

Today, as he bowled along between the low hedges, he passed well-mannered children riding ponies, real village greens, with real, symmetrical ponds, one complete with ducks. It was all so seductive that it took him a while to understand what he would miss if he lived around here. It was only when he went into a pub that he saw it.

The pub was hushed, burnished, almost empty. The four elderly men who were there, too polite to give Francey more than a quick glance as he walked in, spoke over their drinks in subdued tones. They all wore tweeds; one, a spaniel at his feet, rested his chin on a walking stick. Francey ordered a Scotch – forgetting that with the miserable English measures he should have ordered a double – and retired with it to a corner to consult his road map and to see if he could find any more names that tickled his fancy. It was then that it hit him. In an environment as ordered as this, the element of chance was missing. The most humble life in Ireland was led with a hopeful eye to what lay in store just around the corner. Conversely, everyone also allowed for the possibility of chaos. Francey could well imagine that the maps of life for these four men, sitting so peacefully in their corner, had been followed as laid out with little deviation no matter what the bigger world threw at them. World wars, death: he could picture these four ploughing through. It was what made them great. As he stared at the map on his lap, he became convinced there must be a correlation between human characteristics and local landscape.

If he could go to Bangkok he might discover the key to Fleur, but realizing this was wildly impractical – and would arouse suspicion – he resolved instead to read as much as he could about Thailand. He ordered a sandwich, postponing his return to Inveraray Manor for as long as he could, knowing that he would not be able to stop himself telephoning her the minute he got home.

He forgot about landscape, national characteristics, all of it, as, taking shortcuts, he drove home, where, to his disappointment, the telephone was answered by the maid who said her mistress was out and was not expected home until late that evening.

Assuming that the maid would tell Fleur he had called and not wishing to scare her off by seeming too persistent, Francey decided not to call that night but to leave it until the following morning. When Friday dawned, however, he figured it unlikely she would invite him up to London straight away so there was little point. He might as well hold on now, he thought gloomily over his breakfast, until he saw her at the party the following night.

Preparations for this party were so relaxed and unseen that it was difficult to know they were going on at all; this was what it meant to have servants, Francey thought, adding a butler to his ever-lengthening list of planned acquisitions when he got himself settled. His ambitions were beginning to seem as elastic as Hazel's compo, he thought, grinning. He did not feel like driving around on his own again today and, wondering if Dessie could be prised away from his beloved horses to come along for company, went to the stableyard to ask him.

Unlike Francey, Dessie had become a dab hand at the complicated business of grooming and adornment of the horses and had taken to climbing on the animals' backs. Although they were not for riding, they were of such an agreeable temperament that Mick O'Dowd had taught him how to urge them on with knee and heel. So it was that when Francey arrived at the yard, his half-brother, a wide grin on his face and his legs straddled wide across Jumbo's broad bare back, was lumbering around as happy as a small child riding a seaside donkey.

'Hey you,' Francey called, 'Lester Piggott.'

Dessie looked round and waved. 'Want to come up?' he invited.

'Do you fancy a drive? It's a lovely day.'

'Think I'll stay here.' Dessie fondled Jumbo's ears. 'I'm busy now, Francey. There's a lot to do around a stableyard, you know.'

His self-importance made Francey smile. 'Could you use an extra pair of hands, then?'

'I'll ask the gaffer.' Dessie slid off the horse's back, gratifying

Francey with his physical improvement and entertaining him by how quickly he was picking up the patois.

Despite Dessie's assertion about being busy, however, there being no firm prospect for the horses of work or showing, Francey could see little to occupy him in the yard. The accoutrements and harness already shone like gold and silver, all manes and tails were beribboned and the stalls were fragrant with new straw. But Dessie always found something: a gutter overlooked, a trough less than full. His voice thrilling with new-found knowledge and responsibility, he showed off purely for Francey's benefit, explaining the niceties of the Shires' dress code: that horse brasses such as those he was now attaching to Jumbo's martingale, traditionally belonged to the grooms and not to the animals' owners.

'And look at this, Francey – here, Francey, look,' pulling at the sleeve of Francey's coat, 'this fella's girth is more than nine and a half feet. And he weighs nearly a ton and half. Can you imagine? And I suppose you know already that his tail is for swishing flies off but did you know that horses have special skin muscles at the front where the tail can't reach so they can shiver off the flies – I'll bet you didn't know that?'

'You learn something new every day!' Francey grinned. Dessie's enthusiasm was infectious and, in any event, where Francey was concerned his half-brother was preaching to the converted.

The early part of the morning thus passed enjoyably and as he was helping Dessie tease out the feathers around Goliath's mammoth feet, Francey took the opportunity to ask his half-brother about something which had been on his mind. 'Do you ever think about your mother, Dessie?'

'Sometimes.' Dessie seemed more concerned with his work than with the question.

'I mean, how do you feel about her? Do you think we should try to find her, for instance?' Under the pretence of examining closer the hoof on which he was working, Francey squatted the better to see his half-brother's face.

Dessie shrugged. 'I couldn't care less.'

'I don't believe you, Dessie. Whatever she's done, she's your mother.'

'I told you, I couldn't care less.'

Francey, seeing Dessie was becoming agitated, set about calming

306

him. 'All right, quiet down, I do believe you. And don't worry about it, I'm not going to do anything without your knowledge.'

Dessie hesitated. Then, in a flat voice, 'She's probably dead.'

'Don't worry about it now, Dessie, I'm sorry I brought it up. Just so long as you know that I'm available any time you want to talk about it. Now, what about this work we're supposed to be doing?' Francey worked to rekindle the sense of harmony which had existed between them before he had mentioned Kathleen and succeeded in re-establishing his half-brother's mood to the extent that within five minutes, Dessie was again ordering him around, telling him he was making a mess of plaiting Goliath's tail.

Watching Dessie's deft hands unravelling the thick hair, Francey wondered if he should initiate a serious search for Kitty Scollard, dead or alive. He could start by trying to locate a death certificate. Perhaps, he thought then, it might be just as well to wait until Dessie himself suggested something. He made a mental note to sit down by himself at the earliest opportunity to examine the whole concern.

Later that morning, during one of the yard's many teabreaks, Francey found himself revealing his ambitious – and improbable – plan to establish a show-centre for the Shires in Ireland, not just to Dessie but to the rest of the men. He could have predicted Dessie's reaction of uncomplicated excitement but to his considerable surprise, none of the others laughed at him either. 'You have something there,' Mick O'Dowd observed. 'At least the poor beasts would be doing something. The Guv'nor hasn't been next, nigh or near the yard for months.'

'Yeah,' another chimed in, 'we're all a bit worried.'

It had occurred to Francey before now that the Shires were an expensive hobby for George, particularly as, since his wife's death, he seemed more interested in going up to London to stay with his friends than in anything to do with the house or yard. Then he remembered that ages ago he had promised to ask what his father's plans were for the horses. 'I know I said I'd find out for you, I just forgot,' he apologized, 'I'll bring it up as soon as I can. It's early days yet,' he went on, 'but who knows? Maybe my father will want rid of them altogether and he'll let me have them. But it's Ireland I'd want to show them, if I do,' he reiterated cautiously, seeing that most of the men were more than a little interested. He hoped he had not given them false hope.

'We could do it together, Sullivan and Scollard!' Dessie's eyes shone in his thin face. 'What about that, Francey?'

'Right,' Francey agreed, 'rings like chimes, doesn't it?' What had he started? But before he could put a curb on his tongue, he heard himself offering everyone in the yard a job in Ireland if and when the venture took shape.

'That'd be great,' Mick O'Dowd looked around the circle of weathered faces and they all began to discuss Ireland among themselves. After that, no matter how much Francey warned them that nothing might come of the idea, they were not put off.

As Francey stood to leave, Mick O'Dowd pulled him aside. 'Could I have a word?' he muttered.

'Sure.' Francey walked a few yards with him until they were out of earshot of the others. 'What's up?'

'You're having a party tomorrow up at the house.' Mick spat towards a nearby drain then went on to tip Francey off about one of the expected guests, a Colonel Shottley from Oxfordshire, who, in his opinion, had the best Shire stallion in England. 'You could do with new blood,' he went on, delving into detail about legs and feathering and conformation, much of which passed over Francey's head. What had he got himself into? Mick seemed to assume his takeover of the horses. No less than the party, this idea, once spoken, seemed to be taking on a life of its own.

'I'll bear the Colonel in mind,' he said faintly when the other man seemed to have wound down.

'Good,' Mick spat again, 'and by the way,' he added, 'your brother over there's handy enough with the animals. You could do worse than take him on as a partner in your new show. Give us a few months and he'll be nearly as good as meself.'

Francey spilled all this out to Hazel on the way back to the Manor from Leamington railway station the following afternoon. 'Gives them something to hope for,' she said, 'don't worry about it, Francey. For God's sake, you don't have to take on everyone – you're like Charles Atlas, you look as if you've the world on your shoulders.'

'I feel I have,' Francey admitted.

'You're tryin' to do everything too fast.' She touched his knee. 'Take your time. And you're not responsible for all those workmen, no matter what you think. Now, change the subject for God's sake. Tell us what to expect tonight.'

'Well, the servants are getting everything ready, of course, and I try not to know too much.' Francey had to brake to avert calamity as a tiny shrew dashed across the roadway thirty yards ahead. 'Otherwise,' he continued, 'I'd go demented worrying about Dessie.'

Something prevented him mentioning that even more than his fears for Dessie he was worrying about how he would handle the presence of Fleur. Instead, he went on to comment that the English did not seem to observe the formal mourning periods they were used to in Ireland. 'Jool's only dead about four months,' he explained. 'It's just as well, I suppose, Dessie won't be so much on show. It's easier to blend in with a crowd.'

'We'll look after him all right. I'm dying to meet him. Properly, like. The last time he was in a coma or something?'

'Hardly a coma, Hazel.' Already buoyed up by her cheery presence, Francey grinned across at her.

'Whatever,' Hazel wriggled her shoulders in the passenger seat, 'I love parties, glad I came now – d'you like me new outfit?'

'Lovely.' Francey glanced sideways again: he had been so busy thinking about himself and his problems when he had picked her up he had not noticed what Hazel was wearing. Now he saw she looked very well indeed, in a coat of pale turquoise over a matching dress. 'Lovely,' he repeated, 'that colour really suits you. And you did something new to your hair?' It lay close to her head like a sleek cap and seemed less blonde than usual, more the colour of ripening wheat.

'Yeah,' Hazel twinkled over at him. 'Spent a fortune on it, all for you!'

'Compo?'

'Def'ny.'

'It's a good job we're not married to each other, Hazel, we wouldn't have a penny.' Francey chuckled as he described to her how he was spending his money like water, both literally and in his dreams, and how much he was enjoying the experience. It occurred to him that she was the only one he felt he could talk to like this. Hazel, it seemed, did not care whether he had tuppence or ten million. 'You've a great attitude to money, do you know that?'

'Do you think so?'

'I sure do,' he said fervently. 'Everyone should have a true friend like you.'

Francey got a lot more off his chest before they got to the Manor. He confided in her about his trip to London and how Fleur seemed to discombobulate him. 'Oh, I can't describe it,' he said in frustration, 'it's like one minute I'm sure, absolutely sure, that she likes me, and the next I think she thinks no more of me than the cat.' They were waiting at a stop sign for another car to go through a junction and because she was looking over her shoulder at something behind, he could not catch Hazel's eye. 'I was hoping you'd be able to give me some advice?' He touched her knee to get her attention.

'Oh, yes.' Responding to the touch she looked back at him.

'Did you ever feel like that about anyone?'

Hazel smiled. 'I know *exactly* how that is.'

Francey put the car in gear again and moved off. 'So how did you deal with it?'

'I waited,' Hazel replied at her succinct best.

Francey considered this as they drove along the perimeter wall of the Manor. 'Nearly there.' He slowed the car for the cattle grid. 'Obviously it didn't turn out for you?'

'Mmm.' Then: 'Jeez!' Hazel did a little tap dance on the floor of the car. 'Would you look at this! It's as good as the Aras.'

Francey already knew the story about how for a dare, Hazel had talked her way past the Guards to see into the grounds of the President's residence in the Phoenix Park. 'Oh, wait till you see the house,' he replied. 'I doubt if Dev's house is anything as posh as Jool's.' It was funny, he thought, but his stepmother had taken on a fully fledged personality for him even though he had never met her. In a way he did not think of her as dead: he certainly felt her presence in all the rooms of the house. 'How'd it go with your agent?' he asked.

'As it happened he wasn't available today, after all. I'll have to come back again the next time I have a break.'

'Hazel!' Francey was touched. 'You mean to say you came here especially for this?'

'Why not? You know me, I love a good party.'

'Are you sure you're all right about meeting George again after all these years?' Francey let the subject of the agent pass. Hazel's reunion with his father was something they had discussed only in passing and she had not seemed in the least concerned.

310

'Fine,' she said now, 'water under the bridge.'

'You know I haven't told him you're coming?'

'Why not?' She was curious.

'Good enough for him!' Francey retorted but did not go on to reveal the real reason. It was not all that usual, surely, that albeit separated by a lot of time, father and son had both been to bed with the same woman? This had occurred to him after it had been decided Hazel would come. And Francey might have warned George in advance, had even begun to. But his father, on being told a friend from Ireland was coming to the party, reacted with a dismissive, 'Terrific, great, tell Lewis, would you?' and Francey, furious at being patronized, had retired in a huff.

George and Hazel would just have to work it out for themselves. 'Here we are,' he said now as they rounded the last bend of the driveway and the house came into view. 'Well, what do you think?'

Hazel whistled through her teeth. 'And you've the run of this?'

Her reaction to the interior of the house was just as gratifying. Except for the servants, they had the Manor to themselves: George was expected to arrive from London in the late afternoon, Colin and his family at around the same time, and Dessie, as usual, was in the stables. The pace of preparation for the party had speeded up somewhat and when he took Hazel into the dining-room, having saved it for last, Francey saw the butler was supervising the settings for the buffet supper as two maids arranged white china and silver on the sideboard; the floral centrepiece was already in place on the glass table. 'Sorry, Lewis,' Francey apologized, 'I didn't realize you were in here, we'll come back.'

Hazel was having none of that. 'Jeez,' she breathed, pushing past Francey into the glittering room. 'I never saw anything like this in the whole of me twist – howaya, girls!' She smiled at the two maids who were working at the sideboard. She walked over to the window to peer out at the fountain then turned back to look around the room from floor to sloping ceiling. 'Look at this – would you get a load of *that* . . .' She held out her hand to the butler. 'I'm Hazel Slye.'

'How do you do, madam.' The man bowed then signalled something with his eyes to the two girls. 'We can come back later, sir,' he said to Francey as the three of them withdrew from the room.

Hazel, standing goggle-eyed in front of the aquarium, did not seem to notice they were gone. 'This is like the pictures. You'd expect to see Esther bleedin' Williams, wouldn't you?' She moved on to survey the painting on the end wall of the room, the one Francey now knew was his. 'What's it supposed to *be*?' She pursed her lips.

'I'm not sure.' Francey considered the large abstract. To him the painting, titled *Mellifluous* ≠ *6* looked like nothing more than random smudges of dark grey and dull red on a dirty white background but he had been assured it was very valuable.

'Do you like it?' Hazel turned her vivid eyes on him.

'I don't know,' Francey said, 'I'm not used to it yet.'

'If it's worth what you say it is I'd sell it if I was you,' Hazel advised, 'and if you want a nice picture for your walls, I have a contact that'd sell you one for half nothing. He got me a great one of Howth Head.' Francey was about to demur when out of the corner of his eye he caught a yellow flash beyond the fountain. Colin's MGB.

'Would you like — ?' Hazel turned around and caught the stress on his face. 'What is it?'

'They're here,' he said. 'Fleur and Colin, they've arrived.'

Something flickered in Hazel's eyes but it was fleeting and Francey was too caught up in his own reaction to interpret it before she bustled forward to grip him by both arms. 'Steady,' she said. 'Don't forget, I'll be just around the corner. Where's the ladies' in this joint? I've to powder me nose.'

'I'm afraid you'll have to go to your room.'

'All right,' Hazel replied, 'I won't be a sec. Anyway, this dress is wool, it's too hot for this place. Where did this American woman come from did you say, the bleedin' jungle?'

Francey told her he would wait for her in the lobby off the entrance hall but hung around in the drawing-room until he judged the Mannerings had gone through and were safely in the room they customarily used. His jealous heart was already summoning up the image of the two of them going into that bedroom, maybe kissing, maybe even lying down on the bed . . .

To distract himself he toyed with the idea of going to the stables to fetch Dessie but felt obliged to wait for Hazel. He had no doubt but that she could look after herself but on the other hand she was his guest.

When she came back she was dressed in a pale yellow blouse tucked into a short brown skirt and strappy shoes with such high heels that she had to take very small steps so she would not fall off them. Francey's eyes strayed to her legs. 'You'll stop the traffic tonight, Hazel,' he said, and meant it. He was surprised at how classy she looked.

'Oh, this old thing?' She laughed, tucking the blouse tighter into the waistband of the skirt but he could see she was pleased. 'Any sign?' she went on.

'Not yet.' He shook his head, averting his gaze from the way a seam at two strategic parts of the blouse emphasized the fullness of Hazel's breasts as she plopped into the club chair behind her.

'Go on,' she looked up at him, 'what are you waitin' for? Get it over with. Go and get them.'

'What, now?' He could not understand why she was pushing like this.

'What am I here for, dummy?' Hazel insisted. 'You leave it to me. By the time I'm finished with that one,' she laughed, 'she'll be eating out of your hand. I'll charm the pants off her. Better yet,' she added with a jolly grin, 'it'd probably be better for you if I charm the pants off him. Go on now.'

Before he knocked on the door of the Mannerings' room – giving himself a shock from the static electricity as he accidentally touched the metal doorplate – Francey took a few moments to school his face. He was learning fast. A month ago he would have barged in like a schoolboy.

Colin answered the door: 'Oh, hello, Francey,' he said, 'didn't see you when we came in. All set?'

'My friend from Ireland has arrived,' Francey said. 'She'd love to meet you and Fleur – when you're ready of course,' he added, 'no hurry.'

'Are you decent, darling?' Colin called over his shoulder, causing ructions in Francey's heart. Fleur, barefoot, her hair coiled – as he so well remembered – appeared. She was wearing a white terrycloth robe that was several sizes too big for her and Francey's nerves jangled as he pictured what was underneath.

'Francey's girlfriend from Ireland wants to meet us, darling.' Colin put an arm around Fleur's waist and Francey thought he had never before seen such a proprietorial gesture.

'She's not my girlfriend,' he tripped on the words, over-explaining, 'she's just a very good friend. We go way back.'

'Of course.' Fleur's eyes were as expressionless as ever as she

313

looked up at him and there was nothing left for him but to turn away.

'Whenever you're ready,' he said, 'we'll be in the drawing-room.'

But he could not remain seated and paced the room as he and Hazel waited. He should not have let Hazel influence him like this: it would have been much better just to let the meeting between herself and Fleur happen in the course of the party. Worse, he could not banish the image of Fleur taking off that robe in front of Colin and what would happen then . . .

'Ah, here!' After more than five minutes of trying to calm him, Hazel went to the drinks cabinet. 'What you need is a stiff gin-and-tonic, gin is the best medicine for nerves.' Overriding his protests that he hated the taste of the stuff, she mixed the drink. 'Now get that down you, quick!' She stood looking up at him while, grimacing, he drank at least half of it. 'Give it a minute,' she advised, 'and sit *down*. You're makin' me feel like one of the Seven Dwarfs.'

To his surprise, after a minute or so Francey did feel a little calmer. 'I hate him, Hazel,' he said. 'If you saw the lofty way he treats her.'

'Probably like a husband,' Hazel said wryly. 'Anyway, I'm going to see it for meself in a few minutes and make up me own mind. Now drink the rest of that gin!' She sat into a chair near Francey's and continued to admire the furnishings in the room. 'Pity about the fire, though,' she said. 'I hate anything plastic.'

'Oh, Hazel—' Francey had been about to tease her about the stuffed animals in her own flat but swivelled to look towards the door as Colin, followed by Fleur, came into the drawing-room.

Then Hazel startled him so much he almost dropped his glass. 'Well, hello-oo!' she cried in a gushing voice he had never heard before, shooting out of her chair and baby-stepping across the carpet. 'You must be Colin – and this is the famous Fleur!' Before Francey could intervene she was pumping Fleur's hand. 'I'm so-oo pleased to meet you!'

'Hazel,' Francey began as he reached her side but she looked from Fleur to him, vivid eyes glowing.

'Francey here's told me a-aall about you – isn't that right, Francey?' then back to Fleur. 'I've always wanted to go to the Far East, ever since I was a little girl and we had to bring in our pennies for the Foreign Missions.'

314

Chapter Sixteen

Someone turned up the record player and within seconds voices were raised further to compete with the belting of Shirley Bassey. Francey, temporarily alone and pulling at the tight collar of his shirt, wished the night was over, or that he could take off his jacket.

George – or the staff – had gone to a lot of trouble in decorating the rooms: clusters of heart-shaped balloons bounced around high in the overheated air and on most flat surfaces cardboard cupids played hide-and-seek through showers of red roses. The party, which had already spread into the corridor outside, was accelerating into high gear.

Francey, who was standing near the open door, saw that almost everyone present seemed to know each other. Being so tall he could see the room as a whole: it was like looking through a microscope at a molecular organism as groups coagulated and broke up again, helping themselves to tit-bits and drinks from silver trays borne by the servants. He found it simple to distinguish George's London friends from the landed gentry of the shires: whereas the males among the latter sported suits and the women tasteful, if dull, classics, the London crowd were altogether more flamboyant and the women a lot younger, their teeth whiter, their hair and legs longer and their voices loudest of all.

The guests had been punctual, arriving in couples and larger parties, and standing alongside Dessie, Francey had been introduced to so many within the first fifteen minutes that he knew he had no chance of remembering more than a handful of names. Everyone had obviously been well briefed because during the introductions he was conscious of nothing more than politeness. One for the English, he thought; if he and Dessie had been placed in a similarly sensational situation at home, he could not imagine either of them getting away so lightly.

Dessie, also dickied out in a new suit, had stuck close by him during this phase of the proceedings but when Mick O'Dowd and his wife arrived, about twenty minutes after the main influx, he had latched on to them and Francey was given a little more freedom. When his half-brother had asked him the night before if he could invite Mick, Francey had taken it on himself to say yes and had passed on the addition in numbers to the butler without reference to George. He doubted if George would care – or even notice.

He saw now that his father, debonair in a magnificent white dinner jacket and bow-tie and with glass in hand, was holding forth as kingpin of an attentive circle seated on the arrangement of sofas in the centre of the room. In many ways, Francey thought, he regretted having found the real George: the fantasy figure of his childhood had meant so much more to him. On the other hand, the first flush of disillusionment after the row had now been moderated: George was such a transparent old rascal it was impossible to dislike him for long. Francey also knew that he had many more questions for his father and some part of him continued to long for satisfactory answers. It was still possible that in time, perhaps, he and George could forge a half-way decent relationship.

'All alone, head? How's it goin'?' Looking down, he found Hazel at his elbow.

If he had been asked in advance how Hazel would have dressed for a big party, he would have guessed something sparkly, akin to her stage clothes. She had surprised him, however, appearing in a boat-necked, sleeveless sheath in plain cream, elegant and tasteful but short enough to show off her splendid legs, and although she usually jangled with bracelets and chains around her neck, tonight she had contented herself with one thick gold bangle and his butterfly brooch, worn high on her left shoulder. Her hair, still tight to her head, was combed back behind her ears, emphasizing her slim throat.

Francey had already noted that male eyes all around the room followed as she moved about. 'Are you behaving yourself?' He was worried about what might happen in the course of the night: although Fleur had not reacted to Hazel's electric introduction of herself earlier, he felt uneasily that his Irish friend was ticking away like a time bomb.

'Francey!' Hazel looked wounded. 'I'm only here for you.'

'I know,' he relented, 'I appreciate your support – although,' he added ruefully, 'I was expecting it more in the line of help with Dessie.'

'Oh, well, if you don't want me to talk to Fleur any more —'

'Of course I do.' Francey rushed to stave off any perceived insult. 'Have you seen her in the last few minutes?' Although Colin was in the gathering around their father, Francey's most recent scan of the room had shown no evidence of Fleur. 'Gone to the ladies',' Hazel grinned up at him, 'relax, I'm workin' me fingers to the bone there, we're already the best of pals.'

'Do you like her?' Francey lowered his voice and turned his back to deter interruptions.

'That's the twenty millionth time you've asked me that. She's lovely, beautiful, I told you.'

'What about Colin?'

'Harmless,' Hazel said, taking a swig from her vodka and orange juice. 'And before you ask, I haven't a clue yet how yer woman feels about him. Give us a chance, I'm only getting started. She's a bit, well . . .' She searched for the right word '. . . sort of flawless.'

'I know what you mean,' Francey said, then felt disloyal. 'Did you talk to George yet?' getting on to safer ground.

'Savin' that one up,' Hazel said with relish, then, when she saw his face, 'Oh, Francey, for God's sake, will you stop!' She thumped his arm. 'You go and enjoy yourself, you're standin' around as long as a wet week. I'm not going to make a show of you in front of all your new posh friends. I've been at parties before, you know.'

She swung off and before Francey could follow Dessie had brought Mick and his wife across to him. 'Shottley's arrived,' Mick pointed across the room to where a middle-aged man with cropped pepper-and-salt hair was talking to Francey's father.

Stallions were the last thing on Francey's mind but he feigned enthusiasm. 'Oh, good, I'll go and introduce myself later.' Then, during the subsequent small-talk with Mick and his wife, he saw over their heads that Fleur had come back into the room. In a yellow cheong-sam, to Francey she was easily the most beautiful person in the room and, for a second or two, while Mick and Dessie launched once again into their interminable discussions about horseflesh, Francey's chest ached with love and pride as he marvelled that a creature so lovely had lain naked in his arms. The pleasure was

317

not long in evaporating, however, as he saw Hazel hurry over to join her.

He shot a glance towards the sofa and, to his relief, saw that Colin was still engaged in animated conversation with George. Excusing himself from his own group Francey, terrified that in an effort to be helpful Hazel would say something that might have the opposite effect, walked across to join the two women. 'Everything going all right?' He included them both in his smile.

'Well, speak of the devil!' Hazel's answering smile was wicked, confirming his fears. 'I was just starting to fill in Fleur here about how you saved me life. 'You'd want to have seen him, Fleur,' she enthused, turning back to the other woman and launching into an embarrassing paean of praise for Francey's chivalry and strength. In his ears, her Dublin pronunciation of the name – 'flewer' – had sounded suspiciously exaggerated.

Fleur took minuscule sips from her sherry glass as she listened to the recital, but despite what Hazel had said about the two of them having forged a friendship, from where Francey stood the friendship was distinctly one-sided. 'I'm sure poor Fleur's heard quite enough about me for one day,' he intervened when Hazel paused for breath. 'Would you like another drink, Fleur?'

To his chagrin it was Hazel who drained her drink and – 'Thanks a million, love' – with a merry smile, held out her glass.

'Excuse me,' Fleur inclined her head, 'I must go and speak with my husband.'

As she drifted away, Francey grabbed the other woman's arm. 'What are you at, Hazel?'

'I'm trying to build you up with her, of course!' Hazel's expression was injured. 'Fat lot of thanks I'm gettin' for it too.'

'I'm sorry,' Francey apologized and released her arm, 'I'm just on edge. I know you're doing your best and I do appreciate it, but maybe you shouldn't do anything so – so *active*.'

'Don't you trust me?' Staring into the kohl-ringed stare of green and blue, Francey felt obliged to admit that he did. 'Well, then, shut up and let me get on with it.' Like a nanny, Hazel patted him. 'You'll thank me, you just wait and see,' and before he could stop her she had followed Fleur across to his father's claque and was shimmying into a sofa between George himself and another man. She waved genially back at Francey in the manner of the Queen Mother and

318

then, to his horror, pointed at Fleur – who happened to be looking away at the time – following this with a second gesture, a jolly, double thumbs-up.

Someone whose name he did not remember was bearing down on him and Francey instinctively looked for help towards Mick O'Dowd's threesome. Alarm bells rang in his head as he saw that Dessie's cheeks were flushed with colour and he was waving an arm around his head as he told some story. More ominously, there was now a glass in his other hand which contained what looked like whiskey. Within the space of five minutes or so, the evening had begun to turn into a nightmare.

Francey was hesitating as to which group to join when it was announced that supper was served.

Hazel was careful to stay out of Francey's way as the meal got under way in the noisy dining-room. Things were going quite well, she thought, and the fortune she had spent on new clothes had been well justified, if only to see the look on Gorgeous George's face when Francey had introduced them. 'Long time no see!' She had smiled at George, then, giving him no time to come up with anything at all, had passed on to the next introduction as though she was the Queen of Sheba.

Just after the beginning of supper, George came up to her, blocking others' view of her with his substantial torso. 'You're not going to make trouble, are you?'

Hazel assured him that not only was she not going to make trouble, but that her interest in him was less than zero, 'Wouldn't be caught brown bread with ya, George!'

This stung him into the feeble, 'Well, I wouldn't be caught dead with you, either, sunshine.'

At which Hazel converted victory to a rout: as he turned to walk away, she reached up and tweaked his nose: 'Tsk, tsk! How the mighty have fallen! That the best you and your renowned silver tongue can come up with, George?' Not giving him a chance she turned away and accepted her appetizer of fresh salmon from a white-gloved maid and when she turned back he had gone.

As she tucked into her food, Hazel thought about the real business of the night. So far it was going according to plan and she had managed, throughout the evening, to stick like glue to the Siamese twin, despite the latter's best efforts to shake her. Fleur was what one of Hazel's theatre colleagues used to call 'an enigma' and no mistake. Standing now beside her husband on the other side of the room, with the glass table safely between her and Hazel, the look of blankness on her face was off-putting to say the least. The woman gave the word 'undemonstrative' a bad name, Hazel thought. Beautiful all right, there was no denying it, in the way you'd think a sword was beautiful or a bit of Waterford glass: you wouldn't mind having her on your wall or in your china cabinet. But as for being human: Hazel, who prided herself on her talent for assessing human nature, was finding it hard to believe that a man with such an intuitive and warm capacity for love as Francey Sullivan could fall so completely for someone so cold. It had to be for one of two reasons, she decided: what was going on here was either the old cliché about opposites attracting or else Fleur Mannering was exceptionally talented in the physical side of things. If that was the case the situation was not beyond repair. That kind of heat tended to turn to ashes.

Yet looking at the woman now, all buttery demure like Little Miss Muffet, Hazel was finding it difficult to believe that she was a tiger in bed. It was not only that Fleur was outwardly so cool – some of the sexiest people in the world never moved a muscle in public – it was something deeper than that. All Hazel's instincts told her that she was missing something fundamental and if she could just open up her own line of thought, sideways, or upwards or downwards, she could make a breakthrough. She would have bet her compo that all was not quite what it seemed about Fleur Mannering.

When Hazel had planned this she had seen it as a simple exercise: Fleur versus her and may the best woman win. The reality, however, was less like a Boucicault play and more like a Hammer Horror or at least a Bette Davis. And Fleur was a bloody good actress, Hazel had to hand that to her at least: no one in the room could have guessed she had been in the hay with Francey.

But the more Hazel thought about it the more she felt it in her bones that this woman didn't love Francey. And it was cobblers, all that stuff he had been spouting about the difference in their nationalities: love was love and sex was sex no matter where in the world it hit.

Or maybe it was just her own self-interest that was talking –

maybe she was losing her touch, Hazel thought gloomily. She scowled as she saw the middle-aged codger who was bearing down on her; she had chosen to stand behind a huge potted palm for a bit of peace to think.

It was not the first time this geezer had sought her out and he was not at all put off now by her forbidding expression. 'Hello again,' he dreeshed at her through a row of teeth as long and yellow as those on a horse. He was under the weather too. Hazel, well experienced in handling this kind of situation, froze him out but he was having none of it. 'Shottley,' he breathed, 'Colonel, friend of the family. And you don't have to say a thing, eh?'

Before Hazel could decipher this he obviated the need, reaching out an unsteady hand as though to put it on her waist. 'Keep your maulers to yourself, Colonel,' she pushed his hand away, 'this is a new dress and I want to keep it clean if you don't mind.' To her astonishment he reacted by chortling, then tapping the side of his nose with a forefinger as though she had delivered a coded signal of some importance.

Hazel did not wait to find out what he meant but went to the table to where a boy in a tall white hat was carving lamb. She veered off, however, on seeing Francey glance in her direction as though to come over to talk to her. She had noticed he was having a bit of trouble with Dessie, who was drinking a bit, but she could only handle one project at a time.

'Ahh – there you are.' Knowing full well she was acting like a monster, she hailed Fleur and Colin who were standing at the far side of the room.

'Hello again.' In marked contrast to his wife, Colin remained polite, a quality which seemed innate. 'Francey tells us you're a singing star in Ireland,' he continued. 'You must lead a very interesting life.'

'Yeah,' Hazel enthused, 'but not as interesting, I'm sure, as what you and Fleur do. All that travelling – do you travel a lot with Colin, Fleur?' She opened her eyes to their roundest, most innocent extent as she polished off the last morsel of salmon on her plate.

'No,' Fleur replied, her eyes downcast, 'I have my son to take care of.'

'Must be lonely all the same,' Hazel smiled, 'all that time on your own. Francey says you live in London?'

But she failed to discommode the other woman who did not lift her eyes and who remained serene. 'That is right.'

'In a flat, I believe?'

'Yes,' it was Colin again, 'but tell us about yourself, please do.'

Hazel was then forced to answer all the standard, semi-interested queries about her showbusiness career and Ireland. Then, in an attempt to steer the subject back on track by roundabout means, 'You haven't been to Ireland yourself, Colin?' By now all three were at the buffet table being served the next course from the platters of salads, fish, game, and the more conventional meats. 'Salad? Here, let me,' she heaped spoonfuls of shredded green leaves on to Fleur's plate, 'I'm sure Francey's told you all about it, Fleur,' she gushed while watching closely for reaction from her or from Colin. When there was none, save for a non-committal smile from Fleur, she plunged on, 'Well you'd want to see the place he was brought up. Back of beyond, it is,' rabbitting about the Béara peninsula while planning her next attack.

For the best part of ten minutes she plugged away at Fleur, trying to find some way to crack that face. And every time she caught Francey's eye, she gave a large, encouraging smile or a wave, signalling that everything was under control.

She had to admit that the haunted looks he threw at her in return did give her mischievous satisfaction.

Having seen to it that everyone was served, George found himself alone. He glanced around his dining-room with some pride: the enormous space, which nowadays saw such little action, rang with pleasure as his guests enjoyed their supper. Now that he was a free agent and truly lord of the manor, he thought, he must do this more often: have parties, create a bit of a stir in the boring old shires.

They had entertained in Jool's day but a great proportion of their parties had of necessity been a lot more toffee-nosed than this. Charity affairs most of them, populated with bossy committee women down from London with their colourless husbands, they bustled rather than sang. Tonight's mix was a good one, he decided, a few family, a few obligations, tweedy neighbours from the houses around, even old Shottley, all the way from – well, wherever he was from, George could not quite remember. Seeing Shottley again had jogged his conscience about the horses; he had neglected making a decision about what to do about the stables. He had lost interest, somehow: while Jool was alive he had to have a serious hobby to pass the time; now he had his hands full with pursuits which were far more enjoyable. Yes, he thought, he must really do something about those animals. Not yet, though. It would be too bothersome to have all that on his conscience, all those men out of work. And he would have to go to the trouble of finding buyers and so on. So what if the Shires were chewing and shoeing their way through a small fortune every month, he could afford it: Jool's 'house upkeep' money paid for them. He would think about it soon.

Since his wife's death George had been surprised at the amount of brain power and attention to detail one needed to muster simply to keep a house and bank account running smoothly.

And as for the personal side of things, who would have thought that in the space of four months any man could have lost a wife and found two sons? Glancing around the room he saw all three of his; Francey and Dessie were with the head groom and his wife, Colin was with Fleur – and, of all people, Hazel Slye. When he had come down to the party to find Hazel was the 'friend from Ireland' his son had invited, George had had to draw on every ounce of his acting experience not to show how taken aback he was; although it had been the best part of twenty years since he last saw her, he remembered only too well the terms on which they had parted; in fact it did not take much for him to feel again the smarting of his shin where she had kicked him.

He glanced again at her, gesticulating, locked in spirited conversation. George's lips twitched in fond remembrance of Hazel's enthusiasm to learn about sex and her rapid progress; she had been among his better pupils. She had certainly changed, and not for the worse: her figure was, if anything, better than it had been all those years ago and she seemed to have toned down what he remembered as a rather garish taste in clothes.

All in all, George thought, he would not have minded another round with her . . .

As he speculated about Hazel and conducted an automatic and concurrent survey of the other attractive young women in the room, an astonishing thing happened. For the first time in his life, the thought of having to go through a pre-coital gavotte, all that skirmishing and chatting up, rose like a spectre to dismay him. As if that was not enough, his eye then fell on Francey and Dessie, eating together in a corner and in a huddle with Mick O'Dowd and Mick's pretty little wife. George, who openly rejoiced in his ox-like constitution, found that his heart was rattling uncomfortably in his chest. As he tried to deal with this discovery, the noise level in the room seemed to swell until he, who adored social occasions, found it unbearable. Having signalled to one of the staff to come round again with wine, George excused himself to the group nearest him, threaded his way to the door and walked to the nearest bathroom. Safely inside he closed the door and leaned on it, forcing himself to take a series of slow, deep breaths.

Within a minute or two, he was feeling calmer and his heart had resumed its normal, undemanding beat. What was the matter with him tonight?

Hazel's opportunity to have a serious go at Fleur did not present itself until much later in the evening. About an hour after supper, the party relaxed into larger, looser groups, divided roughly by age and inclination. The younger people made use of the dance floor or sprawled all over the furniture while the older, more frumpish lot, stayed involved in more straight-backed confab. Francey's group, which had stuck together throughout the evening and included the leery Colonel Shottley, continued to inhabit the corner of the drawing-room they had made their own. Hazel continued to ignore all hints that she was not welcome, and hung around the Mannerings like an ancestral hex.

At one point, detecting the sweetish aroma of dope wafting towards her from the dance floor she was glad she had all her wits about her and was not stoned; she felt it was just a matter of time before Fleur cracked. Not that Fleur showed a pick of it. The object of Francey's adoration continued to behave as though she was one of those po-faced performers in the Yeats' Noh play that Hazel had once had to sit through in the Peacock Theatre in Dublin for the sake of one of her old flames who was in the cast.

Her chance to make the definitive push on Fleur came at about eleven o'clock when people were less densely packed into the drawing-room and the party had drifted into the corridor and many of the other rooms off it.

Hazel, who was fighting off a headache, was not a Shirley Bassey fan and was glad that her thumping arrangements had been replaced by the gentler strains of singers like Matt Monro, Ruby Murray and Peggy Lee. She was dancing with a man who had asked her so often that she could no longer refuse, when, out of the corner of her eye she noticed Fleur touch her husband on the sleeve, murmur something to him and then walk towards the door. Scanning for Francey, who for once was not to be seen, Hazel apologized to her companion then hurried across the room. 'Hey, Fleur! Hold it there a sec, Fleur.'

'Yes?' The other woman turned round and Hazel had the pleasure of seeing her eyes flicker.

'Would you mind if we had a chat in private?' Hazel moved very close.

'What about?' The alabaster surface of Fleur's forehead was now marred with a tiny ripple as she backed away.

'It's personal,' Hazel said levelly, dropping the act she had sustained all evening.

'Will this take long?' Fleur's frown deepened, 'I am a little tired.'

'I won't keep you a second longer than is necessary, I promise. Let's go to my room – it's not far.' She led the way.

'Ow!' Hazel swore as her touch on the knob of the door to her room gave her another electric shock. 'Someone should do something about all this static electricity, like open a window!' Sucking her fingers, she stood back to usher Fleur in before her and as she closed the door behind the two of them, the sounds of the party behind it shrank to a soothing murmur.

Hazel's room was as large as all the other guest rooms in the Manor; decorated in shades of pink and grey it was illuminated with at least seven lamps, all lit. 'Sorry about the mess,' she made a perfunctory effort to tidy up, removing a pair of stockings from the back of a chair and straightening the bedclothes, 'the maid came in to do it but I sent her away. I like to do the little things for meself,' she confided, housewife to housewife, 'you know how it is, Fleur – and by the way I love your dress, Siamese, is it?'

'Thank you, no, it is not Thai and the room is perfect. Could you get to the point, please?'

Hazel was pleased to see that at last she had pierced through a little bit. 'All right, love.' She engaged Fleur's eyes directly. 'I'd like to know what your intentions are concerning Francey Sullivan.'

When Fleur heard her name called in the corridor and saw it was that awful woman again, she had had to fight, for the first time in many months, not to let her feelings show. She had been hoping to slip away to her room without fuss but she might have known it would have been too much to hope for: the woman was like a leech.

The evening had been even more of a trial than she had feared. Although she had not regarded it as being at all dangerous that one or two of her generous friends had come into close proximity to one another – the most serious rule of the game in which they were all involved was discretion – Colin's half-brother had displayed no such restraint, mooning around her more than once. Diamond watch notwithstanding, Fleur had already decided that she must have no more dealings with him in the flat. At least until he understood the terms.

Francey's behaviour had not been the worst, however: the most appalling aspect of the night had been the conduct of this profoundly irritating Irishwoman. As she stared at her now, in the aftermath of her intolerable question, Fleur experienced an urge rare for her: she would enjoy causing this woman bodily harm. 'I have no idea what you mean,' she said stiffly.

'Yes, you do,' the woman insisted. 'Listen, Fleur, that poor fella's dying for you. And I think you know it. All I'm asking is what you feel about him. Straight.'

Fleur considered her, the short dress, the dreadful shoes, the eyes which might have come from the palette of an artist of the avant-garde. 'It is not your business what I feel or do not feel,' she said softly.

'Oh, yes, it is, sunshine,' the other woman said, 'because you see I've been to bed with him too. Not to put a tooth in it, Fleur, I wouldn't mind it again but the poor devil can't see to wash himself at the moment because of you. You're not a witch by any chance, are you?' this last in a conversational tone, and if it had been designed to startle Fleur it hit its target.

'I beg your pardon?' Fleur played for time.

326

'You heard. It was meant as a half-joke but now I dunno. That fella is bewitched, no mistake about it. So? Do you love him back or what? He seems to think he has a chance.'

Then Fleur saw the possibilities inherent in this conversation. Francey could prove troublesome: if she played the situation correctly, this woman could save her an awkward scene. As Fleur's brain performed a lightning-fast set of calculations, she thought how foolish she had been to grant him a date in the first place and that she would never make such a mistake again. 'I gave him no reason to believe that,' she said now. 'If he chooses to love me it is not my concern.'

'Jesus H. Christ,' the other woman said, 'but you really take the biscuit, do you know that? I'm warning you now, Fleur,' the eyes, which were above Fleur's own solely because of their owner's shoes, narrowed to black slits, 'you don't come near that fella again or I for one,' at this she thrust her head forward so that some of her hair stood on end like the comb of a little white cockerel, 'will be dug out of you.'

Although she had not heard the phrase before, as Fleur stared at Hazel, at the belligerence of the stance, she knew what it meant and that the woman in front of her would not hesitate to carry out the threat. 'As you wish.' She shrugged.

'You don't believe me, do you?' Hazel's lips spread in a thin smile. 'But I can tell you I've never been more serious in me life. You're supposed to have had a deprived childhood or something and that's supposed to give you licence to fuck people around? Well, I can tell you I've survived places in Dublin city where the kids'd take your eyeballs out to play marbles with, so don't mess with me. And don't mess my friends around either. You understand, Mrs Mannering?'

Throughout this speech, by the end of which her adversary was shaking, Fleur employed a trick which had stood her well whenever she had to submit to a client or face anything unpleasant. Mentally, she separated her soul from her body, picturing the former soaring high into the sky so it looked dispassionately at everything going on down below, nothing of which could touch it. 'Please don't swear,' the soul heard the lips say to the person in front of the body. 'Are you finished?' Then the soul watched as the body left the room.

*

327

Francey found himself dancing, or, to be more correct, shuffling around on the dance floor to the strains of Ruby Murray's 'Softly Softly' with a long-haired girl leaning against his chest. He was having a terrible time.

Although in the last few months he had overcome what he had always thought of as his shyness, he continued to hate the artificiality of assembling a random number of males and females in one place, throwing drink and music at them and leaving them to get on with it. He knew most people thought parties attracted magic and even romance but he would have preferred to be anywhere else, even, God forbid, back behind the counter at Ledbetter's.

The little group with which he had spent the last hour was a disaster area: Dessie was drinking; the Colonel was well on the way to being drunk as, with Mick, he traced the bloodlines of heavy horses right back to the crusades and the Battle of Hastings, and his wife continued to sit stony-faced. But what was even more disastrous was that for some time past Francey had not been able to spot either Fleur or Hazel.

The interminable song dragged on while the girl continued to cling to him. She was moving so slowly now, sagging so heavily in his arms that Francey wondered if she was asleep.

Then to his relief, he saw Hazel come into the room and peer round. He waited until she looked in his direction then signalled at her with his eyes, rolling them in Dessie's direction; she gave him a peremptory wave to show she understood and went over to the group.

Shortly afterwards, the song ended. 'Thank you very much,' Francey said, giving the girl no chance to expect anything further, and in a moment he was back in the corner. 'Would you like to get up, Hazel?' He had to find out if she and Fleur had had any further conversations – and if so what about.

'Sure.' Hazel followed him to a quiet corner of the room.

'Well?' Francey asked, as he turned to take Hazel into his arms.

'Well what?' Hazel's expression was uncharacteristically grim.

'You were missing for ages and so was Fleur. Were you talking to each other?'

'I don't want to talk about it now.' Hazel looked up at him. 'There's too much noise in here, Francey.'

328

'You *have* said something to her, I knew it.' Panic caught Francey under his ribs. 'Hazel, how could you —'

'Take it easy, will you? You're standin' on me toes.' She glared up at him.

'Tell me!' Francey gripped her shoulder so hard he could feel the sharp point of the bone.

'Ow! That hurts.' She pushed him away, 'All right,' she said, 'but not here. My room.'

Francey followed her out. He did not care now if Dessie drank Lough Fada dry. The moment Hazel closed the door of the bedroom behind them he seized her again, this time by both shoulders: 'What's happened? Tell me, for God's sake.'

'What makes you think something's happened?' She attempted to free herself.

'Hazel!' he warned.

'Let me go,' she said quietly. 'And sit down, I'm getting a crick in me neck looking up at you.'

'Stop stalling and talk, Hazel.' But he could see she would not open her mouth until he obeyed, so he sat on the edge of the bed.

'Nothing happened,' Hazel began to pace the room, 'well, nothing much. I couldn't get anything out of her.'

'Nothing about what?' Francey was appalled. 'Did you talk to her about me? For God's sake, Hazel, you'd no right.'

Hazel stopped dead in the middle of the room and turned towards him, chin high. 'Who says we were talking about you?' she asked. 'I was just trying to find out what makes that woman tick. On your behalf, certainly, but I'm not so stupid as to come right out with it.'

Some of the wind leaked from Francey's sails. 'Are you sure? Why all the secrecy then?'

'No secrecy,' Hazel said. 'I just didn't think we should be discussing any conversation I might or might not have had with Fleur Mannering in front of all those people out there, do you?'

Francey could see the logic. 'Well, what did you find out?' he asked, less frantic now.

'Lookit,' Hazel came across to him and took his face between her hands, 'I found out nothing, sweetheart. But every bone in me body says I'd be careful if I was you.'

'You mean Colin? I am being careful.' The relief was like a sunrise.

'If you think I have to be careful she must have let you see something. Oh, Hazel—' He grabbed the hand nearest his mouth and kissed it. 'I'm sorry I doubted you.'

'Don't you think you should go back out there? You are one of the guests of honour, after all?' Hazel's eyes were lowered. She was more subdued than he had seen her in a long time.

'Of course, of course.' He jumped up from the bed and took her in his arms for a full-fledged hug. 'Don't be cross,' he begged, 'I'm sorry I spoke to you like that, I was just out of my mind with worry.' He stood her away from him and smoothed the cow's lick over her head. And as she made as if to protest, he hugged her again. 'You're a brick, Hazel – I don't know what I'd do without you. Come on back to the party, I'm worried about Dessie.'

'Oh, Francey, what am I going to do with you?' To his surprise, Francey saw tears stand in Hazel's eyes as she dispensed one of her customary thumps. 'You're like Mrs bleedin' Kennedy of Castlerosse' – naming the figurehead of the daily soap opera on Radio Eireann – 'always worrying about someone. Lookit,' she dashed the tears away, 'this is a party. And I've to be up tomorrow at the crack of dawn so could I go out and enjoy meself for the last hour d'you think?'

'What about—'

'What about no one,' Hazel interrupted, 'what about me? I need a drink, all right?'

The party had entered that penultimate phase where some were beginning to mutter about long drives home while more were dancing cheek-to-cheek while engaged in blissful discovery of one another's bone structure. Francey's group, which seemed to have squatters' rights on the corner they had occupied for most of the evening, was still *in situ*. Dessie, pulling on one of his Woodbines, was staring blankly into space and as he appeared to be no danger to himself or to anyone else at present, Francey let him be.

As soon as he arrived with Hazel, the Colonel, the worse for drink but steady on his feet none the less, immediately asked Hazel to dance. Francey felt duty bound then to ask Shottley's colourless wife, who stood up without uttering a word and, handbag dangling from one crooked elbow, raised her arms so he could take the lead. After a moment or two of small-talk with her, Francey gave up and concentrated on not stepping on her toes; then he became aware that Hazel and the Colonel had stopped in the middle of the floor. He steered

Mrs Shottley around so he could see what was going on. Hazel was facing the Colonel as though thunderstruck.

Fleur lay on one of the twin beds in the room she shared with Colin. She was angry with herself for letting that woman get under her skin. The walls of the Manor were well insulated but their bedroom, although separated from the drawing-room by a little private sitting-room, was not immune from the noise of the party which drummed on in the distance. She and Colin had been to Inveraray Manor too often lately: Colin could come alone the next time. Now that Jool was gone, Fleur saw little need for her own presence here. She concentrated for a few moments, letting the aggravation seep away, picturing it draining down her body and out through the soles of her feet until the centre of herself became calm and clear as usual.

Fleur smiled as Tommy's face floated in to fill the cold, silent spaces in her mind. When Fleur thought about Tommy the feelings were conflicting: they were warm and joyful but also sharp like the point of a dagger – he could so easily be taken away. One step into the roadway in front of a lorry he did not hear, one trip to the swimming baths where he could hit his head on the bottom of the pool. Fleur sometimes did not know where she found the courage to let Tommy out of her sight. She looked at her bedside clock: almost half past eleven. There was an outside chance that Tommy was not yet asleep: although he was supposed to be in bed by ten o'clock on Saturday nights, Fleur knew that the nanny sometimes relented and let him stay up. She longed to make contact.

She was in luck. The nanny called him to the telephone and when he was there, although she knew there was no point in speaking, she initiated their special ritual for saying they loved one another. They had developed a system whereby if she banged her receiver against a hard surface three times, by holding the receiver at his end to the front of his throat, Tommy could sense the vibrations. 'How is he?' she asked the nanny when the girl came on after they had finished.

'He's fine, Mrs Mannering, bold as brass. I don't know what they're teaching him at that school of his . . .' Fleur, knowing by the pace at which the nanny was speaking that she was simultaneously signing to her charge, was stabbed with jealousy. It was she who should be there with her son and not some hired help.

'Say goodnight to him for me,' she requested and hung up.

Still fully clothed, she lay back on the bed and stared up at the ceiling. She had planned to wait for another year or so but, abruptly, Fleur felt she should not postpone things any longer. The time had come for her and Tommy to make their move.

Back in the drawing-room, Dessie had his own plans which involved not only more drink, but a woman. It had been a long time since Dessie had had a woman – he had lost his virginity years ago, quite casually, to one of the girls in the shoplifting gang – and he was looking forward to what was in store. He had no doubt that the girl sitting beside him was game – she hadn't but a tooth in it, as a matter of fact, but he had to be careful. He was sure drippy old Francey wouldn't approve.

Dessie wished his brother wasn't hanging around him like such an old blouse; Francey was seriously getting on his nerves tonight, checking up on him every way he turned. All right, he thought, he was grateful for what had been done for him – and he was *very* glad now that he had not drowned that time. Pity he had put the little dog through it as well, he thought, but he'd make it up to him, and he could get as many dogs as he liked now. He could buy the whole Battersea Dogs' Home if he wanted to. Fizzing with whiskey, Dessie felt better and more confident than he had in years.

Not only dogs but horses. As he listened to more of Mick's stories about the Shires, Dessie nodded while only half listening. He was deciding that Francey's half-cocked plan for the horses could go to hell. Dessie Scollard was going to be no one's second banana: he'd make up his own plans, get his own horses.

One thing was sure, he was glad now that he had come over to meet his father. George was a really good sort, he thought, easy-going, a man's man. He knew how to have a good time too, you could see that. Francey had been nagging him to have a serious, one-to-one talk with their father but Dessie could see no reason for it at all. What good would it do either of them? He was quite happy the way things were and they could only get better. He didn't really want to argue with Francey, though, but he was getting annoyed that his brother always seemed to think he knew everything about everything.

From Dessie's point of view, Francey had a nerve to say some of the things he did about their father. George didn't *have* to be so good to either of them, after all. He had given both of them the run of this fantastic place, the horses. He had given them this fabulous party. Then Dessie realized something was going on in the middle of the room: he looked over to see Francey's friend, Hazel, standing in front of the Colonel. Francey was now going over . . .

As Dessie watched, he saw Hazel's head go down, saw Francey touch her arm, saw the Colonel back off and take the arm of his wife.

While Francey was thus distracted, Dessie told Mick he was going to see a man about a dog. But on the way out of the room, he swiped a three-quarters full bottle of whiskey from under the nose of the fella at the drinks table.

George loved dancing, the feeling of a soft warm body, harmonious movement with a hint of something better to come. Jool, bless her, had had two left feet and it was one of the little luxuries of life he had missed during his marriage, but he was having to work hard tonight to maintain the usual delight. Everything should have been tophole, the party, the music, the lovely RADA student with whom he was dancing and for whom he had high hopes.

But George had never quite recovered his equilibrium after that puzzling episode in the bathroom and although on the surface he was performing his hostly duties with his usual aplomb – and the girl in his arms, a vicar's daughter from Portsmouth, was gazing up at him with soft, doe-like eyes – he could not shake off a feeling of unease. He tried to analyse it but could come up with nothing more than vague feelings that all was not quite right in his world. Blast it, he thought now, kissing his dancing partner's ear. I'm too old to be going through this, then looked up to see Dessie skip through the door with a bottle in his fist. He frowned: that probably meant trouble.

Up to now, George's reason for throwing this party – to avoid facing Dessie one-to-one – had seemed to be working very well indeed. And the bonus was that, as far as he could see any time he checked, the lad had seemed to be enjoying himself perfectly well. Fitting it a treat as a matter of fact, despite Francey's holier-than-thou warnings.

When he saw Dessie slip out, however, George became conscious that here again was that disturbing sense of disquiet.

It was only then he realized that what was wrong with this party, with his unsettled heart, was the presence of those two boys, Francey and Dessie. And it was the two of them together. Everything had been hunky-dory until Francey had dragged Dessie into the picture. He now saw that since the day he had opened his door to the two of them, standing there in the snow like Bambi and his mother, nothing had been the same.

He had had no such problems with Colin and this, he complimented himself, was not entirely due to Jool's influence. Colin was an infinitely adaptable character, which suited George down to the ground. Colin and George accepted the boundaries of their relationship and got on fine with one other. But these other two . . . They demanded attention.

Particularly Dessie.

When Dessie had first come to Inveraray he had acted like his half-brother's shadow but, as the days wore on, he had seemed gradually to be shifting his allegiance so that now, whenever he was not in the stables and around the house, it seemed to George that more and more he was meeting Dessie's gaze.

Now that he thought about it, George could not turn round in his own house these days without meeting those two wide, innocent eyes. It was almost as though he had become Dessie's hero. It was just as well, he thought, that he could go away to London now and then for a breather. Dammit! George thought again. Why did this have to happen to him now?

And yet, and yet . . . Old age with a family around him, like Jool had always dreamed? Maybe it was not so bad to have at least one son who thought you were the bee's knees? Maybe it was time he sorted out his life a little. And maybe Francey did have a point when he was on about neglect and all the rest of it . . .

Pshaw! Catching himself boarding this train of thought proved so disturbing that Gorge almost tripped and had to apologize to his partner. Then he was distracted by the sense of something peculiar happening in the centre of the room. Looking over he saw it was Shottley. And Hazel again. In the centre of it – she hadn't changed.

And there was Francey now, going over to catch Hazel's arm . . .

George was about to perform his duty and go across with the

intention of finding out what was going on but hesitated as he saw the wine-nosed Colonel walk away while Francey engaged Hazel in conversation.

Since Francey seemed to have things under control, George decided to leave it to him. He smiled down at the lovely girl in his arms and concentrated on his dancing.

As it happened, Francey felt he was not handling the situation at all well.

Five minutes after the startled Shottley had retired with his wife to get their coats, Hazel was still refusing to tell him what had happened. 'It must have been something,' Francey pleaded. 'Did he insult you?'

'You could say that,' Hazel muttered at last.

'Do you want me to say something to him? What did he say to offend you?'

'Look, just leave it, Francey, it was nothing, all right?' Unusually for her, the expression in her eyes was unreadable. 'You're a head case, Francey, do you know that?' she said softly. 'You shouldn't be let out.' Francey nagged her for another while but she would not divulge any more. Eventually he had to let her go when, pleading tiredness, she said she wanted to go to bed.

Ten minutes later, Hazel, her face scrubbed and shiny with moisturizer, lay snugly under the bedcovers. She still couldn't believe it. That bloody oul' codger. Thinking she would do business with him. That because he had seen her hanging around with Fleur Mannering all night that she was part of the same circle.

And him not even seeing what beans he had spilled.

Chapter Seventeen

Hour after hour, Hazel wrestled with the problem of how to tell Francey what she had discovered. She felt she could guess how he would react to the revelation that the woman he loved – or lusted after, Hazel could not bring herself to believe what he felt for that woman could be categorized under the word love – was a prostitute. And she was long enough in the tooth to know that in cases like this it was the messenger who often got shot.

Fleur's game would not have occurred to Hazel. But now that she knew, everything fell into place: the understatement, that feeling the woman gave off of being detached, as though the human race was none of her business. It stood to reason. The newspapers in Ireland had been as agog as those in England over the Profumo affair and it was only two months since Christine Keeler had been jailed for something similar to what Fleur was up to: nods, winks, money talks, here's a few names but keep it under your hat and Bob's your uncle.

Not that Fleur Mannering could in any way be thought to conform to the further cliché of being a showgirl or a model: no, this ice queen was in a different league. For a few minutes, Hazel speculated on how good she must be and then had to give it up because the picture of Fleur in bed with Francey was too painful.

Then the practical problems arose. Hazel did not subscribe to the prostitute-with-a-heart-of-gold theory and Mrs Mannering, she would have bet her compo on it, did not come cheap. As far as she could guess by reading between the lines of Francey's accounts of his 'visits' to the London flat, Fleur had been to bed at least twice with him and she had already established that the woman did not love him – so had he paid her? Or whom had he paid?

On and on it went until Hazel thought she might lose her reason.

At half past two in the morning, she jumped out of bed and padded into the bathroom to pour herself a glass of water. She could not believe cash had changed hands directly: for one thing, the

336

woman had too much class, but for another, even Francey would not be so naïve as to think that Fleur would take his money and then fall in love with him, enough to divorce her husband and to marry him.

So how then? Did she have a pimp or a minder? No, Francey would have copped that . . .

It was while drinking the water and looking at her unadorned reflection in the bathroom mirror that it occurred to her that this had been a terrific night's work. The challenge now was how best to turn it to her own advantage. When she came back into the bedroom, Hazel looked with distaste at the rumpled bed. Usually an excellent sleeper, she felt as alert and jittery as a mouse and regretted now that she had not brought a bottle of duty-free booze with her.

During the previous hour and a half or so, she had been aware of muffled sounds of cars leaving, but the drawing-room was out as far as a raid on the drink was concerned: Hazel had been to enough parties in her time to be sure that there were bound to be a few stragglers decorating the furniture there. But there must be a place in this house where the supplies were stored, most likely the kitchen . . .

Going over to the door, which faced the opening into the entrance lobby, she opened it a little and peeped out. The hallway, lit with a single table lamp, was empty and so was the corridor in both directions; and although she held her breath to listen for any signs of life, she heard nothing but the hollow suck of the hot air central heating system. She put on the négligé that went with her frilly baby dolls – fat lot of use they were, she thought – and stole out into the corridor. It was so silent she could hear the nylon rustling against her legs as she crept barefoot along the thick carpet towards the kitchen.

She was concentrating so hard on being quiet that when the door to the second last bedroom clicked open just as she came level, she jumped back in fright: 'Jesus Mary and Joseph.' Her heart thumping, she stared at the girl framed in the doorway.

'I think there's something awful wrong with him.' The speech of the girl, whose wide bare shoulders protruded from the sheet trailing on the floor around her, was slurred; she gazed at Hazel with eyes as opaque as marble.

Hazel did not need to ask who 'him' was. Hurrying in past the girl, she took in the situation in the bedroom, the scrambled bedclothes, the up-ended wine bottle on the floor, the ashtray overflowing with cigarette butts and papers for the dope.

Dessie lay slumped in a semi-sitting position on the bed, his head lolling to one side against a pile of tumbled pillows. His thin body was naked: a bright red stain had spread from his mouth down across the pillowcase and across the sheets. 'He's haem– haem– ' the girl, who had followed Hazel back into the room, could not get her tongue around the word.

Hazel, who had dealt with such dramas before, peered at the stain. 'No, it's not blood,' she said, 'it's wine and other stuff. He's vomited.'

Her next instinct was to go and get Francey but then she thought there was not much he could do any more than she. Dessie had to have medical attention. 'Help me here,' she ordered, so peremptorily that even through the marijuana-induced fog the girl was spurred to react. The two of them pulled Dessie up higher, propping him up so that even if he did vomit again he would not choke. 'Watch him,' Hazel admonished her and went to the telephone where she dialled 999 and asked for an ambulance, giving the address as far as she knew it.

Guessing that Francey would be in the bedroom next door, she knocked and looked in just as two heads attached to two naked and entwined bodies raised themselves from the bed. 'Sorry!' Closing the door, Hazel then tried the bedroom on the other side and in the shaft of light from the corridor, to her relief, saw Francey's blond thatch. 'Francey!' She shook him.

'What is it?' Waking at once, his eyes were round with fright.

Hazel switched on the bedside lamp. 'You're not to worry, everything's under control, but Dessie's in trouble.'

'What kind of trouble?' He sat up.

'Come and see for yourself.' Taken aback by the inappropriate leap in her blood, *for God's sake not now*, Hazel averted her eyes from his splendid nudity as he sprang out on to the floor. She kept them away and while he threw on a dressing-gown, wondered crossly why no one in this house seemed to have heard of pyjamas.

When she led him back to Dessie's room, Francey took in the situation without any further explanation. 'Oh, my God!'

'It's not as bad as it looks,' Hazel assured him, 'but he needs help. I've called an ambulance.'

'I think you'd better make yourself scarce,' Francey turned to the girl who, still draped in her sheet, was swaying in the middle of the

338

floor, 'you can use my room, it's next door – I'll stay here.' When the girl had gone he sat beside Dessie and cradled his unconscious head against his shoulder. 'It's all my fault, I should never have agreed to this party.'

'It's no one's fault.' Hazel pulled her négligé tighter around her: the room was as warm as ever but she felt chilled. 'I was egging you on, we all thought he was doing great. It was just too soon, that's all. Which room is George Gallaher's?'

Francey told her and as she went to fetch him, Hazel thought grimly that if George was up to his old tricks with any of the young girls who had littered the night she would give him short shift. But having knocked on his door and entered in response to his slurred invitation she found that she had been wronging him for once. He was groggy and sleepy but he was alone. She did not give him a chance to ask any questions, informing him briskly of what was happening and leaving him to come or not as he saw fit.

George arrived a few minutes after she got back to Dessie's room and just as the wailing of the ambulance siren could be heard in the distance. Everything happened fast. The ambulance attendants were efficient and consoling, wrapping Dessie in a blanket and transferring him to a stretcher as though he were as easy to handle as a loaf of bread. Francey got dressed to go with him and by the time he was ready Dessie was secured in the vehicle and the doors were being closed.

The siren had woken up the entire household. In varying states of undress, guests and servants clustered around the door, their faces wan in the pulsing play of blue lights from the roof of the ambulance. Colin and George stood by the door and contributed little. Of Fleur there was no sign.

The driver turned the siren on again as the vehicle buzzed off down the driveway. 'Thanks a lot, God,' Hazel mouthed to herself as she watched it go. Dessie's timing was impeccable. Any hopes she might have entertained of sorting out the subject of Fleur with Francey was now of necessity on the back burner.

'Don't worry,' the ambulance man said to Francey as they rattled over the cattle grid at the end of the driveway and revved up on the narrow roadway, 'he'll be all right, he's young, his pulse is strong.

They'll probably pump his stomach and he'll be right as rain in the morning.'

Francey then found himself apologizing for the trouble Dessie was causing. The smell in the confined space of the ambulance was appalling, reminding him of the first time he had taken his half-brother from the cot in Salladerg to his own house in Lahersheen. Despite Hazel's reassurances, he continued to castigate himself for his selfish laxity. He should not have strayed from Dessie's side; and the very minute he saw Dessie was drinking was the time he should have intervened instead of pursuing his own agenda. And who was that girl? How had he not seen that coming?

Then Francey began to get angry. Why him? What had he ever done to the human race that he was its scapegoat? The more he tried and worked and took other people's problems on his own shoulders the more complicated everything became for him; he had been locked into a vicious circle from the moment he had decided to look for George Gallaher. And what had this brought him? Money, for sure, but what else? His adventures with Fleur and the reunification with Dessie notwithstanding, his life was nothing now but heartscald. Francey was beginning to believe he might even have been better off back in Ledbetter's. It might have been boring but at least he had had a modicum of control: was he so much better off riding this emotional roller-coaster? Look at him now: rocketing along in an ambulance at three o'clock in the morning, hunched over on an uncomfortable narrow seat so his head would not hit the ceiling. This was some fun, wasn't it?

After all the self-recrimination and soul-searching, the feeling of anger felt clean, almost exhilarating. So Dessie was going to have his stomach pumped and be all right then, was he? And then what? Maybe he'd take to swallowing broken bottles?

He should have taken Hazel's implied advice long ago. It was still not too late: he should throw the whole lot over – Dessie, George, his mother, Abby and her vocation, the whole shooting match – and go off to a South Sea island or something. He was tired of being Charles Atlas or Mrs Kennedy of Castlerosse or all the other agony aunts with whom Hazel compared him. She was dead right: he had become such a worry-wart that he was in imminent danger of vanishing up his own fundament. They could all watch his dust the minute this latest little episode concerning his half-brother was sorted

340

out. Francey Sullivan was turning over a new leaf and was no longer one of Santy's little helpers. He was going to enjoy himself: he was young, he had money and the world was his oyster. Fleur could come along for the ride, or she needn't – that was up to her. And he was not going to beg.

That was another thing – Francey was working himself up into a fine rage now – he was fed up, tired to the toenails wondering about what Fleur thought, what Fleur was feeling, whether Fleur loved him or whether Fleur did not. He had been a right drip, hanging around her like a humbly persistent bumble bee, afraid to say 'boo' in case she'd be offended and not want to know him any more. No wonder she'd taken him for granted – he had been asking for it. Well, like the rest of them, let Fleur just look out from now on. 'Humble' was not a word that would ever apply to Francey Sullivan again.

Let her stand in towels in front of her husband, he thought, let her drop the towel to the floor, let her do anything she liked with that half-eejit – see if Francey Sullivan cared.

And there'd be no more diamond watches. He could have *bought* a South Sea island for what that cost him. 'Thank you so much,' says she, as cool as a cucumber. *Thanks!* Like the Queen of England.

'We're here, sir.' The ambulance man busied himself over Dessie's prone body. Francey was in such a mental lather he had not noticed the vehicle slowing down. As it came to a halt, the doors were pulled open from the outside and Dessie was transferred into the casualty department of the hospital with the minimum of fuss. He was taken into a cubicle and Francey was left to cool his heels in the waiting-room. He went to fill himself a paper cupful of water from a hand basin, since this appeared to be the only form of refreshment available, and nodded to the room's other occupant, a woman whom he guessed was about fifty. Simmering with resentment and anger, he brought the cup back to a chair and, drumming his fingers on its leatherette armrest, sipped the tepid contents.

His mood persisted until, having been assured Dessie was going to be all right, he left him and got back to the Manor just after seven in the morning.

He found Hazel up and dressed, ready to go for her plane. 'I didn't think you'd get back.' She surveyed him from behind a plate of rashers and eggs in the breakfast room. 'I was just going to order a taxi. How is he?'

'Sorry for himself.' Francey poured a cup of tea and ladled scrambled egg and sausages on to a plate. 'He's been admitted for observation, but he's going to be fine. I'm sick of him, to tell you the truth,' he added, bringing over his meal to the table, 'I'm sick of the whole lot of it. You're right, what you said last night, I've become an old drudge. A few things are going to change around here and I'm going to be the first.'

'Good for you.' She gave him one of her biceps thumps. 'I'm with you on that one. So where are you going to start?'

Francey was loath to admit the embryonic nature of his plans but intimated to Hazel that they involved a long and very expensive holiday. 'Alone?' Her eyes widened with interest, or amused challenge, he could not tell which, but he knew to whom she was referring.

'Who knows?' he retorted. 'Maybe it'll be just you and me'll have to go, Hazel.'

'You bet!' Her cheerful voice was a tonic after the night of angry introspection.

They finished eating without the need to speak further. Although the breakfast room was at the western end of the house, it had been built so the table nestled in a projecting bay and the rays of the just-risen sun slanted through the floor-to-ceiling windows beside the table. Francey assumed that his feeling of chill was due to tiredness, and for once welcomed the additional warmth. As he wolfed his meal it occurred to him that it had not taken long for him to get used to such an opulent lifestyle and not to notice the care lavished on simple things: the silver, spotless linen and sparkling glassware with which the breakfast table was laid, the centrepiece of crocuses and snow-drops, even the unobtrusive presence of the servants.

'I could get used to this!' Picking up his thoughts again, Hazel finished the last mouthful of her coffee and folded her napkin with a satisfied sigh.

She was flying back to Dublin from Birmingham and because it was such a beautiful day, Francey overrode her protests that she would be happy in the train from Leamington and said he would drive her the whole way to the airport. 'What about the hospital?' she asked as they got into the car, but Francey told her he would call in on the way back. 'And anyway,' he renewed his resolve, 'he has a

342

father and another brother, hasn't he? I'll go and see him this morning but from then on it's their turn to row in.'

They set off without having encountered George, the rest of the family, or any of the guests from the night before. Francey was glad he had been so abstemious – until he realized that this, too, was a prissy and unfitting sentiment for his new incarnation as a gay blade.

The trip was uneventful and they arrived at the airport with plenty of time to spare. Hazel checked in and then invited him to have a drink with her until it was time to board. Because it was Sunday morning, they could find nowhere open except a small concession selling coffee and lukewarm tea in plastic cups. 'There's something we're not talking about, isn't there?' Hazel, who had insisted on paying, took him off guard as she plonked his tea on the table in front of him.

Fleur's serene, beautiful face floated in the air between them and Francey saw no point in pretending innocence. 'I'm not sure about what I feel,' he said. 'I'm probably too tired to be rational but when I said to hell with all of them I included her, too. A man can be a fool for only so long, Hazel.'

'But what did she do last night that was to terrible?' One of Hazel's long nails seemed to be giving her trouble. She was concentrating on rubbing the tip of it along the inside surface of one of the fingers on the other hand.

Now that she put it like that, Francey saw that Fleur had done nothing to deserve inclusion in his general condemnation of the human race. She had been guilty just of being herself. Before he could reply, Hazel looked up from her endeavours with her nail. 'I thought that dress was just gorgeous. And did you get a load of the earrings? Francey, I have to hand it to ya, you have terrific taste. The diamonds in those earrings were real, you know. You could probably pay off a mortgage with them.'

Francey was getting uncomfortable. She was so much on his wavelength: could it be possible she had guessed – picked up something – about the diamond watch? He was glad now that Fleur had not worn it last night. This conversation was making him feel that to give such an expensive gift to Fleur and such an insignificant little butterfly to Hazel had been disloyal. 'I thought your dress was lovely too, Hazel.' He smiled at her.

343

'That oul' cream thing? Not in her class, sugar.' She yawned and looked towards the departures board. 'Still a few minutes more before I have to go. They must be loaded,' she added, 'the two of them. Is the flat nice? Do they have a lot of nice things?'

'Beautiful.'

'Go on, describe it to me.'

It was well known that Irish showbands were making a fortune and Francey knew Hazel had plenty of money; it was uncharacteristic of her to be nosy about other people's wealth and possessions except in passing and he wished she would change the subject. He did the best he could, however, telling her about the two-storey layout, the spacious entrance hall, the eastern feel to the drawing-room, all the flowers.

'I can tell she's not a stuffed-animal person.' Hazel smiled but then, without warning, the smile vanished and she gazed into the depths of her empty cup.

'What is it?' Francey was shocked at the change.

'Nothing. I just thought of something, that's all – so go on,' she urged. 'Tell us more.'

Francey did not care that his good resolutions were winging away with the plane taking off from the runway outside. 'Hazel, please – is it something about Fleur?'

'Of course not! Do they have nice furniture?' But the evasiveness in Hazel's eyes, usually so candid, alerted Francey that she was not telling him the full truth. 'I must know,' it became crucial to find out what she was hiding, 'you know how I feel about her. Please, Hazel.'

'That's just it,' Hazel muttered, again concentrating on the cup.

Icicles pierced Francey's heart. It *was* something about Fleur. 'What?' he begged. 'Please, *what?*'

'Lookit,' Hazel at last looked him in the eye, 'I told him I didn't believe him.'

'Who? Told who?'

'That Colonel fella, whatever his name was . . .'

'What did he say?' Francey remembered all too well that strange little scene in the middle of the dance floor the previous night.

'I've said too much already,' Hazel glanced at her watch. 'There's nothing in it – he's a creep, Francey, he tried to give me the come-on—'

'He obviously said something about Fleur.' Francey was mad-

344

dened now. 'You can't start this and not go on, you're not being fair, Hazel.'

'He said nothing at all,' Hazel said, seeming to come to a sudden decision, 'you'll just have to ask Fleur herself. It's none of my business.'

'Ask her what?' Francey gripped the sides of the table. 'I'm not letting you get on that plane until you tell me what you're on about, Hazel. I'm warning you.'

Hazel pursed her lips. 'Keep your hair on.' Through his alarm, however, he could see that she was at last taking him seriously. 'All right,' she said, after a few tense moments, 'all I'll say is that oul' codger seemed to think that Fleur was not as pure as the driven slush, Francey.'

Outraged, Francey sprang to his feet, upsetting the cups on the flimsy table. 'How dare he? I'll kill him.' The thought of Fleur and that awful, red faced, middle-aged man —

'Take it easy.' Hazel appeared unruffled as she, too, stood up and righted the cups. 'Don't be makin' a show of yourself, Francey, there's people looking.'

'I don't care if the world and his mother are looking.' Francey's breath was hurting.

Hazel picked up her handbag. 'There's probably a very simple explanation – maybe he was referring to you? Maybe youse weren't as discreet as youse thought?'

That did take some of the steam off Francey's anger, but he could not imagine how the Colonel could possibly have found out he and Fleur had been lovers.

Then it hit him. It had to have been the servant, that maid. Apart from Hazel, the maid was the only one, besides Tommy – and Colin, of course – who knew he had visited the flat.

Perhaps it was George? It occurred to Francey that his father had been at the table on the occasion Colin had thanked Francey for Tommy's gifts. Could George have put two and two together?

Then Francey recognized the awful fact that in the short term it did not matter who it was who knew. 'I've got to warn Fleur,' he whispered.

This time Hazel did or said nothing to calm his panic. 'I suppose you'd better,' she agreed, glancing again at the departure board. 'Lookit, I have to go, all right?' With assurances that she would be in

345

touch when she came back for the Rollers' Lenten tour, she bussed him on the cheek and tip-tapped her way towards the departure gates.

It was only after she had left that Francey remembered he had not asked her how Fleur's name had come up in the first place during her ill-fated conversation with the Colonel. No matter, he could find that out later. What was most urgent was that he had to let Fleur know that in all probability her maid was a gossip. And, of course, he could not just ring the Manor and ask for her. Dammit, he thought, as he got back to his car, why did everything have to be so complicated?

When he got to the hospital he found Dessie, unkempt as a scarecrow in hospital-issue pyjamas, sitting up in bed. 'Before you say anything, Francey,' his half-brother stubbed out the butt of his Woodbine on the ashtray in his other hand, 'I'm sorry, I'm sorry, I'm sorry. It'll never happen again, I know I was wrong.'

Seeing his woebegone expression, Francey, who had been about to launch into a lecture, modified it. Being the sole visitor in the ward he felt elephantine and conspicuous. 'This time you have to mean it,' he whispered, 'and you'll have to agree to let us get help for you, Dessie. You can't do this on your own.'

'I know,' Dessie's penitence was absolute. 'I know that now, Francey. You'll see – from this day I'm a new man. I'll do anything you say.'

Recognizing that he may not be so malleable in the future, Francey insisted they talk then and there about what form the help should take and whether it should be in Ireland or here in England. At least money was no object and Dessie could afford the best treatment going. He was reluctant to stray too far from his beloved horses, however, so they decided that whether it should be in a clinic of some sort or in private consultation, the best place for him was London. Francey promised to find out what he could in the next few days and then went off to check when Dessie was to be released.

This proved to be straight away but since he had brought none of his brother's clothes, Francey had to make the round trip to the Manor to fetch them. This was more of it, he thought, anger rebuilding as he gunned the Morris through the sunlit lanes: Francey Sullivan – everyone's dogsbody.

His temper was not improved when, on arriving at the house, he found that Fleur and Colin had already left and that his father had left instructions with the staff that he was not to be disturbed. 'Thank you, Lewis, we'll see about that!' Leaving the butler no opportunity to intervene he strode towards the study, scene of the recent painful row.

He barged in after a perfunctory knock to find his father sitting behind the desk, head bowed in both hands over a heap of papers. 'Dessie's being released,' he announced from the threshold, anger causing a quiver in his voice.

'Wha—' George's head jerked up and he stared across the room.

Francey saw his father's eyes were milky with incomprehension and realized he had been asleep. 'Did you hear me?' he asked roughly. 'Dessie's being released from hospital. And I can't look after him today, I have to go to London.'

'What are you talking about?'

Seeing George's bewilderment and the white stubble which covered a lot of his face as he shook off his nap cooled Francey's anger. It was difficult to maintain fury with an old man. 'I've got to go to London,' he repeated in a calmer voice.

The room was in shade and he walked around the desk to open the blinds at one of the windows, releasing a flood of sunlight into the room. 'Oh, God!' George winced at the merciless light. 'Do you have to?'

'I have to. You have to go to the hospital straight away. Dessie has no clothes, I'll give you a few minutes to get ready and I'll have his bag in the hall for you.'

In case he should weaken, Francey turned on his heel and left.

The maids had already been into Dessie's room, he saw: the bed was made up, ashtray clean, and no empty bottle or any other trace of last night's depredations was in evidence. Francey wondered what opinion these silent, efficient girls must hold of the people they served. Not an elevated one, he suspected.

And why should they? Take himself, for instance, he had been so wrapped up in his own affairs he had not even bothered to find out what any of them was named – neither had he ever heard any of them being addressed by name in the house. That, too, must change: the next time he came here he would make it his business to get to know each of the staff as an individual. He packed Dessie's few things in his bag and brought it out to the lobby, then went again to the study.

This time he waited for an invitation before going in. George had shaved and he looked more like his normal chipper self. 'You never gave me the chance to ask how the lad's doing,' he complained but Francey saw that the papers in front of him were now so tidy that the pen he held was clearly a prop.

Hating the notion that his father felt obliged to maintain an act in front of him – hating him for the weakness of it – he walked around the desk to open the rest of the blinds. 'He's doing fine,' he said, his voice curt, 'but if we're not to have a repetition of last night he needs proper attention. It's one of the reasons I'm going to London, to see if I can sort something out.'

'On a Sunday?' Twisting around to watch the operation with the blinds, George put down the pen.

'I'll start first thing in the morning.' Francey had other plans for this evening.

'What'll I do with him all day? When will you be back?' His father's dismay was palpable and Francey did his level best to control himself.

'He's your son,' he replied, 'it'll give you a chance to get to know him. He loves the horses,' he added, then wondered if George had noticed even this about Dessie. 'And since you like them too – or used to – that could be a good place to start.'

George opened his mouth but Francey cut him short. 'I have to be going, his bag's in the hall.' Then he hesitated. 'There's something else . . .'

'More trouble?' With a theatrical sigh, George sat back in his chair.

'I'm not sure,' Francey said, watching him closely: 'I was just wondering if – if you know anything about rumours concerning Fleur?'

'What rumours?' George's eyes remained steady but his body stiffened a little and Francey, sensitized as he was, could not help but imagine he had seen a slight shade of doubt.

'About her and – and – someone else.' He could not bring himself to name the awful Colonel. But he could hardly confide in his father about his own involvement.

'Who is this someone?' It was George's turn to look watchful and Francey, whose stomach contracted, noted he had not thrown out the implied suggestion.

348

'I'm not prepared to say at this point,' he said shakily. 'I just want to know if you've heard anything.'

'No,' George said slowly, 'I didn't. I don't believe everything I hear. You shouldn't either, Francey.' Then, unusually, Francey's father paused to choose his next words. 'Do I take it – that you have, shall we call it, a special interest?'

Francey stared at him. His insides stilled as though his body was at the very brink of a canyon and about to take a leap into the empty air. 'I think Fleur is a wonderful person,' he said, holding his father's gaze, 'and I am very concerned about what people might be saying about her. I want to protect her.'

'She does have a husband for that, you know.' George's violet eyes were without expression.

'I know she does. But we're all her family, too. In my opinion, George,' Francey said, 'she needs us all.'

'I agree.' George's face relaxed and Francey thought he saw a trace of sympathy. But the subtlety of the exchange was at too high a level for him to sustain it any longer. And in any event he was not in the business of forging complicity with his father.

'I'd better be going.' The interview had been not at all what Francey had expected, and if George's reaction was to be believed, his father either knew about himself and Fleur, or there was some substance to the allegations made via Hazel that Francey had not been his lover's first adulterous affair.

After Francey left, George collapsed against the back of his chair. *When troubles come they come not singly* ... As usual, Shakespeare popped up to help him but with no audience except himself, the quote fell flat.

No doubt about it, George Gallaher, he thought, when you set yourself a problem you don't do it by halves. Francey and Fleur? So his suspicions that day he had seen them hugger-muggering at the edge of the wood had been correct. Poor kids, he thought.

Then, staring into space, George realized that he was definitely getting old. Was it only a few months ago that he had thought – and at his wife's funeral, too – that he himself would not have objected to a little turn with Fleur? Only a few weeks ago that he had been having a whale of time in London with his own little friend? Only a few days ago that, had he been asked, he would have replied that of course adultery was the icing on the cake of sex, that the whiff of illegality was what gave a romp its special thrill? When a reaction like sympathy for the plight of Francey and Fleur would have been the very last to occur to him.

Should he intervene like a father? Father-in-law?

This was all too much. With sudden resolution, George stood up. There was life in the old dog yet and it was not yet time to find a patch of sunlight in which to lie down and twitch into the twilight. In the meantime he might as well follow orders and go to fetch the misfit who was the third of this diverse clutch of sons. As he collected the car keys, George had to smile at the irony of the reversal of roles between himself and Francey. Whatever about Colin and the misfortunate Dessie, he thought, it looked like Francey would turn out all right.

Francey did not know the topography of London well enough to find his way around by car so he decided to park at Oxford and take the train. It being a Sunday, the train, when it eventually did come, was a slow one, stopping at many of the stations en route. He dozed a little, but not enough to refresh him.

It was the late afternoon when his taxi deposited him at the hotel off Kensington High Street. The weather had changed and as he paid off the cab, the heavy drizzle woke him up a little; this hotel was many steps up from the one he had occupied before, yet not so luxurious as to be intimidating. He was not yet in the super-playboy league: that was yet to come, he thought, prodding his faltering resolve as he allowed a young boy to take his overnight bag and checking the impulse to insist on carrying it himself.

During the intervals between naps in the train he had been trying to decide how he should approach Fleur. No matter which way he looked at it, he felt he had no option but to go to the flat in person and hope that fate handed him an opportunity of a few moments alone with her or, if it did not, to engineer it. He could not telephone because he already knew from Inveraray that extension lines could be picked up by anyone; and although from the experience with the brooch he thought he could be confident no one opened Fleur's post except herself, to write would delay matters. He had to find out one way or the other.

He did not bother to unpack his bag but went into his bathroom, splashing icy water on his face to shock himself into the full reality of what he was facing. He left the hotel again within minutes of his arrival, taking a taxi from the rank outside and giving Fleur's address. He had not rehearsed what he would say and, as the taxi sped through the wet Sunday streets, eschewed the temptation to do so. Now that the task was upon him, he had recovered his determination and his mind felt open and clear.

A female voice, not Fleur's, answered his bell push and admitted him. When the lift door slid open on the vestibule of the flat he was greeted by the nanny with an apology that neither Fleur nor Colin was in but both were expected shortly. 'Come on in and wait,' she invited, 'have a drink or something, Tommy and I are watching the telly. Yes,' she continued, correctly interpreting Francey's look of surprise, 'he loves it, and it's amazing how much he understands just from the pictures. What he doesn't pick up by himself, I translate for him.'

The television was in a small, warm room, its windows insulated from the afternoon drizzle with cheerful yellow curtains. The little boy was lying full length on his stomach, chin on his hands and surrounded by a litter of toys, including, Francey saw, his own helicopter. Tommy's concentration on the wildlife programme was such that he did not notice Francey's arrival until the nanny tapped him on the shoulder and signed that they had a visitor.

He turned round and smiled – Francey noticed the child had Fleur's smile – and jumped to his feet, holding out his hand for Francey to shake it. That little ceremony over, he flopped back on his stomach and fell back into contemplation of his programme. 'Sorry,' the nanny apologized to Francey. She left the room to fetch Francey's beer.

Francey could not take his eyes off the prone body of the little boy. Here was a factor he had not considered in his long-term goal of winning Tommy's mother for himself. It was such a mundane, comfortable activity: watching television on a wet Sunday afternoon in the home you had known all your life, all your possessions around you, your nanny just a step away, your mum and dad out for a bit but expected back soon.

He had never until now taken into account the nuts and bolts of breaking up this marriage. For sure Colin would not just move aside and allow an interloper to move in with his wife so even if Francey's suit had been, *would be*, successful – Francey was determined not to let the notion go until Fleur herself killed it – he and Fleur would have to live somewhere new. Forgetting his resolve that he was meant to be thinking only of himself from now on, Francey asked himself if he could be the one to remove all this from under this child's feet. And no ordinary child but one who was deaf.

The nanny came back with the drink and he tried to settle in to watch the programme with the other two, seeing nothing on the screen except a series of moving shapes, hearing nothing but indistinct noise.

Colin and Fleur returned less than half an hour later to find the three of them, Francey, the nanny and Tommy, still staring at the flickering pictures. 'Well,' Colin smiled from the door, 'this is cosy.' Francey's gaze flew over Colin's shoulder to where Fleur hovered; unlike her husband's, Fleur's face was as impassive as always as she came in to give Tommy a hug. As mother and child signed to one another, Colin asked Francey as to what they owed the honour of the visit. 'Is Dessie all right?'

Francey brought him up to date on their half-brother's condition and then mentioned why he was officially in London. 'I'd appreciate your help on this one, Colin,' he said. 'I know that in theory George is the one who should be doing most for Dessie but I'm not sure we can rely on him.' All the time he was speaking, Francey's peripheral vision was observing the three-way silent conversation between the child, the nanny and Fleur, whose hair, falling in two dark curtains on either side of her face, concealed her features. The only part of her body visible under the folds of her astrakhan coat was the back of one of her dainty hands, the touch of which he so well remembered.

He could just imagine it on the skin of another man's back . . .

Francey swallowed hard. 'I think our father wishes all three of us would just go away,' he said to Colin, forcing himself to concentrate on the words coming out of his own mouth and to look the other man in the eye.

'Well, wouldn't you?' Colin's grin was lop-sided.

'I see what you mean,' but then Francey's attention was diverted again as Fleur stood up.

'Would you like some tea?' she asked, the perfect hostess.

This echo of the preamble to their lovemaking startled him into stuttering, 'Y-yes, please.'

'I'll have it brought. Come, Tommy,' she signed, and the little boy took her hand as the two of them left.

'I'll just go to my room, if you'll excuse me.'

The nanny went too, leaving Francey with the man he had cuckolded.

'Come into the drawing-room,' Colin invited, 'we'll be more comfortable in there.'

'Oh, but this is lovely,' Francey protested, but was then obliged to follow his half-brother down the hallway and up the stairs towards the scene of his crime. This whole idea had been a mistake: he had not been able to hold on to his sense of purpose, he was too flustered and was bound to betray that he knew this place better than if he had just dropped by with a toy for the boy.

'I need to go to the bathroom.' He bought time.

'Sure.' Colin indicated a door opposite the drawing-room. 'When you're finished, we'll just be in here,' pointing towards the door Francey knew all too well.

In the bathroom, he washed his hands and slowed himself down. 'Pull yourself together,' he said to his reflection, deciding that if he could not manage time with Fleur within the next ten minutes he would leave.

As he came out of the bathroom, however, she was coming up the stairs. And she was alone.

'Fleur,' he intercepted her when she was about two-thirds of the way up. 'Thank God,' he whispered, taking her arm. 'We have to talk.'

She frowned. 'Here is not a suitable place for talk.'

'Well, where then?'

'There is nowhere at present,' she went as though to pass him but he tightened his grip on her arm.

'You don't understand, we have to.'

She glanced towards the drawing-room. 'Please leave my arm alone. We must not meet again as we were, not ever.' Delicately, she prised off his fingers. 'I hope you understand. Now, if you'll excuse me, we must not stand here like this.' She mounted the last few stairs.

To compound Francey's horror, Colin popped his head out

through the drawing-room doorway just as Fleur got to the top of the stairs. 'I thought I heard voices. Everything all right, old chap?'

From the top step, Fleur smiled down at Francey as though she, too, was waiting to hear what he had been talking about.

'I think I left something in the bathroom.' Somehow Francey managed to climb back again to the top of the staircase and walk towards the room he had just vacated. Once inside, he sat on the edge of the bath; his face felt as cold as the porcelain beneath his hands. Her discarding of him had been as elegant, precise and brutal as the dissection of an insect with a needle.

He sat there until he became aware that someone was knocking on the door. 'Are you all right in there?' Colin's muffled voice seemed anxious.

'Sure.' Francey forced himself to speak. 'I'll be out in a sec.' He ran water into the washbasin, letting it fill and drain out again. He did this twice. And then filled it up a third time.

'You've been in there an awfully long time. Are you sure you're all right, old chap?' Colin opened the door a fraction and peered in.

'I'm fine,' Francey pretended to be washing his face. His hands were shaking so much he slopped water out on to the floor. Blindly, he groped for a towel.

'Here, let me – you're an awful colour, Francey, let me get you a brandy.' Colin picked up the towel from the floor.

'I'm all right,' Francey croaked. 'It's just lack of sleep. I was up all night at the hospital.'

'Of course.' Colin hesitated. 'Is there anything I can do?'

'About Dessie? No.' Francey's intention had been to reiterate that Dessie was a joint problem for all three of them, himself, Colin and George, when something in Colin's demeanour stopped him. 'Sorry, what do you mean?'

'It wasn't anything Fleur said to you, by any chance?'

'I beg your pardon?' Francey's heart, already tested, almost stopped. 'Of course not,' he breathed.

Colin studied the towel he held. 'It's just that, you see . . . she was with you on the stairs there and I thought . . .'

Francey noticed that the dark green tiles in the bathroom were self-patterned with fleur-de-lis. Before he could come up with anything, Colin looked up from his towel. 'She's a wonderful person. Really.' A curious little grimace crossed his face as though he had just remembered something he regretted very much. 'I'll go and get your brandy.' He crossed to the door but hesitated and turned back again. 'She's – never mind . . .' He reconsidered what he had been about to say. 'Come down when you're ready,' he said, 'no rush.'

Chapter Eighteen

After Fleur's conversation with him, more precisely, after Colin left the bathroom, Francey had become numb. He managed somehow to go into the drawing-room and to take tea with his brother, Fleur and their son but the china cup in his hands felt like a piece of cactus. If Fleur noticed anything amiss, she showed no sign and Colin made all the running in what conversation there was, about Dessie, their father and Inveraray.

All the way back to the hotel, her words repeated themselves in his brain: *We must not meet again as we were, not ever*, over and over and over again like a children's nursery rhyme or the rhythm of a song he had heard on the wireless and could not get out of his mind for the rest of the day. His mind danced to it, skipped to it; like a little girl with a two-handled rope.

From his room he rang down and asked for a bottle of whiskey but even the large glassful he drank after the waiter's immediate departure could not cut through the thick ice around his feelings. Everything in the room looked a little off colour or of the wrong texture. The curtains were as coarse as thatch, the sateen bedspread as loose as water. Even the quality of the air in the room seemed wrong: grainy, as if it were not lit from the window but infused with a thicker, alien substance.

It was not until he was half-way through his third whiskey that the truth of what had happened overcame him. Everything was gone, all his plans – no, not all his plans but all his self.

She had rejected him, his humiliation was absolute. No, she had not rejected him: it had been worse than that. She had treated him as though he never was.

He tried to become angry, again to catch hold of the swaggering bravado which had risen to energize him in the ambulance the previous night. Had helped him face his father with such brio. Had that only been last night? He could not remember, the whiskey was doing its work, blurring the edges of time . . .

He knew he had not slept and he was feeling drunk now so it could have been any time in the last century that he had dreamed of a South Sea island. With Fleur. Without Fleur.

Without Fleur . . . *as we were, not ever* . . . The pain rose through his body until he could not bear it, his chest was about to shatter.

Quick: focus on South Sea island, palms, warm skin burrowing into white sand, turquoise sea . . . Francey poured himself another glass of whiskey but lucidity flashed for a moment and he saw himself as others must see him, a pathetic giant in a rented room, throwing good dreams after bad.

He drank until the whiskey bottle was three-quarters empty and he was too drunk to pour any more into the glass.

He stayed in bed all next day. Goaded beyond endurance by the unfortunate housekeeping staff who continued to blunder into his room, he roared down the telephone that he was not to be disturbed any more. He had never had a hangover like this one. *Men With Little Hammers* – somewhere in the Folly was a book by that title and for the first time Francey knew what it signified. Yet, despite the physical pain and sickness, he felt cleansed. It was as though his body had far too much to do in looking after itself to have any resources left to deal with grief or self-pity and between bouts of heavy sleep, he half welcomed the hangover as a type of catharsis.

And when at last he felt able to stagger out of bed and into the shower, the pain had retreated to the extent that at least he was able to walk without holding his head sideways. Hair of the dog, is what Hazel would have advised, yet as Francey speculated about the whiskey remaining in the bottle, his gorge rose at the thought of drinking it. He stood under the shower for twenty minutes, alternately raising and lowering the temperature of the water. By the time he got out, he felt weak and shaky but almost human. He contacted room service and ordered steak and chips.

For the next few days Francey wandered around the seedier parts of London like the homeless man he was. He might have been living in an hotel, with all the food he could eat, clean linen on his bed, staff at his beck and call, but he felt as rootless and directionless as if he was living on a piece of wasteground or under a railway bridge.

He put himself in Dessie's shoes: whereas nothing could compensate for the desperate poverty and hopelessness of a derelict, from the bits and pieces he had gleaned from his half-brother he recognized one or two small compensations, among them that a man could drop all pretence of being anything other than he was. So people looked at you? You did not need to look at them at all.

And whereas Francey could feel nothing but pity for those he saw eating out of newspaper at the back doors of restaurants, at least their condition gave him pause for thought. He was sure that any expectations had been knocked out of them long ago and they were therefore no longer in line for crushing disappointment.

Some part of him knew he was in shock and therefore not being rational, but for the first time since he was born, Francey did as his instincts bid him, allowing himself to feel miserable, walking his pain out of his system, walking all day until his feet were sore. Avoiding conversation, even the most trivial, he sat alone and ate chips from rundown cafés and drank in seedy, dangerous pubs, always ending up in a place he did not know from Adam. Then, not drunk but not sober, he sought out a taxi or a bus to travel back to the bright lights of Kensington High Street and the hotel. If the staff thought it peculiar that he came in each evening looking and smelling like a hobo, they did not show it.

Each night he telephoned Inveraray Manor to talk to Dessie who, penitent and obedient, was awaiting his first appointment, set up by George, with a Harley Street consultant. This luminary was going to assess what kind of counselling or other treatment Francey's half-brother needed.

Dessie was doing fine, he assured Francey every time. And although Francey listened hard, thinking it ironic in light of his own recent excesses, he could detect no untoward symptoms of drink or other substances in his half-brother's speech.

On the fourth day of his wanderings, the Thursday after Fleur's disposal of him, Francey was walking across an open space somewhere in the East End. The area, a graveyard for up-ended cars, was full of warehouses, many of them sealed up. He thought he spotted the distinctive chassis of a Jag and was going over to check when something moved nearby. Looking closer, he saw it was a bundle of rags. Except, just like Dessie when first he found him, it was human.

'Are you all right?' He went over to the bundle, which was lying on a piece of cardboard in a patch of withered vegetation. The whites of a pair of eyes rolled in a face more like a filthy relief map than a human face. 'Are you all right?' Repeating the question louder, Francey leaned over the person – he could not tell whether it was male or female – and touched his or her shoulder.

'I'm very cold.' The reply was whispered.

'Here.' Francey took off his coat. He put an arm under the creature and lifted it up and saw, when some of the rags fell away, that it was a man, his beard as long and awful as Dessie's had been.

'Are you from the council?' The man shivered like a birch leaf as he allowed Francey to insert his arms into the sleeves of the coat.

'No, I'm from Ireland.' Francey almost chuckled at the non sequitur but then stopped, afraid he would have to explain it.

'I was Irish once.' The man hunched down into the expensive coat as if it was a flour sack. 'Thanks, mate.'

'Are you hungry?'

The man looked at Francey as though he were from Mars and then the black creases in his face deepened with cunning. 'I could do with a few smokes, a few gargles. You know how it is, pal,' he exaggerated an Irish accent, 'ball o' malt?'

'What part of Ireland are you from?' The drizzle which had dogged Francey all day had turned to rain now: its cold fingers inserted themselves under the collar of his jacket and shirt as he squatted in the mud beside the tramp.

'Can't remember,' the man replied.

'What's your name?' From his inside pocket, Francey pulled out his wallet and checked to see how much money he had left.

The derelict's eyes were riveted on the wallet. 'Malachy.'

Another king of Ireland. 'Come with me, Malachy,' Francey attempted to hook him upright. 'We'll get you something to eat.'

'Can't,' the tramp said, then, wheedling, 'it's me feet, d'you see.' His hand snaked from the sleeve of Francey's coat towards the wallet. 'But if you could leave me a few bob, mate, I'm sure I'd be better in a little while and I'll get it meself.'

Francey, whose thighs were trembling with the strain of squatting for so long, was relieved to stand. 'Whatever you say, Malachy.' He removed every note from the wallet except a single tenner and gave the money to the astonished tramp who looked at the bundle in his hands as though it was a bomb.

'How much is here?' He looked up at Francey.

'Couple of hundred.' Francey turned away, sickened by what he was doing. 'Not enough.'

He looked back before he walked behind one of the warehouses to see that his friend had been joined by another. Both were standing upright. The skirts of Francey's coat were flying around 'his' tramp's feet as they bashed hell out of one another.

Next day, Francey went home to Ireland to be with the family for Abigail's entrance into the convent.

Up to the final episode in Fleur's flat, the last thing he would have wanted to do was to go back to the claustrophobia of Lahersheen, and during the week after it he been in such a state of shock he had wanted contact with no one at all, not even Hazel.

After the scene with the tramp, which had shocked a sort of sense into him, he had telephoned home purely to let his mother know he was still alive. It was Abigail, however, who answered the phone. 'I've never asked you to do anything for me before, Francey,' her soft voice came and went over the telephone wire, 'but Mam will need a bit of support for a few days. It's not like I'm going to Timbuctu or anything, but it's a bit soon after Mossie's death.'

'Then why not wait a bit?' But Francey was wavering. Suddenly the prospect of having somewhere safe and familiar, a place to lick his wounds and where he would have to make no efforts at all to be understood, was quite appealing. Whether Abigail picked up his lack of resolve or not, her response to his plea was firm. 'I've waited as long as I can, Francey. It's time now.'

And so he agreed.

More to bolster his spirits than to swank, on arrival at Cork airport next day he hired a Ford Consul which was the biggest car available, so that by the time he turned in through the farmyard gates, everyone on Béara knew Francey Sullivan was home again and they were all waiting for him in the kitchen: his mother, Abby, Margaret, Connie, and Tilly.

After the initial chat, grateful for the uncomplicated rhythms of the kitchen, Francey brought them all up to date about Dessie. Over the course of the next hour, although his mother's eyes were hollow, Francey was pleased to hear her use Mossie's name in conversation as it cropped up, referring to him quite naturally. 'Hazel Slye rang this morning, by the way.' She refilled his cup during a comfortable lull in the conversation. 'I told her you'd be here for a few days so she said she'd ring again next week.'

'Hazel rang? What about?' Francey was taken aback at the comfortable and familiar use of the name.

'What's the matter with you?' his mother seemed surprised at his expression. 'It was nothing to do with you. She's rung a few times since Mossie's died. Just to find out how things are going. Take that look off your face.' She gave his shoulder a little push. 'Why shouldn't we talk to each other? She's a very nice person.'

'I know she is.'

It was news to Francey that Hazel was telephoning his home regularly. Why had she not mentioned it? 'Where was she ringing from?' he asked, uncertain about how he felt. In many ways it seemed as though it was not just his love life but even his friendships which had slipped out of his control.

'She was ringing from home, I suppose,' his mother pushed pins deeper into her hair, 'but it's no use trying to get her now, if that's what you were thinking of doing. 'She's gone to England with the band since about an hour ago.'

Of course, the Lenten tour.

When Hazel did ring again a few days later, Francey was reluctant to talk to her in front of the others. Not for the first time did he wish the telephone was not in the kitchen where everyone lived for every hour of the day except for time spent sleeping. 'It's about time this house had a parlour,' he complained as he took the receiver from Margaret.

'Well, Mr Moneybags,' she retorted, 'why don't you build us one then?'

'Look, if you want money you can have it all, I don't want it.' Francey was at the end of his tether with the gibing about his wealth. He was planning to give a substantial sum to each of his sisters but had not yet got around to it and the way Margaret was behaving about it he was beginning to believe he might not bother after all. Since the lift of spirits on his arrival, he found himself locked again into his own troubles and was now just about surviving living at home. He could not wait until Abby went into the convent so he could escape again.

'That sounded interesting.' Hazel's voice was faraway.

'Sorry, it was just the normal joys of family life – you can get no privacy here, even to talk on the telephone.' Francey took the opportunity to send her a signal that she should not ask him about anything personal. In any event if he had been alone, he was not yet ready to talk about Fleur. 'Where are you, Hazel?'

She told him they were in Glasgow and were criss-crossing Scotland before going down into England, then mentioned that they would be playing a date in Birmingham during the first week in March. 'That's not all that far away from the family seat,' she said, 'so if you're around, why don't you drive up to the dance and say hello? It'd be fantastic to see you.'

'I might.' Francey hesitated: he did not know what his plans were now but there was no way on earth he wanted to be anywhere near Inveraray if Fleur was there.

'Oh, come on,' she urged, 'what happened to the new devil-may-care Francey? Where's he gone?'

Francey had been asking himself the same thing. At present the pain was still coming in waves and he was finding it difficult not to waver in his resolve to change his life. When Francey-and-Fleur was a possibility, he might have been mad at her but the wrath was ritual. Now anger with Fleur would have been a luxury. Nevertheless he found Hazel's joshing tone impossible to resist. 'Oh, that oul' Francey? He's up in Nellie's room behind the wallpaper,' repeating one of her own adages.

'Something happen?' Hazel's voice was careful now.

'Nothing, nothing, just one step forward, two steps back,' Francey acknowledged truthfully, 'but I'm going forward again as of today. I'll try to come to that dance, Hazel,' pushing the conversation away from controversy. To his relief she got the message and fell again into chat, as though Fleur Mannering's spectre was not perched like a Valkyrie on the telephone lines between them.

When he could get a word in edgeways, Francey asked if she would like to speak to his mother. 'You've been talking to her, I hear?'

'Why not? Is that a problem for you, Francey?' Hazel was blithe.

'She's a human being, isn't she? I like her, we like each other as it happens, and she's going through a bit of a rough patch.'

There was no reply to that and promising again to consider going to the dance in Birmingham if he happened to be nearby, Francey handed over the telephone and flopped into a chair by the window to resume reading his book. Then he caught Abigail's brown eyes on him. 'What is it, Abby?'

'Is she the special intention?' Abigail pitched her voice so the others would not hear.

'Who, Hazel? Of course not.' To his surprise, Francey found he was annoyed that Abby would think otherwise, more annoyed than perhaps the question warranted. 'Hazel's a great friend,' he insisted, 'but that's all she is.'

Abigail made no comment but lowered her eyes to the never-ending task of sewing Cash's name-tapes on to her trousseau. 'I'm going out.' Francey threw his book aside and, springing to his feet, picked his coat off the back of the door.

'Will you be back for dinner?' His mother interrupted her conversation with Hazel and covered the mouthpiece of the telephone.

'I might.' He slammed the door behind him.

What the hell was going on now? Francey gunned the engine of the big Ford and nearly ran over Rex as he shot out of the farmyard. Why was he so upset that Hazel Slye had become such a bosom friend of his family? And which was worse? This, or Abigail's misconception about his relationship with the singer? Already regretting his bad behaviour, he decided that it was neither: it was just that he was still out of sorts. He would have to have patience: it would be a long time before he recovered his equilibrium after what Fleur had done to him.

He drove to Castletownbere and parked the Consul in the square opposite MacCarthy's. Why not? he thought and went into the pub. Although it was still morning, and Lent to boot, a fair few were propping up the bar counter behind the grocery. Francey stood in beside them and ordered a pint. Although each of the men nodded hello, he knew none of them and when the pint came he took it to the seat facing the bar and savoured it sip by sip.

MacCarthy's was the type of establishment – fast disappearing in a drive towards modernity in Ireland – that Francey loved. Its old wooden shelves and thick brown counters exuded timeless sagacity: this place had seen the British Army and Navy being replaced by native forces; it had hosted wakes and weddings for generations past and in the way of human experience there was little its old walls could regard as new. It was possible to leave your grocery list on the front counter of MacCarthy's and then to enjoy your drink in the back or in the snug just inside the door while the list was being filled. Patronized by farmers' and fishermens' wives as well as the men themselves, it was the place where everyone caught up on the news or rode out the storms or waited for the tide to be right. There were always collections being taken up, raffle tickets to be bought and anyone looking for anyone else could leave a message and be sure it would be delivered.

Francey ordered a second pint and sat down with it to contemplate his future, this time once and for all. This time he had to make decisions and not just flirt with the possibilities as he had been doing on and off since last October. So much had happened in that short span of time that it was difficult sometimes to accept that it had been less than five months.

What was abundantly clear was that this rudderless existence would have to stop. His lack of direction, his reactive rather than active way of living had to be why his emotions were exposed and flapping in the wind like a line of washing. He had too much time to think about love and hurt and betrayal, about himself. South Sea islands notwithstanding, it had been more than three months since he had done an honest day's work: no wonder he did not know which end of him was up.

He looked at the weatherbeaten men in front of him: they seemed peaceful and calm, men confident of their place in the world and, to Francey's mind, could not in a million years have understood the selfish and destructive passions with which he had been engaged.

So what of the future? Throughout the past few days his mother had been hinting that she wanted to leave the farm to go back to live in the city and that if he wanted to take over now was the time. He could think of nothing he would like to do less. That was one decision made at least.

Decision number two was more difficult. What *did* he want to do? In his present mood, his dream of bringing the Shires to Ireland seemed far-fetched and too self-indulgent for words; in any event, in that department he had been outshone by Dessie. Francey saw that it would be far better for all concerned if he helped Dessie set up with the horses in whatever way he wanted. A riding school, perhaps with the Shires around the place as glorified pets?

Shed the Shires. That was decision number two.

But as he continued to mull over his options, Francey was forced to conclude that a dreamer and an ex-counter clerk from a builders' supply premises was qualified for precious little, and although out of his small change he could buy a shop of his own or even a pub if he wanted to, that way of life did not appeal to him.

Yet the thought of living on his money like a gentleman went against every tenet of his instinct and upbringing.

Hazel had mentioned helping him find something in the music business. Maybe the next time they made contact he could remind her of the offer? Even driving a van for the High Rollers or any of the other showbands would be preferable to this aimless hanging around. At least to tide him over until he knew what he wanted. Francey finished his pint and went out into the bright day.

He walked down on to the quayside where the nets were spread out for tending. But even here were reminders of his own failures: most of the fishing craft bore names of women – the *Nora Ann*, the *Máire Rua*, the *Stella Marie* – probably, Francey thought, in celebration of wives or daughters. At one point during the long days of distress after Fleur had filleted him, as though to punish himself further, Francey had summoned up the images he had entertained of their life together had things gone as he had wished. None had included a boat, of course, but these flowery scripts on the painted wooden hulls in front of him were potent reminders of what togetherness meant.

Because it was so big and comfortable they decided to use Francey's Ford to drive Abigail to her convent.

Every action that Sunday took on a special significance, a 'lasttimeness'. They took Abby to Sunday Mass in Eyeries for the last time, ate their last Sunday fry together and Abby took Rex for the last walk.

Then, having loaded her trunk into the boot and installed his silent mother, Margaret and Connie, Francey watched from the yard through the open door as Abby who had asked to be left alone in the house for a few minutes, walked around the kitchen as though to memorize every detail in it. She took down the ancient alarm clock from the mantelpiece and then replaced it, straightened the chairs around the table from which she had eaten so many meals and on which she had done her homework since the age of six. Abby would never again be allowed to set foot inside her home; she could, she had told them, if the occasion arose, look in through the windows from the outside.

Unable to bear the poignancy of it, Francey turned away and sat in behind the wheel. After a bit, his sister, face set, came out, pulled the door shut after her and got into the car without a backward glance.

The convent, which was in the north of the county, was a large square building set in rolling parkland. Francey parked the car on the gravel in front of the hall door and went round to the back to lift out Abigail's trunk. 'Are you the only new convict?' he asked, surveying the rows of blank windows. 'There're two other girls,' Abby's tight voice was so unlike her sunny self that Francey, who had veered between sadness and treating this whole adventure in a rather cavalier manner, repented his flippancy. 'Do I give in this dowry or do you take it?' His tone was gentler as he pulled the envelope containing the cheque out of his pocket.

'I'm sure they'll tell us.' Abigail straightened the jacket of her good costume and swallowed. 'Come on,' she exhorted them all, 'let's get this over with.' She rang the bell on the front door which was immediately opened, revealing a group of beaming nuns, at least ten or eleven in number, and of all ages.

The next half-hour passed in acute discomfort for Francey as he and his family were ushered into the parlour and served with refreshments by two of the nuns, who were introduced as the Reverend Mother and the Mistress of Novices. Abigail was taken away to dispose of her belongings and the dowry transferred hands without fuss, the Mistress of Novices taking it on behalf of the Bursar.

Abigail was brought back and the time had arrived to say goodbye. It was a serious goodbye because during her time as a postulant and then as a novice, they would be allowed to see little of her.

When Francey's turn came to give her a hug, he discovered his face was wet with tears. Although in childhood he had been closer to Johanna, he had always thought of Abby as his baby sister, his to mind and love and play house with. Her gentle presence was the best of Lahersheen. 'Take care,' he whispered into her soft curls, 'we'll all miss you. And don't be afraid to change your mind.'

'Oh, Francey,' her own face was distorted, 'I'll miss you all, too. I'll pray for you and your special intention. God bless.'

Francey took Connie and Margaret out of the parlour so their mother could say goodbye in privacy.

Hazel telephoned from Liverpool at about eight o'clock that evening and Francey's spirits lifted at the sound of her voice. The band was having a night off, he could hear the sounds of a party in the background. 'I wish I was there,' he said, only half joking, 'sounds like you're all having a great time.' For once he was alone in the kitchen, his mother had retired to bed early, Margaret was out on a call and Connie had gone to the house of one her schoolfriends to compare notes on homework.

'You're welcome any time, you know that.' Hazel's voice became muffled as she covered the receiver and shouted at the others to pipe down – that she could not hear her ears. 'Sorry about that,' she was back on the line, 'so why don't you come over for a few days? It's a good tour, we're doin' great business. Let your hair down, Francey, you'd enjoy it.'

'I can't – well, not just yet,' Francey was not sure why, 'but I might come over soon.'

'Any news? Can you talk?' Hazel dropped her voice as much as the background noise would allow. Knowing quite well what she meant, Francey hesitated, then decided he had bottled up everything long enough.

Hazel listened without comment as, omitting his own devastated reaction, he related to her what had transpired between himself and Fleur on the staircase of the Kensington flat. 'And there's poor Abby,' he realized he had sounded very sorry for himself and tried to lighten up the mood, 'wearing holes in her kneecaps, still praying for something which can't come true now.'

'Oh, I dunno,' Hazel's tone was reassuring, 'where there's life

367

there's hope. You put her on the spot, she could have misunderstood. Maybe you should have another go, talk to her again —'

'No!'

'All right, all right, don't bite the nose off me.' Hazel again covered the mouthpiece to shout down a loud, concerted guffaw behind her.

It all sounded so normal, so *lighthearted* that inside his body Francey felt his own soul as thick as lead. 'I will come over,' he said with sudden decision when Hazel came back on the line again. 'I've one or two things still to straighten out but after that I'll see you. Give me your schedule.' He wrote down the locations and dates she gave him and, promising to pass on her love to his mother, hung up.

Next day Francey surprised even himself with the speed of his decision-making. His mood was transmitted to the others in the house and by nightfall, as they were sitting around the table for their tea, everything was arranged.

Since there was little doubt that from September Connie would have a place at University College, Cork, his mother had announced that she would like to live nearby. Francey was so intent on being businesslike that he concetrated on the details and left consideration of the implications of this until later. When his mother demurred about his buying her a house of her choosing and his insistence on paying Connie's fees, he pushed both issues with such vehemence that it did not take her long to give in. The next business was Margaret: they decided that since she was staying in the area, she would continue to live in the farmhouse but that the farmland around it would be leased on conacre and any remaining animals sold.

'What happens to Rex?' Connie demanded at the end of this.

'I'll be in and out all day, he'll be all right,' Margaret reassured her. 'Anyway, I could do with a dog for company . . .'

'Maggie!' Francey laughed for the first time in what to him seemed like years, 'You're getting sentimental in your old age,' then had to duck as she threw a piece of tomato at him.

It was still bright outside and they had not turned on the electric light; the kitchen was slowing to its night-time pace, chores complete, peace descending. They all felt reluctant to get up from the table and dawdled over their last cups of tea, wondering about Abby and what she was doing right at this minute.

This was when it occurred to Francey that he had just passed another landmark in his life: as his family scattered with remarkable suddenness, the emotional foundations of his life were under assault. 'Are you sure this is what you want to do, Mam?' he asked her. 'What about your friends, Tilly, all the neighbours?'

Even the farmhouse would never be the same again: although it would remain in family hands, it would never again be home.

'I've the rest of my life to live too.' His mother's tone was definite as though this was something she knew would come up and was prepared to deal with. 'I've never talked about this but I do miss the social life of the city, public transport, shops at the corner, the cinema, things like that. And yes, I'll miss Tilly very much – you too, Maggie – but I'll come back to visit as much as I can. And I hope you'll all visit me. With all of you pursuing your own lives I'll be free now, after all.

'I never belonged here,' she added calmly, a revelation which was as shocking in its own small way to Francey as Fleur's rejection of him. Mammy and Lahersheen had always been inseparable in his mind and it had not occurred to him that she might be marking time in the farmhouse. It had been all right for him to move on, but the thought of her doing the same was unsettling.

Later that evening, before they went to bed, Francey discussed this turn of events with Margaret. She was sympathetic but firm.

'Take Jackie Kennedy,' she said. 'Like her, mammy has her whole life ahead of her. And when is the last time you've looked at her – *really* looked at her? She's a beautiful woman, Francey. It's not beyond the bounds of possibility she could even marry again.'

When it was put like that, Francey could not disagree but somehow the notion of his mother cavorting like a young person was going to take a lot of getting used to.

Before he and Maggie left the kitchen he wrote her a cheque, the equivalent of the dowry he had given the convent for Abby. Overwhelmed, Margaret looked at the amount: 'What am I going to do with all this? Francey, you're too good. I hope you didn't think I was hinting all those times.'

'Buy yourself a proper car, a yacht, do anything you like with it,' now that such momentous change was in train, Francey was impatient, 'but for God's sake enjoy it. Don't put it in a glass case and

369

throw sugar at it.' This, he realized, was another of Hazel's favourite sayings: he had absorbed more from her than he had thought. 'Anything else you need, just ask,' he added.

'Don't laugh – I might get meself a man. Mammy and meself might go hunting in pairs.' Francey laughed but this time, instead of throwing something at him, Margaret chuckled along. 'It's good to hear you laugh, Francey,' she said, 'I was getting a bit worried about you, we all were.'

'I was beginning to take life too seriously,' Francey admitted, 'but that's all going to change.' Wondering how many times he had said or thought that in the last six months, he went on to tell her about his plans to join Hazel and the High Rollers on the road for a few days.

'Good,' Margaret remarked when he had finished. 'We all like Hazel.'

'What is this?' Francey became annoyed again. 'First Abby and now you, she's a friend, no more.'

'Yeah, yeah!' Margaret got up from her chair and put the cheque into her handbag. 'I'm going to take your advice, I can't wait to spend this.'

Francey sighed and thought it better to say nothing more about Hazel Slye.

He caught up with the High Rollers in Birmingham late the next evening.

Despite Hazel's mentioning its proximity to Inveraray Manor, he had no intention of going anywhere near the house but planned to stay at a hotel in Birmingham city centre. His conscience had pricked him, however, and he had telephoned Inveraray from a public telephone at Cork airport to find that George was away in London and that when the butler put the call through to the stableyard, Dessie was too busy to come to the phone. Smiling, Francey had asked the hand who answered to pass on a message that he would telephone again tomorrow and, with a light heart, boarded his plane.

For the first time in many days, weeks, perhaps even months, Francey felt like a young man as, having checked into his hotel, he explored the city. Birmingham was not a pretty place in his estimation, but it was vibrant, filled with young people and on this fresh, sunny

370

day, even the cacophony of pneumatic drills from the numerous roadworks and building sites added to the impression of movement and life.

Everywhere he saw that the High Rollers' advance people had been busy: their handbills were plastered all over the construction hoardings and he could not walk down any street in the centre of the city without being far from Hazel's merry gaze. Whenever Fleur's face rose before his mind or if he saw a girl who reminded him of her, he put the image away by concentrating on other things: an ornate birdcage going past him on the carrier of a bicycle, a pair of slacks in a shop window, the way most of the girls here had hair as short as Hazel's. This new ability was progress of a sort, he supposed. And it went further: on seeing a couple kissing, observing the ecstatic fusion of one body into another, he was able to face the recognition that, at the height of his obsession with her, his love for Fleur had felt perilously close to suffering.

Francey felt as though he was on holiday: as he walked back towards his hotel to eat, for the first time in what seemed to be a long, long time, he realized that in the next few hours, days even, he had no one to put before himself, no duties in prospect, no task except to go to a dance where he would have the chance to enjoy himself. As a privileged insider he could lounge around the bandstand and would not even have to endure the ordeal of asking girls up.

His hotel room had a television set and, fascinated by the novelty, he ate his dinner in front of it and then took a short nap before showering and changing into his good clothes. It was well after ten o'clock, when, infused with pleasant anticipation, he headed for the ballroom. He got there at about a quarter to eleven and found that being the headliners, the Rollers were not due on stage for another fifteen minutes and that a local beat group was doing the warm-up for them. The hall was already full, however, and he knew by the accents in the queue, which still snaked past the cash office and out through the door, that most of the punters were Irish.

Having sized him up, the doorman directed him to a small lounge bar area where he said Hazel could be found. She was there, all right, perched on a stool at the counter at the far side of the room, legs crossed, fag-end in mouth and the sequins on her minidress and matching boots flashing in the multicoloured lights above the bar. Delighted to see her, Francey waved.

371

He was sure she must have seen him but instead of returning the greeting, Hazel turned to the counter to stub out her cigarette in an ashtray. He faltered in mid-stride and then decided he had become paranoid. 'Hello, Hazel.' He tapped her on the shoulder.

'Well, look what the cat brought in!' With a wide smile she surveyed him from top to bottom. 'How'ya, Francey!'

'You did invite me.' He grinned.

'Hey, fellas!' Hazel waved her hand around the group which spread along the bar on either side of her. 'Yiz all remember Hercules?'

Francey knew the term was not pejorative: except for Hazel's friend Vinnie, he had not seen any of these men since the accident with the minibus. 'How'ya, head!' They crowded round, offering drinks, clapping him on the back. He saw that only one of them bore visible scars: a livid weal from hairline to just above his cheekbone.

'I thought you said these ballrooms were kips?' he said to Hazel when the brouhaha had died down. 'This is very posh.'

'Ah, but this is England,' Hazel fluttered her false eyelashes, 'you've a different class of bengal here. You've to watch the door, of course, they'd do you soon as look at you, just like home, but the facilities are better. I even have a dressing-room.'

She insisted on buying him a drink, then introduced him to a number of people, the ballroom proprietor, the promoter and a few women who were done up to the nines and who seemed to be attached to individual members of the band. 'Before you put your foot in it,' Hazel muttered under her breath to him as she paid for his drink, 'don't ask those girls any questions, just smile and keep your mouth shut.'

'Give me some credit,' Francey was indignant that she thought him so naïve. 'I wasn't going to say a word.'

'Yeah?' Hazel thumped him with affection then saw over his shoulder that they were being called on. 'Drink up,' she ordered, 'you could make yourself useful setting up – or do you want to stay here and wait until we get going?'

'I'd like to come out and help.' The implicit acceptance that he was now part of the group was pleasing. He was amused to notice a phial of Gold Spot breath freshener being passed from hand to hand among the musicians as they all straightened their ties and walked towards the flunkey who was beckoning them through the door.

The girls touched up their hair and lipstick as they followed in a little self-conscious bunch and Francey would have been amused at them, too, if it had not occurred to him that he was in a somewhat analogous position walking out behind Hazel. Not quite, he told himself with a certain degree of smugness: unlike those girls, he had no designs on any of the band members.

The beat group, five lanky boys whose thin shoulders and spots were indicative of their youth, were just clearing the big stage as Francey helped the Rollers' drummer lug his bulky equipment on. 'Good luck, mate,' one of them said to Francey as they passed and Francey, pleased, did not disabuse him.

The noise in the ballroom thundered like the roar of the sea in his ears while the drummer performed expert manoeuvres with wing nuts, extending metal legs and little bolts. The area in front of the stage was already packed ten deep and, loving it all, particularly the ripple of expectation that passed through the crowd as they watched the set-up, Francey was delighted he had come. He was having fun, a commodity which had been in short supply during recent months.

He went off stage when the gear was ready, standing alongside Hazel in a holding area during a short hiatus in which the musicians drew metaphorical breath. A portentous announcement boomed through the Tannoy and, to a huge roar from the crowd, the men bounded through the dividing curtains and up on to the stage. Hazel let them go, then gave Francey one of her quick thumps, raised her head, counted 'one-two-*three*' and vanished, too.

Francey thrilled as the bellow from outside reached a crescendo.

He slipped out through the curtains and stood with his back to the wall of the ballroom, watching as with well-rehearsed fluency, the High Rollers picked up their instruments and launched without preamble into their opening routine, a five-minute medley which included a little dixieland, some rock 'n' roll, a fast polka and ending up with a lightning-fast arrangement of an Irish jig. The cheer at the end was so loud Francey felt his eardrums might split.

From then on, the band could do no wrong as, for two and a half hours, they lathered the punters with solos, duets, trios, even sextets, cover versions of chart numbers from Lonnie Donegan, Petula Clark, Kenny Ball, Cilla Black, Dionne Warwick and Hazel's favourite, Brenda Lee. They covered Elvis, Cliff Richard and Louis Armstrong, the Platters, even Bing Crosby and the Irish tenor John McCormack.

The rhythm guitarist switched to a banjo to lead an Irish dancing miscellany which set the place ablaze and, following that, when the dancers were sweating and panting under the condensation which dripped on their shoulders from the overhead struts of steel, Hazel let them catch their breath, stopping the show with an a cappella version of Gounod's 'Ave Maria'. Then, just when the crowd was feeling reverential and respectful of her artistry, she hopped them up again by swinging into the Everlys' 'Cathy's Clown' as a duet with the sax player.

It was wonderful to experience the dance from the unusual perspective Francey now enjoyed, and to increase his sense of relish, various girls had come up to where he stood to ask him up, a phenomenon previously unknown – even during a Ladies' Choice. He decided that his mood must be showing on his face and revelled in the luxury of being able to refuse without hurting their feelings, pointing with regret at the stage and muttering, 'I can't', a ploy which, without being a lie, gave them the impression that he was some crucial cog in the machinery of the band and could not desert his post.

But more than any other emotion, Francey was lost in admiration for Hazel. Having gone so late to the dance in Dublin, he had never seen her work in this way and he could see why there were as many men as girls packed into the sardine crowd in front of her. Hazel was not just talented and good-looking, her act was knowing and sexy. She had backcombed her hair so it looked longer and thicker than it was and frequently raked it with her nails, a studied movement that drew attention to her lithe body as she bopped alongside the rest of the band in choreographed synchronization. She took great care, however, not to stray to the edge of the stage within reach of grasping hands, and a little worm of pride that he had been the one she had chosen to take to bed with her began to puff itself up inside Francey's heart.

He never took his eyes off her from then on. About half an hour before the dance was due to end, Hazel, eyes closed, bent over the microphone as though it was a lifeline, was wailing through a torchy version of 'Anyone Who Had A Heart' when she miscalculated and came too close to the edge.

Before Francey's horrified eyes her feet were grabbed and she was pulled into the crowd, bobbing among them like a silver cork on a dark sea for a moment before vanishing. The three musicians at the front stopped playing and ran to rescue her, diving off the front of the stage.

But Francey was there before them; elbows and fists flying, he waded into the mêlée around Hazel and found her on the floor, struggling to get away from the clutches of a large, red-faced youth who was attempting to kiss her. While others, both men and women, pushed and shoved as though in a rugby scrum, Francey grabbed the suit collar of the young man and plucked him off her as easily as if he were a kitten and then picked Hazel up and, pushing through the crowd, carried her off to the side and safety. 'Are you all right?' he asked as he put her down.

'Thanks,' she did not seem at all frightened or upset, 'that's the third time that's after happenin' this month. Feckin' animals.' With that, pulling her hair straight and then her dress, she hopped back up on the stage, waited for the musicians to get back up and the act resumed where it had left off.

After the dance, no one in the band, least of all Hazel who was concerned only that two of her nails had been broken, seemed to take the incident seriously. Adrenalin pumping, they repaired to the little lounge bar, which was now crowded and doing a roaring trade in pints and double shorts. 'You could have been hurt,' Francey remonstrated as he brought a large gin and tonic over to where she was signing autographs for those fans privileged enough to be allowed into the bar for a brush with the band.

'We're all used to it – thanks, love,' she switched autograph books, 'there's only a few of us girls singing and it happens to us all. Happens to the men too – I'll just have to be more careful.'

'You need a bodyguard like Frank Sinatra, Hazel.' One of the girls in the crowd around her had an accent as rich as Hazel's own. Giggling, she indicated Francey. 'Yer man here'd scare the bejasus o'wa King Kong.'

'You might have something there,' Hazel glanced with amusement at Francey, 'I doubt if he's in the market, though.' Again she switched books.

'Who's your manager?' Francey did not want to let the subject go. 'He shouldn't be letting this happen —'

'That yoke?' Hazel scoffed. 'He's back at his big fat desk in Dublin. He doesn't care as long as the chicken necks keep comin' in and he can live in his big house and drive his Merc – thanks, love.'

She smiled and took the next piece of paper offered. 'We're not his only act, he has about ten of us, has to keep an eye on us all.'

She scribbled the last of the autographs and repaired with Francey to the counter to join some of the band and the promoter. 'I still think he should be with you, or somebody should.' Francey held her back, pulling at her elbow.

'Well, if you're all that concerned about it,' Hazel looked up at him her eyes teasing, 'why don't you take it on yourself like that young one over there suggested? Roadie, huh? Now forget it, all right?' She turned away. 'It's just one of the hazards of the job. Remind me to ask for danger money . . .' Seeming to forget all about it, she became immersed in high-octane banter with the rest of the group.

The outcome of that night, however, was that for the next two weeks Francey travelled with the High Rollers as relief driver for the wagon, security watchdog and general factotum. He learned to watch out for the frauds and scams that were apparently endemic in the business, checking to see that all punters came in through the official portals of the halls and that the promoters were not selling tickets at any other entrances, in car parks, or on the charter buses in order to swindle the band out of some of the door percentage. Any time the question came up in his own mind about why he was doing this, Francey rationalized that he was getting good training in the business end of showbiz, which should stand to him when his own time came. And he did not care that the absentee manager refused to pay him for his unofficial duties, insisting to Hazel and the others that he was travelling with them for the fun of it.

Which he was.

Leaving Dessie with George was proving to have been a good move, benefiting both. George, while still not a saint and absent from Inveraray a lot of the time, was at least honouring his commitment to bring Dessie to and from his appointments with his counsellor, a task he probably would have delegated if Francey was still there and willing to take it on. Maybe George was at last growing up.

Dessie himself, although sometimes jittery and defensive, seemed without doubt to be on the emotional mend, happy in the yard in what he now referred to as his work. Francy had had a quiet word with Mick O'Dowd who reassured him that his half-brother really was useful about the place and was not in the way or making a nuisance of himself.

In personal matters, Francey bided his time. He was so busy and active he hoped that, bit by bit, he was getting over Fleur Mannering. He suffered setbacks: sometimes, when sleep eluded him, the hateful phrases of her dismissal played like a stuck record in his ears and he was still afflicted with dreams of her but, by and large, although her rejection still hurt, the pain lessened a little each day.

He did not know, however, how he would react if he met her face to face and at present had no intention of letting that happen; and although he still had it in mind to discuss with Hazel what Shottley had said to her that night, subsequent events had made this irrelevant and he felt that to bring it up now would be to pick at the scab.

If Hazel wondered why he was not pressing the issue, she did not say so. In fact Francey was finding Hazel to be uncharacteristically reticent and tactful about Fleur: when she had recognized his distress during one tentative attempt to raise the matter, he had been astonished at the speed at which she had let the subject drop, adding only the reassurance that she was ready to talk about it any time he felt the need. These blips aside, and in spite of the constant travelling, the sameness of the hotels, the repetitiveness of the band's jokes and chat, during these two weeks in March, Francey grew almost happy.

And as he got to know the more intimate details of life on the road, he also saw with some surprise that whereas most of the men took full advantage of opportunities presented, Hazel always went to bed alone.

Chapter Nineteen

Not having been to Inveraray Manor since the ill-starred party on St Valentine's Day, and notwithstanding her decision never to go there again, if she could avoid it, Fleur found she had to go one more time.

Colin's father, who late in life had apparently discovered the meaning of paternal duty, had got it into his head that, for Dessie's sake, they should mark Saint Patrick's Day. Always the one for the grand gesture, he had asked that she and Colin, who was at home for once, should come down to Warwickshire for a special dinner. Francey had been invited too but he was still away in the north, continuing his ridiculous and irresponsible vagrancy with that dreadful little woman's danceband.

As it happened, however, Fleur was glad Colin's half-brother was away – it was one potential complication she did not have to face and not just where Francey himself was concerned: she would not have been surprised to find that if he had come along, he would have had the woman in tow.

She and Colin were going to take Tommy, who was out of school with a cold, and where Tommy went, his nanny went too. Fleur was a little worried as to how Tommy would react to being separated from the nanny when they took off for their big adventure but, on balance, was sure that he would so enjoy his new life in the sunshine with her that he would settle. Anyhow, they had so much money now that he could have a new nanny, or even send for the existing one if the girl would follow them.

But this was for the future because of course no one knew her plans were complete except Fleur and her friend in Hatton Garden, through whom she had secured a four-year lease on a villa in Little Cayman. She had picked this particular place not for its status as a tax haven but because it boasted an expensive convent school catering to the rich, one class of which was reserved for children with disabilities.

With Colin's unsuspecting collaboration – he and Fleur had discussed a possible holiday in the South of France – Tommy had been transferred from his passport to hers; the rest of their papers were in order, or at least as much in order as they had ever been, and were stashed in the safe in her boudoir. The airline tickets were booked and ready to be picked up at the airport. Although she had had to give the correct names, Fleur, covering every angle in case the agent decided to telephone her home with some query, had not given him her real address, explaining she was travelling a lot at present and would be out of contact until the day of the flight. In case the agent or airline had to be in touch or became worried that she would not turn up and gave their seats away, she had telephoned every day since making the booking to reconfirm them.

Fleur had kept Jool's pearls because she knew they suited her but she had made the final trade-in of the rest of the jewellery inherited from the old lady along with her own range of diamonds and, in exchange, now owned three magnificent, blue white flawless solitaires, each approximately four carats in weight and together worth the best part of half a million pounds. She had sewn these into a pouch, as long and narrow as a finger, that she had made from black silk, fixing this in turn into the inner lining at the bottom of her mother's beaded purse. She arranged the pouch along the seam in such a way that unless someone was snooping on definite information, the natural assumption would be that the lumps made by the gems were caused by the large pieces of jet and crystal with which the outside of the purse was encrusted. The lining was so worn it was doubtful that anyone would suspect its recent mending.

All that was left to do was to withdraw all the cash from her private deposit account and to make arrangements with her bank to forward the incomes for herself and Tommy to the account she had already opened – with the help of her jeweller friend – on the island.

She had planned the departure to the airport with military precision, allowing two clear hours along the way for the financial business, a precaution she deemed necessary in case there were any nosy parkers in the bank who, given the amounts involved, might feel they had to seek approval for the transactions from superiors – or even her husband.

The latter was not a problem: Colin was going to Singapore early in the morning and would be none the wiser until after he came back, or at least until he telephoned. By that time she and Tommy would be well ensconced in their new home.

The closer she got to takeoff – less than thirty-six hours away now – the more nervous Fleur became that something would go wrong and, just prior to leaving for the dinner at Inveraray, the afternoon of 17 March found her in the boudoir, double-checking everything in the safe. This pernickety behaviour was unlike her, she knew, but the scale of this adventure put in the shade every other plan she had ever hatched; compared with it, even the successful scheme to escape from the Lily Garden had been child's play.

The beauty of it lay in its simplicity: she was doing nothing illegal, stealing nothing from her husband or anyone else. Whenever she thought about the moral aspect of her project, which was seldom, Fleur saw nothing amiss. All she was doing was taking her own hard-earned profits and her son and going to live an independent life in a different climate. No one would suffer, except Colin, perhaps, for a while, because he thought he loved her, but romantic love was a plaything for the bourgeoisie; the only love that counted was the love of a mother for her son. Colin could find a new games mistress.

Having checked the documents and felt along the bottom of the beaded purse for the umpteenth time to reassure herself that the diamonds were still there, she was in the process of replacing everything when she heard someone come into the drawing-room. Quickly, she closed the small trap-door concealing the safe, kicked the silk rug over it and pulled down the bedspread just as the person knocked at the boudoir door. 'Who is it?' The imminence of her departure was making her so jumpy her voice sounded peculiar to her.

'It's Colin.' The voice was faint through the thick door. 'We're ready to go, Fleur, may I come in?'

'I'll come out.' Fleur stood up and unlocked the door to find Colin already wearing his coat. 'Tommy's already in the car.' Then he glanced downwards: 'Your mother's purse?'

Fleur realized she was still holding it. 'Yes.' She looked at it as though she herself was surprised and pleased to see it. 'I had misplaced it but I found it again just the other day. I thought I would show it to Tommy since it was his grandmother's.'

'I haven't seen that for years!'

Fleur could have killed herself for her carelessness. 'Shall we go?'

As she passed him in the doorway, she admonished herself to take care: this mistake was not serious but it was indicative of what could happen if she did not keep her wits about her in the next twenty-four hours. It was bothersome that having told the lie she now had to take the purse with her to Inveraray, but she knew it would be secure enough.

Hazel smiled as widely as her face would allow while Francey chatted, his voice raised so he could be heard above the reverberations of the wagon's engine, to the other band members. After two weeks of playing the best friend/favourite sister role with him she was feeling the strain but was determined to see it through, at least until the end of the tour, or Francey's stint on it. Then she would see what her next move could be. At present, she rejoiced to see the animation on his face, a great improvement on the stress that had marked it for the first days after the dance in Birmingham. And it had been a while since she had caught that glassy expression, which she knew signified his raking over the coals again about what might have been with the Siamese twin.

Hazel dared to hope that he was getting over the woman, although she considered it ominous that he would not go to the Saint Patrick's Day dinner for his brother. She would have preferred it if seeing Fleur would not matter to him one way or the other.

The Catholic Church in Ireland granted a dispensation from Lent for Saint Patrick's Day and three-quarters of the country went dancing. This year, however, the Rollers' management had negotiated a lucrative deal with a chain of ballrooms in centres of high Irish population in Britain and it would not have paid the band to go home. Therefore, they were on their way to Coventry where they were, uncommonly for them, sharing the night with another of the bands on their management's books. Normally the Rollers, as headliners, would have come on last but in this instance, because they were travelling on to Brighton for the following night and because they were stopping off in Cricklewood for a bit of private Paddy's night crack with another band, they had negotiated that the lesser band would start and finish the date in Coventry so that they themselves would come on at ten thirty and end at a quarter past midnight.

The road to London would take them within twenty miles of

Little Staunton and if Francey had gone to his family party, they could have detoured to pick him up. It would have been relatively early – before half-past one in the morning – and he would not even have had to stay the night under his father's roof. But he had been firm in refusing to discuss the possibility and Hazel, whose campaign was calibrated as finely as the mechanism of a watch, knew better than to push it.

She had been able to watch him at close quarters for such a concentrated period – even when he did not realize it – that she was getting to know Francey as well, if not better, than he knew himself. The change in him since he had approached her that first night in the Dublin ballroom had been nothing short of spectacular: in that period of less than six months, a new Francey had appeared right before Hazel's eyes as though she was in a photographer's darkroom watching a print develop from raw materials.

The Francey who was emerging, despite his self-deprecation about 'one step forwards, two steps back', was no longer an insecure, overgrown boy. Hazel felt that this one could no longer be manipulated and that he had hardened quite a bit. She reckoned this was no bad thing. While she did not want him to bury the sweetness at the core of his nature and, which was one of his most attractive attributes, the Francey she had brought to bed with her had been far too easily put upon. This one was no longer naïve or a pushover for every dog and divil with a sob story. If Fleur had done that for him with her andramartins, she had done him an unwitting favour.

The big drawback, of course, was that now he had swung too much the other way and was behaving like a monk. While all around them people were messing out of their skulls, Francey's demeanour would have done a Carthusian proud. From her vantage point on stage every night, Hazel was able to keep an eye on him and was partly relieved, partly amused at his steadfast, if charming, refusals to entertain any of the numerous invitations, both overt and subtle, he received from the girls who thronged around his self-designated patrol zone around the stage.

Hazel, who at no point had seen the punters as potential rivals, was also beguiled at his zeal to protect her from being pulled into the crowd again. She had once been to a concert by a rising young rock 'n' roll group called the Rolling Stones who attracted screaming adulation, even frenzy. Francey's behaviour was reminiscent of that of the gorillas who prowled the front of the auditorium during the Stones' act to guard them against their fans.

She had never come to any harm and if the truth be known she had incorporated a sort of teasing will-she-won't-she-fall sideplay into her act. But if being a gorilla made Francey happy, she reasoned, why not let him at it?

The musician who was driving pulled the wagon into a layby just outside Sheffield so that he could relinquish the wheel to someone else and they could all take a small walkabout. Hazel got out with the rest and slugged water from the bottle she always carried in her kitbag: one of the showbiz commandments drummed into her from infancy was that to keep skin unlined you had to drink gallons of it. 'Want some?' She offered the bottle to Francey.

'Thanks.' He drank, gave the bottle back to her and, with a huge yawn, stretched his arms above his head, making Hazel, who was wearing flat shoes for travelling, feel the lack of every inch above her four foot eleven.

'For God's sake put your arms down,' she complained. 'Do you want to make a show of me? You look like Stonehenge.'

'I feel like it.' Francey grinned. 'I think my joints are calcifying from all the time I'm spending in that bloody wagon. I hope I'm OK to drive – it seems like years since I slept two consecutive nights in the same Uncle Ned.'

It was a source of mischievous delight to Hazel that Francey was using the band's road lingo so self-consciously, but he was so proud of being one of the gang she would not have dreamed of teasing him about it. 'If you're tired then let someone else drive,' she retorted.

'Absolutely not, it's my turn and I want to play my part.'

'Suit yourself.'

'That's big of you, Queenie.' He ruffled her hair with affection.

'Don't do that,' she warned, smacking his hand away with exasperation.

'Sorry.' He leaned down and, to Hazel's chagrin, compounded the insult by bussing her on the cheek.

Just you wait, Francey Sullivan, she thought as she climbed back into the wagon and resumed her seat, *I'll take that out on your glorious hide some night in the not too distant future.*

The erotic thought sent shivers down her spine and she had to take another drink from her water bottle in case it showed.

When Colin and Fleur rattled across the cattle grid at the end of the driveway into Inveraray Manor, they were treated to the sight – not seen since before Jool's death – of George driving a pair of Shires towards them.

With Dessie standing behind him, George, perched on the high seat of the rulley and wearing full driving regalia, bowler hat, apron and all, looked like a woodcut illustration from a book published at the turn of the century.

'Well, well!' Colin slowed the car and looked sideways at Fleur in an effort to implicate her in his amusement but she looked away from the oncoming team and out over the fields. From the time that the date of her leaving had been set, she had found it difficult to maintain her domestic charade with Colin and almost everything he said or did now irritated her. Then, from the back seat, Tommy made excited noises and indicated by pulling at her back that he wanted to get out so she was forced to speak to Colin after all, asking him to pull up.

Tommy ran straight to the rulley and clambered, with Dessie's help, on to its flat bed, and then, as Colin negotiated the car around the vehicle, Fleur's son waved down at her with such joy that her vexation dissipated.

Dessie was itching to get his hands on the reins of the team. He was still more than a little in awe of his father, however, and did not like to ask him straight out. He smiled at Tommy as George turned the team at the gates, getting the child's attention by touching his shoulder. He was relaxed in the little boy's company. Having met him only once before, he felt that, in some way he could not define, they had understood one another right away; the only possible explanation for this had to be that although their upbringing and backgrounds could not have been more dissimilar, each recognized in the other a fellow traveller: each laboured under a handicap, Tommy had his deafness, Dessie his background and alcoholism.

He was in no doubt now about the latter. He had been sober for weeks and his counsellor in London, whom sometimes he hated, sometimes he loved, had become his truly best friend. He saw the therapist twice a week and they were beginning to explore areas which were painful for Dessie but which his counsellor said he had to think about and experience, no matter how horrible a process this was, before he could start to deal with the way he drank. Much of the agony had to do with Dessie's mother. The counsellor kept picking and picking away, even when Dessie refused point blank to talk about it, even when he got furious. Bit by bit, though, she was bringing him towards the decision that he would have to try to find out what had happened to Kathleen Scollard. Even if she was dead that would be something to deal with, a line to be drawn so that he could get on with the rest of his life. Dessie had mentioned this tentatively on the telephone to Francey, who had volunteered to help as soon as Dessie felt ready.

But Dessie was angry a lot of the time, and fearful, and many, many times he cried in the counsellor's office and he always came away feeling washed out. Yet somehow she was helping him build up towards making plans, *real* plans. In the near future, for instance, Dessie accepted that one of the first practical tasks he faced was to learn to read and write; the counsellor expressed the view that he should have no problem at all with this once he put his mind to it and had offered to arrange a literacy tutor for him. She also thought his work with the horses valuable and seemed to understand how he felt about the great beasts. Holding on to Tommy's little arm now, standing beside his father and watching the flippety-floppety movements of the colourful ear-caps on Samson and Goliath as they clopped along the tarmac like the champions they were, Dessie felt warm and happy. Confident enough to ask his father if he could drive.

'If you think you can manage.' George pulled up the horses and passed him the reins and the apron, then showed him how to put them on and to fix the leather strap about his waist to secure himself to the seat. 'Here you are,' he then placed the bowler hat on his head, 'to the manner born. Home, James!'

Dessie clucked his tongue and was thrilled to feel the pull between his fingers as the horses responded. It was one thing to ride on the back of one of the animals as it ambled around the yard like a swaying armchair, quite another to feel the awesome strength and power as two of them working together took up the slack on the harness.

'You're doing well, sonny,' George remarked a couple of minutes later as, solid tyres rumbling under them on the tarmac, they bowled along the driveway at a steady pace. 'Keep this up and I'll let you take the four-in-hand.'

'I'd love that.' Dessie's blood was racing with excitement. Never having been one to pay much attention to his surroundings, he could feel the warmth of the spring air which flowed past his face and although it was after five o'clock in the afternoon, noticed the great stretch in the evenings as the sun was just now beginning to drop; he even saw that at some point during the past few days, while no one had been looking, two yellow daffodil rivers had seeped up through the edges of the paddocks along the driveway.

High on the throne-like seat, with the little boy now and then catching on to his right leg for balance and his approving father standing on his left Dessie felt like the king of the world. Samson and Goliath seemed to be having a great time too, he saw, as with heads raised, they high-stepped towards the house at a fast trot.

They were coming up to the lake and Dessie did not feel secure enough yet to steer the team around it at the same time as trying to communicate with the little boy so he hauled on the reins. 'Easy.' George reached up and eased the pressure. 'You don't have to pull so hard. They're trained to react to the smallest signal.'

'Can Tommy have a go now?' Dessie loosened the strap around his waist.

'I'm not sure he'd be strong enough,' George looked doubtfully at his grandson, 'why don't you take him up on your lap with you?'

They lifted Tommy up and Dessie held his hands over the reins while they walked the horses around the lake. Tommy's mother and nanny were standing at the door to watch.

'Please be careful,' Fleur called out as Samson suddenly tossed his head and almost overbalanced Tommy at the other end of the leather. Dessie held him tighter between his arms and the two successfully negotiated a second circumnavigation of the water. 'Well done!' the nanny called, signing to Tommy, but the child was too intent to notice.

'Can we go down the driveway again?' Dessie appealed to his father.

'I've to make a telephone call.' George looked at his watch. 'Do you think you can manage by yourself?'

'I won't take them any faster than a walk,' Dessie promised.

Leaving him with a firm instruction that he was not to attempt to turn the team at the gateway but to dismount and lead them around by hand, George got off the rulley and walked towards the front door. He, Fleur and the nanny watched as Dessie settled Tommy in between his thighs; they waited until the rulley rumbled off at a slow walk down the driveway, then all three went into the house.

Ten minutes later, Fleur was shaking out the dress – green for the occasion that was in it – she planned to wear for the dinner when she was struck with sudden fear. Tommy. Something had happened to Tommy.

'What's the matter? Where are you going?' Colin called after her in alarm as she dropped the dress on the floor and ran out of the room.

Fleur did not call back any answer as she flew down the corridor and into the entrance lobby. The door refused to open: heart pounding, she tore at the Yale lock then realized that in her panic she was turning the snib the wrong way.

At last the door came in and she ran out.

She saw the rulley was at the far side of the lake, both horses calmly stepping out, Tommy safe in his uncle's lap.

'Come down from there!' In the residue of her panic, Fleur ran towards the vehicle and forgetting either to sign or to speak so he could lip-read, shouted at Tommy. He looked at her in surprise. 'Come on, *down*!'

This time she did sign but Dessie intervened. 'He's all right, Fleur, I'm minding him.'

'I insist he gets off right away.' Fleur reached up but Tommy was too high up for her to grasp. 'Stop this cart right now!' she screamed at Dessie, having to run beside the rulley as the horses, although still only walking, were so large that they covered a lot of ground with each stride.

Dessie finally did as she had asked and silently helped the reluctant Tommy to dismount. 'What did I do?' he asked as she clasped Tommy to her.

'Nothing.' Then Fleur saw the hurt on Dessie's face. 'I am sorry,' with her fingers she combed her son's fine hair and then held him tighter, 'I just became afraid.'

'He was safe, Fleur,' Colin's half-brother insisted, 'I know how to mind a child.'

387

'I know you do. Come on, Tommy, time to go inside.' She tried to walk Tommy away but he resisted, signing to her that he wanted to stay with Dessie and the horses, explaining that they were on their way back to the stableyard.

Fleur, whose fright had subsided somewhat, looked at his determined young face. She was still reluctant to let him go but he had begun to assert himself lately and she did not want a scene. 'If you promise to be inside the house in fifteen minutes,' she signed, 'and you may not drive any more, agreed?'

Tommy's black hair flopped over his eyes with the vigour of his reply: 'Twenty minutes?' he signed, and Fleur knew by the set of his lips that she would have to agree or face a long, exhausting argument. When they got to Little Cayman she would have to spend a little time on retraining Tommy who, until recently, used to be so tractable. *'Here, blow your nose'* – his cold was still in runny evidence. She handed him a handkerchief and waited while he blew, then helped him scamper back up on to the bed of the rulley.

Although she renewed her apologies to Dessie, Fleur's heart began again to race with irrational fear as she watched the sedate progress of the vehicle bearing her son towards the side of the house and the stables. She knew she was overreacting – no doubt because their departure was so near. So much could still go wrong: Tommy's cold could get worse, could even develop into pneumonia; he could break an arm or a leg – or worse – by falling down from that cart . . .

To her intense irritation, Fleur saw Colin hurry towards her from the front door. 'Is everything all right?'

'Everything is fine,' she forced a wry smile, 'it was just a mother's foolishness.'

Dinner that night was less of an ordeal than she had feared. George had gone to the trouble of stocking up on Guinness stout and insisted that everyone except Dessie try some. He was in top form, chatting and joking and putting himself out to be as entertaining as possible. As a result, the pre-dinner drinks were prolonged and the little party did not sit down to eat until nearly ten o'clock. They all wore green, or something green, in honour of Saint Patrick of whom none of them, including Dessie, proved to have the remotest knowledge. Fleur herself hated green, considering it unlucky, and despised the dress she had bought at the last minute in one of the boutiques on the King's Road. But on her last night in England she did not want to draw attention to herself, even to the extent of inviting conversation or comment. She had gone along with the prevailing mood even so far as to knot a green bow-tie around the reluctant Tommy's neck.

The serving staff had got into the spirit of the day: the maids wore little bows of green in their caps and even Lewis sported a lapel ribbon of green satin. They had excelled themselves with the food and table decorations: a little spray of wilting shamrock – which Fleur suspected was clover – had been placed by each table setting, a centrepiece had been constructed from conifer branches and dyed carnations and a large, green-iced cake sat on the sideboard. The starter was lettuce soup and the main course corned beef and cabbage which, George assured everyone, was the national dish of Ireland and which was accompanied by every green vegetable on which the cook could lay her hands.

The guest of honour sat at the top of the table, puffing on those appalling cigarettes of his, but even he seemed to be making an effort tonight. At least he was smoking only between courses and not all the time. Fleur noted that since she had seen him last, Colin's half-brother had put on weight and his hair had lengthened. He was quite presentable now, she decided, remembering that she had entertained and been entertained by far worse, and watching his pleased face, she was forced to conclude that for once, and from whatever motive, Colin's father had made the correct decision in organizing this party.

When the staff were removing the plates after the main course, George stood to make a little speech, so fluent and gracious that Fleur knew it had to have been rehearsed. She had to admit, however, that this newly responsible George was an improvement on the old one.

But then, having sat down, he could not leave well enough alone. Now that he had the floor he could not resist holding it, launching into his favourite Irish joke, a long one about the Irish farmer who borrowed a bull from a neighbour to service one of his cows and did not return it: 'And when the neighbour went to see what had happened he found the poor creature yoked up to a plough and plodding up and down a mucky field with the farmer wielding a whip behind him and shouting "I'll teach you there's more to life than romance!"'

He threw back his head, booming his huge laugh and wiping tears of mirth from his face, 'I do like that one,' he spluttered, 'I heard it from an Irishman, of course' – and he was off again, reminiscing about his days on tour in Ireland.

Listening to him, Fleur wondered how his son, puffing furiously on his cigarette, really felt about George's constant, and rosy, references to his adventures in Ireland and elsewhere. How either of his Irish sons felt about it for that matter. After all, it was during the wartime period he now found so nostalgic that he must have fathered both of them in such dubious circumstances.

And as for Colin, how had he come to terms with being left out of George's sudden conversion to fatherhood as soon as his youngest had appeared? She had not discussed George much with Colin: after the first months of living together when, wide-eyed, she had allowed him to believe she revered every syllable which fell from his lips, they had come to talk less and less about anything serious. Colin seemed happy enough to substitute sex, of which he could not get enough and of which Fleur was an amenable provider, for verbal communication, so she had little idea of what he felt about George, but suspected he felt lonely and left out – especially since Jool had died and these other two had turned up.

Having served each of them with a dish of green ice-cream, one of the maids then brought the cake, which was in the shape of a shamrock, to the table and set it along with a cake slice in front of the guest of honour so he could cut it. Dessie, blushing, stubbed out his cigarette and without the ceremony which was expected of him, plunged the slice into the centre of the confection so hard and at such an awkward angle that it crumbled and fell apart. 'Let Lewis do it,' George signalled to the butler and then, to cover Dessie's embarrassment, proceeded with another anecdote.

'Did you enjoy your food?' As the butler signalled to the maid, Fleur detached herself from the scene and signed the question at Tommy who was beginning to fidget at her side. After his return from the stables she had kept him with her, making the nanny's presence redundant. The girl, seated at the child's other side, slipped him a tissue now as Tommy signed back to his mother that because of his cold he was finding it difficult to taste anything.

Fleur felt his forehead. It was hot, which could be due to the cold, or even the central heating, as always at an uncomfortably high level. 'Would you like to go to bed straight after your pudding?' she signed.

390

He nodded.

As soon as he had finished the ice-cream and his portion of cake, Fleur asked that the two of them be excused and took him away to his room. She helped him undress and stood over him while he brushed his teeth, then supervised his getting into bed.

Fleur knew that Tommy, although sensible beyond his age in many respects, had been so coddled by herself and everyone else in the family circle, particularly the old American lady, that he was emotionally younger than his years. For instance, when in bed in this room, he loved to assemble a regiment of soft toys on either side of him, lording it over them like a little colonel. He did this now, selecting the night's line-up from the huge population of brightly coloured and expensive animals with which the room was populated. Seeing his cheeky, self-satisfied smile, Fleur had to smother her impulse to tell him to make the most of this tonight, that this was the last time he would see this child's paradise, which had been created for him. Instead, she leaned over and kissed him. 'Go to sleep now . . .'

'Will you ask Dessie and Grandfather if I can drive the horses again tomorrow?' he signed back.

'We'll see.' Fleur knew they were due to leave in the early morning and tomorrow, of all days, she wanted no delay. 'Here's your book, now blow your nose.' She handed him the book and a tissue from the night-stand, then, 'Night night,' kissing him again on the forehead, left him.

When she got back to the dining-room, Colin looked up from his plate. 'Is he all right?'

'He is fine. It is just a little cold.' She sat down again and toyed with her demi-tasse of coffee. She was becoming seriously impatient now and did not care a fig about George's party. She sipped her coffee and prayed for speedy deliverance.

The others, she noticed, were continuing with the green theme, the glasses in front of them containing large measures of chartreuse or crème-de-menthe – all except Dessie whose glass was full of what looked like Coca-Cola. Fleur had no intention of drinking any alcohol tonight. Needing a clear head, she had refused even the wine that had been offered during the meal.

She noticed, however, that for him Colin had drunk rather a lot. His eyes were brighter than normal and his cheeks were flushed as he accepted a refill from the butler.

391

Fleur had to endure a further hour and a half of more Irish jokes, of the descent of the party towards inebriation, of the resultant singalong. Even the nanny, whom Fleur had never seen drinking to any extent, got into the spirit of the evening and rendered a wobbly version of 'Flow Gently Sweet Afton', and when Dessie, glassy-eyed and smoking like a steam engine between glassfuls of Coca-Cola, was prevailed upon to sing, he gave them 'Daisy, Daisy' in a clear, halting tenor.

If she had cared at all, Fleur thought as she observed the way his hands trembled with nerves, she might have warmed to him. She could see why Tommy had. Dessie was little more than a child. She herself refused to sing or to perform when George attempted to persuade her. To her relief the party seemed to be running down but then, at about half-past midnight, a move to the drawing-room for a game of charades was mooted and taken up with enthusiasm by all except Dessie to whom the idea had to be explained. Fleur saw her chance and begged to be excused.

Colin said he would come with her but she smiled her most brilliant and trusting smile at him and insisted that he should stay. He gave in and followed the nanny and Dessie out of the room.

Fleur was about to leave after them when George, who had hung back to check something at the far side of the room, called after her, 'Have you a moment, Fleur?'

'I am very tired.' Fleur made her voice sound decisive. Whatever it was he wanted she was in no mood for any confidences about George's problems.

'This won't take long.' As he walked towards her, Fleur realized that, despite all the dinner-table bonhomie to which she had long been accustomed, George had seemed a little different tonight. More circumspect somehow. 'What time are you leaving in the morning?' he asked when he came up to her, then glanced over her head through the doorway as if to check they were not being overheard.

'Early, as soon as we can.' Fleur was puzzled by the expression in his eyes.

'I'd like a word with you about something before you go. In private.'

'As you wish.' But Fleur was not as calm as she appeared. As she hurried away, although she knew it was impossible, Fleur worried that George had somehow learned of her imminent departure. So much could still go wrong.

Tommy's room was beside the one she shared with Colin and, on impulse, as she passed the door, she peeped in to check on him. All she saw on the bed was a scattering of stuffed animals.

Tommy's bathroom was empty too.

Chapter Twenty

Thank God, Dessie thought, as he saw everyone making a move to leave the table: he was bursting to go to the bathroom and thought he had never consumed so much liquid in his life. He wished his old friend, Petey, was here tonight: how he would have laughed to see the nobs all dressed up in green and having green soup and all the rest of it. Not that he did not appreciate it, he was genuinely grateful for all the trouble his father had gone to and he hoped he had not made too much of a cobbler's with the cake that time. But as the talk and the singing became looser he found, for the first time in weeks, that the longing for a real drink was becoming acute, especially since everyone else seemed to be having such a good time.

He could have used a few bevvies before the song. He had been mortified to have to sing in front of everyone and 'Daisy' had been the only thing he could remember the whole words to. It had been Petey McCann's anthem.

Petey certainly would have got a great kick out of the fish in the aquarium: he had gone on and on about all the lakes in Cavan and how when he was a youngster he was able to tickle trout and even salmon. Dessie was not so hot on water at present: having been seated on the side of the table which faced the aquarium, the sight and sound of all that gurgling and pouring, not only in the fish tank but down the wall to his left, were not helping the discomfort in his bladder.

The nanny was great, he thought, stealing little glances at her while trying to hold back from jigging like a child in his chair. Some day, Dessie had promised himself – and his counsellor did not think he was stupid to think this – he might have a real girlfriend of his own. A nice girl like this one, not just a used-up one like the slags he had been able to go to bed with in filthy flats and allotment sheds.

He had to endure another five minutes of agony, pretending to know what they were talking about as they explained the game they were going to play in the drawing-room, something to do with acting out words of songs and poems. Oh, yes, Petey would have had a right laugh at this party all right . . .

He saw that Colin's wife was leaving before the rest of them. She was a funny little bird, that one, beautiful but not someone you'd want for your girlfriend. There was something about her that made you go a bit cold inside. Their kid was great, though, lovely little fella. Spoiled, of course, but who wouldn't with a deaf kid? When he thought about it, Dessie understood Fleur's screaming match about the horses earlier. Anything could happen to a deaf kid, just crossing the road.

At last amid the hubbub of everyone standing up from the table he was able to escape to the bathroom. When he came out, he was surprised to see Fleur again, her hair streaming out behind her, running towards him from the far end of the corridor. She looked as if she'd seen a ghost.

Tommy just could not sleep. Every time he lay down, his nose filled up and the space behind it hurt. And he was too hot. He flung some of the stuffed animals off his bed as if it was their fault. He blew his nose for about the one hundred zillionth time and then jumped out of bed to get himself a drink of water from the bathroom. There was a window beside the mirror over the sink and because the moon was bright and also because he had not bothered to put the light on, he could see through it, out towards the play yard and the wood.

Sipping his water, Tommy thought for a moment he actually heard the voice of his grandma Jool. She wasn't saying much, just telling him he was a good boy like she used to do. He wished he had known that day she brought him to the stables that she was going to die; if he had known, he might have stored it up better. He was in the habit of storing up feelings. Just like voices.

He had a repertoire of voices in his head: in his imagination, they sounded like swords, ranging in size from big to tiny. His mummy's voice sounded like the small pretty sword carried by Sir Lancelot in the picture book about the Knights of the Round

Table, his daddy's like King Arthur's big one, his nanny's like Sir Gawain's. His grandad's sounded as big and rich as Ali Baba's curved scimitar.

His grandma Jool's voice had been long and straight with a wide flat blade, the kind of voice you could trust. He was finding it difficult to imagine that he would never see her again. He wondered what dying felt like: his mummy and his teacher had told him that when you die you go to heaven but, as far as Tommy could see, that was a fib. They were always telling you these fibs because they thought you were not old enough to know the truth.

He had seen with his own eyes on the television that when you died you went down into a grave, not only on the films but on the news and from President Kennedy and the earthquake in Yugoslavia last year. In one way Tommy was glad his mummy had not let him come to see his grandma Jool be put down into the ground, but he had been curious and would have liked to see it. He missed her a lot. Sometimes at night, like now, he thought he heard her voice in his head. She had learned to sign but her voice was there too.

Something moved outside, beyond the trampoline. For half a second Tommy allowed himself to imagine it was Grandma Jool come back to bring him again to the little wood she had made for him with the yellow brick road. He shaded his eyes with his hand and leaned his forehead against the window-pane to get a better look but then sneezed and bumped himself. He had a triple sneeze then, one of the worst.

He went back into the bedroom and looked at the bed with the toys all over the place. He was not a bit tired, not a bit. And he had never been in the wood by himself at night. It would be fun, an adventure.

His mummy would never know if he sneaked out just for a few minutes.

Living in London gave Tommy no scope for adventure. This one could be like something out of the *Eagle*, a real boy's adventure where the adults wouldn't know a thing about it. About to throw on his clothes again, Tommy stopped. He thought he heard Grandma Jool's voice again. Could people in heaven see what you were doing?

Anyway, even if she could see him she couldn't be upset because, after all, she was the one who made the yellow brick road for him in the first place. And he would only stay a minute. No, a second. Just one second.

Excited now, he got dressed and put on his shoes and coat, then opened his bedroom door just a crack, enough to see out and to check that the coast was clear.

He had to tiptoe all the way down the corridor, past all the bedroom doors, past the front lobby. They were still in the dining-room, the door was not fully closed and through the little gap he could see a tiny part of the table and the sleeve of his grandad's green jacket; he held his breath until he was safely past.

The normal way out to the back was through the kitchen but, at the last minute, Tommy remembered the servants would be in there and had to backtrack, past the danger zone of the dining-room, all the way back to the hall. His shoes had leather soles and they made a lot of noise as he crept across the marble floor towards the door.

He dared not shut it behind him in case it made a noise but he pulled it until it was as closed as it could be without the lock being engaged.

Another second or two and he was running like the wind around the side of the house. The feeling of freedom and adventure was tremendous – he could hear it inside his ears as he ran, a sort of zinging sound. It was the kind of sound he imagined the highest stars made, or the lights from lighthouses. All he was sorry about now was that he had not brought some tuck. Boys in the *Eagle* planned things properly and always had tuck along with them.

As he ran past the big, silent stable block he hesitated. That had been fab today, driving Samson and Goliath: maybe instead of going to the little wood he should go and say goodnight to the horses. That would be something real to do instead of just walking along a silly old pile of bricks.

Tommy had been afraid of the horses until he got big, nearly eight, but then Grandma Jool had brought him into the yard one day in her arms and held him really tight while they went around the stalls and fed the Shires with lumps of sugar and big carrots. It had been a bit scary at first, their lips were so big and whiskery, but once you got used to it, they were very gentle.

But tonight Tommy discovered that the stableyard, once he let himself into it, was a different place from what it was in the daytime.

All the stalls were closed up like blind men and everything was a sinister grey and black like a Boris Karloff film, instead of all the different colours that he could usually see. It was a windy night and although everything was clean and tidy as usual, a piece of paper was blowing around the centre of the yard, in circles, rising up and falling again and reminding Tommy of a big white bird with a broken wing.

He was almost turning back when he remembered that *Eagle* boys had pluck and didn't lose their nerve just because there were no lights on. He was ashamed of himself: he was letting the side down. He had come here to see the horses, *dared* himself to do it and he was going to do it.

One horse would do, he thought, and he needn't stay long.

But as he struggled with the stiff bolts on the nearest stall, Tommy was having to make great efforts to bolster his determination. Some stupid dare this was: he was cold and he had forgotten to bring tissues or a handkerchief so his nose and his eyes were streaming and he was having to wipe them on the sleeve of his coat and he knew his nanny would be annoyed. He kept sneezing too, making things worse . . .

The size of the task he had set himself was shrinking every second. All he would have to do to save his honour would be to get these bolts open, go inside for one second, a millionth of a second, and give the horse one pat. If the truth be told, Tommy was now wishing that instead of being here, he was safely tucked up in his warm bed with his little zoo of animals all around him.

Hurry up, he thought to the bolts.

At last the second one gave and he was able to pull open both halves of the door.

He peered into the dark interior of the stall. He did not even know which horse this was but under the terms of the dare he had set himself that didn't matter.

Whichever one it was was standing quietly facing the back wall. Through the gloom he could see the white hair around its legs and a bit of white around the top of its tail. But as he moved forward to give the horse's rump the ordained pat, the wind from outside stirred up the chaff in the stable, causing him to sneeze, a double one.

Amazon started, then lashed out with one of her hind hooves, catching Tommy on the side of the face.

As he fell she kicked again, this time with both hooves, connecting hard with his head so he shot backwards. Nostrils flaring, she looked around as the irritant that had invaded her sleep landed six feet away in the soft straw of her bedding. His falling made only a rustling sound but Tommy was dead before his skull hit the floor of the stall.

'Yowsa, fantabulous, wow-*eee*!' Hazel felt on top form as she burst through the doorway which separated the dance floor from the backstage area. 'That was some night, eh, boys? Come on, come on, let's get a move on, we've a party to go to.' She rushed around collecting her bits and bobs and flinging them any old way into her vanity case.

Some of the punters had managed to squeeze their way in and milled around in the crossover chaos as the Rollers made way for the next band, each set of musicians lugging bulky equipment through the tiny space. 'Where's my bodyguaa-a-ard?' Hazel sang, calling over to Francey whose great pale head floated like a harvest moon above everyone else's.

'I'm here.' He turned towards her and, seeing the way his blond hair hung in tendrils about his face Hazel smiled. Because of the night that was in it, they had done more than their usual quota of céilidhe music and the place was jumping. Even with no band on right now, through the wall, she could hear the punters la-la-ing another round of 'The Walls of Limerick' with the aid of their own gob music.

'Do you want something?' Francey had reached her.

'Nothin' much, just want to get going.' She pulled his head down and smacked him one on the lips. 'Happy Saint Paddy's day, chicken! Thanks a lot for the great mindin' – whe-eee!'

'Diddley-eye, dee-eye dee-eye di, diddley eye dee eye dee eye.' Chirping her own gob music and unable to restrain her feet which insisted on performing the first sixteen bars of a hornpipe, Hazel placed both hands on Francey's chest for ballast. 'Medals for it, I have.' She loved the bounce of her breast and the silver fringes of her dress, of her feet pattering against the floor through the unsuitable boots. 'Feis Maitiú, nineteen thirty-eight – ' she gasped, 'bet ya didn't know that now, *didja*?' She finished the sequence and let him go.

'You're full of surprises.' Francey grinned. 'Are you quite finished? I've to pack the wagon.'

'Finished, finished,' Hazel carolled. '"Oh, what a be-oo-tiful evening."' Trilling a pastiche of the *Oklahoma!* opening at the top of her voice she pirouetted away to sign the inevitable autograph book.

She had calmed down a little before they all climbed into the wagon and, for a change, was one of the first outside in the car park. 'This is ridiculous,' she said to Francey and Vinnie, the others who were waiting, 'what's keeping them?'

'Patience, Queenie,' counselled the High Roller, 'we're only off less than ten minutes.'

'Did you make your phone call?' Hazel turned to Francey. She was in the habit of monitoring his daily contact with Inveraray Manor and had a special reason tonight because of Fleur being there for the dinner party.

'I couldn't get through.' Francey looked away and she knew immediately he was lying. She was in two minds as to whether to push it and decided on balance that she should. 'Go on inside,' she gave Francey a little shove, 'tell the others we're going without them if they don't come on. And try that call again.'

'It's too late now.' Francey looked at his watch.

'Balderdash!' Hazel knew what he was at but in her own plan to detach him from the Siamese twin it was important he should make a start in treating the woman as a has-been with whom contact was not as traumatic as it still clearly was. 'It's not even twenty-five past twelve,' she brooked no further argument, 'they'll be still up – it's a party, isn't it? Go on, and wish them a happy St Paddy's Day from me, too.'

She waited until he left and then lit a cigarette. 'Watch it, Hazel,' cautioned Vinnie as he held a lighter flame to the tip of her cigarette. 'Don't push that one too far.'

'I know what I'm doing.' Quiet now, Hazel drew deep on the cigarette and exhaled the warm, pungent smoke through her nose.

'As long as you do.' The High Roller climbed into the wagon, turned on the small light over one of the tables and spread out his *News of the World*.

Hazel leaned her back against the side of the wagon. It was a mild night for March, although the wind kept blowing the smoke from her cigarette into her eyes until she turned sideways. The car park was not well lit and through the shadows she could make out the courting couples only by straining her eyes. Poor sods, she thought. It had never ceased to amaze her that while back in Ireland everyone thought that England was a hotbed of sex and freedom, outside London the kids here were every bit as shy and tentative – and as short of passion pits – as those in Bohola or Cahirciveen. More even. At least at home no provincial ballroom was far from a field and it was a rare night that the headlights of the wagon did not land on couples hard at it in the ditches of the Irish countryside. And the boys in the band picked up one-night stands or even mistresses in Ireland with even greater ease than they did here.

Hazel was tired of all that. Francey was her last big project and if she failed with him she planned to retire from the romantic play-ground. As always happened when she was as high as a kite in the immediate aftermath of a show, the euphoria faded fast to be replaced by introspection and even depression. Tonight was no exception and as she climbed into the wagon and went to the back seat – the one nearest the door – she had favoured since the accident, she felt quite drained. Leaving her lamp off, she lit a second cigarette from the butt of the first and curled up with it, watching through the window for Francey's return with or without the other members of the band.

One difficulty with the Francey-project was that he might consider she was after his money. Hazel could not care less about money. She owned her flat and had a nest egg put by, enough to keep her for a few lean years, and what was more she had her compo coming. Somehow, if they did get as far as discussing a future together, she had to come up with a way to convince him it was not his millions she wanted although she already knew that, where money was concerned, Francey was a bit like herself. But she figured it was early days yet: in her experience, you never could tell how money would affect people.

One way or another, she had to pay attention to her future. She

401

could already see the writing on the wall for the High Rollers: it was not because of the others snapping at their heels – the Rollers would continue to outclass the opposition – it was that in showbusiness fashions change. Having been in it in various manifestations for so long, Hazel could read the wind and accepted, unlike many of her contemporaries in Ireland, that groups like the Beatles and the Rolling Stones were not just a passing phenomenon. Those five spotty boys who had played support to the Rollers in Birmingham had been so young that they should probably still be in school, but she had recognized that the music they bashed out had pulsated with energy and a sort of raw jungle call to their own contemporaries.

Three, or maybe four, more good years on the road is what Hazel reckoned she had left – if she was lucky. Maybe even that was being too optimistic: those Beatles had come from nowhere; their rise had seemed to happen so fast it had put the serious frighteners on the big orchestras and dancebands which had thought themselves impregnable, at least over here in Britain. And what happened in Britain always happened in Ireland sooner or later.

Hazel spotted Francey coming towards the wagon with all six of the stragglers and crushed out the butt of the second cigarette in the ashtray set into her table. She called to Francey to join her, patting the seat beside her own. 'How'd you get on on the phone?'

'No reply,' he said in a way which defeated her because she knew he was telling the truth . . .

Gingerly, Dessie led Amazon out of her stall. She was still jumpy, pulling on the halter that he had, with difficulty, managed to secure around her head.

As he continued to coax her out into the yard, he kept his eyes averted from the corner of the stall where Fleur, showing the whites of her eyes like a wild animal, rocked her dead son in her arms. She had refused to allow him to be moved, or to let anyone else near him, even Colin who was now sobbing helplessly in the arms of his own father, surrounded in the yard by the rest of the guests from the ill-fated party.

Dessie was determined that no one should take it out on Amazon. The awfulness of the child's death could not take away from the fact that it was not the horse's fault. What had Tommy been doing in here in the middle of the night, anyway? Everyone knew that Amazon was touchy and she was near her time too. Only that afternoon, when they had finished driving the rig, Dessie had used a crude form of pantomime to communicate with the kid about the foal that was coming soon. He had also tried to warn him, never thinking he might have good reason to, that until then Amazon had to be treated with kid gloves.

When he and the rest of the people in the house had begun to search for the child after Fleur had reported him missing, it had been his suggestion they try the stables. And it had been Dessie who had found him: Amazon would not let anyone else into her stall. Fleur had got by only because she had rushed in with no thought for her own safety and Dessie, halter in one hand, had managed to catch hold of the horse's thick mane with the other.

'There now, girl,' he hushed the mare as she danced a little while passing the crowd around Colin. No wonder she was nervous: it was not only the invasion of her privacy but the behaviour of some of the guests who clearly did not know how to act around horses. Also the wind had freshened to the extent that it could nearly be considered a gale and all the lights were on so that the yard was as bright as the Covent Garden market.

All the horses, calm though they were by nature, were probably reacting by now, Dessie thought. As if to prove his point, as he led Amazon past Trojan's stall, the top half of the door shook as the horse banged against it with his head in an effort to open it to see what was going on.

Dessie took his charge into a disused stall in a corner of the yard, used to store feed and bales of bedding. He closed the door behind them, turned on the light and rubbed her down with a wisp of straw. Then, as he fed her a handful of horse nuts, he thought how this need not have happened at all: the grass had come on in the last few weeks and they had been planning to turn out the horses into the paddocks within the next couple of days. Too late for wishing, as Petey would have said. Dessie wished Mick O'Dowd would get here. One of the maids had gone to telephone him. Mick would know what to do next.

He removed Amazon's halter and hung it on a nail just outside the door. When he was confident she was calm enough to be left alone again he bolted her in and then had to try to screw up the courage to rejoin the crowd clustering around the entrance to the stall inside which Fleur obviously still held the little boy. Animals were so much easier to deal with than people.

It was dark in the corner where Fleur huddled, rocking her son to and fro in her arms. He was so cold. She held him as tight as she could, trying to make him warm again. And there was something wrong with his neck: his head was flopping backwards as it had when he was a baby, the fine, silky hair falling away from his face. Fleur attempted to tidy it: it was due to be cut.

'You're lovely, you're my darling baby,' she whispered to him, 'you're my life and my joy, you're everything I ever dreamed about.' Ignoring the anxious white faces which, hanging like a monstrous wreath of fungus on the door frame, peered in at her, she kissed his pale face. They were not going to get him. They had tried already but she would not give him up.

At least his cold was better, she thought, his nose was not running any more. That was one small blessing.

His eyes were open, such lovely eyes, black like olives, but she could not get them to look at her, they were looking up behind her shoulder. 'Look at me, my little darling, look at me.' She wept now, the tears pouring as she tried to hold his head so the eyes would look straight into hers but his head kept falling.

Desperately, she loosened the collar of his coat which must be too tight against his throat with his head hanging back like that.

The light from the door darkened as someone attempted to come into the little refuge she had created for the two of them in the corner. Outraged, Fleur looked up. It was George.

Then the stable was abruptly flooded with an obscenity of light as he pressed the light switch inside the door.

'Put it off!' Although Fleur knew it was she who had spoken she did not recognize the voice. 'Put if off!' Half-rising, snatching up her child to protect him, she spat with fury at Colin's father. The light was so bright, she knew it would hurt Tommy's eyes.

When George had turned off the light and retreated to the door, Fleur sat down again in the straw, this time with her back to the entrance to shield the two of them from the others. She settled her son in a more comfortable position against her shoulder. 'There now,' she whispered, 'my little darling flower, I love you,' signing the words right in front of his eyes so he would be sure to read them properly. 'Just hold on a little longer,' she begged, 'we'll be in the sunshine tomorrow.'

She waited for him to sign something back, anything, one gesture to indicate he understood. 'My little darling flower,' she said it again, 'please answer me, little squirrel, please . . .'

Again she waited. Just once more would do.

'Please, Tommy,' her own nose was running now, 'please –' She buried her face in the soft hair, at the place where the fontanelle used to be: her lips could feel where the bones had joined. 'Please.' Some of the hair was getting in her mouth and it was getting wet but what she was asking was so urgent it did not matter, she could clean it up later. 'Please wake up, just for a few minutes.' She rocked over him, harder, forcing him to listen. 'Please, just once more, once will be enough, I will not be greedy, I promise.' She crushed Tommy's head into her breast. 'Just a minute then? Thirty seconds, please, you're such a good boy, you're so clever. All I want is thirty seconds. You can go then. Thirty seconds – you can't go without saying goodbye to Squeaky.' This was the small colourful clown, the figure from a broken jack-in-the-box and in tatters now, that Tommy had loved since babyhood. 'Tommy?' She shook him a little. 'We forgot to bring Squeaky, he is still at home waiting for us, we must say goodbye to him.'

But no matter how she begged and cried, Tommy's eyes remained open and he did not answer.

They were behind her now, the intruders, she could sense them, more than one. Through the door, when she flashed a furious look at them over her shoulder she saw the pulsing lights of an ambulance. Like a cat, she hissed at them to go away, to leave her and Tommy alone.

But they would not go away, there was another there now with George, a man she did not recognize in a dark coat. He was wearing a trilby hat and, for some reason, Fleur saw this hat as the most enormous threat of all. The trilby made the man look like an army person, or a policeman come to arrest her son, to take him away from her for ever as though he had done something wrong. 'Go away,' she shrieked, 'go away, all of you.'

The man in the dark coat and hat introduced himself as Doctor something or other but Fleur was so intent on holding on to Tommy and on not letting anyone else lay a finger on him that she did not hear the name. He was squatting down now, speaking to her in a low voice like you would talk to a mad person. Did they think she was mad? 'Go away!' She spat at the man the way she had earlier spat at George.

He did not react to the spittle running down his face, or wipe it off the collar of the coat. He was continuing to speak to her in that low, insulting voice. Fleur covered Tommy's face with one hand so he would not have to look at this stranger while she herself attempted to stare him down, focusing all her concentration until she felt it cutting like a narrow beam of light through the white disc of his face. Using every ounce of her being, she willed the man to go away and leave them. But no matter how she concentrated, every time she checked he was still there.

He was reaching out to take Tommy from her while George took hold of her shoulders. She fought both of them, fought with nails and teeth and feet, all the while trying to hold on to her son. But they were winning . . .

There was a third one now. Colin. She had always known she could not trust Colin. He, too, was trying to tear her apart from her son, he was just as bad as the others, just like all the others. Fleur heard her voice again, high-pitched and screaming, like the cry of a seagull or one of the vultures she remembered from her childhood. She kicked and bit and scratched with the hand that was not protecting Tommy but there were too many of them and they were too big. When Tommy was wrenched away from her it was as though they were disembowelling her, not only of her intestines but of everything, even the insides of her eyes.

Tommy's body was put into the ambulance and for several minutes after the vehicle had left, Fleur continued to fight as though possessed. George tried to hold her as the doctor tried to give her an injection but she fought so hard, flailing and twisting against his grip that the doctor was unable to use the syringe and finally had to give up.

And then, just as though someone had thrown a switch to cut off the flow of manic energy, Fleur became still, closed her eyes, and went limp. The doctor, a local from Little Staunton, tried to rouse her without success. He told George that, as she was breathing perfectly and her pulse was steady, she was in no immediate danger and that he was loath, under the circumstances, to remove her to hospital. He handed over a supply of sedative tablets which he said might be useful if she became hysterical again.

Then, leaving several telephone numbers where he could be contacted during the rest of the night, he drove off, following the ambulance to the hospital where the post-mortem would be carried out on Tommy's body in the morning.

Since Colin had gone to the hospital in the ambulance, it fell to George to carry Fleur back to the house. For once he was not thinking of the trouble he was being caused but was crying, a phenomenon he had not experienced since the first night he had left home, all those years ago, and understood the enormity of what he had done.

Making no attempt to hide the tears, he laid Fleur on the bed in the room she shared with Colin and pulled up the bedcover. Then he watched beside her, riven with pity for what she faced when she woke up. He waited for the best part of a quarter of an hour but when Fleur showed no sign of movement, convinced that deep sleep was the best and most merciful panacea for her, George tiptoed out of the room.

Fleur was not sleeping. After they took Tommy away from her, the rage in her brain turned to ice. They would not keep her from him. She would go to the hospital to be with him, but not yet.

She fixed her eyes on a small irregularity in the ceiling above the bed, on a little knot in the plaster, beside the exposed white beam. For five or ten minutes – who counted the minutes now? – Fleur laid her plan. The horses would have to be the first to pay.

She heard someone approach, closed her eyes again and breathed deeply; as she heard the door of the bedroom open, she willed her eyelids not to move. It was George, she knew by the sound of the breathing. Fleur moaned a little as though dreaming and turned her head away from the direction of the door. After a few interminable seconds, George moved away and the door closed.

Instantly Fleur got off the bed and went to the door, counting to ten before she opened it. The corridor was empty although she heard a murmur of voices from behind the door of the drawing room. She crossed the corridor and within seconds was in the tiled lobby. The front door was ajar, she did not even have to open it.

Keeping to the wall of the house she flitted towards the garages. Colin's car was parked carelessly in front of George's and since it was never locked while they were down here – there was no need even to take the keys from the ignition – it was a matter of a moment to open the boot. She knew Colin always kept a spare can of petrol.

Then she had to waste valuable time by going back to the car and opening the glove compartment where she knew there were several books of matches, collected from restaurants over the years.

Fleur was torn as to which way to go: the direct route was back the way she had come but the front door was open and she might be seen by someone passing it on the inside; on the other hand she could not remember whether or not the curtains had been pulled across the enormous windows of the drawing-room. On balance, she thought it was less dangerous to risk being seen by the butler or one of the servants at the far end of the house.

Walking as quickly as she could and looking neither right or left, Fleur trusted herself to fate. She got round the side of the house without being challenged and, having to lean into the considerable wind, broke into a run as soon as the stable yard, still all lit up, came into view.

When she got into it, she saw no sign of anyone and the doors on all the stalls, even the fatal one, were shuttered and blank. Not that it would have made any difference who saw her. Her determination to wipe out everything in her path was absolute. Unless they shot her she would not be deterred.

She went straight to the doors behind which Tommy had been attacked and opened the stiff bolts, not without difficulty. Hooking them open against the outside wall so the wind would not slam them shut, she went inside, and keeping her eyes averted from the corner where she had fought for Tommy, proceeded to sprinkle some of the petrol into the straw bedding. Although the stalls were made of brick and concrete, she saw that her task would be simplified by the construction of the stables themselves. The walls between the one in which she stood and the next one in the row did not go fully to the roof – there was a gap of four or five feet – and she remembered that this was the case throughout the yard. To make it even easier, she saw that, just as in the house, the roof beams were exposed.

To make absolutely sure the fire would spread, however, Fleur poured petrol on some hay in the feeding net suspended high in a corner beside the dividing wall. Then she placed the petrol can carefully behind her outside the door – she would need it in the house – and struck a match.

She had intended to toss the light in through the stable door but the strength of the wind defeated her and to get a match to burn at all she had to go back into the stall and shield the tiny flame with her body.

The ploy worked and she tossed it into the straw, pausing only long enough to see the first wisps catch.

By the time she had picked up the petrol can and had reached the gate to look back, the fire, fanned by the wind from the open door, was well alight.

Fleur hurried back towards the house. The wind was behind her now, blowing the thin silk of the green dress up around her thighs. She endeavoured to keep it down around her knees as she walked but, lumbered with the petrol can in one hand, found it difficult. Hoping that no one was looking out to see her immodesty, she abandoned the attempt and concentrated on getting back to the front door as quickly as possible.

She stowed the petrol can behind the conifer in one of the ornamental tubs outside the door and got into the outer lobby without incident but then heard the clicking of two pairs of heels on the marble of the inner hallway and had to dive into the anteroom to hide behind one of the pillars. She held her breath as she heard the footsteps, obviously those of two women, pass on towards the drawing-room and pause. Then one set hurried towards the front door. From her hiding place Fleur did not dare look out but saw the edge of a black dress swirl by before the door was closed with a thump. It was a maid, noticing that the door had been left open and doing her duty.

It seemed as though the girl was passing by without further ado but then she stopped again. Fleur squeezed tighter against the wall behind her pillar as she heard the maid ask her companion if she could smell anything.

'No,' the other replied, coming forward too.

'I thought I smelt oil or something,' the first girl went on, 'must be my imagination.'

Then, to Fleur's relief, they both left the lobby and went towards the drawing-room. She ran to her bedroom, went straight to the bathroom and locked herself in.

The bathroom window, like the windows of all bedrooms in this house except George's, faced the back of the house. Fleur watched through it until she saw the orange glow begin to rise from the stable block.

Then she waited.

Sure enough, pandemonium ensued in the house. First the telephone rang in the corridor outside and then she heard people running up and down the corridor, raised voices, shouting . . . from both women and men . . .

She counted to a hundred before going back into the bedroom.

Through the window in here she could see that the glow in the sky was brighter now.

The next step was easy. Fleur knew they would all be over at the stables or on their way there. Just to be sure, however, she again checked the corridor.

After that it was a matter of walking calmly to the front door, retrieving the petrol can and going the length of the internal corridor, opening all doors and sprinkling some of the contents inside every room and all along the floor of the corridor itself. Thanks to the central heating, she knew that the house was as dry as tinder, and with all the carpets and draperies, the exposed beams, the mock timbering on the front, she would not even need kindling. She worked only the eastern side of the house as far as the entrance lobby, leaving herself an escape route and trusting the fire to complete the task for her.

Beside her on a side table just outside the drawing-room, one of the three telephones in the corridor rang. Fleur, who was striking her first match, ignored it. She tossed the flare on to the patch of petrol-soaked carpet inside the master bedroom, threw a second one into the study, then a third into the drawing-room. She waited until she saw fire lick at all three sites and then moved on to the next, walking backwards along the corridor. The telephone had stopped ringing before she got as far as the lobby, and by this time, eight small fires were beginning to grow in front of her and the one in George's bedroom was going well.

Not wanting to be caught, she aimed two more matches on to the carpet in the corridor on the other side of the lobby. Sure she had done enough, she did not wait for these last two and walked away from them, across the lobby and out into the night.

She shut the door after her, walked to Colin's car and started it. She was not an experienced driver and the gears crunched as she put the lever into first. The vehicle stalled as she turned it towards the driveway but she restarted it and, again grinding the gearbox, drove off without looking back.

Chapter Twenty-One

Dessie, whose hearing was acute, was the first to hear the horses' agitation. He and Mick were sitting hunched over a cuppa in the tack-room, discussing the awful business of the previous half-hour. If he had not felt so wretched, he might have enjoyed the unaccustomed night-time feel of the place, the island of light from the single bulb overhead, the cosiness of the electric heater that insulated them against the gale outside. He did not know how he could face going back into the house, but one way or another, he told Mick, he was not going to let Amazon take the blame for what had happened.

Then, through the wind's howl, he thought he heard the mare kick against the side of the spare stall which was the one nearest to where they were sitting.

Leaving Mick, he went out into the yard to quiet her down – and then Dessie saw the reason for Amazon's commotion, and why all the others were kicking as well.

Flames were shooting through the open doorway of the stable at the far end where the tragedy had occurred.

And in the next instant, Dessie saw to his horror that smoke was also filtering through the cracks around the door of the stall beside the first one. He ran back inside, shouting, 'Fire! Fire!' then, having yelled at Mick to hurry, 'I'll get Trojan out.'

With Mick not far behind him, the latter having paused just long enough to pick up two of the yard's fire extinguishers, Dessie sprinted across the cobblestones towards the blaze.

When he pulled open the doors, the smoke that billowed round his head was so dense he could just about make out the star on Trojan's tossing forehead as the Shire plunged about at the back of the stall. Coughing and half blinded as he was, however, Dessie could tell that the horse was not yet sufficiently panicked to be out of control.

412

He retreated a little, took off his jacket and put it over his head. Then, plucking a halter off the hook on the outside wall and using the armhole of the suit as an air pocket, he made his way in. Despite the protection his eyes stung so badly he had difficulty in keeping them open but he saw that the bedding in the corner of the stall was on fire, the flames starting to race across the floor. He would have only a few seconds.

Keeping his head low and making the little burring sounds he had learned from Mick, he walked the few steps towards the horse, ignoring the pain in his foot as one of Trojan's massive hooves glanced off the toe of his shoe. He seized the Shire's mane and, although the animal pulled away hard, managed to slip the halter over his head. 'Come on, come on,' he urged, hauling on the lead rein.

Trojan refused to budge, straining backwards towards what he had clearly decided was the safety of the stall's back wall. The flames were now well advanced, no longer little curls and splutters but full blown and several inches tall, drawn forwards by the wind towards the open door; Dessie knew he would have to leave right away if he himself was not to be burned. Acting on instinct, or remembering something Petey had told him about spooked horses and racecourses, he took one last breath from the relative purity of the armhole and ripped the jacket off; then, while hanging with all his weight on the halter, he pulled the horse's head down low enough to fling on the jacket, covering the animal's eyes.

Confused, Trojan hesitated, just enough for Dessie, whose lungs were already starting to hurt, to seize this one last chance. 'Come on, *move!*' He gagged on the words then threw himself backwards as if competing in a tug-of-war.

Trojan shook his head to try to dislodge the blindfold but took one tentative step forwards. Dessie lost his balance and almost tumbled backwards into the fire, which was now all around his feet. He managed to right himself, however, and again leaned backwards. The horse took one more step, then a third . . .

The two escaped through the door just as all the little rivulets and rings of fire joined up together, whooshing out through the door after them as though in vengeful pursuit. Coughing and spluttering as the air hit him, Dessie left the jacket in place while he led the horse across the yard and tied him to one of the halter rings at the furthest

413

point from the fire outside Amazon's temporary holding pen. She was worked up now, the door of the stall shivered under her repeated assaults.

Dessie took no time to soothe her but rushed back across the yard to help Mick who was leading the prancing Goliath out of the stall next to Trojan's. 'We're fine here,' Mick shouted as Dessie went to take Goliath's halter. 'The next one's empty but it won't be long before it reaches Jumbo. You go along there and do what you can. I'll get the next one.'

In the face of the wind and all the combustible material, the extinguishers proved inadequate to put out the fire but with their aid, the two of them managed to control it sufficiently to free both Jumbo and John, the remaining two on the side of the yard along which the fire was taking hold. 'We'll have to get help, it's going to take more than these things,' Mick yelled above the wind and the crackling of the flames, now pouring from the door of the first stall. He cast aside the extinguisher he held, shouting, 'You take care of that lot,' as he raced towards the tack-room. 'Turn them out into the paddocks and come back for the others. Don't worry about padlocking gates or anything, go, go – run! I'll set up the yard hose too.'

Dessie, whose feet were as raw and painful as his lungs, untied the halters of the four horses which, wheeling and jostling each other, were fretting in their corner. He clucked his tongue at them and willed them to follow as he leaned into the reins, walking backwards so that he could look into their eyes. Somehow, either because they felt there was safety in numbers or because they trusted him, the ploy worked and as meekly as lambs, all four of the huge beasts clopped after him as sparks from the roof timbers of the stalls showered like sparklers on to the cobblestones around them.

Once outside the yard Dessie broke into a run as he took them towards the nearest field, the gate of which was about two hundred yards down a lane. When he opened it the horses needed no urging to go through and he had to jump aside or be trampled as they pushed past one another in to the field.

Pausing only to shut the gate and not bothering about the lead reins which trailed in the grass from the nosebands of all four of the animals, Dessie rushed back to the yard to find Mick in the process of leading Samson, Ulysses and Richard which, now they found them-selves in good hands, were as docile as the first four. 'I've phoned up

414

to the house,' the head lad shouted on seeing him, 'they're calling the brigade. Do you think you can manage Amazon by yourself? I'll come back and start with the hose.'

'Sure!' Dessie ducked a wind-borne piece of burning straw and ran. He noticed smoke curling out from the last doorway in the row at the far side and knew it would not be long now before the entire yard, including the tack-room and the staff quarters, would go up. Before going in to Amazon, he picked up the yard hose, turned the tap to which it was attached and doused himself all over in case he was delayed with the mare and the fire ran even faster than it was running already. Then he unhooked the halter from the nail on which he had so recently hung it and opened the stable door.

Amazon showed him the whites of her eyes as she stood facing him in the rear of the stall, feet planted, ears back. Knowing there was no time to waste, Dessie again went with his instincts. He raised both arms, cruciform fashion, not quite knowing why but feeling that by doing so he was showing the mare he had nothing to hide and was on her side. He burred at her, as he advanced, rolling his tongue against the hard place behind his top front teeth. Amazon pawed the ground, first with the right hoof, then the left.

In Dessie's view she was not panicked, merely angry. This, he thought, was a good sign. As if to prove his point, she snorted, then kicked a little with both hind feet, connecting with the partition to the next stall, then did it again for good measure.

'Good girl, good girl,' while continuing to keep his left hand in the air to distract her, Dessie moved his right hand, the one carrying the halter and lead rein cautiously towards her head. 'Now listen,' he said to her when he was just inches from her, 'you have to come, you have to prove you're not the monster they all think you are.'

Amazon pawed again and then her ears flicked a few times as though she was considering what he said. She lowered her head and, 'Good girl,' Dessie's hand slipped the halter over it before she could raise it again. He pulled.

Caught, Amazon threw up her head, just once and then became quiet. She let him take her outside just as though her previous bad humour had been a try-on.

Dessie led her as fast as he dared, the two of them having to run the gauntlet of the burning hay and straw, which, like an assault of barrage balloons, was now swirling in greatly increased quantity on the wind. Now that she had decided to co-operate, Amazon seemed less perturbed by the fire blizzard than was her minder.

As he took her through the arched gateway, Dessie saw a crowd of people, led by his father and the butler, Lewis, running towards him. George was gesticulating and shouting something at him but his words were whipped away and Dessie did not wait but concentrated on the task in hand, trotting beside the mare down the lane towards the rest of the horses. He saw Amazon safely into the sanctuary of the field, then went around to take off all the halters, an easy task because with the exception of Amazon, all the horses were bunched together in the corner of the field furthest from the fire.

Dessie was trudging back towards the gate when his knees gave and he had to sit down on the grass. He felt as though he might vomit and, lowering his head to his knees, hunched himself into a little ball. The spasm of nausea eased but his heart continued to race as he replayed the last forty-five minutes in his imagination. Then he felt a nudge on the side of his head and looked up to find it was Amazon, mane and tail streaming out behind her, ears pricked. Having got his attention, she nudged him again.

Dessie felt his legs would not hold him if he made any attempt to stand up. The pain in his feet was getting stronger, they were beginning to throb and he did not dare to look at them for fear of what he might see. 'You're a great girl.' He stroked the mare's muzzle. Amazon whiffled and then snatched a mouthful of grass.

As she munched it, the two of them watched the fireworks display beyond the clipped hedging at the boundary of the field. Because Dessie could hear little except the gale that whistled past his ears, the bubbles of flame and sparks bursting above the stable block against the orange sky seemed too spectacular to be real.

He waited until he felt a little stronger and then took Amazon into another field so she could have a bit of peace; as she was so close to foaling he did not want her to be annoyed by the other horses. As he led her towards this new field, he saw that the roof of the house, too, was blazing. Dessie had no resources left to do anything about it: he would have to leave it to others. He could already hear sirens in the distance.

Although the place to which he took Amazon was quite close to the blaze in the house, she did not seem to mind, turning her back on it. And even though it was the middle of the night, she trotted away from him and straight away started to graze on the juicy new grass. Dessie let her go: he did not have the energy to follow her to take off her halter. His lungs were not so bad any more but his feet were killing him – and, despite all the smoke he had inhaled, Dessie thought that he could badly do with a ciggie.

For five minutes, the high-speed battle raged, High Rollers versus the Shades, another Irish band racing them to London. Both groups had planned to meet up at the party in Cricklewood. The Shades were coming from Birmingham and their wagon had shot past the Rollers' at a point on the London road about six miles south of Coventry. The Rollers' driver had risen to the challenge and, since his Mercedes engine was newer and bigger than that on the Shades' Commer, easily outpaced his rival. He passed them, cut in in front of the Commer then waggled his steering wheel in triumph, throwing the card game in the cab of the Merc into disarray and provoking a yell of indignation, mixed with fear, from Hazel. He ignored her and when he was about a hundred yards ahead of his rival, the Rollers' driver let his vehicle fall back, daring the Commer to come up again, then speeding up when the dare was accepted, repeating this exercise over and over. The contest ended abruptly, however, when a police car gave chase.

They were lucky: the officer in charge had just returned from a successful salmon-fishing expedition to the West of Ireland and because the roads were clear and it was Saint Patrick's Day let both drivers off with a stern warning.

The Shades' wagon moved off immediately after the police car but two of the Rollers needed to answer a call of nature.

'Turn on the radio there,' Hazel called out from the back while they waited for the men to return. The driver complied, tuning in to the velvety tones of an announcer reading the south-easterly gale warnings. 'For God's sake,' Hazel complained, 'we know all about the feckin' gales, we can hear them, can't we? Find us a bit of music, wouldja? This is like a wake, not a party.'

'In a minute, Queenie, I want to hear the news first.' The driver leaned over to release the door catch as the two men came back from behind their bushes. He gunned the engine over the pips that announced the news.

417

Seated across the aisle from where Francey sat with Hazel, the Roller nicknamed the Intellectual, because he wore glasses, shuffled the cards to restart the game and shouted at the driver to turn up the volume – he, too, wanted to hear the news. The wagon's auxiliary speakers were at the back of the cab and Francey listened idly to the catalogue of war, disaster and political shenanigans from Cambodia, Cyprus, the United Nations and London. Mods were still fighting Rockers, the Queen and her new son were doing well – he heard nothing to interest him. Lulled by the motion of the vehicle, the driver of which was now keeping to a respectable pace, he felt himself drifting off into a pleasant, unspecific daydream.

He had been wondering all night whether he had made the right decision in not going to his father's Saint Patrick's Day party. Hazel's suggestion, that he go and be picked up again, had been reasonable, but Francey had not trusted his own behaviour in the presence of Fleur and her husband. He was confident Dessie would not hold his absence against him; the only subject which interested Dessie was the welfare of the horses. But anything that helped Dessie get well and stay on the straight and narrow was welcome.

He was tired and the night was just beginning. He closed his eyes in the hope that he could have a little nap when, from the speaker just behind him, he thought he heard the words 'Little Staunton'. He snapped to attention to hear that every fire brigade for miles around Little Staunton was being deployed in an effort to fight a huge fire at Inveraray Manor.

'Stop the wagon!' Hazel had heard it too.

'What?' the driver glanced over his shoulder. 'For crying out loud, Queenie, why didn't you go when we stopped only five minutes ago —'

'Stop!' Hazel yelled again.

'All right, keep your hair on.' The driver swerved into the verge.

Waiting for more information, Francey sat rigid in his seat. But the newsreader said nothing more, simply that any 'further details' would be included in future bulletins. Then he went on to repeat the gale warnings.

Francey became aware that Hazel was talking to him. 'What do you want to do? Do you want to ring?'

'I have to go there.'

'Of course, and I'm coming with you.'

Hazel ordered the driver to take them as fast as possible to Leamington Spa. The musician immediately offered to drive the whole way and some of the others were anxious to help, too, but Francey refused all offers. Hazel's determination to accompany him was unshakable, however, and he was already too terrified about what he might find to waste any time in fighting her.

It took them about twenty minutes to get to the outskirts of the city and they drove around until Hazel spotted a taxi with a lighted sign on its roof parked outside a small office. This vehicle was nearly as old as its young driver and although the latter, awed by the significance of his task, did his best, the journey to the Manor seemed to take for ever.

When the car turned at a crossroads a mile outside Little Staunton, Francey's stomach somersaulted: they were still nearly two miles from the house but across the fields, low in the sky, he could already see the orangey glow. He found Hazel's hand in his own and squeezed it tightly as the driver careened his jalopy around the sharp bends in the narrow roads.

They were within a quarter of a mile from the house when the driver had to pull the taxi close to the edge of the narrow road to let a police car, siren and lights in use, scream past them. As it did so, Francey caught sight of the side of Colin's face. There was something wrong with this: his half-brother was supposed to have been at the dinner party with Fleur. He had little time to speculate, however, as within minutes they were turning in through the gates of the Manor.

In the last hundred yards of the driveway, they passed a lot of cars, including his own, and others Francey recognized as belonging to the family, parked willy-nilly.

But he could not take his eyes off the awful display of pyrotechnics being given by the house.

It was ablaze along more than half of its length, mostly to the right of the front door. The area around the lake beetled with frantic activity as dark figures scurried between the police and fire vehicles and two ambulances. And while Francey could see that a few of the firemen had climbed on to the roof over the kitchen and dining room, he detected that neither the jets of water arcing from their hoses nor those of the men on the ground seemed to be having much effect.

On the drawing-room side of the house, long streamers of flame, fanned by the high winds, leaped high from the tops of most of the

419

windows and from the half-timbering on the roof. The gale was blowing from right to left, which was not in the firefighters' favour, and where the fire was fiercest, Francey saw that some of the external brickwork had collapsed, exposing the awful fact that the bricks were merely cladding and that Jool, following in her national tradition, had built her house with a timber frame. To judge by the way the blaze had already taken hold, Francey feared it would not be long before the whole house was engulfed.

The cacophony, as he jumped out of the taxi, was horrific: the shouts and yelling, the sharp, gunfire reports as windows blew out, the humming of the fire equipment – in Francey's ears as loud as pneumatic drills – the high-pitched swish of the water pressuring through the hoses. Most of all, the crackling and roaring of wind-driven flames consuming their prey.

Having told Hazel to stay well back, he was running towards the nearest group of fireman playing water on the drawing-room when, on hearing an enormous explosion, he instinctively ducked and covered his head. One of the huge picture windows had blown outwards, releasing a fireball.

When Francey looked up again he saw that the men in front of the drawing-room had dropped their hoses and had scattered in disarray.

Three lay on the ground.

Francey, forgetting his own fear, rushed towards them and helped carry one, whose face was burned, to an ambulance.

As the vehicle screamed off down the driveway, Francey went back in search of the family. He found his father, Colin and Tommy's nanny with Hazel now standing alongside them, transfixed. George Gallaher was restraining Francey's half-brother who, yelling and shouting what sounded like gibberish, appeared to be struggling to run towards the house.

Francey ran straight to George. 'I got here as soon as I heard.'

No one in the shocked group reacted with surprise on seeing him. 'She's in there, Francey, please do something.' While continuing to battle against his father's grip Colin attempted to claw at his half-brother.

'Who's in there?' Francey's horror intensified.

'We've just discovered we can't find Fleur.' It was George who replied. 'She was in the bedroom and no one has seen her since the fire was discovered. We were so busy in the stables we realized it only when Colin got back. Lewis has gone to tell the firemen. Have you heard—?' George tightened his grip on Colin and seemed to think better of what he had been going to say.

Francey jumped the gun. 'Where's Dessie?'

'He's still around at the stables as far as I know. They're gutted.' It was the nanny.

'Are you sure he's all right?' Francey yelled.

'I haven't seen him lately,' the girl shouted, trying to make herself heard above all the noise, 'but I think so. I saw him leading one of the horses into a field away from the fire.'

With that, Dessie himself came into view. Barely recognizable, with blackened face and torn, sodden clothes, he was limping badly as he came towards them from the burning end of the house. He was barefoot.

'Dessie?' As Francey ran towards him, he saw by the flickering light that the skin on both of his half-brother's feet had blackened and peeled away. 'What happened? You're injured—'

'Oh, Francey!' Dessie's face crumpled. He threw his arms around Francey's waist and wept like a baby against his chest.

'What about Fleur? *What about Fleur?*' Behind him, like a banshee, Francey heard Colin's scream.

'Where is she exactly?' As gently as possible given the urgency of what was going on, Francey put Dessie aside and turned to his father.

'Don't be mad, you can't do anything about her now—'

'It would be suicide—'

George and Hazel roared together but Colin, his voice rising even further with sudden hope, shrieked that Fleur was probably still asleep in the bedroom beside the drawing-room.

Francey looked towards the inferno at the end of the house. He instructed himself not to think about consequences or even about the condition of Fleur herself and had taken a few steps towards the house when, with a crash, a section of the roof over the drawing-room fell in. Flame and sparks shot to a height of thirty-five feet before falling back to burn furiously.

'Nothing and no one could be surviving in there,' George breathed.

'We could go in from the other side – it's not too bad at the dining-room end.' Dessie pulled at Francey's sleeve.

421

Francey looked to the far side of the house. Dessie was right, the dining-room and kitchen were still intact. And although the relentless stride of the fire towards it seemed unstoppable now, Francey saw the blaze had a fair way to go.

There was still a chance for Fleur – who knew? The front door was alight and rather than risk coming out that way, she might have escaped up to that end of the house and could be trapped in there behind the sealed windows. There were a number of bathrooms up there too. Bathrooms meant water.

Water: the dining-room, the water-wall, the aquarium, she could well be in there . . .

Before Francey could develop the idea, he heard his father's shout behind him: 'For God's sake, don't let him go in there!' and whirled around but he was too late. Colin had taken advantage of George's momentary distraction and had wriggled out of his grasp. Picking up one of the concrete balls from the parapet of the ornamental lake and carrying it like a rugby ball, Francey's half-brother was running with it like a player evading the opposition, weaving through the fire tenders and all the men.

'*Stop him!*' The communal shout was too late. Evading capture and using all his strength, Colin hurled the heavy ball against one of the breakfast-room windows, shattering it. Then, kicking the hole wide, he dived through and vanished.

For a second or two, the spectators, even the firemen, were too shocked to react. Then some of the latter rushed forward as though to follow him but stopped just short of entry to consult with their commanding officer.

'Stay here!' Shoving Dessie roughly towards their father in case he, too, came up with any grandiose ideas, Francey raced towards the house, unheeding of calls for him to stop. He was vaguely aware that the firefighters were rushing to get into different clothing and strapping objects on to their backs, as he sped past them and plunged through the shattered window.

Except for the shards of glass, and that it was lit only with overspills of light from the emergency equipment outside, the interior of the breakfast room looked incongruously normal, but the sound of the fire was like an oncoming train. Immediately Francey felt the intensity of the heat.

He saw no sign of Colin.

The door to the room opened inwards from a small lobby which ran at right angles to the central corridor; at the other side of the lobby, a similar door, used for serving, opened into the dining-room. This door was closed.

Francey decided arbitrarily to give himself four minutes in the house, that this should allow him ample time for rescue and would lie well within the margins of safety. That settled, the minutes splintered into seconds, each a whole and indivisible resource as his brain narrowed the focus of its attention.

He felt no fear; he felt nothing at all. He set himself just three tasks. Get Fleur. Get Colin. Get himself out.

First of all, where? His brain ticked off options. It was unlikely that even if Colin had gone through into the dining-room and discovered Fleur there that he would have closed the door after him.

It followed they were not in there.

It was more likely that in his hysterical state Colin had headed straight for their bedroom at the drawing-room end.

He, Francey, had to follow.

As Francey opened the door of the breakfast-room and went out into the little lobby, he encountered clouds of acrid black smoke, wafting towards him from round the corner, from the corridor proper. Covering his mouth and nose with one elbow, he risked a look.

It was like staring into the mouth of a furnace.

A solid wall of fire burned from wall to wall of the corridor. Every colour from bright yellow to darkest red, it scrolled black at the edges, puffing along, gathering into its maw all the satellite fires which extruded from the open bedroom doors in its path.

What was more immediately disturbing, however, were the advance parties of fire which rampaged along the exposed ceiling beams, cohorts which dropped blobs of flame onto the carpet below all the way down to Francey's end of the corridor. The heat was almost unbearable and although he reckoned he had been in the house now for less than one of his four minutes, rivers of sweat coursed from his forehead into his eyes.

He dashed them away. Colin was lying face down on the floor a few feet beyond one of the three doors to the dining-room, the *trompe l'oeil* door just beyond the aquarium. His outstretched hand was only a few feet from the marching wall. Small fires burned behind him although, as far as Francey could see, he was still clear.

Somewhere Francey had read that to survive a fire you must stay low. He dropped into a crouching position and ran for Colin, grabbed one of his half-brother's feet and started to drag him backwards towards the 'safe' end of the corridor.

Unfortunately, in the few seconds this took, the blaze had leapfrogged again and the small carpet fires behind him had joined up. He could not drag Colin through it and he knew that to stand up and carry him would be too dangerous.

Instead, he shouldered at the door of the dining-room and, having pulled Colin inside, kicked it shut again.

In here, although the air was smoky and just as scorching as outside, all was relative calm. The fish were in darkness, the water wall moribund. All the electricity was obviously off but as far as Francey could see, there was so far no structural damage, although through the soles of his shoes he could feel the heat of the lucite on the floor. Would it melt? Would the glass of the table?

Francey, reckoning he had been in the house about two, maybe two minutes and a half now, eschewed the luxury of speculation. Although he was beginning to have difficulty with his breathing, he still felt strong and capable. All he had to do to get himself and Colin out was to break one of the windows.

He had forgotten something. Fleur? Where was Fleur? He had one and a half minutes to find Fleur. He glanced through the window and saw the firefighters, dressed like scuba divers, moving towards the breakfast-room. Good. Help was coming.

Francey dragged Colin away from the door and towards the water wall. Although the water was no longer running, at least it was damp and made of marble. Dumping his burden at its base, he made for the door of the room to go back out to look for Fleur.

When he opened it, a mountain of black smoke erupted all over him.

Immediately, Francey dropped again to the floor, kicking the door shut but now feeling sick, groggy and disoriented. He crawled over to the door to the lobby which was at one end of the water wall but despite pulling at it, could not get it to open. It felt hot to the touch and he assumed the fire had taken hold outside.

Francey crawled the short distance back to Colin as he considered what to do next. It had been a mistake to open the first door. The air in here was now so smoky that breathing was more difficult than ever. He knew his indecisiveness was costing him some of his precious seconds; he must be coming close to the end of his self-imposed four-minute time limit. And it had seemed like a good round figure – Roger Bannister, all the rest of it . . .

To his horror through the thick air, he saw a huge, jagged crack appear high in the wall at the far end of the room. The crack instantly glowed red and orange.

Francey scrambled to his feet. He now had to make an act of faith that wherever Fleur was in the house she was safe. He could not go out there any more. The most pressing thing was to get out of here with Colin.

The window.

He looked around for something to throw at the window. The air was getting thicker, to walk through it felt like trying to swim through a sea as thick as a blanket. He was getting weaker too. He picked up a chair and threw it towards the window but it fell short. He got another one and made a huge effort. This one connected but bounced harmlessly off the heavy double glazing. Francey lowered his forehead to breathe: his lungs seemed capable only of taking in tiny amounts of air. The lucite under his hands felt hot and greasy and even through the pungency of the smoke it smelled strange. A piece of flame dropped from the ceiling on to one of the upholstered chairs beside him; mercifully, it did not burn but as it smouldered it released clouds of thick, brownish smoke which seemed to add to Francey's breathing difficulties and disorientation.

Then he had one last idea: if he couldn't break the glass in the window, he could at least break the glass in the aquarium. All that water . . . he could release all that water . . .

Pushing one of the chairs in front of him, Francey was crawling over to the aquarium when the whole world seemed to explode around his ears. The explosion went on and on and on and when it finished there were more sounds, strange, high-pitched ones he could not connect up.

He managed to raise his head sufficiently to see that the fire had raced along the ceiling beams and was dropping with fizzing noises all around him. But there was something else.

Francey thought he was hallucinating. Through the smoke and fire, a huge, two-headed beast was prancing towards him from the window he had not been able to break. It was screaming and shouting at him and was being followed by smaller monsters with humped backs.

As soon as he saw Francey go into the house, Dessie, too, had run. The pain in his feet vanished as he raced back around the side of the burning drawing-room to the field where he had left Amazon. He felt he would have one chance.

Amazon's head was protruding over the hedge beside the gate into the field. Dessie wasted no time in throwing open the gate and hauling himself on to her back – miraculously, his calves and ankles seemed to have developed springs. He leaned over Amazon's neck, caught hold of her halter with one hand and urged her through the gate with his knees.

Down the little lane and back round the side of the house they trotted, Dessie whispering into her ear all the time. When they got round to the front, he slid off and led her across to the dining-room. The roof over the kitchen was now well alight and in a sort of pincer movement, the dining-room was threatened now from both sides. Out of the corner of his eye Dessie saw some of the firemen had finished strapping themselves into their bulky equipment and were making their way towards the broken breakfast-room window but he thought that now the only safe way in was through the massive plate glass of the dining-room.

'*What's that horse doing here?*' He ignored the shout, which came somewhere from his right. Amazon was starting to dance and buck a little but he kept talking to her, keeping eye contact as he turned her around and pushed her back towards the dining-room. 'Good girl, you're absolutely beautiful, you're my good, good girl . . .' He kept her head low, pushing at her forehead with his chest. She resisted a little but Dessie forced her, made her, willed her to keep backing, backing . . .

She was dancing harder now, prancing, giving little kicks, tossing at the lead rein but he caught hold of the tuft of mane at her poll and pulled on it with one hand, staring as mesmerically as he could into

426

her eyes. He got her to within feet of the plate glass when one of the firefighters reached him, brandishing something.

Amazon plunged and kicked, almost getting away, but Dessie managed to hold on as she backed away, rearing a little, then plunging again and this time her backwards kick connected with the glass. She kicked twice more in quick succession, the second assault shattering the window, which was what Dessie had hoped for. Then Amazon finally took fright. She reared high now, kicking wildly in all directions, backing through the massive hole she had made, the larger pieces of glass crunching under her. The firemen scattered but Dessie, afraid she would cut herself on the jagged contours of the window still remaining, went with her, managing to hold on, all the time talking, 'Don't, darlin', don't,' talking, talking . . .

He hauled her head down but Amazon resisted, straining backwards into the room. Thinking he could control her better from her back, Dessie managed to vault on to her back but he was too late and she speeded her backing up, just avoiding a particularly vicious spear of glass and went into the room, hooves skidding on the greasy surface. As the two of them almost came a cropper, Dessie heard the firemen come in behind him but was too intent on keeping his own balance, and on preventing Amazon from falling, to look round.

Again, leaning full length along her neck, he hauled on her head. With a high-pitched, terrifying whinny, Amazon turned until she was facing into the room – although this had not been Dessie's intention – and with feet sliding and slipping, took a few steps in. She was wholly inside before she realized what a mistake she had made. She wheeled and, still whinnying and with Dessie hanging on, made for the outside.

When Amazon felt firm ground under her, she broke into a gallop and flew across the gravel, veering around the lake and scattering everyone in her path. With Dessie clinging on to her mane and head collar she did not slow down until she was half-way down the driveway.

Francey felt himself being grabbed and the next thing he knew the back of his head was resting on something soft and his lungs were being seared by air so clean and cold they felt they were being sliced.

427

He saw Colin being taken away on a stretcher and dimly, through all the commotion, he saw Hazel's anxious face hovering above his own. 'Fleur?' he croaked.

'Someone else is looking after it.' Hazel crouched over him and took his unresisting hand. 'Oh, Francey, Francey,' she wept, 'you were in there for hours, I thought – if it hadn't been for Dessie –'

'Not hours. Four minutes?' Francey's throat hurt but he felt it imperative that she should know how organized he had been. He managed to lift his head to see that the roof was ablaze along its entire length now. Then he saw Dessie. His half-brother had a lead rein in his hand, at the other end of which was one of the Shires.

Amazon, impervious to the fire or to the fuss all around her, pulled hard to get at the fresh grass in the verge along the driveway.

Chapter Twenty-Two

Francey was released from hospital next morning but Colin was kept for observation for a further twenty-four hours. Considering what they had been through, both were in remarkably good health. Dessie had refused point blank to stay in overnight and had gone back to the Manor.

Because his father was closeted with the police and insurance investigators, and because the burn dressings on Dessie's feet meant he had to keep them raised and could not wear shoes, it was Hazel who came in George's chauffeur-driven car to pick up Francey. It was also she who broke the news to him about Tommy's death.

Before he could react, Hazel took one of his hands in both of hers. 'I'm afraid there's more, Francey.'

They were sitting on a little bench in the hospital entrance hall and he saw that Hazel was watching his face. 'There's no easy way to say this,' she squeezed his hand, 'but there's good grounds for thinking the fires were set deliberately. And it seems now that Fleur was not in there. They searched and searched but they didn't find her.'

She paused to let the implication sink in. 'No one knows where she is now,' she added then, 'she came to the hospital last night, around the time the fire was at its height, and tried to take Tommy away from the mortuary, but they stopped her and she ran off. She hasn't been seen since. Their car is gone, too.'

It was too much to take in. 'Are you saying that Fleur did it?' Francey's voice was so hoarse it was hardly audible. Hazel's words seemed to be coming towards him from behind a layer of cotton wool. On admission to the hospital he had been given sedatives which had knocked him out completely; he had slept for hours and could fall asleep again now with no difficulty.

'Now I'm not saying that,' Hazel swallowed, 'but I'm afraid the way it looks now, everything points to her. I'm sorry,' she whispered, 'but they've found the remains of a petrol can inside the house. And Colin used to keep a petrol can in the boot of that car.'

Francey did not know what to think. The trauma of the night before was still so fresh that he could not grasp the notion that Tommy had died, much less that Fleur had set fires.

How could Tommy have died? And why would Fleur set fires? In his befuddled perception, both concepts seemed as preposterous as the pattern of the polished chequerboard tiles on the floor and the swing doors which kept moving backwards and forwards as people entered and left the hospital foyer. Even the way the sunlight lit the back of Hazel's head looked weird. Nothing had any reality except the lurid, red-bordered images, now shrunk and silent as though someone was turning the pages of a snap album, which continued to wheel through the fog in the forefront of his imagination.

'She was very upset about Tommy's death, naturally,' Hazel offered as though reading his mind.

From somewhere in the recesses of his brain it occurred to Francey that he should ask how Tommy died but then, once again, the notion that he was dead at all was so ludicrous that it was easier to say nothing. He looked at the serious wavering face before him and decided that he would let it take over, to wait for it to say or do something else.

'Are you all right? Francey, you're as white as a sheet.' Hazel was still holding his hand. 'I'm afraid I have to go on to Brighton – you know we have a show there tonight – but I'll come up early tomorrow morning to see you again. We've no gig tomorrow and Friday's Leeds so I'll be able to hang around for a bit.'

'Will you stay at the Manor?' Francey shook his head to try to clear away some of the fug.

Hazel looked down at his hand. 'There's no more Manor, Francey.'

Francey stared at her: how could he have forgotten?

'They're all staying at one of the inns in Little Staunton,' she went on gently. 'We've booked you in there too and the doctor is going to come to have a look at you later on.'

It was time to go. Francey made an effort to stand up but one of his feet slipped on the tiles and he would have fallen if she had not steadied him. 'The Rolls is outside.' Hazel linked him under one elbow.

Francey looked down at her: this, too, seemed bizarre, for him to be leaning on such a tiny little body as hers. But before he could extricate himself, she had tugged at him and he was forced to put one foot in front of the other or he might fall.

Francey was helped out of the little hospital as though he were an old man.

He slept in the comfortable back seat of the car and all that day he drifted in and out of sleep in the bedroom in which they put him. People came and went from time to time but he only half took in what they were saying. He woke up at one point to find George sitting at the end of his bed, saying something about 'my three sons' a phrase that seemed outlandish. The bedspread on the cramped bed was covered with roses as big as cabbages and, in his half-asleep condition, Francey thought he saw some of the roses come alive and crawl up over his father's chest and head. Knowing it had to be an illusion, he attempted to focus but his eyes were heavy and woolly and would not respond properly. It was so much easier to lapse again into a nice doze.

He was ravenously hungry when eventually he woke properly. Then he remembered the full horror of what Hazel had told him about Tommy and Fleur. About what they had *alleged* about Fleur.

He saw through the window of the room that the sky was pink and red and, for a moment, feared the worst. But then he looked at his watch and seeing it was just after six o'clock, deduced that the colouring in the sky was the natural phenomenon of sunset.

Someone – Hazel? – had caused his travelling bags to be placed in his room. Francey, having to keep his head low in order not to hit it off the ceiling and refusing to dwell on anything except the urgent call of his stomach, dressed quickly and descended the stairs to the little lobby of the hotel. The first person he saw was Lewis, who told him that his father had gone to visit Colin and in Fleur's absence to make funeral arrangements for his grandson – but that Dessie was in the bar. 'And Miss Slye left this for you, sir.' The butler took an envelope out of his pocket.

Hazel's note said only that he was to get as much rest as he could and that she would see him early the following day. She also gave him the name and telephone number of the Rollers' hotel in Brighton if he should want her.

In spite of everything else on his mind, he was relieved to find Dessie nursing a Coca-Cola and not drinking alcohol as he had feared.

'Tell me about Fleur – and Tommy.' Having ordered two sandwiches to tide himself over until dinner, Francey brought his own drink over to sit beside him.

'It wasn't Amazon's fault.' Dessie, whose bandaged feet were raised on a footstool, went immediately on the defensive and it took a while to prise out of him what had happened to the little boy.

Although he had not been close to Tommy, Francey was nevertheless upset. He could appreciate what Fleur must have felt – must be going through, he reminded himself, *if* the allegations were correct. But not feeling up to it at present, he postponed an examination of how he felt either about Fleur or about the allegations against her.

Dessie, however, could throw no light on her whereabouts; neither could he elaborate much about why everyone thought it was she. As far as Francey could tell, not only did his half-brother not know a great deal about what had happened, he did not care – so long as his beloved horses were all right. 'What's going to happen to them, Francey?' he asked now. 'Thank God it's nearly summer and they can be out for a while but Mick came in to see me earlier and he's as worried as I am.'

Francey forebore to point out that with a little boy dead, his mother missing and a mansion presumably in ruins, the horses were unlikely to be high on most people's agendas. 'Are your feet sore?' he asked. 'And I never thanked you for rescuing me, for rescuing the two of us, Colin and me both. You saved my life, Dessie.'

'I didn't rescue you,' Dessie looked surprised, 'it was Amazon. That's why nothing can happen to her. You know, I don't think any other horse would have been able to do what she did, it's the breed, you see. My feet are grand, thank you. They're a bit sore but the doc gave me some great pills. More pills!' He grinned. 'Just when you thought I was safe!'

Francey grinned back. After what had happened in the last twenty-four hours, the anticlimactic nature of this exchange, the log fire crackling in the grate beside them, the chintz furnishings and the quiet to-ing and fro-ing of the young woman behind the bar, was both soothing and disturbing. Francey felt he should not be able to smile, or to enjoy so much this cheese and pickle between these two slices of bread or the mild taste of this beer. And yet, while he ate and drank, and the two of them talked to one another in desultory fashion, he felt that in the short time he had known his half-brother, this was

432

the first time he had felt close to him. It was the very nothingness of the conversation that seemed so intimate. What was more, the nature of the relationship between them had changed: it was no longer one of benefactor and dependant but of equals.

The Inveraray household had taken over most of the bedrooms in the inn. George had not yet returned from his visit to Colin in the hospital and the nanny had apparently gone back to London, but about half an hour later when Francey helped Dessie hobble into the dining-room for dinner, he found they were sharing the place with the butler and six of the live-in staff. Not at their table, however. Although Francey invited them, Lewis, speaking on behalf of the staff, insisted they would not dream of joining the half-brothers and so Francey, feeling that he had trespassed across some invisible line, did not insist.

The inn had no other guests and, as Dessie and George's staff ate mostly in silence, the atmosphere was subdued throughout the meal. This did not bother Francey who, busy with his own thoughts and still so hungry he could not get the food into him fast enough, was not in the mood for talking.

When they had finished, he helped Dessie up to his room and then went back downstairs in search of the butler to ask him what had happened to his car. He discovered that, as far as Lewis knew, it was still out at the house. 'The police have cordoned off the area, sir,' the butler warned, but Francey did not heed him. The retrieval of the car was only part of the reason why he wanted to go out to the house. Having been carted off to hospital at the height of the fire, he felt impelled to witness the full extent of the devastation for himself.

He took a taxi and asked the driver to let him off at the entrance gates, feeling that the walk up the driveway would clear his head and prepare him a little for what he was about to see.

At first, there was little sign that anything was different. As if to atone for its behaviour of the night before, the weather was calm; lit by a large, tranquil moon, the daffodil heads under the rails at the edge of the driveway on both sides barely stirred and the only trace of last night's pandemonium were the tyre tracks ground here and there into the grass.

His own car was the first vehicle Francey encountered. Parked behind Jool's Jaguar just before the last bend in the driveway, it started at the first turn of the key. Letting the engine die again, he got out and walked towards the bend. On the journey out here, he had tried to imagine the ruin, picturing something like the shell of the burned-out coastguard post on the shoreline below the road near Eyeries, a hulk of jagged chimney stacks and blackened walls. Maybe it was still smoking . . .

As he rounded the bend he saw that a police car had been pulled across the top of the driveway. Its internal light was on and he could see the man inside pouring liquid from a Thermos flask into a cup. Behind it virtually nothing was left except an enormous, irregularly shaped mound of charred rubble. Francey had forgotten that the house was timber-framed and that the only fireplace was the gas one in the drawing-room which, presumably, had not needed a full-scale chimney.

Shocked, he walked towards the police car. As he got closer, in the distance behind the rubble he could see the stable block, which, having been built of concrete and stone, looked more like what he had expected. It was too far away from where he was, however, for him to assess the extent of the damage.

'Evenin'!' The police officer, seeing him coming, addressed Francey through his open window. He drained his cup and screwed it back on to the top of his flask and then got out of the car. 'I'm sorry, sir,' he said, 'but this is as far as you can go.'

'I'm Mr Gallaher's son.' Francey continued to look over the man's head towards the slag heap which used to be Inveraray Manor. 'I was involved in the fire here last night.'

'Has anyone talked to you yet?' The policeman looked keenly at him.

'Do you mean the police?' Francey shook his head. 'Not yet. I was in hospital until a short time ago.'

'I'm sure we'll be in touch, sir, but you can't go any further than this. I'm sorry.'

Francey was about to argue but changed his mind. The man was only doing his job and he could come back again in daylight. 'I'll be taking my car,' he said then, in case the policeman thought he was stealing it, 'the Morris Oxford.'

This seemed to be in order and wishing the man a goodnight, Francey, after one last look, walked back down the driveway.

But as he attempted to start the car again his hands started to tremble, so badly that he did not trust himself to drive but sat staring through the windscreen at the back of Jool's Jaguar. What had he expected? That he could just come out here and walk around and go away again without being affected? He sat there for a while, trying to control himself.

'Are you all right, sir?' It was the policeman again, tapping on the side window of the car.

His hands still shaking, Francey rolled down the window: 'Yes – yes, thank you, officer,' he made an effort to pull himself together, 'I – I hadn't realized quite how bad the damage was going to be.'

'Are you sure you're fit to drive?' The policeman squatted beside the car so his face was level with Francey's. 'I can call up someone to drive you if you like.'

'No, I'm fine, really, it was just the shock.' Francey attempted to smile. To prove to the man he had recovered, he turned the key in the ignition, successfully this time, and put the car into gear.

The policeman stood up. 'Mind how you go.'

'I will, thanks, officer.' Francey brought the Oxford through a ragged three-point turn and drove slowly away.

When he was sure he was safe from the policeman's scrutiny and hearing, he stopped the car at the side of the driveway about forty yards inside the gates. He could not weep; his emotions ran too deep for tears. Although the only sound in the car was of the rattling of the keys in the ignition as the wheel reacted under his shaking hands, in his mind Francey heard his own voice call names: Fleur's, Tommy's, Dessie's, Mossie's, Neeley Scollard's, Kathleen's, his mother's, even George's and his own. And Hazel's.

It was as though he had layered up the emotions during the tumult of the past six months, not only the tragic and hurtful but the happy and the bittersweet, too, packing them all into a heap as dense as the ruin behind them.

All was now disintegrating. *Shut up! Shut up!* Francey screamed at himself in silence. If he could just hold on for one minute, two minutes, this would pass.

The spasm did ease after a few minutes and he released his grip on the steering wheel finger by finger. His wrists, palms and knuckles hurt but other than that he felt temporarily free, as though he was floating.

He was just about to drive off again when another pair of headlights turned slowly in through the gates and came towards him at a snail's pace. Instantly, thinking this was a gawker, Francey's mood changed again and boiled with resentment; he needed a scapegoat and he despised such ghoulishness.

He flashed his own headlights full in order to blind the driver of the other car but the reaction caught him off guard. Instead of flashing back or dimming, the lights of the other car went off completely. Then the vehicle veered into the side, stalled and cut out.

Francey, still angry, jumped out of his own car to intercept the intruder. On coming close to the car, however, he stopped dead. He was looking through a windscreen at Fleur.

'What are you doing here?' Furiously, he pulled open the door of the Rover, which he recognized as Colin's, but on seeing the state Fleur was in, was so taken aback that his rage drained away. She looked as though she had not washed or combed her hair for a week. The dress she wore was creased and stained, and she had a cut over her eye. 'What happened to you?' Francey asked and then immediately regretted the question. What had *not* happened to her? Whatever she had done or not done subsequently, this was a woman whose child had just died.

When she got out of the car, in spite of her bedraggled appearance she seemed calm, far calmer than he, and much more in control than she should be for someone who had lost her son and who had allegedly burned down a mansion. The muscles of her face, normally so controlled, were working, however, as though she was trying to make a decision. 'I had to wait until after it was dark,' she said, 'is it possible to get into the house?'

Francey stared down at her. Was she acting? Or could it be feasible that they were all wronging her and she genuinely did not know what had happened? This was no time for subterfuge, or speculation. 'Is it true, Fleur?' he asked. 'Did you burn it?'

'Yes.' She stared up at him, eyes half concealed under her tousled hair. 'But now I need to fetch something.'

Francey, flummoxed, could not believe what he was hearing. 'What?' He was upset at the way his voice would not come out clean. 'What do you need to fetch?'

'May I trust you?' Fleur continued to look up at him and Francey, who could not have replied if one of the Shires was pulling words out of him, could only nod.

436

'I brought three diamonds to this house yesterday,' Fleur said in a monotone. 'They were sewn into a little black purse. I left them behind but I need them now.'

She was mad, Francey decided. Grief had unbalanced her mind. 'Why do you need them now?' He tried to match her tone but again it came out all wrong. This was a woman he had loved, loved . . .

'They are no doubt watching my bank,' Fleur said. 'I need money.' Then, for the first time, she showed some emotion. 'Please help me, Francey—' Her voice broke. 'I was going – I mean, Tommy and I were going—' She gulped, then: 'They would not allow me to take Tommy home with me. They took him away from me and they would not allow me to take him back.' She put a hand on Francey's arm to strengthen her appeal but removed it as though realizing she had committed an indiscretion. 'I have my passport and papers, I managed to get into the flat through a back way. I know they might put me in gaol for what I have done, Francey. I will kill myself rather than have that happen. I cannot apologize for what I did because it would not be honest. You see, I would probably do it again if – if—'

She could not continue but Francey, who felt like a stone, was unable to help her out.

Fleur took a long, shaky breath. 'And if I go to the bank,' she continued at last, 'they will find me. To buy a flight I must have those diamonds. Will you help me?'

Francey had no doubt that she would carry out her threat to kill herself. 'How do you know they are watching your bank, Fleur?' He tried to gain some time to think. 'You must be imagining it. And anyway, I'm sure they would make allowances for—'

Again it hung unspoken in the air between them: the death of the child.

'They just want to question you,' Francey managed, then, conversationally, 'What about Colin? Have you thought about him, Fleur? He must be out of his mind with worry.'

'I am finished with this family,' Fleur cried. 'I am finished with England and I need to go right away, tomorrow. Please, will you help me?'

Francey thought of Colin's headlong dash into the jaws of the fire, of his own efforts, of Dessie's. 'What about the funeral?' he asked. 'Don't you even want to stay around for your own son's funeral?'

'Please do not talk about Tommy.' Again Fleur almost lost her composure. 'Tommy is dead, he has moved on. A funeral will not help him.'

Francey tried to decide what to say or do next, and sought inspiration in the quiet fields. 'There's nothing left of the house, Fleur,' he said. Then the absurdity of the negotiation struck him. Aside from the agony she had caused him, she had deliberately gutted a multi-million-pound palace. What was he doing talking to her as if she were a sane human being? 'For Christ's sake, Fleur!' he cried as passionately as his hoarseness would allow. 'Don't ask this of me, don't, please don't.'

Fleur looked at the ground and then gave an almost imperceptible shrug. 'Goodbye, Francey, I must go to get my diamonds.' She began to walk away from him up the driveway.

Francey, who wanted to shake her, instinctively walked after her. 'Can't you get it into your head that it's just a heap of rubbish?' he called. 'You'd never find a bulldozer in there much less three diamonds. We could all have been killed,' he was in step with her by this time, 'we very nearly were.'

'Tommy was killed.' Fleur stopped and looked away as if that was the end of the conversation while Francey tried to hold on to his own sanity. In the dim, quiet light of the sky, in spite of her dishevelled state, in spite of what she had done to him and to them all, she still looked beautiful to him.

And now he hated that beauty.

Behind him, the ticking over of the engine of Francey's car became louder in the silence. And clearly within it, Francey abruptly heard the words of the old lady's letter to him: *So look after them all . . . specially little Tommy and his mother. I've a funny feeling they're the ones who'll need you most . . .* The words had thrilled him at the time, he had taken them to be a good omen.

While Fleur waited, continuing to stare at the ground, he shook his head as though to dislodge Jool Gallaher's exhortation but then, remorselessly, her letter came back at him with a cliché he had heard all his life at Lahersheen, one he had smiled at as he read the letter, the one about the Lord making the back for the burden. *Go away*, Francey thought savagely, *this has nothing to do with me any more*. But the more he fought them, the more Jool's words hounded him.

He looked down at this woman he had loved so completely and recognized that to hate Fleur was akin to hating a wounded blackbird.

'Goodbye, Francey.' Having sensed his internal struggle and decided the battle was lost, Fleur began to move again when, about a hundred yards away, Francey saw twin cones of light pierce the sky above the perimeter wall as another car approached the estate. From the vantage point of his height, he saw the quick blue reflection of an unlit roofbar and knew it was another police car. Perhaps it was passing by; on the other hand perhaps it was coming to relieve or to consult with the officer at the top of the driveway.

Francey's natural inclination towards action took control. 'Police! Quickly!' Before Fleur could say anything, he had scooped her into his arms and had run with her towards the Morris. Opening the back door he threw her inside. 'Get down as low as you can – on the floor.' Then he shot into the driver's seat and gunned the engine, spinning the wheels with the effort to get the car moving.

He was too late, the police car was already turning in through the gates.

'Evening.' He let the engine die down and wound open his window as the panda stopped beside him.

'Good evening, sir,' the officer in the passenger seat put on his cap and got out. 'I'm George Gallaher's son,' Francey said swiftly through the window opening before the man could ask any awkward questions, 'as I was telling your colleague in the other car,' he jerked a thumb over his shoulder in the direction of the house, 'I was here last night but I've been in hospital and this is the first opportunity I've had to inspect the damage.'

'I see.' The policeman hesitated. 'Is this one of the family cars, sir?' He directed the beam of his torch across the driveway at Colin's Rover.

Thanking God that Fleur had not taken the distinctive MGB, Francey adopted a look of concern. 'I was wondering that myself, officer,' he said, hoping that in an effort to still the commotion in his blood he did not sound too fulsome, 'I've never seen it before. I thought it might be one of those sightseers, or even a looter, that's why I stopped here. There seems to be nobody in it though,' he added, holding his breath as the policeman walked over to the Rover, opened the door and took the keys from the ignition.

'Well he can't have got far, whoever he is,' the officer weighed the keys in his hand, 'and he's going nowhere now. Don't worry, sir, we'll find him. And please accept my sympathies.'

'Thank you.' Francey rolled up his window as he drove off. Warning Fleur to stay low, he drove for nearly three miles before stopping in a gateway along a stretch of straight road. 'All right,' he said, checking the sky around for signs of approaching headlights, 'you can come out now.' He heard the faintest of rustling and then, in the rear view mirror, saw that Fleur was sitting on the back seat. 'What now?' He was resigned to his fate.

'I am in your hands.' Fleur's tone was dull, hopeless. Even if he had not been touched, Francey now knew he had already implicated himself to the extent that he had to follow this through as far as he could. 'Have you any friends you could go to for the night?' he asked but, to his dismay, she shook her head.

'I have a friend in Hatton Garden but he is away. You are my only friend now.'

Francey thought bitterly that six weeks ago he would have given his entire fortune to hear that phrase on her lips. 'Well, you'd better come into the front seat,' he said. 'It looks peculiar you being in the back like that. And we have to get away, we're drawing attention to ourselves loitering around here.'

Fleur climbed into the front and covering her face as though she was crying, hunched into the seat, a posture which rendered her tinier than ever. 'I'm really sorry about Tommy,' Francey said gently, although he did not trust himself to touch her. She nodded but did not remove her hands from her face. If she was weeping, she was doing so without making a sound and he could not bear to look at her any more.

'Was that your own car you were driving?' he asked as he put the Morris in gear.

'Colin's.' Her voice was muffled from behind her hands.

With Fleur's husband in hospital, Francey was thinking rapidly now. It would not take long before the police figured out who had been driving the Rover. And because of the bad luck they had had in encountering the second police car, he was also sure that his own involvement would be suspected sooner rather than later. He was hardly inconspicuous. If Fleur was to be got safely out of the country it would have to be with the assistance of a third party.

440

He noted grimly that, whether he liked it or not, he had begun to think of himself and Fleur as being in this together. Thank you, Grandma, he thought, this is for you – this was your idea, so get me out of this . . .

Francey decided he was becoming as unhinged as his passenger – talking to dead people. He almost laughed at the situation in which he found himself. His absent sister Johanna, who loved bizarre stories and gloried in the telling of them, would have had a great night's outing on this one. 'If I'm to help you out, Fleur,' he said now, 'you must do exactly as I say, all right?' She looked so woebegone as she nodded acquiescence that Francey almost forgot he hated her.

They came to a crossroads in one of those picture-book villages he had so enjoyed during his meanderings around Warwickshire. This one was unfamiliar but he saw it had a telephone box in a relatively hidden location, tucked into a right angle made by two walls beside the post office. The pub sign across the road was illuminated but as far as he could see no one was about. 'Sit tight,' he said to Fleur, making a quick decision. 'I've to use the telephone. I'll be back in a minute.'

He took Hazel's note out of the breast pocket of his jacket and called out the number she had given him to the operator. It was just after five past eight. With any luck he would catch her – the band would not yet have left for the venue.

There followed the interminable palaver with coins when the hotel answered and then the nervous wait while the receptionist tried to contact her. He could have cheered when he heard her breathless Dublin accent. 'Francey? What's after happenin'?'

'I don't have much time and I'm in a coin box. Hazel, please listen to me. I have a very, very great favour to ask of you and if you can help me out I'll be in your debt for ever.'

'I told you when you rescued me that it was me owed you, Kemo Sabay!' But he could tell that Hazel's lightness masked doubt. Nevertheless he had no option but to trust her so he outlined the events of the evening and what he now planned to do.

Hazel did not hesitate. 'I'll meet you as soon as I can after the gig,' she said. 'Go to the Lorna Doone Hotel in Eaton Square, I'll book you in.' Then Francey heard her hesitate. 'Will I ask for one room for yiz or two?' Her voice was matter-of-fact.

'Two.' Francey's reply was more vehement than he had intended.

441

'Right,' Hazel said, 'you can trust them there but once you're in keep her out of sight. I'll do the necessary and I'll be there as quick as I can. Probably before three.'

Francey then telephoned the inn at Little Staunton and asked for Dessie. He told his half-brother that he was feeling much better and that in case anyone was looking for him, the police or anyone, he emphasized, Dessie was to say that he was going to Leeds to wait for Hazel and the band and that he would be back in time for Tommy's funeral.

Fleur was silent throughout the car journey to London and Francey, too mixed up to try to talk to her, concentrated on driving. As before, he felt uneasy about the notion of trying to find his way around the huge city and when they came to Watford, followed a signpost which indicated a railway station. Railway stations meant taxi ranks.

He parked nearby, then, to cover the ruined dress which might attract undue attention, he gave Fleur his sheepskin jacket, instructing her to put it over her shoulders like a cloak. 'And you'd better clean up that cut on your face a little. Have you a comb?'

Fleur shook her head so he took his own from his pocket and passed it to her along with a tissue from the glove compartment of the car. He waited until she had tidied herself up a little then, with the sheepskin trailing around her ankles, took her in search of a taxi.

The hotel was small, similar to the one in which Francey had stayed when he had first organized his financial affairs. Hazel had been true to her word and the reservations had been made. The man behind the desk made no comment as he signed them in, merely remarking when handing over the keys that Miss Slye would be in touch as soon as she got in. Francey noted that he had an Irish accent.

He saw Fleur to her room, instructed her to stay there and to try and get some sleep and then went to his own.

As he collapsed on to the narrow bed, he wondered what he could be charged with – conspiracy to arson? Accessory to arson? Whatever . . . He was in deeply now. And so, to give her credit, was Hazel. The thought gave him comfort. After ten minutes or so, the tension and emotion of the past few hours caught up with him and he fell into a light sleep. He woke some time later to the sound of gentle knocking on his door.

Hazel . . .

He jumped off the bed and, still a little groggy, ran to the door.

It was not Hazel who stood there, however, but Fleur. 'May I come in?' She still wore the sheepskin around her shoulders.

Francey pulled the door wider. 'Can you not sleep?'

Fleur waited until he had closed the door behind them then walked to the bed and sat on it, letting the jacket fall away. 'I will have no money to pay you back for your help. At least for a time.'

'That doesn't matter,' Francey began, then, recognizing what she was offering, trailed off in shock. He gazed at her waif-like, serious face. 'I'm sorry, Fleur,' he said as quietly as he could, 'thank you but no.'

'Are you sure?' Her expression did not waver.

Francey did not at first trust himself to speak. Then, 'Go back to your own room, Fleur.' As she passed him in the doorway he kept his eyes averted. After she had left, he stared at the closed door, as if by deciphering the dents and scratches caused by years of use, he could gain some key to what had happened.

He was angry not with her but with himself. By his previous behaviour towards her he had begged for such treatment. He had been the prize chump of all chumps. Like a caged bear, Francey paced the too-small room. He felt like smashing the little window, pulping the flowered plastic lampshade, splintering the cheap wooden dressing-table. He caught sight of himself in the mirror, a huge, shambling, white-headed patsy.

Remembering that the hospital had given him the remains of his prescription to take home with him in case he could not sleep, Francey went into his kiosk-sized bathroom and, for the first time in his life, elected to take a tranquillizer. Although the label on the bottle said he was to take two of the tablets, after some hesitation, he put the second one back into the bottle. He wanted to calm himself but had no desire to become the vegetable he had been this morning.

He took his shoes, socks and jacket off, loosened his trousers and got into bed and when Hazel did tap on his door a couple of hours later, he was sleeping deeply.

Despite the medication, he must have been listening subconsciously for her knock because he woke without difficulty and leapt across the room, opening the door to find her standing in the dingy hallway. She had come directly from the Rollers' gig and was in full regalia, the rhinestone-covered boots looking incongruous under the ordinary cloth coat she wore. She had already dropped off a bag containing clothes and toiletries with Fleur: 'We're the same height and roughly the same size,' she explained to Francey. 'She doesn't seem to like me taste very much but as far as I'm concerned she can just feckin' well lump it.'

Francey could not believe how relieved and happy he was to see her. 'I'm sure she's really grateful.' He smiled at her. 'How'd you get here?'

If Hazel was surprised by the warmth of her welcome she did not show it. 'Vinnie drove me.' She gazed around the room. 'Sorry this place is so small, by the way. Yeah,' she went on, parking herself on the side of the bed, 'Vinnie's a pal.'

'He certainly is.' It dawned on Francey that perhaps there was more between Hazel and Vinnie, who seemed to be around her a lot, than friendship. He was unsure of how he felt about this; as far as he knew the saxophonist was a married man but, in the circumstances, felt he was in no position to make prissy moral judgements or to pry.

Although the earlier incident with Fleur bit at his tongue, as he and Hazel mapped out the plan for tomorrow, he forced himself to pay attention to the details. Admiring the practicality of Hazel's approach and her incisive replies to his own suggestions, he saw that she was treating the situation as though Fleur was an urgent parcel they had to dispatch with all speed and discretion. Francey found it the best way to take the emotion out of his own predicament.

'You sure you want to go through with this?' Hazel asked at one point.

'I'm sure.' Francey had already decided, with Hazel around to make it so simple, that the act of helping Fleur to escape the law did not appear to compromise him much. 'And, anyway, it's not as if anyone got killed,' he added, 'except poor Tommy, of course. And that was nothing to do with the fire. It's only a house, for God's sake, bricks and mortar – and with the way things are, I'm sure the family won't even miss it out of small change.'

'Right.' Hazel patted his hand, beside her on the coverlet. She had brought along a naggin of whiskey, which they were sharing; since the bathroom had only one glass, she used that and Francey swigged out of the bottle. Strangely, the alcohol did not react badly with the pill he had taken; instead, he felt energized and alert. Bathed by the glow from the single, tacky bedside lamp and with the two of them side by side on the bed, which was the only form of seating in the small room except for a stool meant for suitcases, he began to feel very close to Hazel as she went on to explain that as far as she could gather from Fleur – 'Bit unforthcoming, isn't she?' – the latter had been planning to go to Little Cayman.

The plan now, however, was for Fleur to lie low for a while in Canada. 'She has a British passport,' Hazel continued, 'and she can always go to the Caribbean later – lucky bitch! – sometime in the future when the fuss dies down.'

'Did she agree to that?' Francey was surprised. 'There's a huge difference between the Cayman Islands and Canada. She was always talking about the cold.'

'She has no choice,' Hazel said shortly.

When they had sorted it all out, he tried to tell her how much he appreciated her instant and unquestioning take-up of his appeal but she brushed him off: 'I told you, I owe you.' As she stood up, Hazel reached over and chucked one of his cheeks. 'After this, though,' she fluttered her eyelashes humorously only inches from his face, 'we're quits, all right? From tomorrow's gig on, it's every man – and woman – for himself!'

'All right.' Francey's heart lightened further as he gave her a hug. She responded with a swift kiss to his cheek and he lumbered to his feet to see her through the doorway.

After she left he lay, sleepless again, with his hands behind his head. The booze had now taken effect, but not unpleasantly. He had a feeling that everything was going to work out. He still found it hard to accept that Fleur would be able to stay away from the funeral of her own son but Hazel had probably hit the nail on the head: it was no doubt to do with Fleur's background where life and death were viewed differently. And even Fleur herself had pointed out that all the flowers and tears in the world would be of no help to Tommy now.

The more he thought about it the more he understood why Tommy's mother had done what she did. Who could say how he himself would react – how any parent would react – in similar circumstances? No jury in the country would convict a mother who had just held the body of her dead, only son. The more he thought about it, the more Francey came to believe that what he and Hazel were doing was not abetting crime or perverting justice, or whatever the legal terminology was. He now agreed with Hazel that they would be quite safe, and that despite Fleur's own fears her crime was not of such enormity that the police would have placed a dragnet around the capital. Hazel had said, quite rightly, that the police had more to be doing catching real criminals than looking out for distraught, half-crazed mothers who torched the mansions of millionaires – millionaries who spent half the time away from home and who couldn't care less about their bloody houses because all they had to do was order a new one.

Having Hazel around made all the difference to this crisis.

Love was a funny thing, Francey thought then. There he was – or had been – head over heels about Fleur and feeling sick all the time, whereas Hazel, with whom he was *not* head over heels, was the one in whose company he always felt warm and secure, not to mention amused. Turning over to catch a few hours' sleep, Francey sighed. It was all so confusing; being a backwards, inexperienced hopeful had been so much simpler.

On the night before she got married to her ex-husband, Hazel had gone for a few jars with some of her women friends. Among all the ribaldry and vulgar jokes, one of the women, an ex-hoofer who now worked in Jacob's biscuit factory and who, as far as Hazel could see, had made the only decent marriage she had ever come across, gave her a piece of advice she had never forgotten. 'Listen,' the woman had taken a sup from her pink gin, 'the thing to remember in marriage is, when you have an advantage, don't use it.'

Something about the adage had struck a chord in Hazel and when times were bad, when she could not help feeling superior, or more experienced, or even more intelligent than the man she married, she had tried to put it into practice.

It had not worked, of course, but it was still a precept she took out and dusted off every now and then. This was one such occasion.

It would have been so easy to tip off the police.

Or to do nothing at all and to let justice take its course.

Or even to reveal to Francey, who had become disillusioned anyway – she had picked that much up from him this evening – just what he was dealing with. But Hazel knew that in the long term he would not thank her for it. Even if he never found out that Fleur was what she was, what harm?

Lying on her bed, Hazel watched the smoke from her cigarette curl up and then spread out along the top of the frilled curtain pelmet in her bedroom. The poor bitch had enough to contend with now without being locked up, she thought. Hazel, who had lately begun to think about having a child of her own before it was too late, tried to imagine what it would be like to have one and then lose it. It must be the most awful, dreadful bereavement, worse than the longest prison sentence.

She sat up and stubbed out the cigarette. Her initial agreement to help Francey get the woman out of the country might have sprung from selfish motives but Hazel now saw that by speeding Fleur on her way she would be doing everyone a favour, even the unfortunate woman herself.

Chapter Twenty-Three

Next morning, while at Heathrow everything was moving with the precision of a military manoeuvre for the co-conspirators, the fire and insurance investigators were continuing their dispiriting task of sifting through the rubble and debris. Because the house was so large and the insurance claim, which the company was likely to dispute, was probably going to be in seven figures, the investigations were painstaking. There seemed little doubt now about the origins of the fire. The petrol can found the day before was not the only clue: it appeared that the blaze had sprung up almost simultaneously at several sources on one side of the house.

The only part of the rubbish heap from which anything recognizable had been pulled was the area the investigators knew to have been the dining-room. From here they recovered a huge, massively heavy glass table on steel legs, the frames of a set of dining chairs, also steel, and an abstract oil painting which had apparently hung near a fish tank. When the tank shattered, the rush of water from it had saved the glass of the table from melting and had also saturated the painting; although the canvas was covered in grime and the frame beyond repair, the work could be restored.

'Hey, look at this.' One of the men working on the site at the far end picked up an oddly shaped lump of a whorled, glittering substance which looked like fused plastic. Black with white streaks, the heat had shaped it into an object which resembled a zebra-striped, irregularly shaped hen's egg. The man who had found it handed it to his supervisor who consulted the floor plan of the house he held in one hand. 'One of the bedrooms,' he said, turning the object over in his hands. 'Maybe it was an ornament, or a fancy doorknob or something.' Picking off and discarding three small bits of gravel, so filthy they resembled tiny pieces of coal, which had adhered to the surface of the object to ruin its symmetry, he rubbed it on his sleeve. Then he held it up to the sunlight under which it glowed with a subdued sheen. 'Nice,' he said, 'but I don't think it's anything to worry about, certainly not valuable, but just to be safe, put it aside for the moment and we'll have it checked against the inventory.'

The object's finder complied and continued to sift through the layers of ash.

Francey, Hazel and Fleur had timed their arrival at Heathrow to coincide with when they thought the staff would clock in for work at Francey's bank in the City.

Immediately on arrival, he went to the airport's Lloyd's counter and asked to speak to the manager. He explained that he wanted to draw a substantial sum of cash from his account at his own branch and asked if he could have the money transferred out here. It took a little to-ing and fro-ing and Francey himself had to speak to his own manager on the telephone but, after twenty minutes or so, he was walking away from the counter with a wad of high-denomination notes in his inside pocket. Feeling like a spy in a thriller he met Hazel near the Aer Lingus desk and gave her enough cash to pay Fleur's transatlantic fare.

It had been Hazel's idea that in case Fleur was right and the authorities were looking out for her, she should travel to Canada via Dublin and New York on Aer Lingus, transferring on to the Canadian carrier at Kennedy. No one, she had reasoned, would suspect she would go to Ireland – 'Who the hell'd emigrate there?' – and as a transit passenger in New York, the immigration people there would not bother her.

While Hazel was booking and paying for the tickets, Francey took a look round the concourse to see if there was any overt police activity. Seeing nothing unusual, he went to join Fleur who was sitting, as instructed, at a little table in the snack bar. Although Hazel had been correct in saying that she and Fleur were of equal height, her figure was considerably more opulent and her clothes hung loosely on the other woman's bird-like frame. Fleur's hair was neat but unwashed, hanging in thick strings on either side of her elfin face. She looked like the refugee she was.

She did not see Francey's approach but continued to stare into space over her untouched cup of tea. After another quick glance around to make doubly sure there were no furtive-looking characters

449

with walkie-talkies in the vicinity, he sat down opposite her and, 'This is to tide you over,' handed her the rest of the money he had drawn. 'Put it away, quickly – don't let anyone see it.' If the truth be known, Francey was more concerned about what Hazel might think about his milksop generosity rather than anyone else becoming suspicious. For the first time since he had known her, Francey saw Fleur's eyes fill with tears. 'It's only money,' he was embarrassed now, 'you've a few minutes before your flight, do you want another cup of tea?' Without waiting for her reply he got up and went over to the counter.

Hazel was with Fleur by the time he got back but she would not hear of any tea or coffee or any more time wasting. 'Come on, Fleur,' she said crisply, 'put your hair under the hat like I told you.' Obediently, Fleur took out a floppy beret into which she folded her hair. The result gave her the appearance of a sad fifteen-year-old. Francey could tell that even Hazel noticed it. 'Come on,' she said softly, 'time we were getting this show on the road.'

Francey felt he should be able to think of something memorable or apposite to say, but nothing came to mind and he simply put out his hand to shake Fleur's. 'Goodbye,' he said formally, holding her hand only as long as was strictly necessary and then, on impulse, scribbled the telephone number of the house in Lahersheen on the back of the transaction slip from the bank. 'If you ever need to get in contact, I can always be found through this number.'

As Fleur took the slip, Francey glanced at the stony-faced Hazel and muttered, 'I'll see you outside later?' The plan was that since he was so conspicuous it was she who would accompany Fleur to the departure gate. She did not respond and, feeling her disapproval wash over him like a cold wave, he averted his eyes and felt rather than saw her nod of assent as she bid Fleur to accompany her towards the gate.

Francey watched as the two went towards the departure gates, both dressed in Hazel's clothes, Hazel carrying Fleur's single, pathetic piece of luggage, also donated. Although he waited until they vanished around a corner, neither looked back.

Then Francey had to bite back his own tears as he saw a middle-aged woman say goodbye to a group of weeping children and a man who was presumably her husband. He had never been able to watch these sad departures – or, even worse, the reunions – whether at airports, railways platforms or bus stations, without being in danger of breaking down himself. He turned away, realizing that throughout

450

the morning he had been so concentrated on getting through one self-assigned task after another, he had allowed himself no time for emotion. Neither had he examined what was going on in his life. The capers of last night and this morning would have done justice to one of the stories in one of Abby's *Argosy* magazines, he thought. He had always been surprised at his gentle sister's gory taste in reading matter.

Francey decided to telephone Lahersheen. He needed the reassurance of a familiar voice, and he would be less obvious standing by the wall at the banks of telephones than he was out here, sticking up like a telegraph pole over the heads of all the normally sized people in the hall.

The Lahersheen number was engaged at his first and second tries and when he did get through on the third, as it was dinner-time at home he was not surprised to hear Margaret's voice. But her voice was unusually sharp, even for her. 'Francey!' she yelled. 'Thank God, we were trying to get you all morning. Are you all right? We were frantic.'

It had never occurred to Francey that news of the fire would have crossed the Irish Sea. 'How did you know?'

'Tilly Harrington's first cousin in Birmingham saw it on the television news.' Margaret went on to berate him for not being in touch, complaining that they had telephoned every police station for miles around Coventry and, although the police had put them in touch with Dessie this morning, he had told them Francey was in Leeds. 'What the hell are you doing in Leeds?' she demanded.

But all Francey could think of was that, inadvertently, his family had let the Coventry police know that Fleur had an Irish connection. 'I can't talk now,' he said abruptly, 'I'll telephone later this evening. Love to Mam.' He hung up on Margaret's spluttering reply.

The next ten minutes were torture as Francey watched for Hazel to return from the departure gate. If she did not come soon, it meant that all was lost for Fleur, and he was sure he would not be immune from retribution. Hazel would be in trouble too – she had every right to disapprove of him.

Why, oh why had he been such a softy? He was a doormat, that's what he was – weak, weak . . .

He pulled out his paperback – he was reading *Lucky Jim* – from his inside pocket but could not concentrate and had to close it. He jumped with relief when he saw Hazel's jaunty blonde head bob towards him. 'Did everything work out?' He fell on her as she came within earshot.

'Keep your hair on, smooth as milk.' Obviously having forgiven him for his earlier transgression, she grinned up at him. Quickly, Francey filled her in.

Thick as the wall . . . Hazel thought with affection as, walking beside him towards the taxi rank, she listened to Francey's tumbling words. She did not mean this, of course, knowing that underneath all those layers of tender-heartedness burned a keen intelligence.

Now that Fleur was safely out of the way, it was time to step up her own strategy. On balance, Hazel thought the possibility of the police being as hot on Fleur's trail as Francey and Fleur feared was pretty remote. She had never met a Flash Gordon on any police force and in her experience cops moved more at the speed of the tortoise than the hare.

It was not her concern any more, and she was going to make damned sure it did not remain an obsession of Francey's. She did not tell him how Fleur's iron mask had slipped during the last few moments before boarding, bringing home to Hazel that whore or not, the poor girl had suffered a great deal. If the truth be told, Hazel's heart had thawed at the end. She had even given her a last-minute hug, and Fleur went off not only with Francey's telephone number but with Hazel's too.

But all that namby-pamby stuff was behind Hazel now and she was damned if she was not going to make the most of her opportunities with Francey now she had been presented with a clear field. On the other hand she knew she still had to be careful: to judge by the way he was talking about his former lover, he still nursed a small spark, so, in response to his queries as to how Fleur had behaved, Hazel replied in non-committal and non-specific fashion, telling him only that she had been fine and that everything had gone well. Even the flight had been on time. 'Come on,' she said then, reaching for his elbow, 'it's a lovely day and I'm free until nine o'clock tomorrow night. So are you. We deserve some kind of treat after all our good works.'

'A treat, what's that?'

Watching carefully, Hazel saw that, although his eyes remained

452

troubled, Francey smiled a little. 'Fun, Francey,' she urged, 'a little bit of fun for a change. Just the two of us, what do you say? We could go to a pub somewhere out in the country and have a few pints and a few laughs. The boys aren't expecting to see me until we meet up at the hotel before the gig tomorrow night.'

'Well, all right, but just let me make one phone call,' Francey looked hunted, 'I want to make sure Dessie is all right.'

Hazel frowned at his expression. It was on the tip of her exasperated tongue to tell him to screw his telephone calls but she bit back the words. 'Go on,' she encouraged him, 'but don't be long. It isn't often we get a bit of blue sky in these latitudes!'

As he went off to find a public telephone, Hazel sat on a concrete parapet beside one of the slip roads into the car park and drummed her fingers on her thigh. Francey's over-developed sense of responsibility would have been almost amusing if it did not pull at him so much. This was something she would have to address after—

After what? With a shock Hazel recognized that she already had them riding into the sunset. And that she was already perishing on the rock on which she had foundered with her first husband. Francey was worry-wart Francey, his sense of looking after others was part and parcel of his marshmallow heart. She would be an idiot to attempt to change him. There and then, Hazel uttered a quick prayer that if this worked out the way she hoped it would, she could be given the strength to desist from trying to rearrange people's personalities.

Anyway, she already understood her man well enough to know that any such attempt would be doomed to failure. Soft and tolerant he might be, but now and then Hazel had glimpsed in Francey something that caused her to wonder how far he could be pushed in a direction which did not suit him.

Ten, fifteen minutes went by and still there was no sign of him. Hazel looked at her watch for the umpteenth time. She tried to resign herself to the likelihood that someone was probably bending his ear again.

It took a long time for Dessie to come to the telephone at the inn in Little Staunton and when he did he was even more incoherent than usual.

Having disposed of the matter of the messages from Lahersheen,

453

eventually Francey divined that the solicitor, Mr Solomons, had been the one leaving the most urgent messages for him. Dessie went off at a tangent then, something about money and the horses. 'Say that again, slow down,' Francey interrupted.

Dessie paused and Francey could hear him taking a breath. 'I'm going to be richer now,' Dessie said carefully. 'Mr Solomons talked to me too. He said it'll take a while but that Tommy being gone changes everything in . . .' he paused again, 'our Dad's wife's will.'

Before Francey could react, he heard muffled voices and then his father came on the line. 'Is that you, Francey?'

'Yes.' Francey had paid no attention to the 'what ifs' and 'where-ases' in Jool's will. Now he wished he had.

'Where are you?' George asked then.

'I'm in a telephone box,' Francey said warily. His father's questions promised something he was not all that sure he wanted to hear.

'Dessie tells me you're in Leeds,' George went on. 'Francey, how soon could you get back here? Take a taxi if you like, I'll pay. But Colin's coming out of hospital this morning – I've to go and fetch him within the next half-hour – and I'm stuck here with Dessie and what with the police asking about Fleur and the funeral to arrange and the solicitor and the insurance people and everything else I'm swamped. Jool was always the one who took care of business.'

'Are the police there now?' Francey, having registered that his father's voice bore no trace of its customary suave tones, gripped the receiver.

'No, not since last night, they went into the flat in London but found nothing. They're worried now that Fleur might have – well, not to put a tooth in it, they wonder if she's the type to harm herself. That's all we need.' George's voice took on an aggrieved cast then recovered a little. 'By the way, I don't know if Dessie told you but it looks like you're the only one to have anything saved from the wreckage. That painting Jool left for you.'

'That's good.' It was all Francey could think of to say.

'So what time do you think you'll get here?' His father sounded almost light-hearted now.

Francey thought of Hazel waiting outside, of what they had planned to do. Of fun. 'I'm sorry but I can't come, George,' he said.

'I beg your pardon?' George asked, and Francey could clearly hear his father's gasp of astonishment. 'I said I can't come, George,' he said, 'I'm sorry. But I have other plans. I'll certainly be there for the funeral.'

'But Dessie – what about—' George seemed lost.

'Dessie's your son, George. You and he will get along fine.'

'You can't do this to me now . . .' But as George went around the houses with him Francey remained adamant. He repeated that he was sorry George was upset but that there was not much he could do about it. He had other plans and that was that.

As he listened to George come to the realization that he would, indeed, have to manage things on his own, Francey reflected that perhaps for the first time he himself had made a grown-up choice.

The extraordinary aspect of the whole affair was his lack of guilt, even where Colin was concerned. Whereas he acknowledged Colin's need for tenderness and care, Francey did not feel inclined to take him on at present; and as for Dessie, a few cigarettes and a chat with the horses was all that his half-brother asked of life. 'You won't have to worry too much about Dessie,' he said to his father when he could get a word in. 'He'll be able to look after himself.'

Hearing nothing but breathing at the other end of the line he added, 'Did you hear me, George?'

As he waited for the response, which was slow in coming, he warned himself not to allow treacherous compassion to gain purchase in his heart. It was time George Gallaher found out that fathering three sons required more than throwing parties. This one's for you, Mammy, he thought . . .

'If there's nothing else, I'll say goodbye now,' he said when George seemed to have nothing more to say, 'but I'll stay in touch by telephone. See you at the funeral. Put Dessie back on, please.' He had to put more coins in the slot. As he did so he imagined George's face.

'How are your feet?' he asked when the line cleared and Dessie came back on.

'Grand, grand. I hear you're not coming down?' Dessie did not sound as put out as George and Francey softened.

'Not for the present,' he replied, 'but I'll be talking to you on the telephone. I want you to do something for me, something special?'

'Sure, Francey, if I can.'

'Colin is coming out this afternoon, apparently, and you have to help George take care of him. He's going to need you, Dessie.'

455

'Of course, Francey, don't worry a bit. I'll look after him all right. The two of us will.'

'How are you getting on with our father?'

'Great, great!' Dessie clearly meant it. 'He's very nice, Francey, very nice to me. And he's explaining a lot to me, about the money and all . . .' Francey grinned as Dessie went on about George. He could well imagine how Dessie would haunt their father. 'Have you managed to get out to see the horses?' he asked, then was sorry he had. Dessie had been out all right, twice, in a taxi; there never were animals like them on the face of the earth, Mick and himself and a few of the other lads were getting their heads together to know could they sort out some decent housing for the horses before the autumn, heavy horses like Shires were the only breed you could trust in an emergency like war, or a fire . . .

Francey's money ran out while Dessie was still in full flow. As he walked back to Hazel he decided that he could stop worrying about him. Dessie's personality, not to say his confidence, was enlarging by the day. It would be good for George and himself to have to look to one another and take care of Colin.

Hazel, who had been holding her face up to the unseasonably warm sun, opened her eyes as its blissful radiance was blotted out. Francey was looming over her, a look on his face she could describe only as stunned. 'What is it?' she asked, squinting up at him. 'Don't tell me. Your auntie's died now and you have to be a pallbearer. No – that's not it – you're opening a hostel for the homeless and we all have to contribute?'

'Something like that,' Francey rushed to correct himself, 'but don't worry I said no. I said I was staying here with you.'

'With me? You mentioned me?' Hazel was incredulous.

'No,' Francey grinned, 'I didn't tell anyone. I just said no. Hazel, I feel great!'

'Serio? You really said no?'

'M-mmm,' Francey nodded.

'Good for you.' Hazel jumped off the concrete ledge. 'Let's go.'

'There's just one thing.' Francey restrained her and seeing his face was grave again, Hazel thought, Uh-oh, here we go again.

'Go on,' she said with resignation, 'what is it?'

'It seems now that with poor little Tommy gone, I'm richer than ever,' he said, with an expression which fell so comically between rueful and wicked that Hazel felt she had to give him a real hard thump.

George, slumped in a chair in the small reception area of the inn, stared into space. He was having grave difficulty in coming to terms with what had happened. Why could Francey not have done his bit to help out?

Until the last two days, since he had left home half a century before, the only real trauma George had had to face had been Jool's death and funeral and even that had been relatively easy; she had died with as little fuss as she had lived and he had left a lot of the organization of the aftermath to the undertakers and the solicitors. Money bought a lot.

Now, in the space of a few hours, everything had collapsed and although there was still money – more than ever – unless he, too, ran away like his daughter-in-law, even cash provided no escape from what was facing him.

For the first time in his life George faced the fact that if he was to be a man, he had to fulfil others' emotional need of him: Colin would need him, Dessie would need him.

And just when he himself needed someone. Because, too late now, George missed Tommy dreadfully.

The identification in the morgue had been a nightmare, the white smooth body on the slab, so pale and unmarked, with no trace of life or violent death. The silky black hair, shining under the lights, had been George's undoing and he had not been able to look at his grandson for more than a second before turning away in tears. He had wept more in the past thirty-six hours than he had in all his previous sixty-three years. And regret, which all his life had been a foreign country to him, plucked and darted at him incessantly. He had been careless with the gift of a grandson. Now he was paying for it.

He raised dull eyes to see Dessie coming towards him across the lobby. 'Francey says he'll see us in a few days.'

George levered himself up from his chair. 'Will you come with me to fetch Colin in the hospital?'

457

'Of course.'

George, who had not really expected Dessie to agree, was surprised by the readiness of the response. 'Are you feeling up to it?' he asked doubtfully. 'What about your feet?'

'You'll have to have a bit of support,' Dessie gazed earnestly at him, 'and Colin is going to need all the help he can get now. Poor Colin,' he added, his voice sad, 'he's going to need us all. We're all going to have to pull together on this one. Francey'll be back soon,' he repeated, 'but I'm here.'

'Yes.' Embarrassed at his own want, George put his arm around Dessie's thin shoulders.

The gesture proved too much for him, however. It smacked too much of too many bad plays. But as he dropped the arm, he looked straight into his youngest son's eyes. 'I suppose we'll all rub along together all right?'

'Sure we'll give it a try,' Dessie nodded vigorously. 'Will I call a taxi or will you? Or will we take the chauffeur?'

Francey and Hazel were buying a Morgan.

They had been on their way to Watford to pick up Francey's Morris Oxford when, on passing through some town there it was in the window of a showroom, glossy, red, wire wheels and beckoning like a siren, the apotheosis of what he had always wanted. 'Oh, God,' he groaned, craning through the taxi's rear window to see it for as long as he could.

'What?' Hazel too had twisted around in her seat to scan the traffic behind.

'There's a car I've always wanted back there in a garage.'

'Stop!' Hazel tapped the taxi driver on the shoulder.

'We couldn't!' But excitement had dawned as Francey realized that indeed he could.

The entire transaction took less than an hour. They did not demur at the price and the salesman, who knew a good prospect when it walked into his premises with a cheque book already in its hand, arranged the insurance and to pick up the Oxford from where Francey had parked it. Francey assured the man he would come back some other day to arrange its sale, and fifty-four minutes after they had walked into the showroom, Hazel and he were on their way with a complimentary bottle of champagne stowed between Hazel's feet and a road map spread over her lap.

It was such a beautiful day that Francey left the top down, revelling in the wind and the sporty roar of the car's engine. The squared-off bonnet in front of him looked like the most beautiful shape in the world, the walnut of the dashboard the most opulent. Compared to the Oxford's stately perambulations, this beautiful machine was so lively and so low to the road that her handling took a lot of getting used to.

'For cryin' out loud, Fangio, take it easy, don't kill us,' Hazel shouted as at a stop sign, the brakes proved far more responsive than the Oxford's. Then she grinned at him to take the harm out of the criticism and Francey, remembering the night he had first heard the name of the racing driver, grinned back.

Francey turned the car northwards, then found he was bound for the area he most wanted to avoid. 'Ah, no,' he stabbed at the map across her knees, 'try to get me away from the Coventry-Birmingham direction.'

'Right,' Hazel pored over the map, 'take the next right and we can go to – let's see – Cambridge. I've always wanted to see Cambridge.'

They took the smaller back roads, meandering along at a relatively easy pace until he got used to the driving and, with each mile, Francey felt himself relax. It was lovely to be out, free, all the words he had lost from his vocabulary recently. And in the car of his dreams, too. The countryside, which was not as pretty as that around Little Staunton, might nevertheless on this day have been drawn by a child to illustrate spring: green fields, white lambs, primrosed verges and budded hedgerows, birds in pairs and white woolly clouds puffing across a high blue sky. 'Terrific, isn't it?' After half an hour or so, Francey gunned the engine and opened her up a little.

For the fun of it, he resumed his name-collecting, initiating Hazel into the sport by shouting them out as soon as he spotted one that took his fancy so that she could add them to his notebook. Of the present batch, Maggots End was his favourite until Hazel, tiring of his more esoteric taste, began a game of her own with the names she liked.

In her mouth, the names became double-meaning and suggestive until every sign and signpost, whether for village, suburb or crossroads, became hilariously sexy: *Much Had*ham, *Bull's* Green, all the *Greats* shrinking to *Littles* and *Ends*. She found a place called Roost Green, then *Stump* Cross, *Cherry* Hinton.

'This is great,' she cackled, 'and they've the cheek to think our names are funny? *Com*-berton,' she intoned, '*Throck*-ing . . . Done any good *throck*-ing lately, Francey?' This last sent her into paroxysms of mirth, so infectious that Francey found himself roaring along with her as they continued to hurl the unfortunate Throcking between them, using it in ever more outlandish ways.

Francey knew their behaviour was juvenile and silly but it had been so long since he had acted this way that he was thoroughly enjoying himself. He even cracked a private joke at poor Fleur's expense and, considering how he had persisted in seeing her as defenceless, at his own, too: '*To Kill a Throcking Bird* . . .' he chortled, thumping the steering wheel.

'I don't get it?' Hazel's eyebrows knitted even as she continued to laugh.

'Oh, nothing, it was stupid. Hold on to your knickers!' he yelled as they swooped over a hump-backed bridge so that she left her seat and then set about him with a retaliatory handbag.

'I'm starving, let's eat,' he announced as they coasted into a pleasing little village called Bishop's Slipper.

'So am I, but let's not eat, let's throck first!' This set both of them off again and Francey continued to chuckle until he turned off the engine in the car park of a small pub-cum-inn opposite the village shop. 'See you later.' He stroked the warm bonnet as he left the car and went inside.

As it was mid-afternoon, the bar was closed but the obliging woman at the reception desk of the inn section said she would see about getting them something to eat, returning after ten minutes or so with a tray laden with tea and coffee, Scotch eggs and the inevitable cheese and pickle sandwiches.

'I'm going to buy a house in Dublin,' Francey announced as he dived into the sandwiches. Then, chewing on his pickle, he gazed through the window into the sunny yard of the inn. 'And maybe a little flat somewhere in London. I'm fed up hanging around in hotels. Dammit, I know George doesn't deserve it but I'm going to have to be around a bit. For Dessie, too.'

'Good for you,' Hazel said, helping herself to an egg. 'And when you're settled, are you going to do that thing with the horses?'

'Did I not tell you? I think Dessie's the natural there. That was a lovely idea while it lasted but I've realized lately it's not what I really want to do. I'll give Dessie all the help he wants but he won't really need it. He has Mick O'Dowd, after all, and as much money as me. No. I want something different. I'm applying to go to university.'

It was something on which Francey had just decided but it rang so true in his head that he knew he had at last found something he wanted to do. Something not only possible but so attractive that the back of his neck had tingled as he said it.

'With all that money?' Hazel was disbelieving. 'That's like going back to school! Why wouldn't you just sit back and enjoy yourself?'

'It's fun at first,' Francey explained, 'the money, I mean, but it's a responsibility too and I'll have to take real advice as to what to do with it. I can only sleep in one bed at a time, you know, and wear one pair of trousers.'

'You're not going to do something stupid like give it away?'

'No,' Francey replied thoughtfully, 'but I'm going to have to spread some of it around. All I have is a Leaving Cert, Hazel. If I'm to benefit from this fantastic opportunity, I'm going to have to settle down and do something useful.' Feeling shy, as though he were telling a shameful secret, he glanced across at her. 'I want to *be* something or someone and I never thought I could. Now I can. And, anyway, I feel that it's my duty to do something constructive. University is a start.'

'God, I have to admire you.' Francey saw by the look in her eyes that she meant it. 'Your mother'll be delighted. What'll you study?'

'That's easy,' Francey poured himself some tea. 'English. Don't laugh, Hazel, but I might even be a writer some day.'

'Why would I laugh? You're always readin' bleedin' books!'

They let the conversation lapse while Francey examined the bubbling, happy feeling in the pit of his stomach. It was not right he was so happy in the wake of the chaos of the past few days.

'Don't be havin' second thoughts, now!' Hazel put a warning hand on his arm.

'How did you know?'

'Women's intuition!' Hazel tapped the side of her nose.

461

'You're a wonder, Hazel!' Eschewing doubt, Francey wolfed another sandwich, 'I'm having a great time,' he said happily, 'it's like being on holiday.'

'I'm glad. Let's both take a holiday, let's not talk about anything serious today.'

'So what'll we talk about? I can think of nothing new to say about throcking.' He nudged her playfully.

'Can you not?' Something about Hazel's reply stopped him in mid-chew. He glanced at her and remembered where he had seen that look before and in an instant the food in his mouth became tasteless.

'Hazel?'

'I've to go to the ladies',' she said, and stood up, almost knocking over her cup of coffee in her haste to get out from behind the small table.

Slowly, Francey put down the half-eaten sandwich. He did not need to ask what was going on. The look on Hazel's face had shot an electric current through his skin and, in half a second, the rules of engagement, of friendship, had rotated 180 degrees.

He looked around at the ordinary, slightly worn furnishing of the little bar, the evenness of the slats on the shutter that closed off the counter, the old-fashioned spirit measures under the bottles. The sun was splitting the stones outside, even if it was only March. Passion was alien to such a setting and yet here it was, staring at him. And this time there could be no blaming of drink.

And was it just passion? He thought of all the happy conversations with Hazel, all the fun, the companionship. How much he admired her guts and verve, how warm she made him feel about himself.

Francey began his old game of abacus-clicking. Was it Hazel he was attracted to or was he attracted to Hazel because, to put it bluntly, he had not made love to anyone for such a long time? Was it the old *Finian's Rainbow* number that Mick Harrington used to sing at the parties in every kitchen in Lahersheen, the one about when he was not with the girl he loved he loved the girl he was with? Was it love or just sex? And if it was love, how come he hadn't seen it before?

Had he not seen it before because sex with Fleur had blinded him? Was it in that arena where love versus sex had happened?

This was as far as he could get with his analysis checklist because Hazel was coming back, serene now, and looking cool, as though the

462

temperature in the room had not shot up by a minimum of fifty degrees.

She was wearing tight white slacks – shades of Fleur – but there the comparison ended. The ends of Hazel's slacks were tucked into little white ankle boots and over it, she wore a tight black blouse of some sort of stretchy fabric which criss-crossed under her breasts, drawing attention to them and displaying her considerable cleavage. 'Y'all right?' she eased herself behind the table again and as she did so, had to bend over a little so the tops of her breasts plumped out over the V of the blouse. Francey could not take his eyes off them.

Hazel had decided during her sojourn in the ladies' that she was going to play this very carefully. She loved him and all that jazz, she was sure about that – and she was fairly sure that all she had to do was let him *discover* that he loved her. Sex had a lot to do with it but it could ruin it too. She had never played sexual come-on games with anyone, believing them stupid and unnecessary. Coyness was foreign to her nature and she saw no point in pretending to let yourself be won over or conquered: you either liked a bloke or you didn't.

She did worry a little that she might have given Francey the impression that she was promiscuous, although she lost no sleep over this because she herself knew the truth. Which was that with the exception of one or two understandable lapses such as the periods immediately post-husband and post-Francey, her sexual exploits had been by the standards of the circles in which she moved, modest.

She stared at herself in the mirror: there was also the little matter of the difference in their ages. It certainly did not bother her and she was almost sure it did not bother him. As far as Hazel was concerned all relationships were like raffles. You pulled the lucky numbers or you didn't – and if you did you had to make damned sure the ticket stayed lucky. If this worked out for her – for them – she was going to give it her all.

She knew well what had happened between them out there, had meant it to happen, and she sensed now that this next hour would be very important, if not crucial. Everything was right, the place, the time, the mood, even the weather, God bless it. No one on earth knew where they were. If she couldn't organize something now, she and Francey probably did not have a future together.

463

Hazel felt surprisingly calm, considering what was at stake. 'Oh, well.' Speaking aloud to her reflection, she spat on a finger and smoothed one of her eyebrows. 'We'll always have Ballsbridge!' Smiling disparagingly at the weakness of her own wit, she shimmied her blouse tighter inside her waistband and then left for the fray.

'You're lookin' at me!' she said now as she resumed her seat.

Francey reached out and took her hand.

Hazel had to fight the impulse to giggle. He looked so shocked. 'Talk to me,' she said.

'What can I say? I'm poleaxed, Hazel.'

'I see.' Hazel felt the air between them crackle and grow thick, like electric soup. Although every nerve in her body screamed to dig her nails into the back of his hand, to grab it and bite it, she remained steady. 'So what are we going to do about it?' she asked conversationally, forcing her hand to stay loose under his. 'Or shall we just drive on, d'you think?'

'What can we do about it?' Francey ran the index finger of his free hand along the thin fabric which covered one of Hazel's thighs then rested his hand gently on it.

Her whole body jumped within itself but again she managed to hold on. 'I dunno,' she shrugged, 'you tell me.'

'How do you feel about it? Do you think I've an awful nerve? You know all about me – about Fl –'

'You know all about me, too.' Hazel moved in before he could say the name. 'Nothing serious, remember?'

'This is serious, Hazel.'

'Oh?' She let the syllable hang there, like a pear ready to drop from a tree.

'I can't think of anything to say that doesn't come from a book or a song.'

Hazel waited while the air grew thicker still. She could feel it judder now, just as hot summer air shimmered like water above a ribbon of flat tarmac. 'I know all the songs, you can't surprise me.'

'I think what I'm thinking now would surprise you.'

'Why don't you try me?' The bonds of her restraint were in grave danger of shredding like cheap twine and Hazel crossed one leg over the other. This was a mistake because in concentrating on *not* feeling him near her she had forgotten his hand on one thigh and it was now trapped between both. She felt the beat of both of their pulses but could not for the life of her uncross her legs again. 'No one's listening except me and I'm no squealer.' She attempted to laugh.

'I love you, Hazel.'

Hazel took a long breath while the blood inside her head erupted with jubilation. 'I bet you say that to all the girls,' she managed, then, just to be certain, 'Sure I'm old enough to be your – well – your older sister . . .'

'I've said it to only one other. And I wasn't telling the truth. I thought I was.' He gripped her thigh. 'And I don't give a tinker's about your age. I was wondering about you and Vinnie, though.'

Hazel's exultation would stay bottled no longer. 'Oh, Francey!' she yelled. 'Ya big lunk! Of course you love me and I love you, I love you, love you, love you.' She threw her arms around his neck and kissed him. 'I thought I'd never hear you say it, though. I was going to *die* if you didn't say it soon.'

She kissed him again, pulling his hair, his ears, anywhere she could get a handhold. 'Vinnie?' she asked breathlessly on coming up for air. 'He's a *pal*, I told you that.' She had to pull away because the woman, having heard her shout and thinking they were calling for service, came into the bar. On seeing the two of them wound around one another she stopped dead at the end of the bar. Hazel rejoiced in her embarrassment. 'We're in love,' she announced, kissing Francey's hand. 'It's all right, missis, this is my fiancé. We've just got engaged.'

'Congratulations.' The woman hesitated and then retreated leaving Francey gazing at Hazel with a look of such comical consternation that she burst out laughing. 'For God's sake,' she reassured him, 'I had to say something. I didn't mean it. Anyway, me divorce isn't through yet.'

'I mean it.' Francey sprang off the narrow bench seat on which they were sitting and knelt on one knee on the wooden floor. Before he could utter the words, Hazel flicked him on the shoulder.

'Jesus, Mary and Joseph,' she raised her eyes to heaven, 'even kneelin' down you're bigger than me!'